C KU-756-954

L'ASSOMMOIR

ÉMILE ZOLA was born in Paris in 1840, the son of a Venetian engineer and his French wife. He grew up in Aix-en-Provence where he made friends with Paul Cézanne. After an undistinguished school career and a brief period of dire poverty in Paris, Zola joined the newly founded publishing firm of Hachette which he left in 1866 to live by his pen. He had already published a novel and his first collection of short stories. Other novels and stories followed until in 1871 Zola published the first volume of his Rougon–Macquart series with the sub-title *Histoire naturelle et sociale d'une famille sous le Second Empire*, in which he sets out to illustrate the influence of heredity and environment on a wide range of characters and milieux. However, it was not until 1877 that his novel *L'Assommoir*, a study of alcoholism in the working classes, brought him wealth and fame. The last of the Rougon–Macquart series appeared in 1893 and his subsequent writing was far less successful, although he achieved fame of a different sort in his vigorous and influential intervention in the Dreyfus case. His marriage in 1870 had remained childless but his extremely happy liaison in later life with Jeanne Rozerot, initially one of his domestic servants, gave him a son and a daughter. He died in 1902.

MARGARET MAULDON was born in Buenos Aires, read French and Spanish at Cambridge University, and now lives in the United States. She has taught French in several universities, most recently in Amherst at the University of Massachusetts, and she has worked as a translator since 1987.

ROBERT LETHBRIDGE is Professor of French at Royal Holloway, University of London.

ZOLA IN WORLD'S CLASSICS

L'Assommoir
Translated by Margaret Mauldon
With an introduction and notes by Robert Lethbridge

The Attack on the Mill and Other Stories
Translated with an introduction and notes by Douglas Parmée

Germinal
Translated and edited by Peter Collier
With an introduction by Robert Lethbridge

The Masterpiece
Translated by Thomas Walton
Revised and edited by Roger Pearson

Nana
Translated with an introduction and notes by Douglas Parmée

Thérèse Raquin
Translated with an introduction and notes by Andrew Rothwell

THE WORLD'S CLASSICS

ÉMILE ZOLA

L'Assommoir

Translated by
MARGARET MAULDON

With an Introduction and Notes by
ROBERT LETHBRIDGE

Oxford   New York
OXFORD UNIVERSITY PRESS
1995

Oxford University Press, Walton Street, Oxford OX2 6DP

Oxford New York
Athens Auckland Bangkok Bombay
Calcutta Cape Town Dar es Salaam Delhi
Florence Hong Kong Istanbul Karachi
Kuala Lumpur Madras Madrid Melbourne
Mexico City Nairobi Paris Singapore
Taipei Tokyo Toronto

and associated companies in
Berlin Ibadan

Oxford is a trade mark of Oxford University Press

Translation, Note on the Translation © Margaret Mauldon 1995
Introduction , Select Bibliography, Explanatory Notes
© Robert Lethbridge 1995
Chronology © Roger Pearson 1993
First published as a World's Classics paperback 1995

British Library Cataloguing in Publication Data
Data available

Library of Congress Cataloging in Publication Data
Zola, Émile, 1840–1902
[Assommoir, English]
L'Assommoir / Émile Zola; translated by Margaret Mauldon; with an
introduction and notes by Robert Lethbridge.
p. cm.
includes bibliographical references.
1. Paris (France)—Social life and customs—19th century—Fiction.
2. Working class women—France—Paris—Fiction. 3. Married
women—France—Paris—Fiction. I. Mauldon, Margaret. II. Lethbridge.
Robert. III. Title.
PQ2496.M38 1994   843'.8—dc20   94–11779

ISBN 0-19-282983-1

1 3 5 7 9 10 8 6 4 2

Typeset by Pure Tech Corporation, Pondicherry, India
Printed in Great Britain by BPC Paperbacks Ltd.
Aylesbury, Bucks

INTRODUCTION

IT requires an imaginative leap of a substantial kind to appreciate fully the impact of *L'Assommoir* on its nineteenth-century reading public. At first sight, it may not seem inevitable that this story of a woman's struggle for happiness in a working-class district of Paris should have provoked so disproportionate a reaction. Yet both its subject and its treatment guaranteed the novel a *succès de scandale*. Its commercial success, indeed, persuaded Zola's generous publisher to offer the writer the revised contract ultimately responsible for his considerable wealth. More significant is the fact that the novel's appearance constituted a literary event in its own right.[1] It initiated a long and passionate debate about the legitimate scope and formal procedures of modern literature. Only in this context can Zola's preface, dated 1 January 1877, be understood. For rather than being a mere editorial gesture, this statement (see pp. 3–4) is just one of the very great number of similar declarations he was forced to make in response to attacks (made during the prior serialization of the novel in the press) which tell us a great deal about the cultural and political climate in which he was working. From within that same polemical context, Zola would elaborate the theoretical principles of Naturalism, as a direct consequence of *L'Assommoir*'s reception. Its notoriety encouraged readers to unearth Zola's earlier work. And its qualities, as well as its far-flung reverberations, marked the beginning of his reputation as the most important European writer of his generation. That such contemporary concerns now seem to us like a distant echo is as unsurprising as *L'Assommoir*'s recent designation as a 'landmark of world literature'.[2] Its 'classic' status, however, depends less on the wisdom of hindsight than on a recognition, sustained and enriched by more than a century of critical interpretation, that it is *because* it is the most

[1] See, in a series significantly entitled 'Les Grands Evénements littéraires', Léon Deffoux, *La Publication de L'Assommoir* (Paris: Malfère, 1931).

[2] Through its inclusion in the series of that name; see David Baguley, *Emile Zola: L'Assommoir* (Cambridge: Cambridge University Press, 1992).

finely-crafted of all Zola's novels that *L'Assommoir* retains its ability to shock and its unsettling affective tenor, its capacity to move us, in other words, in powerful and contradictory ways.

As part of the strategy designed to refute charges that he had compromised his aesthetic integrity, Zola's preface to *L'Assommoir* draws attention to its place within a larger artistic project. Although his Rougon–Macquart cycle was only subsequently increased to the twenty novels mentioned here, it is perfectly true that a study of Parisian working-class life does figure in the outline of the series he submitted to a prospective publisher in 1869. From the start, this series was conceived as a historical panorama of the Second Empire, not merely complementing what Balzac had done for the Restoration and the July Monarchy, but also asserting (beyond such a chronological distinction) an originality of its own. A set of private notes headed 'Differences between Balzac and myself' simply confirms, it could be argued, Zola's acute awareness of working in the shadow of *La Comédie humaine*. But in sketching the future *L'Assommoir* at so early a date, the ambitious young novelist was thereby marking out as his own a terrain barely touched by his predecessors.

His prefatory claim that *L'Assommoir* was 'the first novel about the common people that does not lie' (p. 3) was not calculated to gain the unqualified assent of writers like the Goncourt brothers. Their *Germinie Lacerteux* (1864), much admired by Zola, sought (as its authors put it) to give to the 'lower classes' their rightful place in the domain of the novel. But their focus on the physiological destiny of a maidservant remains angled through the barely-concealed revulsion of the character's aristocratic mistress. And, not unlike some of Balzac's incidental evocations of the urban poor, the portraits and settings of *Germinie Lacerteux* anticipate only in superficial ways the working-class milieu into which the reader of *L'Assommoir* is plunged.

The 'differences' between Zola and the writers who precede him are by no means limited, in any case, to the appropriation of fictional subjects. He was at pains to point out that it was his approach to his material which differentiated his work from other representations of the social world. That approach is inscribed in the subtitle he gave to his series: 'A Natural and Social History of a Family under the Second Empire'. Zola was thereby making explicit the seminal influence of Hippolyte Taine (1828–93), whose 'humble disciple' he admitted to being. In particular, his project is indebted to the Positivist philosopher's isolation of three principal determinants on human behaviour: heredity, environment, and the historical moment. By tracing the destiny of a single family and its descendants, Zola felt he could give due weight to biological imperatives, lent added intellectual credibility in France by the 1865 translation of Darwin's *On the Origin of Species*. That is to suggest neither that Zola uncritically subscribed to theories of heredity being popularized at the time, nor that these are systematically illustrated in his Rougon–Macquart novels. Preliminary notes for the series as a whole, drawn up in 1868–9, make it clear that he considered heredity a conveniently scientific substitute for the outmoded concept of Fate. Above all, it was intended that the twin focus on the Rougon and Macquart branches of the family would endow Zola's fictional world with an internal coherence. This would be afforded not only by blood ties and comparative experiences, but also by reappearing characters less arbitrarily related than in Balzac's exploitation of the same technique.

Consistent with such aims, all the Rougon–Macquart novels contain cross-references which serve, or seek, to enhance the illusion of overlapping books and lives. *L'Assommoir* is no exception to this rule. We are alerted, for example, to its heroine's provincial origins (p. 31) and to her courtship with Lantier prior to their arrival in Paris (p. 19), which are described in the opening novel of the series, *La Fortune des Rougon* (1871). Her two children by him, Étienne and Claude, are given apprenticeships (pp. 245, 96) which prepare them, above all, for central roles in *Germinal* (1885) and *L'Œuvre* (1886) respectively. That Claude had already appeared as a young artist in *Le Ventre de Paris* (1873), the third novel of the series (whereas *L'Assommoir* is the seventh), is confusing only for a reader who works systematically through the Rougon–Macquart on the mistaken assumption that it is organized as an unfolding family saga. That its members inhabit spheres more clearly delineated than the exactitudes of chronology is confirmed by the failure of Gervaise's sister (also one of the principal characters of *Le Ventre de Paris*, and thus living barely a mile away in the proximity of Les Halles) to attend any of the ceremonial occasions of *L'Assommoir* (see p. 74). This also underlines the general rule, throughout *Les Rougon–Macquart*, whereby characters have such nominal relationships that the juxtaposition of separate biographical 'chapters' is not mutually enriching, as these remain subordinate to the requirements of autonomous texts. On the other hand, the second half of *L'Assommoir* does more than simply announce what is in effect its sequel; for the chapters devoted to Gervaise's daughter's introduction to prostitution lead directly to *Nana* (1880), the novel which bears her name.

This is not the only feature of *L'Assommoir* which encourages a degree of caution before applying to the novel the generalizations frequently encountered in summary accounts of the underlying principles of the Rougon–Macquart. In few other novels of the series, it has to be said, are references to heredity so prevalent. Authorial scepticism notwithstanding, a tainted genetic inheritance is repeatedly invoked as a factor loading the dice against the characters' efforts to avoid a virtually preordained degeneration. To descend from Antoine Macquart (see p. 39) is to repeat an alcoholic destiny which has the force of an ancestral curse. But Coupeau too replays a parental scenario (p. 429), even to the extent of falling off a roof as his father had done before him. Only Goujet seems able to resist this pattern (p. 106), while remaining as vulnerable as the others to the workings of historical circumstance and social milieu.

Certainly in no other Zola novel is the influence of the latter so insistently foregrounded. *L'Assommoir* is not just *set* in a *quartier*; it is the story *of* a *quartier*, with its human figures subject to its utterly material determinants and collective moral horizons. Whereas, in Balzac, habitat and inhabitant are mutually reflective, Zola takes this one stage further by detailing how the environment in which characters live fashions their personality traits and leaves its mark on their bodies. And this includes the less tangible but even more insidious texture of communal values which shapes the individual's life. When the preface to *L'Assommoir* refers to the 'filth of promiscuity' (p. 3), the associative move between literal and figurative dirt catches that double shaping of a 'downfall' which Zola speaks of as 'inexorable'. The novel is not uniformly melancholic; its ribald strain and comic moments have enchanted many a reader. But if *L'Assommoir* is often held up as evidence of Zola's pessimistic vision, it is because of the sheer weight of his deterministic equations in this book; for these seem to nullify every effort to escape fatalities located not in the edicts of vengeful gods but in the very substance of the stage on which characters progressively decline, 'ultimately to degradation and death'. This sombre certainty is even encoded in the title of the novel. Colombe's bar, the Assommoir, is taken from one of the same name in Belleville (a working-class area in north-eastern Paris); it was so well-known that an *assommoir* came to be used generically for any such cheap establishment in which (in keeping with the literal meaning of the verb *assommer*) one was 'smashed' or 'bludgeoned' by drink. But Zola also extends its metaphorical sense, beyond the effects of alcohol, to embrace everything which serves to 'crush' the human spirit, starting with contextual forces.

The properly historical coordinates, on the other hand, are perhaps less precisely aligned in *L'Assommoir* than in some of the other Rougon–Macquart novels. This is partly as a result of the impression (or perhaps the illusion) we have that it takes place in a self-enclosed world, not just in an outlying area of the city but also far removed from political dates and officially recorded events. There are in fact a sufficient number of discreet reference points to allow us to reconstruct the novel's chronology. The wedding in Chapter III, for example, supposedly takes place on 29 July 1850; by the *coup d'état* of December 1851 (p. 108) Nana has been born and baptized; by this reckoning Chapter IV extends from 1851 to 1854, and Chapter V from 1855 to 1858; Chapters VI and VII both take place in 1858; Chapter VIII takes us up to 1860; Chapter IX covers the period December 1860 to the beginning of 1862; Chapters X and XI can be dated 1863–5 and 1866–8 respectively; and it is possible to calculate that the text closes in 1869, at the very end of the Second Empire. In this respect, however, the subtitle of the series applies only loosely to *L'Assommoir*, and its reception, indeed, confirms that its picture of the working class was neither exclusively modelled on, nor limited by, conditions prevailing during the imperial regime of Napoleon III. Here again, Zola's preface is instructive, for his highlighting of 'the poisonous atmosphere of our industrial suburbs' (p. 3) has a topical rather than a narrowly historical resonance. Such a lack of precision, of course, serves only to enlarge the target of the novel's concerns. For it deals with one of the major consequences of the Industrial Revolution in France, namely the teeming slums which grew up around the great cities, populated by labourers newly arrived from the provinces in search of work and by those displaced from renovated urban centres. In that sense, the characters of *L'Assommoir* are the products of an era, as well as of a milieu more specifically described, giving substance to his notion of a 'social history' beyond the 'brackets' of the Second Empire alone.

Yet what the reception of the novel also reminds us of is that to study such a sociological phenomenon, whether in fiction or in a treatise, was to open up what was known as 'the question of the working class', a nineteenth-century topic so fraught with ideological tensions that a declared neutrality or objectivity of stance was seldom taken at face value. Before *L'Assommoir* Zola had already gained a certain notoriety as a writer unwilling to disguise physiological realities with conventional euphemisms. It is not by chance that it was this particular novel which radically changed both the tenor and the stakes of the critical debate at the heart of French cultural life for at least the next decade. For it was to accusations of the gross exaggerations of *L'Assommoir* that Zola mounted a defence based on the argument that the veracity of his descriptions was supported by published sources and his own empirical observations of the social worlds represented in his novels. Polemical pressures so vitiated Zola's accounts of his own achievement (with the strategic analogy of the novelist and natural scientist hardening into a militant Naturalism) that by 1880, in his best-known theoretical work, *Le Roman expérimental*, he was going so far as to claim that the documents assembled by Naturalist writers like himself were entirely responsible for the structure and content of their work: they both preceded the elaboration of character and plot, and were transposed so directly that the creative imagination was virtually redundant. Scholars with access to the preparatory notes for his novels have since shown the more dogmatic statements to be highly misleading, and intelligible only in a climate in which Zola was violently attacked for his depiction of unaesthetic physical appetites and social conditions. *L'Assommoir* was the test case, and as his opponents insisted that obscenity and bias resulted from a perverse and politically motivated representation of reality, so Zola found himself denying that any such distortion had taken place; quasi-scientific evidence, he asserted, was the cornerstone of his objective realism.

As far as the documentation of *L'Assommoir* is concerned, we know (from the preparatory dossier of the novel preserved in the Bibliothèque Nationale in Paris) that Zola had recourse to a number of books which provided him with specialist information. He consulted medical texts describing the pathology of chronic alcoholism; he copied out long lists of working-class slang, culled mainly from Alfred Delvau's *Dictionnaire de la langue verte* (1866); and he carefully annotated Denis Poulot's *Question sociale. Le Sublime ou le travailleur comme il est en* 1870 *et ce qu'il peut être* (1870). From this he drew details of the habits and leisure activities of the working class as well as a range of proletarian types. And, notebook in hand, Zola visited the future setting of the novel, returning with vivid sketches of streets, shops, dance-halls, and taverns. Yet such research merely supplemented a personal experience which considerably pre-dates the preparation of *L'Assommoir*. For when he himself had first arrived in Paris from Aix-en-Provence in 1859, he had lived in some of the poorest streets of the Latin Quarter, and over the next ten years had moved to a succession of less than salubrious addresses. In 1869 he had conceived his novel about the working class as 'the novel in the Batignolles', the very district (on the edge of the present-day seventeenth *arrondissement*) in he which he was then living. Only when he set to work on *L'Assommoir* in August 1875 did he decide to set it somewhat

further east, in an area of the city in which not even impover-
ished artists set up home. In addition to a familiarity with such
neighbourhoods, Zola's career as a journalist since the early
1860s had also brought him into contact with the burning issues
of the day, amongst which were figuring with increasing
prominence the unattended problems posed by urban poverty.
A number of his own articles in the opposition press after 1868
forcefully evoke the dehumanizing squalor of parts of the
capital, and his bourgeois readers' implied ignorance of such
unpalatable realities anticipates the deliberately eye-opening
perspectives informing *L'Assommoir*. What might be termed
this 'prehistory' of the novel explains both its inclusion in his
1869 prospectus for the Rougon–Macquart series and why he
was able to imagine its outline well before embarking on his
documentation. From the earliest stages of his planning, the
disintegration of a family is built into its narrative direction; and
notes dating from 1871–2 already contain in embryo many of
the novel's major scenes, framed by the intention to dramatize
the humble pleasures and intolerable suffering of working men
and women. To restore Zola's documentation to its secondary
position in the genesis of *L'Assommoir* is to underline further
his creative achievement. For whether we compare it with
other texts on the same theme, with his annotations, or even
with the most meticulous of his chapter-plans, there remains a
remarkable imaginative distance between preliminary draft and
finished novel.

On 13 April 1876, barely eight months after Zola had started
work on *L'Assommoir*, its serialization began in *Le Bien public*,
only to come to an abrupt halt at the beginning of June. The
last seven chapters appeared not in this daily newspaper, but in
a weekly literary review, *La République des lettres*, between 9
July 1876 and 7 January 1877. The reason for this extraordinary
transfer in mid-publication was, as Zola himself explained, that
the novel had revealed itself to be too disappointingly uncom-
mitted for the left-wing *Bien public*, founded by the radical
politician Yves Guyot. *La République des lettres*, on the other
hand, was a highbrow journal (directed by the writer Catulle
Mendès) amongst whose contributors were to be found

the avant-garde of contemporary novelists and poets. The curious circumstances of *L'Assommoir*'s publication are thus properly symptomatic, uneasily positioned as it has often been seen to be between political equivocation and artistic self-sufficiency.

In 1876–7 the novel was thought to be so ambiguous that, while conservative critics were divided over whether Zola was a dangerous socialist or providing them with evidence that uneducated workers were unfit to vote, their left-wing opponents lamented the fact that *L'Assommoir* painted the working class in so unflattering a light. Marxist critics of the 1930s simply accused its author of a dereliction of intellectual duty in failing to insert appalling social conditions within the dynamic of class conflict. Even today it is not uncommon to find analyses of the novel which criticize Zola not just for a paternalist discourse characteristic of the 'respectable bourgeois' (p. 4) he professed to be, but also, and perhaps above all, for leaving politics *per se* out of *L'Assommoir* altogether. For this apparent omission is often cited as being consistent with the ideologically suspect position of explaining proletarian suffering in the language of environment and heredity rather than in terms of the causal mechanisms of political systems.

The reader cannot help noticing, indeed, that political realities in the novel seldom *seem* more than a distorted echo in the shape of apocryphal stories (p. 242), unseen riots (p. 108), unconfirmed sightings of the Emperor (p. 375), and reports of vacuously radical meetings attended by Lantier off-stage (p. 245). This is partly a consequence of the pedagogic divisions of Zola's series, organized as 'studies' of different strata of society. More problematic is a note of 1872 in which he envisages within his novel-cycle, to go alongside *L'Assommoir*, 'a second novel about the working class of a particularly political nature', thus signalling the postponement of the latter until the writing of *Germinal*. It is implicitly repeated in the work-notes for *L'Assommoir* when he refers to the fact that 'the novel about Gervaise is not the political novel, but the novel of working-class manners'. That such a distinction is not clear-cut, however, is suggested by the last (and rarely cited) part of this interior monologue when Zola admits to himself that 'there will

necessarily be a political dimension, but in the background and
to a limited extent.'

It can be argued, in fact, that as well as reflecting that
afterthought, *L'Assommoir* is a highly coded text, whose political dimension is suppressed and repressed, and yet which is
nowhere more visible, paradoxically, than where it seems to be
representationally out of sight. That argument is less opaque if
we move back from its appearance in volume form in January
1877, and think of it rather as a text of 1875, by the end of
which its first three chapters had been completed. Only in the
light of that factual readjustment is it possible to consider
L'Assommoir as a book determined by the very specific prevailing conditions of its writing, themselves identifiable in its
textual fabric: in its thematized and disguised allusions, and in
its ironic devaluations and telling silences.

For it is worth remembering that at this time, and certainly
in 1875, writing was a highly problematic activity. If the
Commune of 1871 had convinced Zola that working-class
politics would have to figure in his series at some stage, this
revolution also provided the founders of the Third Republic
with the most authoritarian of mandates to impose law and
order. During what is thus known as the 'Ordre moral'
(translated by Marshal MacMahon into its most severe phase
after May 1873), all writers were viewed as potentially subversive, and scriptural repression was taken to obsessive lengths. At
the ludicrous end of the spectrum, Casanova's *Memoirs* were
judged to be 'politically incorrect' and even La Fontaine's
Fables were banned; at the other, proscription, exile, and
censorship were the order of the day. It is hardly necessary to
fill in the details of emblematic constructions like the Sacré
Cœur, or the continuing state of emergency which justified the
deportation of yet another shipload of *communards* to New
Caledonia as late as February 1876. The pertinence of the
systematic constraints placed on writing at this time is that
these are inseparable from the strategic forms adopted by
intellectual expression from within a culture for which Stend-
hal's famous warning (of politics in a novel being like a
pistol-shot in the middle of a concert) seemed to have a
renewed topicality. An understanding of that informing context

suggests that structural imperatives alone are insufficient to explain Zola's decision not to give politics a central place in *L'Assommoir*. As he wrote many years later: 'it was only at the time of *L'Assommoir* that, being *unable* to include in that book the political and, above all, the social role of the worker, that I resolved to leave that subject for another novel'.[3] To underline the impotence of 'being unable' is also to focus on the pragmatism which marks the novel's elaboration.

What characterizes the response of writers to such forbidden territory is what might be called a strategy of displacement— literally, of course, to or from London or Geneva, and especially Belgium (where the editor of *La République des Lettres* had it in mind to publish several instalments of *L'Assommoir* of a transgressive kind), but also, more interestingly, a displacement to the domain of the historian. This is simply because the historian has the prestige of his work enhanced—spuriously or not—by a scientific apparatus which allows the recounting of acceptable revisionist versions of an archival past. Thus an authorized text of 1873 is *Les Crimes politiques de Napoléon III* (by J.F.G. de Vezzani); a grander example is Taine's *Origines de la France contemporaine*, the first volume of which appeared in 1875-6. While the subtitle of Zola's series registers genuine historical ambitions, at least one sharp-eyed reviewer of the early *Rougon–Macquart* quickly grasped that it also cleverly testified to apparently objective credentials. If the Second Empire's demise had deflated the polemical thrust of *La Fortune des Rougon* (which recalled the criminal beginnings of that regime), the novel's 1871 preface was careful to guarantee that both text and series would deal with 'a dead reign'. Four years later, Zola could get away with his study of imperial politics, *Son Excellence Eugène Rougon*, for the same reason, its satirical intentions being overlaid with the official anxiety which had allowed its author to publicize *La Fortune des Rougon* in the press as 'virtually a topical work, at this time of Bonapartist conspiracy'. It is exactly in this kind of superimposition of

---

[3] In a letter to Jacques van Santen Kolff of 6 Oct. 1889 (my emphasis); see Zola's *Correspondance*, ed. B.H. Bakker (Montreal: Les Presses de L'Université de Montréal, and Paris: Éditions du CNRS 1978–), vi. 422–3.

time-frames which effects an allegorization of history that the displacement of political reflection can both assert and deny its interdiction.

Zola's work-notes for *L'Assommoir* reveal that he originally thought of giving his characters rather more defined political attitudes than they are left with in the novel we now read. They also alert us to unsuspected aspects of the text. Monsieur Poisson is not merely the representative of imperial authority; he is also the figure representing the Emperor himself in caricatural form, as André Gill recognized in his own caricatural duplication of this particular 'Badinguet' (p. 242) for the illustrated edition of *L'Assommoir* in 1878. From the character's physical features (which are remarkably similar to those in Zola's other portraits of Napoleon III in *Les Rougon–Macquart*), to his unthinking respect for the printed word (p. 243), to the apocryphal inversion of the Emperor as *sergent de ville* (i.e. a policeman) in London (p. 242) and Poisson's status as Bonapartist spokesman and defender, such substitutions appear to secure within a satirical perspective a politics of the past. They are underscored by images of imperial debauchery and Lantier's prediction of its central protagonist's imminent demise: 'I haven't told you, Badingue,' he shouted, 'I saw your boss yesterday in the Rue de Rivoli. He looks as haggard as the devil, I wouldn't give him more than six months' (p. 375). So too, in Zola's notes at least, there is an attempt to integrate political chronology and family destinies: Coupeau's decline is charted from 1850 to 1869, and 'the downfall of a family' (using the historically specific term *débâcle*) is calibrated with critical dates such as 1866, when Nana symbolically rejects domestic authority: 'I want to situate her episode in 1866, when the downfall began. And it will be at that moment that the important parts of the book will take place.'

On the one hand, therefore, *L'Assommoir* is a self-censoring text. Zola ultimately leaves out his early reminder to himself to include 'a photograph of a man killed on the barricades in forty-eight, sustaining the family's revolutionary hatred'. There is no mention of the fact that in 1848 barricades had been erected in the Rue de la Goutte d'Or itself, less than two years before the novel begins. Instead it transposes and relegates to the margins its overt 'political dimension'. And wisely so, it should be stressed, given Zola's reputation as a dangerously radical neo-Communard, and the radically dangerous subject he intended to treat. On the other hand, the very imprecision of the novel's historical references may well have contributed to *L'Assommoir*'s reception, not least because the period 1871-5 bore an uncanny resemblance, in the collective imagination, to the post-1848 political history it was now officially free to reject.

One way to negotiate this provocative terrain—which is the journalistic equivalent of historical allegorization—was to adopt the indirections of what the proscribed writer Jules Vallès called the 'allusionists'. This was a practice in which Zola himself had served an invaluable apprenticeship on the staff of opposition newspapers surviving on the precarious line between self-regulation and the Censor's terminal displeasure. Such an art of allusion is, of necessity, equivocal, both recuperable to the safety of historical distance and yet connotative for the present. And in *L'Assommoir* it takes a number of inventive forms. A passing mention of Eugène Sue's election to the Assembly in 1850 (p. 7), for example, refers to a 'red-scare' panic of such a long time ago, all but forgotten were it not for Victor Hugo's analogous re-entry on to the democratic stage on 30 January 1876. This is also true of other dates in the text, like the *coup d'état* (p. 108). At one level, these function as chronological markers; but they are resonant ones, nevertheless, within the contemporary questioning of political freedom and the power of the State. The novel's anti-clerical mockery ('that bunch of Latin-spewing fakes' (p. 307)) lies in the shadow of the law of 12 July 1875 reinforcing the status of the Church. So too, in the interpolated socio-political comments mouthed by the characters, there is the possibility of slippage. This applies to Legitimist pretensions (p. 87) and more disguised hopes for the restoration of the Monarchy up until 1877, or Coupeau's castigation of every kind of regime: 'Let 'em have anyone they fancy, a king, an emperor, nothin' at all, it won't stop me earnin' me five francs' (p. 87). And there is slippage too between the figurative (Lantier and Virginie 'as if they were on thrones' (p. 372) as they watch Gervaise scrubbing) and the burlesque (Coupeau 'sitting on the throne' (p. 337) in the asylum), with royalism as the target of both. The public meetings to which only Zola's notes refer become the dispersed locations of Lantier's absences; but they are also reassembled in the novel's recurrent *fêtes*, the metaphor of February 1848, and especially, of course, of the joyous disorder of the Commune. Linked to this aspect of *L'Assommoir* are its songs, many of which are not only highly coded and subversive refrains, but also often drawn from a repertoire banned both during the Second Empire and the period 1872–6. Singing, at this time, was not an innocent activity; for the Commune itself was sufficient to remind the authorities of the dangers of collective grievances being articulated in harmony. Even the Vendôme column scaled by Gervaise and her friends (p. 80) seems like a less than innocuous tourist destination, as Bec-Salé's later swagger ('he could have pounded the Vendôme column as flat as a pancake' (p. 167)) makes clear; readers of *L'Assommoir* were unlikely to have forgotten that its destruction on 16 May 1871 was one of the most ritualized moments of the very revolution the 'Ordre moral' was designed to erase from public consciousness. And if that is preceded by an equally memorable fictional visit to the Louvre, we should not make the mistake of thinking of the characters' outing from the slums as simply an excursion to a splendid art gallery. For the scene represents a visit to the historic and political heart of France as it was; and in a highly political space, both before and after 1870, the wedding-party confronts that most politicized of paintings, Géricault's *The Raft of the Medusa*, whose subject and compositional structure make of it a mirror of *L'Assommoir* itself.

That particular episode is brought to an end by powerful voices (p. 79), by the forces of law and order, in a text in which disorder is only just kept in check. Monsieur Poisson's is far from being the the sole authoritarian profile. Such agents are discreetly spaced across the book as a whole, variegated through museum guards, bailiffs (p. 283) and institutional officials who speak to Gervaise in a 'rough' manner likened to that of a 'policeman' (p. 429). They are the representatives of the official order, reflected in 'a big engraving' on the Coupeaus' walls 'of some field marshal cavorting about, baton in hand, between a cannon and a pile of shot' (p. 98). Under *Marshal*

MacMahon's 'Ordre moral', that seems at least as double-edged as Lorilleux's grotesque championing of 'le bon ordre'. As far as the police themselves are concerned, at a deceptively anecdotal level Zola shows them upholding the moral codes of the street (p. 314) and keeping the pavement clear (p. 315); they are the guardians of property (p. 370), picking up shoplifters (p. 301) and the 'trash' of society (p. 374), closing down shady cafés (p. 408), functioning as the last line of defence against incest (p. 275) and domestic violence (p. 191). Their presence in *L'Assommoir* is so pervasive that the 'all-seeing eye' becomes a forceful image in its own right. Even in quite different contexts, the gaze and features of other characters—themselves collectively 'scared of the law' (p. 272)—are compared to those of policemen. It seems hardly a coincidence that two policemen should appear at the end of Gervaise's feast. But it is also interesting that they do not negate the disorder they police. The feast remains a moment in the experience of the working-class characters beyond political control: 'Paris belonged to you. . . . Right now, fr'instance, wasn't it true they didn't give a damn about the Emperor?' (p. 216). And this could well be juxtaposed to the question asked of *L'Assommoir* by Albert Millaud, one of Zola's most vituperative critics: 'What would M. Zola say if a dramatist paraded . . . every form of human infamy for four acts, leaving it to the fifth to fill the stage with policemen? It's highly probable that the audience would have walked out without waiting for the expiatory conclusion.' It may well be significant that Zola leaves the reader of this novel with the prediction that 'the policeman was going to lose his job' (p. 433).

Nor does it seem by chance that *L'Assommoir* should parody censorship itself, just after Zola had published an article on the subject in *Le Sémaphore de Marseille* (July 1875). It is, after all, the overarching allusion of all the 'allusionists' sidestepping the Censor. The censoring activities of the aptly-named Madame Lerat are thus precisely those of the official arbiters Zola would often accuse of 'a preoccupation with filth verging on the sadistic'. She warns against moral dangers with as little effect as she defends Nana's virtue, and both represents and imposes a linguistic propriety at odds with her prurience: 'as long as you avoided crude words you could say anything you liked' (p. 357). Anticipating his own language's reception while performatively challenging such hypocrisy, here again Zola offers his readers the most unreassuring of reassurances.

L'Assommoir also has to be considered within that more far-reaching strategy which seeks to protect the freedom of contemporary artistic expression by maintaining the distinction between politics and literature. Even when proposing his novel-series to his publisher in 1868-9, Zola had been careful to spell out his intention to be 'merely an observer and artist rather than a socialist'. Thus all his attempts to offer reassurance about a study of the working class—from the bourgeois self-portrait in the novel's preface to its stress on philological experimenta-tion—invoke exclusively artistic criteria. He insists that 'my political opinions are not at issue', that the terrible suffering depicted needed no further commentary, that 'I am just the clerk of the court refusing to draw any conclusions from the evidence recorded'. While this last statement is addressed to the radical Guyot, it echoes the defence mounted against the conservative Millaud in September 1876: 'My novels refuse to come to any conclusions because I believe that it's not the business of the artist to do so.'

But to isolate that formula within repeated denials of *parti pris* is to be reminded of one other crucial influence on the author of *L'Assommoir* in the autumn of 1875, namely Zola's re-reading of Flaubert's *L'Éducation sentimentale* (1869). In the major study of it which he composed that November, Zola refers to his discovery of 'a new poetics', based on what he calls Flaubert's 'apparent disinterestedness'; as he puts it: 'you will search in vain for any conclusion or moral lesson drawn from the facts'. Between *L'Éducation sentimentale* and *L'Assommoir* there are a number of suggestive parallels. The most obvious is to be found in the final meeting between Goujet and Gervaise, where Zola's work-notes ('her hair is white. Too late') direct us to the corresponding encounter between Frédéric and Mme Arnoux; nor should we forget Flaubert's own ever-present *sergents de ville*, who are known as 'les assommeurs'. For *L'Éducation sentimentale* functions, above all, as a model of writing about politics, with its cynical opportunists and political agitators, its revolutionary dreamers and its own proletarian euphoria embraced by an authorial irony which highlights different political points of view while overtly subscribing to none.

What is less certain is whether, in Zola's case too, an aesthetic of impersonality could be construed as an attitude of genuine indifference. The contemporary divorce between politics and culture begs the sort of questions which later persuaded a writer as committed as Vallès that Zola, by contrast, was a man of letters. Indeed, in an 1879 review of the former's *Jacques Vingtras*, Zola expresses the view that Vallès himself should have left 'politics to those who are failed artists', on the comprehensively Flaubertian grounds that 'politics, in these disturbing times, is the preserve of the impotent and the mediocre'. In *L'Assommoir*, Zola's analogous *reductio ad absurdum* of every political voice in the spectrum has often been criticized, even when qualified by the recognition that he thereby underlines the working–class political apathy registered by his principal historical sources. To insist upon that apathy in a novel about alcoholism is nevertheless to refuse to subscribe to the premise of the Commissions d'Enquêtes (into the causes of the Commune) investigating the links between literal and political intoxication.[4] And it should also be noted that the antithetical distribution of political attitudes among his fictional characters provides Zola with a remarkable freedom. For if it undercuts Lantier's self-serving radicalist clap-trap, it simultaneously devalues his allowable derision at the expense of 'a hopeless bunch of republicans [in the Chamber], those bleeding parasites on the left' (p. 264). The effect of these self-cancelling ironies is to delineate an authorial silence. That may be thought of as a ludic detachment; but it is certainly a refusal to play with the profoundly meaningless political labels of the time. 'Politics is nothin' but a big joke!' (p. 87). Coupeau's unthinking phrase is also, perhaps, Zola's own considered view.

---

[4] See Susanna Barrows, 'After the Commune: Alcoholism, Temperance and Literature in the Early Third Republic', in *Consciousness and Class Experience in Nineteenth-Century Europe*, ed. John M. Merriman (New York: Holmes and Meier, 1979).

The very intensity of the political outrage provoked by *L'Assommoir* is testimony to the unease created by these kinds of strategies. It was a hostility not moderated by the self-imposed editorial cuts the serial-contract allowed, Zola's supplementary prefatory reassurances, delays in the publication of the novel in volume-form as a result of the Censor's misgivings, or its sale being prohibited in station bookstalls. It should also be said that the polemical fury which promoted Zola to the rank of 'leader of the literary Commune' (according to one review of *L'Assommoir*) has had massive consequences for the way in which he is still read, notably in the separation of the mythico-poetic from the socio-political (a separation consecrated by the reception of *Germinal*)—which is to read his novels reassuringly out of context. In the particular case of *L'Assommoir*, published at that decisive turning-point of 1876-7, immediately prior to the resumption of political debate, it does seem inappropriate to condemn Zola for leaving politics in the margins.

We might ask instead to what extent his strategies are in fact the only way of writing about politics in a period in which political discourse is still impossible; impossible not only because of official constraints on the freedom of expression, but also because of the paradox that while (as Zola protests) 'politics is invading every aspect of daily life', with republican factions opposing each other in the name of the Republic, at the same time the floating political labels of the moment conspire to create an absence of substantive differentiation. And the kind of stance which perfectly corresponds to that crisis of definition may well be the authorial silence or indeterminacy we find in *L'Assommoir*. The most eloquent response to the proscribed celebration of the Fourteenth of July is Gambetta's analogous silence, refusing to publish his *République française* on that very day. That is not to suggest that, in Zola's case, this is a fully thought-out position; nor is it to deny that there are residual tensions and contradictions in the 'writing-in' and the 'writing-out' of the political margins of *L'Assommoir*. But discernible here, in the confrontation between his consciously non-political novel and the political context it refuses to take seriously, is a conjunction of discursive registers; and it seems to have been one, moreover, intuitively recognized by outraged critics of every party as being less a reflection of politics than the politics of a reflection.

At more than a hundred years' distance from the 'sound and fury' of *L'Assommoir*'s reception, today's reader of Zola's novel is more likely to be wholly engrossed in the vicissitudes of its heroine's personal story. And, indeed, no other volume in the Rougon–Macquart is so deliberately organized as a fictional biography, as is suggested by the fact that its original title was *The Simple Life of Gervaise Macquart*. Yet that should not cause us to lose sight of the fact that *L'Assommoir* has a historical interest of another kind, not least as one of the nineteenth-century's greatest novels about Paris itself. It provides us with a remarkable record, not just of the way of life of the urban poor (so detailed as to constitute a document of exceptional anthropological value), but also of a city now virtually transformed beyond recognition. The very processes of that transformation are alluded to within the novel. By its end, the encroaching geometry of Baron Haussmann's rebuilding of the capital is changing Gervaise's familiar territory into a 'huge crossing' (p. 406) of luxurious boulevards driven outwards through the city-walls, giving Paris its modern shape and leaving both the character and the reader with a sense of a world that has been lost.

The Rue de la Goutte d'Or still exists, of course, though the Rue Neuve which runs into it had its name changed to the Rue des Islettes in 1877. The appellation 'la goutte d'or' (or 'drop of gold') derives from the fifteenth-century hamlet on the same site, reputed for its golden white wine; and it is quite possible that Zola was aware of the tradition in his choice of these particular streets as the location for his study of a family turning to drink. The area in which the novel takes place corresponds to the south-eastern quarter of today's eighteenth *arrondissement*, hemmed in by the Gare du Nord and the edges of Montmartre, and bounded by the thoroughfares of the Rue Polonceau, the Boulevard de la Chapelle and the Boulevard Barbès, thus forming an enclave as it did during the Second Empire. It remains a bustling neighbourhood of the underprivileged, but now populated by North African immigrants. In newspaper reports on crime in the French capital, it is often singled out as being infested by drug-dealers; it is certainly not an area where readers of this translation will be made to feel welcome if they venture into it with camera in hand. The probable model for the Hôtel Boncœur is next door to 'Le Maghreb' and the site of old Colombe's Assommoir is occupied by a Tati department store.

The more fundamental difference is that, at the time the novel takes place, the district lay outside the city-boundary constituted by the octroi wall. Between the latter and the military fortifications (p. 71), beyond which lay the Saint-Denis plain, there was a heterogeneous zone of urban construction, cheap housing crammed along uncobbled streets, workshops and small factories, waste ground, places of popular entertainment, cemeteries and allotments, and even vestiges of countryside separating the sprawling suburbs from a Montmartre still rural enough to be considered a village. In the opening paragraphs of *L'Assommoir*, Gervaise looks out over the intersection of Paris proper and these outlying suburbs, and might be thought to be dominating the scene were it not for her apprehension of the city's 'heart of darkness'. Her disorientation at the end testifies not simply to a modified topography but also brings to a close her attempts to resist a fearful presence. Only once does she venture inwards, when she visits the Louvre after her wedding, and as this is signposted by 'monstrous creatures' (p. 75), so the ensuing labyrinthine experience is integral to a novel cast as an epic struggle between Gervaise and a devouring Parisian monster (p. 7). At the point, in Chapter XII, at which she registers her defeat, she nostalgically recalls outings within her own community's legitimate space, reminding the reader too of an urban reality only otherwise captured in sepia photographs or in Renoir's *Le Moulin de la Galette*. If that particular open-air dance-hall is mentioned in *L'Assommoir* (p. 256), so are countless others now forgotten, along with once well-known cafés, restaurants, taverns, theatres, wine-merchants, toll-houses, prisons, hospitals, slaughterhouses, the very markers of a mid-nineteenth century experience lived at an irremediable remove from the Paris we think we know.

Zola's achievement is to have constructed from this patently verifiable experience a work of art. His first biographer and devoted friend, Paul Alexis, recounts a discussion with him on the beach at Saint-Aubin during the planning of *L'Assommoir* in the summer of 1875. 'You see that,' Zola remarked pointing to the gentle curve of the horizon, 'I need something like that ... something utterly simple, a clear straight line'. He never lost sight of that ambition. It was in the interests of such clarity too, it could be argued, that the political dimension of the novel was much reduced. For the same reason he ultimately abandoned the ending he had first imagined, with its wildly melodramatic duel between Lantier and Goujet immediately following on from Gervaise's throwing vitriol at the former while Virginie, his mistress, lay dying in the courtyard. Instead he kept before him the reminder to himself to chart the *progressive* downfall of Gervaise Macquart, plotted and foretold in an inherently credible pattern of gradation. The reader pressed up close to her hopes and fears, to the prosaic details of the unbearable suffering she endures, may be only intermittently aware of *L'Assommoir*'s formal qualities. And yet it is precisely the novel's artistry, its thematic structuring and calculated symmetries, which makes its human drama so compelling. For what Zola has done is to shape the unadulterated realities of nineteenth-century working-class existence into a work characterized by an exceptional unity of design.

Amongst those realities, for example, few are more vividly conveyed than the filth and stench of the milieu Gervaise inhabits. This is a world of open sewers and overflowing drains, its streets turned to mud by the rain, its workshops filled with choking dust, its bars thick with rancid smoke. Nor is Zola's claim that *L'Assommoir* is the first novel which 'smells of the common people' an empty one. For it is pervaded by fetid odours: of unwashed bodies, vomit, bad breath, alcohol, the discharges of slaughterhouse and corpses. That this is the breeding-ground of respiratory diseases is as self-evident as the proximity of the Lariboisière Hospital, its halls reeking of illness and feverish secretions. It is in every way appropriate, therefore, that Zola should have chosen a laundress as his protagonist. For a quest for human dignity is thus enacted at the level of a desired cleanliness. It has also been shown, however, that the laundry itself occupies a double-edged place in the contemporary hygienist discourse which Zola's text so faithfully replicates in its detailing of a 'poisonous atmosphere'.[5] If recourse to it is morally positive, it is nevertheless singled out, in medical treatises on occupational hazards, as the particularly dangerous site of bacterial infection and noxious vapours. From such facts, as dreadful as they are banal, the novelist makes of Gervaise's shop the symbolic location of equally contradictory forces, a paradise of cleanliness regained as surely as the very conditions of that ideal imply its ultimate loss.

Gervaise's quest, however, is not limited to this doomed attempt to overcome the material squalor of her working-class environment. For it is inseparable from a larger dream, oft-repeated during the novel and ironically recalled at the point it can no longer be sustained: 'to be able to get on with her work, always have something to eat and a half-decent place to sleep, bring up her children properly, not to be beaten, and die in her own bed' (p. 421). The central element of this, translating as it does the French 'avoir un trou un peu propre pour dormir', overlays an escape from filth with the multiple connotations of a womb-like refuge, a beatitudinous state invulnerable to the pressures of the outside world. This is an unconscious obsession on the character's part, to the extent that when a sanctuary is threatened (as when the laundry is invaded by the neighbourhood (p. 187), or the intimacy of her feast in Chapter VII is opened up to the street), Gervaise seeks another, finding in Goujet's smithy 'her only refuge' (p. 189). But it is also the preoccupation which governs the narrative itself. It makes of *L'Assommoir* the novel of Gervaise's successive abodes, from her room in the Hôtel Boncœur (Chapters I–III), her home in the Rue Neuve (Chapter IV), her laundry (Chapters V–IX), the sixth-floor flat to which the Coupeaus have to move when they lose the shop (Chapters X–XIII), all the way to 'Père Bru's tiny hole' (p. 439) where she ends her days. These are the variations on the snug enclosure equated with Gervaise's happiness, ephemerally realized in the heavenly hues of a shop 'the colour of the sky' (p. 130) only to be cruelly travestied in a den under the stairs.

Such displacements chart a rise and fall symmetrically consistent with what one of Zola's contemporaries, his fellow-novelist George Moore, recognized as *L'Assommoir's* 'pyramid size'. And one of the finest modern studies of it has shown that its triangular shape (built around the apex of the seventh of its thirteen chapters) is enhanced by a thematic structure which provides a more subtle graph of Gervaise's struggle.[6] For if her ideal articulates an antithetical symbolic code (work, cleanliness, and self-control on the one hand, idleness, filth, and indulgence on the other), the novel not only moves from positive to negative values corresponding with the character's decline, but also inserts within the first half of the book the telling signs of a demise of which Gervaise herself is blissfully unaware. In that sense, *L'Assommoir* is shadowed by a tragic irony which reminds the reader, even in the midst of apparent triumphs, of its uncompromising title.

This can be more readily grasped if the other characters are also viewed as properly structural features of the work. Lantier, for example, is the epitome of the anti-values of the novel, with his laziness, his voracious appetites, and his trunk with its 'smell of a sloppy man' (p. 242). By contrast, Goujet is a model of abstinence and hard work, living in a home marvelled at by Gervaise, 'astonished at how clean it was' (p. 106). Zola's dispensing with his original idea of a duel between these two rivals for her affections leaves intact their function as the conflicting paths of Gervaise's destiny, while allowing the reader to measure the development of the Coupeau family against the opposing poles they represent. Thus Coupeau himself falls, not just from a roof, but from an exemplary industriousness to drunken idleness, anticipating Gervaise's own metaphorical descent from the values she once held dear. The minor characters too serve to reflect the curve of her life.

[6] See David Baguley, 'Event and Structure: the Plot of Zola's *L'Assommoir*', *Publications of the Modern Language Association*, XC (1975), 823–33.

The destitute housepainter, Père Bru, whose occupation ('whitewashing ceilings' (p. 188)) is clearly analogous to Gervaise's, becomes the mirror of her misfortune. And if Lalie Bijard also spends her brutalized life trying to keep things clean, her suffering and martyrdom similarly prefigure Gervaise's fate. Bazouge, the undertaker, the very incarnation of filth, with his invitations to renounce her quest in the enforced idleness of death, is a figure who both attracts and repulses her. Less obviously, perhaps, the lazy Virginie Poisson is Gervaise's double, taking over her lover and laundry (and letting it go to ruin for the same reasons), so that the fight between the two women in the wash-house at the beginning of the novel can be seen as symbolic of an inner struggle, with Gervaise's initial victory preparing us for the inevitability of the revenge which awaits her.

Inserted within the rising and falling movement of the novel as a whole, there is a thematic interplay of details no less foreboding. In the depths of her despair, towards the end of Chapter XII, Gervaise takes 'her final walk, between the blood-drenched yards where the slaughtering went on and the dimly-lit wards where death laid out your stiffened corpse in a common shroud' (p. 414). Yet that space that 'had encompassed her life' is the object of her gaze in the novel's opening pages, with the landmarks of hospital and slaughterhouse as unambiguously ominous as the stream of dirty water in the alleyway or the stain left by Lantier in the washbasin (p. 33). Even as she starts her new life with Coupeau in Chapter III, a less idyllic future is prefigured, and not just in the storm which threatens to spoil her wedding-day (pp. 70-1), or her first encounter with Bazouge and his ominous predictions (p. 95). For the visit to the Louvre, in the same chapter, provides us with a particularly suggestive example of the ways in which even episodes apparently removed from the claustrophobic darkness of the Rue de la Goutte d'Or reinforce the novel's overall design.

Indeed, one could go rather further and argue that the Louvre scene mirrors the texture of *L'Assommoir* as a whole. Superficially there is a blatant opposition between the official history and the daily grind: between monumental cleanliness and *faubourg* squalor, domestic constriction and public space; between 'clear and shiny' parquet floors (p. 76) and the encrusted boards Gervaise scrubs humiliatingly on her hands and knees; between the 'place full of gold' (p. 55) *not* found in the Rue de la Goutte d'Or and the lavish display of 'gilding' (p. 76) in the Louvre. But the wedding-party's itinerary is also reduplicative. Their destination, reached down the same alimentary canal which swallows up the workers, and traversed back and forth along its East-West axis, merely magnifies Gervaise's 'intersection' (p. 134) of work and leisure in her own *quartier*. The enormous building she inhabits there, with its entrails likened to 'the very heart of a city' (p. 46), has its own 'interminably bare' walls (p. 44) and a 'dim courtyard with its paving stones so badly worn it could have been a public square' (p. 126). This microcosm of the city, 'the size of a small town, with its streets of stairs and passages that went stretching on and criss-crossing for ever' (p. 126), thus reflects the Louvre topography the characters are unable to negotiate. That disorientation is precisely anticipated by Gervaise's guided visit to the Lorilleux 'down the endless spiral' of 'echoing corridors' (pp. 53–4): 'the wall turning round and round and those glimpses of people's homes following one upon another were making her head spin'. Monsieur Madinier's charges in the Louvre hurry past as many rooms and images barely sighted until overcome by 'a confusion of people and things in such a busy riot of colours that everyone was beginning to get a nasty headache' (p. 77). Unifying thematic patterns, working across the spatially alternating warp of street and interior which structures *L'Assommoir*, are thereby woven from a common fund of metaphor.

The Louvre episode, however, is privileged by its position at the end of the novel's exposition, and it echoes with 'the trampling of a stampeding herd' (p. 78) with which the text opens (p. 7) and draws to a close (p. 408). The scene looks both forward and back, generated by passages just written and itself obliquely evoked in retrospect, as Gervaise repeats her labyrinthine wanderings in the midst of coloured posters which catch her eye (p. 411). It stands between complementary ceremonies of a wedding and a funeral, equally mistimed, gaped at, marked by a misunderstanding of protocol and the incomprehension of a dead language, leaving their participants summarily dismissed, out on the street. It was to an unpromising tomb in Père Lachaise that the wedding-party had also thought of going (p. 72), and the bride-to-be is likened to a neighbour recently deceased (p. 60). The clocks of mortality which chime through *L'Assommoir* strike four o'clock at the Louvre to signal only the first of those expulsions threatened by Monsieur Marescot (p. 322) and, more terminally, by Bazouge. If the episode's pivotal status is underscored by the comparison between the Salon Carré and a church (p. 76), it is fitting that Coupeau should rail against his enforced immobility as being 'stuck there like a mummy' (p. 121). For there are telling shudders (pp. 75, 78) in the presence of archaeological relics and lifeless creatures with 'death masks'. Related to such dissolution, the most striking note introduced by the visit to the Louvre remains the unmaking of people and things. The episode is later replayed with astonishing precision, even in its tempo, in the spectacle of Nana and her friends (pp. 153–4), racing 'helter-skelter' and 'barging sideways through groups' (p. 351) as the wedding-party had flown on through the Tuileries gardens. Their progress is charted in the fragmentation of physical unity and collective purpose, and in a dismemberment which corresponds to their own metonymic focus on bodily parts in the paintings they see. In the references to corporeal mutilation (pp. 192, 252) and broken statues (p. 242), and in the disintegration of conviviality (p. 92), dirty laundry (p. 245), and Gervaise herself (p. 277), the accelerating disorder unleashed here ripples outwards through the novel.

What is more, many of *L'Assommoir*'s principal motifs are encoded in the artistic works foregrounded by the text, notably in the triptych formed by Géricault's *Raft of the Medusa*, Veronese's *Wedding at Cana*, and Rubens's *Kermesse*. These have been identified as a 'translation into art of certain of the narrative's obsessive themes',[7] aligned into an ambiguous spec-

---

[7] Phillip Duncan, 'Oracular Paintings in Zola's *L'Assommoir*', in *French Literature and the Arts*, ed. P. Crant, University of South Carolina French Literature Series, V (1978), 173–8.

trum ranging from voracity to transcendence, and interrelated by the eating which marks the successive phases of Gervaise's destiny. This interpretation only makes sense if we view the great feast of Chapter VII as an occasion when Gervaise herself is figuratively consumed; and it depends crucially on the *Raft of the Medusa* being associated with cannibalism, the most shocking feature of the 1816 event on which it is based, but one eliminated from the final version of the painting. What is certain is that the Géricault confirms the predictive mal-evolence, in the shape of sphinxes and funereal gloom, which immediately precedes it. In an enduring image of human despair marginalizing a remote glimpse of hope, this painting points not only to a bleak future but also to the illusory 'escape' to the Louvre during which it is seen. As far as the Veronese is concerned, however appropriate it may seem in the context of a wedding, it only assumes its importance in contradistinc-tion to the Rubens. The latter's celebration of carnality and inebriation, irrecuperable to moral judgement, social forms, and temporal constraints, will be concretized in the banquets of *L'Assommoir*, both on the day of the wedding and (especially) in Chapter VII. But the *Kermesse* refers us to other textual moments too. Also well-known under its alternative title of *The Village Feast*, it speaks of Gervaise's ideal of pastoral liberation, grotesquely mimed in her courtship with Goujet on the 'last remaining strip of green' behind Montmartre (pp. 251–5). Amongst the 'smutty details' spotted by Boche, 'someone puking' (p. 78) looks forward to Coupeau's fateful vomiting, as the 'red faces' jumping about (p. 231) at the end of the novel's central chapter seem to step out of Rubens's frenzied dance. The two textual segments are linked by the scandalized reaction to Clémence's 'showing off everything she'd got' (p. 232) and the sarcastic 'Well! This 'ere's a fine lot, I must say' which greets the double 'voiding' of the *Kermesse*. Approached in their 'funny carnival costumes' (p. 74), the Louvre opens up the carnivalesque dimension of *L'Assommoir* noted by the most stimulating of its commentators, inspired by Bakhtin.[8] If the

[8] See David Baguley, 'Rite et tragédie dans *L'Assommoir*', *Les Cahiers naturalistes*, LII (1978), 80–96.

characters remain bewildered by masterpieces perceived only at
the level of overt subject, the reader is alerted to their significance by the narrative sequence of the guided tour. For we are
taken from the upright configurations of the sacred in the
Wedding at Cana to the circular dynamic of the *Kermesse*. It is
the rhythm internal to both orgies of gluttony and characteristic
of the degradation between and beyond them. Whether or not
Gervaise's miraculous six extra bottles (p. 217) catches the
biblical allusion,[9] the progressive desacralization ensures that
the thirteen at dinner (twelve went to the museum) replace
Christ with a goose as the object of reverence, and that her final
meal with Goujet is a travesty of the Last Supper. As they go
rollicking through the Louvre 'clump[ing] their heels on the
noisy floors' (p. 78), it is the rhythm of the visitors' disrespect
and the rising cadence of Zola's own description.

   Such textual reverberations, most consciously declared
through ironic recall, serve to bind together disparate narrative
segments. Their prefigurative weight makes it decidedly and,
through accretion, increasingly unlikely that Gervaise's ideal
will be realized. That is not to deny that the chapters elaborat-
ing her fresh start in life (in the appropriately named Rue
Neuve) have an almost lyrical energy. 'Four years of hard work'
(p. 95) are filled with laughter, friendship, and solidarity, the
purposeful enjoyment of uncomplicated times. Yet long before
the culmination of this joyous mood in Chapter VII, there is no
mistaking the presages of doom. The fragility of Gervaise's
hopes is brought into dramatic relief by Coupeau's accident;
and, above all, it is her own willing exposure to the anaesthe-
tizing effects of that other *assommoir* which her laundry itself
becomes which signals future reversals. Nowhere does Zola
underline this more explicitly than when she weakly submits to
her husband's drunken attentions: 'She relaxed in his arms,
dazed by the slight vertigo from the piles of washing and not
in the least put off by Coupeau's boozy breath. And the
smacking kiss they gave one another full on the mouth,
surrounded by all the filth of her trade, was like a first step

---

[9] See John 2: 1–10, on 'the six stone water jars . . . turned into wine!'.

along their slow decline into depravity' (p. 144). Though we may feel that such authorial didacticism is redundant, the tragic force of *L'Assommoir* depends on this 'fatal flaw' in its heroine to complement her status as the passive victim of external circumstances.

The tension between these agents in her downfall is most clearly visible in her saint's day feast. For if preparations for the high point of her fortunes are overshadowed by threats of imminent disruption, Lantier's fortuitous return is less insidious than the self-respect forfeited by allowing Coupeau to bring him in, turning a customer away, resorting to the pawnshop in order to purchase more wine, and surrendering to both a physical and moral torpor induced by uninhibited indulgence. Thrift, propriety, and willpower are corroded, not by envy or malice, but by the very goodheartedness which makes Gervaise so sympathetic a character. This is thus another chapter which perfectly synthesizes *L'Assommoir*'s extended design, moving from a precarious harmony to the abdication of all semblance of control.

The second half of the novel takes this movement to its logical conclusion. It is punctuated by more discontinuous reassertions of Gervaise's original ambitions, but these now form the benchmark of her decline. When she is drawn to Lantier's bed, for example, it is bitterly ironic that it is Coupeau lying in his vomit across her own which revives her quest for cleanliness (p. 269). So too attempts to exert parental discipline on Nana, by reference to the family values Gervaise had championed, are gradually overtaken by indifference. More consistently, but equally integrative in terms of the novel's organic unity, each and every element of her ideal is inverted. She wallows in filth ('the dirt itself was like a cosy nest it was lovely to snuggle into' (p. 282)) and idleness; she goes into debt and lets both her person and her surroundings fall apart; she starts to drink inside Colombe's Assommoir, where previously she had remained outside on the pavement; sleeping with Lantier precisely contradicts her earlier disapproval of infidelity (p. 50); she is beaten often; she becomes the object of communal derision where once she had held her head up high.

Nor can the reader fail to notice how even the weather takes a turn for the worse. Earlier gay and sunlit scenes give way to grey skies and rain-drenched streets, as surely as the Coupeaus' dingy room is a sad reminder of their bright apartment. Seen from the distance of critical analysis, such novelistic techniques and repetitions may seem as artificial as they are heavy with symbolic import. Such is our involvement in Gervaise's plight, however, not least as a result of a narrative perspective increasingly angled through her own point of view, that the sombre colours seem utterly in keeping with *L'Assommoir*'s development. For this traces a decomposition more pervasive than the heroine's progressive loss of human dignity. If the stages of Coupeau's alcoholism, interspersed by remissions which merely postpone his death throes, prefigure Gervaise's animalization, this drama is contextualized by others: the deaths of Maman Coupeau, Lalie Bijard, Père Bru, and Madame Goujet; the definitive departures of Lantier and Nana; the breakup of a family and a community. The book becomes an unremitting catalogue of misery, starvation, and pain, recounted in the most distressingly minute detail. While Gervaise's attempts to prostitute herself are the pathetic counterpoint to Nana's rising star, the supreme humiliation is to be found in her death. But even here, it should be noted, Zola takes care to bring full circle his novel's dominant themes. As the grotesque obverse of her quest, Gervaise consumes filth and becomes a rotting object (p. 439), while her soliciting Bazouge to carry her off makes of her original ideal of a clean place in which to sleep a death-wish ultimately realized. She ends her days in suffering utterly disproportionate to the causes of her personal failure. The tragic dimension of *L'Assommoir* is inseparable from our sense of a preordained design taken to such a conclusion and the paradoxical 'satisfaction' generated by the text's inner necessity.

One of the many reasons why *L'Assommoir* is so fiendishly difficult to translate is Zola's extensive use of working-class slang. French editions of the novel invariably include a glossary to assist the modern reader in this respect. But this is not a problem which simply reflects a historical distance from a language which was once familiar. For contemporaries too were so unprepared for this that several reviewers suggested that the novel was accessible only to a working-class audience. Zola's admission, in his preface, that 'people were angered by words' (p. 3) is something of an understatement. Critics denounced not only unintelligible colloquialisms, but also verbal obscenities and sexual puns equally unprecedented in a nineteenth-century novel. Masked behind the hysteria of this reception there was, indeed, a discernible anxiety, crystallized in Edmond de Goncourt's recognition of Zola's 'deliberate refusal to write in a literary style'. And the latter's denial, in terms of *L'Assommoir*'s philological appeal to 'linguistic researchers' (p. 3), is undoubtedly less eloquent than the now-famous inscription in the copy of the novel he sent to Flaubert: 'en haine du goût' points to the book itself as nothing less than 'a challenge to good taste'. It remains to be asked whether in fact *L'Assommoir* is as radical, in cultural terms, as this might suggest.

To put this question in another way (reformulating it within the novel's own terms of reference), where does *L'Assommoir* situate itself in relation to the artistic tradition exemplified by the works in the Louvre? For if, as has already been suggested, its representation functions as a matrix of thematic and symbolic codes, it is also an emblematic space in which *L'Assommoir* defines its own originality. And central to this is its potential destabilization of our own vantage-point. While the language of the novel is the most visible question mark over the cultural certainties from which we read, other popular forms assert their validity. There is an alternative pictorial tradition, for example, in the contemplation of images on the street (pp. 355, 409). The walls of Goujet's room are 'covered in pictures' (p. 279): 'all over the walls, pictures, cut-out figures, coloured prints secured with four nails, and portraits of all kinds of people taken from illustrated papers' (p. 106); and he cuts some out for Gervaise, as the youngest Bijard children do for themselves (pp. 398–402). The 'not very good painting' (p. 107) of Goujet's father is morally instructive. Others are merely decorative: on wallpaper, cardboard boxes, and shop-fronts. They allow the characters to visualize, even in the most rudimentary form, their dreams and experiences. Exemplified by Lantier's engravings (p. 243), they are as authoritative as books but less demanding than reading: 'in the evenings it tired [Goujet] to read, so he'd amuse himself looking at his pictures' (p. 106). What it is important to notice is that these offset the imagistic complex in the Louvre. The contrast, however, is one of register rather than representation, a substitution of one set of portraits, busts (p. 242), and rustic icons (p. 134) for another. Between the Pascal and the Béranger on the one hand, and the Géricault and the Rubens on the other, there is a symmetry ('the one serious, the other smiling' (p. 98)) not confined to the top of Gervaise's cupboard.

Our implied superiority is, at best, insecure. From a world apart, Gervaise and her friends stumble through a totally unintelligible script, symbolically announced to us by the 'Phœnician characters' (p. 76) they cannot decipher. They are mocked, it can be argued, from the point of view of the regular visitor with whom the reader is complicitous. Our enjoyment of the episode is certainly enhanced if we inhabit a cultural frame of reference wide enough to embrace Monsieur Madinier's incompetence within Zola's elliptical, ironic structure. But our unambiguous mirth at his expense does depend on knowing that Titian's *Young Woman at her Toilet* (with Venetian auburn rather than yellow hair) is not *La Belle Ferronnière* (by Leonardo), and that the lady in question was reputed to be the mistress not of Henri IV (p. 77), but, at best, of François I and, more probably, of Ludovico Sforza. Without those cultural keys the reader of *L'Assommoir* may be left unsure whether he or she stands above or within this 'comic' scene.

On the other hand, those keys pale into insignificance beside the glossaries designed to allow us to decode a language which invades the point of view of the 'literate' as problematically as the hilarity which enters the Louvre. For two cultural frames are not merely juxtaposed in an implicit hierarchy. As many critics have noted, their interpenetration ultimately contests the narrative voice, eroding the distinction between free indirect speech and authorial stance. In the light of the redirected laughter in the Louvre which transforms incomprehending spectators into amusing spectacle, the 'No, it wasn't possible, nobody had ever read that scribbling' (p. 76) is as doubly ironic as Augustine 'laughing at things she'd no business understanding' (p. 147). For are we not ourselves implicated in the text's punning possibilities? To deny *that*, from a standpoint analogous to the Louvre's guardians of decorum, is to belittle the 'most amazing innuendos' invented by Madame Lerat's charges who 'twist the word's sense round' (p. 359) at her expense, and to refuse to admit that we would like to know the answer to her question about Lantier's chance meeting with Nana: 'In what sense d'you mean saw her?' (p. 389). And we might well ask where Zola himself stands in relation to Lantier's self-indulgence, in the midst of the laundresses, 'revelling in their crude language, egging them on to be vulgar while watching his own language carefully' (p. 246). Amidst *L'Assommoir*'s rising tide of uncertainly attributable 'crude language', Gervaise poses (for the reader too) a different question: 'When he started to talk dirty she never knew if he was joking or not' (p. 315). As the labels on whirling images destabilize the visitors from the Rue de la Goutte-d'Or, so to enter their private linguistic space is to be confronted by proliferating nicknames (of people, shops, bars, and dance-halls), exuberant semantic slippage, and a concatenation of song titles. To read the 'tableaux' of *L'Assommoir* from the perspective of the Louvre, in other words, is to stumble through a text parading its signs, self-consciously overdetermined on the one hand (starting with its title) and sense-defying on the other.

   Further examples of meanings declared would include onomastic underlinings. In a novel in which eating is a major preoccupation, Mademoiselle Remanjou's name plays with the verb *manger*; just as obviously, Madame Lerat is as vicious as any rodent, and it is all the more ironic, therefore, that she should live on the monastic Rue des Moines. At the other extreme, there is a provocative authorial delight in a working-class slang so arcane in the original French that only an impenetrable translation would do it justice. Or, at the very least, it requires editorial amplification to capture the knowing play (in the case of Monsieur Poisson, for instance) on *poisson* as both drink and pimp, according to Delvau's *Dictionnaire de la langue verte*, recurring as it does in *Un poisson d'quatr' sous* (translated here as 'A few sous' worth of rum' (p. 230)), in the exuberantly sung 'What a Pig of a Boy'.

The songs of *L'Assommoir*, either alluded to or partially cited, serve to bring this critical problem into sharper relief, occupying as they do a place in the novel more consciously devised than illustrative purposes (of the immemorial habits of labouring men and women) would have warranted. At one level, they allow Zola to engage in indirect commentary. Gervaise's 'washerwoman's song', for example, ironically refers to her own 'heart's black pain' (p. 31) at the very moment of 'ferocious glee' which leaves Virginie's rump so black and blue. Many of the songs thus function as an accompaniment to the narrative itself, not least the wickedly appropriate 'My Nose is where it Tickles Me' (p. 268) which takes Lantier back to Gervaise's bed as she is overcome by an insidious sensuality at odds with moral rectitude. The entire singing episode of Chapter VII is deliberately organized in counterpoint, as news of approaching temptation, in the shape of Lantier's return, is interpolated between songs of seduction ('The Volcano of Love or The Irresistible Trooper' (p. 221)) and resistance ('Pirate Ship Ahoy!' (pp. 222–3)). A similar alternation contrasts the sobriety of 'Abd-el-Kader's Farewell' (p. 224) and the intoxication of 'The Wines of France' (p. 223). We should not forget, however, that these are but the sanctioned pauses in the accelerating rhythm of a transgressive repertoire. For between the serious and the salacious, on the one hand, and respectful silence and a deafening roar, on the other, the chapter as a whole charts the progression of an unbridled laughter. And its disruptive potential is already asserted in the telling disturbance of those muslin curtains between room and street (pp. 222, 229) which separate the private and the public.

Within the domestic space of 'The Simple Life of Gervaise Macquart', the correlation of performer and performance ensures that the songs are angled as mirrors in which characters either locate themselves or are reflected for the reader in individuated echoes. The strains of exotic Spain or Arabia (p. 223) open up 'golden vistas' which had remained encased with 'the little gods of the Orient' (p. 79) in the Louvre; and they anticipate the more prosaic flight to Belgium in Goujet's proposal to Gervaise of an elopement 'like what goes on in novels' (p. 254). The informing desire of a rural idyll is a recurrent motif: in Coupeau's 'Hey, Ho, the Baby Lambs' (p. 112) and 'Oh, I do Love Pickin' Strawb'ries!' (p. 114), and, especially, in the mawkish 'Build your Nest': 'it reminded you of the countryside, and the dainty little birds, and dancing under the trees, and the nectar-laden flowers' (p. 224). Of these inconsequential negations of an urban destiny, none is more grotesquely redolent than the title of the last. For it picks up, of course, Gervaise's lifelong dream of 'a cosy nest' (p. 282) so precariously placed between the literal and the figurative. Nor is it by chance that Nana should sing of a limping beast of burden (p. 296). There will be no dignified surrender such as that exemplified by Abd-el-Kader's submission to colonial power (p. 224). Gervaise's 'Oh! Let Me Sleep' (p. 223) looks forward to a wish finally granted by Bazouge as the novel closes ('Go to bye-byes, my pretty one!'); but not before 'she was upset by his song, "There Once were Three Pretty Girls"' (p. 328) which had made her the victim of 'The Volcano of Love'. Her appeals to God go unheard; bereft of familial structures, 'alone and abandoned' (p. 407), she had earlier listened to 'The Child of the Lord' with justified trepidation: 'she felt as if the song was about her own suffering, as if she were that lost, forsaken waif whom the Lord would take into his care' (p. 226).

It is only when such private concerns spill over on to the street, however, that recourse to this idiom represents a different kind of threat. The songs of *L'Assommoir* speak of its characters' dislocated experience and may be partially comprehensible to us only in the fragments not distorted by colloquial expression. But for the diverse inhabitants of the Rue de la Goutte d'Or 'who all knew the song, joined in the chorus' (p. 230), to be transmitted from one working-class generation to the next, the singing is a declaration of coherence (in every sense). The banquet is thus contrasted with the wedding-feast which had broken up in rancour because of the absence of a chorus-leader. In a novel apparently so far removed from the political stage, it is here that the authorities' fear of the café-concert is related to the spectre of the barricade. For the most coded songs, voicing unregulated inebriation and sexuality, establish a community invulnerable to political control.

The raucous invasion of the muted high culture of the Louvre
had been brought to an end by the powerful voices ('les voix
puissantes', as the French text has it) of the guards. Within the
characters' own linguistic space, however, patriotic intonations
are drowned out; and historical reality and symbolic significance
coincide in the aborted appearance of the policemen, 'thinking
it must be a riot' (p. 231).

The assault on the parameters of 'taste' is not limited, of
course, to the novel's songs. Nor are they the only moment
within it where *L'Assommoir* seems to anticipate the official
suspicion with which it would be greeted. In a number of ways,
however, they both capture its own preoccupations and mirror
our reading of the novel as a whole. Thematically resonant, they
are also spaced in alternating registers and moods, overlaying
the ribald and the pathetic. But the internal arrangement of the
songs at the banquet, itself so structurally significant, reflects a
textual progression rather than a biographical curve, moving
from moral commentary and identifiable narrative tableaux to
an increasingly unintelligible script.

This reaches its climax in the sense-defying, disarticulated
grammar of Coupeau at Sainte-Anne. His babble remains only
intermittently comprehensible to us, separated as we are from
his inchoate laughter and imaginative world. But the rising
cadence of the novel's central chapter is stopped short of that
verbal delirium which it also prefigures. It is sectioned off by 'a
conniving little nod' (p. 231), exchanged by the representatives
of law and order; but also (it could be said) between policing
author and readers in search of ordered meanings. In both cases
the gesture serves to restore an ironic complicity. From the
same vantage-point as that from which the story as a whole will
be brought to a close, our sense of an ending survives inherently
redundant refrains continuing into the night. But to move past
the songs as permissive spectators of a colourful linguistic
episode is to 'overlook', precisely, their activating power. For
Zola's juxtapositions are seldom more problematic than when
the subversive orthography and lexical arbitrariness of 'Qué
cochon d'enfant' (see note to p. 230) assume an autonomous
cultural legitimacy; sung not to, but for and by, the community,
and simultaneously excluding those outside it. The hostility

engendered by *L'Assommoir* cannot be understood without reference to this perceived threat to the hierarchy between orality and the institutionally inscribed (or uncontrollable laughter and 'common' sense); but also, of course, to the distinction separating their class-related audiences.

There were few more acute observers of the symptoms of such cultural crisis than the poet Stéphane Mallarmé. His reaction to *L'Assommoir* focuses on contemporary anxieties about readership. 'Those who accuse you of not having written for the common people', he wrote to Zola on 3 February 1877,[10] 'are in a sense quite wrong, but no more so than those who regret that you have abandoned an established ideal'. This is not to adumbrate a fallacious history of the leisure-habits of the proletariat. It is to locate the novel's modernity in its troubling admixture of codification: 'your admirable linguistic experiment, thanks to which the often inept expressions forged by poor devils assume the value of the most beautiful literary formulations.' More inevitably perhaps, given the perspective of a 'man of letters' (as Mallarmé puts it), the recuperative tribute, 'You have contributed to literature something absolutely new', leaves an enlarged category intact. It can be suggested, however, that *L'Assommoir* does more than just accommodate 'beauty in popular form'. If it is 'worthy of its age', it is also because the novel encodes the dissolving boundaries of the popular and Art.

It seems inconceivable that Zola himself was not acutely aware, during the writing of the novel, of what he was doing in this respect. If Madame Lerat's linguistic concerns are specific, the Louvre signals more general preoccupations. For an artist to confront directly, within his work, the norms of the pantheon of art, is an open invitation to the reader to measure *L'Assommoir* against traditional criteria. Less overtly perhaps, the scenes at Sainte-Anne are complementary in so far as it is here that the visit to the Louvre finds itself reflected in another mode: 'Yet another vast public building, with grey courtyards and endless corridors' (p. 337). In an epilogue which structurally

[10] The letter is cited in full in Henri Mitterand's Pléiade edition of *L'Assommoir* (Paris: Gallimard, 1961), 1566–7.

corresponds to the end of *L'Assommoir*'s exposition, Sainte-Anne remains the only other 'escape' developed beyond a passing reference, and getting there is as much a 'real expedition' as the wedding-party's excursion. It is as regulated as the Salon Carré, with its own institutional guards and officials. Within it, Coupeau confirms the fate which awaits Gervaise as one of those dehumanized beasts in the Assyrian Gallery described as 'monstrous creatures, half-cat, half-woman' (p. 75).

Over and above this kind of thematic recall, however, these pages allow Zola to return to the problem of representation posed by his copyists in the Louvre, 'with their easels set up in the middle of the crowd, coolly painting away' (p. 77). The foregrounded detail ('what actually interested them the most') is enlarged beyond the anecdotal by the contemporary debate on artistic originality, and the untroubled copying contrasts with *L'Assommoir*'s self-conscious dimension. The curiosity of the seated observer at Sainte-Anne, with notebook in hand, reflects both the 'curious bystanders' (p. 77) who draw up their chairs to watch the wedding-party pass by and Zola's 'literary curiosity to gather together the language of the people and present it in a carefully fashioned mould' (p. 3). Gervaise engages in a similar mimetic activity, reproducing in a *tableau* (translated here as an 'imitation' (pp. 429, 432, 439)), and for assembled spectators of her own, her husband's terrifying 'performance' (p. 432); as opposed to 'comics imitating what Coupeau was doing; only they imitate it badly' (p. 425), Gervaise 'did Coupeau to perfection' (p. 432). *L'Assommoir* too was to be, according to Zola's notes, a 'terrifying tableau', and its reception is anticipated in this startling moment of textual introspection: 'they'd accused her of overdoing her imitation!' (p. 429), even more precisely echoed in the French term *exagérer*. Alongside all those representations contemplated by the characters, the novel's preface asserts the power of its 'images'. Between the Louvre and Sainte-Anne, it can be argued, Zola explores the hall of mirrors in which such images of experience imagined are threatened by the insertion of a museum wall between art and life. The writer and critic Paul Bourget caught the structure of *L'Assommoir* exactly: 'it's as if the paintings of life were aligned in a gallery'; but also the paradox: 'Don't you think', he asked Zola, 'that you provoke in us a sense of curiosity which militates against the naturalness of the story.'[11] On the one hand, the novel subverts what Zola saw as the desire of a writer like Théophile Gautier to 'immobilize language in a hieratical stasis'; on the other, Bourget puts in a more polite form the charges, expressed by contemporary socialists such as Arthur Ranc, of 'art for art's sake'. If Zola's distaste for the sculptured shapes in the Louvre (with 'their rigid hieratical poses' (p. 75)) is self-evident, the writer's 'carefully fashioned mould' remains double-edged.

The same ambivalence can be detected in the process whereby art and experience seem to parody each other in *L'Assommoir*. Coupeau's zinc-cutting is that of an 'artist'; Goujet's toil produces 'a real masterpiece' as he fashions rivets 'so finely wrought they deserved to be put in a museum' (p. 166); Maman Coupeau fits into her coffin so perfectly that she is 'just like a picture in a frame' (p. 305). Such comparisons operate from both ends of the cultural divide. The songs of the novel may articulate a poetry of common experience, but are themselves cast in the ambiguities of Zola's metaphorical configurations. He uses the term *chanson* for 'gossip' (p. 48), the 'never-ending lament' (p. 402) of Gervaise's empty stomach, and Coupeau's 'bawling-out' (p. 425). To the extent that idiom is concretized, we may be left unsure of the differentiated status of the 'poetry' and the 'experience'. Nowhere is this more evident than in the extended references to music. The background instrumentation of moral degeneracy (pp. 51, 89, 408) is used in precisely the same way as Zola exploits the texts of the songs as commentary. Cornets and fiddles seem to be mocked by Veronese's cultural heroes listening to the foregrounded players in *The Wedding at Cana*. But a 'minuet' of long ago and the vulgarity of a 'sleazy bar routine' (p. 168) gradually create a complementary rhythm of their own within this oppositional framework. A superimposition is effected in the obscenities sung by drunks 'looking exactly like choristers' (p. 411). Sacred modulations become

---

[11] In a letter of 2 February 1877, cited by Deffoux 111–12.

'the belly's vespers' (p. 284) as the church organ is reproduced in 'a dirge of misfortune' (p. 322). There are the sonorities of running water (p. 63), drumming fists (p. 50), and a workshop with its own 'refrain' (p. 46). _L'Assommoir_ puts us in touch with the 'music' of Coupeau's comic snoring (p. 291); but also, in the other mode equally characteristic of its songs, with that of crying children (p. 11), heartless gravediggers (p. 307), and diseased chests (p. 335).

To the extent that such conflations are parodic, Zola seems to register an awareness that revelations of the undisclosed may be transformed into another spectacle of scissored images: as unresponsive to suffering as the children's cutting; as inward-looking as Poisson's arabesques; as proliferating as those on Goujet's walls are increasingly obscured; as hallucinatory as the verbiage at Sainte-Anne which dissolves the boundaries of significance and sense. The confidence of Poisson's 'It was printed in a book, so he couldn't deny it' (p. 243), in other words, is not one to which Zola unequivocally subscribes. _L'Assommoir_ nevertheless overcomes those hesitations. Delineated structures and the stabilizing reference points of thematic patterns ensure that we can both understand, and share the writer's compassion for, Gervaise's plight. As she looks at the insubstantial image of herself, in a savage Paris veiled by driving snow, many readers will feel that art and life have come together. If a texture of garbled utterances accommodates a point of view excluded from our own, the extremes of Coupeau's self- reflecting 'new kind of music' (p. 387) are held in check by Zola's orchestration of his fiction. That still leaves the novel at odds with the 'classical' movements of Goujet's 'clear melody' (pp. 168–9). But it is in its confrontation with such problems of definition, less in its subject than its enactment, that _L'Assommoir_ retains its distinctive hybrid resonance.

Robert Lethbridge

NOTE ON THE TRANSLATION

L'Assommoir is a notoriously difficult text to translate. No translation, however faithful its rendering of the novel's gutter slang and obscenities, could possibly recreate the impact of that language on the nineteenth-century reader. Today readers have become accustomed to slang and are no longer shocked by obscenity. It follows that much of the original power of *L'Assommoir* to command attention by its unorthodox and audacious language is lost forever—and lost, of course, not simply in translation but to readers of the original as well. The difficulty of appropriately translating Zola's vocabulary, however, goes far beyond questions of changing sensibility and taste. Intelligibility is an issue. Some of the working-class slang that Zola wove so methodically into the fabric of *L'Assommoir* created problems of comprehension even for his own contemporaries, and has long been out of currency. The glossary included in the Pléiade edition is sufficient proof that some 'translation' is needed even for French readers. But readers of an English version should not need an English slang dictionary; I have aimed at a clearer, more accessible 'read', using slang that is not, as in the French original, outmoded or obscure.

In translating slang and idioms I set out to determine as accurately as possible the meaning of the French term. I turned first to Delvau's 1866 *Dictionnaire de la langue verte* from which Zola culled many of his more picturesque expressions, but in which the coyly periphrastic definitions often need careful interpretation. My search for precise meaning usually required further dogged detective work with other dictionaries and reference works. The next step was to look for an English equivalent of the French which, while still in current use, would preferably not be of recent vintage and would, ideally, convey the vigour of the original without introducing incompatible English or American cultural connotations. In fact, I looked for forceful, timeless, culturally unmarked slang. In this frustrating endeavour my most valuable resource was Eric Partridge's *Dictionary of Slang and Unconventional English*, with which I have spent countless fascinating hours. Translation inevitably involves compromise, and I am aware that in seeking greater intelligibility I may have sacrificed, in my version, some of Zola's pungent stylistic vitality.

As the novel progresses, Zola increasingly confines the reader to the grim world of the *Rue de la Goutte-d'Or*. One way he achieves this is by eroding the distinction between narrative voice and interior monologue, creating a claustrophobic universe where these voices penetrate each other, recounting and reacting to the life of the slum in the idiom of the slum without any relief from an outside viewpoint or a different stylistic level. I have tried to reproduce this relentless effect by keeping within an insistently working-class register. Mindful that Zola aimed at a 'spoken' rather than a 'written' style, not only in the dialogue but throughout the novel, I have where appropriate made the narrative sequences more colloquial by using verbal contractions instead of the full conventional forms—'didn't' rather than 'did not' and so on. Every translator faces the temptation to tidy up the text under translation, but I wanted to reproduce the rather jerky rhythm of Zola's prose and so chose to copy his punctuation and to keep his short sentences, rather than to combine several sentences together for greater elegance or fluency. I have also preserved the many somewhat tedious repetitions. In translating dialogue I have largely avoided phonetic renderings of incorrect speech, which are often difficult to read. Although all the characters are poorly educated, Coupeau is the only one who cannot even sign his name; Zola noted that he had 'no education'. Accordingly I have made his speech sloppier and less grammatical than that of his family and friends, and I have also tried to reproduce the gradual degradation of Gervaise's speech that so vividly mirrors the breakdown of her moral being.

This translation of *L'Assommoir* is based on the text published in vol. ii of the Pléiade edition of *Les Rougon–Macquart*, edited by Henri Mitterand (Paris: Gallimard, 1960-7), which includes interesting and useful notes and background material.

I am deeply indebted to Robert Lethbridge for his encouragement and generous advice and help throughout the long months I have been working on this project. My grateful thanks go to him and to my husband Jim Mauldon, who as well as helping me in countless practical ways has been an eagle-eyed and judicious reader. Finally I should like to thank Amherst College for the use of their excellent library and computing facilities.

Amherst, Massachusetts Margaret Mauldon

SELECT BIBLIOGRAPHY

THE most authoritative French edition of *l'Assommoir* appears in vol. ii of *Les Rougon–Macquart* in the Bibliothèque de la Pléiade (Paris: Gallimard, 1961); the scholarly apparatus, by Henri Mitterand, includes a synopsis of the novel's genesis and composition, a useful glossary, notes on the text, and successive amendments from the manuscript to the final version of *L'Assommoir* in volume form. Much of this documentation is reproduced in the Folio edition (Paris: Gallimard, 1978). Another good paperback of the original French text is to be found in the Garnier-Flammarion series (Paris: 1969).

The best general study of Zola's life and work remains F.W.J. Hemmings, *Émile Zola* (2nd edn., London: Oxford University Press, 1966; reissued Oxford Paperbacks, 1970). A very readable biography is Philip Walker, *Zola* (London: Routledge and Kegan Paul, 1985). Recently reissued in paperback (1993) is Robert Lethbridge and Terry Keefe (eds.), *Zola and the Craft of Fiction* (Leicester: Leicester University Press, 1990); the Introduction to this collective volume surveys modern critical approaches to Zola's techniques as a novelist. Challenging interpretations of the Rougon–Macquart cycle as a whole are Michel Serres, *Feux et signaux de brume: Zola* (Paris: Grasset, 1975), and Auguste Dezalay, *L'Opéra des Rougon–Macquart* (Paris: Klincksieck, 1983). Students of Zola's writing will also learn much from the three volumes of essays by Henri Mitterand: *Le Discours du roman* (1985), *Le Regard et le signe* (1987), and *Zola: L'Histoire et la fiction* (1990) (all published Paris: Presses Universitaires de France).

The most substantial monograph on *L'Assommoir* is Jacques Dubois, *L'Assommoir de Zola: société, discours, idéologie* (Paris: Larousse, 1973). There are four excellent short studies of the novel in English: Lilian Furst, *L'Assommoir: A Working Woman's Life* (Boston: Twayne, 1990); Roger Clark, *Zola: L'Assommoir* (Glasgow: University of Glasgow French and German Publications, 1990); Valerie Minogue, *Zola: L'Assommoir* (London: Grant and Cutler, 1991); David Baguley, *Émile Zola: L'Assommoir* (Cambridge: Cambridge University Press, 1992). The last of these, in the Landmarks of World Literature series, contains a 'Guide to Further Reading' (pp. 111–16) which constitutes the most comprehensive available summary of secondary work on the novel; it both signals the level at which such work is pitched and includes detailed bibliographical references. One of the few items not mentioned, but of particular interest to those concerned with the problems of translating *L'Assommoir*, is Baguley's article in a special issue of the *Cahiers de traductologie* (no. 5): 'Après babil: l'intraduisible dans *L'Assommoir*', in *La Traduction. L'Universitaire et le praticien*, ed. Arlette Thomas and Jacques Flamand (Ottawa: Éditions de l'Université d'Ottawa, 1984), 181–90. Too late for inclusion was Robert Lethbridge, 'Reflections in the Margin: Politics in Zola's *L'Assommoir*', *Australian Journal of French Studies*, XXX (1993), 222–32. Those looking for a single stimulating essay, at once essential and accessible, should read Baguley's own 'Event and Structure: The Plot of Zola's *L'Assommoir*', *Publications of the Modern Language Association*, XC (1975), 823–33.

As far as the setting of the novel is concerned, an indispensable work of reference is Jacques Hillairet, *Dictionnaire historique des rues de Paris*, 2 vols (Paris: Minuit, 1963). More localized is *La Goutte d'Or, faubourg de Paris*, eds. Marc Breitman and Maurice Culot (Paris: Hazan, 1988), including a first-rate study by Philippe Hamon on the sites of *L'Assommoir*.

CHRONOLOGY

1840   (2 April) Born in Paris, the only child of Francesco Zola (b. 1795), an Italian engineer, and Émilie, née Aubert (b. 1819), the daughter of a glazier. The Naturalist novelist was later proud that 'zolla' in Italian means 'clod of earth'

1843   Family moves to Aix-en-Provence

1847   (27 March) Death of father from pneumonia following a chill caught while supervising work on his scheme to supply Aix-en-Provence with drinking water

1852–   Becomes a boarder at the Collège Bourbon at Aix. Friendship with Baptistin Baille and Paul Cézanne. Zola, not Cézanne, wins the school prize for drawing

1858   (February) Leaves Aix to settle in Paris with his mother (who had preceded him in December). Offered a place and bursary at the Lycée Saint-Louis. (November) Falls ill with 'brain fever' (typhoid) and convalescence is slow

1859   Fails his *baccalauréat* twice

1860   (Spring) Is found employment as a copy-clerk but abandons it after two months, preferring to eke out an existence as an impecunious writer in the Latin Quarter of Paris

1861   Cézanne follows Zola to Paris, where he meets Camille Pissarro, fails the entrance examination to the École des Beaux-Arts, and returns to Aix in September

1862   (February) Taken on by Hachette, the well-known publishing house, at first in the dispatch office and subsequently as head of the publicity department. (31 October) Naturalized as a French citizen. Cézanne returns to Paris and stays with Zola

1863   (31 January) First literary article published. (1 May) Manet's *Déjeuner sur l'herbe* exhibited at the Salon des Refusés, which Zola visits with Cézanne

1864   (October) *Tales for Ninon*

1865   *Claude's Confession*. A *succès de scandale* thanks to its bedroom scenes. Meets future wife Alexandrine-Gabrielle Meley (b. 1839), the illegitimate daughter of teenage parents who soon separated, and whose mother died in September 1849

1866   Forced to resign his position at Hachette (salary: 200 francs a month) and becomes a literary critic on the recently launched daily *L'Événement* (salary: 500 francs a month). Self-styled 'humble disciple' of Hippolyte Taine. Writes a series of provocative articles condemning the official Salon Selection Committee, expressing reservations about Courbet, and praising Manet and Monet. Begins to frequent the Café Guerbois in the Batignolles quarter of Paris, the meeting-place of the future Impressionists. Antoine Guillemet takes Zola to meet Manet. Summer months spent with Cézanne at Bennecourt on the Seine. (15 November) *L'Événement* suppressed by the authorities

1867   (November) *Thérèse Raquin*

1868   (April) Preface to second edition of *Thérèse Raquin*. (May) Manet's portrait of Zola exhibited at the Salon. (December) *Madeleine Férat*. Begins to plan for the Rougon-Macquart series of novels

1868–70   Working as journalist for a number of different newspapers

1870   (31 May) Marries Alexandrine in a registry office. (September) Moves temporarily to Marseilles because of the Franco–Prussian War

1871   Political reporter for *La Cloche* (in Paris) and *Le Sémaphore de Marseille*. (March) Returns to Paris. (October) Publishes *The Fortune of the Rougons*, the first of the twenty novels making up the Rougon-Macquart series

1872   *The Kill*

1873   (April) *The Belly of Paris*

1874   (May) *The Conquest of Plassans*. First independent Impressionist exhibition. (November) *Further Tales for Ninon*

1875   Begins to contribute articles to the Russian newspaper *Vestnik Evropy* (*European Herald*). (April) *The Sin of the Abbé Mouret*

1876   (February) *His Excellency Eugène Rougon*. Second Impressionist exhibition

1877   (February) *L'Assommoir*

1878   Buys a house at Médan on the Seine, forty kilometres west of Paris. (June) *A Page of Love*

1880   (March) *Nana*. (May) *Les Soirées de Médan* (an anthology of short stories by Zola and some of his Naturalist 'disciples', including Maupassant). (8 May) Death of Flaubert. (September) First of a series of articles for *Le Figaro*. (17 October) Death of his mother. (December) *The Experimental Novel*

1882   (April) *Pot-Bouille*. (3 September) Death of Turgenev

1883   (13 February) Death of Wagner. (March) *Au Bonheur des dames*. (30 April) Death of Manet

1884   (March) *La Joie de vivre*. Preface to catalogue of Manet exhibition

1885   (March) *Germinal*. (12 May) Begins writing *The Masterpiece* (*L'Œuvre*). (22 May) Death of Victor Hugo. (23 December) First instalment of *The Masterpiece* appears in *Le Gil Blas*

1886   (27 March) Final instalment of *The Masterpiece*, which is published in book form in April

1887   (18 August) Denounced as an onanistic pornographer in the *Manifesto of the Five* in *Le Figaro*. (November) *Earth*

1888   (October) *The Dream*. Jeanne Rozerot becomes his mistress

1889   (20 September) Birth of Denise, daughter of Zola and Jeanne

1890   (March) *The Beast in Man*

1891   (March) *Money*. (April) Elected President of the Société des gens de lettres. (25 September) Birth of Jacques, son of Zola and Jeanne

1892   (June) *The Débâcle*

1893   (July) *Doctor Pascal*, the last of the Rougon–Macquart novels. Fêted on a visit to London

1894   (August) *Lourdes*, the first novel of the trilogy *Three Cities*. (22 December) Dreyfus found guilty by a court martial

1896   (May) *Rome*

1898   (13 January) 'J'accuse', his article in defence of Dreyfus, published in *L'Aurore*. (21 February) Found guilty of libelling the Minister of War and given the maximum sentence of one year's imprisonment and a fine of 3,000 francs. Appeal for retrial granted on a technicality. (March) *Paris*. (23 May) Retrial delayed. (18 July) Leaves for England instead of attending court

1899   (4 June) Returns to France. (October) *Fecundity*, the first of his 'Four Gospels'

1901   (May) *Toil*, the second 'Gospel'

1902   (29 September) Dies of fumes from his bedroom fire, the chimney having been capped either by accident or anti-Dreyfusard design. Wife survives. (5 October) Public funeral

1903   (March) *Truth*, the third 'Gospel', published posthumously. *Justice* was to be the fourth

1908   (4 June) Remains transferred to the Panthéon

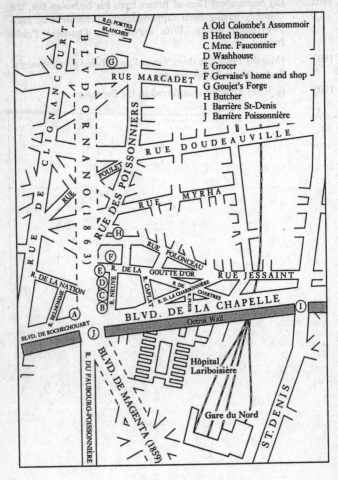

A Old Colombe's Assommoir
B Hôtel Boncoeur
C Mme. Fauconnier
D Washhouse
E Grocer
F Gervaise's home and shop
G Goujet's Forge
H Butcher
I Barrière St-Denis
J Barrière Poissonnière

Street-plan of the setting of *L'Assommoir*

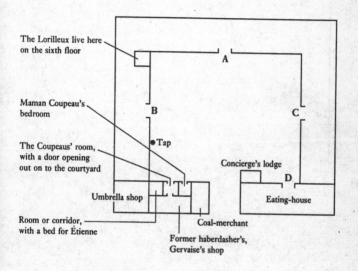

The Lorilleux live here on the sixth floor

Maman Coupeau's bedroom

The Coupeaus' room, with a door opening out on to the courtyard

Room or corridor, with a bed for Étienne

A

B

C

D

● Tap

Concierge's lodge

Eating-house

Umbrella shop

Coal-merchant

Former haberdasher's, Gervaise's shop

Zola's plan for the building in the Rue de la Goutte d'Or

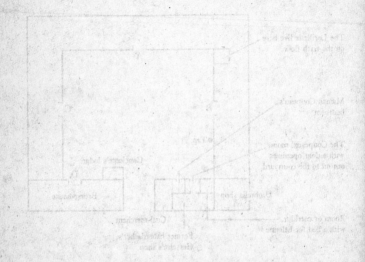

The Lavatories are
in the attch floor

Maria Orsieani's
bedroom

The Company room
with a door opening
out on to the courtyard

Printing shop

Room of oracles
with a slit for letters

The Grand Master's
bedroom

Grand Master's Lodge

Reception room

Cellaonium

Former Master's den
(later attick Store)

Zook's plan for the building in the Rue de la Sourdière d'Or

L'Assommoir

PREFACE

THERE will be some twenty novels in the Rougon–Macquart series. I decided on the overall plan in 1869 and I am following it with the utmost rigour. *L'Assommoir* appeared at its appointed time and I wrote it, as I shall write all the other novels, without deviating for one second from my direction. That is the source of my strength. I have a goal before me.

When *L'Assommoir* was serialized in a newspaper, it was attacked and denounced with unprecedented ferocity, and charged with all manner of crimes. Is it really essential that I explain here, in just a few lines, what my authorial intentions were? I wanted to depict the inexorable downfall of a working-class family in the poisonous atmosphere of our industrial suburbs. Intoxication and idleness lead to a weakening of family ties, to the filth of promiscuity, to the progressive neglect of decent feelings and ultimately to degradation and death. It is simply morality in action.

L'Assommoir is without any doubt the most chaste of my books. Often I have had occasion to write about far more horrifying evils. It is only the novel's form that caused alarm. People were angered by words. My crime is to have had the literary curiosity to gather together the language of the people and present it in a carefully fashioned mould. Ah yes, the novel's form, there lies my crime! Yet there exist dictionaries of this language, scholars study it and take pleasure in its vigour and its powerful, unexpected images. This language is a feast for linguistic researchers. But even so, no one understood that my intention was to carry out a strictly philological enterprise, one which I believe is of the greatest historical and social interest.

In any case I am not defending myself. My novel will be my defence. It is a work of truth, the first novel about the common people that does not lie and that smells of the common people. And readers should not conclude that the common people as a whole are bad, for my characters are not bad, they are only ignorant and ruined by the conditions of sweated toil and poverty in which they live. But I ask nothing more than that my novels be read, and understood, and seen clearly in the context of the entire series, before people subscribe to the ready-made, distorted and odious opinions about me and my works that are circulating. Oh, if people only knew how my friends laugh at the astounding tales dished out for the entertainment of the populace! If they only knew what a respectable bourgeois is this blood-sucking vampire, this savage novelist, a man dedicated to learning and to art, living in quiet seclusion, whose sole ambition is to leave behind him a body of writing as comprehensive and as alive as he can make it. I deny none of the stories about me, I go on writing, trusting that time and the good faith of the public will finally reveal me as I am, cleared of all the nonsense that has been heaped upon me.

Paris, 1 January 1877   Émile Zola

CHAPTER I

GERVAISE had waited up for Lantier until two in the morning. Then, shivering all over from sitting half-dressed in the cold air from the window, she'd dropped off into a feverish doze, lying across the bed, her cheeks soaked with tears. Every night for a week now, as they left the Veau à deux têtes,* where they had their dinner, he'd sent her home to bed with the children, and not come in himself until the small hours. He said he was looking for work. That particular evening, while she was watching for his return, she thought she'd seen him go into the Grand-Balcon* dance hall, whose ten blazing windows lit up with a sheet of flame the black expanse of the outer boulevards;* and she'd caught sight of little Adèle, a burnisher by trade who ate at their restaurant, walking five or six paces behind him, her hands dangling as if she'd just dropped his arm so they wouldn't be seen passing together beneath the glaring lights of the doorway.

When Gervaise woke up at about five o'clock, her back stiff and aching, she burst into tears. Lantier hadn't come in. Never before had he stayed out all night. She went on sitting on the edge of the bed, under the faded bit of chintz hanging from a rod tied to the ceiling with string. And slowly, her eyes dimmed by tears, she looked round the wretched furnished room, at the walnut chest with one drawer missing, at the three cane-bottomed chairs and the greasy little table on which stood a chipped water jug. An iron bedstead had been brought in for the children; it blocked the chest of drawers and took up two-thirds of the room. Gervaise and Lantier's trunk lay wide open in a corner: it was completely empty except for a man's old hat right at the bottom, under a pile of dirty shirts and socks; while hanging over furniture against the walls were a tattered shawl and a pair of gutter-shredded trousers, their last remaining things that the old-clothes dealers wouldn't touch. In the centre of the mantelpiece, between two zinc candlesticks which didn't match, lay a bundle of pale pink pawn tickets. The room was the hotel's best, on the first floor at the front, looking on to the boulevard.

The two children, meanwhile, were fast asleep, their heads side by side on the same pillow. Eight-year-old Claude had thrust his little hands outside the cover and was breathing slowly, while Étienne,* who was only four, lay smiling, with one hand round his brother's neck. When their mother's brimming eyes came to rest on them, she began to sob again and stuffed a handkerchief into her mouth to muffle the faint cries she couldn't control. And, with bare feet—for she hadn't thought of putting her old slippers back on— she took up her vigil again, leaning on the window sill and scanning the distant pavements.

The hotel stood on the Boulevard de la Chapelle, to the left of the Barrière Poissonnière.* It was a ramshackle, two-storey building, its lower half painted a purplish red, its shutters rotted by the rain. Above a lantern with cracked panes one could just make out, between the two windows, 'Hôtel Boncœur,* prop. Marsoullier' in large yellow letters, bits of which had crumbled away with the damp plaster. The lantern obstructed Gervaise's view and she craned her neck, her handkerchief to her lips. Looking to the right, towards the Boulevard de Rochechouart, she could see groups of butchers in blood-stained aprons hanging about in front of the slaughterhouses, and occasionally a stench came to her on the cool breeze, a pungent smell of slaughtered animals. Looking to the left, her eyes ran down a long, ribbon-like avenue, coming to rest almost opposite at the white mass of the Lariboisière Hospital* which was then under construction. Slowly, from one edge of the horizon to the other, her gaze followed the line of the octroi wall* from behind which, in the night, she could sometimes hear the screams of someone being murdered, and she peered into its secluded corners, its dark recesses black with damp and filth, fearful of discovering Lantier's body there, his belly gaping with knife wounds. When she looked up, beyond that grey, unending wall which girded the city with a band of barren space, she could see a great glow, a blaze of dusty sunlight already filled with the rumble of the city's awakening. But her gaze kept returning to the Barrière Poissonnière, and she stretched her neck, growing dizzy as she watched men, animals, and carts flowing in an uninterrupted stream between the two squat booths of the toll-house, making their way down from the heights of Montmartre and La Chapelle.* It was like the trampling of a herd, a mob which would stop suddenly, spreading out and overflowing on to the roadway, a measureless procession of men going to work, carrying their tools on their backs and their loaves under their arms: and the throng went on being swallowed up by Paris, sinking into it, never ending. When Gervaise thought she recognized Lantier among all those people, she'd lean further forward, at the risk of falling out; then she'd press her handkerchief harder on to her mouth, as if seeking to bite back her pain.

A young, cheerful voice made her leave the window.

'So, the boss hasn't made it back, Madame Lantier!'

'Well no, Monsieur Coupeau,' she replied, trying to smile.

He was a roofer who lived right at the top of the building, in a tiny, ten-franc room. His tool-bag was on his shoulder. Finding the key in the door he'd dropped in, as neighbours will.

'You know,' he went on, 'I'm workin' over there now, at the hospital . . . Right lovely weather for May, eh? Real nippy this morning.'

And he looked at Gervaise's red, tear-stained face. When he saw that the bed hadn't been slept in he shook his head gently; then he went over to the bed where the children, with their rosy cherubic faces, still lay sleeping and, lowering his voice:

'Well now! the boss has been misbehavin', has he? . . . . Don't go gettin' upset now, Madame Lantier. He's mad keen on politics; the other day, when they voted for Eugène Sue*— who's a good chap, so I've heard—he was that pleased he nearly went crazy. I'll bet he's spent the night with some mates pullin' that bastard Bonaparte* to bits.'

'No, no,' she murmured, making an effort. 'It's not what you think. I know where Lantier is . . . But, Lord knows, we've our troubles same as other folk!'

Coupeau winked, to show he wasn't taken in by this lie. And off he went, after offering to fetch her milk, if she didn't feel like going out: she was a lovely woman, a fine woman, and could count on him, if she was ever in trouble. As soon as he'd gone, Gervaise went back to the window.

The herd was still trampling past the barrier in the chill of the morning. You could recognize the locksmiths by their blue smocks, the masons by their white overalls, the house-painters by their coats, with their long smocks showing underneath. From far away the colour of this throng was nondescript and chalky, of a neutral tone made up chiefly of faded blue and dirty grey. Now and then a workman would stop to relight his pipe, while around him the others would go plodding on, with never a laugh or a word to a mate, their cheeks ashen, their faces strained towards Paris which swallowed them one by one down the gaping mouth of the Faubourg-Poissonnière.* All the same, some men did slow to a halt at the two corners of the Rue des Poissonniers, in front of two bars where the shutters were being taken down; and, before going in, they hung about on the kerb casting sidelong glances at Paris, their arms slack, succumbing already to the idea of doing nothing all day. Groups of men were standing in front of the counters, buying each other rounds, oblivious of everything else as they crowded into the bars, spitting, coughing and downing tot after tot to clear out their throats.

Gervaise was keeping an eye on old Colombe's bar, on the left side of the street, where she thought she'd seen Lantier, when a stout bare-headed woman in an apron called to her from the middle of the road.

'My word, Madame Lantier, you're up early!'

Gervaise leaned further out.

'Goodness, it's you, Madame Boche! Oh, I've ever so much to do today!'

'Yes, that's the way it is—work don't do itself.'

And a conversation began between window and pavement. Madame Boche was concierge of the building in which the Veau à deux têtes restaurant occupied the ground floor. More than once Gervaise had waited for Lantier in Madame Boche's lodge to avoid sitting down alone at table with all those men having dinner round her. The concierge told her that she was just popping over the way to the Rue de la Charbonnière, to catch a particular tailor before he got up—her husband simply couldn't get him to mend his frock-coat. Then she talked about one of her lodgers who'd come home with a woman the night before, and had kept everyone awake till three in the morning. But as she chatted she stared at the young woman with intense curiosity, and she seemed to have come there, to have stationed herself under the window, solely in order to find something out.

'Monsieur Lantier's still in bed, then?' she suddenly enquired.

'Yes, he's asleep,' answered Gervaise, unable to stop herself blushing.

Madame Boche saw her eyes filling with tears and, no doubt satisfied, was setting off, cursing men as a bunch of lazy devils, when she turned back to shout:

'This is your morning for the washhouse, isn't it? I've something to wash, I'll keep a place for you by me, and we can have a nice chat.'

Then, as if suddenly overcome with pity:

'You poor dear, you really shouldn't stay there, you'll catch your death . . . You're quite blue.'

Gervaise stuck it out at the window for two solid hours more, until eight o'clock. The shops had opened. The flow of smocks moving down from the heights had stopped, and only a few latecomers were now striding past the barrier. In the bars, the same men were still standing around, still drinking, coughing and spitting. The workmen had been followed by the girls, burnishers, dressmakers, flowergirls, who, pulling their thin garments tightly round them, went scampering along the outer boulevards; they came in groups of three or four, chattering excitedly, giggling and flashing bright glances all round; now and then there would be one quite alone, a thin girl, pale and serious, who, skirting the streams of muck, kept close to the octroi wall. Next came the office workers, blowing on their fingers, eating their little rolls as they walked: skinny youths, in outgrown clothes, with rings round their sleep-bleary eyes, or else tiny old men doddering along, their faces pale and worn from long hours in the office, checking their watches to regulate their pace within a couple of seconds. The boulevards had relapsed into their morning peace; the locals who were comfortably off strolled about in the sunshine; bare-headed mothers wearing grubby skirts sat on benches rocking their long-clothed babies in their arms or changing their nappies; swarms of runny-nosed, half-dressed brats lurched and crawled about on the ground whining, laughing and crying. And then Gervaise felt she was suffocating; faint with anguish, she lost all hope; it seemed to her it was the end, their days were over, Lantier would never come back. Her vacant gaze wandered from the old slaughterhouses black with blood and stinking filth to the pale new hospital where she could see, through the yawning holes soon to be rows of windows, empty wards in which the Reaper would do his work. Her eyes were dazzled by the brilliance of the sky opposite, behind the octroi wall, as the sun rose ever higher above the vast awakening of Paris.

She was sitting on a chair, her hands idle in her lap, no longer crying, when Lantier walked calmly in.

'It's you, it's you!' she cried, trying to throw her arms round his neck.

'Yes, it's me, so what?' he replied. 'Now don't go and start your carrying on, mind!'

He'd pushed her away. With an angry gesture, he hurled his black felt hat across the room on to the chest of drawers. He was a young fellow of twenty-six, small, very dark and good-looking, with a little moustache which by habit he continually twirled. He was wearing a workman's overall and a dirty old frock-coat pulled in at the waist, and he spoke with a strong Provençal accent.*

Gervaise had sunk back on to her chair uttering gentle, disjointed complaints.

'I couldn't sleep a wink . . . I thought something awful must have happened to you . . . Where've you been? Where'd you spend the night? My God! Don't ever do that again, I'd go mad . . . Auguste, tell me, where've you been?'

'I went to see someone, for Christ's sake!' he said, shrugging. 'It was gone eight when I got to that friend of mine at La Glacière,* the chap who's going to open a hat factory. We didn't finish till late so I thought I'd best stay the night . . . You know I can't stand being spied on, so get off my back!'

The young woman began to sob again. Lantier's raised voice and the rough way he was crashing into the chairs had roused the children. They sat up, half-naked, pushing their hair back with their little hands; hearing their mother cry, they started up a frightful wailing, weeping like Gervaise even though their eyes were hardly open.

'Oh! Now we've got a concert!' shouted Lantier furiously. 'I'm warning you, I'm off again! And this time I'll be gone for good! Shut up, won't you? Bye-bye, I'm going back where I came from.'

He'd already picked up his hat from the chest. But Gervaise rushed forward, stammering:

'No! No!'

And she quieted the children, caressing away their tears. She kissed their hair and settled them down again with loving words. The children, easily soothed, lay chuckling on the pillow, amusing themselves pinching one another. In the meantime their father, without even taking off his boots, had flung himself on the bed; he looked dead beat and his face was blotchy from a sleepless night. He didn't fall asleep, but lay with wide-open eyes, gazing round the room.

'Lovely place this is, I must say!' he murmured.

Then, after looking at Gervaise for a moment, he added nastily:

'Given up washing, have you?'

Gervaise was only twenty-two. She was tall and rather thin, with delicate features already worn by her hard life. With her hair uncombed and her feet in slippers, shivering in her white bodice on which the furniture had left traces of its dust and grease, she looked as if the hours of anxiety and tears she'd just endured had added ten years to her age. Lantier's remark jolted her out of her timid, resigned mood.

'You're not being fair,' she said with more spirit. 'You know quite well I do the best I can. I'm not to blame 'cos we've landed here . . . I'd like to see how you'd manage, looking after the two kids in a room where there isn't even a stove so we can have hot water . . . When we got to Paris, instead of throwing your money around, you ought to have fixed us up somewhere right away, like you promised.'

'Hey, just a minute!' he shouted. 'You did your share, getting through our nest-egg: it's a bit rich your turning your nose up now at our little fling!'

But she went on, as if she hadn't heard him:

'Anyway, if we really put our backs into it, we can still make a go of things. Yesterday evening I went to see Madame Fauconnier, the woman who has that laundry in the Rue Neuve; she's taking me on starting Monday. If you go in with your friend at La Glacière, we'll be back afloat in six months' time; it'll take that to rig us out and rent a little place, somewhere we can call home . . . Oh my! It'll mean no end of work . . .'

Lantier, looking bored, turned his face to the wall. At that, Gervaise flared up.

'Yes, that's the trouble, everyone knows you aren't exactly panting to work. You're bursting with ambition, you'd like to be got up like a gent and parade about with tarts in silk skirts on your arm. That's it, isn't it? I'm not fine enough for you any more, now that you've made me pop all me dresses . . . Now listen, Auguste! I didn't mean to say anything about it, I would've waited a bit, but I do know where you spent last night; I saw you go into the Grand-Balcon with that trollop Adèle. You certainly know how to pick 'em! She's a fine one, that one, no wonder she puts on such fancy airs . . . She's been to bed with the whole restaurant.'

Lantier leapt off the bed. His eyes had turned black as ink in his ashen face. Small though he was, his temper was ferocious.

'Yes, yes, with the whole restaurant!' she repeated. 'Madame Boche is going to kick 'em out, her and her great gawk of a sister, because there's always a queue of men on the stairs.'

Lantier raised his fists; then, resisting the urge to hit her, he grabbed her by the arm and shook her violently, so that she fell on to the children's bed. They started to bawl again. And he lay down once more, muttering grimly, like a man resolved on something he'd been wavering about,

'You don't know what you've just done, Gervaise . . . You've made a big mistake, you'll see.'

The children continued sobbing for a moment. Their mother, still bent over the edge of the bed, held them both in her arms, repeating again and again in a monotonous voice:

'Oh! if it weren't for you, my poor babies, if it weren't for you, if it weren't for you! . . .'

Lantier lay quietly, no longer listening, his gaze fixed on the scrap of faded chintz above his head, his mind gripped by a single idea. Although his eyelids were heavy with weariness, he stayed like that for nearly an hour without falling asleep. When he finally turned over and propped himself up on his elbow, his face hard and determined, Gervaise had nearly finished tidying the room. She'd just got the children up and dressed, and was making their bed. He watched her sweep the floor and dust the furniture; the room still looked dark and wretched with its smoke-blackened ceiling, its paper peeling off in damp patches, its wobbly chairs and chest of drawers on which her duster only caked and spread the grime. Then, while she was having a good wash, after pinning up her hair in front of the little round mirror that hung from the window latch and which he used for shaving, he seemed to be studying her bare arms, her bare neck, all the bare parts of her he could see, as if making mental comparisons. He pressed his lips together in distaste. Gervaise limped with the right leg but it hardly showed except when she was tired and gave way to the ache in her hips. That morning, worn out by the night she'd spent, she was dragging her leg and leaning on the wall.

The silence was complete, they'd not exchanged another word. He seemed to be waiting. Gervaise, sick at heart but trying not to show it, hurried through her work. As she was making a bundle of some dirty clothes which had been tossed into a corner behind the trunk, he opened his mouth at last and asked:

'What's that you're doing? . . . Where're you going?'

At first she didn't reply. Then, when he angrily repeated the question:

'You've got eyes, haven't you? I'm going to wash this lot . . . The kids can't live in muck.'

He waited while she picked up two or three handkerchiefs. After another silence he spoke again:

'Got any money?'

At that she stood up and looked him in the face, still holding the children's dirty shirts in her hand.

'Money! And where d'you suppose I might've pinched some money? You know perfectly well I got three francs the day before yesterday on me black skirt. We've had lunch twice on that, and it soon goes, at the pork-butcher's . . . No, of course I haven't got any money. I've got four sous* for the washhouse. I don't earn money like some I could mention.'

He took no notice of this remark. He'd got off the bed, and was inspecting the few rags hanging round the room. Finally he took down the trousers and the shawl, opened the chest of drawers and added a bodice and two women's chemises to the pile, and, flinging the whole lot into Gervaise's arms:

'Here, take these to the pop-shop.'

'You wouldn't like me to take the kids too? If they'd lend us something on the kids, that'd be a real load off our backs, wouldn't it!'

All the same she did go to the pawnshop. When she came back half an hour later she put a five-franc piece on the mantelpiece, adding the pawn ticket to the others, between the two candlesticks.

'That's what they gave me,' she said. 'I tried for six, but nothing doing. Oh, they'll never go broke . . . And there's always a crowd in there!'

Lantier didn't immediately pick up the five-franc piece. He'd have preferred it in change, so he could leave her something. However when he saw the remains of some ham wrapped in paper and a bit of bread lying on the chest of drawers, he made up his mind and slipped the coin into his waistcoat pocket.

'I didn't go to the dairy because we owe them for a week,' explained Gervaise. 'But I'll be home early and while I'm gone you can fetch a loaf and some fried chops and we'll have lunch . . . Get a litre of wine as well.'

He made no objection. Peace seemed to be restored. The young woman went on making up the bundle of dirty clothes. But when she reached for Lantier's shirts and socks in the bottom of the trunk he shouted at her to leave them alone.

'Don't touch my things, d'you hear! I don't want them to go!'

'What d'you mean, you don't want 'em to go!' she exclaimed, pulling herself up. 'You're not thinking of putting these filthy things on again, are you? They've got to be washed.'

She stared at him anxiously, seeing only hardness in his handsome face as if nothing, ever again, would soften him. Losing his temper, he snatched the clothes from her hands and flung them back into the trunk.

'Do as I say for once, damn it! Haven't I told you I don't want them to go!'

'But why?' She turned pale as a dreadful suspicion dawned on her. 'Right now you don't need your shirts, you're not going anywhere . . . Why don't you want me to take 'em?'

He hesitated a moment, disconcerted by the blazing look she'd fixed on him. 'Why? Why?' he stammered. 'Lord! you'll be going round saying that you look after me, that you do my washing and my mending. And that makes me see red, that does. You look after your things, I'll look after mine. Laundresses are there to be used.'

She begged him, protesting she'd never complained, but he slammed the trunk shut and sat down on it, shouting 'No!' in her face. Surely he could please himself what he did with his own clothes! Then, to escape from her searching gaze, he went back to the bed and lay down on it, saying he was sleepy and she wasn't to pester him any more. This time he really did seem to fall asleep.

For a while Gervaise hesitated. She felt tempted to kick the parcel of laundry out of the way and sit down to her sewing. In the end Lantier's steady breathing reassured her. She took the blue-bag, for whitening the laundry, and the piece of soap left from her last wash and went up to the children who were playing quietly by the window with some old corks; kissing them, she said in a low voice:

'Be very good now, and don't make a noise. Daddy's sleeping.'

As she left the room, the only sound breaking the deep silence beneath the blackened ceiling was the soft laughter of Claude and Étienne. It was ten o'clock. A ray of sunlight came in through the half-open window.

On the boulevard, Gervaise turned left and went along the Rue Neuve de la Goutte-d'Or. She gave Madame Fauconnier a little nod as she passed her shop. The washhouse was about half-way up, at the point where the street began to climb. Three huge, cylindrical zinc water tanks, firmly riveted to the roof of a flat building, showed round and grey against the sky, while behind them rose the drying room, a lofty second storey with sides formed by thin-slatted shutters, through which the fresh air could blow and you could see washing hung out to dry on brass wires. To the right of the tanks, the narrow flue from the steam engine puffed out jets of white smoke to a raucous, regular beat. Without hitching up her skirts—for she was used to puddles—Gervaise went in through the entrance which was cluttered with large jars of bleach. She already knew the manageress, a frail little woman with unhealthy-looking eyes who sat in a glassed-in booth with ledgers in front of her, surrounded by cakes of soap on shelves, bottles full of blue-bags and pound packets of bicarbonate of soda. As she passed, Gervaise asked for her wooden beater and scrubbing brush, which she'd left there after her last wash. Then she took her number and went in.

It was an enormous shed with a level ceiling, exposed beams resting on cast-iron pillars, and big clear glass windows. Pallid daylight shone freely through the hot steam hanging in the air like a milky fog. Clouds of vapour rose up here and there and spread out, their bluish haze blotting out what lay beyond. The place was filled with a clinging dampness, like fine rain, smelling of soap, a stale, dank, persistent smell overpowered at times by the sharper fumes of bleach. Washing tubs lined either side of the central aisle and rows of women stood at them, their sleeves rolled right up to their shoulders, their necks bare, their skirts hitched up showing their coloured stockings and heavy laced boots. They were beating away like mad, laughing, leaning back to yell something above the uproar, then bending low over their tubs again, a foul-mouthed, coarse, ungainly lot, soaking wet as if they'd been in a downpour, with red, steaming skin. Water was streaming everywhere around and under them, hot water from buckets lugged over and emptied in one go, cold water from open taps pissing down, splashes from beaters, drips from rinsed washing, puddles they were sloshing about in that ran off over the sloping flagstones in little trickles. And, amidst the shouts and the rhythmic thumping and the gentle patter of rain, in that tempest of noise muffled by the wet ceiling, the steam engine, covered with a fine white dew, puffed and snorted away over on the right without ever stopping, as if the frenzied vibration of its fly-wheel was regulating the whole outrageous din.

Gervaise, meanwhile, walked slowly down the aisle, glancing to left and right. One hip was thrust out to balance the bundle of washing slung over her arm, so her limp was worse than usual as she wove her way through the rushing, jostling women.

'Hey, dearie, over here!' bellowed Madame Boche in her strident voice.

When the young woman had reached her, down at the far end on the left, the concierge, who was furiously rubbing a sock, began talking disjointedly without stopping what she was doing.

'You get in here, I've kept your place for you . . . Oh, this won't take me very long. Boche hardly dirties his things at all . . . How about you? You'll be done soon too, won't you? Your bundle's ever so small. We'll have got through this lot by noon and then we can go and have a bit of lunch . . . I used to take my washing to a laundress in the Rue Poulet, but what with her bleach and her scrubbing she ruined everything. So now I do it myself. It's all money in me pocket. There's only the soap to buy . . . . Goodness, you should've put those shirts to soak. My word, those kids of yours are proper little devils, they must have been sitting in soot.'

Gervaise was undoing her bundle and spreading out the boys' shirts; when Madame Boche advised her to wash them with some soda she replied:

'Oh no, hot water'll do: I know a thing or two about washing clothes.'

She'd sorted the washing and set the few coloured things to one side. After filling her tub with four pails of cold water from the tap behind her, she dumped in all the white things; then hitching up her skirt and tucking it between her thighs she got into a sort of upright box which reached to her waist.

'So you know a thing or two about washing, eh?' repeated Madame Boche. 'Back home you were a laundress, weren't you, dearie?'

Gervaise had rolled up her sleeves, revealing her lovely fair-skinned, youthful arms, scarcely reddened even at the elbows; she began to work the dirt out of her things. She'd spread a shirt out on the narrow washboard which was worn and bleached by the constant contact with water; she rubbed the shirt with soap, turned it over, then rubbed it on the other side.

Before answering she took her beater and began to beat, so her words came as shouts, punctuated by powerful, rhythmic blows.

'Yes, that's right, laundress . . . Since I was ten . . . That'll be twelve years ago now . . . We used to go to the river . . . It smelt a lot sweeter than this . . . You should've seen it, a spot under the trees, and the water running clear as clear . . . You know, in Plassans* . . . You don't know Plassans? . . . Near Marseilles?'

'My word, that's the stuff!' exclaimed Madame Boche, amazed at the vigour of the beating. 'What a girl! I bet she could straighten out an iron bar with those lady-like little arms of hers!'

They went on talking at the tops of their voices. Sometimes the concierge, unable to hear, had to lean over. Every bit of the whites was beaten, and no two ways about it! Gervaise plunged the clothes back into the tub and then fished them out one at a time to soap and scrub them again. Holding the garment on the washboard with one hand, with the other she used a short scrubbing brush to force out a dirty froth which hung down in long dribbles. Then, because scrubbing didn't make much noise, they moved closer together and began to talk more intimately.

'No, we're not married,' Gervaise went on. 'I don't make a secret of it. Lantier's not such a kind bloke that you'd want to be married to him. Believe me, if it weren't for the kids . . . I was fourteen and he was eighteen when we had our first. The other one came four years later . . . It's the old story. I wasn't happy at home, and Père Macquart used to kick me up the backside over every little thing. So, goodness me, you look around for a bit of fun ... We might've got married, but, I don't know why really, our families weren't keen.'

Her hands were turning red in the white suds; giving them a shake, she said:

'This Paris water's awful hard.'

Madame Boche, by now, was only washing half-heartedly. She kept stopping, making the soaping last so she could stay and listen to this tale which she'd been burning to hear for the past two weeks. Her mouth hung half-open in her fat face; her prominent eyes were gleaming. Pleased at having guessed right, she was thinking:

'Yes, I knew it, the girl's talking a deal too much. There's been a real blow-up.'

Then, aloud:

'So he's not being kind to you?'

'Don't talk to me about it!' replied Gervaise. 'Back home he treated me fine, but since we've been in Paris I don't know what's got into him ... His mother died last year, you see, and left him a tidy bit, about seventeen hundred francs. He was dead set on going to Paris. So, being as how Père Macquart was still clouting me whenever he fancied, I said I'd come too, and we did, with the two kids. He was supposed to set me up as a laundress and he would work as a hatter, that's his trade. We'd have been so happy ... But, you see, Lantier has big ideas, he likes spending money, all he ever thinks about is having fun. He's not much good, really ... So we went to the Hôtel Montmartre, in the Rue Montmartre.* It was all dinners, and carriages, and the theatre, a watch for him and a silk dress for me, 'cos he's not a bad chap, when he's in the money. Well you see we went the whole hog, and after two months we were stony-broke. That's when we came to the Hôtel Boncœur and this bloody awful life began ...'

She stopped short, a lump in her throat, trying to fight back her tears. She'd finished scrubbing her things.

'I'd better fetch me hot water,' she murmured.

But Madame Boche, much put out by this interruption in the flow of confidences, called over the laundry boy who was passing by.

'Charlie dear, be ever so kind and bring this lady a pail of hot water, she's in a hurry.'

The boy took the pail and came back with it full. Gervaise paid him—it was one sou per pail. She poured the hot water into the tub and soaped the washing one last time by hand, bending over the washboard right into the smoky steam, which clung in grey vaporous threads to her golden hair.

'Better use some crystals, I've some here,' said the concierge helpfully.

And she emptied the remains of a bag of soda she'd brought into Gervaise's tub. She also offered her some bleach, but that the young woman refused, saying it worked best on grease spots and wine stains.

'I think he's fond of a bit of skirt,' began Madame Boche, returning to the subject of Lantier without mentioning his name.

Gervaise, bent double, with her clenched hands deep in the washing, merely shook her head.

'Yes, yes,' persisted Madame Boche, 'I've noticed one or two little things . . .'

But when she saw Gervaise suddenly stand up, white in the face, staring at her, she protested:

'Oh no, I really don't know anything, he likes a bit of fun, that's all . . . Those two girls who room with us, Adèle and Virginie, you know who I mean, he likes having a bit of a joke with them, there's no more to it than that, I'm sure.'

The young woman went on standing in front of her, her face drenched in sweat and her arms dripping wet, staring at her with a steady, penetrating gaze. So then the concierge, annoyed, thumped herself on the breast with her fist and gave her word of honour. She shouted:

'I tell you I don't know a thing!'

Then, calming down, she added in soothing tones, as if speaking to someone who had no use for the truth:

'Well, I think he has honest eyes. He'll marry you, dearie, you can take it from me.'

Gervaise wiped her forehead with her wet hand. She took another piece of washing out of the water, shaking her head again. For a moment, both were silent. Around them, the

washhouse had quietened down. It was striking eleven. Half the
women were perched on the edge of their tubs, an open bottle
of wine at their feet, eating sausage stuck into chunks of bread.
Only the housewives who'd come in to wash the family smalls
were hurrying, one eye on the clock which hung above the
office. Now and then you could still hear the occasional thump
of a beater, amid quiet laughter and chatting muffled by the
sound of greedily munching jaws; while the vibrating, throbbing voice of the steam engine, as it laboured on without pause
or respite, resounded more and more loudly until it seemed to
fill the vast hall. But not one of the women heard it; it was like
the very breathing of the washhouse, a scalding breath that blew
the ever-present steam into a cloud which hovered in the air
beneath the rafters. The heat was becoming unbearable; rays of
sunlight streaming through the high windows on the left lit up
the steamy vapour with opalescent bands of the softest rosy-
grey and blue-grey. And, since people were beginning to
grumble, the attendant, Charles, went from window to window
pulling down the heavy canvas blinds, and then crossed to the
other side, the shady side, and opened some fanlights. He was
cheered and applauded amid great gales of laughter. Soon,
however, even the last few beaters stopped. The women, their
mouths full, hardly stirred except to gesture with the open
pocket-knives they held in their hands. The silence was so
complete that at regular intervals the scraping of the stoker's
shovel could be heard, far away in the back, as he scooped up
coal and shovelled it into the furnace of the steam engine.

Meanwhile Gervaise was washing her coloureds in the hot
sudsy water she'd saved. When she'd finished she drew up a
trestle and threw all the clothes over it; they dripped on to the
floor, making bluish puddles. Then she began rinsing. Behind
her, the cold water tap ran into an immense tub that was fixed
to the floor; two wooden bars for supporting the washing
stretched across it. High above the tub were two other bars
where things were left to finish dripping.

'Well, it's nearly finished, and a good job too!' said Madame
Boche. 'I'll stay and give you a hand with the wringing.'

'Oh, please don't bother, thanks all the same,' replied Gervaise, as she worked the coloureds about in the clean water,

kneading them with her fists. 'If there were sheets, now, I
wouldn't say no.'

But all the same she had to accept the help of the concierge.
Together, each holding one end, they were wringing out a skirt,
a badly-dyed brown wool affair from which came yellowish
water, when Madame Boche exclaimed:

'Goodness, if it isn't that great tall Virginie! Whatever does
she think she's doing here I'd like to know, with her fiddling
little bits of washing done up in a hanky?'

Gervaise had looked up quickly. Virginie and she were the
same age but Virginie was taller, with dark colouring and a
pretty, though rather long, face. She wore an old black dress
with flounces, with a red ribbon at the neck, and her hair was
carefully coiled into a chignon secured by a blue chenille net.
She paused for a moment in the middle of the central aisle and
screwed up her eyes as if looking for someone; seeing Gervaise,
she passed close by her with her nose in the air, insolently
swaying her hips, and chose a place in the same row, five tubs
away.

'Whatever can have got into her?' went on Madame Boche,
lowering her voice. 'She doesn't ever wash so much as a pair of
cuffs! . . . My she's a lazybones and no mistake, let me tell you!
A seamstress as doesn't even mend her own boots. They're a
pair, her and her sister who's a burnisher—that hussy Adèle—
well more often than not *she* doesn't turn up at the workshop.
They've no father nor mother as anyone knows of, and what
they live on is a mystery, though I could tell you a thing or two
. . . So what's that she's scrubbing, eh? A petticoat? Well it fair
turns my stomach, that petticoat does, I bet it's seen some fine
goings-on!'

It was clear that Madame Boche was trying to please
Gervaise. The truth was that she often had coffee with Adèle
and Virginie, when the girls had a bit of money. Gervaise didn't
answer, but hurried on, her hands working feverishly. She'd
just dissolved her blue in a little three-legged tub. Now she was
soaking her whites, stirring them around for a bit in the tinted
water which had crimson glints where it reflected the light: after
gently squeezing the clothes, she arranged them over the
wooden bars up above. During this entire operation she made

a show of keeping her back to Virginie. But she could hear sniggering, and was conscious of her sidelong glances. It seemed as if Virginie had come just to provoke her. When Gervaise happened to turn round for a moment, they stared hard at one another.

'Take no notice of her,' muttered Madame Boche. 'You're not thinking of having a set-to, surely! . . . There's nothing going on, I tell you. She isn't the one, anyway!'

At that moment, as the young woman was hanging her last piece of washing, the sound of laughter came from the entrance.

'It's two kids asking for their mum,' shouted Charles.

All the women leaned forward. Gervaise recognized Claude and Étienne. As soon as they caught sight of her, they began to run through the puddles towards her, the heels of their untied shoes clattering on the flagstones. Claude, the elder, was holding his little brother by the hand. The women uttered fond little cries on seeing the two boys passing by, looking rather scared but smiling nevertheless. They stopped in front of their mother and stood with their hands still clasped, lifting up their golden heads.

'Did Daddy send you?' asked Gervaise. But, as she was bending down to tie Étienne's shoelaces, she saw their room key with its brass tag swinging from Claude's finger.

'Goodness, you've brought me the key!' she exclaimed, very surprised. 'Why?'

The child, seeing the forgotten key on his finger, seemed to recollect and announced in his shrill voice: 'Daddy's gone.'

'He's gone to buy the lunch, and he told you to come here for me?'

Claude glanced at his brother and hesitated, nonplussed. Then he went on, without stopping for breath: 'Daddy's gone . . . He jumped out of bed, put everything in the trunk, and took it down and put it on a cab . . . He's gone.'

Gervaise, who'd been crouching down, stood up slowly, her face white, and put her hands to her cheeks and temples as if she could feel her head exploding. All she could find to say was 'Oh, my God! . . . Oh my God! . . . Oh my God! . . .' over and over again in a monotonous voice.

Madame Boche meanwhile, very excited at finding herself
mixed up in this affair, was also questioning the child.

'Come on, my lad, tell us everything . . . So he locked the
door and told you to bring the key, did he?'

Lowering her voice, she added in Claude's ear, 'Was there a
lady in the cab?'

Once more the child looked nonplussed. Then, triumphantly,
he launched into his story again from the beginning:

'He jumped out of bed, put everything in the trunk . . . He's
gone . . .'

At that Madame Boche gave up, and Claude pulled his
brother over to the tap. They amused themselves turning the
water on and off.

Gervaise couldn't cry. Gasping for breath, she leant against
her tub with her face in her hands. She kept giving little
shudders. Sometimes she'd heave a great sigh, ramming her
fists harder into her eyes, as if she longed to vanish forever into
the blackness of her desolation. It was like a dark deep pit down
which she was falling.

'Buck up, dearie, what the hell!' muttered Madame Boche.

'If you only knew! If you only knew!' she whispered at last.
'This morning he made me take my shawl and my chemises to
the pawnshop, it was so he could pay for that cab . . .'

And she began to cry. The thought of her trip to the
pawnshop, by reminding her of one of that morning's events,
forced out the sobs which had been choking her. That particular trip was an outrage, the very worst of the agonies which
made up her despair. Tears streamed down over her chin which
her hands had already wetted, but she never even thought of
bringing out her handkerchief.

'Hush, pull yourself together, people are looking at you,'
Madame Boche kept repeating as she fussed about her. 'How
can you be in such a taking over a man! . . . You're still in love
with him, aren't you, you poor dear? Only a moment ago you
could have killed him, and just look at you now, crying your
eyes out over him! . . . My God, what fools we are!'

Then she turned all maternal.

'A pretty little thing like you, if you'll pardon the liberty . . .
Now I can tell you everything, can't I? You'll remember I

passed your window this morning, well now, I already had my suspicions then . . . Just imagine, last night when Adèle came in, I could hear a man's step along with hers. I wanted to know who it was, so I looked up the stairs. The party in question had already got to the second floor, but I'm certain it was Monsieur Lantier's coat I saw. Boche kept a lookout this morning and saw him come down as cool as you please. It was Adèle he was with, you understand. Virginie has a gentleman now that she visits twice a week. Only thing is, it's not at all nice, it isn't, for they've only one room between 'em, with an alcove for the bed, and I can't think where Virginie slept.'

She stopped for a moment and turned round, then whispered in her gruff voice:

'Look at her over there, she's laughing 'cos you're crying, the heartless bit of goods. I'd take my oath this laundry of hers is all eye-wash . . . She's packed off the other two and then come here so she could tell 'em how you're taking it.'

Gervaise lifted her hands from her face and looked. When she saw Virginie surrounded by three or four women, whispering and staring in her direction, she was filled with blind fury. Trembling in every limb, she turned and moved a little forward, reaching down and groping on the ground with her arms; finding a pail of water, she grabbed it in both hands and pitched it straight at the tall girl.

'Bitch!' screamed Virginie. She'd jumped back, so only her boots were wet. The women of the washhouse, all agog now because of Gervaise's tears, crowded round to see the fight. Some who hadn't finished their bread yet climbed on to the tubs. Others rushed up with their hands still all soapy. A circle formed.

'Oh! The bitch!' repeated Virginie. 'Whatever's got into her, she must be off her rocker!'

Gervaise stood still, her chin thrust out and her face contorted, at a loss for an answer. She hadn't yet learned how to bawl insults in the Parisian style. The other girl went on:

'Just look at her, she's sick of fucking the provinces, soldiers had her for a mattress by the time she was twelve, she's left a leg back home there . . . Rotted away, it did! . . .'

There was laughter. Virginie, emboldened by her success,

came two steps nearer, drew herself up to her full height and yelled even louder:

'C'mon, a bit closer, let's have a look at you, I'll give you wot for! Listen, you'd no business coming here, pesterin' us! ... I don't even know the old bag! If she'd got me just now I'd 'ave pulled up her skirts in a jiffy; you'd have seen all right. Why don't she say what I've done to her? Hey, you trollop, what is it I've done?'

'Don't go on like that,' Gervaise stammered. 'You know all right ... They saw me husband, last night ... And shut your trap or I'll strangle you, for sure.'

'Her husband! Oh, that's rich, that is! Madame's husband! As if she could catch a husband with a bandy leg like hers! Not my fault if he's dumped you. I ain't pinched him, have I? Here, feel me pockets ... D'you want me to tell you? You were making his life a misery, you were, he's too good for you ... Let's hope he'd got his collar on! Has anyone found madame's husband? There's a reward ...'

The laughter began again. Gervaise could still only mutter, almost in a whisper:

'You know all right ... You know all right ... It's your sister, I'll strangle her, your sister ...'

'OK, so go and have it out with her,' sneered Virginie. 'It's my sister, is it? Maybe so, my sister's got a lot more class than you ... But what's it to do with me? Can't a body do some washing in peace any more? Leave me alone, d'you hear: I've had enough!'

But Virginie, drunk with jeering and quite carried away, returned to the attack herself after half a dozen whacks with her beater. Three times she began, then stopped, then began again:

'Yes, all right, it's my sister. There, does that satisfy you? ... They're mad about each other. You should just see 'em billing and cooing! ... An' he's walked out on you and your bastards. Darling little brats with faces all over scabs! One of 'em's a policeman's, ain't he? An' you got rid of three others, so as not to have all that extra baggage coming here ... It was your precious Lantier told us that. He's told us some pretty tales, he's had all he wants of you, you bag of old bones!'

'Bitch, bitch, bitch!' screamed Gervaise, beside herself, once more trembling uncontrollably.

She turned round and groped on the ground again; finding only the little tub, she grasped it by its feet and hurled the blue-tinted water at Virginie's face.

'The slut! She's ruined me dress!' Virginie shrieked. One shoulder was soaked and her left hand dyed blue. 'Just you wait, you shit!'

She in turn seized a pail and emptied it over the young woman. At that, a battle royal began. Each would run down past the tubs, grab a pail full of water, and run back to fling it at the other. Shouts and screams accompanied every drenching. Gervaise, too, was answering back now.

'Take that, you filthy bit o' trash. Got yer! That'll cool yer arse.'

'Fuckin' bitch! This'll rinse off your muck. Have a wash for once.'

'Yea, how 'bout a good soak, you'll be tastier for yer customers, you tart.'

'Here we go! Wash your mouth out an' get cleaned up for your beat tonight on Belhomme* corner.'

Eventually they had to fill the pails from the taps. The foul exchanges continued while they waited. At first their aim was bad and the pailfuls of water hardly touched them. But they were getting their eye in. Virginie was the first to catch one full in the face; the water, pouring in at her neck, streamed down her back and her bosom and piddled out from underneath her dress. She was still stunned from that when a second caught her from the side, smacking her sharply on the left ear and soaking her chignon, which unravelled like a ball of string. Gervaise got it first in the legs; a pailful flooded her shoes and splashed up to her thighs, then two others drenched her round the hips. Soon it was impossible to keep track of the score. Both were shivering and streaming with water from head to foot, their bodices sticking to their backs, their skirts clinging to their buttocks; they seemed to have grown stiffer and skinnier, as they stood there dripping all over like a pair of umbrellas in a downpour.

'They don't 'alf look funny!' croaked one of the bystanders.

The washhouse was having a grand time. The spectators had moved back to avoid being splashed. Applause and repartee could be heard above the swoosh of pails being emptied in one go. The ground was awash, and the two women were paddling about, up to their ankles in water. It was then that Virginie decided to play dirty: she suddenly grabbed a pail of boiling soda ordered by someone nearby, and flung it at Gervaise. There was a scream. People thought Gervaise had been scalded. The boiling water, however, had barely caught her left foot. Maddened by the pain, she seized a pail without filling it and flung it with all her might at Virginie's legs, knocking her down.

The women all spoke at once:

'She's bust 'er leg!'

'Well, the other one tried to boil her alive!'

'After all the blonde's in the right, ain't she, if the other's pinched her bloke!'

Madame Boche kept exclaiming and raising her arms in the air. She'd prudently taken refuge between two washtubs, while Claude and Étienne, crying and gasping in terror, hung on to her skirts, screaming over and over again between their sobs, 'Mummy! Mummy!' When she saw Virginie on the ground, she ran up to Gervaise and pulled her by the skirt, repeating:

'Here, get on home now. Do be sensible . . . You've given me quite a turn, I declare! I've never in me born days seen such a rough-up.'

But she had to step back and return to the safety of the tubs, with the children. Virginie had jumped at Gervaise's throat. She was squeezing her neck, trying to strangle her. Gervaise freed herself with a violent thrust and grabbed the ends of Virginie's hair, tugging as if to pull her head off. Once more the battle was joined, but silently, without any screams or insults. They didn't try to wrestle, but each went for the other's face, pinching and clawing with open hands and hooked fingers at any flesh she could grasp. The tall brunette's red ribbon and blue chenille net went flying; her bodice had split at the neck, showing a lot of skin and most of one shoulder, while the blonde was half naked, one sleeve of her white bodice ripped off somehow or other and a tear in her chemise revealing the naked curve of her waist. Scraps of material were flying about. It was on Gervaise that the first blood was drawn, three long scratches from her mouth to under her chin; she closed her eyes at each attack, afraid of having an eye put out. Virginie was not bleeding yet. Gervaise, who was aiming for Virginie's ears, became infuriated by her lack of success, but in the end she did manage to grab an earring, a yellow glass pear-shaped thing; she pulled, the ear split, and blood began to flow.

'The sluts are murderin' each other! Get 'em apart!' several voices cried.

The women had closed in. They were forming into two camps, with some of them egging on the combatants as if they were a couple of dogs fighting, while others, more timid, trembled and turned away their heads, saying they'd had enough, it was making them feel queer, it really was. The fight nearly became a general brawl: people were calling each other names—heartless bitch, good-for-nothing; bare arms were being raised threateningly and three slaps rang out.

Madame Boche, meanwhile, was searching for the laundry boy.

'Charles . . . Charles . . . Where's he got to?'

She found him in the front row, his arms crossed, watching. He was a great big chap, with a huge neck. He was laughing and enjoying the bits of naked flesh the two women were displaying. The little fair one was as plump as a partridge. What a joke if her chemise split open!

'Hey!' he muttered, giving a wink, 'she's got a birthmark under her arm.'

'So this is where you are!' exclaimed Madame Boche on catching sight of him. 'Come on, help us separate 'em! You could do it ever so easy, you could.'

'Oh, no, not me, thanks ever so. Not if it's just me on me own,' he replied calmly. 'And get me eye scratched out like t'other day, eh? I'm not paid for that, I'd never be finished . . . Come on, no need to be scared! A bit of blood-letting'll do 'em good. Soften 'em up like!'

The concierge said something then about fetching the police. However the manageress, the frail young woman with sickly eyes, wouldn't hear of it. She kept repeating:

'No, I can't have that, it'll give the place a bad name.'

The fight was continuing down on the ground. All of a sudden, Virginie got to her knees; she'd just picked up one of the beaters and was brandishing it. Her voice had changed into a raw snarl:

'Now here's a treat for you! C'mon, let's have your dirty duds!'

Gervaise also quickly reached out her hand and grabbed a beater, holding it up like a club. Her voice too had grown harsh:

'Oh, so it's a proper laund'ring you want, eh? Here, gimme your hide, I'll make ribbons of it!'

They knelt there for a moment, glaring at one another. With their hair falling over their eyes, all muddy, their breasts heaving and their faces puffy, they waited, watching warily and catching their breath. Gervaise struck first, her beater glancing off Virginie's shoulder. And then she flung herself sideways to avoid the other's beater as it brushed her hip. Once into their stride, they pounded each other vigorously, rhythmically, like laundresses pounding dirty clothes. When a blow landed on flesh, it sounded muffled, as if it had landed in a tub of water.

Around them, the women were no longer laughing; several had left, repeating that it turned their stomach; the others, those who stayed to watch, craned their necks, their eyes glinting cruelly as they remarked on what a lot of guts the hussies had. Madame Boche had taken Claude and Étienne away; their sobs could be heard in the distance, mingling with the echoing thuds of the beaters.

Suddenly, Gervaise gave a howl. Virginie had just hit her with all her might on her bare arm, above the elbow; a red patch appeared and immediately began to swell. So then she hurled herself at Virginie. Everyone thought she meant to murder her.

'Stop! Stop!' people shouted.

But her face was so terrifying that no one dared go near. With extraordinary strength she seized Virginie round the waist and forced her over so her face was pushed down on to the flagstones and her bottom was in the air; despite her struggles, Gervaise pulled her skirts all the way up. Underneath were drawers. Slipping her hand into the slit she tore them off, exposing bare thighs and bare buttocks. Then Gervaise raised her beater and began to beat, just as she used to beat in Plassans, on the banks of the Viorne,* when her employer did the washing for the garrison. The wood smacked into the flesh with a wet thud. With each blow, a red weal appeared on the white skin.

'Oh! Oh!' muttered young Charles, round-eyed with amazement.

At first there was more laughter. Soon, however, cries of 'stop! stop!' began again. Gervaise didn't hear, didn't tire. Keeping her eyes on her work, she bent low over it, determined not to miss one single spot. She wanted every inch of this flesh beaten, beaten and scarlet with shame. And she began to speak, full of ferocious glee as she remembered an old washerwoman's song:

> Bang! Bang! Margot's wash she's thwacking,
> Bang! Bang! With her beater smacking,
> Bang! Bang! Washing out the stain,
> Bang! Bang! Of her heart's black pain.

And she went on: 'This one's for you, this one's for your sister, this one's for Lantier . . . Mind you give it 'em when you see 'em. Wait! I've not finished. This one's for Lantier, this one's for your sister, this one's for you. Bang! Bang! Margot's wash she's thwacking . . . Bang! Bang! With her beater smacking . . .'

They had to drag Virginie out of her grasp. The tall brunette, her face tear-stained and purple with mortification, grabbed her washing and fled, defeated. Gervaise, meanwhile, slipped her arm back into the sleeve of her bodice and fastened her skirt. Her arm was hurting, and she asked Madame Boche to put her bundle of washing up on her shoulder. The concierge kept talking about the fight and how she'd felt while she was watching it, and suggested examining Gervaise, just in case.

'Something could easily be broken . . . I heard a crack . . .'

But the young woman wanted to leave. She paid no attention to the commiserations or the wordy congratulations of the women standing round her in their aprons. Carrying her washing she made for the door, where her children were waiting for her.

'Two hours, that'll be two sous.' The manageress, already
back inside her glassed-in box, stopped her.

Two sous? Why? She couldn't grasp that she was being
charged for using the wash-house. She handed over the two
sous. And, limping badly under the weight of the damp clothes
hanging from her shoulder, dripping wet, her elbow black and
blue and her cheek bleeding, she set off, with Claude and
Étienne, tear-stained and still racked by sobs, each dragging on
a bare arm as they trotted along at her side.

Behind her, a tremendous sluice-like noise once again filled
the washhouse. The women had finished their bread and
drunk their wine and, their faces flushed, were now pounding
away with extra vigour, enlivened by the barney between
Virginie and Gervaise. Along the rows of tubs, once again, you
could see a frenzy of moving arms, and sharply outlined
puppets with lopsided shoulders and bent backs, that jerked
sharply up and down as if on hinges. Conversations were
being carried on between one end of an aisle and the other.
Voices, laughter and smutty talk mingled in with the tremendous gurgling of the water. Taps were spewing, pails were
spurting, a river was flowing beneath the washtubs. It was
the dog-tired stage of the afternoon, with the washing beaten
into a pulp. In the huge hall, the clouds of steam were
turning reddish-brown, except where circles of sunlight, shining through the holes in the blinds, formed golden balls. Even
the air you breathed was thick with a stifling, soapy-smelling
warmth. Suddenly the hall was filled with a white fog; the
enormous lid of the copper in which the washing was boiled
rose automatically along a central ratchet, and from the gaping
mouth of the copper, set deep inside a brick casing, rose swirls
of vapour which smelt cloyingly of potash. Meanwhile, alongside, the dryers were hard at it; in the cast-iron cylinders
bundles of washing yielded up their water with each turn of the
flywheel; and as their steel arms laboured on unremittingly, the
machines puffed and steamed, making the building shake still
more violently.

When Gervaise set foot in the alley beside the Hôtel Boncœur, her tears began again. It was a dark, narrow alley, with
an open channel for sewage running along the wall; the familiar

stench brought back memories of the fortnight spent there with Lantier, memories of a fortnight's misery and quarrels which now filled her with bitter regret. From this moment, she felt, the world had forsaken her.

Upstairs, the room was bare and filled with sunshine from the open window. The sunlight with its beam of golden dancing dust showed up the wretchedness of the blackened ceiling and the torn paper drooping from the walls. All that remained, hanging from a nail by the fireplace, was a woman's little neckerchief, all twisted like a piece of cord. The children's bed had been dragged into the middle of the room to free the chest, whose drawers were open and quite empty. Lantier had washed and finished up the pomade, two sous' worth of pomade on a playing card; the bowl was full of the greasy water from his hands. He'd forgotten nothing, and it seemed to Gervaise there was a gaping hole in the corner where the trunk used to be. Even the little round mirror hanging from the window latch had gone. Filled with foreboding, she looked at the mantelpiece: Lantier had taken the pawn tickets, the pale pink bundle no longer lay there, between the two zinc candlesticks which didn't match.

She hung her washing over the back of a chair, and stood looking all round, staring at the furniture, so dazed that she could no longer even cry. She had one sou left of the four she had saved for the washhouse. Then, hearing Claude and Étienne laughing, for they'd already cheered up, Gervaise went over to them at the window and put her arms round their necks; oblivious, for a brief moment, of everything else, she gazed down at the grey road along which that very morning she'd watched the workers of Paris awaken to their toils, and the mammoth labours of Paris begin. At this time of day a fiery haze arose from the much-travelled cobbles and hung over the city behind the octroi wall. It was on to these streets, into this stifling furnace, that she was being cast out alone with her babies; and she looked along the outer boulevards, to the left and to the right, her eyes pausing at either end, filled with a nameless dread, as if, from now on, her life would be lived out within this space, bounded by a slaughterhouse and a hospital.

CHAPTER II

THREE weeks later, at about half-past-eleven on a lovely sunny morning, Gervaise and Coupeau the roofer were having a brandied plum together at Père Colombe's bar, the Assommoir.* Coupeau had been smoking a cigarette outside on the pavement when Gervaise crossed the road after delivering some laundry; he'd made her come in with him and now her big square laundry basket lay beside her on the ground, behind the little zinc table.

Père Colombe's Assommoir stood at the corner of the Rue des Poissonniers and the Boulevard de Rochechouart. The sign bore the single word 'Spirits' written in tall blue letters right across it. There were some dusty oleanders growing in two half-barrels at the entrance. The enormous counter with its rows of glasses, its water vat and its pewter measures stretched along to the left of the entrance, and the vast room was decorated all round with huge casks painted pale yellow and highly varnished, with hoops and spigots of shining copper. Higher up were shelves displaying bottles of liqueurs, jars of brandied fruit and carefully arranged flasks of all kinds; they concealed the walls, reflecting their vibrant splashes of apple green, pale gold and soft reddish-brown in the mirror behind the counter. But the real attraction of the place, standing beyond an oak balustrade in the glassed-in rear courtyard, was the still, which the customers could see working, with its long-necked alembics and its tubes coiling down into the ground, a veritable devil's kitchen in front of which boozing workmen would hang about and day-dream.

Now, at this stage of the lunch hour, the Assommoir was empty. Père Colombe, a stout man of forty wearing a sleeved waistcoat, was serving a little ten-year-old girl who'd asked for four sous' worth of spirits in a cup. Sunshine flooded in through the door, warming the wooden floor which was permanently wet with the spit of smokers. And from the counter, from the casks, from the entire room, a smell of spirits rose up, an alcoholic vapour which seemed to make even the dust-motes spinning about in the sunlight dense and drunken.

Coupeau, meanwhile, was busy rolling a fresh cigarette. He looked spick-and-span in his smock and little peaked cap of blue cloth, and his white teeth gleamed when he laughed. With his protruding lower jaw, slightly flattened nose and fine brown eyes, his face reminded you of a cheerful, good-natured dog. His thick curly hair stood up on its own. At twenty-six, his skin was still soft. Opposite him Gervaise, in a black cloth jacket, her head bare, was finishing her plum, holding it by its stem with her fingertips. They were sitting close to the street, at the first of the four tables set alongside the casks in front of the counter.

When the roofer had lit his cigarette, he put his elbows on the table and, leaning forward, gazed for a moment in silence at the young woman's pretty face. That morning, her fair skin had the milky transparency of fine porcelain. Then, referring to something private between them, he asked simply, keeping his voice low:

'So it's no? You're sayin' no?'

'But of course it's no, Monsieur Coupeau,' Gervaise replied calmly, with a smile. 'You're not going to start on about that here, surely. And you did promise to be sensible, didn't you . . . If I'd known, I'd have refused your offer of a drink.'

He said nothing more, and went on leaning close, staring at her with bold, inviting tenderness, entranced by the corners of her lips, tiny pale pink corners, slightly wet, which revealed the bright red of her mouth when she smiled. Nevertheless she didn't draw back, but continued looking unruffled and affectionate. After a silence, she spoke again:

'I'm sure you don't really mean it. I'm an old woman, I am; I've a great big boy of eight . . . Whatever would we do together?'

'Lor,' murmured Coupeau with a wink. 'Same as everyone else!'

But she answered, with a gesture of irritation: 'Oh! If you think it's always fun . . . It's clear you've never had to run a home. No, Monsieur Coupeau, I've got to stick to what matters. Fun and games don't get you anywhere, you know. I've two mouths to feed at home, and they're hearty eaters, let me tell you! How d'you suppose I'll ever manage to bring up

me little chicks if I spend me time larking about? And then,
well it's like this, me bad luck's really taught me a lesson. You
know, when it comes to men, I just don't fancy 'em any more.
It'll be a good while before I'm caught again.'

She explained herself dispassionately, sounding very wise and
calm as if she were talking about something to do with laundering, like why she wouldn't starch a shawl. You could see she'd
worked it all out in her head, after long and careful thought.

Coupeau kept repeating tenderly:

'You're makin' me very unhappy, very unhappy . . .'

'Yes, I can see that,' she replied, 'and I'm very sorry on your
account, Monsieur Coupeau. You mustn't take it amiss. If I
wanted a bit of that, lord, I'd sooner it was with you than
anyone else. You seem like a nice chap, you're kind. We'd try
it out together, wouldn't we, and see how long it lasted. I'm not
being stuck-up, I'm not saying it couldn't have happened . . .
Only, what would be the point, since I don't want to? I've been
at Madame Fauconnier's for a fortnight now. The kids are at
school. I've a job, I'm quite happy . . . Best leave things as they
are, eh?'

She bent down for her basket.

'You're keeping me chatting, when they'll be expecting me
at Madame's . . . You'll find someone else, Monsieur Coupeau,
of course you will, someone prettier than me, who won't have
a couple of brats to drag about.'

He was looking at the clock set in the mirror. He made her
sit down again, exclaiming: 'Wait a bit! It's only twenty-five to
twelve! . . . I've still twenty-five minutes. Surely you're not
afraid I'll do something silly—we've got the table between us
. . . Come on, d'you hate me so much you won't even have a
little chat?'

Not wishing to be unkind, she put her basket down and they
talked like old friends. She'd had her lunch before setting out
with the laundry and he'd bolted down his soup and beef that
day so he could watch for her. While answering his questions
in a pleasant way Gervaise kept looking through the windows,
between the jars of brandied fruits, at all the activity in the
street, which was amazingly crowded with people now it was
the lunch-hour. Along the two pavements, jammed into the

narrow space between the houses, came an endless rush of
striding feet, swinging arms and jabbing elbows. The latecomers, workmen who hadn't been let out on time, raced along
with giant strides, their faces bad-tempered and hungry, and
went into the baker's across the road, reappearing with a pound
loaf under their arm before going into the Veau à deux têtes,
three doors further on, for the six-sous set meal. Next to the
baker there was also a fruiterer who sold fried potatoes and
mussels with parsley, and a continuous stream of working girls
in long aprons emerged carrying bags of chips and cups of
mussels; other girls—pretty, bare-headed, dainty-looking—
were buying bunches of radishes. Leaning forward, Gervaise
could see another shop, a pork-butcher's, crowded with people,
where children came out holding, wrapped in greasy paper, a
breaded chop, a sausage or a piece of hot black pudding.
Meanwhile, along the road which even in fine weather was
always slimy with black mud because of the trampling throng,
little groups of workers were already coming out of the eating
houses and setting off in twos and threes; sluggish with food,
they dawdled about, slapping their open palms on their thighs,
calm and slow amid the jostling of the crowd.

A group had gathered at the door of the Assommoir.

'What about it, Bibi-la-Grillade,'* asked a croaky voice, 'ain't
you goin' to stand us a round o' rotgut?'

Five workmen came in and stood by the bar.

'Hey, here's that old crook Colombe,' continued the voice.
'Now we want the real old stuff, mind, and in proper glasses,
not thimbles!'

Père Colombe was serving them placidly. Another lot of three
workmen arrived. The overalls would gather slowly into groups
at the pavement corner, stop there for a little while, then push
their way between the dust-grey oleanders into the bar.

'Don't be silly! What a dirty mind you have!' Gervaise was
saying to Coupeau. 'Of course I loved him . . . Only, after the
horrible way he left me . . .'

They were talking about Lantier. Gervaise hadn't seen him
again; she believed he was living with Virginie's sister, at La
Glacière, at that friend's who was supposed to be starting a hat
factory. In any case, she'd no intention of chasing after him. At

first she'd been dreadfully hurt and had even thought of throwing herself into the river but now she'd made herself see sense and felt it was all for the best. If she'd stayed with Lantier she mightn't have been able to bring up her kids, he went through money so fast. He could come and see Claude and Étienne, she wouldn't kick him out. Only, as far as she was concerned, she'd sooner be chopped into little bits than let him touch her with the tip of his finger. She said all this very decisively, like a woman who has her whole life clearly planned, while Coupeau, still driven by his desire for her, kept making jokes and dirty remarks out of everything, asking her the crudest questions about Lantier, but so cheerfully and with such a gleaming white smile that she never even thought of taking offence.

'I bet you knocked him about,' he said finally. 'Oh, you're a bad 'un! You beat everybody up.'

She interrupted him with a long laugh. Still, it was true, she *had* beaten up that hulking great Virginie. That day, she'd have been more than happy to strangle somebody. She began laughing even more when Coupeau explained that Virginie was so mortified at having displayed everything she'd got, she'd left the neighbourhood. Gervaise's face, however, still kept its childlike sweetness; she showed him her chubby little hands, declaring she wouldn't harm a fly; she only knew about beating up because she'd been at the receiving end herself so damn often. That started her talking about her girlhood in Plassans. She'd never been one for the men; men bored her; when Lantier had taken her, at fourteen, she thought that was nice because he said he was her husband and it was like playing house. Her only weakness, she assured him, was being very soft-hearted, liking everybody, getting desperately fond of people who then put her through endless misery. So, when she loved a man, she wasn't interested in all that nonsense, what she dreamt of was simply living together happily ever after. When Coupeau started to snigger and mentioned her two kids, whom she certainly hadn't hatched out under the bolster, she rapped him on the knuckles, adding that of course she was made the same way as other women; only it was wrong to imagine women were always mad keen on you-know-what;

women were taken up by their homes, they worked their fingers to the bone in the house and went to bed at night too worn out not to fall asleep straight away. Besides, she was like her mother, a tireless worker who'd died in harness after serving as beast of burden to Père Macquart for over twenty years. She was still very thin, while her mother had had a pair of shoulders on her broad enough to stave in a door, but just the same she took after her in the way she got desperately fond of people. And even her bit of a limp came from the poor woman, whom Père Macquart was forever beating half to death. Time and again her mother had told her about the nights when Macquart came home blind drunk and made love so brutally that he almost broke her bones, and certainly she, Gervaise, with her gammy leg, must have been started on one of those nights.

'Oh, it's hardly anything, it doesn't show at all,' said Coupeau, to please her.

She shook her head; she knew quite well it showed; she'd be bent double by the time she was forty. Then with a little laugh she added gently:

'You've funny tastes, to fancy a girl who limps.'

So then, leaning closer to her with his elbows still on the table, he became less guarded in his flattery, as if trying to make her drunk with words. But she went on shaking her head, not letting herself be tempted, although she found that coaxing voice beguiling. She listened to him with her gaze fixed on the street, apparently absorbed once more by the ever-increasing crowds. Now, in the empty shops, they were sweeping up; the fruiterer was taking the last panful of fried potatoes off the stove and the pork-butcher was tidying up the jumble of plates on his counter. Groups of workmen were emerging from all the eating houses; great strapping fellows with beards were pushing and slapping each other about, playful as kids, their heavy nailed boots making a scraping noise as they went sliding over the cobbles; others, their hands deep in their pockets, were enjoying a quiet smoke, blinking their eyes as they gazed at the sun. They poured on to the pavement, the roadway, the gutters, streaming out of open doorways like a slow-running tide, coming to a stop amid the passing carts, making a trail of workmen's overalls and smocks and old coats which looked all faded and colourless in the rays of golden light which filled the street. Factory bells could be heard in the distance; however the workmen weren't hurrying but kept stopping to relight their pipes; then, after calling to each other from bar to bar, they finally made up their minds to get back to work and slouched off, dragging their feet. Gervaise amused herself watching three men, one tall and two short, who stopped and turned round every few paces; in the end they came back down the street, heading straight for Père Colombe's Assommoir.

'Well now,' she murmured, 'those three must be proper lazy-bones!'

'Hey,' said Coupeau, 'I know the tall one, it's Mes-Bottes,* a pal o' mine.'

The Assommoir had filled up. People were talking very loudly, sometimes shouting to break through the hoarse rumble of voices. At times a fist would bang down on the counter and make the glasses ring. The drinkers were crowded together, standing in little clusters with their hands crossed on their bellies or tucked behind their backs; over by the casks there were some groups who had to wait a quarter of an hour before being able to order their drinks from old Colombe.

'Why, if it isn't old nose-in-air Cadet-Cassis!'* shouted Mes-Bottes, giving Coupeau a great whack on the shoulder. 'Quite the gent, what with 'is cigarettes and 'is fancy shirts! So, we're trying to make an impression are we, standing the lady friend a little treat?'

'Hey! Piss off!' answered Coupeau, very put out.

But the other just laughed. 'Right! Very snooty, aren't we, mate? Well, once a moron always a moron . . .'

He turned his back, after staring at Gervaise with a frightful leer. She drew away, rather scared. The atmosphere, thick with pipe-smoke, alcohol fumes and a strong smell of male bodies, was making her choke and she began to cough a bit.

'Oh, drinking's foul!' she muttered.

And she told him that years ago, in Plassans, she used to drink anisette with her mother, but one day it had nearly killed her, so now she couldn't bear to touch spirits.

'Look,' she said, pointing at her glass, 'I ate me plum, but I'm leaving the syrup because it would make me ill.'

Coupeau couldn't understand either how people could swallow spirits by the glassful. There was no harm in having the odd plum. But as for rotgut, absinthe and all that other muck—thanks very much, they could keep it! His mates could chaff him as much as they liked, he stayed outside when those piss-tanks dropped into the boozer. Old man Coupeau, who'd been a roofer like him, had bashed his head in when he fell on to the pavement of the Rue Coquenard* from the eaves of number 25, one day when he'd had a few, and the memory of that kept 'em all sober in his family. Whenever he himself went along the Rue Coquenard and saw the spot, he'd sooner drink water out of the gutter than have a glass of wine in a bar, even if it was free. He ended by remarking:

'In our line of business, you need steady legs.'

Gervaise had picked up her basket. However she didn't get up, but held it on her lap, with a far-away, dreamy look on her face as if the young workman's words had stirred in her some dimly-felt thoughts about life. And she went on slowly, with no apparent transition:

'My God! I'm not ambitious, I don't ask for much . . . My ideal would be to get on with me work in peace, always have something to eat and a nice little place to sleep—you know, just a bed, a table and two chairs, that's all . . . Oh! I'd also like to be able to bring up me kids to be decent folk, if I could . . . There's another ideal I have, and that's not to be beaten, if I ever took up with anyone again; no, I wouldn't want to be beaten . . . And that's all, really, that's all I want.'

She considered, searching her mind for other wishes but could find nothing else that was important. Nevertheless she did go on, after a little hesitation:

'Oh yes, at the end, you might want to die in your own bed . . . After slogging away all me life, I'd really like to die in me own bed, at home.'

Gervaise got up. Coupeau, who strongly approved of what she'd been saying, was already on his feet, for he was worried about the time. But they didn't leave immediately; she was full of curiosity to see the big copper still which was working away under the transparent glass roof of the little courtyard at the back, behind the oak barrier. Coupeau, who'd followed her, explained how it worked, pointing out the different parts of the machine and showing her the huge retort from which came a trickle of crystal-clear alcohol. The still, with its weirdly-shaped containers and its endless coils of piping, had a gloomy look about it; there was no steam escaping from it, and you could just hear a kind of breathing, like a subterranean rumbling, coming from deep within; it was as if some midnight task were being glumly performed in broad daylight by a strong, taciturn worker. Meanwhile, Mes-Bottes, with his two mates, had come over and was leaning on the oak balustrade, while they waited for a free spot at the counter. His laugh sounded like a pulley that needed greasing as, nodding his head, he gazed fondly at the boozing machine. Christ almighty! wasn't she a sweetheart! There was enough in that great big copper belly to keep your whistle wetted for a whole week! He'd have liked it, he would, if they'd solder the end of the tubing between his teeth, so he could feel the rotgut—still warm, it'd be—filling him up, flowing on and on right down into his heels, like a little stream. Lor! he'd never have to budge again, it'd be a bleeding good exchange for the thimbles that rat Colombe dished out! His pals were all laughing and declaring that that sod Mes-Bottes didn't half have the gift of the gab. The still worked silently on, with no flame visible, no cheerful play of light on its lack-lustre copper surface, sweating out its alcohol like a slow-flowing but relentless spring which would eventually flood the bar-room, spill over the outer boulevards and inundate the vast pit that was Paris. Gervaise gave a shudder and stepped back; trying to smile, she murmured:

'I know it's silly, but that machine really gives me the shivers . . . Drink always gives me the shivers . . .'

Then, coming back to her cherished vision of perfect happiness:

'Well, aren't I right? It'd be so much better to work, put food on your table, have a little place of your own, bring up your kids and die in your own bed . . .'

'An' not get beaten,' added Coupeau cheerfully. 'But I'd never beat you, I wouldn't, if only you'd say yes, Madame Gervaise . . . You needn't be scared, I never drink, an' anyway

I love you too much. Come on, how 'bout tonight, let's keep each other's tootsies warm.'

He'd lowered his voice and was murmuring in her ear as, holding her basket in front of her, she made her way through the crowd. But she went on refusing, shaking her head several times. Nevertheless she did turn round to smile at him, and seemed pleased that he didn't drink. She'd certainly have said yes to him if she hadn't promised herself never to take up with a man again. At last they reached the door and went out. Behind them the Assommoir was still packed, with the hoarse rumble of voices and the fumes from all those rounds of booze wafting out into the street. They could hear Mes-Bottes calling Colombe a dirty swindler and accusing him of only half filling his glass. He himself was a real brick, one hell of a fellow, as good as they came. The boss could go fuck himself, he wasn't going back to that dump of a workshop, he felt like having a wander. And he suggested to his two companions that they go to the Petit bonhomme qui tousse,* a boozer near the Barrière Saint-Denis,* where you could get it neat.

'Ah! You can breathe here,' said Gervaise, when they were on the pavement. 'Well, goodbye and thank you, Monsieur Coupeau . . . I'd better hurry.'

She was going along the boulevard. But he'd taken her hand and was keeping it in his, saying:

'Why don't you come with me, round by the Rue de la Goutte-d'Or, it's hardly out of your way at all . . . I've got to drop by my sister's before I go back to work . . . We can keep each other company.'

In the end she accepted, though she did not take his arm, and they walked slowly up the Rue des Poissonniers side by side. He told her about his family. His mother, Maman Coupeau, used to make waistcoats for a living but now she went out charring because her eyesight was failing. She'd turned sixty-two the third of last month. He was the youngest. One of his sisters, Madame Lerat, a widow of thirty-six, was a flower-maker by trade and lived in the Rue des Moines, in the Batignolles.* The other sister, aged thirty, had married a chain-maker, a sarky sod called Lorilleux. It was her he was going to see, in the Rue de la Goutte-d'Or. She lived in the big building on the left. He usually had his meal with the Lorilleux in the evening; it saved all three of them money. In fact, he was on his way there now to tell them not to expect him that night because he'd been invited to eat at a friend's.

Gervaise had been listening, but she suddenly interrupted him to ask with a smile:

'So you're called Cadet-Cassis, are you, Monsieur Coupeau?'

'Oh,' he replied, 'It's a nickname my mates have given me, 'cos I usually have a cassis when they drag me into a bar . . . Might as well be called Cadet-Cassis as Mes-Bottes, eh?'

'Of course, it's not bad at all, Cadet-Cassis isn't,' the young woman declared.

And then she asked him about his work. He was still at the same place, the new hospital, behind the octroi wall. Oh, there was no lack of work, he'd certainly be there for the rest of the year. There were yards and yards of gutters to do!

'You know,' he said, 'I can see the Hôtel Boncœur when I'm up there . . . Yesterday you were at the window and I waved my arms about, but you didn't see me.'

They'd already walked some hundred paces along the Rue de la Goutte-d'Or when he stopped and said, raising his eyes, 'Here's the place. I was born further along, I was, at number 22. But still, isn't this building a damn great pile of bricks! It's as big as a barracks inside.'

Looking up, Gervaise studied the façade. On the street side, the building had five stories, each with a straight row of fifteen windows whose black shutters with their broken slats lent an air of desolation to the vast expanse of wall. Below, four shops occupied the street level: to the right of the door, a large, squalid eating house, and to the left, a coal merchant's, a haberdasher's and an umbrella shop. The place seemed all the more colossal because it rose up between two low, wretched little structures which pressed against it on either side; and, squared off like a roughly cast block of mortar, mouldering and crumbling from the rain, the huge, crude cube of the building stood out above the surrounding rooftops against the pale sky. On its unplastered, mud-coloured sides, as interminably bare as prison walls, rows of projecting bricks stuck out like a lot of

decaying jaws gaping impotently in the void. But what especially interested Gervaise was the door, an enormous arched
affair which reached up to the second floor, giving access to a
deep covered entryway, beyond which the dim light of a great
courtyard could be seen. Down the centre of this entryway
which, like the street, was paved, ran a gutter flowing with very
pale pink water.

'Well come in,' said Coupeau. 'No one's goin' to eat you.'

Gervaise preferred to wait in the street. However, she
couldn't resist going as far as the concierge's lodge on the right.
There, on the threshold, she looked up once more. On the
inside, each of the identical four walls stretched up six stories,
symmetrically framing the vast square of the courtyard. The
walls were grey, peeling away in leprous yellow patches and
streaked where moisture dripped from the roof; they rose
straight, without any moulding, from the paving stones to the
roof slates, broken only by the downpipes which were attached
at each storey where rusty stains surrounded the gaping cast
iron drain heads. The shutterless windows revealed naked panes
of greenish glass, the colour of muddy water. Some of them
were open, with blue-checked mattresses hanging out to air; in
front of others, lines were strung with drying clothes, a whole
household's wash, the man's shirts, the woman's camisoles, the
kids' pants; there was one on the third floor where a baby's
nappy was spread out, caked with filth. From the top floor to
the bottom, the crowded tenements were bursting at the seams,
expelling bits of their misery through every crack. On each side,
at ground level, the wall was pierced by a tall narrow entrance
cut directly, without a doorframe, into the plaster. This led to
a hallway with walls criss-crossed by cracks beyond which a
slimy staircase with an iron rail spiralled upwards; there were
four of these stairways, indicated by the first four letters of the
alphabet painted on the walls. The ground floors had been
made into huge workshops with grime-blackened windows; you
could make out the flames from a locksmith's forge; further on,
the sound of a carpenter's plane could be heard, while the pale
pink stream which ran through the entryway was gushing out
from a dyeworks near the concierge's lodge. The courtyard,
messy with puddles of dye, woodshavings and charcoal clinkers,

had grass growing round its edges and in cracks between its paving stones; a glaring brightness filled half of it, as if it had been cut down the middle by the line where the sunlight ended. On the side which was in the shade, round a tap which kept one spot permanently damp, three little hens with muddy feet were pecking at the earth, hunting for worms. And Gervaise let her eyes move slowly from the top of the building down to the ground and back up again, astonished at the sheer size of it, feeling herself inside the core of a living organism, in the very heart of a city, intrigued by the building as if she were in the presence of some gigantic human being.

'Is there anyone you're looking for?' called the concierge inquisitively, appearing at the door of the lodge.

But the young woman explained she was waiting for somebody. She turned back towards the street but then, as Coupeau was taking his time, she went inside again, fascinated, wanting to see more. The place did not strike her as ugly. There were some cheerful little touches among the odds and ends hanging from the windows: a wallflower blooming in a pot, a cage of canaries—she could hear them twittering—and shaving mirrors which flashed sparkling circles of light into the dark interiors. Down below, a carpenter was singing, accompanied by the regular buzzing of his plane, while from the locksmith's shop came a loud silvery ringing noise made by hammers beating in rhythm. Then, at almost every open window, outlined against a background of dimly perceived poverty, you could see the heads of laughing, grubby children, or women sewing, their tranquil profiles bent over their tasks. Work was starting up again after the lunch hour; with the menfolk gone off to their jobs outside, the building was settling back into this deep stillness, broken only by noises from the workshops or the lulling sound of a refrain that went on and on, never changing, for hours on end. The courtyard was a bit on the damp side, though. Gervaise thought that if she lived there she'd have liked to be at the back, where it was sunny. She'd taken a few steps into the courtyard and could smell the frowsty smell so typical of places where the poor live, a mixture of age-old dust and rotting rubbish. Still, as the acrid odour of the dyewater predominated, she thought it wasn't nearly as nasty as at the

Hôtel Boncœur. And she was already choosing the window she would have, one over in the left-hand corner which had a little window-box planted with scarlet runners, whose slender stalks were beginning to twine round a framework of string.

'I've kept you waitin', haven't I?' said Coupeau, all of a sudden right behind her. 'There's always a fuss when I'm not havin' dinner with 'em, an' especially today as my sister's bought some veal.'

And as she'd given a little start of surprise, he in his turn glanced about him, saying: 'You've been lookin' at the building. It's always completely let, from top to bottom. There are three hundred tenants, I believe . . . If I'd any furniture I'd have been on the lookout for a small room . . . It'd be all right here, wouldn't it?'

'Yes, it'd be all right,' murmured Gervaise. 'Down in Plassans, in our street, there weren't so many people . . . Look, isn't that nice, that window on the fifth floor, with the scarlet runners?'

Then, in his persistent way, he asked her again if she wouldn't say yes. As soon as they had a bed, they could rent something here. But she hurried off, walking quickly through the entryway, begging him not to start his nonsense again. The building could collapse before she'd ever sleep under the same blanket with him. Nevertheless, when Coupeau left her in front of Madame Fauconnier's shop, she let him hold her hand for a moment, out of friendship.

For a month Gervaise and the roofer remained on the best of terms. He thought she was damn plucky, killing herself at work, looking after her kids, still finding time in the evening to do all kinds of odds and ends of sewing. Some women were bad lots, all they thought about was having a good time and lining their bellies, but, bloody hell! she wasn't a bit like them, she took life too seriously. Then she'd laugh, and protest modestly. She hadn't always been so good, worse luck. She'd mention her first baby, at only fourteen, and the litres of anisette she and her mother used to get outside of, in the old days. She'd learnt something from life, that was all. It was a mistake to suppose she was strong-willed; on the contrary, she was very weak, she let herself be pushed around, because she hated to hurt anybody. Her dream was to live with decent people, because if you're with bad people, she said, it was like being hit on the head, it bashed your brains in, it smashed you flat in two shakes if you were a woman. She came out in a cold sweat when she thought about the future, saying she felt like a coin someone had tossed in the air that might land heads or tails depending on how the pavement lay. Everything she'd seen so far, all the bad examples she'd had round her as a child, had taught her a right good lesson. But Coupeau would make fun of her gloomy thoughts and buck her up, while at the same time trying to pinch her bottom, and she'd shove him away, slapping his hands, while he bellowed with laughter and declared that for a weak-minded woman she wasn't exactly a pushover. As for him, he liked a bit of fun, he didn't worry his head about the future. Lor'! One day followed another, and that was that. You'd always find a roof somewhere, and a bite to eat. The neighbourhood seemed all right to him, apart from a bunch of drunks that could be cleared out of the gutters. Coupeau wasn't a bad fellow, sometimes he said very sensible things, and he was even a bit of a dandy, parting his hair carefully on the side, and wearing nice neckties and patent leather shoes on Sundays. And along with that he was as bright and cheeky as a monkey, with a Parisian working-man's love of leg-pulling and a gift of the gab which went charmingly with his boyish looks.

As time passed the pair of them did all sorts of good turns for one another at the Hôtel Boncœur. Coupeau would fetch her milk for her, run her errands and deliver her bundles of laundry; and in the evening, as he came home from work first, he often took the kids for a walk on the outer boulevards. In return for these kindnesses Gervaise would climb up to the little attic room where he slept and go through his clothes, sewing buttons on to his overalls and mending his heavy cloth jackets. They began to feel very much at home with one another. She was never bored when he was there, he amused her with the gossip he'd heard, and the unending stream of wisecracks from the Paris streets which were still a novelty for her. But Coupeau was becoming increasingly aroused by this continual brushing against Gervaise's skirts. He was hooked, good and proper! It began to get him down. He joked as much as ever, but inside he was so upset, his guts all knotted up, that he didn't think it funny any more. He went on with his nonsense, asking her every time he saw her: 'When's it goin' to be?' She knew what he meant, and promised it for when the moon was blue. Then, to tease her, he'd turn up in her room with his slippers in his hand, as if he were moving in. She'd make a joke of it, managing to get along very well without blushing despite the suggestive remarks he continually made when he was with her. As long as he didn't get rough, she didn't mind what he did. She only lost her temper with him once, when he pulled out some of her hair, trying to make her kiss him.

But towards the end of June Coupeau's high spirits vanished. He became very touchy, very moody. Gervaise, uneasy at the look in his eye, barricaded herself in at night. Then after a fit of the sulks which had lasted from Sunday until Tuesday, he suddenly came and knocked on her door about eleven o'clock on the Tuesday night. She didn't want to let him in but his voice was so gentle and trembly that in the end she pulled away the chest of drawers she'd shoved against the door. When he came in she thought he must be ill, he seemed so pale, with reddened eyes and a blotchy face. He stood there, stammering, shaking his head. No, he wasn't ill. He'd been crying for two hours, up there in his room; crying like a child, with a pillow stuffed into his mouth, so the people in the next room wouldn't hear. He hadn't slept for three nights. It couldn't go on like this.

'Listen, Madame Gervaise,' he managed to say, barely able to control his tears. 'This has got to stop, hasn't it? We'll get married. I really want to, I've made up my mind.'

Gervaise was astonished. She became very solemn. 'Oh, Monsieur Coupeau,' she murmured, 'whatever can you be thinking of! You know perfectly well I've never asked for that . . . It was just that I didn't want to . . . Oh, no, this is a serious matter now; please think it over carefully.'

But he went on nodding his head, with an air of unshakeable determination. He'd thought it all out. He'd come down now because he absolutely had to have a decent night's sleep. Surely she wasn't going to send him back upstairs to cry! As soon as she said yes, he wouldn't bother her any more, she could go to bed in peace. He simply wanted to hear her say yes. They could talk about it tomorrow.

'I'm certainly not going to say yes just like that,' replied Gervaise. 'I don't want to have you blaming me, one day, for making you do something silly . . . Look, Monsieur Coupeau, you shouldn't be so dead set on the idea. You yourself don't really know how you feel about me. If you went a week without seeing me, you'd get over it, I bet you would. Men often get married just for one night, the first, but then there's night after night, and the days go on and on, a whole lifetime of them, and they get terribly sick of it all . . . Please sit down, I'd like to talk this over straight away.'

And so, until one in the morning, they argued about getting married, sitting in that dark room lit by a single smoky candle they forgot to trim, and keeping their voices low so as not to awaken Claude and Étienne who lay with their heads on the same pillow, breathing softly. Gervaise kept coming back to them, making Coupeau look at them: she'd be bringing him a funny sort of dowry, she really couldn't saddle him with two kids. And then, she felt ashamed on his account. Whatever would the neighbours say? Everyone knew about her lover, and what had happened; it wouldn't seem very nice, their getting married barely two months later. Coupeau's answer to all these reasonable objections was to shrug his shoulders. A fat lot he cared what the neighbours thought! He didn't poke his nose into other people's business, for one thing, he'd be afraid of getting it dirty! All right, so she'd lived with Lantier first. What was so bad about that? She wasn't a loose woman, she wouldn't bring men home like so many women did, women who were better off than she was. And Christ, as for the kids, Claude and Étienne would grow up, and they'd bring 'em up decent, wouldn't they? He'd never find anybody else as plucky, or as good, or with so many fine qualities. Anyway, all that was nothing to do with it, she could have walked the streets, been an ugly, lazy slut with a string of filthy brats, it wouldn't have mattered to him: he wanted her.

'Yes, I want you,' he kept repeating, pounding his knee with his fist. 'D'you hear me, I want you . . . There's nothin' more to be said, is there?'

Little by little Gervaise began to weaken. She was giving way to her treacherous heart and senses, overcome by the atmosphere of animal desire she felt enfolding her. Now she was venturing only diffident objections as she sat with her hands limp in her lap, her face alight with tenderness. A warm breeze from the lovely June night outside wafted in through the half-open window, so that the tall, glowing wick of the smoking candle would suddenly flare up; the only sounds to break the deep silence of the sleeping neighbourhood were the childish sobs of a drunk lying on his back in the middle of the boulevard, and, from a far-off restaurant, a fiddle playing a popular dance tune at some late-night revelry, a little melody which carried crystal-clear, sharp and thin as the sound of a harmonica. Coupeau, seeing Gervaise vaguely smiling and silent, at a loss for further arguments, had seized her hands and was pulling her towards him. She was in one of those unguarded moods which she feared so much, when her defences were down and she was so deeply stirred she couldn't refuse or hurt anybody. But Coupeau didn't understand that she was giving herself to him, and all he did, to take possession of her, was to squeeze her wrists hard enough to crush them; the slight pain made each of them give a sigh, as if it eased their longing somewhat.

'You are sayin' yes, aren't you?' he asked.

'My, you do badger me!' she murmured. 'You really want me to? All right, then, yes . . . My God, we may be making an awful mistake.'

He'd stood up and, grabbing her by the waist, gave her a rough kiss on her face, just anyhow. Then, as the kiss had been quite noisy, he was the first to look anxiously at Claude and Étienne, tiptoeing up to them, lowering his voice.

'Shh! We must be good,' he said. 'Musn't wake the kids . . . See you tomorrow.'

He went back up to his room. Gervaise, trembling all over, stayed sitting for about an hour on the edge of her bed, forgetting to undress. She was touched, and thought that Coupeau had behaved very well: for there'd been a moment when she'd really believed that it was all over, that he was going to spend the night with her. Down below, the drunk under the window was groaning more hoarsely, like an animal that's lost. The popular air played by the distant fiddle had died away.

During the following days Coupeau tried to persuade Gervaise to go with him one evening to his sister's, in the Rue de la Goutte-d'Or. But she was very shy and seemed terrified at the prospect of this visit to the Lorilleux. She could clearly see that deep down the roofer was frightened of the couple. Of course he certainly wasn't dependent on his sister, who wasn't even the eldest. Maman Coupeau would gladly give her consent, for she never refused her son anything. However, it was believed in the family that the Lorilleux earned as much as ten francs a day and that gave them real power. Coupeau would never have dared get married unless they first accepted his wife.

'I've told 'em about you an' they know our plans,' he explained to Gervaise. 'Lor! what a baby you are! Come with me this evening . . . I've warned you, haven't I, that you'll find me sister a bit starchy. And Lorilleux ain't always that friendly either. The real trouble is they're fed up, because if I get married I won't be eatin' with 'em any more and that means one less way of savin' money. But it doesn't matter, they won't kick you out . . . Please, do it for my sake, it's got to be done.'

These remarks frightened Gervaise even more. One Saturday evening, however, she did agree to go. Coupeau went to fetch her at half past eight. She'd got all dressed up in a black gown, a shawl of very fine wool patterned with yellow palm leaves and a white bonnet edged with narrow lace. During the six weeks since she'd started work, she'd saved the seven francs for the shawl and the two fifty for the bonnet; the dress was an old one, which she'd cleaned and turned.

'They're expectin' you,' Coupeau told her, as they were going round by the Rue des Poissonniers. 'Oh, they're beginnin' to get used to the idea of me bein' married. They seem in a very good mood this evening . . . And then, if you've never seen gold chains bein' made, you'll enjoy watchin'. As it happens, they've a rush order to do by Monday.'

'They've got gold there?' asked Gervaise.

'You bet they have—there's gold on the walls, on the floor, everywhere.'

In the meantime, they'd passed through the arched entryway and crossed the courtyard. The Lorilleux lived on the sixth floor, staircase B. Coupeau laughed as he told her to hold tight to the rail and not let go. She looked up, blinking her eyes, and saw the towering void of the stairwell, lit by three gaslights, one on every other floor; the last one, way up above, looked like a star flickering in a black sky, while the other two cast long, strangely-shaped shafts of light up and down the endless spiral of the steps.

' 'Struth! what a pong of onion soup,' said the roofer as they reached the first landing. 'No doubt about it, someone's been havin' onion soup.'

In fact staircase B, dingy and dirty, with its greasy stairs and rail and its flaking walls with the plaster showing through, did indeed still smell fiercely of cooking. On each landing, noisy echoing corridors led off into the distance, with yellow-painted doors opening off them, blackened round the latch by dirty hands; while at the level of the window a sink gave off a sickly dank stench which mingled with the pungent smell of cooked onion. From the ground floor to the sixth you could hear the clattering of dishes, saucepans being rinsed, stewpots being scoured with spoons. On the first landing Gervaise noticed, through a half-open door on which the word 'Draughtsman' was written in big letters, two men sitting in a cloud of pipe-smoke at an oilcloth-covered table from which dinner had been cleared; they were talking nineteen to the dozen. The second and third landings were more peaceful; the only sounds filtering through the cracks in the woodwork were the rocking of a cradle, a child's muffled crying and a gruff female voice murmuring quietly on and on like running water, with no words audible. Gervaise could read the names on cards nailed to doors: 'Madame Gaudron, wool-carder', and further on: 'Monsieur Madinier, cardboard boxes'. On the fourth floor a fight was in progress, with the floor shaking from stamping feet and furniture being knocked over amid a frightful racket of curses and blows, but this didn't prevent the neighbours opposite playing cards with their door wide open to give them more air. But when she reached the fifth floor Gervaise had to stop to catch her breath; she wasn't used to climbing, and the wall turning round and round and those glimpses of people's homes following one upon another were making her head spin. Besides, there was a family blocking the landing; the father was washing dishes on a small earthenware stove near the sink while the mother, sitting with her back against the railings, was cleaning up their little tot before putting it to bed. But Coupeau was urging Gervaise on. They were almost there. When at last he got to the sixth floor, he turned to her with an encouraging smile. She'd raised her head, wondering where a piping voice she'd been hearing ever since the bottom of the stairs could be coming from, a clear and penetrating voice that dominated the other sounds. It was a little old woman who lived up there under the roof and sang while she dressed thirteen-sous dolls. Then, as a tall girl was carrying a pail of water into a nearby room, Gervaise also caught a glimpse of an unmade bed with a man in shirt-sleeves sprawled there, waiting and staring into space; when the door closed again she read a handwritten visiting card on it which said: 'Mademoiselle Clémence, iron-ing'. By the time she reached the very top Gervaise's legs were buckling under her and she was gasping for breath, but she felt an urge to peer down over the railing: now, it was the ground-floor gaslight which looked like a star, shining at the bottom of a narrow, six-storey well; and it seemed that all the smells, all the teeming, reverberating life of the building rose up to her in a single blast of scalding air, striking her anxious face as she leaned insecurely over, as if on the edge of an abyss.

'We're not there yet,' said Coupeau. 'Oh, it's quite an expedition!'

He'd turned left, into a long corridor. He turned twice more, again to the left, then to the right. The corridor branched into others, narrowing as it went on and on, its cracked and peeling walls occasionally lit by a dim gas jet; and the identical doors, evenly spaced as in a prison or convent, almost all stood wide open, revealing yet more scenes of hardship and toil which were bathed in a reddish glow that warm June evening. At last they reached a short corridor in total darkness.

'Here we are,' said Coupeau. 'Careful now. Hang on to the wall: there are three steps.'

In the dark, Gervaise took about ten more paces, cautiously. She stumbled, and counted the three steps. But Coupeau, at the end of the corridor, had just pushed open a door without knocking. A bright light fanned out over the floor. They went in.

It was a very narrow room, a sort of tunnel, which seemed like an extension of the corridor itself. A faded woollen curtain, tied back for the present with string, divided the tunnel in two. The first part contained a bed pushed into a corner where the attic ceiling sloped down, a cast-iron stove still warm from dinner, two chairs, a table and a cupboard with its cornice sawn off to make it fit between the bed and the door. The workshop was set up in the second part of the room: at the back, a small forge with its bellows; to the right, a vice fixed to the wall, under some shelves littered with scraps of iron; to the left, beside the window, a tiny workbench cluttered with pincers, wire-cutters, and miniature saws, all greasy and very dirty.

'It's us!' yelled Coupeau, going up to the wool curtain.

But at first there was no answer. Gervaise, feeling very agitated, and particularly excited by the thought of being in a place full of gold, stood behind Coupeau, stammering and nodding her head at random by way of greeting. The very bright light from the lamp burning on the workbench and the charcoal blazing in the forge made her still more flustered. However, after a while, she was able to see that Madame Lorilleux was small, sandy-haired and rather stout; armed with a large pair of pliers, she was pulling with all the strength of her short arms at some black wire which she'd passed through the holes of a draw-plate fixed to the vice. Lorilleux sat at the workbench. He too was short, but with thinner shoulders, and, nimble as a monkey, he was working with the tip of his pliers at something so tiny that it seemed to disappear between his knotty fingers. It was he who glanced up first, raising his nearly bald head, a long, sickly-looking head, pale yellow like old wax.

'Ah! It's you, good, good,' he murmured. 'We're in a hurry, you know. Don't come into the workshop, you'd be in our way. Stay in the room.'

He took up his minute work again, his face once more suffused by the greenish glow from a globe filled with water through which the lamp cast a bright circle of light on to his work.

'Sit down!' Madame Lorilleux shouted in her turn. 'And is this the lady? Fine, fine!'

She'd coiled up the wire and now took it over to the forge where she revived the fire with a large wooden fan, then put the wire to heat again before passing it through the last holes of the draw-plate.

Coupeau pulled up the chairs and settled Gervaise at the edge of the curtain. The room was so narrow that he wasn't able to sit beside her. He put his chair behind hers, leaning over her shoulder to explain the work in progress. Gervaise, taken aback by the odd reception the Lorilleux had given her and embarrassed by their sidelong glances, couldn't hear what he was saying because of a buzzing in her ears. She thought the woman looked very old for her thirty years, surly and slovenly, with her mousy hair hanging down over her unbuttoned bodice. The husband, only a year older than his wife, seemed like an old man to Gervaise, with his thin-lipped, mean mouth; he was in his shirt-sleeves, and wore down-at-heel slippers on his bare feet. But what dismayed her most was the smallness of the workshop, its spattered walls, the tarnished metal of the tools, the overall impression of litter, blackness and grime, like a scrap-iron yard. The heat was stifling. Drops of sweat appeared on Lorilleux's greenish complexion, while his wife decided to remove her bodice and worked on with bare arms, her chemise clinging to her sagging breasts.

'Where's the gold?' Gervaise asked in a whisper.

She peered anxiously into every corner, searching, amid all that filth, for the splendour she'd dreamed of.

But Coupeau had begun to laugh.

'The gold?' he said, 'Look, there's some there, an' there, an' some more under your feet!'

He pointed first to the drawn wire his sister was working, and then to another lot which hung on the wall near the vice and looked just like a coil of ordinary wire; then, getting down on all fours he picked a scrap up off the ground, from underneath the wooden slatting which covered the workshop floor, a tiny fragment like the point of a rusty needle. Gervaise protested. It wasn't gold, it couldn't be, not that nasty black metal, as ugly as iron! He had to bite the scrap and show her the gleaming dent left by his teeth. And he went on with his explanations: the employers provided the gold wire, already alloyed, and the craftsmen began by passing it through the draw-plate to get it down to the right thickness, being careful to reheat it five or six times during the operation so that it wouldn't break. Of course you needed a strong grip and lots of practice! His sister wouldn't allow her husband to touch the draw-plates because of his cough. She had splendid arms for the job, he'd seen her draw gold as fine as a hair.

Meanwhile, Lorilleux was doubled up on his stool, overcome by a fit of coughing. In the middle of this he said, half-choking and still without looking at Gervaise, as if his statement were solely for his own benefit:

'What I do is make column-chain.'

Coupeau made Gervaise get up. She should go a bit nearer, so she could see. The chain-maker grunted his consent. He was winding the wire prepared by his wife round a mandrel, a very thin steel rod. Next, with a saw, he delicately cut along the length of the mandrel so each turn of the wire made a link. Then he soldered them. The links were placed on a big piece of charcoal. He dampened them with a drop of borax from the bottom of a broken glass beside him before quickly heating them with the horizontal flame of the blow-pipe till they glowed red. Having done this to a hundred or so links, he went back again to his fine work, leaning on the edge of a small board which had been polished smooth by his hands. With his pliers he twisted each link, gripping one side as he poked it into the link above which was already in place, then reopened it with an awl, doing this with such continuous regularity and so fast, links being added to links, that under Gervaise's very eyes the chain was gradually growing longer without her being able to see or understand exactly how it was done.

'This is column-chain,' said Coupeau. 'There's small-link, fetter, curb and rope. But this is column; it's all Lorilleux makes.'

The chain-maker gave a complacent chortle. Continuing to squeeze together links which were invisible between his blackened fingernails, he shouted:

'Listen, Cadet-Cassis! I worked it out this morning. I started when I was twelve, didn't I? Well, d'you know how much column I must have made by today?'

He raised his pale face, blinking his reddened eyes.

'Eight thousand metres, d'you hear! Two whole leagues! There! A piece of chain two leagues long! Enough to go round the neck of every woman in the neighbourhood . . . And, you know, it's getting longer all the time. I'm going to get from Paris to Versailles,* I hope.'

Disappointed, Gervaise had gone back to her seat; it was all so ugly. She smiled to please the Lorilleux. What bothered her the most was the fact that they hadn't said a word about her marriage, a subject of the utmost importance to her and certainly the only reason she'd come. The Lorilleux continued to treat her as an inquisitive outsider Coupeau had brought along. When at last a conversation did get started, they talked solely about the tenants in the building. Madame Lorilleux asked her brother whether, on their way up, they'd heard the people on the fourth floor fighting. Those Bénards were at it hammer and tongs every day: the husband came home pissed as a newt, but the wife was no angel either, she was forever yelling the filthiest things. Then they discussed the draughtsman on the first floor, that great lout Baudequin, a real show-off, never out of debt, smoked non-stop; he and his friends were always shouting their heads off. Monsieur Madinier's cardboard business was on its last legs; he'd sacked two more workers yesterday and it would be a good thing if it went bust, because it ate up every sou, so the two kids were left to go about bare-arsed. Madame Gaudron had a funny way of carding her mattresses; she was expecting again, which at her age was really hardly decent. The landlord had just given notice to the Coquets, on the fifth floor; they owed three quarters' rent, added to which they insisted on lighting their stove out on the landing; in fact, the Saturday before, when the old girl on the sixth floor, Mademoiselle Remanjou, was going down with her dolls, she'd arrived just in time to prevent the Linguerlot kid from being burnt alive. As for Mademoiselle Clémence, who took in ironing, well, she lived as she thought fit, but you really couldn't criticize her, she adored animals and had a heart of gold. Still! It did seem a shame, didn't it, a lovely girl like her going with all those men! One thing was sure, some night she'd be walking the streets.

'Here, this one's done,' said Lorilleux to his wife, handing her the piece of chain he'd been working on since lunch. 'You can do the finishing.'

And he added, with the persistence of a man who won't give up his little joke:

'That's another four and a half feet. I'm getting closer to Versailles!'

Before finishing the chain Madame Lorilleux reheated it again, then passed it through the final draw-plate for adjustment. Next she pickled it, putting it into a small long-handled copper pot full of dilute nitric acid which she warmed on the forge fire. Coupeau urged Gervaise forward again, to watch this last operation. When the chain was pickled, it turned a dull dark red. Now it was finished, ready for delivery.

'It's delivered rough-finished,' said Coupeau, continuing to explain. 'The polishers rub it up with cloth.'

But Gervaise felt she'd had all she could take. The heat had grown worse and worse and was suffocating her. They kept the door shut because the slightest draught gave Lorilleux a cold. So, as there still had been no mention of their marriage, she decided they should go, and gave Coupeau's coat a little tug. He understood. In any case, he too was beginning to be embarrassed and annoyed by this show of silence.

'Well, we'll be off,' he said. 'We'll let you get on with your work.'

He waited for a moment, shuffling his feet, hoping for some word, some allusion to the marriage. In the end, he decided to raise the matter himself.

'Look here, Lorilleux, you're to be the witness for my wife, we're countin' on it.'

Pretending to be surprised, the chain-maker raised his head and gave a disagreeable little laugh, while his wife abandoned the draw-plates and took up a position in the middle of the workshop.

'Oh, so you really mean it?' he murmured. 'You never know, with old Cadet-Cassis, whether he's pulling your leg.'

'Ah, I see, this is the lady,' said his wife, staring at Gervaise. 'Goodness, it's not for us to give you advice . . . Still, it's a queer idea, to get married. However, if it's what you both want . . . If it doesn't work, you'll have no one but yourselves to blame, that's all. And it's not often that it works, no, not often . . .'

Lingering over these last words, she shook her head, her gaze travelling from the young woman's face to her hands, to her feet, as if she'd have liked to undress her and inspect the texture of her skin. Apparently, she found her better than she'd expected.

'My brother can please himself,' she went on in a dryer tone. 'Of course, the family might perhaps have preferred . . . People always make plans. But things work out so strangely . . . For my part, I don't intend to argue about it. Even if he'd brought us the lowest of the low, I'd have said to him: "go ahead, marry her, but stop bothering me." Still, after all, he wasn't badly off with us. He's got plenty of flesh on him, you can see he wasn't starving. Always a hot meal, right on the dot. I say, Lorilleux, don't you think Madame looks like Thérèse, you know who I mean, the woman across the way who died of consumption?'

'Yes, she does look rather like her,' replied the chain-maker.

'And then there's your two children. Yes, well, on that head, I did say to my brother: "Lor'! I just don't understand how you can marry a woman who has two children . . ." You mustn't mind if I think of his interests, after all, it's quite natural. And then you don't look at all strong, either. Don't you agree, Lorilleux, that she doesn't look at all strong?'

'No, she doesn't, not at all.'

They didn't mention her leg. But Gervaise understood, from their sidelong glances and pinched mouths that that was what they were talking about. She stood before them, wrapped in her thin shawl with its yellow palm leaves, answering in monosyllables as if she were being tried in front of judges. Coupeau, seeing how upset she was, shouted:

'That's got nothing to do with it . . . What you're sayin' is a lot of bosh . . . The wedding's to be on Saturday the 29th of July. I've worked it out on the almanac. Is that agreed? Does it suit you?'

'Oh, that suits us,' said his sister. 'You didn't have to consult us. I won't stop Lorilleux being a witness. Anything for a quiet life.'

Not knowing what to do with herself, Gervaise hung her head, poking her toes into one of the squares of the wooden slatting which covered the workshop floor; then, afraid she'd disarranged something in withdrawing her foot, she bent down and felt about with her hand. Lorilleux hurried over with the lamp and inspected her fingers suspiciously.

'You've got to be careful,' he said, 'tiny bits of gold can stick to your soles and get carried off without your realizing.'

It was quite a business. The employers didn't allow for a milligram of waste. And he showed her the rabbit's foot with which he brushed the specks of gold from the board he worked on, and the leather apron where the gold fell, which he kept spread over his knees. They swept the workshop carefully twice a week; they saved the sweepings and burnt them, then sifted the ashes, finding twenty-five or thirty francs' worth of gold every month.

Madame Lorilleux never shifted her gaze from Gervaise's shoes.

'No offence intended,' she murmured with an ingratiating smile, 'but Madame could take a look at the soles of her shoes.'

And Gervaise, scarlet in the face, sat down again and raised her feet to show there was nothing there. Shouting a curt 'goodnight!', Coupeau had opened the door. He called to her from the corridor. She followed him out, stammering some polite nothings: she hoped they'd meet again and all get on well together. But the couple were already back on the job at the far end of their dark burrow of a workshop, where the little forge shone like a last remaining piece of coal burning white-hot in the fierce heat of a furnace. The wife, her chemise slipping down off one shoulder, her skin reddened by the glow from the blazing charcoal, was pulling at a fresh wire, and with each straining effort her neck swelled up, its muscles rippling and

standing out like pieces of cord. The husband, huddled over in
the green light cast by the globe of water, was starting another
piece of chain, bending the link with his pliers, gripping it on
one side, poking it into the link above and reopening it with the
awl, on and on like an automaton, never wasting a movement
even to wipe the sweat from his face.

When Gervaise emerged from the passages onto the sixth-
floor landing, she couldn't help saying, with tears in her eyes:

'It doesn't bode too well for our happiness!'

Coupeau shook his head furiously. He'd get his own back on
Lorilleux for this evening! Did you ever see such a miserly
bugger! As if they'd make off with three grains of his flippin'
gold dust! All that to-do was nothing but sheer close-fistedness.
Maybe his sister had imagined he'd never get married, so she
could go on saving four sous on his dinner? Anyway, it was
going to be the 29th of July just the same. To hell with the pair
of 'em!

But Gervaise was still feeling down-hearted as she went down
the stairs, and plagued by foolish terrors which made her peer
anxiously into the long shadows cast by the banisters. At this
hour the stairwell was deserted and asleep, lit only by the
gaslight on the second floor, whose turned-down jet gleamed
like a tiny night-light in that murky pit. From behind the closed
doors came a heavy silence, the exhausted slumber of workers
who'd gone to their beds straight from the supper table. Still,
someone was laughing quietly in the ironing girl's room, and a
gleam of light shone through Mademoiselle Remanjou's keyhole. They could hear the little snipping sound made by her
scissors; she was still cutting out gauze dresses for her thirteen-
sous dolls. Downstairs at Madame Gaudron's a child went on
crying. The stench from the landing sinks seemed stronger, in
the midst of this vast, dark, silent stillness.

Then, out in the courtyard, while Coupeau was calling in a
sing-song voice for the concierge to open the door, Gervaise
turned round to look at the building one last time. It seemed to
have grown bigger under the moonless sky. The grey façades,
as though cleansed of their leprous patches and painted over by
darkness, stretched wide and high, looking even barer now they
rose up quite flat, stripped of the rags which by day hung out

to dry in the sun. The shuttered windows slept. A few here and there were like eyes, brightly lit, so that in some spots the walls appeared to squint. Above each entrance, lined up from bottom to top, the windows of the six landings shone palely white, making a tall, narrow column of light. A beam of lamp-light coming from the cardboard box workshop on the second floor cast a yellow streak across the courtyard paving-stones, piercing a hole in the black shadows which engulfed the ground-floor workshops. And from the damp reaches lying deep in those shadows, the sound of water falling drop by drop from the dripping tap by the well rang out in the silence. Then it seemed to Gervaise as if the house was on top of her, crushing her, ice cold against her shoulders. Another of her foolish, childish terrors, that she'd smile about later.

'Look out!' shouted Coupeau.

To get out through the entryway she had to jump over a large puddle which had drained from the dyeworks. That day the puddle was blue, a deep blue like a summer sky, and it sparkled with stars reflected from the concierge's little night lamp.

CHAPTER III

GERVAISE didn't want a fancy wedding. Why spend the money? Besides, she still felt a bit bashful and couldn't see the point of drawing attention to the marriage all over the neighbourhood. But Coupeau protested that you couldn't get married just like that, without a bite to eat together. He didn't give a damn what the neighbours thought. Oh, something quite simple, a bit of a jaunt in the afternoon to pass the time before a spot of dinner in some little restaurant or other. And no music afterwards, definitely not, no clarinets to make the ladies' backsides jiggle about. Just a friendly glass or two, then everyone home for bye-byes.

Joking and fooling, Coupeau finally managed to get round her when he swore there'd be no larking about. He'd keep his eye on the booze, and see no one got pissed. So he made arrangements for a simple meal at five francs a head, at Auguste's

Moulin-d'Argent* in the Boulevard de la Chapelle. It was a
cheap little establishment with a dance floor under the three
acacias of its courtyard, behind the back shop. They'd be quite
OK in a room on the first floor. He spent ten days mustering
guests from his sister's building in the Rue de la Goutte-d'Or:
Monsieur Madinier, Mademoiselle Remanjou, Madame Gaudron and her husband. He even persuaded Gervaise to agree to
two of his mates, Bibi-la-Grillade and Mes-Bottes; it was true
Mes-Bottes liked his tipple, but his appetite was so terribly
funny that he was always included in outings so they could
enjoy the look on the landlord's face as he watched a dozen
loaves disappear into that bottomless pit.

Gervaise, for her part, promised to bring her employer,
Madame Fauconnier, and the Boches, who were very decent
folk. That would mean they'd be fifteen at table, which was quite
enough. When there are too many of you, it always ends in rows.

Coupeau, however, was dead broke. Although he'd no wish
to show off, he did want to do the thing properly. He borrowed
fifty francs from his boss. With that money he bought the ring
first, a twelve-franc gold ring which Lorilleux picked up
wholesale for him, for nine. Then he ordered a frock-coat,
trousers and a waistcoat from a tailor in the Rue Myrrha, whom
he paid only twenty-five francs on account: his patent leather
shoes and his hat would still do. When he'd put aside the ten
francs needed to pay for his meal and Gervaise's (the children's
would be on the house), he had exactly six francs left, the cost
of a poor man's mass. He personally had no use at all for Holy
Joes, and it broke his heart to hand over his six francs to those
piss-tanks who didn't need *his* money to keep from dying of
thirst. But whatever anyone said, a wedding without a mass just
wasn't a wedding. He went to the church himself to haggle, and
spent an hour bickering with a little old priest in a dirty cassock,
who was as fly as a barrow-man. He felt like fetching him a
good one. In the end, as a joke, he asked him whether he hadn't
a bargain-priced mass tucked away somewhere, not too shop-
soiled, that would be just the job for a nice young couple.
Grumbling that God would take no pleasure in blessing their
union, the old priest finally agreed to say mass for five francs.
At any rate, he'd saved one franc. He had one franc left.

Gervaise also wanted to do the thing properly. As soon as the marriage had been decided on, she began working extra hours in the evening, and managed to put aside thirty francs. She'd set her heart on a little silk cape marked at thirteen francs in the Rue du Faubourg-Poissonnière. She treated herself to that, then for ten francs bought from the husband of a laundress who'd died in Madame Fauconnier's house, a dress of dark blue wool which she remade completely to fit her own figure. The remaining seven francs went on a pair of cotton gloves, a rose for her bonnet and shoes for Claude, her eldest. Luckily the kids' smocks were presentable. She spent four nights cleaning everything and seeing to even the tiniest holes in her stockings and chemise.

On the Friday evening, the eve of the big day, when Gervaise and Coupeau came home from work, they still had masses to do which kept them hard at it till eleven o'clock. Then, before going to sleep each in their own bed, they spent an hour together in Gervaise's room, very thankful that all the fuss was over at last. Despite their determination not to break their necks just for the sake of the neighbours, they'd ended up taking things very seriously and wearing themselves out. They were dead beat by the time they said goodnight. All the same, they heaved a great sigh of relief. Everything was settled now. Coupeau's witnesses were Monsieur Madinier and Bibi-la-Grillade, while Gervaise had Lorilleux and Boche. They were to go quietly to the town hall and the church, just the six of them, without trailing a whole lot of people along. The bridegroom's two sisters had even declared that they would be staying at home since their presence was not required. Maman Coupeau, by contrast, had burst into tears, saying that sooner than miss it she'd set off ahead of them and hide in a corner, so they'd promised to take her with them. As for the rendezvous for the whole party, that was to be at one o'clock, at the Moulin-d'Argent. From there they'd go out to Saint-Denis* to work up an appetite; they'd go by train and come back by shanks's pony along the main road. The party was shaping up very nicely, not a great big booze-up but just a quiet, pleasant little outing.

While he was dressing on the Saturday morning, Coupeau was overcome by misgivings as he eyed his one-franc piece. It had struck him that it would be only polite to stand the witnesses a a glass of wine and a slice of ham to tide them over till dinner. And then there might be unexpected expenses. One franc wasn't enough, that was clear. So, after taking Claude and Étienne along to Madame Boche, who was to bring them to the dinner in the evening, he raced round to the Rue de la Goutte-d'Or and asked Lorilleux outright to lend him ten francs. Having to do this really stuck in his craw, for he could just imagine the face his brother-in-law would make. Lorilleux grumbled and sneered in a mean way, then finally lent him the two five-franc pieces. But Coupeau heard his sister muttering that 'this was a nice beginning'.

The ceremony at the town hall was to be at ten-thirty. It was a beautiful morning, with the streets baking hot under a blazing sun. So as not to attract attention, the bridal pair, Maman Coupeau and the four witnesses divided into two groups. Gervaise led the way on the arm of Lorilleux, followed by Monsieur Madinier with the old lady; on the other pavement, twenty steps behind, came Coupeau, Boche, and Bibi-la-Grillade. The three of them were dressed in black frock-coats, and walked along with their shoulders hunched and their arms dangling; Boche had yellow trousers; Bibi-la-Grillade wore no waistcoat and was buttoned up to the neck, showing just a tiny bit of a screwed-up necktie. Only Monsieur Madinier wore a proper tail-coat, with square-cut tails, and the passers-by stopped to look at him escorting Coupeau's stout mama in her green shawl and black bonnet with red ribbons. Gervaise, in her dark blue dress, with a narrow little cape round her shoulders, looked very sweet and bright as she listened patiently to the jibes of Lorilleux who, despite the heat, was engulfed in a vast sack-like overcoat; and, from time to time, as they rounded a corner, she would turn her head slightly and give Coupeau a little smile. He seemed ill at ease in his new clothes, which looked all shiny in the sunlight.

Even though they walked very slowly, they arrived at the town hall a good half-hour too soon. Then, as the mayor was late, it was nearly eleven o'clock before their turn came. They waited on some chairs in a corner of the room, staring at the high ceiling and completely bare walls, keeping their voices low and politely scraping their chairs out of the way every time an office boy went past. But under their breath they called the mayor a lazy bugger who was very likely having his gout 'massaged' by that blonde piece of his, or then again maybe he'd swallowed his official sash. However, when the magistrate appeared, they got to their feet respectfully. They were told to sit down again. They then sat through three weddings, crowded out by the posh wedding-parties, with brides in white, and little girls with curled hair, and bridesmaids in pink sashes, and endless processions of gentlemen and ladies all dolled up to the nines, looking very prim and proper. Then, when they were called, they almost couldn't be married after all, because Bibi-la-Grillade had disappeared. Boche found him down below, in the square, smoking his pipe. And what snooty customers they were in that dump, not giving a damn about you if you didn't have cream-coloured gloves to wave about under their noses! And the formalities, the reading of the Code,* the questions and the signing of the documents were got through so fast that they were left staring at one another, convinced that they'd been gipped of more than half the ceremony. Gervaise, stunned and on the verge of tears, was pressing her handkerchief to her lips. Maman Coupeau was in floods. They took great care over signing the register, tracing their names in large clumsy letters, all except the bridegroom who made a cross as he couldn't write. Each of them gave four sous for the poor. When the office boy handed him the marriage certificate, Coupeau, at a nudge from Gervaise, forked out a further five sous.

It was a tidy step from the town hall to the church.* On the way the men had a beer, and Gervaise and Maman Coupeau a cassis with water. Their route lay down a long road which was in full sun without the tiniest bit of shade. The verger was waiting for them in the middle of the empty church; he hustled them over to a little chapel, asking them furiously if they were trying to make fun of religion, arriving so late. A priest came striding over to them, his demeanour surly, his face pale with hunger, with a server wearing a dirty surplice trotting along in front. The priest rattled through his mass, mumbling the Latin phrases, turning, bowing, spreading open his arms at top speed, while he cast sidelong glances at the bride and groom and their witnesses. The bridal couple, very disconcerted, stood before the altar, not knowing when they were supposed to kneel, or get up, or sit down, and waiting for signals from the server. The witnesses remained respectfully on their feet the whole time, while Maman Coupeau, once more overcome by tears, sobbed into the missal she'd borrowed from a neighbour. By now it had struck noon, the last mass had been said, and the church was filling with the sound of sacristans tramping about as they noisily put chairs back in place. Apparently the high altar was being made ready for some saint's day, for you could hear the decorators hammering as they nailed up the hangings. And, at the back of the far chapel, amid a cloud of dust from the verger's broom, the surly-looking priest rapidly passed his shrivelled hands over the bowed heads of Gervaise and Coupeau, seemingly uniting them in the middle of a removal, in the interval between two proper masses while the Good Lord was otherwise engaged. When the members of the wedding party had once more signed a register in the vestry and were back outside in the bright sunshine of the porch, they stood there for a moment in bewilderment, breathless from having been rushed along at such a spanking pace.

'So that's that!' said Coupeau with an awkward laugh. He was shifting about uneasily on his feet, for he didn't think it at all funny. Nevertheless he went on: 'Oh well, they don't waste any time. Over an' done with in two shakes. It's like goin' to the dentist's: you haven't time to say "ouch!"—you're spliced without feelin' a thing.'

'Yes, yes, a lovely job,' sneered Lorilleux. 'They cobble you together in five minutes, and it lasts a lifetime. Well poor old Cadet-Cassis!'

Coupeau, who was looking pleased with himself, was thumped on the back by the four witnesses. Meanwhile Gervaise, smiling through her tears, was kissing Maman Coupeau and replying to the old lady's stammered remarks:

'Never fear, I'll do all I can. If it doesn't work out, it'll not be my fault. No, that it won't, for I'm only too anxious to be happy meself . . . Anyway, it's done now, isn't it? It's up to him and me to get on together and put our backs into it.'

Then they went directly to the Moulin-d'Argent. Coupeau had taken his wife's arm. They walked fast, laughing, as if carried away, a couple of hundred paces in front of the others, heedless of the houses, and the passers-by, and the traffic. The deafening noises of the street rang in their ears like peals of bells. When they reached the Moulin-d'Argent, Coupeau immediately ordered a bite to eat—two litres of wine, some bread and slices of ham, no need for plates or tablecloth—in the little glassed-in room on the ground floor. Then, seeing that Boche and Bibi-la-Grillade were really tucking in, he ordered a third bottle and a piece of brie. Maman Coupeau wasn't hungry, she was too overcome to eat. Gervaise was dying of thirst and drank large glasses of water barely tinged with wine.

'This is my treat,' said Coupeau, going straight over to the counter where he paid four francs twenty-five.

By now it was one o'clock and the guests were arriving. Madame Fauconnier was the first to appear: plump and still good-looking, she wore a dress in a pale cream flowery print, with a pink scarf and a bonnet decorated with a great many flowers. Then Mademoiselle Remanjou, slender as a reed in her inevitable black dress which it seemed she must wear even in bed, arrived at the same time as the Gaudrons. Monsieur Gaudron was a great big brute of a man, whose slightest movement seemed about to split his brown jacket, while his enormous wife paraded her pregnant belly in a vivid purple skirt which accentuated its roundness. Coupeau explained that they didn't have to wait for Mes-Bottes, who was going to meet the party on the way to Saint-Denis.

'My word,' shouted Madame Lerat as she came in, 'we're in for a good soaking! That's going to be fun.'

She called everyone over to the street door to look at the sky to the south, above the city, where inky-black thunderclouds were rapidly building up. Madame Lerat, the eldest of the Coupeaus, was a tall, spare, masculine woman with a nasal voice; her frumpy puce dress hung on her, and its long fringes made her look like a skinny poodle emerging from the water. She was waving her parasol about like a baton. When she'd kissed Gervaise, she went on:

'You simply can't imagine, the blast of heat on the pavements really hits you . . . It's like having flames thrown at your face.'

Everybody then declared that they'd seen the storm coming for quite some time. When he left the church, Monsieur Madinier had had no doubts about what was going to happen. Lorilleux said his corns had kept him awake since three that morning. Anyway, it was bound to break, it had been much too hot for three days now.

'Oh yes, it's probably goin' to pour,' agreed Coupeau, standing in the doorway and anxiously scrutinizing the sky. 'We're just waitin' for me sister, an' if she came, we could set off.'

Madame Lorilleux was indeed late. Madame Lerat had dropped in at her place to pick her up, but she'd found her only just putting on her stays and they'd had a row. 'So,' whispered the tall widow in her brother's ear: 'I walked out on her. She's in such a temper! . . . Well, you'll see.'

And they had to hang about, cooling their heels for another quarter of an hour in the bar, pushed and jostled by all the men who were dropping in for a quick one at the counter. From time to time Boche or Madame Fauconnier or Bibi-la-Grillade would go outside to the edge of the pavement and gaze up at the sky. There wasn't a spot of rain coming down but it kept getting darker; gusts of wind, scudding along the ground, were raising little eddies of white dust. At the first rumble of thunder, Mademoiselle Remanjou crossed herself. Everyone was staring anxiously at the clock over the mirror: it was already twenty to two.

'Here it comes!' yelled Coupeau. 'The angels are weepin'.'

As a squall of rain swept the road, women raced for cover, holding up their skirts with both hands. It was in the middle of that first downpour that Madame Lorilleux finally appeared in the doorway, out of breath, out of temper, and struggling with her umbrella which wouldn't close.

'Did you ever see the like!' she spluttered. 'It caught me just as I was leaving. I felt like going back in and changing. That's what I bloody well should have done . . . My, this isn't half a lovely wedding! I told you so, didn't I, I wanted you to put it off till next Saturday. And now it's raining because you wouldn't listen to me. Well that's fine by me, just fine! Let the heavens open!'

Coupeau tried to calm her, but she shut him up. *He* wouldn't have to put his hand in his pocket if her dress was ruined. Madame Lorilleux was wearing a black silk dress in which she couldn't breathe; the bodice was too small, dragging at the buttonholes and straining across the shoulders, while the sheath-like skirt hugged her thighs so tightly that she had to walk with tiny little steps. The women of the party were looking her up and down with pursed lips, deeply interested in her outfit. She gave no sign of seeing Gervaise, who was sitting beside Maman Coupeau. She called to Lorilleux and demanded his handkerchief, then went into a corner of the bar and, one by one, carefully wiped the rain drops from the silk.

Meanwhile, the downpour had abruptly stopped. It was getting even darker, it was almost like night, a leaden night cut across by great sheets of lightning. Bibi-la-Grillade kept saying with a laugh that for certain sure it was going to piss cats and dogs. Then the storm broke with tremendous violence. For half an hour it came down in bucketfuls while the thunder roared without interruption. The men, standing in the doorway, gazed at the grey curtain of rain, at the overflowing gutters, at the fine spray which flew up where the rain splashed the puddles. The women were sitting down, rather scared, their hands over their eyes. Gulping a bit with fright, they were no longer chatting. When Boche tried out a joke about the thunder, saying Saint Peter was sneezing up there, no one smiled. But, as soon as the thunderclaps came less often and then faded into the distance, the company grew impatient again and annoyed by the storm, swearing and shaking their fists at the clouds. A light, incessant rain was falling now from the ash-grey sky.

'It's gone two,' cried Madame Lorilleux. 'We can't spend the night here, now, can we?'

When Mademoiselle Remanjou suggested setting off for the country just the same, even if they got no further than the moat round the fortifications,* the group protested: the roads would be in a lovely mess, and they wouldn't even be able to sit on

the grass; and besides, it didn't look as if it was over, there
could be another dousing on the way. Coupeau, who was
watching a soaking wet workman walking calmly along in the
rain, muttered: 'If that old sod Mes-Bottes is waitin' for us on
the Saint-Denis road, he won't be gettin' sunstroke.'

That raised a laugh. Nevertheless, they were all growing
crosser. In fact it was a real pain in the neck. They'd have to
think of something. They surely didn't want to hang around
staring into each other's mugs till dinner time! So for the next
fifteen minutes, while the rain fell persistently, they sat racking
their brains. Bibi-la-Grillade wanted to play cards; Boche, by
nature given to anything sly and smutty, knew a very funny
little game, called 'confessor'; Madame Gaudron thought they
might go down to the Chaussée Clignancourt for some onion
tart; Madame Lerat would have enjoyed telling stories; Gaudron wasn't bored, he was perfectly happy to stay put, and only
added that they should sit down to eat straight away. There
were cross exchanges and bickering over each suggestion; this
was stupid, that would send them all to sleep, people would
think they were a lot of brats. Then, when Lorilleux, determined to put his oar in, proposed simply walking along the
outer boulevards to Père Lachaise* where they could see the
tomb of Héloïse and Abélard* if there was time, Madame
Lorilleux could control herself no longer and blew up. She was
going to clear off, that was what she was going to do! Was this
some kind of joke? She'd got all dressed up, she'd got wet
through, and all to hang about in a bar! No, no, she'd had all
she could take of this sort of wedding, she'd sooner be in her
own home! Coupeau and Lorilleux had to block the doorway.
She kept repeating:

'Get out of my way! I tell you I'm off!'

When her husband had managed to calm her, Coupeau went
up to Gervaise, who was still sitting in a corner chatting quietly
to her mother-in-law and Madame Fauconnier.

'You haven't suggested anything, have you,' he said, not yet
daring to address her by the familiar 'tu'.

'Oh, whatever you like,' she replied with a laugh. 'I'd like
anything. We can go out, or not, it's all the same to me. I'm
perfectly happy, there's nothing more I want.'

And indeed her face was aglow with tranquil joy. Ever since the guests had arrived she'd chatted to each in turn, her voice rather soft and full of feeling, her manner contained. She'd kept out of the arguments. During the storm, she'd gazed fixedly at the lightning, as if seeing by its sudden flashes of light important events far away in the future.

Up to now, however, Monsieur Madinier had not suggested anything. He was leaning on the counter with his coat-tails spread, conscious of his status as an employer. He spat in a leisurely way, rolled his large eyes and said:

'Well now! We could go to the museum . . .'*

Stroking his chin and blinking, he cast an enquiring glance round the group.

'There are ancient statues, and drawings, and paintings, all sorts of things. It's very instructive . . . Perhaps you've not been there? Oh it's certainly worth seeing, at any rate once.'

The wedding guests looked at one another uncertainly. No, Gervaise had never seen it, nor had Madame Fauconnier, nor Boche, nor the others; Coupeau rather thought he'd gone one Sunday but he couldn't really remember now. They were still hesitating, however, when Madame Lorilleux, who was deeply impressed by Monsieur Madinier's importance, declared the proposal very proper, very suitable. Since they'd given up the day anyway, and were all dressed up, they might as well see something instructive. Everyone agreed. Then, as it was still raining a little, they borrowed some umbrellas from the proprietor, old blue, green and brown things which customers had left behind, and set off for the museum.

The party turned right and went into Paris down the Faubourg Saint-Denis. Once again Coupeau and Gervaise took the lead, hurrying ahead of the others. Monsieur Madinier was now escorting Madame Lorilleux, as Maman Coupeau had stayed in the bar because of her legs. Next came Lorilleux and Madame Lerat, Boche and Madame Fauconnier, Bibi-la-Grillade and Mademoiselle Remanjou, with the Gaudrons at the very end. There were twelve of them, again making quite a crocodile along the pavement.

'Oh, we'd nothing to do with it, believe me,' Madame Lorilleux was explaining to Monsieur Madinier. 'We don't know where he picked her up, or rather we know only too well; but it's not our place to say anything, is it? My husband had to buy the wedding ring. First thing this morning we had to lend them ten francs, otherwise it would all have fallen through . . . A bride who doesn't produce a single member of her family at her wedding! She says she's got a sister in Paris who's a pork butcher, so why didn't she invite her?'

She broke off to point to Gervaise, who was limping badly because of the sloping pavement.

'Just look at her! I ask you! Banban!'* The nickname Banban ran through the group like wildfire. Laughing meanly, Lorilleux said that was what she should be called. But Madame Fauconnier sprang to her defence: they were wrong to make fun of her, she was as neat as a band-box and could get through work like nobody's business when need be. Madame Lerat, never at a loss for a suggestive remark, called Gervaise's leg a 'love pin', adding that lots of men liked such things, though she refused to explain further.

The wedding party emerged from the Rue Saint-Denis and crossed the boulevard.* After waiting a moment because of the stream of carriages, they ventured on to the road, which the storm had turned into a sea of liquid mud. It was starting to rain again so the group put up their umbrellas, and under those pathetic gamps which swayed about in the men's hands the ladies walked, holding their skirts high; the crocodile straggled out over the mud, stretching from one pavement to the other. As they crossed, a pair of louts yelled 'roll up and see the freak show!'; passers-by rushed over and grinning shopkeepers rose to their feet to watch through their windows. In the midst of that milling throng, against the grey, wet background of the boulevard, the line of couples stood out like a string of garish splashes of colour: Gervaise's deep blue dress, Madame Fauconnier's flowery cream print, Boche's canary yellow trousers; the rigid discomfort of wearing one's Sunday best made Coupeau's shiny frock-coat and Monsieur Madinier's square-cut tails look like funny carnival costumes, while Madame Lorilleux's smart outfit, Madame Lerat's fringes and Mademoiselle Remanjou's tatty skirts mixed together different styles, as they went trailing along one behind the other in the reach-me-down finery of the poor. But what raised the biggest laugh were the mens' hats, ancient hats carefully preserved, their lustre deadened by dark cupboards, their shapes replete with comedy, tall, bell-shaped or pointed, with extraordinary brims, curled or flat, too wide or too narrow. The smiles grew even broader when, at the very end, to bring the spectacle to a close, Madame Gaudron the wool-carder appeared in her bright violet dress, with her vast pregnant belly well to the fore. Meanwhile, the wedding party was not in any hurry, for they were all good-naturedly enjoying the attention and laughing at the jokes.

'Oy! 'ere comes the bride!' cried one of the louts, pointing at Madame Gaudron. 'Wot a shame, she's got a bun in the oven an' no mistake!'

The whole group shrieked with laughter. Bibi-la-Grillade, turning round, said that the kid certainly had a point. Madame Gaudron, preening herself, laughed harder than anyone else; after all there was nothing to be ashamed of, quite the opposite; there was more than one lady casting envious glances in her direction, who'd have been pleased to change places with her.

They'd turned into the Rue de Cléry. From there they took the Rue du Mail. In the Place des Victoires they all came to a halt. The bride's left shoelace was undone and while she was retying it at the foot of the statue of Louis XIV,* the waiting couples gathered closely round her, joking about the bit of calf she was showing. At last, after going down the Rue Croix-des-Petit-Champs, they reached the Louvre.

Monsieur Madinier politely requested permission to conduct the party. The place was very big, and you could get lost; besides, he knew the best spots, because he'd often come with an artist, a most intelligent fellow whose drawings were bought by a big box-making company to decorate their boxes. When the wedding party entered the Assyrian Gallery,* on the lower level, they all gave a little shiver. Christ, it wasn't exactly warm! The room would have made a first-rate cellar. Slowly, tilting up their chins and blinking their eyes, the couples walked along between the giant stone statues, the silent gods of black marble in their rigid hieratical poses, and the monstrous creatures, half-cat, half-woman, whose pinched noses and swollen lips made their faces look like death masks. They thought them all

very ugly. People worked stone a hell of a lot better these days.
An inscription in Phœnician characters left them flabbergasted.
No, it wasn't possible, nobody had ever read that scribbling!
But Monsieur Madinier, who'd already reached the first landing
with Madame Lorilleux, was calling to them, shouting under
the vaulted ceiling:

'Come along! Don't bother about those contraptions . . . It's
the first floor you want to see!'

They were awe-struck by the stark severity of the staircase.
They were even more intimidated by a magnificent usher in a
red waistcoat and gold-braided livery who seemed to be waiting
for them on the landing. Most respectfully, walking as quietly
as possible, they entered the French Gallery.

Then, never stopping, they hurried through the sequence of
small galleries, their eyes filled with the gold of the frames,
while the pictures—far too many to be looked at properly—
raced past them. You'd have had to spend an hour in front of
each one to understand them. Gawdalmighty, what a lot of
pictures! They went on forever! Must be worth a tidy sum.
Then, at the end, Monsieur Madinier suddenly halted them in
front of the *Raft of the Medusa** and explained what it was
about. They stood stock still in mute astonishment. When they
set off again, Boche voiced the general opinion: it was tip-top.

In the Gallery of Apollo,* what amazed the group most was
the floor, which was clear and shiny like a mirror, and reflected
the legs of the benches. Mademoiselle Remanjou kept her eyes
closed, because she felt as if she was walking on water. They
shouted to Madame Gaudron to be careful to set her feet down
flat, because of her condition. Monsieur Madinier wanted to
show them the gilding and painting on the ceiling, but looking
up gave them a crick in the neck and they couldn't see anything
properly. Then, before going into the Salon Carré,* he pointed
to a window, saying:

'It was from that balcony that Charles IX* fired on the
people!'

Keeping an eye on the stragglers at the back of the procession, he signalled a halt in the middle of the Salon Carré, where
in hushed tones suitable for a church he murmured that
everything in that room was a masterpiece. They did the rounds

of the Salon. Gervaise asked what the *Wedding at Cana** was about; it was silly not to put the subjects on the frames. Coupeau halted in front of the Mona Lisa, she reminded him a bit of one of his aunts. Boche and Bibi-la-Grillade were sniggering as with sidelong glances they drew each other's attention to the naked women. They were particularly struck by Antiope's thighs.* And, last of all, the Gaudrons, the husband open-mouthed and the wife with her hands on her belly, stood gaping in maudlin incomprehension in front of Murillo's *Virgin.**

Having completed the tour of the Salon, Monsieur Madinier suggested they should begin again: it was well worth it. He was very attentive to Madame Lorilleux, on account of her silk dress, and each time she interrupted him he answered her gravely, with great self-assurance. She was interested in Titian's mistress,* whose yellow hair she thought quite like her own, and he told her it was La Belle Ferronnière,* a mistress of Henry IV, about whom there'd been a play at the Ambigu.*

Next the party embarked on the long gallery which houses paintings of the Italian and Flemish schools. More pictures, and still more pictures, of saints, of men and women whose faces meant nothing to them, of very dark landscapes, of animals gone yellow, a confusion of people and things in such a busy riot of colours that everyone was beginning to get a nasty headache. Monsieur Madinier had stopped talking and was now slowly leading the way. The line of couples trailed along behind him, keeping in the same order, craning their necks and staring upwards. Centuries of art passed before their bewildered ignorance: the subtle frugality of the primitives, the splendours of the Venetians, the rich, radiant life of the Dutch. But what actually interested them the most were the copyists, with their easels set up in the middle of the crowd, coolly painting away; an old lady standing on a tall ladder, wielding a whitewash brush over the delicate sky of an enormous canvas, impressed them especially. Little by little, however, the word must have spread that a wedding-party was visiting the Louvre; painters rushed over, their mouths twitching with laughter; curious bystanders sat down on benches ahead of the group, the better to enjoy the sight, while the attendants watched tight-lipped, restraining their witticisms. And the wedding-party, weary now and no longer so intimidated, dragged their hob-nailed boots and clumped their heels on the noisy floors, sounding, in the bare and tranquil orderliness of the galleries, like the trampling of a stampeding herd.

Monsieur Madinier was keeping quiet: he had a surprise up his sleeve. He strode directly over to Rubens' *Kermesse*.* There, still saying nothing, he simply rolled his eyes salaciously in the direction of the picture. The ladies, when they'd got right up close, gave little shrieks then looked away, scarlet in the face. But their menfolk, sniggering, made them stay with them while they searched the canvas for smutty details.

'Take a look at this!' Boche kept repeating. 'This is worth a fortune. Here's someone puking. And there's someone watering the dandelions. And that one—oh! as for that one! . . . Well! This 'ere's a fine lot, I must say.'

'Let's be on our way,' said Monsieur Madinier, tickled pink by his success. 'There's nothing more to see on this side.'

The party turned back and they retraced their steps through the Salon Carré and the Gallery of Apollo. Madame Lerat and Mademoiselle Remanjou were complaining that their legs were giving up on them. Their guide, however, was determined to show Lorilleux the antique jewels. These were quite close, at the back of a little room; he could find them with his eyes shut. Nevertheless he led the group off in the wrong direction, through seven or eight cold, deserted galleries containing nothing but plain glass cases displaying rows of countless broken pots and repellent little figurines. They were all shivering and bored to tears. Then, trying to find a way out, they ended up among the drawings. This meant another endless trudge; the drawings went on for ever, there was room after room of them, without anything funny, just scrawled-on pieces of paper in glass cases against the walls. In quite a dither but unwilling to admit he was lost, Monsieur Madinier led the party to a staircase and made them climb to the next floor. This time they wound up in the Maritime Museum, surrounded by models of instruments and cannons, relief maps and ships the size of toys. Finally, after a long quarter of an hour's walk, they reached another staircase and went down it, only to find they'd landed back among the drawings. In total despair now they roamed haphazardly through the galleries, couple following couple, all of them trailing behind Monsieur Madinier who was mopping his brow, beside himself with rage at the authorities, whom he accused of changing the placement of the doors. Attendants and visitors watched their passage with amazement. In less than twenty minutes, they were sighted anew in the Salon Carré, in the French Gallery and alongside the glass cases where the little gods of the Orient repose. Never would they get out again. With their feet killing them and all hope abandoned, the wedding guests were making a tremendous racket as they meandered along, leaving Madame Gaudron's belly far behind.

'Closing time! Closing time!' shouted the powerful voices of the attendants.

They very nearly got locked in. One of the attendants had to lead them to an exit. Then, in the Louvre courtyard, after they'd retrieved their umbrellas from the cloak-room, they breathed again. Monsieur Madinier recovered his composure: he should have turned left; of course, he remembered now that the jewels were to the left. In any case, the whole party professed themselves pleased to have seen it all.

It was striking four. There were still two hours to fill before dinner. They decided to go for a little walk to pass the time. The ladies were worn out and would have been glad to sit down, but as no one offered to buy a round of drinks they set off again along the embankment. There, they were caught in another downpour heavy enough to spoil the ladies' outfits in spite of the umbrellas. Madame Lorilleux, pierced to the heart by every raindrop that wet her dress, suggested sheltering under the Pont-Royal:* indeed she announced that if the others wouldn't come she'd go down all by herself. So the wedding-party climbed down under the Pont-Royal. It was awfully nice there. In fact, you could say it was a bloody brainwave! The ladies spread their handkerchiefs on the cobbles and sat down on them, knees apart, pulling with both hands at the blades of grass growing between the stones, and watching the dark water flow past, just as if they were in the country. The men amused themselves shouting very loudly so as to awaken the echo from the arch which faced them; Boche and Bibi-la-Grillade took turns hurling insults into space, yelling 'Pig!' and laughing madly when the echo sent it back to them; then, when they'd gone hoarse, they picked up some flat stones and played ducks and drakes. The downpour had stopped but they were all enjoying themselves so much that no one thought of moving on. The Seine bore along patches of oil, old corks, vegetable peelings, rubbish of all kinds which would swirl round for a moment, held back by an eddy in the sinister black waters darkened by the shadow of the arch, while overhead on the bridge passed the rumble of omnibuses and cabs and the tumult of the city, of which they could see nothing save rooftops, as if from the bottom of a hole. Mademoiselle Remanjou sighed, remarking that if there'd been some greenery, it would have reminded her of a spot on the Marne* where she used to go, back in about 1817, with a young man she was still mourning for.

Monsieur Madinier, however, pronounced it time to leave. They crossed the Tuileries garden, where their orderly progress in couples was upset by a little crowd of children playing with hoops and balls. Then, at the Place Vendôme, as the wedding-party was staring up at the column,* Monsieur Madinier was inspired to make a gallant gesture to the ladies: he invited them to climb to the top to see Paris. They thought his suggestion great fun. Yes, yes, they absolutely *must* go up, it would be ever such a good laugh. Besides, it would be really interesting, to people like them who'd always kept their feet on solid ground.

'I can't see Banban daring to go up that, with that pin of hers!' muttered Madame Lorilleux.

'I'd like to go up,' said Madame Lerat, 'but I don't want there to be a man behind me.'

And up they went. The twelve of them climbed the narrow spiral staircase in single file, stumbling on the worn steps and holding on to the walls. Then, when it became pitch dark, there were gales of laughter. Little shrieks came from the ladies. The men kept tickling them and pinching their legs. But it wouldn't do to mention it—better pretend it was mice! Besides, it didn't amount to anything; they knew just where to stop, to keep things decent. Then Boche thought of a joke that everyone took

up. They called out to Madame Gaudron, as if she'd been left
behind, asking her whether her belly could get through. Just
imagine! If she'd been stuck there, unable to go up or down,
she'd have plugged up the hole and no one would ever have
been able to get out! And their mirth at this pregnant woman's
belly was so prodigious that the column began to shake. Boche,
now well away, declared they were aging fast, inside this
chimney stack; did it never end then, did it go right up to
heaven? And he tried to scare the ladies, exclaiming that the
column was swaying. Coupeau, meanwhile, said nothing; he
was behind Gervaise, with his arms round her waist, and he
could feel her yielding to him. When they suddenly emerged
into the light, he was kissing her on the neck.

'You're a nice pair, I must say; don't let us stop you, will
you!' said Madame Lorilleux in a scandalized voice.

Bibi-la-Grillade was glaring furiously. He kept muttering:

'What a racket you made! I couldn't even count the steps.'

Monsieur Madinier, however, was already on the roof pointing out the important landmarks. Madame Fauconnier and
Mademoiselle Remanjou flatly refused to leave the stairway: the
very thought of the street down below made their blood run
cold; the most they would do was take a quick peep or two
through the little door. Madame Lerat was bolder, and went
right round the narrow platform, sticking close to the bronzed
dome. But still, it really was damn thrilling, when you thought
that all it would take was one false step. Bloody hell, that'd be
quite a cropper! The men, rather white, gazed down at the
square. You could be in mid-air, cut off from everything. No
two ways about it, it turned your guts to water. But Monsieur
Madinier was advising everyone to look up, straight ahead into
the far distance; that stopped you feeling dizzy. And he went
on pointing out the Invalides, the Panthéon, Notre-Dame, the
Tour Saint-Jacques* and the heights of Montmartre. Then, it
occurred to Madame Lorilleux to ask whether you could see the
Moulin-d'Argent on the Boulevard de la Chapelle, where they
were going to have their dinner. They spent ten minutes
searching for it and squabbling as each of them picked out a
different spot. All around them stretched the vast greyness of
Paris, hazy-blue in the distance, its deep valleys surging with

rooftops; the whole of the right bank lay in shadow, beneath a huge, ragged, copper-coloured cloud; a broad ray of sunlight, streaming out from the cloud's gold-fringed edge, glittered and sparkled on the myriad windows of the left bank, lighting up that part of the city so that it stood out against a perfectly clear sky, washed clean by the storm.

'It wasn't worth coming up here just to have a row,' said Boche furiously as he started down the stairs.

The wedding-party went down in sullen silence, broken only by the clatter of shoes on the steps. At the bottom, Monsieur Madinier tried to pay, but Coupeau protested, quickly putting twenty-four sous—two for each person—into the hand of the attendant. It was nearly half-past five; they had just enough time to get back. They set off along the boulevards and the Faubourg-Poissonnière. However Coupeau, feeling the outing shouldn't finish in that way, hustled them all into a bar for a glass of vermouth.

The meal had been ordered for six o'clock. They'd been waiting at the Moulin-d'Argent for twenty minutes when the wedding-party arrived. Madame Boche had entrusted her lodge to a lady who lived in the building, and was sitting chatting to Maman Coupeau in the first-floor room where the table was laid. She'd brought the two boys, Claude and Étienne, who were chasing about under the table, amid a jumble of chairs. When Gervaise came in and caught sight of the kids, whom she'd not seen all day, she took them on her knees, caressing them and giving them great big kisses.

'Have they been good?' she asked Madame Boche. 'I just hope they haven't driven you batty.'

And while Madame Boche was telling her the side-splitting things the little devils had said during the afternoon, she picked them up again and clasped them tight, overcome by a frenzy of tenderness.

'It's a bit queer though, for Coupeau, really,' Madame Lorilleux was remarking to the other ladies, at the far end of the room.

Gervaise's calm smiles of that morning had not deserted her. Now the outing was over, however, she felt very down-hearted at times, as she sat looking at her husband and the two

Lorilleux in her thoughtful, contained way. Coupeau, it seemed to her, was a coward in dealing with his sister. Only the evening before he'd been shouting and swearing to put that pair of mud-slingers in their place, if they let him down. But face to face with them—she could see it only too clearly—he was just a doormat, hanging on their words, in despair if they seemed annoyed. And quite simply this made her worry about the future.

Now they were waiting only for Mes-Bottes, who hadn't yet turned up.

'Oh, hell!' cried Coupeau. 'Let's sit down an' get started. He'll roll up, you'll see; he's got a nose like a bloodhound, he can smell a good spread from miles away . . . Hey, he must be havin' fun, if he's still moonin' about on the road to Saint-Denis!'

In great good spirits the whole party took their places amid much noisy scraping of chairs. Gervaise was between Lorilleux and Monsieur Madinier, and Coupeau between Madame Fauconnier and Madame Lorilleux. The other guests sat where they fancied, because it always led to grudges and arguments if you arranged the seating. Boche slipped in beside Madame Lerat. Bibi-la-Grillade's neighbours were Mademoiselle Remanjou and Madame Gaudron. As for Madame Boche and Maman Coupeau, at the far end, they took charge of the children so they could cut their meat and pour out their drinks, not letting them have much wine of course.

'Isn't anyone going to say grace?' asked Boche, while the ladies were arranging their skirts under the tablecloth, for fear of stains.

But Madame Lorilleux didn't care for that kind of joke. The vermicelli soup, which was almost cold, disappeared very fast, to the loud sucking of spoons. There were two waiters serving, wearing short grease-stained jackets and not-too-white aprons. Broad daylight streamed in through the four windows opening on to the acacias in the courtyard; after the stormy day the evening was clear and balmy. The reflections from the trees in this damp spot filled the smoky room with a green light, setting the shadows of the leaves dancing over the faintly musty-smelling tablecloth. At either end of the table hung a flyblown

mirror, so that the table seemed to stretch on for ever, laden
with its thick yellowing china crazed with black where dirty
washing-up water had left grease in the knife-scratches. Each
time a waiter came up from the kitchen the door at the far end
swung open and a powerful smell of burnt fat wafted in.

'Let's not all talk at once,' said Boche, as they bent low over
their plates, not speaking.

They were drinking the first glass of wine and eyeing the
progress of two meat pasties which the waiters were serving,
when Mes-Bottes came in.

'Well, well, you're a bunch o' rotten sods, you are!' he
shouted. 'There I was, hoofing it up and down the road
for three mortal hours, and a copper even asked to see me
papers . . . How could you play a lousy trick like that on a pal!
You might at least have sent someone to get me with a cab.
Really, y'know, joking apart, I think it's a bit thick. And what's
more it was raining that hard I got water in me pockets . . . I
swear you'll find enough fish there for a fry-up.'

They were all busting their sides laughing. That bastard
Mes-Bottes was quite plastered; he'd already sunk his couple of
bottles, just, of course, so as not to be got down by all that
frog-piss the storm had spewed on to his person.

'Well, if it ain't milord Spindleshanks!' said Coupeau. 'Sit
you down over there, by Madame Gaudron. As you see, we've
been waitin' for you.'

Oh, that didn't bother him, he'd soon catch the others up!
And three times he called for more soup, putting away platefuls
of vermicelli into which he cut great big hunks of bread. Then,
when they'd got started on the pasties, he aroused the deep
admiration of everyone at the table. What a guzzler! The
startled waiters had to make a chain to pass him bread, and he
swallowed the thin slices in one mouthful. Eventually he grew
annoyed and asked for a loaf to be put by his place. The
proprietor, in quite a state, appeared for a moment at the door.
The party had been expecting this and it set them roaring
afresh. That'd give mine bloody host something to think
about! But wasn't that Mes-Bottes one hell of a bloke! Didn't
he once eat twelve hard-boiled eggs and drink twelve glasses of
wine while the clock was striking twelve? It's not every day

you run across such a champion eater. And Mademoiselle Remanjou, rather moved, watched him as he chewed, while Monsieur Madinier, searching for the right word to express his almost reverent admiration, declared such a capacity extraordinary.

Silence fell. A waiter had just placed on the table a fricassee of rabbit, in a huge dish deep enough to hold salad. Coupeau, a great leg-puller, came out with a good one.

'Hey, waiter, this rabbit's come off the roof, it has . . . It's still miaowin'.'

And indeed a faint miaowing, perfectly imitated, seemed to be coming from the dish. Coupeau was doing it in his throat, without moving his lips; it was a party trick of his whose success was certain, so that he never ate out without ordering a fricassee. Then he purred. The ladies, overcome with laughter, were dabbing their faces with their napkins.

Madame Fauconnier asked for the head; she only liked the head. Mademoiselle Remanjou adored the bits of bacon. And, as Boche was saying he preferred the little onions, when they were nicely browned, Madame Lerat pursed her lips, murmuring:

'Well yes, naturally.'

Although she was as dried-up and skinny as a bean-pole, and led the monotonous, sheltered life of a working woman, and though no man had so much as set foot in her home since she was widowed, Madame Lerat continually displayed an obsession with smut, a mania for words with double meaning and for suggestive allusions so obscure that only she could understand them. As Boche leant towards her, whispering in her ear that he wanted an explanation, she went on:

'Obviously, two little onions . . . Surely I need say no more.'

But the conversation was turning serious. They were all talking about their work. Monsieur Madinier was enthusing about the cardboard box business; there were some real artists in that line, and he mentioned special gift-boxes—he'd seen the models—which were absolute marvels of luxury. Lorilleux, however, was sneering; he was very vain about working with gold, it was as if he could see it shining from his fingers and his entire person. In fact, as he kept repeating, in the olden days jewellers used to wear swords, and he cited the example of Bernard Palissy,* without knowing who he was. For his part Coupeau was describing a weathercock, a masterpiece made by one of his mates; it consisted first of a column, then a sheaf of corn, then a basket of fruit, then a flag: the whole thing very life-like and made of nothing but bits of zinc cut out and soldered together. Madame Lerat was showing Bibi-la-Grillade how to make a rose-stem, turning the handle of her knife over and over between her bony fingers. Their voices rose and mingled together; through the hubbub you could hear the piercing voice of Madame Fauconnier, who was complaining loudly about her workers, saying that only the day before a slut of a girl had gone and burnt a pair of sheets.

'You can say what you like,' yelled Lorilleux, banging his fist down on the table, 'gold is gold.'

The silence which followed this truism was broken only by the piping voice of Mademoiselle Remanjou, saying:

'Then I pull their skirts up and sew up the inside . . . I stick a pin in the head to hold the cap . . . And that's that, they fetch thirteen sous.'

She was explaining about her dolls to Mes-Bottes, whose jaws were slowly working away like a grindstone. He'd nod his head, not listening, keeping an eye on the waiters, lest they carry away a dish before he'd had a chance to scrape it clean. They'd eaten a veal stew and some green beans. Now the roast was being brought in, two skinny chickens lying on a bed of cress which the heat of the oven had faded and dried up. Outside, the last rays of the setting sun touched the upper branches of the acacias. The greenish light inside the room was thick with the vapours rising from the table, stained now with wine and sauce and littered with a mess of cutlery and china, while all along the wall lay dirty plates and empty bottles the waiters had dumped there, looking like so much rubbish swept up and tipped from the tablecloth. It was very hot. The men took off their frock-coats and went on eating in their shirt-sleeves.

'Madame Boche, please don't stuff them like that' said Gervaise, who wasn't saying much but kept her eye, from a distance, on Claude and Étienne.

She got up and went to have a little chat, standing behind the children's chairs. Kids had no sense, they'd eat all day long without ever saying no; and she herself served them some chicken, a little off the breast. But Maman Coupeau said they could surely give themselves a belly-ache, just this once. Madame Boche, in a whisper, accused her husband of pinching Madame Lerat's knees. Oh! he was a sly one, always after a bit of skirt. She knew she'd seen his hand disappear. If he started that again, Jesus Christ, she'd think nothing of dotting him one on the head with a carafe.

In the silence, they could hear Monsieur Madinier talking politics.

'Their law of May 31st* is an absolute disgrace. Now, you have to have two years' residence. Three million citizens have been struck off the roll! . . . I've heard that really and truly Bonaparte is very upset, because he loves the people,* he's proved that more than once.'

As for him, he was a republican, but he admired the prince, because of his uncle, the likes of whom they'd never see again. At this Bibi-la-Grillade flared up: he'd worked at the Elysée Palace,* he'd seen Bonaparte as near as Mes-Bottes was, there across the table: well that bastard of a president looked just like a police spy, he did really. People said he was going to tour the country down by Lyons,* it would be good riddance and no mistake if he broke his neck overturning in a ditch. As the discussion was turning nasty, Coupeau had to intervene.

'You're a lot of babes in arms, getting that excited over politics! . . . Politics is nothin' but a big joke! What difference does it make to folks like us? . . . Let 'em have anyone they fancy, a king, an emperor, nothin' at all, it won't stop me earnin' me five francs, an' eatin' an' sleepin', now will it? . . . No, it's all balls!'

Lorilleux nodded. He'd been born the same day as the Count of Chambord,* the 29th of September 1820. This coincidence seemed very significant to him, filling him with a vague dream in which his personal fortune and the king's return to France were connected. He didn't say precisely what his hopes were, but let it be understood that something very wonderful indeed

would then come his way. So, each time he wanted something
beyond his means, he would postpone it till later, 'when the
king came back'.

'As a matter of fact,' he said, 'I saw the Count of Chambord
one evening . . .'

Every face turned towards him.

'I did indeed. A big man, wearing an overcoat; he looked ever
such a nice chap . . . I was at Péquignot's, a friend of mine who
sells furniture in the Grande-Rue de la Chapelle . . . The Count
of Chambord had left an umbrella there the day before. So in
he came, and he said, just like that, quite simply, "Would you
kindly give me back my umbrella?" Lord, it was him alright,
Péquignot gave me his word of honour.'

Not one of the guests expressed the slightest doubt. They'd
reached the dessert. The waiters were clearing the table amid a
noisy clatter of crockery. Madame Lorilleux, who until then
had been very proper and lady-like, suddenly let fly with a
"bloody bastard!" because one of the waiters, in removing a
plate, had let something wet drip on to her neck. It must
certainly have stained her silk dress. Monsieur Madinier had to
inspect her back, but he swore there was nothing to be seen. In
the centre of the tablecloth, now, lay a salad bowl containing
egg pudding, flanked by two plates of cheese and two of fruit.
The pudding, with its overcooked egg-whites floating on yellow
custard, was greeted by an admiring silence: it had not been
expected, and was thought quite classy. Mes-Bottes was still
eating. He'd demanded another loaf. He finished the two
cheeses and as some custard still remained, he asked for the
bowl to be passed and cut big hunks of bread into the bottom,
as if it were soup.

'The gentleman is truly amazing,' remarked Monsieur Madinier, filled anew with admiration.

Then the men got up to fetch their pipes. They stood for a
moment behind Mes-Bottes, slapping him on the back and
asking him if he was feeling better. Bibi-la-Grillade lifted him
up in his chair, but, Christ almighty!, the bastard had grown
twice as heavy. For a joke, Coupeau said their mate was only
just getting into his stride, and that now he'd keep on eating
bread like that all night. Horrified, the waiters disappeared.

Boche had gone downstairs for a moment, and on returning described the wonderful expression on the face of the proprietor; he was deathly pale, down there behind his counter, while his lady wife, very shaken, had just sent out to see if the bakers were still open; even the cat looked done for. Really, it was a hoot, well worth the price of the dinner, they must never have a meal out without that guzzle-guts Mes-Bottes. And the men, smoking their pipes, gazed at him with envious eyes: after all, to be able to eat that much, you must have the constitution of an ox!

'I wouldn't like the job of keeping you filled,' said Madame Gaudron. 'No, thanks very much!'

'Come on dearie, give over teasing,' answered Mes-Bottes, with a sidelong glance at his neighbour's belly. 'You've taken in a deal more'n wot I have!'

There was applause and cries of 'bravo!': nothing you could you say to that! It was quite dark now, and in the room three gas-jets blazed, casting great circles of murky brightness amid the pipe smoke. After serving the coffee and brandy, the waiters had just taken away the last piles of dirty crockery. From below, under the acacias, the strains of the band starting up—a cornet and two violins playing very loudly—and rather shrill female laughter rose through the warm night air.

'Now let's have a burnt brandy!' bellowed Mes-Bottes, 'two litres of rotgut, plenty o' lemon an' not too much sugar!'

But Coupeau, seeing Gervaise's anxious face across the table, stood up and said they wouldn't have any more to drink. They'd got through twenty-five litres, one and a half apiece if you counted the kids as grown-ups, and that was already more than enough. They'd had a bite to eat, friendly-like, without any to-do, because they thought a lot of each other and wanted to celebrate a family occasion together. It was all very nice and they were enjoying themselves, and now they mustn't get disgustingly sozzled, not if they wanted to show respect for the ladies. In a word, and this was his point, they'd got together to drink the health of the newly-weds, not to drink themselves under the table. This little speech, delivered in a sincere voice by the roofer, who put his hand on his heart at the end of every sentence, met with strong approval from Lorilleux and

Monsieur Madinier. But the others, Boche, Gaudron, Bibi-la-
Grillade and especially Mes-Bottes, all four of them well away,
laughed derisively, declaring thickly that their throats were
bloody dry and needed watering.

'Them as are thirsty, are thirsty, and them as aren't, aren't,'
Mes-Bottes pointed out. 'So, we're going to order the burnt
brandy . . . We're not shoving it down anyone's throat. The
nobs can send for some sugared water.'

And as Coupeau began protesting again, the other, who was
standing, slapped himself on the backside and shouted:

'See here, you can kiss that . . . Waiter, two litres of old
brandy!'

Then Coupeau said that was fine, only they'd settle for the
meal right away. That would prevent arguments. No need for
decent folk to pay for boozers. And, indeed, Mes-Bottes, after
a long hunt through his pockets, could only produce three
francs seven sous. Anyway, why'd they left him hanging about
on the road to Saint-Denis? He couldn't just let himself drown,
so he'd broken into his five-franc piece. It was all their fault. In
the end he handed over three francs, saving the seven sous for
tomorrow's tobacco. Coupeau, enraged, would have hit him,
had not Gervaise in a great fright entreated him not to, pulling
him back by his coat. He decided to borrow two francs from
Lorilleux, who refused but then passed him them in secret, as
of course his wife would never have agreed.

Meanwhile, Monsieur Madinier was going round with a
plate. The unaccompanied ladies, Madame Lerat, Madame
Fauconnier, Mademoiselle Remanjou, were the first to place
their five-franc pieces discreetly on it. Then, the gentlemen got
together by themselves at the far end of the room and worked
things out. There were fifteen of them: so that would come to
seventy-five francs. Once the seventy-five francs were on the
plate, each man added five sous for the waiters. It took a quarter
of a hour of dogged calculations before everything was settled
to everyone's satisfaction.

But when Monsieur Madinier, who wanted to do the paying
himself, had asked for the proprietor, the company was dumb-
founded to hear the latter say with a smile that that didn't
nearly settle his bill. There were extras. And as the word

'extras' was greeted with furious protests, he went into details: twenty-five litres, instead of twenty, as had been agreed; the egg pudding, which he'd added, thinking the dessert seemed rather skimpy; and finally a small carafe of rum, which had been served with the coffee, in case anyone fancied a spot. At this, a violent quarrel ensued. Coupeau, taken to task over the arrangements, floundered about: he'd never said anything about twenty litres: as for the pudding, too bad—that was part of the dessert, and it was the proprietor's own idea to produce it: and the carafe of rum, what a lot of eye-wash, it was just an excuse to pad the bill, slipping liqueurs on to the table so people wouldn't realize.

'It was on the coffee tray,' he shouted, 'so, it should count as part of the coffee . . . Now piss off! Take your money, an' I'll be damned if we ever set foot in this dump again.'

'It's six francs more,' the proprietor insisted. 'Give me my six francs . . . And I'm not even counting the three loaves that gentleman had, mind!'

In a fury, the whole pack of them surrounded him, making wild gestures and yapping incoherently. The ladies, in particular, shed their customary reserve and flatly refused to add another centime. This was a nice wedding, this was, thank you very much! Mademoiselle Remanjou declared she wouldn't be seen dead at one of those dinners ever again, not she! Madame Fauconnier hadn't liked her food at all; at home, for her forty sous, she'd have had a tasty little dish you'd smack your lips over. Madame Gaudron complained bitterly that she'd been put right down at the crummy end of the table, beside Mes-Bottes, who'd not paid her the slightest attention. In short, affairs like these always ended badly. When you wanted people to come to your wedding, well you should damn well invite them, shouldn't you! And Gervaise, feeling ashamed, had taken refuge beside Maman Coupeau near one of the windows, but said nothing. She was sure all these recriminations were being laid at her door.

In the end Monsieur Madinier disappeared with the proprietor. They could be heard arguing down below. Then, after half an hour, he came back up, saying that he'd settled the matter by handing over three francs. But the wedding-party was still annoyed and exasperated, and kept on reverting to the question of the extras. And the hubbub got a lot worse when Madame Boche suddenly turned violent. She'd been keeping her eye on Boche, and had copped him squeezing Madame Lerat's waist in a corner. So, with all her might, she hurled a carafe at him, smashing it against the wall.

'It's easy to see your husband's a tailor, Madame,' said the tall widow, pursing up her lips in a suggestive way. 'He doesn't half like a bit of skirt! . . . And yet I fetched him some whopping great kicks, under the table.'

The evening was ruined. People were getting crosser and crosser. Monsieur Madinier suggested a sing-song but Bibi-la-Grillade, who had a fine voice, had just vanished; Madamoiselle Remanjou, leaning on a window sill, spotted him galloping about under the acacias with a large, bare-headed girl. The cornet and the two fiddles were now playing 'Le Marchand de moutarde',* a quadrille with a lot of hand-clapping in the country-dancing style. This brought on a stampede: Mes-Bottes and the Gaudrons rushed down and even Boche himself slipped away. Looking down from the windows, they could see the couples whirling about among the leaves, which had been turned an artificial garish green by the lanterns hanging from the trees.

The night was breathlessly still, as if stunned by the intense heat. In the dining-room a serious conversation was under way between Lorilleux and Monsieur Madinier, while the ladies, needing an excuse to vent their ill-humour, inspected their dresses for stains.

Madame Lerat's fringes must have dipped into the coffee. Madame Fauconnier's off-white dress was covered in sauce. Maman Coupeau's green shawl had fallen off a chair, and had just been found in a corner, all screwed up and trodden on. But it was Madame Lorilleux who was really fuming. They could say what they liked, she knew there was a stain on the back of her dress, she could feel it. And finally, by twisting about in front of a mirror, she managed to see it.

'There! I told you so!' she shouted. 'It's chicken gravy. The waiter'll have to pay for the dress. I'll have the law on him . . . Oh! that's the last straw. I'd have done better to stay at home in bed . . . I'm off this very minute. I've had it up to here with their lousy wedding!'

And off she went in a fury, her rapping heels making the staircase shake. Lorilleux ran after her. All he could get her to say was that she'd wait for five minutes on the pavement, in case they decided to leave together. She should've done what she wanted, and gone home after the storm. She'd get even with Coupeau for this day's work! When her brother heard how angry she was, he seemed really dismayed, and Gervaise, not wanting him upset, agreed to leave immediately. So they quickly exchanged good-night kisses, and Monsieur Madinier undertook to see Maman Coupeau home. Madame Boche was to have Claude and Étienne for the first night; their mother need have no fear, the kids were already fast asleep on their chairs, overcome by gorging on the pudding. The newly-weds were finally setting off with Lorilleux, leaving the rest of the group in the dining-room, when a fight broke out down below, on the dance-floor, between some of their party and another lot: Boche and Mes-Bottes, who'd been canoodling with a lady, didn't want to give her back to a couple of soldiers she belonged to, and were threatening to clean up the whole affair, to the ear-splitting accompaniment of the cornet and two fiddles playing the polka from *Les Perles*.

It was barely eleven. On the Boulevard de la Chapelle and throughout the whole of the Goutte-d'Or district the fortnight-ly pay-day, which happened to fall that Saturday, had set off a tremendously noisy, boozy spree. Madame Lorilleux was stand-ing waiting under a gas-lamp, some twenty paces from the Moulin-d'Argent. She took Lorilleux's arm and walked ahead, not turning round, at such a fast pace that Gervaise and Coupeau were quite out of breath trying to keep up. From time to time they had to step into the road to avoid a drunk lying sprawled on the pavement. Lorilleux looked back, wanting to patch things up.

'We'll see you right to your door,' he said.

But Madame Lorilleux said loudly that she thought it funny to spend your wedding night in that filthy hole the Hôtel Boncœur. Oughtn't they to have put the wedding off and saved a franc or two, so they could buy furniture and spend the first night in their own place? They'd be ever so comfortable, wouldn't they, the two of them crammed into a ten-franc garret where there wasn't even any air?

'I've moved out of that room, we're not stayin' up there,' objected Coupeau timidly. 'We're keepin' Gervaise's room, it's bigger.'

Madame Lorilleux, beside herself, turned round sharply.

'Well if that doesn't beat everything!' she cried. 'So you're sleeping in Banban's room!'

Gervaise went quite white. That nickname, used to her face for the first time, struck her like a blow. Moreover, she knew perfectly well what her sister-in-law's exclamation implied: Banban's room meant the room where she'd lived for a month with Lantier, where bits and pieces of her former life still lingered. Coupeau didn't understand this, but was just offended by the nickname.

'You shouldn't call other people names,' he replied crossly. 'Perhaps you don't know they call you Queue-de-Vache,* round here, because of your hair. There, you don't like that, do you? . . . Why shouldn't we keep the first-floor room? The children won't be there tonight an' we'll be fine.'

Madame Lorilleux said no more and retreated into a dignified silence, raging inwardly at being called Queue-de-Vache. Coupeau, to comfort Gervaise, squeezed her arm gently, and even managed to cheer her up, whispering to her that they were setting up house with precisely seven sous, three big coins and a little 'un, which he jingled, his hand in his trouser pocket. On reaching the Hôtel Boncœur, they said good night rather curtly. Just as Coupeau was pushing the two women close together, telling them not to be such idiots, a drunk who had seemed about to pass to their right, suddenly veered left and flung himself between them.

'Hey, it's Père Bazouge!' said Lorilleux. 'He's certainly had a skinful this evening.'

Frightened, Gervaise flattened herself against the door of the hotel. Père Bazouge was an undertaker's assistant of about fifty. His black trousers were splashed with mud, his black coat was slung over his shoulder and his black leather hat dented and squashed from some fall.

'Don't be scared, he won't hurt you,' Lorilleux went on. 'He's our neighbour; the third room in the corridor leading to our place . . . He'd be in a fine mess if his employers saw him like this!'

Old Bazouge, meanwhile, was offended by Gervaise's alarm.

'Well now!' he stammered, 'we don't eat you, y'know, in our line of business! C'mon, dearie, I'm as good as the next man . . . 'Strue I've 'ad a few! When business is good you might as well oil the wheels. It wasn't you, no, nor any of your lot, as could've brought down the party just the two of us carried from the fourth floor to the pavement—forty-odd stone 'e weighed— and no bones broken neither. Me, I like folks as is cheerful.'

But Gervaise was retreating further into the doorway, over- come by a fierce urge to cry which was ruining her quiet happy day for her. She forgot all about kissing her sister-in-law, she begged Coupeau to make the drunk go away. At that Bazouge, as he lurched about, sketched a gesture full of philosophical contempt.

'That won't stop you from goin' the same way, dearie . . . Perhaps you'll be 'appy to go, one day . . . Yes, I know some women who'd thank me, if I came for 'em.'

And, as the Lorilleux were trying to take him with them, he turned round and mumbled a final remark, between two hiccups:

'When you're dead—mark me words now—when you're dead, it's for a long, long time.'

CHAPTER IV

THERE followed four years of hard work. In the neighbourhood Gervaise and Coupeau were known as a happy couple who kept themselves to themselves, didn't fight, and regularly took their Sunday walk over Saint-Ouen* way. The wife put in twelve- hour days at Madame Fauconnier's, and still managed to keep her home clean as a new pin and get a meal for all her family morning and evening. The husband wasn't a boozer, brought his fortnightly pay straight home, and would smoke a pipe at his open window before going to bed, to get a breath of air. They were held up as an example because they were so nice. And, as they earned nearly nine francs a day between them, people reckoned that they must be putting by quite a tidy bit of money.

But, especially at the beginning, they had to slog like anything to make ends meet. Their wedding had saddled them with a debt of two hundred francs. And they hated the Hôtel Boncœur; they thought it a horrid place, frequented by some very shady customers, and they dreamed of being in their own home, with furniture of their own that they'd really look after. Time and again they worked out the sum they'd want: it would come, in round figures, to three hundred and fifty francs, if they were to have somewhere to stow their things right away, and the odd saucepan or casserole they might need. They'd given up hope of setting aside so large an amount in less than two years, when they had a stroke of luck: an old gentleman in Plassans asked them for Claude, the older child, so he could put him in school there; a generous whim on the part of an eccentric art collector who'd been deeply impressed by some daubs of human figures the kid had once done. Claude was already costing them a packet. When they only had the younger boy, Étienne, to support, they were able to save the three hundred and fifty francs in seven and a half months. The day they bought their furniture, from a second-hand dealer in the Rue Belhomme, they took a turn on the outer boulevards before going home and their hearts were filled with joy. There was a bed, a bedside table, a marble-topped chest of drawers, a cupboard, a round table covered with oilcloth and six chairs, all in old mahogany; not counting the bedding, linen, and kitchen utensils, all as good as new. For them this was like a solemn, definitive initiation into life, something that in making them householders gave them standing among the well-established people of the neighbourhood.

For two months they'd been thinking about where they ought to live. What they wanted more than anything was to rent a place in the big building in the Rue de la Goutte-d'Or. But there wasn't a single vacancy there and they had to abandon their old dream. To tell the truth, Gervaise didn't really mind;

she was very frightened by the idea of having the Lorilleux as next-door neighbours. So they looked elsewhere. Coupeau very sensibly didn't want to be too far away from Madame Fauconnier's, so that Gervaise could easily pop back home any time she liked. And eventually they made a lucky find, a big room with a little one off it and a kitchen, in the Rue Neuve de la Goutte-d'Or, almost opposite the laundry. It was a small two-storey house with a very steep staircase at the top of which there were just two apartments, one on the right, one on the left; the ground-floor was occupied by a man who hired out cabs that were kept in sheds in a huge courtyard stretching along the street. The young woman was delighted, and felt she was back in the country; no neighbours, no tittle-tattle to worry about, a nice peaceful spot that reminded her of a little street in Plassans behind the ramparts; and as a crowning stroke of luck she could see her window from her work-table, without leaving her ironing, if she craned her neck.

They moved in April on the quarterly rent day. Gervaise was then eight months pregnant. But she was very spunky, and would say with a laugh that the child helped her when she was working; she could feel its little hands pushing, inside her, giving her strength. And she didn't half tell Coupeau where to go, when he tried to make her lie down and pamper herself a bit! She'd lie down when the pains got bad. That would be quite soon enough, because now, with another mouth to feed, they were going to have to put their backs into it and no mistake. And it was she who cleaned the place before helping her husband to arrange the furniture. She worshipped those pieces of furniture, she dusted them with maternal solicitude and was broken-hearted at the sight of the tiniest scratch. If she banged into them when she was sweeping she'd stop dead, as shocked as if she'd hit herself. She was particularly attached to the chest, which she thought handsome, solid, a thing of consequence. She had a dream that she didn't dare mention, to own a clock and stand it right in the middle of the marble top, where it would look to wonderful advantage. If there hadn't been a baby on the way she might perhaps have risked buying her clock. But, with a sigh, she put it off till later.

The couple were absolutely delighted with their new home. They put Étienne's bed in the little room, where there was still space for another child's cot. The kitchen was no bigger than your hand and pitch dark; but if you left the door open you could see fairly well and in any case Gervaise wasn't going to be cooking for thirty people, all she needed was somewhere to make her stew. As for the larger room, it was their pride and joy. First thing in the morning they'd close the white calico curtains round the bed recess and the room was instantly transformed into a dining room, with the table in the centre and the cupboard and the chest facing each other. Because the fireplace burned as much as fifteen sous' worth of coal in a single day, they'd blocked it up; a little cast iron stove that stood on the marble slab kept them warm for seven sous when it was really cold. And then Coupeau had decorated the walls as best he could, promising himself he'd make improvements later on; a big engraving of some field marshal cavorting about, baton in hand, between a cannon and a pile of shot, took the place of a mirror; on the chest, family photographs were arranged in two rows on either side of a gold-coloured china bowl that had once been a holy water stoup and now served for storing matches; while on the top of the cupboard a bust of Pascal* complemented a bust of Béranger:* the one serious, the other smiling, they seemed to be listening to the ticking of the cuckoo clock hanging nearby. It really was a beautiful room.

'Guess how much we pay here?' Gervaise would ask each visitor.

And when people guessed their rent to be higher than it was, she'd cry exultantly, thrilled to be so comfortably settled for so little money:

'A hundred and fifty francs, that's all! They're giving it away, aren't they!'

The Rue Neuve de la Goutte-d'Or itself had a lot to do with their contentment. Gervaise practically lived in it, being forever on the go between her own place and Madame Fauconnier's. In the evenings Coupeau, now, would go down and smoke his pipe on the doorstep. The rough cobbled street, without a pavement, climbed steeply. At the top, on the Rue de la Goutte-d'Or side, there were some dismal shops with dirty windows, cobblers,

coopers, an unsavoury-looking grocer's, a wine merchant's that
had gone bust and whose shutters had been closed for weeks
and were covered with bills. At the other end, in the direction
of Paris, some four-storey houses blocking any view of the sky
all had their ground floors occupied by laundries that were
clustered together in a row side by side; the only exception was
a small-town style barber's shop-front, painted green and full
of delicately-coloured flasks, that livened up this gloomy spot
with the bright gleam of its spotlessly clean copper dishes. But
the cheerful part of the street was the middle, where the
buildings, fewer in number and not so tall, let in air and
sunlight. The sheds belonging to the cab-hire business, the soda
water factory next door and the washhouse across the road
created a great open space full of quiet, in which the faint voices
of the washerwomen and the regular beat of the steam engine
only seemed to reinforce the stillness. Plots of land stretching
a long way back from the street and alleys leading off between
dark walls made it seem like a village. And Coupeau, who
enjoyed watching the few passers-by stepping over the continuous stream of sudsy water, said it reminded him of a place he'd
been taken to by one of his uncles, when he was five. Gervaise
was especially enchanted by a tree that grew in a yard immediately to the left of her window, an acacia with just one single
branch, whose sparse greenery was sufficient to lend charm to
the entire street.

The young woman had her baby on the last day of April. The
pains came on in the afternoon, about four o'clock, while she
was ironing a pair of curtains at Madame Fauconnier's. She
didn't want to leave straight away, but stayed there twisting
about on a chair and doing a little ironing when the pains let
up a bit; the curtains were wanted urgently and she was
determined to finish them; besides, it might just be a belly-ache,
and you shouldn't make a fuss about a belly-ache. But just as
she was talking of starting on some men's shirts, she turned
quite white. She had to leave the laundry and cross the road,
bending right over and holding on to the walls. When one of
the women who worked there offered to go with her Gervaise
refused, but instead asked her to fetch the midwife from the
Rue de la Charbonnière, close by. After all, the house wasn't

on fire, was it? She'd probably be at it the whole night long. It wasn't going to stop her getting Coupeau's supper once she was home; then she'd see about lying down on the bed for a minute or two without even bothering to undress. Half-way up the stairs she was taken so bad that she had to sit down right where she was; and she stuck both fists in her mouth to stop herself yelling, because the thought of being found there by any man climbing up the stairs mortified her. The pain passed and she managed to open the door, very relieved and sure it must have been a false alarm. That evening she was planning to make mutton stew with some best end of neck. Every-thing went fine while she was peeling her potatoes. She was browning the mutton in a pan when the sweating and the griping pains started again. She stirred the gravy, pacing back and forth in front of the stove, blinded by big tears. Even if she was having a baby that wasn't any reason, was it, for letting Coupeau go hungry? At last the stew was simmering over a banked-down fire. Gervaise came back into the room, sure she had the time to lay a place at one end of the table. But she had to put the wine bottle down again ever so quickly; she couldn't make it as far as the bed, and collapsed on to a mat on the floor, where she gave birth to her baby. When the midwife arrived a quarter of an hour later that was where she saw to her needs.

The roofer was still working at the hospital. Gervaise would-n't hear of his being bothered. When he came home at seven he found her in bed, well wrapped up, looking very pale against the pillow. The baby was crying, lying swaddled in a shawl at her feet.

'Oh, my poor wife!' said Coupeau as he kissed Gervaise. 'An' not an hour ago there I was larkin' about, while you were yellin' your head off! . . . Well you certainly don't waste any time, do you, you produce the goods just like sneezin'.'

She gave a faint smile and murmured:

'It's a girl.'

'Right!' answered the roofer jokingly, to cheer her up. 'I'd ordered a girl! . . . And that's exactly what I've got! So d'you do everythin' I ask?'

And, picking the child up, he went on:

'Let's see what you look like, you dirty little miss . . . What a dark little mug. Oh, don't you worry, it'll lighten up. You must be a good girl now, and not chase after the boys, but grow up sensible like your Papa and Mamma.'

Gervaise lay gazing solemnly at her daughter, her wide-open eyes slowly shading over with sadness. She shook her head; she'd have liked a boy, because boys could always get by and didn't run so many risks in the Paris she knew. The midwife had to take the babe from Coupeau's hands. Also, she forbade Gervaise to talk; it was quite bad enough having so much noise round her. Then the roofer said he must let Maman Coupeau and the Lorilleux know; but he was absolutely starving, and wanted his supper first. The newly-delivered mother was very upset to see him serving himself, running into the kitchen to get the stew, eating it out of a soup-plate, not being able to find the bread. In spite of the midwife's orders Gervaise lay there fretting and twisting about in the sheets. It was so silly, too, that she hadn't been able to lay the table; the pains had knocked her on to the ground like a blow from a club. Her poor hubby would be fed up with her for lying there taking her ease when he was making such a poor supper. At any rate, she hoped the potatoes were properly done. She couldn't remember now whether she'd salted them.

'Will you be quiet!' shouted the midwife.

'Oh, that'll be the day, when you can stop her gettin' all worked up!' said Coupeau, his mouth full. 'If you weren't here I bet she'd get out of bed to cut me me bread . . . Just you stay there on your back, you silly goose! Don't wear yourself out, or it'll be a fortnight before you're on your feet again . . . It's very good, your stew is. Madame's goin' to have some too. That's so, ain't it, Madame?'

The midwife refused, but wouldn't say no to a glass of wine; it had given her quite a turn to find the poor woman with her baby on the mat. Eventually Coupeau went off to tell the family the news. He came back half an hour later with the whole lot of them, Maman Coupeau, the Lorilleux and Madame Lerat, whom he'd found visiting the Lorilleux. The Lorilleux, faced with how well the young couple were doing, had become as nice as could be, praising Gervaise to the skies, though always hinting with tiny gestures—a jerk of a chin or a blink of an eye—at reservations, as if they were deferring their real verdict till later. After all, they knew what they knew; but they didn't want to go against the opinion of the whole neighbourhood.

'I've brought you the whole gang!' cried Coupeau. 'Couldn't help it! They all wanted to see you . . . Now don't start yackin', it's not allowed. They'll just stay here and look at you quietly, nobody's goin' to mind. And I'm goin' to make 'em some coffee, real good stuff!'

He disappeared into the kitchen. Maman Coupeau, after kissing Gervaise, went into ecstasies over the size of the baby. The other two women had also planted smacking kisses on the new mother's cheeks. And the three of them stood in front of the bed, exclaiming a lot and going into details about confinements, all sorts of strange confinements, but saying it was no worse than having a tooth pulled. Madame Lerat examined the baby all over, declaring it well formed and adding, meaningfully, that *this* one would grow up to be a fine woman; and as she thought the head rather pointed she gently kneaded it, in spite of the baby's cries, to make it rounder. Madame Lorilleux angrily snatched the baby from her; that was enough to give an infant every defect you could think of, messing about with it while its skull was still so soft. Then she tried to decide who it was the baby took after. There was nearly a row. Lorilleux, peering past the women, kept saying the kid didn't look at all like Coupeau; maybe a bit round the nose, but even there! It was its mother all over again, with different eyes; there was no doubt about it, those eyes didn't come from *their* family.

Meanwhile Coupeau had not reappeared. They could hear him in the kitchen struggling with the stove and the coffee-pot. Gervaise was getting all worked up; it wasn't a man's job, making coffee; and she kept calling instructions to him, in spite of the fierce shushing of the midwife.

'Tell that dummy to shut up!' said Coupeau, coming in with the coffee-pot in his hand. 'What a pest she is! She just can't help carryin' on like that . . . We'll drink this in glasses, OK? 'Cos you see, the cups are still in the shop.'

They sat down round the table, and the roofer insisted on serving the coffee himself. It smelt amazingly strong, it wasn't any of your nasty rubbishy stuff. When the midwife had sipped her glassful she left; everything was going nicely and she wasn't needed any longer; if there was trouble during the night they could send for her in the morning. While she was still on the stairs Madame Lorilleux started calling her a tippler and a good-for-nothing. She put four sugars in her coffee and set you back fifteen francs for letting you have your baby all by yourself. But Coupeau stuck up for her; he'd gladly hand over the fifteen francs; after all, those women spent their youth studying, they were right to charge a lot. Then Lorilleux got into an argument with Madame Lerat; he claimed that in order to have a boy you had to turn the head of your bed to the north, whereas she, shrugging her shoulders, called that a lot of nonsense, and cited a different formula that consisted of hiding under the mattress a bunch of fresh nettles you'd picked in sunlight—but the wife mustn't know. They'd pushed the table close to the bed. Until ten o'clock Gervaise lay there in a daze, smiling, her head turned sideways on the pillow, gradually overpowered by a feeling of immense weariness; she could see and she could hear, but no longer could she find the strength to venture a gesture or a word; she felt as though she was dead, but it was a very pleasant death, in which she was happy to watch the others living. From time to time a little cry would come from the baby, amid the loud voices chatting interminably about a murder committed the day before in the Rue du Bon-Puits, at the far end of La Chapelle.

Then, when they felt it was time to go, they talked about the christening. The Lorilleux had agreed to be godparents. In private they griped about this, but if the Coupeaus hadn't asked them they'd have looked pretty silly. Coupeau didn't see why the baby had to be christened at all; it wouldn't give her ten thousand a year, would it, and it might give her a cold. The less you had to do with priests the better. But Maman Coupeau called him a heathen. And the Lorilleux, although they didn't go to church to take communion, prided themselves on being religious.

'It could be on Sunday, if you like,' said the chain-maker.

Gervaise nodded her agreement and everyone kissed her and told her to keep well. They also said goodbye to the baby. They each leant over that poor little trembling creature with smiles and fond words, as if it could understand. They called it Nana, the baby name for Anna, her godmother's name.

'Goodnight, Nana . . . Now be a good girl, Nana . . .'

When at last they'd gone, Coupeau drew his chair close up against the bed and finished his pipe, holding Gervaise's hand in his. Deeply moved, he smoked his pipe slowly, saying a word or two between puffs.

'Well, old girl, did you find 'em a pain in the neck? I couldn't stop 'em comin', you know. After all, it's their way of showin' they're fond of us . . . But it's nicer on our own, ain't it? I really needed to be alone with you like this for a bit, I did. I thought the evening would never end! . . . You poor old thing, did it hurt real bad? Those little shrimps, when they come into the world, they don't have a notion how bad it hurts. It must feel like you're bein' split in two . . . Tell me where it hurts an' I'll kiss it better.'

He'd slipped one of his big hands gently under her back and, pulling her nearer, was kissing her stomach through the sheet, full of a simple man's emotion in the presence of this still painful fecundity. He kept asking whether he was hurting her, he'd have liked to make her better by blowing on the pain. And Gervaise was very happy. She swore she wasn't in any pain at all now. All she could think of was getting up as soon as possible, because this wasn't the time to be sitting about with idle hands. But he told her not to worry. Wasn't it up to him to support the little one? He'd be a real good-for-nothing if he ever left her saddled with that kid to take care of. It didn't strike him as all that clever to be able to make a baby; the difficult part was bringing it up, wasn't it?

Coupeau hardly slept at all that night. He'd damped down the fire in the stove. He had to get up every hour to give the baby spoonfuls of warm sugary water. But that didn't stop him leaving for work in the morning as usual. He even used his lunch hour to go and register the birth at the town hall. Meanwhile Madame Boche had been alerted and she came over to spend the day with Gervaise. But after ten hours of deep sleep the latter was making quite a fuss, grumbling that she was stiff all over from staying in bed. She'd be ill if they didn't let her get up. That evening when Coupeau came home she unburdened herself to him: of course she trusted Madame Boche, but it drove her wild to see a stranger making herself at home in *her* room, opening the drawers and touching her things. The next day when the concierge came back from running an errand she found her up and dressed, sweeping the room and busying herself with her husband's dinner. And she absolutely refused to go back to bed. Whoever did they think she was! It was all very well for fine ladies to seem exhausted. When you're not rich, you haven't the time. Three days after having her baby she was ironing petticoats at Madame Fauconnier's, banging away with her irons and drenched with sweat from the fierce heat of the stove.

On the Saturday evening Madame Lorilleux, as godmother, brought over her christening presents: a thirty-five-sou bonnet and a christening robe trimmed with tucks and narrow lace, that she'd got for six francs because it was shop-soiled. The following day Lorilleux, as godfather, presented the new mother with six pounds of sugar. They were doing things properly. Nor did they turn up empty-handed that evening, at the meal given by the Coupeaus. The husband arrived with a bottle of vintage wine under each arm, while the wife came carrying a large custard tart bought at a very well-known pastrycook's in the Chaussée Clignancourt. But the Lorilleux went and talked about their generosity all over the neighbourhood; they'd spent almost twenty francs. When Gervaise heard about the way they'd gossiped she was furious, and no longer gave them any credit for their politeness.

It was at this christening dinner that the Coupeaus became really close friends with their neighbours across the landing. The other apartment in the little house was occupied by two people, a mother and son, the Goujets as they were called. Until then they'd just exchanged a nod on the stairs or in the street and nothing more; the neighbours seemed a bit stand-offish. Then, as the mother had carried up a pail of water for her the day after the birth, Gervaise felt it was appropriate to invite them to the meal, especially as she thought them very nice. And there, of course, they got to know each other.

The Goujets came from the Nord.* The mother repaired lace; the son, a blacksmith by trade, worked in a factory that made bolts. They'd lived in the other rooms on that landing for five years. The silent tranquillity of their lives concealed a real tragedy in their past; one day in Lille the father, in a fit of drunken rage, had beaten a fellow-worker to death with an iron bar, and had then strangled himself in prison with his handkerchief. After this calamity the widow and her child had fled to Paris, where, under the ever-present burden of their tragic history, they tried to make amends for it by a life of scrupulous integrity and unvarying gentleness and courage. There was even a hint of pride involved, for they began to see themselves as better than other people. Madame Goujet, always dressed in black, her brow framed by a nun-like head-dress, had a calm, white, matronly face, as if the pale shades of the lace and the meticulous work of her fingers had bestowed upon her some of their serenity. Goujet was a colossus of twenty-three, a splendid man with a rosy face, blue eyes and the strength of Hercules. At the workshop he was known as Gueule-d'Or* on account of his handsome golden beard.

Gervaise immediately felt a great liking for these people. The first time she went into their home she was astonished at how clean it was. No two ways about it, you could blow anywhere you liked, you wouldn't raise a speck of dust. And the tiled floor shone as brightly as a mirror. Madame Goujet took her in to see her son's room. It was decorously neat and white, like a young girl's: a little iron bed with muslin curtains, a table, a washstand, a small bookshelf hanging on the wall; then, all over the walls, pictures, cut-out figures, coloured prints secured with four nails, and portraits of all kinds of people taken from illustrated papers. Madame Goujet said with a smile that her son was a great big baby; in the evenings it tired him to read, so he'd amuse himself looking at his pictures. An hour passed in a flash while Gervaise was with her neighbour, who'd settled down to her lace-making again in front of a window. Gervaise took a great interest in the hundreds of pins holding the lace, happy just to be there, smelling the good clean smell of Madame Goujet's home, where her delicate occupation created an atmosphere of harmonious silence.

The Goujets seemed even nicer when you knew them better. They worked very long hours and put away more than a quarter of their earnings in a savings account.* In the neighbourhood they were greeted respectfully and people talked about their thrift. There was never a hole to be seen in Goujet's clothes, and his overalls were spotlessly clean. He was very polite, even rather timid, in spite of his broad shoulders. The laundresses at the end of the road got a lot of fun out of seeing him walk past with averted eyes. He didn't like their coarse language and thought it disgusting that women should be always talking smut. One day, however, he'd come home drunk. Madame Goujet's only reproach was to confront him with his father's portrait, a not very good painting that they dutifully preserved, hidden away in the bottom of the chest. After that lesson Goujet drank only moderately, although he wasn't put off wine, because the workman needs wine. On Sundays he'd go out with his mother on his arm; usually they went over Vincennes* way, but sometimes he'd escort her to the theatre. He adored his mother. He still spoke to her as if he was a little boy. With his square-shaped head and body thickened by the heavy work he did, he reminded you of a large animal; a bit slow on the uptake, but a good chap all the same.

At first Goujet was very ill-at-ease in the presence of Gervaise. Then, after a few weeks, he became used to her. He'd watch out for her and carry up her parcels, treating her with the blunt familiarity of a brother, cutting out pictures especially for her. But one morning he turned the door-handle without knocking and caught her half-naked, washing her neck; for a week after that he didn't look her in the face, so that in the end he made her blush as well.

Cadet-Cassis, with his Parisian gift of the gab, thought Gueule-d'Or a bit dim. It was fine not to get sozzled or chat up girls in the street but after all a man should be a man, or he might just as well put on skirts right away. He'd tease Goujet in front of Gervaise, accusing him of making eyes at all the women in the neighbourhood, an accusation which that fine figure of a man would vehemently deny. That didn't prevent the two workmen from being friends. They'd call for one another in the morning and set off together, and sometimes they'd have a glass of beer before coming home. Ever since the christening dinner they'd used the familiar 'tu', because saying

'vous' all the time is so longwinded. That was the extent of
their friendship when Gueule-d'Or did Cadet-Cassis a tremendous service, one of those extraordinary good turns you remember all your life. It was the second of December.* The roofer,
just for fun, had had the bright idea of going down to see the
rioting; the Republic, Bonaparte and the whole outfit left him
cold, but he adored gunpowder and thought the shooting a
great joke. He got stuck behind a barricade and could easily
have been copped, if the smith hadn't happened along at
exactly the right moment to protect him with his big frame
and help him slip away. Going back up the Rue du Faubourg-
Poissonnière, Goujet walked fast, his face serious. He dabbled
a bit in politics and was a republican, but a moderate one, for
the sake of justice and universal happiness. But he hadn't joined
in the shooting. He gave his reasons: the people were tired of
being the pawn of the middle class, and getting hurt in the
process; February and June* were valuable lessons, so from now
on the workers were going to leave the bourgeois to themselves
to do as they thought best. Then when he'd reached the Rue
des Poissonniers, up on the heights, he turned his head and
looked at Paris; all the same, what was going on down there was
a dirty business, and one day the people might be sorry they'd
stood by and done nothing. But Coupeau sniggered, calling
them silly asses to risk their skins just in order to save those
bloody idlers in the Chamber their twenty-five francs.* That
evening the Coupeaus invited the Goujets to supper. During
dessert Cadet-Cassis and Gueule-d'Or gave each other smacking kisses on the cheeks. Now they were friends for life.

For three years the lives of the two families on either side of
the landing passed without incident. Gervaise brought up her
baby girl without ever missing more than two days' work a week
at the most. She'd become a good skilled worker, and earned
up to three francs. So she decided to start Étienne, now nearly
eight, at a little school in the Rue de Chartres, where she paid
five francs. Even though they had two children to keep, the
Coupeaus managed to put aside twenty or thirty francs each
month. When their savings reached a total of six hundred
francs, the young woman became obsessed by an ambitious
dream and could no longer sleep; she wanted to set up in

business, rent a little shop and herself employ some girls. She'd worked it all out. After twenty years, if business was good, she'd be able to buy an annuity and they could go and live on it somewhere in the country. But she didn't dare take the risk. She said she was looking for a shop, to give herself time to think it over. The money wasn't coming to any harm in their savings account; on the contrary, it was producing offspring. In three years she'd allowed herself only one of the things she'd set her heart on, and bought herself a clock; it was made of rosewood, with twisted columns and a brass pendulum, and even so she was taking a year to pay for it, in twenty-sous instalments every Monday. It annoyed her when Coupeau said he'd wind it up; only she could take off the glass shade and reverently dust the columns, as though the chest's marble top had been transformed into a chapel. She hid the savings book behind the clock, under its glass cover. And often, when she was thinking about her shop, she'd stand there in a dream, staring at the hands moving round the clock face, as if she were waiting for a particular, very special moment to make up her mind.

The Coupeaus went out almost every Sunday with the Goujets. These were pleasant little outings, a meal of fried fish at Saint-Ouen or of rabbit at Vincennes, served without fuss in the garden of some restaurant. The men would drink their fill and come home in fine form with their ladies on their arms. Before they went to bed that night the two families would tot up the cost and divide it between them, and there was never any argument over the odd sou. The Lorilleux were jealous of the Goujets. After all it did seem funny for Cadet-Cassis and Banban to go out with strangers all the time when they had family of their own. Yes, well, they didn't care a rap, did they, for their family! Now that they'd saved up a few sous they didn't half give themselves airs! Madame Lorilleux, fed up at seeing her brother get away from her, started bad-mouthing Gervaise again. But Madame Lerat stuck up for the young woman, telling in her defence some extraordinary tales of attempts on her virtue on the boulevard at night, in which Gervaise, like the heroine of some play, had boxed the ears of her assailants. As for Maman Coupeau, she tried to make them all get on together, and to keep in her children's good books; her eyesight was failing more and more, she'd only one charring job left now and was grateful when one or the other of them slipped her the odd five francs.

On the day of Nana's third birthday Coupeau came home to find Gervaise in a state of great agitation. She refused to explain why, saying there was nothing whatever the matter with her. But, as she was setting the table all wrong and kept standing still with the plates in her hand, deep in thought, her husband insisted on being told.

'Well, all right, it's this,' she finally admitted, 'that little draper's shop in the Rue de la Goutte-d'Or is for rent . . . I saw it an hour ago when I went to buy some thread. Quite a shock, it was.'

It was a nicely kept shop in the very same big building where they used to dream of living. There was the shop and a room behind, as well as two other rooms to left and right, in fact just what they needed; the rooms were a bit small, but the layout was good. The only trouble was, she thought it too dear; the proprietor had mentioned five hundred francs.

'So you went an' looked at it an' asked the price?' said Coupeau.

'Oh, you know, just out of curiosity!' she replied, feigning indifference. 'You look at places, you go in wherever there's a sign up, it doesn't commit you . . . But that one's definitely too expensive. Anyway, it might be a silly thing to do, to set up on me own.'

Still, after dinner she came back to the subject of the draper's shop. She drew a plan of the rooms on a corner of a newspaper. And little by little she talked it through, estimating the size of different areas and arranging the rooms as if she was going to have to move her furniture in the next day. Then Coupeau, seeing how desperately she wanted it, encouraged her to go ahead; she'd never find anything in good condition for less than five hundred francs; anyway, they might get the rent reduced. The only fly in the ointment was going to live in the same building as the Lorilleux whom she couldn't stand. But she said crossly that she didn't hate anybody; in the heat of her passion she even defended the Lorilleux; they weren't really so bad,

they'd all get along fine. And after they were in bed and
Coupeau was fast asleep, she went on planning the arrangement
of the rooms although she still hadn't definitely decided on
renting.

When she was alone the next day she couldn't stop herself
lifting off the glass cover and studying the savings book. Just
think, her shop was in there, in those messy pages covered with
nasty scrawls! Before setting off for work she consulted Madame Goujet, who was very much in favour of her going into
business; with a husband like hers, a reliable type who didn't
drink, she was sure of being able to do well and not go broke.
At lunch-time she even went up to see the Lorilleux to ask their
advice; she didn't want to look as if she was hiding something
from the family. It was a dreadful blow for Madame Lorilleux.
What! So Banban was going to have a shop now! Though cut
to the heart, she managed to stammer something, aware that she
ought to seem delighted; the shop was convenient, and Gervaise
would certainly be right to take it. Still, when she'd pulled
herself together a bit, she and her husband both mentioned the
dampness of the courtyard, and how gloomy the ground-floor
rooms were. Oh, it was a good spot for rheumatism! Still, if
Gervaise had made up her mind, nothing they said would
prevent her from renting the place, would it?

That evening Gervaise acknowledged openly, with a laugh,
that it would have made her ill if anyone had stopped her
having the shop. Nevertheless, before signing on the dotted
line, she wanted to take Coupeau to look at it and try to get the
rent lowered.

'All right, tomorrow, if you like,' said her husband. 'Come
an' fetch me about six at the house where I'm workin' in the
Rue de la Nation, an' we'll go home by way of the Rue de la
Goutte-d'Or.'

Coupeau was then finishing the roof of a new three-storey
house. It so happened that he had to lay the last sheets of zinc
that very day. As the roof was almost flat, he'd installed his
workbench, a large board on two trestles, up there. A beautiful
May sun was setting, turning the chimney-tops to gold. And,
high up against the clear sky, the workman was calmly cutting
the zinc with his shears, leaning over his workbench like a tailor

cutting out a pair of pants in his own workshop. Against the
wall of the neighbouring house his assistant, a fair, slender
youth of seventeen, was keeping up the fire in the brazier by
operating an enormous pair of bellows, which sent out a shower
of sparks with every puff of air.

'Oy, Zidore, put the irons in!' shouted Coupeau.

The assistant shoved the soldering irons right into the middle
of the glowing coals, which looked pale pink in the bright light.
Then he worked the bellows some more. Coupeau was holding
the last sheet of zinc. It was to go on the edge of the roof, near
the guttering; just there the slope became steep, with a yawning
drop to the street below. The roofer, wearing cloth slippers,
apparently completely at home, moved forward shuffling his
feet and whistling the tune of 'Hey, Ho, the Baby Lambs'. On
reaching the steep bit he let himself slide, then braced himself
with one knee against the brickwork of a chimney, half hanging
over the gap above the street. One of his legs was dangling.
When he leaned back to shout to that bone-idle Zidore, he'd
catch on to a corner of the brickwork, because of the pavement
down there below him.

'C'mon, you bleedin' slowcoach! . . . Gimme the irons! 'Sno
good starin' at the sky, you weedy bugger, the job won't do
itself!'

But Zidore was in no hurry. He enjoyed gazing at the
nearby roofs and at a thick column of smoke rising up from the
depths of Paris, over by Grenelle;* it might easily be a fire.
However he came and lay down on his stomach with his head
over the gap, and passed Coupeau the irons. Then the latter
began soldering the zinc sheet. He'd crouch down or he'd
reach forward, always managing to keep his balance as he
squatted on one haunch or perched on one toe or hung on by
one finger. Coupeau had the most fantastic nerve; as cool as a
bleeding cucumber, he was, rubbing shoulders with danger,
thumbing his nose at it. He knew all about it. It was the
street that was afraid of him. As he was never without his pipe,
he'd turn from time to time and calmly spit down into the
street.

'Hallo! Madame Boche!' he suddenly called out. 'Oy! Madame Boche!'

He'd just noticed the concierge crossing the road. She looked up and recognized him. And a conversation got going between the roof and the pavement. She stood with her hands tucked under her apron and her nose in the air. He was on his feet now, his left arm round a flue pipe, bending over.

'You haven't seen me wife?' he asked.

'No, I haven't,' replied the concierge. 'Is she somewhere about?'

'She's comin' to pick me up . . . An' is everyone well at home?'

'Oh yes, thanks, everyone but me, and you can see how ill I am! I'm off to the Chaussée Clignancourt for a nice leg of mutton. The butcher near the Moulin Rouge* won't sell it for less than sixteen sous.'

They were raising their voices because a cab was passing. In the broad, deserted Rue de la Nation, their shouted conversation had brought only one little old woman to her window; and that old woman stayed there leaning out, enjoying the tremendous thrill of watching this man on the roof opposite, as if she hoped to see him fall at any moment.

'Well cheerio!' yelled Madame Boche again. 'I don't want to keep you.'

Coupeau turned round and took the iron Zidore handed him. But just as the concierge was moving away, she saw Gervaise on the other pavement, holding Nana by the hand. Madame Boche was already looking upwards to tell Coupeau, when the young woman silenced her with an emphatic gesture. And, in a low voice, so as not to be heard up above, she explained what she was afraid of: she worried that if she appeared suddenly she'd give her husband a shock that could make him fall. In four years she'd only fetched him once from work. Today was the second time. She couldn't stand seeing it, her heart seemed to stop beating when she looked at her man up there between the sky and the earth, in places where not even sparrows dared go.

'I'm sure it can't be very nice,' murmured Madame Boche. 'As mine's a tailor I don't get frights like that.'

'Just imagine, in the early days,' went on Gervaise, 'I'd be in a panic from dawn to dusk. I was always picturing him on a stretcher with his head bashed in . . . I don't think about it so much now. You get used to anything. You've got to earn your daily bread . . . Still, it's bread that costs ever so dear, 'cos you're risking your bones more often than others do.'

She fell silent, hiding Nana in her skirt, afraid the child might cry out. In spite of herself she watched, white-faced. Just then Coupeau was soldering the far edge of the sheet, near the guttering; sliding down as far as possible, he still couldn't reach the very end. So then, moving unhurriedly as workmen do, very easily and deliberately, he did a risky thing. For a moment he was right over the pavement, no longer holding on, calmly getting on with the job; and from below you could see the tiny white flame sputtering under the soldering iron as a careful hand moved it along. Gervaise, quite silent, choking with terror, had raised her clasped hands in an involuntary gesture of supplication. She drew in her breath, noisily: Coupeau had just climbed back up on to the roof, not hurrying, taking a moment to spit one last time into the street.

'Oh so you're keepin' your eye on me, are you!' he called cheerfully on catching sight of her. 'She was bein' silly, wasn't she, Madame Boche, an' didn't want to call out . . . Wait for me, I'll be done in another ten minutes.'

All he had left to do was put a zinc cover on the chimney, a trivial little job. The laundress and the concierge stayed where they were on the pavement, chatting about the neighbourhood and keeping an eye to see that Nana didn't paddle in the gutter, where she was hunting for little fish; and the two women kept looking up at the roof, smiling and nodding, as if to say they didn't mind hanging about. Across the road the old woman was still at her window, watching the man and waiting.

'Whatever does that old trout think she's doing, spying on him like that!' said Madame Boche. 'And what an ugly mug!'

Up above they could hear the strong voice of the roofer singing 'Oh, I do Love Pickin' Strawb'ries!' Now, leaning over his workbench, he was cutting the zinc like an artist. Using a pair of compasses he'd traced a line and was cutting out a large fan with a pair of curved shears; then, with his hammer, he gently bent this fan into a pointed mushroom shape. Zidore was using the bellows again on the coals in the brazier. The sun was sinking behind the house, in a great pink light that slowly grew paler, turning a soft lilac. And, right up in the sky, at this tranquil moment of the day, the silhouettes of the two workers stood out, enormously enlarged, alongside the dark rectangle of the workbench and the weird outline of the bellows, against the translucent background of the air.

When the chimney cover was cut, Coupeau shouted:

'Zidore! The irons!'

But Zidore had just vanished. Swearing, the roofer looked all round for him, calling his name through the open attic skylight. At last he caught sight of him on a neighbouring roof, two houses away. The young devil was sauntering about, having a good look round, his thin fair hair blowing in the breeze as he blinked his eyes at the vastness of Paris.

'Hey, you lazy bugger! Where d'you think you are, in the country?' said Coupeau furiously. 'Think you're Monsieur Béranger, do you, writin' verses? Let's have those irons now! Did you ever see the like, traipsin' about on rooftops! Why not bring your girl up right away, for a kiss'n'cuddle! Gimme those bloody irons, you soddin' nitwit!'

He finished the soldering and called to Gervaise:

'There, that's that . . . I'll be right down.'

The flue he had to cap was in the middle of the roof. Reassured, Gervaise went on smiling as she watched him moving about. Nana, suddenly very tickled by the sight of her father, was clapping her little hands. She'd sat down on the pavement, the better to see what was going on up there.

'Daddy! Daddy!' she shouted at the top of her lungs, 'Daddy, look!'

The roofer tried to lean forward but his foot slipped. Then suddenly, stupidly, like a cat falling over its own paws, he slid down the gentle slope of the roof, unable to stop himself.

'Christ!' he cried in a muffled voice.

And he fell. His body made a shallow arc as it fell, turning over twice, crashing on to the middle of the road with the dull thud of a bundle of linen flung from high up above.

Paralysed with shock, her throat rent by a terrible scream, Gervaise stood there with raised arms. Passers-by rushed up and a crowd gathered. Madame Boche, weak-kneed with horror, took Nana in her arms so as to hide her face and stop her seeing. Meanwhile, across the street, the little old woman was calmly shutting her window, as if satisfied.

Eventually four men carried Coupeau to a chemists' on the corner of the Rue des Poissonniers; he stayed there for almost an hour, lying on a blanket in the middle of the shop, while someone fetched a stretcher from the Lariboisière hospital. He was still breathing, but the chemist kept shaking his head. Gervaise, now, was kneeling on the floor in a daze, sobbing continually, blinded by the tears streaming down her face. Her hands would reach out in an involuntary gesture and very gently feel her husband's limbs. Then she'd draw back, looking at the chemist who'd forbidden her to touch; but a few seconds later she'd begin again, unable to stop herself making sure that Coupeau was still warm, and believing she was helping him. When the stretcher finally arrived and there was talk of setting off for the hospital, she got to her feet, saying fiercely:

'No, no, not the hospital! . . . We live on the Rue Neuve de la Goutte-d'Or.'

They explained to her that the illness would cost her a great deal of money if she kept her husband at home, but it was no use. She reiterated stubbornly:

'Rue Neuve de la Goutte-d'Or, I'll show you which door . . . What's that got to do with you? I've money . . . He's my husband, isn't he? He's mine, and that's what I want.'

And they had to carry Coupeau to his home. When the stretcher made its way through the throng crowded in front of the chemist's shop, the local women were talking excitedly about Gervaise: it was true she limped, poor thing, but she was very spunky all the same; she'd save her husband all right, whereas in the hospital the doctors just let the patients who were too sick peg out, to save themselves the trouble of curing them. Madame Boche, after taking Nana to her home, had come back and, still quivering with agitation, was going into interminable details about the accident.

'I was on my way to get a leg o' mutton, I was standing right there and I saw him fall,' she kept repeating. 'It was because of his little girl, he wanted to see her, then pow! Oh, God forbid I should ever see the likes of that again! . . . Well, I must be off to buy me bit of mutton.'

For a week Coupeau was in a bad way. The family, the neighbours, everybody, expected him to kick the bucket at any moment. The doctor, a very expensive doctor who charged five francs a visit, feared there might be internal injuries; this opinion caused great alarm, and the neighbours went round saying that the roofer'd had his heart-strings broken by the jolt. Gervaise alone, pale from lack of sleep, serious and determined, just shrugged her shoulders. Her hubby had broken his right leg; everyone knew that; it would be put right, that was all there was to it. As for the rest, the broken heart-strings, that was nothing. She'd mend his heart for him. She knew all about mending hearts, with care, and cleanliness, and unvarying devotion. And her conviction was wonderful, she was certain she would cure him just by remaining at his side and touching him with her hands when he was feverish. She never had a moment's doubt. For a whole week she stayed constantly on her feet, saying little, withdrawn into her determination to save him, forgetting the children, the street, the entire city. When on the evening of the ninth day the doctor finally declared the patient no longer in danger, she fell into a chair, her legs like jelly, tired to death, sobbing her heart out. That night she agreed to sleep for a couple of hours, with her head resting on the foot of the bed.

Coupeau's accident had thrown the family into total disarray. Maman Coupeau did spend the nights with Gervaise, but she'd be asleep on her chair by nine o'clock. Every evening, going home from work, Madame Lerat came the long way round to hear the latest. At first the Lorilleux had come two or three times a day, offering to sit up with Coupeau and even bringing an armchair for Gervaise. But it wasn't long before there were quarrels over how to care for the sick. Madame Lorilleux claimed she'd saved enough people in her time to know how you should set about it. She also accused the young woman of pushing her aside, of keeping her away from her brother's bed. Of course Banban was right to want to take care of Coupeau, because after all if she hadn't gone to pester him in the Rue de la Nation, he wouldn't have fallen. The only thing was, the way she was looking after him, she was sure to finish him off.

When she saw Coupeau out of danger, Gervaise stopped guarding his bedside with such jealous ferocity. Now that they could no longer kill him she could let others come near him without worrying. The family made themselves at home in the room. The convalescence was going to be a very long one: the doctor had mentioned four months. So then, during the long hours when the roofer lay sleeping, the Lorilleux told Gervaise how stupid she was. What good had it done to have her husband at home? In the hospital he'd have been back on his feet in half the time. Lorilleux would gladly have got ill, gone down with some bug or other, to prove whether he'd hesitate for even a second to go into Lariboisière. Madame Lorilleux knew a lady who'd just left the hospital; well, she'd had chicken to eat twice a day. And the pair of them worked out for the twentieth time what the four months of convalescence would cost the household: first of all there were the lost days of work, then the doctor, the medicines, plus good wine and rare meat later on. If the Coupeaus did no more than just run through their little nest egg, they should consider themselves damned lucky. But they'd probably get into debt. Of course that was their affair. But most definitely they shouldn't rely on the family, which wasn't rich enough to keep a sick man in his own home. Tough luck, wasn't it, on Banban; she'd just have to do like everyone else, and let her husband be taken to the hospital. Her pride was the crowning touch to her character.

One evening Madame Lorilleux was spiteful enough to ask suddenly:

'Well, what about your shop, when are you going to rent it?'

'Yes,' sniggered Lorilleux, 'the concierge is still expecting you.'

Gervaise was stunned. She'd forgotten all about the shop. But she could see what malicious glee the Lorilleux felt at the thought that the shop had now gone to blazes. And indeed from that evening on they never missed a chance of needling her about her vanished dream. If someone referred to an unrealizable wish, they'd say it would come true when Gervaise was owner of a splendid shop with frontage on the street. And they had some good laughs behind her back. She tried not to think that badly of them, but it was a fact that the Lorilleux now seemed very pleased about Coupeau's accident, which prevented her from setting herself up as a laundress in the Rue de la Goutte-d'Or.

So then she herself tried to treat it as a joke and show them how gladly she parted with the money so that her husband could get better. Each time that she took the savings book from under the clock's glass cover, she'd say brightly, if they were in the room:

'I'm off, I'm going to rent me shop.'

She hadn't wanted to take out all the money at once. She asked for it a hundred francs at a time, so as not to have to keep such a lot of cash in her chest of drawers; and then she was hoping vaguely for some miracle, for a sudden recovery that would make it possible not to withdraw the entire sum. On her return from every trip to the savings bank she'd work out, on a scrap of paper, how much money was still left in their account. It was simply a question of knowing where they stood. No matter how big the hole in their nest-egg grew, she'd smile calmly, and in her sensible way note down the details of this devastation of their savings. Wasn't it already a comfort to be spending this money so wisely, to have had it available just when disaster struck? And without a single regret, she'd carefully put the book back under the cover, behind the clock.

The Goujets behaved with great kindness to Gervaise during Coupeau's illness. Madame Goujet would do absolutely anything for her; she never once went out without asking if she needed some sugar or butter or salt; she invariably gave her the first of the broth whenever she made a stew, and if she saw that Gervaise had too much to do she'd even take over the cooking or give her a hand with washing the dishes. Every morning Goujet would collect the young woman's pails and fill them at the fountain in the Rue des Poissonniers, and that saved a couple of sous. Then, after dinner, if the room wasn't overrun with family, the Goujets would come and keep the Coupeaus company. For two hours, until ten o'clock, the smith would smoke his pipe and watch Gervaise taking care of Coupeau. He wouldn't utter ten words the entire evening. He'd sit there with his big fair face sunk down between his enormous shoulders, very touched by the sight of her pouring tisane into a cup and stirring in the sugar without making any noise with the spoon. He'd feel deeply moved as he watched her tucking in the bedclothes and cheering up Coupeau in her gentle voice. He'd never ever known such a fine woman. And her limp even seemed to add to her appeal, for because of it she was all the more deserving, slaving away the whole day long at her husband's bedside. There were no two ways about it, she never sat down for more than the fifteen minutes it took to have a meal. She was forever rushing over to the chemist's, and sticking her nose into nasty things, and working like a slave to keep that room where they did everything in apple-pie order; and never a grumble, always pleasant, even on those evenings when she'd almost fall asleep on her feet with her eyes wide open, she was so exhausted. And, in that atmosphere of devotion, surrounded by furniture littered with medicine bottles, the smith began to feel a deep affection for Gervaise, as he watched her loving and caring for Coupeau in this way, with her whole heart.

'Well, old chap, so you're patched up again,' he said one day to Coupeau, now on the mend. 'I never had a moment's doubt, your wife's just like the good Lord!'

He was going to be married. At least, his mother had found a very suitable young girl, a lace-maker like herself, whom she very much wanted him to marry. So as not to upset his mother Goujet had agreed, and the wedding date had even been fixed for the beginning of September. The money for setting up house had been sitting in their savings account for ages. But he'd shake his head when Gervaise spoke to him about this marriage, saying softly in his slow way:

'Not all women are like you, Madame Gervaise. If they were all like you, we'd marry ten of them.'

Meanwhile Coupeau, after two months, was able to get up a bit. He didn't walk far, just from the bed to the window, and even so Gervaise had to support him. There he'd sit down in the Lorilleux's armchair, with his right leg stretched out on a stool. That joker, who used to make fun of people who broke their legs in icy weather, was very galled by his accident. He couldn't take it philosophically. He'd spent two months in bed swearing and driving everyone up the wall. What kind of a life was it anyway, lying there with one of his pins all tied up and as stiff as a salami! Oh, he'd soon know the ceiling by heart; there was a crack in the corner over the bed that he could draw with his eyes shut. And then when he got settled in the armchair it was a different moan. How long was he going to be stuck there like a mummy? The street wasn't all that much fun, no one ever went by, and it stank of bleach the whole day long. No, he was absolutely bored stiff, and he'd have given ten years of his life just to know how the fortifications were doing. And, invariably, he'd start railing violently against fate. His accident wasn't fair, it wasn't; it shouldn't have happened to him, a good worker, not an idler or a boozer. Now if it had been somebody else, he might perhaps have understood.

'Old man Coupeau,' he'd say, 'broke his neck one day when he'd been boozin'. I'm not sayin' as he deserved it, but at least you could understand how it happened . . . But there I was, hadn't had me supper, felt as calm as can be, hadn't a drop of booze in me body, an' I go and fall when I'm turnin' round to smile at Nana! Don't you think it's a bit much? If there is a good Lord up there, he's got a funny way of doin' things. No, I'll never be able to swallow this.'

And when he'd got back the use of his legs, he still felt a smouldering resentment against his work. What a bloody awful way to earn a crust, having to spend your days up in the guttering like a cat. The rich knew what they were doing, all right! They sent you to your death but they themselves hadn't the guts to risk climbing a ladder, they just settled down comfortably by their fireside and didn't give a damn what happened to the poor. He even got to the point of saying that everyone should do their own roofing on their own house. Hell! If things were really fair, that was how it should be: if you don't want to get wet, you get under cover. Next, he was sorry he hadn't learnt a different trade, a pleasanter, less dangerous one, cabinet-making for example. That also was old man Coupeau's fault: fathers had this idiotic way of shoving their kids into their own trade, regardless.

Coupeau walked with crutches for a further two months. At first he managed to get down to the street and smoke a pipe by the door. Then he could go as far as the outer boulevard, dragging himself along in the sunshine and spending hours sitting on a bench. His high spirits were returning, and his devilish gift of the gab blossomed during these long idle outings. And, along with his renewed zest for life, came delight in doing nothing, with his limbs relaxed and his muscles sinking into a sweet lethargy; it was as if he was being slowly taken over by sloth, sloth that was using his convalescence to get inside his skin and permeate his body with a titillating languor. He'd come home in fine fettle, joking and saying this was the life, and why in the world couldn't it last like this for ever? When he could manage without crutches he went on longer expeditions, dropping by building sites to see his old mates again. He'd stand idly around in front of the houses being built, laughing derisively and shaking his head; and he'd make fun of the workmen who were hard at it, sticking out his leg to show them where working your damnedest got you. These hours spent jeering at the labour of others satisfied his grudge against work. Of course he'd go back to it, he'd have to: but as late as possible. Oh, it was in a hard school that he'd learnt not to be too enthusiastic. And, anyway, a bit of mooching about was ever so nice!

When Coupeau was bored in the afternoons he'd go up to visit the Lorilleux. They felt very sorry for him and tempted him to come and see them by all kinds of blandishments. During the early years of his marriage he'd got away from them, thanks to Gervaise's influence. But now they were winning him back again, by teasing him because he was scared of his wife. Wasn't he a real man then! Nevertheless the Lorilleux did show great circumspection, praising Gervaise's good qualities to the skies. Coupeau, without yet making an issue of it, would swear to Gervaise that his sister adored her, and he'd beg her not to be so nasty to her. The couple's first quarrel, one evening, happened because of Étienne. The roofer had spent the afternoon with the Lorilleux. When he came home, as the meal wasn't ready and the kids were whining for their supper, he'd suddenly turned on Étienne and given him a couple of well-placed clouts. And he'd gone on grousing for an hour: that brat wasn't his, he didn't know why he put up with him in his home; one of these days he'd kick him out. Until then he'd accepted the boy without much fuss. The next day he was talking about his dignity. By three days later he was kicking the kid's bottom morning and evening, so that the boy, when he heard him on the stairs, would escape to the Goujets', where the old lace-maker kept a corner of the table for him to do his homework.

Gervaise had been back at work for quite a while. She no longer had to bother taking off and replacing the cover of the clock; their savings had been completely eaten up; and she had to slog really hard, slog for four, as there were four mouths to feed. And just her to support the lot. When she heard people say they were sorry for her, she was quick to come to Coupeau's defence. Just think! He'd suffered so much that it wasn't surprising if he'd turned a bit sour. But that would pass when he was completely better. And if they hinted that Coupeau seemed quite OK now and could perfectly well return to work, she'd protest. No, no, not yet! She'd no wish to have him back in bed. She knew just what the doctor had said, didn't she? It was she who stopped him going back to work, telling him each morning to take his time and not push himself. She even slipped the odd franc into his waistcoat pocket. Coupeau accepted this as quite natural; he complained of all kinds of aches and pains so he'd be pampered; when six months had gone by he was still convalescing. Now, on the days he spent watching others working, he'd be pleased to go and drink a glass of wine with his mates. It was quite nice, really, in the bar, they'd have a good laugh, and just stay a few minutes. No need to feel ashamed of that. Only phonies claimed they were dying of thirst when they went in. In the past people had been quite right to tease him, since a glass of wine had never killed anybody. But, he declared proudly, thumping his chest, he drank nothing but wine; always wine, never spirits; wine made you live longer, it didn't upset you, it didn't make you drunk. Several times, however, after a day spent loafing about from building site to building site and from boozer to boozer, he'd come home a bit pissed. Gervaise shut her door on those

occasions, pretending she herself had a terrible headache, so the
Goujets wouldn't be able to hear Coupeau's drivel.

Gradually, though, the young woman grew depressed. Every
morning and evening she'd go along to the Rue de la Goutte-
d'Or to look at the shop, which was still for rent; and she'd do
this furtively, as if it was a childish act, unworthy of a grown
woman. That shop was once again beginning to obsess her; at
night, when the light was out, she lay awake wide-eyed, taking
a kind of illicit pleasure in dreaming of it. Once again she did
her sums, two hundred and fifty francs for the rent, one
hundred and fifty for buying and installing the equipment, one
hundred set aside to live on for two weeks, a total of five
hundred at the very least. If she didn't actually talk about it all
the time, that was because she was afraid it might seem she was
sorry they'd used up their savings on Coupeau's illness. Often
she'd turn quite pale because she'd very nearly let her dream
slip out, and she'd stop herself in mid-sentence, as embarrassed
as if she'd had an unclean thought. Now she'd have to work for
four or five years before she could save so large a sum. What
made her unhappy was the very fact that she couldn't set up in
business right away; then she'd have been able to support the
household without counting on Coupeau, leaving him plenty of
time to get back his taste for work; she'd have felt quite easy in
her mind, certain of the future and free of the secret fears that
sometimes gripped her when he came home very cheerful,
singing and telling some funny story about that bastard Mes-
Bottes, whom he'd treated to a drink.

One evening when Gervaise was at home alone, Goujet
dropped in but didn't leave straight away as he would normally
have done. He'd taken a seat and was watching her while he
smoked. He seemed to have something important to say; he was
thinking about it and mulling it over, without being able to
decide just how to phrase it. Eventually, after a heavy silence,
he made up his mind, removed his pipe from his mouth, and
said in a rush:

'Madame Gervaise, would you allow me to lend you some
money?'

She was leaning over one of the drawers of the chest, looking
for some dusters. She stood up, very red in the face. So he must

have seen her that morning, standing in a trance in front of the shop for almost ten minutes. He was smiling uneasily, as if his suggestion might give offence. But she refused vehemently: she'd never accept money without knowing when she'd be able to pay it back. And then, it really was much too large a sum. And when in dismay he kept urging her, she finally blurted out:

'But what about your marriage? I can't take money you've saved for your marriage, now can I?'

'Oh! Don't worry about that,' he answered, blushing in his turn. 'I'm no longer going to be married. It was just an idea, you know . . . I'd much rather lend you the money, really I would.'

Then they both dropped their gaze. Something very sweet passed between them that they didn't put into words. And Gervaise accepted. Goujet had already warned his mother. They crossed the landing and went to see her right away. The lace-maker was looking serious, rather sad, with her calm face bent over her embroidery frame. She didn't want to go against her son, but she didn't approve of Gervaise's plan and gave her reasons very clearly: Coupeau was going to the bad, Coupeau would fritter away all the takings from her shop. Madame Goujet couldn't forgive the roofer for having refused to learn to read, during his convalescence; the smith had offered to show him how, but the other had sent him packing, saying that learning made people waste away. This had almost caused a rift between the two workers: each now went his own way. But Madame Goujet, seeing her great big boy's imploring looks, was very nice to Gervaise. It was agreed that they'd lend their neighbours five hundred francs; the loan would be repaid in twenty franc installments every month, for as long as it took.

'Well, well, so the smith's sweet on you,' laughed Coupeau when he heard the news. 'Oh, it don't worry me, he's such a dummy . . . He'll get his money back. But if he was dealin' with riff-raff he'd be taken for one hell of a ride, he would really.'

The Coupeaus rented the shop the very next morning. All day Gervaise ran back and forth between the Rue Neuve and the Rue de la Goutte-d'Or. Watching her racing nimbly along, so elated that she no longer limped, people in the neighbourhood said that she must have had an operation.

CHAPTER V

As it happened, the Boches had moved from the Rue des
Poissonniers on the April quarterly rent day and taken over the
lodge of the big building in the Rue de la Goutte-d'Or. Now
wasn't that a piece of luck! One of Gervaise's worries had been
that after living so peacefully without a concierge in her little
place in the Rue Neuve, she'd be back under the thumb of some
spiteful creature who'd make trouble over a drop of spilt water
or a door closed too noisily at night. Concierges are such a nasty
lot! But with the Boches it would be a pleasure. They knew one
another and they'd always get along. In short, they'd be like
family.

On the day when the Coupeaus went to sign the rental lease,
Gervaise felt her heart swell as she passed through the tall
entryway. So she was actually going to live in this enormous
building, the size of a small town, with its streets of stairs and
passages that went stretching on and criss-crossing for ever.
The grey façades with rags drying at the windows in the
sunlight, the dim courtyard with its paving stones so badly
worn it could have been a public square, the rumble of work
that filtered through the walls, all filled her with intense
agitation, with joy at finally being on the point of realizing her
ambition and with fear that she would fail and find herself
crushed underfoot in this vast struggle against hunger, whose
nearness she could sense. She felt she was doing something very
daring, that she was flinging herself right into the heart of a
moving machine, as the locksmith's hammers and the cabinet-
maker's planes banged and whirred in the depths of the
ground-floor workshops. The water from the dyeworks running
through the entrance that day was a very soft apple green. She
smiled as she stepped over it; the colour, she thought, was a
happy omen.

The appointment with the proprietor was in the Boches'
lodge itself. Monsieur Marescot, a wealthy cutler from the Rue
de la Paix,* had once worked as a knife-grinder on the city
pavements. It was said that now he was worth several millions.
He was a man of fifty-five, strong and bony, with a ribbon in

his buttonhole; he liked to flaunt his huge ex-workman's hands, and loved taking away his tenants' knives and scissors to sharpen them himself, just for the pleasure of it. He had the reputation of not being stuck-up, because he spent hours with his concierges in the dark recesses of their lodges, going through the accounts. That was where he did all his business. The Coupeaus found him sitting at Madame Boche's greasy table, hearing how the seamstress on the second floor, staircase A, had refused to pay, and used foul language to boot. Then, when they'd signed the lease, Monsieur Marescot shook the roofer by the hand. For his part, he liked workers. In his time he'd had more that his share of difficulties. But anything was possible if you worked. And, after counting the two hundred and fifty francs for the first two quarters and stowing the money away in his capacious pocket, he told them about his life and showed them his decoration.

Gervaise, meanwhile, was rather nonplussed by the attitude of the Boches. They pretended not to know her. They fussed round the proprietor, bowing obsequiously, hanging on his words, nodding approval whenever he spoke. Madame Boche suddenly rushed out to chase away a pack of kids paddling about in front of the communal tap which had been left running and was flooding the paving stones; and when she walked back across the courtyard, erect and stern in her full-skirted dress, she glanced unhurriedly at every window, as if to ascertain that all was in order in the building, her pursed lips asserting the authority vested in her now that she had control over three hundred tenants. Boche was again talking about the second-floor seamstress: in his opinion she should be evicted; he worked out how much was owing, with the important air of a steward whose stewardship might by compromised. Monsieur Marescot agreed about the eviction but wanted to wait till the mid-term rent day. It was hard, turning people out into the street, and furthermore it didn't put a single sou into the owner's pocket. And Gervaise gave a little shiver, wondering whether she too would be turned out into the street one day if some misfortune prevented her from paying. The smoke-filled lodge, damp and murky and crowded with dark furniture, reminded her of a cellar; all the light from the window fell on to a tailor's work-table standing in front of it, spread with an old coat waiting to be turned; while Pauline, the Boches' little carrot-haired four-year-old, sat quietly on the floor, watching a piece of veal braising and revelling in the powerful aroma of cooking that enveloped her as it floated up from the pan.

Monsieur Marescot was offering his hand to the roofer again in farewell, when the latter raised the subject of redecorating, reminding the proprietor of an earlier conversation when he'd promised he'd discuss the matter. But Monsieur Marescot grew angry; he hadn't promised anything, and anyway redecorating was never done in the case of a shop. He did however agree to go and look at the place, followed by the Coupeaus and Boche. The draper had departed taking with him all the fittings of racks and counters; the shop was completely bare, revealing its blackened ceiling and cracked walls from which hung strips of ancient yellow wallpaper. There, in the empty, echoing rooms, a furious argument broke out. Monsieur Marescot shouted that it was up to the shopkeepers themselves to decorate their shops; after all a tradesman might fancy doing his place up all in gold and he, the landlord, couldn't pay for gold; then he described the way his own shop in the Rue de la Paix was set up, he'd spent more than twenty thousand francs on it. Gervaise, with a woman's obstinacy, kept repeating what seemed to her an irrefutable argument: if it was a home and not a shop, he'd have it repapered, now wouldn't he? So, why not consider the shop as a home? All she was asking for was for the ceiling to be whitewashed, and fresh wallpaper, nothing else.

Boche, meanwhile, stood by inscrutable and aloof; he stared about, gazing at the ceiling, never saying a word. In vain did Coupeau try to catch his eye; apparently he didn't want to take advantage of his considerable influence over the landlord. In the end, however, he did indulge in a change of expression, a thin little smile accompanied by a nod. And just then Monsieur Marescot, looking exasperated and unhappy, and spreading out his fingers convulsively like a miser who sees his gold being snatched away, gave in to Gervaise and promised the ceiling and the paper, on condition she'd pay for half the paper. And he immediately took himself off, not wanting to listen to anything else.

Then, when Boche was alone with the Coupeaus, he slapped them very effusively on the back. Well, he'd pulled that off nicely, hadn't he! If it hadn't been for him they'd never have had their paper or their ceiling. Had they noticed the way the landlord had glanced at him for his opinion and had suddenly agreed when he saw him smile? Then he confided to them that he was the real boss of the building; he decided who should be given notice, he let to the people that he liked, he collected the rents, keeping them in his chest for anywhere up to two weeks. That evening the Coupeaus decided to send the Boches a couple of bottles of wine, as a polite way of saying thank you. It was worth a present.

The following Monday the workmen started on the shop. Buying the paper turned out to be quite a business. Gervaise wanted a grey paper with blue flowers, to lighten and perk up the walls. Boche offered to take her so she could make her choice. But he had strict orders from the landlord that he mustn't spend more than fifteen sous a roll. They stayed in the wallpaper shop for an hour, and Gervaise kept reverting to a very pretty chintz at eighteen sous; she became quite desperate because she thought all the others were horrible. Eventually the concierge gave in; he'd fix it, if need be he'd count in an extra roll. On her way home Gervaise bought some cakes for Pauline. She didn't want to appear unappreciative, it was always worth your while to do her a good turn.

The shop was supposed to be ready in four days. The job took three weeks. At first the plan had been simply to wash down the paintwork. But this paintwork, originally a purplish-red, was so dingy and dirty that Gervaise let herself be persuaded to redo the whole shop-front in pale blue with yellow accents. After that the redecoration seemed to go on and on. Coupeau, who was still not working, turned up first thing every morning to see how it was progressing. Boche abandoned the frock-coat or trousers he was making new buttonholes for, and came over from the lodge to supervise his workmen. All day long the pair of them would stand there staring at the painters, their hands behind their backs, smoking and spitting and criticizing every single brush-stroke. The removal of a nail would prompt endless commentaries and deep reflections. The painters, two great big good-humoured chaps, were constantly getting off their ladders and planting themselves in the middle of the shop, where they'd stand about for hours nodding and joining in the discussion while gazing at the job they'd started. The ceiling was whitewashed fairly quickly. It was the wood-work that seemed to take forever. It just wouldn't dry. About nine o'clock the painters would show up with their pots of paint, put them down in a corner, take a quick look round, then vanish; they wouldn't come back. They'd gone for a bite to eat, or else they'd a little job to finish round the corner in the Rue Myrrha. Other times, Coupeau would invite the whole gang out for a quick one: Boche, the painters, and any mates who might be passing; one more afternoon gone to blazes! Gervaise was working herself up into quite a state. Then suddenly, in a couple of days, it was all finished, the paintwork varnished, the paper hung, the rubbish carted away. The workmen had done a slap-dash job, treating it as a joke, whistling on their ladders and singing loudly enough to drive all the neighbours round the bend.

They moved in straight away. During the first few days Gervaise felt a childlike joy when she crossed the road on her way home from some errand. She'd linger, smiling at the sight of her home. From far away, in the centre of the black row of the other shop-fronts, her shop seemed to her full of light, so cheerful and new, with its pale blue sign on which the words 'High Quality Laundering' were painted in big yellow letters. In the window, which was closed at the back with little muslin curtains and papered in blue to show off the whiteness of the linen, there were mens' shirts displayed and womens' bonnets hung by their ribbons from brass wires. She thought her shop was pretty, the colour of the sky. When you went inside there was still more blue; the paper was a copy of a Pompadour* chintz, showing a trellis entwined with morning-glories; the workbench was a huge table with a thick cover; it took up two thirds of the space and was draped in a piece of cretonne printed with big bluish leaves, that hid the trestles. Gervaise would sit down on a stool, panting slightly with pleasure, delighted by how beautifully clean it was and gazing fondly at all her new equipment. But invariably her eyes went first to the cast-iron stove, where ten irons could heat at the same time, arranged round the grate on sloping stands. She'd go over to it and kneel down to have a look, always afraid that her half-witted little apprentice would wreck the stove by stuffing it with too much coke.

The accommodation behind the shop was just what they needed. The Coupeaus slept in the first room, where they cooked and had their meals; a door at the back opened on to the building's courtyard. Nana's bed was in the room on the right, a sort of large closet lit by a round sky-light near the ceiling. As for Étienne, he shared the room on the left with the dirty washing, which lay about on the floor all the time in huge piles. There was, however, one drawback, which at first the Coupeaus wouldn't admit: water pissed down the walls, and you could no longer see properly after three in the afternoon.

The new shop caused a sensation in the neighbourhood. People said the Coupeaus had gone about it all far too fast and were sure to land in Queer Street. They had indeed spent all the Goujets' five hundred francs on setting up the shop, without even keeping something in reserve to live on for the first fortnight, as they'd intended. On the morning when Gervaise took down the shutters for the first time she had exactly six francs in her purse. But that didn't worry her, the customers were rolling up and business looked most promising. A week later, before going to bed on the Saturday, she sat up for two hours doing sums on a scrap of paper and then woke up Coupeau to tell him, her face shining with joy, that there was pots of money to be made if they were sensible.

'Well now!' Madame Lorilleux proclaimed all over the Rue de la Goutte-d'Or. 'My dimwit of a brother puts up with some very funny goings-on! . . . So now Banban's two-timing him—I call that the crowning touch. Suits her to a T, doesn't it?'

The Lorilleux and Gervaise had had a frightful dust-up. At first, while the shop was being redecorated, they'd almost died of fury; simply seeing the painters from a distance made them cross over to the other side of the road, and they'd go back home grinding their teeth. That good-for-nothing with a blue shop, now wasn't that more than enough to make decent folks just give up! Also, on the second day, the apprentice had been

flinging out a bowlful of starch at the precise moment when
Madame Lorilleux was emerging into the street, and the latter
stirred up the entire neighbourhood, accusing her sister-in-law
of getting her assistants to insult her. All relations were severed
and they only exchanged terrible glares when they passed one
another.

'Oh, they're leading a lovely life!' was Madame Lorilleux's
refrain. 'We know where she got the money for that place from.
She earned it from the blacksmith . . . And they're a nice lot,
they are, too! Didn't the father cut his own throat with a knife
to avoid the guillotine? Or, at any rate, something nasty like
that!'

She accused Gervaise quite openly of sleeping with Goujet.
She lied, claiming she'd caught them one evening together on
a bench on the outer boulevard. The thought of this affair and
of the pleasures her sister-in-law must be enjoying exasperated
her still more: she had an ugly woman's regard for respectability. The same deeply-felt complaint sprang to her lips each
day:

'But what in the world is there about that cripple, that makes
her so adorable! Nobody falls for me, do they?'

So next she went round telling endless tales to all the
neighbours. She told them the entire story. To be sure, on the
wedding day, she'd felt ever so funny about it! She'd a sharp
nose, she could smell already how it was going to turn out. And
later on, heavens, well Banban had been so cajoling and
two-faced that for Coupeau's sake she and her husband had
agreed to be godparents to Nana, even though it had cost a
packet, a christening like that one. But now, you see, well now
Banban could be at death's door and needing a glass of water
but she certainly wouldn't be the one to give her it. She
couldn't stand impudent hussies, or bitches, or shameless
women. As for Nana, she'd always be welcome if she came up
to see her godparents; after all, you couldn't blame the kid for
the way the mother carried on, could you? Coupeau shouldn't
need advice; in his place any other man would have stuck his
wife's arse into a tub of cold water and boxed her ears; however
that was his business, and all they asked was that he make
certain his family was respected. God almighty! If Lorilleux had

caught her, his wife, in the act, it wouldn't have passed off quietly, he'd have thrust his shears into her belly.

However the Boches, who took a very dim view of quarrelling in the building, pronounced the Lorilleux in the wrong. It was true that they were quiet, respectable people, who worked the whole blessed day and payed their rent on the dot. But in this affair, to put it bluntly, jealousy was driving them crazy. What's more they were such nit-pickers. And as for being close-fisted! People who'd hide their bottle of wine when you went up to see them, so they wouldn't have to offer you a glass; in a word, a nasty type. One day Gervaise had just brought the Boches some cassis and soda water and they were all drinking it in the lodge, when Madame Lorilleux stalked stiffly by, pretending to spit as she passed the concierges' door. Every Saturday after that, when Madame Boche swept the stairs and passages, she'd leave some rubbish in front of the Lorilleux's door.

'Lord!' cried Madame Lorilleux, 'Banban's always giving those pigs something to guzzle! Birds of a feather, that's what they are! . . . But they'd better not bother me! I'd complain to the landlord . . . Why just yesterday I saw that crafty Boche rubbing up against Madame Gaudron's skirts. Going after a woman of that age, who's got half a dozen kids, well I call it filthy, just filthy. If I catch them carrying on in that disgusting way again, I'll warn Mère Boche so she can give her hubby a good thrashing . . . That'd be a laugh, now wouldn't it!'

Maman Coupeau still saw both households; she agreed with everybody and even managed to get herself invited to dinner more often than usual, by listening sympathetically to her daughter one evening and to her daughter-in-law the next. For the present Madame Lerat was no longer seeing the Coupeaus because she'd had a row with Banban about a Zouave* who'd slashed his mistress's nose with a razor; Madame Lerat had defended what the Zouave had done, saying she considered it very loving to slash someone with a razor, though she hadn't explained why. And she'd made Madame Lorilleux still more angry by assuring her that Banban didn't think twice about referring to her as Queue-de-Vache, in conversation, in front of maybe fifteen or even twenty people. Lord! yes, the Boches and the neighbours now all called her Queue-de-Vache.

While all this backbiting was going on Gervaise would stand, calm and smiling, at the door of her shop, greeting her friends with a little affectionate nod. She loved to put down her iron for a moment and come there to smile at the street, her heart swelling with the pride of a shopkeeper who has a bit of pavement for her very own. The Rue de la Goutte-d'Or belonged to her, and so did the nearby streets, and so did the whole neighbourhood. When she stood there gazing out, in her white bodice with her arms bare and her blond hair flying about from the bustle of work, she'd look to the right and then to the left, towards both ends of the street, her glance taking in the passers-by, the houses, the road and the sky; to her left the Rue de la Goutte-d'Or plunged away, peaceful and deserted, with women chatting quietly in their doorways as if it were a country lane; to her right, close by, the Rue des Poissonniers declared itself by the hurly-burly of vehicles and the continual trampling of the crowd which surged back and forth over that busy working-class intersection. Gervaise loved the street, the jolting of the wagons over the potholes in the big bumpy cobbles and the way the pedestrians rushed down those narrow pavements broken by steeply-sloping pebbled sections; the three metres of gutter in front of her shop seemed to her tremendously important, a broad river that she liked to imagine as very clean, a strange, living river, with waters tinted by the building's dyeworks in the most delicate of shades, amid the surrounding black mud. Then she was intrigued by the shops, by a huge grocer's with an array of dried fruits hanging in small-meshed nets, and by a place selling hosiery and linen for workers, where blue overalls and smocks, displayed with legs and arms spread out, swayed in the slightest breeze. She'd catch glimpses of majestic, imperturbable cats lying purring on counter corners in the fruiterer's and the tripe shop. Her neighbour, Madame Vigoureux, would return her greeting; a plump little woman with a dark face and shining eyes, she'd hang about all day giggling with the men, leaning against her shop-front that she'd had painted in a complicated design of logs on a purplish-red ground, to look like a rustic chalet. Her other neighbours, the Cudorge ladies—mother and daughter—who owned the um-brella shop, never showed their faces; their shop-window was dark and their permanently closed door adorned by two little zinc umbrellas thickly coated with bright red paint. But before she went back inside Gervaise would always glance across the road at a great white windowless wall that had an enormous carriage entryway, through which you could see a blacksmith's forge blazing in a courtyard cluttered with carts and drays that stood about with their shafts in the air. On the wall the word 'Farrier' was inscribed in huge letters surrounded by a fan of horseshoes. All day long the hammers could be heard pounding on the anvil, while showers of sparks would light up the dim shadows of the courtyard. And at the bottom end of the wall, in a hole no bigger than a cupboard, tucked away between a scrap merchant's and a chip shop, there was a clockmaker, a very correct gentleman in a frock-coat, who was always poking about in watches with dainty little implements as he sat at a work-table covered with delicate objects reposing under glass; while behind him the pendulums of two or three dozen very small cuckoo clocks swung in unison, amid the poverty-stricken grime of the street and the rhythmic din from the farrier's yard.

The neighbourhood thought Gervaise was ever so nice. Of course there was plenty of tittle-tattle about her, but everybody agreed that she had big eyes and a sweet little mouth with lovely white teeth. In a word she was a pretty blonde, and had it not been for the misfortune of her leg she'd have been classed as a real beauty. She was now twenty-eight, and had grown plumper. Her delicate features were somewhat coarser and her gestures had taken on a pleasing languour. Nowadays she'd sometimes fall into a dream as she sat on the edge of her chair waiting for her iron to heat, and her face, with its vague smile, would be suffused by an expression of greedy delight. She was becoming greedy, everybody said so: but it wasn't a really bad fault, quite the opposite. When you earned enough to treat yourself to something very special you'd be a half-wit to live on potato peelings, now wouldn't you? The more so since she always worked hard, killing herself to satisfy her customers, spending entire nights on the job, behind closed shutters, when something was needed urgently. As they said in the neighbourhood, she was born under a lucky star: whatever she turned her hand to went well. She did the washing for the building—Monsieur Madinier, Mademoiselle Remanjou, the Boches; she even took customers away from her former employer, Madame Fauconnier, some city ladies who lived in the Rue du Faubourg-Poissonnière. Starting with the second fortnight she'd had to take on two assistants, Madame Putois and Clémence, the tall girl who'd once lived on the sixth floor; that made three persons she had in her shop, if you counted her apprentice, little squint-eyed Augustine, who was as ugly as sin. Success like that would certainly have turned the head of anybody else. You could understand it if she treated herself to a dish she really fancied on a Monday, after slaving away all week long. In any case she needed it; she'd have turned into a useless mess and slopped about watching the shirts iron themselves if she hadn't occasionally got her teeth into something so delectable that the very thought of it made her lick her lips.

Never had Gervaise been so obliging. She was as gentle as a lamb, as good as bread. Apart from Madame Lorilleux, whom she called Queue-de-Vache to get her own back, she didn't hate a soul, she found excuses for everyone. When she was enjoying a little self-indulgent laze after a good lunch followed by coffee, she'd feel an overpowering need to forgive the whole world. She'd say: 'We should forgive one another, shouldn't we? If we don't want to live like savages.' When people remarked on her kindness, she'd laugh. That would have been the last straw, if she'd been unkind! She'd protest that it was no credit to her if she was kind. Hadn't all her dreams come true, was there anything left for her to wish for? She recalled her ideal of long ago, when she was on her uppers: to work, have something to eat, have a little place of her own, bring up her kids, not be beaten up, and die in her own bed. Now she'd achieved more than her ideal; she had everything, but better. As for dying in her own bed, she'd add jokingly, she was counting on doing that but as late as possible, of course.

It was especially towards Coupeau that Gervaise behaved very nicely. Never a harsh word, never a grumble behind her husband's back. In the end the roofer had gone back to work, and as the place where he was then working was at the other end of Paris, she'd give him forty sous every morning for his lunch, his little nip, and his tobacco. The only thing was that two days out of six Coupeau would stop on the way, drink up the forty sous with a pal, then come back for lunch with some story or other. And on one occasion he'd not even gone very far, but instead had treated himself, along with Mes-Bottes and three others, to a fancy binge—snails, a roast, vintage wine— at the Capucin* in the Barrière de la Chapelle; then, as his forty sous weren't enough, he'd sent the bill to his wife via a waiter with a message that he was in jug. Gervaise laughed and shrugged her shoulders. What harm was there if her hubby was having a bit of fun? You shouldn't keep your man on too tight a rein if you wanted peace at home. One thing led to another and before you knew it, you'd come to blows. And Lord! You had to understand that Coupeau was still suffering with his leg, and then again the others sometimes led him on, so he had to do what they did for fear of looking like a creep. Anyway, it didn't matter; if he came home a bit lit up he'd go to bed, and two hours later you'd never know a thing.

Meanwhile the weather had turned scorching. One Saturday afternoon in June, when there was heaps of work to be done, Gervaise had herself filled the stove full of coke; ten irons heated round it while the flue-pipe roared. At that time of day the sun was shining straight into the shop-front and a fiery reflection bounced off the pavement, dancing about in big iridescent patches on the shop ceiling; and that blaze of light, tinged with blue by the wallpaper covering the shelves and the inside of the window, filled the air above the work-table with a blinding brightness, like sunlight filtered through fine linen. The heat in the place knocked you back. They'd left the street door open but there wasn't a breath of wind; the laundry hanging up to dry on wires near the ceiling steamed, turning stiff as a board in under three-quarters of an hour. In that sweltering furnace-like heat a deep silence had reigned for several minutes, broken only by the muffled tapping of the irons which the thick calico-covered padding on the work-table deadened.

'My goodness!' said Gervaise, 'We're going to melt away today! Makes you want to take off your chemise!'

She was crouching on the floor beside a bowl, busy starching some linen. In her white underskirt, with her sleeves rolled up and her bodice slipping off her shoulders, her arms and neck bare, she looked all rosy, and was sweating so much that the little curls of her tousled blond hair stuck to her skin. She was carefully dipping bonnets, men's shirt fronts, whole petticoats, and the ruffles on women's drawers into the milky water. Then she'd roll up the garments and place them in the bottom of a square basket, after wetting her hand in a pail of water and shaking it over the parts of the shirts and drawers that hadn't been starched.

'This basket's for you, Madame Putois,' she went on. 'Can you hurry up a bit? It's drying right away, in an hour we'll have to do it all over again.'

Madame Putois, a small thin woman of forty-five, wasn't sweating a drop as she got on with the ironing, buttoned up into an old brown jacket. She hadn't even taken off her bonnet, a black bonnet with green ribbons that were turning yellow. She stood rigidly in front of the work-table which was too high for her, her elbows in the air, pushing her iron about with the jerky movements of a puppet. All of a sudden she exclaimed:

'Oh no, Mademoiselle Clémence, put your bodice on again! You know I can't stand indecency. While you're about it, why not show off everything you've got. There's already three men stopped across on the other side.'

Clémence muttered that Madame Putois was a stupid old cow. She was suffocating, so why not get comfortable? Not everybody had skin like sandpaper. Besides, could you really see anything? And she raised her arms, so that her lovely big breasts thrust against her chemise and her shoulders seemed about to burst through her short sleeves. Clémence was living it up to such a degree that she'd be done for by the time she was thirty; after a night on the tiles she didn't know which end was up, she'd fall asleep at work, feeling as if her head and her belly were stuffed with rags. But she was kept on nevertheless because there wasn't another girl who could iron a man's shirt as stylishly as she did. She had a knack with men's shirts.

'This is mine, after all, ain't it,' she finally declared, slapping herself on the bosom. 'And it don't bite, it don't do nobody no harm.'

'Clémence, put your bodice on again,' said Gervaise. 'Madame Putois is right, it isn't decent . . . People'll take my shop for something it's not.'

So the great tall girl got dressed again, grumbling. What a lot of bellyaching! Hadn't the passers-by ever seen a pair of boobs, then! And she worked off her anger on the apprentice, that cross-eyed Augustine, who was standing beside her ironing plain things like stockings and handkerchiefs; she pushed her, bumping her with her elbow. But with the peevish, shifty nastiness of an ill-favoured drudge Augustine spat on the back of her dress, without anyone seeing, in revenge.

Meanwhile Gervaise had just started on a bonnet belonging to Madame Boche that she wanted to do extra carefully. She'd prepared some hot-water starch so as to make it look like new. She was gently passing the *polonais*—a special little iron curved at each end—round inside the lining, when a woman walked in, a bony creature with a face covered in red blotches and skirts that were soaking wet. She was a head washerwoman with three girls working under her in the Goutte-d'Or washhouse.

'You've come too soon, Madame Bijard!' shouted Gervaise. 'I said this evening . . . This is putting me out terribly, your coming now!'

But as the washerwoman began to fret, saying she was afraid she wouldn't be able to get the things hung up to drip that day, she agreed to give her the dirty washing right then. They went to get the bundles from the room on the left where Étienne slept, and returned with enormous armfuls that they piled up on the floor at the back of the shop. The sorting took a good half-hour. Gervaise made piles all round her, throwing all the men's shirts together, and all the women's chemises, then the handkerchiefs, the socks, the cloths. When she picked up something belonging to a new customer she'd mark it with a cross in red thread, so she'd recognize it again. In the warm air a stale stench rose up as the dirty laundry was turned over and over.

'Oh my, that don't half niff!' said Clémence, holding her nose.

'Lord, if it was clean, people wouldn't give us it,' Gervaise calmly pointed out. 'It does smell a bit fruity . . . We said fourteen chemises, didn't we, Madame Bijard? . . . fifteen, six-teen, seventeen.'

She went on counting out loud. She was used to filth, and didn't find it in the least disgusting; she plunged her bare pink arms right in among shirts yellow with dirt, cloths stiff with grease from washing-up water and socks eaten away and rotted by sweat. But, amid the penetrating fumes that hit her in the face as she bent over the piles, a kind of languor came over her. Sitting doubled up on the edge of a stool and leaning towards the floor, she was stretching out her hands to left and right more and more slowly and smiling vaguely, her eyes dreamy, as if this human stench was making her drunk. And it seemed as though that was where her laziness first began, that it came from the stifling reek of dirty clothes poisoning the air round about her.

Just as she was shaking out a baby's nappy that she didn't recognize because it was so soaked with piss, Coupeau came in.

'Jeez!' he mumbled, 'what a sun! It don't half beat down on you!'

The roofer grabbed hold of the work-table to stop himself falling. It was the first time he'd got so totally plastered. Until then he'd come home slightly tipsy, nothing more. But this time he'd had a punch in the eye, a friendly bash that had landed there by chance in some scuffle or other. His curly hair where a few white threads already showed must have brushed a dusty nook in some dubious bar, because there was a spider's web draped on a lock at the back of his neck. However he was still just as full of fun, and though his features looked somewhat drawn and older and his lower jaw stuck out more, he still loved the whole world, as he put it, and his skin was still soft enough to be the envy of a duchess.

'Lemme tell you what happened,' he went on, turning to Gervaise. 'It was Pied-de-Céleri, you know who I mean, him that's got the wooden leg . . . Well he was standin' treat be-cause he's goin' away, back home . . . Oh, we were all doin' OK, an' if it weren't for this bloody sun . . . Out in the street, they're all bein' took bad. 'Strue! People are staggerin' about . . .'

And, when Clémence began to laugh because he'd thought the whole street looked drunk, he himself burst out laughing so uproariously that he almost choked. He kept shouting:

'Yea, the bloody pisspots! Killin', they are . . . But it ain't their fault, no, it's the sun . . .'

Everyone in the shop was laughing, even Madame Putois who didn't care for drunks. Open-mouthed, choking with mirth, Augustine was cackling like a hen. Gervaise, however, suspected that Coupeau hadn't come straight home but instead had dropped in for a visit to the Lorilleux, who gave him nothing but bad advice. When he'd sworn to her that he hadn't, she laughed too, very indulgently, not even telling him off for having lost another day's work.

'Lord, doesn't he sound daft!' she muttered. 'How can he say such daft things!'

Then, in a motherly tone:

'How 'bout going to bed? You can see we're busy, and you're in our way . . . That makes thirty-two handkerchiefs, Madame Bijard, and two more, thirty-four . . .'

But Coupeau didn't feel sleepy. He stayed where he was, swaying back and forth like a pendulum and grinning in an obstinate, irritating way. Gervaise wanted to get rid of Madame Bijard so she called Clémence over and made her count the laundry while she listed it. And then, as she picked up each piece of washing, that great big no-gooder began making crude or filthy remarks, drawing attention to the wretched poverty of the customers, the fortunes of their beds, cracking washer-women's jokes about every hole and every stain she came across. Augustine pretended not to understand but didn't miss a thing, dirty-minded kid that she was. Madame Putois pursed her lips; in her view it was silly to say things like that in front of Coupeau; a man has no business looking at dirty washing; it's one of those things that nice-minded people avoid letting you see. As for Gervaise, preoccupied with getting her job done, she seemed not to hear. As she wrote she scrutinized every bit of laundry so as to identify it, and never once did she make a mistake, but put a name to each piece, recognizing it by its smell or its colour. Those table napkins belonged to the Goujets; you could see with half an eye that *they'd* never been used to wipe the bottom of a saucepan. That pillowcase was undoubtedly the Boches', because of the pomade Madame Boche plastered all her linen with. And she didn't have to stick her nose into Monsieur Madinier's flannel waistcoats, either, to know that they were his; the man stained anything woollen, his skin was so greasy. And she knew other details, very personal things about how clean everyone was, about what was underneath the silk skirts that neighbourhood women wore out in the street, about the number of stockings, of handkerchiefs, of shirts that people got dirty in a week, about the way people tore certain garments, always in exactly the same spot. So she had masses of stories to tell. Mademoiselle Remanjou's chemises, for example, were the subject of endless commentaries; they wore out round the top, so the old girl must have pointed shoulders; and they were never dirty, even if she wore them for a fortnight, which proved that at that age you're like a piece of wood that it'd be hard to get even a tiny drop of anything out of. Every time they sorted the laundry in the shop, they undressed the entire Goutte-d'Or neighbourhood in this way.

'My, this one's yummy!' cried Clémence, opening a fresh package.

Gervaise had stepped back, suddenly filled with tremendous revulsion.

'That's Madame Gaudron's parcel,' she said. 'I don't want to do her washing any longer, and I'm trying to think of an excuse . . . I'm not any fussier than the next person, I've handled really disgusting clothes in me time; but honestly, that stuff, well I just can't. I'd puke all over the floor. What in the world does the woman do, to get her things into such a state!'

She begged Clémence to hurry up. But the girl went on with her remarks, sticking her fingers into holes and commenting on the items concerned, which she'd wave about like so many flags of filth triumphant. Meanwhile the heaps surrounding Gervaise had grown bigger. Now, still sitting on the edge of her stool, she was almost invisible among the shirts and the petticoats; sheets, drawers, tablecloths lay before her in an avalanche of squalor; and in there, in the centre of that spreading mire, her arms and her neck still bare, with little whisps of her blond hair

still sticking to her temples, Gervaise looking rosier and more
languid than ever. Her calm manner had returned and she was
once more smiling her responsible, careful employer's smile,
forgetting about Madame Gaudron's washing and no longer
conscious of its smell as she poked about in the piles to make
sure all was in order. Cross-eyed Augustine, who adored
throwing shovelfuls of coke into the stove, had just filled it
so full that its cast-iron plates glowed red. The shop seemed
to be ablaze as the rays of the sun, now low down in the sky,
beat on the window. Then Coupeau, whom the fierce heat was
making tipsier still, was filled with a sudden burst of affection.
Deeply moved, he walked up to Gervaise with his arms spread
wide.

'You're a good li'l wife,' he mumbled. 'Now give us a li'l
kiss.'

But he got tangled up in the petticoats lying in his way, and
nearly fell down.

'What a pain in the neck you are!' said Gervaise placidly. 'Do
be quiet, we're almost finished.'

But no, he wanted to kiss her, he must kiss her because he
loved her so much. As he mumbled he was stirring up all the
petticoats and stumbling over the piled-up shirts; in his determination to get to Gervaise his feet got caught in the laundry
and he fell his length, with his nose right in among the
dishcloths. Gervaise was beginning to lose patience and gave
him a push, shouting that he would muddle everything up. But
Clémence and even Madame Putois told her she was wrong.
After all, he was being nice. He wanted to kiss her. She could
certainly let him kiss her.

'Believe me, you're lucky, Madame Coupeau!' said Madame
Bijard, whose drunkard of a husband, a locksmith, beat her
black and blue every evening when he came home. 'If mine was
like that when he's hit the bottle it'd be a pleasure!'

Gervaise had calmed down and was already sorry she'd been
so sharp. She helped Coupeau back on to his feet. Then,
smiling, she proffered her cheek. But the roofer, untroubled by
the presence of the others, grabbed hold of her breasts.

' 'Sno two ways about it,' he muttered, 'your laundry pongs
to high heaven! But I love you jus' the same, d'you see.'

'Leave me be, you're tickling me,' she cried, laughing more loudly. 'What a great ass you are! Was there ever an ass like you!'

He'd got hold of her and wouldn't let her go. She relaxed in his arms, dazed by the slight vertigo from the piles of washing and not in the least put off by Coupeau's boozy breath. And the smacking kiss they gave one another full on the mouth, surrounded by all the filth of her trade, was like a first step along their slow decline into depravity.

Madame Bijard, meanwhile, was tying the clothes up in bundles. She chatted about her little girl, a two-year-old named Eulalie, who already had the mind of a grown woman. She could be left by herself; she never cried or played with matches. Eventually Madame Bijard took away the bundles of laundry one by one, her tall frame bent double under the weight, purple blotches mottling her face.

'I can't stand this any more, we're roasting,' said Gervaise, wiping her face before starting again on Madame Boche's bonnet.

Then, noticing that the stove was red hot, they threatened to box Augustine's ears. The irons were turning red as well. What an absolute little devil that kid was! You couldn't turn your back without her getting up to some dirty trick. Now they'd have to wait for a quarter of an hour before using the irons. Gervaise banked down the fire with a couple of shovelfuls of ashes. She also had the bright idea of hanging a pair of sheets over the wires in the ceiling, like blinds, so as to block the sun. After that it was very pleasant in the shop. The temperature was still pretty warm but it was like being inside a bed recess, there was this white light and you felt you were shut into your own little place away from everybody else, although you could hear, from behind the sheets, people hurrying along the pavement; and you were free to make yourself really comfortable. Clémence took off her bodice. As Coupeau still wouldn't go to bed they said he could stay, but he had to promise to sit quietly in a corner, because now it was a matter of getting seriously down to work.

'Whatever can that little rat have done with the *polonais* now?' grumbled Gervaise, meaning Augustine.

They were always having to hunt for the little iron, finding it in the oddest places, where the apprentice, they maintained, hid it out of spite. Gervaise finally finished the lining of Madame Boche's bonnet. She'd already roughly done the lace, stretching it by hand and perking it up with a quick stroke of her iron. It was a bonnet whose very fancy brim consisted of narrow ruffles alternating with strips of embroidered insertion. So she was concentrating, working silently and carefully, ironing the ruffles and the insertion with an iron called a 'cock' that was egg-shaped and fixed to a wooden handle.

Silence had fallen. For a moment all you could hear was a dull thudding, muffled by the cover on the work-table. At both sides of the enormous square table Gervaise, her two assistants and the apprentice all stood leaning over their work, with shoulders rounded and arms continually moving back and forth. Each had her 'square' to her right, a piece of flat brick covered with scorchmarks from over-heated irons. In the middle of the table stood a shallow dish full of clear water with a rag and a small brush soaking in it near the edge. A bunch of large lilies flowered luxuriantly in a jar that had once contained brandied cherries, its cluster of big snowy blossoms making the room look like a corner of a royal garden. Madame Putois had begun attacking the basket of linen prepared by Gervaise, table napkins, womens' drawers, bodices, and pairs of sleeves. Augustine was dawdling over her stockings and her dusters with her nose in the air, fascinated by a huge fly that was buzzing about. As for Clémence, she'd got to her thirty-fifth shirt, counting from that morning.

'Wine, only wine, never rotgut!' announced the roofer suddenly, evidently feeling this declaration was called for. 'Rotgut's bad for me, mustn't touch it!'

With her leather and metal holder Clémence took an iron from the stove and put it up to her cheek to feel if it was hot enough. She rubbed it on her "square", wiped it on a cloth hanging from her belt, then set to work on her thirty-fifth shirt, beginning with the shirt-front and the two sleeves.

'I dunno, Monsieur Coupeau,' she said after a minute, 'there's nothing wrong with a little drop of rotgut. I think it makes me sexy . . . And anyway, y'know, the sooner you kick the bucket the better. I never kid myself, I know I'll not make old bones.'

'Aren't you a pain, always nattering about dying!' interrupted Madame Putois, who disliked gloomy conversations.

Coupeau had got to his feet in annoyance, thinking he was being accused of drinking spirits. He swore on his own head and on that of his wife and of his child that there wasn't a drop of spirits in his body. Moving close up to Clémence, he breathed into her face so she could smell him. Then when he was right up against her bare shoulders, he began to snigger. He wanted to see. Clémence, after doing the pleats in the shirt back and ironing the two sides, had got to the cuffs and the collar. But as he kept pushing against her he made her iron in a crease and she had to take the brush from the dish and smooth out the starched cloth.

'Madame!' she cried, 'please stop him carrying on like that with me!'

'Leave her alone, you're being silly,' Gervaise said calmly. 'Can't you see we're in a hurry?'

Well, suppose they were in a hurry, so what? It wasn't his fault. He wasn't doing anything wrong. He wasn't touching, he was just looking. Was he forbidden now to look at the lovely things the good Lord had made? That tart Clémence hadn't half got an amazing pair of knockers! She could put herself on show and charge a couple of sous a feel, it'd be cheap at the price! The assistant, meanwhile, no longer objected, but instead laughed at these very crude compliments from a pisspot. And she even started cracking jokes with him. He was teasing her about her men's shirts. So, she was always into men's shirts, was she? Yes indeed, in fact she lived in 'em. Christ! She knew her way round 'em alright, she knew just how they were made. She'd handled plenty of 'em, hundreds and hundreds! All the fair chaps *and* all the dark ones in the neighbourhood went about with her work on their backs. But she was still getting on with her ironing, her shoulders shaking with laughter; she'd pressed in five wide pleats on the back, working her iron through the shirt-front opening, then she folded the front part down again and pressed that as well into broad pleats.

'Look, that's their flag!' she said, laughing even louder.

Cross-eyed Augustine exploded, she thought this remark so funny. She was told off. Just fancy, a kid like her laughing at things she'd no business understanding! Clémence passed her her iron; the apprentice finished up the irons on her dishcloths and her stockings when they were no longer hot enough for the starched things. But she took hold of this one so clumsily that she gave herself a "cuff", a long burn on the wrist. Bursting into tears, she accused Clémence of deliberately burning her. The assistant, who'd gone over to get a very hot iron for the front of the shirt, quickly calmed her down by threatening to iron both her ears if she didn't shut up. Meanwhile Clémence had slipped a woollen cloth under the shirt-front and was slowly passing her iron over it, so the starch would have time to come to the surface and to dry. The shirt-front was turning as stiff and as glossy as shiny cardboard.

'Bloody hell!' swore Coupeau, who was shuffling about behind her with a drunkard's persistence.

He stood up on tiptoe, laughing, sounding like a badly greased pulley. Clémence was leaning heavily over the work-table, her wrists turned inwards, her elbows held high and wide apart, her neck bent with the effort she was making, and all of her bare flesh seemed to swell, her shoulders lifting rhythmically as the muscles under the fine skin slowly pulsated, while her breasts, damp with sweat, bulged in the rosy shadows of her gaping bodice. So then he reached down with his hands, wanting to touch.

'Madame, Madame,' shouted Clémence, 'make him leave me alone, for God's sake! . . . If this doesn't stop I'm going. I won't be insulted.'

Gervaise had just placed Madame Boche's bonnet on a hatstand covered with a cloth, and was meticulously goffering the lace with the small iron. She raised her eyes at precisely the moment when the roofer was once again reaching down and fumbling about in Clémence's bodice.

'Really, Coupeau, you *are* being silly,' she said in rather a bored voice, as if she were scolding a child who persisted in eating jam by itself without any bread. 'You must come and lie down.'

'Yes, go and lie down, Monsieur Coupeau, that's the best thing,' declared Madame Putois.

'Well,' he babbled, still giggling, 'you bloody lot are a dead loss! . . . So now we can't even have a bit o' fun, eh? I know what a woman likes, I do, an' I've never done 'em no harm. You give a lady a li'l pinch, right? But you don't go no further, it's just a way of showin' you appreciate 'em . . . An' anyway, when you show off your goods, it's so people can make a choice, ain't it? So why's that big blonde showin' everything she's got? No, it ain't right!'

And, turning towards Clémence:

'Y'know, me love, you didn't oughter put on those fancy airs . . . It's 'cos there's others here . . .'

But he wasn't able to say another word. Without being rough, Gervaise took hold of him with one hand and put her other hand over his mouth. He struggled, but just in fun, as she pushed him towards the back of the shop to the bedroom. Freeing his mouth, he said he'd love to go to bed but that the big blonde must come and keep his tootsies warm. Then they heard Gervaise taking off his shoes. She was undressing him and shoving him about a bit in a motherly way. When she pulled at his trousers he laughed uproariously, letting himself go as he lay there sprawling in the middle of the bed, but then he began to wriggle, declaring she was tickling him. Finally she tucked him up very carefully like a child. Was he nice and comfy? Without replying, he called to Clémence:

'C'mon me love, I'm waitin' for you.'

Just when Gervaise came back into the shop, cross-eyed Augustine was getting a terrific slap from Clémence. It was over a dirty iron that Madame Putois had picked up from the stove; quite unsuspecting, she'd dirtied an entire bodice with it; and because Clémence, accused of not cleaning her iron, had defended herself by blaming Augustine and swearing to high heaven that, in spite of the layer of burnt starch stuck to its bottom, the iron wasn't hers, the apprentice, outraged by such unfairness, had openly spat on Clémence's dress. So she'd got one hell of a slap. Augustine blinked back her tears and cleaned the iron with a bit of candle, but each time she had to pass behind Clémence she'd save up her saliva and spit, hiding her glee when it trickled all down the skirt.

Gervaise went back to goffering the lace on the bonnet. And, in the sudden silence, they could hear Coupeau's slurred voice emerging from the depths of the back shop. He was still in a cheerful mood, laughing away all on his own and coming out with the odd remark.

'Me wife's sush a dummy! . . . Ever sush a dummy, puttin' me to bed! . . . 'Sreal daft, innit, in broad daylight, when you don't wanna go bye-byes!'

But, quite suddenly, he gave a snore. Gervaise sighed with relief, pleased that at last he was resting, sleeping off his booze-up on a couple of good mattresses. And in the silence she began to speak in a slow, steady voice, never raising her eyes from the little goffering iron that she was moving briskly back and forth.

'I'm sorry, but he doesn't know what he's doing, there's no point in being cross. If I got nasty with him it wouldn't help. I prefer to string him along and get him off to bed; at least then it's over right away and I can relax . . . And you know, he's not a bad man, and he's ever so fond of me. You saw just now he was absolutely dead set on giving me a kiss. And that's really nice, 'cos there's masses of 'em, masses, when they've had a few, that want to chase after women . . . He comes straight back here. He likes to kid around with me girls but it doesn't go no further than that. D'you understand, Clémence, you mustn't take offence. You know what a man's like when he's pissed; he'd kill his mother and his father and wouldn't remember a blessed thing about it . . . Oh, I forgive him with all me heart. Lord! He's no different from the rest of 'em!'

She said these things mildly, dispassionately, inured already to Coupeau's binges, still feeling a need to justify her own tolerance but seeing no harm, now, in the way he pinched the thighs of girls working in her shop. When she stopped speaking silence fell once more and remained unbroken. Madame Putois, each time she took a garment, pulled out the basket tucked away under the cretonne curtain hanging round the work-table; then, when the garment was ironed, she'd reach up with her short arms and put it on a shelf. Clémence had just finished the pleats of her thirty-fifth man's shirt. There was a great pile of work to do: they'd calculated that it would mean staying up ironing till eleven o'clock, if they hurried. Now that there were no more distractions, everyone in the shop was slogging away, ironing for all she was worth. The bare arms moved back and forth, bright streaks of pink against the white of the clothes. They'd refilled the stove with coke and as a ray of sunlight, stealing between the sheets, fell directly on to it, you could see the fierce heat rising up in the sunbeam, like an invisible flame that quivered in the tremulous air. The heat became so stifling under the skirts and tablecloths hung up to dry near the ceiling that cross-eyed Augustine ran out of spit and let a bit of her tongue dangle from her mouth. The place smelled of over-heated metal, of starch and water gone sour, of scorched irons, a stale bath-tub aroma to which the four women, their arms slaving away, added the coarser smell of their sweat-drenched necks and coils of hair; while the bunch of big lilies, wilting in its jar of greenish water, gave off a very pure, strong scent. And, from time to time, amid the sounds of the ironing and of the poker scraping about in the stove, Coupeau's snores would roll out as uniformly as the ticking of some huge clock that was regulating the tremendous labours of the laundry.

On the mornings after his booze-ups the roofer would have a hangover, a dreadful hangover that meant his thatch would lose its curl, his mouth would taste foul and his mug would be all puffy and screwed up the whole day long. He'd get up late, not budging till about eight, and then trail about in the shop, hawking and spitting, unable to make up his mind to go to work. Another day lost. In the morning he'd complain that his pins were filled with cotton wool, and he'd call himself a blockhead for bingeing like that, because it really loused up your constitution. Also you ran into a lot of bums who wouldn't leave you alone; you did the rounds swigging drink after drink whether you wanted to or not; you got into all kinds of messes and you finished up absolutely plastered. No, dammit all, he wouldn't ever do it again; he'd no intention of pegging out in some bar, in the prime of life. But after lunch he'd feel more like himself and would clear his throat to show the old voice was still in fine shape. He'd start denying that he'd been pissed the night before; a trifle lit up, maybe. They didn't make chaps like him any more, sound as a bell, a grip like iron, able to drink whatever he wanted without turning a hair. Then, all afternoon, he'd hang around the area. When he'd made himself a thorough nuisance to the assistants, his wife would give him a franc to get him out of the way. Off he'd go to buy his tobacco at the Petite Civette,* in the Rue des Poissonniers, where he'd generally have a brandied plum if he ran into a pal. Then he'd polish off his one-franc piece at François's, on the corner of the Rue de la Goutte-d'Or, where they had a nice little wine, quite young, that tickled your gullet. It was a real old-style bar, dark and low-ceilinged, with a smoky room alongside where they served food. And he'd stay there till evening, playing 'tourni-quet' for tots of wine; François let him have tick and had given his solemn word never to send the bill to his old lady. You just had to wet your whistle a bit, didn't you, to clear out all that foul stuff from the day before. One glass of wine soon leads to another. Anyway, he'd always been one of the boys, didn't go in for chasing skirts, loved a bit of fun, of course, and got a tad tipsy occasionally, but nicely, 'cos he took a dim view of those sods who were always boozing, whom you never ever saw sober! He'd come home on his best behaviour and as merry as a lark.

'Has your sweetheart been round?' he'd sometimes ask Gervaise, to tease her. 'We never see 'im nowadays, I'll have to go an' fetch 'im.'

The sweetheart was Goujet. He did indeed avoid coming too often, for fear of being in the way and of causing talk. But he grasped at any excuse, he'd bring round the laundry, or pass in front of the shop again and again. There was a corner at the back of the shop where he liked to sit for hours, never stirring, smoking his little pipe. After dinner in the evening, once every ten days or so, he'd chance it and settle down in his corner; he never said much at all, but sat in silence with his eyes on Gervaise, only removing his pipe from his mouth to laugh at everything she said. When they worked late in the shop on Saturdays he'd lose all count of time, evidently finding it was more fun there than at the theatre. Sometimes the women went on ironing till three in the morning. A lamp hung on a wire from the ceiling, its shade casting a big circle of bright light which made the piles of washing look like soft white snow. The apprentice would put up the shop's shutters, but the July nights were scorching so they left the street door open. And, as the night went on, the women would unfasten their bodices so as to be comfortable. Under the lamp's glowing light their delicate skin looked golden, Gervaise's especially, for she'd grown plumper, and her silky-smooth fair shoulders gleamed, while round her neck there was a crease like a baby's with a tiny dimple in it that he could have drawn from memory, he knew it so well. Overwhelmed by the tremendous heat of the stove and by the smell of the clothes steaming under the irons, Goujet would become slightly dizzy, his mind slowing down while he kept his eyes fixed on those women who hurried through their ironing, swinging their bare arms back and forth as they spent the night sprucing up their neighbours' Sunday best. All around the shop the nearby houses were settling down to rest, as the deep silence of sleep gradually descended. Midnight struck, then one o'clock, then two. The cabs and the passers-by had all gone. Now, in the dark, deserted street, only the doorway of the shop sent forth a ray of light, like a strip of yellow cloth unrolled across the ground. Sometimes, from far away, a step could be heard and a man would approach; and when he crossed over the strip of light he'd crane his neck, surprised by the sound of ironing, carrying away with him a fleeting vision of women with their bodices unbuttoned, glimpsed through a reddish haze.

Goujet, seeing that Étienne was a worry to Gervaise and wanting to save the boy from Coupeau's kicks, had taken him on to work the bellows in his bolt factory. The trade of nailsmith, though not held in any great esteem because of the dirtiness of foundries and the tediousness of forever hammering the same pieces of iron, was a profitable trade where you could earn as much as ten or twelve francs a day. The kid, now twelve, could soon be apprenticed if the occupation suited him. And so Étienne had become another link between Gervaise and the blacksmith. The latter would bring the child home and report on his good behaviour. Everyone kept telling Gervaise, jokingly, that Goujet had a crush on her. She knew that perfectly well, and she'd blush like a young girl, with a bashful flush that coloured her cheeks a bright apple red. Oh, the poor dear boy, he wasn't any trouble! He'd never said anything about it, never done anything unseemly, never uttered an improper word. There weren't many as decent as him. And, without wanting to admit as much, she was filled with a great joy at being loved in that way, like a holy virgin. When something really upset her, she'd think of the blacksmith and be comforted. If they were left alone together it didn't embarrass them in the least; they'd look each other right in the face, smiling, not needing to tell each other how they felt. Their attachment was a sensible one, far removed from anything sordid, because it's so much better to keep your peace of mind if you can arrange things so you're happy like that.

Towards the end of the summer, however, Nana started turning the household upside down. At six she was becoming a proper little devil. So as not to have her underfoot the whole time, her mother took her every morning to a small school in the Rue Polonceau, run by a Mademoiselle Josse. There she pinned together the backs of her schoolmates' dresses, filled the teacher's snuffbox with ash and thought up other more unsavoury pranks better left unmentioned. Twice, Mademoiselle Josse kicked her out, then took her back on account of those six francs every month. The minute school was over Nana got her revenge for having been shut up indoors by making a hell of a racket under the archway and in the courtyard, where the assistants, unable to bear the din, would send her to play. There she would join forces with Pauline, the Boches' daughter, and with Victor, the ten-year-old son of Gervaise's former employer; Victor, a great lump of a boy, loved larking about in the company of very small girls. Madame Fauconnier, who'd remained on good terms with the Coupeaus, would herself send him there to play. In any case, in the building there was an amazing profusion of small kids, swarms of them who'd come rushing down the four staircases at any moment of the day and scatter over the courtyard like flocks of shrill, rapacious sparrows. Madame Gaudron alone had nine she could let loose, some fair and some dark, their hair uncombed, their noses unwiped, their little trousers pulled up to their eyes, their socks

falling over their shoes and their torn jackets revealing patches
of white skin beneath the grime. Another woman on the fifth
floor, who delivered bread, had seven. They streamed out of
every room. And in that seething mass of pink-nosed riff-raff
that got cleaned up whenever it rained, there were tall ones like
bean-poles and fat ones who already had pot-bellies like grown
men and there were tiny ones, so tiny they must surely have
escaped from their cribs, who could barely stand, didn't
understand a thing and crawled about on all fours instead of
running. Nana ruled this gaggle of brats; she queened it over
girls twice her size, and would only relinquish some of her
power to Pauline and Victor, those bosom companions who
backed her up in everything. That damn kid was always
carrying on about playing mother, she'd take the clothes off the
smallest kids and then put them on again, she'd insist on
inspecting the others all over and having a feel, behaving as
despotically and as freakishly as a sick-minded adult. Any game
they played under her command landed them in trouble. The
gang would paddle about in the coloured waters from the
dyeworks, and emerge with legs dyed blue or red up to
the knee; then they'd race off to the locksmith's, where they'd
pinch nails and iron filings, from there to the woodworker's to
fling themselves on to the carpenter's shavings, huge piles of
shavings that were tremendous fun, where you bounced about
with your bum in the air. The courtyard belonged to them, it
echoed with the clatter of their tiny boots as they tumbled
helter-skelter about, it echoed with the piercing cries of their
voices rising up each time the gang took off again. Some days
even the courtyard wasn't big enough. Then they'd plunge
down into the cellars, reappear, climb up one of the staircases,
race along a passage, come down again, go up another staircase,
follow another passage, on and on without tiring for hours on
end, screaming all the time, the vast building shaking as if from
a stampede of dangerous wild animals let loose from every one
of its recesses.

'Those brats are the bloody limit!' Madame Boche would
shout. 'Really, you'd think that people had nothing better to do
than have all those kids! . . . And then they go and complain
that they've not got enough to eat!'

Boche liked to say that children flourished on poverty like toadstools on a dunghill. The portress screamed at them all day long, threatening them with her broom. In the end she locked the cellar doors, because she found out from Pauline, whose ears she'd boxed, that Nana'd hit on the notion of playing doctor down there in the dark; that little monster dispensed 'remedies' with sticks.

Now one afternoon there was a fearful row. You could see it coming, of course. Nana'd thought up a very funny little game. She'd stolen one of Madame Boche's clogs from the lodge. She tied a string to it and started to pull it about like a carriage. Then Victor had the idea of filling the clog with apple peelings. They formed up in a procession. Nana marched at the head, pulling the clog. Pauline and Victor walked to her left and right. Then the entire pack of kids followed in order, the big ones in the front, then the little ones, pushing and shoving; a baby in petticoats, no taller that your boot top, wearing a bashed-in padded cap over one ear, brought up the rear. And the procession was singing something doleful, full of 'ohs' and 'ahs'. Nana had explained that they were going to play at funerals; the apple peelings were the corpse. When they'd gone right round the courtyard they began all over again. They thought it a riot.

'What in the world can they be doing?' muttered Madame Boche; ever watchful and suspicious, she'd come out of the lodge.

And, when it had sunk in:

'But it's my clog they've got!' she screamed furiously. 'The little wretches!'

She dished out clouts to left and right, slapping Nana on both cheeks and giving Pauline a kick for being such a great softy as to let her mother's clog be pinched. Just then, Gervaise was filling a pail at the courtyard tap. When she saw Nana with a bloody nose, sobbing her heart out, she went for the concierge in no uncertain fashion. Whoever heard of hitting a child as if you were hitting a bullock? Anyone who did that must be completely heartless, must be the lowest of the low. Madame Boche, of course, answered back. When your child was trash of that sort you kept her under lock and key. Eventually Boche himself appeared at the lodge door, shouting to his wife to come inside and not have anything more to do with shit like that. The breach was irreparable.

Truth to tell, for the past month things had no longer gone at all well between the Boches and the Coupeaus. Gervaise had a very generous nature and was always giving them bottles of wine, cups of bouillon, oranges, pieces of cake. One evening she'd taken the remains of a chicory and beetroot salad over to the lodge, knowing that the concierge would sell her soul for a bit of salad. But the next day she'd turned quite white on hearing Mademoiselle Remanjou describe how Madame Boche, in front of several people, had thrown out the chicory in disgust, remarking that, thank the Lord, she hadn't yet been reduced to living on other folks' leftovers. From that moment on Gervaise stopped giving them any presents at all: no more bottles of wine, no more cups of bouillon, no more oranges, no more pieces of cake, no more anything. You should just have seen the Boches' faces! For them it was as if the Coupeaus were robbing them. Gervaise realized where she'd gone wrong; after all, if she'd never been so silly as to give them so much, they wouldn't have got into bad habits and they'd still be being nice. But now the concierge went round saying that hanging was too good for her. When the October rent day arrived, she carried on endlessly about Gervaise to Monsieur Marescot, the landlord, because the laundress, who spent every blessed sou on nice things to eat, was a day late with the rent; so that Monsieur Marescot, himself none too polite either, walked in to the shop without even taking off his hat and demanded his money—which incidentally was handed over on the spot. Naturally the Boches had made overtures to the Lorilleux. Now it was with the Lorilleux that they did their tippling in the lodge, amid affecting displays of reconciliation. It was only because of Banban that they'd had a row at all, she was capable of making mountains quarrel. Ah, now the Boches knew what she was like, they understood how much the Lorilleux must have to put up with. And when she went past they all made a point of sniggering, through the door.

One day, however, Gervaise did go up to see the Lorilleux. She went because of Maman Coupeau, who was now sixty-seven. Maman Coupeau's eyes were completely gone. And her legs weren't any good either. She'd just been forced to give up her last remaining charring job, and looked like dying of hunger if no one helped her out. Gervaise thought it shameful that a woman of that age, with three children, should be abandoned in this way by both God and man. And as Coupeau refused to speak to the Lorilleux, telling Gervaise that she herself could bleeding well go on up, up she went, gripped by a sense of outrage that made her heart swell in her bosom.

Once she was up on the top floor she barged in like a whirlwind, without knocking. Nothing had changed since that first evening when the Lorilleux had given her such a sour reception. The same faded and tattered wool curtain divided the living area from the workshop; the narrow tunnel-like place might have been built to house an eel. At the back of the room Lorilleux was bending over his workbench, squeezing together the links of a piece of column-chain one by one, while Madame Lorilleux was standing in front of the vice, pulling a gold thread through the draw-plate. The little forge shone pink in the bright daylight.

'Yes, it's me!' said Gervaise. 'Quite a surprise, eh, seeing as how we're at daggers drawn? But as I'm sure you can guess, I've not come on account of me nor of you . . . It's on account of Maman Coupeau that I'm here. Yes, I've come to see whether we're going to leave her to look to other people's charity for a crust of bread.'

'Well that's a fine beginning!' muttered Madame Lorilleux. 'Some people certainly have an infernal nerve!'

And, turning her back, she again began pulling the gold thread, behaving as if she was unaware of her sister-in-law's presence. But Lorilleux had raised his pale face, exclaiming:

'What's that you're saying?'

But he'd heard perfectly well, and he went on:

'Tittle-tattle again, I s'pose! She's a nice one, Maman Coupeau is, going to all and sundry pleading poverty! However she did have her dinner here the day before yesterday. We do what we can, we do. We're not rolling in it. But if she's going round to everyone else telling tales she can just stay right there with 'em, because we can't stand spies.'

He picked up his piece of chain again and, turning his back as well, added almost regretfully;

'When everyone agrees to give five francs a month, we'll give five francs.'

Gervaise had calmed down, chilled by the snooty expressions on their faces. She'd never set foot in their room without feeling uncomfortable. Keeping her eyes down and fixed on the squares of wooden slatting where the scraps of gold fell, she stated her case in a reasonable manner. Maman Coupeau had three children: if each of them gave five francs that would only come to fifteen, and that really wasn't enough, you couldn't live on that; they'd have to make it at least three times that sum. But Lorilleux protested. Where was he supposed to steal fifteen francs a month from? People were very odd, they imagined he was rich because he had gold in his place. Then he started pitching into Maman Coupeau: she wouldn't give up her coffee in the morning, she was fond of a little nip, she had fussy tastes, like someone with money. Lord! Everybody liked their comforts, but if you hadn't managed to put one sou aside, you did same as other folks and tightened your belt. In any case, Maman Coupeau wasn't yet old enough to give up work; she could still see awfully well when it was a matter of helping herself to a tasty titbit in the bottom of the dish; in a word, she was a crafty old girl and just wanted to take things easy. Even if he'd had the means, he wouldn't have thought it right to support someone in idleness.

Meanwhile Gervaise managed to keep her tone conciliatory as she calmly discussed these unconvincing arguments. She tried to appeal to their feelings. In the end, however, the husband didn't even answer her. The wife was standing in front of the forge now, busy pickling a length of chain in the small long-handled pot that contained dilute nitric acid. She still pointedly kept her back turned as if she was miles away. And as Gervaise went on talking she watched them, with their twisted bodies and their patched, grease-stained clothes, doggedly getting on with their work amid the black dust of the workshop; their confining, mechanical occupation had made them dull and unbending like worn-out tools. Then, quite suddenly, she was overcome with rage and shouted:

'Alright, keep your money, I'd much rather! I'll take in Maman Coupeau, d'you hear! I took in a stray cat the other night, I can certainly take in your mother. She won't want for anything, she'll have her coffee and her little nips! . . . Christ! What a lousy awful family!'

This time Madame Lorilleux did turn round. She was brandishing the pan as if about to throw the nitric acid in her sister-in-law's face. She spluttered:

'Get out of here, or I'll not answer for the consequences . . . And don't count on those five francs, either, 'cos I won't give you a single sou, not a single sou! . . . Five francs, yes, of course! Maman would be like your maid, and you'd pamper yourself with my five francs! If she goes to you, you can tell her this: if she's at death's door I won't give her so much as a glass of water. Now piss off! Get out of here!'

'What a horrible woman!' cried Gervaise, banging the door violently behind her.

She moved Maman Coupeau in with them the very next day. She put her bed in the large cubicle where Nana slept, lit by a round skylight near the ceiling. The move didn't take long, as Maman Coupeau's furniture consisted solely of this bed, an old walnut cupboard that they put in the dirty clothes room, a table and two chairs; they sold the table and had the chairs' rush seats redone. And on her very first evening there the old lady was wielding the broom and washing the dishes, in short making herself useful, very happy that her troubles were over. The Lorilleux were beside themselves with fury, especially as Madame Lerat had just made it up with the Coupeaus. One fine day the two sisters, the flower-worker and the chain-maker, had come to blows over Gervaise: Madame Lerat had dared to approve of Banban's behaviour towards their mother, and then, seeing Madame Lorilleux's annoyance and unable to resist needling her, went on to talk about the laundress's magnificent eyes, eyes you could set a bit of paper alight with; and thereupon the pair of them, after exchanging slaps, vowed never to meet again. Now Madame Lerat spent her evenings in the shop, where (though she didn't admit it) she found Clémence's smutty talk very entertaining.

Three years went by. There were several more occasions
when they all squabbled and then made it up again. Gervaise
couldn't care less about the Lorilleux, the Boches or anybody
who didn't see eye to eye with her. If they didn't like it they
could lump it, right? The main thing was, she was earning as
much as she wanted. The local shopkeepers had come to have
a high regard for her because, to put it in a nutshell, there
weren't many customers as good as she, paying on the nail and
never haggling or bellyaching. She bought her bread from
Madame Coudeloup in the Rue des Poissonniers, her meat from
big Charles, a butcher in the Rue Polonceau, while her groceries
came from Lehongre's in the Rue de la Goutte-d'Or, almost
opposite her shop. François, the wine merchant at the corner
of the street, delivered her wine to her in fifty-litre crates. Her
neighbour Vigoureux, whose wife's bottom must have been
black and blue from being pinched by all the men, supplied her
coke at the same price he paid the Gas Company for it. And
you could certainly say that the shopkeepers were most scrupulous in their dealings with her, because they knew there was
everything to be gained by keeping in her good books. So when
she was out and about in the neighbourhood, hatless and in her
slippers, she'd be greeted on all sides; she felt right at home
there, for the nearby streets seemed just a natural extension of
her own home, with its front door opening straight on to the
pavement. Sometimes, now, she'd spin out her errands, enjoying being outside surrounded by people she knew. On those
days when she was too busy to prepare something for supper
she'd buy ready-cooked food and chat to the cook-shop man
whose place was on the far side of the building, in a vast room
with huge dusty windows through whose grime you could see
the dull light of the courtyard beyond. Or perhaps she'd stop,
her hands laden with plates and bowls, and pass the time of day
in front of some ground-floor window, where she'd catch a
glimpse of the cobbler's room with its unmade bed and its floor
covered with a litter of rags, a couple of battered cradles and a
pot of cobbler's wax full of filthy water. But the neighbour for
whom she felt the most respect was still the clockmaker, the
dapper gentleman in the frock-coat who was always poking into
the watches with his dainty little implements; and often she'd

cross the road to say 'good morning', laughing with pleasure at
seeing, in that shop no bigger than a cupboard, those jubilant
little cuckoo clocks with their hurrying pendulums all beating
time, though never quite together.

CHAPTER VI

ONE autumn afternoon, after delivering some washing to a
customer in the Rue des Portes-Blanches, Gervaise found
herself at the bottom of the Rue des Poissonniers just as dusk
was falling. It had rained that morning, the air was very mild,
and a smell hung about the greasy cobbles; Gervaise, burdened
by her big basket, walked along slowly, her body slack as she
climbed up the street; she was panting slightly, and conscious
of a vague sensual craving that her tiredness intensified. She'd
have loved something really good to eat. Looking up and seeing
the name-plate of the Rue Marcadet, she suddenly had the idea
of dropping in on Goujet at his forge. Time and again he'd
suggested she should stop by some day if she felt like seeing
how they worked with iron. Naturally, in front of the other
workers, she'd ask for Étienne, she'd make it look as if she'd
made up her mind to come just on account of the boy.

The bolt and rivet factory must be nearby, at this end of the
Rue Marcadet, though she didn't know exactly where; especially as a lot of the numbers were missing on these shacks
separated by strips of waste land. Nothing could have induced
her to live in this broad, dirty street which was black with coal
dust from the surrounding factories and full of broken cobble-
stones and ruts brimming with stagnant water. Along both of
its sides stretched rows of sheds, big glass-roofed workshops,
and grey, unfinished-looking structures showing their brickwork and wooden frames—a jumble of rickety buildings flanked
by disreputable lodging houses and sleazy little taverns, with
occasional gaps through which you caught a glimpse of the
countryside. All she could remember was that the factory was
near a rag and scrap-metal merchant's place, a sort of open
sewer at street level where, according to Goujet, stuff worth

hundreds of thousands of francs was just lying about. And, amid the din of the factories, she tried to get her bearings; fierce jets of steam kept pouring out of the narrow flues on the roofs; from a sawmill came repeated screeching noises as if a piece of calico was being suddenly torn, while button factories made the ground shake with their rumbling, pulsating machinery. As she was gazing in the direction of Montmartre, uncertain whether she ought to walk on further, a gust of wind blew down the soot from a tall chimney, filling the street with its filthy stink; and she was standing with closed eyes, struggling for breath, when she heard the sound of rhythmic hammering: without realizing it, she was actually just opposite the factory, which she then recognized by the yard full of junk next door.

But even so she still hesitated, not knowing how to get in. There was an entrance through a break in the fence, and this seemed to lead into a demolition site full of piles of rubble. As a pool of muddy water barred the way, two planks had been flung across. Eventually she decided to risk the planks, and, turning left, found herself in the middle of a weird forest of upside-down carts with their shafts in the air, and crumbling hovels whose beams and rafters were still standing. A long way off, piercing the darkness amid the lingering gleams of murky twilight, she could see a fire glowing red. The sound of hammering had stopped. She was moving forward cautiously towards the light when a workman, his goatee bristling on his coal-blackened face, passed close beside her, his pale eyes giving her a sidelong glance.

'Please sir,' she asked, 'it's here, isn't it, that a kid called Étienne works? . . . He's my boy.'

'Étienne, Étienne,' repeated the workman huskily, swaying to and fro; 'Étienne . . . No, don't know 'im.'

From his open mouth there wafted out a boozy smell like that of freshly-broached old casks of brandy. And, as this meeting with a woman in a dark corner was beginning to make him a bit too free and easy, Gervaise stepped back, murmuring:

'But it is here that Monsieur Goujet works?'

'Oh yes, Goujet does!' said the workman, 'I know Goujet! . . . If it's Goujet yer after . . . Go on down to the end.'

And, turning round, he yelled in his cracked tinny voice:

'Hey, Gueule-d'Or, here's a lady askin' for yer!'

But his shout was smothered by a great noise of hammering. Gervaise went down to the end. She reached a door and stuck her head in. The room was huge, and at first she couldn't see anything at all. Over in a corner the forge fire, nearly out, gave off a pale gleam like starlight, increasing the effect of encroaching darkness. Great shadows drifted about. At times black shapes passed in front of the fire, blocking that last remaining point of light, shapes of men prodigiously enlarged, whose colossal limbs you could just make out. Not daring to go further, Gervaise called softly from the door:

'Monsieur Goujet, Monsieur Goujet . . .'

Suddenly, everything was lit up. As the bellows roared a jet of white flame had spurted out. The shed sprang into view, enclosed by planking partitions, with holes that had been roughly plastered over and corners shored up with brickwork. Coal dust flying about had left a wash of grey soot all over the vast room. Spider's webs, weighed down by years of accumulated dirt, hung from the beams like a lot of rags stuck up there to dry. Round the walls, on shelves, hanging from nails or thrown into dark corners, was a jumble of old iron implements, bashed-in utensils and enormous tools; she could make out their jagged, lustreless, hard shapes. And the dazzling white flame grew ever larger, lighting as if with a ray of sunshine the beaten earth floor where the shining steel of four anvils, securely set in their blocks, took on a silvery sheen spangled with gold.

Then Gervaise saw Goujet in front of the furnace, recognizing him by his handsome yellow beard. Étienne was working the bellows. Two other workers were there as well. She saw no one but Goujet; she moved forward and stood in front of him.

'Goodness! It's Madame Gervaise!' he cried, his face beaming. 'What a lovely surprise!'

But, seeing his mates were giving him funny looks, he pushed Étienne towards his mother, saying:

'You've come to see the boy . . . He's a good kid, he's beginning to get his hand in.'

'Well,' she said, 'what a business it is getting here . . . It seems like the back of beyond . . .'

And she described her journey. Then she asked why they didn't know Étienne's name in the workshop. Goujet laughed and explained that everyone called the child Zouzou because he had his hair cropped short, like a Zouave. While they were chatting together Étienne stopped working the bellows and, in the darkening workshop, the flames of the forge fire died down to a rosy glow. The blacksmith, very moved, gazed at the smiling young woman, so sweet and fresh-looking in that light. They'd both stopped speaking as they stood there in the shadows, but then he seemed to recollect where he was and broke the silence:

'Excuse me, Madame Gervaise, but I've something I must finish. Stay there, won't you? You're not in anyone's way.'

She stayed. Étienne had grabbed hold of the bellows once more. The furnace was blazing, sending out showers of sparks, especially as the kid, to show his mother what he could do, was producing a tremendous gale of air. Goujet waited, tongs in hand, watching an iron bar heating. The bright glare lit him up mercilessly, without a shadow. His sleeves were rolled up and his shirt open at the neck, showing his bare arms and his bare chest and his delicate pink skin covered with curly golden hair; and, with his head a little sunk between his heavy, thickly-muscled shoulders, his face watchful and his pale eyes fixed steadily on the flame, he looked like a giant at rest, tranquil in his strength. When the iron bar was white-hot he grasped it with the tongs and cut it into even pieces, hitting it gently on the anvil with his hammer as if he were cutting glass. He then put the pieces back in the fire, removing them one at a time to shape them. He was making hexagonal rivets. He put each piece into a heading frame, levelling down the metal that formed the head, flattening the six sides, then tossing each finished, red-hot rivet on to the ground, where its vivid glow died away against the blackness; and he was hammering continuously as he did this, swinging the five-pound hammer with his right hand, each hammer-blow completing a detail as he turned and fashioned his iron with such mastery that he could work while chatting and looking at people. A silvery ringing came from the anvil. He was completely at ease, not sweating at all, hammering away quite naturally, with no more apparent effort than when he cut out pictures at home, in the evening.

'Oh, these are little rivets, twenty millimetres,' he said in answer to Gervaise's questions. 'You can do as many as three hundred in a day . . . But it takes practice, because your arm soon seizes up . . .'

And when she asked whether his wrist didn't get stiff by the end of the day, he had a good laugh. Did she take him for a young lady? His wrist had had a pretty rough time of it for the past fifteen years; he was made of iron now, he'd spent so long working with his tools. But yes, she was right: a gent who'd never made a rivet or a bolt and who fancied playing around with his five-pound hammer would give himself the devil of a cramp in a couple of hours. It didn't look like anything at all, but it often finished off even really tough blokes in just a few years. Meanwhile the other men were hammering away as well, all together. Their big shadows danced in the light, red flashes cut through the darkness as pieces of iron were taken from the fires, sparks showered out under the hammers, blazing like sunbeams from the tops of the anvils. And Gervaise, caught up in the rhythm of the forge, felt happy and had no thought of leaving. She was making a wide detour to reach Étienne without risking getting her hands burnt, when she saw the dirty, bearded workman she'd spoken to in the yard come in.

'So you found 'im, did yer, lady?' he asked in his jeering, drunkard's voice. 'Hey, Gueule-d'Or, it was me, y'know, as told the lady where to find yer . . .'

His name was Bec-Salé,* alias Boit-sans-Soif, and he was one hell of a chap, a crackerjack bolt-maker who always kept his iron well-oiled with a daily litre of rotgut. He'd been out for a quick one, because he felt too dry to wait till six. When he discovered that Zouzou was called Étienne he thought that was too funny for words and laughed, showing his black teeth. Then he recognized Gervaise. Why just yesterday he'd been drinking with Coupeau. She could ask Coupeau about Bec-Salé, alias Boit-sans-Soif, he'd tell her straight out: 'he's one of the best!' Oh that bugger Coupeau! Ever such a nice chap, always ready to stand a round even if it wasn't really his turn.

'I'm right pleased to know you're 'is wife,' he kept saying. 'He deserves a pretty wife. Hey, Gueule-d'Or, don't you think the lady's pretty?'

He was being rather fresh and pushing up against the laundress, who picked up her basket and held it in front of her to keep him away. Goujet, annoyed, realized that his fellow worker was teasing him because he and Gervaise seemed so friendly, and shouted:

'Come on, you lazy bum! What about the forty millimetre bolts? . . . Are you up to it now you've had a skinful, you bleeding soak?'

The smith was referring to an order for some large bolts that required two strikers at the anvil.

'Right away, if you like, you great baby!' replied Bec-Salé, alias Boit-sans-Soif. 'Still sucks 'is thumb, 'e does, and pretends 'e's a man! You may be big but I've beaten plenty bigger'n you!'

'Right you are, we'll do it now. Come on, just us two.'

'I'm ready, Mister Know-it-all!'

Excited by the presence of Gervaise, they were challenging one another. Goujet put the ready-cut pieces of iron into the fire, then fixed a large-gauge heading frame to an anvil. From against the wall, his mate fetched two twenty-pound sledge-hammers, the two big sisters of the workshop, that the workers had named Fifine and Dédèle.* And he went on swanking, talking about half a gross of bolts he'd forged for the lighthouse at Dunkirk, real gems, so finely wrought they deserved to be put in a museum. Christ, no! He wasn't afraid of competition: you could comb every joint in the capital and not find another worker to equal him. They were going to have some fun, they'd soon see what was what.

'The lady can decide,' he said, turning towards the young woman.

'No more talk!' shouted Goujet. 'Put some vim into it, Zouzou! It's not hot enough, boy.'

Then Bec-Salé, alias Boit-sans-Soif, asked:

'We'll strike together, right?'

'No we won't! We'll each do our own, mate.'

This announcement had a chilling effect on Bec-Salé who,

despite his bluster, suddenly found his mouth was dry. Forty-millimetre bolts made by one man on his own—that had never been done, especially as the bolts were to have round heads, which would be hellishly difficult, a real masterpiece in fact. The three other men in the shop had dropped their work to watch, and a tall, gaunt chap wagered a litre of wine that Goujet would be beaten. Meanwhile the two smiths each picked a sledgehammer; they did this with their eyes shut, because Fifine weighed half a pound more that Dédèle. Bec-Salé, alias Boit-sans-Soif, had the good luck to put his hand on Dédèle, and Gueule-d'Or got Fifine. And, as they waited for the iron to become white-hot, Bec-Salé, quite his swaggering self again, struck poses beside the anvil, making eyes at Gervaise while he stood there tapping his foot like a gent who was going to fight a duel, and making believe he was swinging Dédèle through the air. Jesus! This was what he was really good at: he could have pounded the Vendôme column as flat as a pancake!

'Right, get started!' said Goujet, himself putting one of the bits of iron, as thick as a girl's wrist, into the heading frame.

Bec-Salé, alias Boit-sans-Soif, arched his back and swung Dédèle with both hands. Small and emaciated, with a little beard and wolfish eyes that gleamed beneath his untidy mop of hair, he threw himself body and soul into each blow of the hammer, springing off the ground as if catapulted by his own energy. He was an excitable chap who'd set upon his iron in a rage at finding it so hard; he'd even grunt with pleasure when he thought he'd landed an especially wicked blow. Perhaps it was true that for other men strong drink weakened the muscles, but he needed booze, not blood, in his veins; the drop he'd just had was warming his body like a boiler, he felt as powerful as a bleeding steam-engine. So that evening it was the iron that was afraid of *him*; he was pounding it softer than a plug of tobacco. And you should just have seen Dédèle waltzing about! She did the *grand entrechat*, kicking her tootsies into the air and showing her undies like a floozie at the Elysée-Montmartre;* because you couldn't fiddle about, you see, iron is such a wily devil it cools straight away just to show what it thinks of the hammer. In thirty strokes Bec-Salé, alias Boit-sans-Soif, had forged the head of his bolt. But he was panting, his eyes were

bulging out of their sockets, and he was in a furious temper at
hearing his arms make cracking sounds. So then, all worked up,
leaping about and bellowing, he let fly with a couple more
blows, just to put his aches and pains in their place. When he
removed it from the heading frame, the bolt was misshapen, its
head badly set like a hunchback's.

'There, lovely job, eh?' he said just the same in his cocky
way, showing his work to Gervaise.

'Oh, I'm not an expert, Monsieur,' replied the laundress
rather coolly.

But she could clearly see, on the bolt, the last two strikes
made by Dédèle's heel, and she was quite delighted, screwing
up her mouth to keep from laughing because now Goujet had
every chance of winning.

It was Gueule-d'Or's turn. Before he began, he gave the
laundress a look full of confident affection. Then, without
hurrying, he stood back from the anvil and brought down the
hammer from high above with long, steady swings. His movements were classical: precise, balanced and flowing. In his
hands Fifine's dance was no high-kicking, showing-all-she'd-
got sleazy bar routine, no, she was raising her head then bowing
low to the rhythm like some noble lady of long ago, gravely
leading a minuet. Fifine's heels beat out the measure soberly,
and they sank with studied artistry into the red-hot iron of the
bolt's head, first flattening the metal in the centre, then shaping
it with a series of blows of rhythmic precision. And of course
it wasn't brandy that Gueule-d'Or had in his veins, it was
blood, pure blood that was coursing powerfully right through
into his hammer and regulating his task. What a superb figure
of a man, when you saw him at work! The light from the great
fire in the furnace shone directly on to him. His short hair
curling over his low brow and his handsome yellow beard
falling in little ringlets glowed with light, illuminating his whole
face with their threads of gold, so you could truly say that his
face was made of gold. What's more his neck was like a pillar,
and as white as a child's; his chest was huge, broad enough for
a woman to lie on; his sculptured shoulders and arms might have
been copied from those of some statue of a giant, in a museum.
When he braced himself to swing the hammer you could see his

muscles swell into mounds of flesh that rippled and hardened under the skin; his shoulders, his chest and his neck expanded; he seemed to give off light, becoming beautiful, all-powerful, like a benevolent god. Twenty times already he'd swung Fifine, keeping his eyes on the piece of iron, taking a breath at each blow, with only two great drops of sweat running down his temples. He was counting: twenty-one, twenty-two, twenty-three. Fifine calmly went on making her patrician curtseys.

' 'E don't 'alf fancy 'imself!' Bec-Salé, alias Boit-sans-Soif, muttered sneeringly.

And Gervaise, standing opposite Gueule-d'Or, smiled fondly as she watched him. Lord! Weren't men idiotic! Wasn't it a fact that those two were hammering those bolts just to impress her? Oh, she knew what was going on, they were fighting over her with their hammering, they were like two great red cockerels strutting about in front of a little white hen. Did you ever hear of anything so funny! But sometimes the heart declares itself in the strangest ways. Yes, it was for her, this thundering of Fifine and Dédèle on the anvil; it was for her, all this pounding of iron; it was for her, this forge blazing away with its roaring fire and showers of bright sparks. They were forging a love there, fighting for her, each seeking to prove it was he who could forge the best. And, to tell the truth, deep down this delighted her, for women love compliments. The blows of Gueule-d'Or's hammer, especially, called forth an answer from her heart; they rang there as if on the anvil, in a clear melody that kept time with the eager pulsing of her blood. It seemed nonsense, but she felt that something was being hammered into her heart, something solid, like a bit of the iron bolt. Before she'd come in there, while she was walking along the damp pavements in the twilight, she'd felt a vague longing, a need for something tasty to eat; but now she was satisfied, as if Gueule-d'Or's hammer blows had nourished her. Oh, she had no doubt at all that he would win! It was to him that she would belong. Bec-Salé, alias Boit-sans-Soif, was too ugly in his dirty smock and overalls, jumping about like a monkey who'd escaped from his cage. And she waited, very flushed, but loving the tremendous heat and revelling in being shaken from head to foot by Fifine's final blows.

Goujet was still counting.

'And twenty-eight!' he cried, at last putting down the hammer. 'It's done, take a look.'

The head of the bolt was clean and polished, without a single burr, a real jeweller's job, as round as though it had been cast in a mould. The workmen nodded as they looked at it: you could get down on your knees and worship that perfect bolt, you really could! Bec-Salé, alias Boit-sans-Soif, did try to laugh it off but got all flustered and finally returned to his anvil, looking fed up. Gervaise, meanwhile, had moved very close to Goujet, as if to see better. Étienne had put down the bellows, the forge was again filling with shadows, with a dying red glow, which changed suddenly to pitch darkness. And the smith and the laundress found it was very sweet to be sheltered by this darkness, in this shed black with soot and filings and smelling of old iron; they couldn't have felt more alone had they met by arrangement deep in the greenery of the Bois de Vincennes.* He took her hand as if he had won her.

Then, outside, they did not exchange one word. He found nothing to say, except that she could have taken Étienne home had there not been another half-hour's work to do. She was finally leaving when he called her back, wanting to keep her with him for a few more minutes.

'Come over here, you haven't seen everything . . . No, really, it's very interesting.'

He led her to the right, into another shed where his boss was installing a lot of machines. She hesitated before crossing the threshold, filled with an instinctive fear. The huge room was shaking with the vibration of the machines; great shadows, streaked with fiery red, floated about. But he reassured her with a smile, swearing that there was nothing to be afraid of: only she must take great care not to let her skirts trail too close to the gear-wheels. He walked in front and she followed, in that deafening din made up of all kinds of hissing and rumbling noises, among those clouds of smoke peopled by dimly seen creatures, black figures rushing hither and thither and machines that waved their arms about, she really couldn't tell which was which. The walkways in between were very narrow, you had to step over obstacles and avoid holes and move out of the path of a trolley. You couldn't hear yourself speak. She still couldn't see anything, it was all dancing about. Then, aware of a sensation above her head like the brushing of great wings, she raised her eyes and stopped, staring at the driving-belts, long ribbons that hung across the ceiling in a gigantic spider's web with every thread being spun on and on for ever; the steam-engine was in a corner, tucked away behind a little brick wall; the driving-belts seemed to move on their own, drawing their momentum from the depths of the shadows, as they slid continuously by with the even, gentle flow of a night bird's flight. But she very nearly fell when she tripped over one of the ventilator pipes, which spread out across the beaten earth floor delivering their blasts of harsh air to the little forges beside the machines. And that was what he showed her first: he opened the air vent into one of the furnaces and big flames fanned out from all four sides, making a dazzling, jagged-edged collar barely tinted with red; the light was so bright that the workmen's little lamps looked like spots of shade in sunlight. Then, raising his voice to explain, he moved on to the machines: the mechanical shears that ate through iron bars, biting off a piece each time they snapped shut and spitting out the bits behind, one at a time; the big, complicated bolt and rivet machines, which forged heads with one turn of their powerful screws; the trimming machines with cast-iron fly-wheels, spheres of cast-iron that beat at the air madly each time the machines were trimming a piece; the thread-cutting machines, worked by women, cutting threads on the bolts and their nuts, their gear-wheels of steel shining with oil as they clicked round. In this way she could follow the entire operation, from the iron bars propped against the walls to the finished bolts and rivets, heaped up in boxes in all the corners. She smiled and nodded to show she understood, but nevertheless she felt a bit on edge, uneasy at being so small and delicate in the midst of these big, rugged metal-working machines, and from time to time she'd turn round, chilled with fear, at the dull thud of a trimmer. She was growing accustomed to the darkness and could make out the places where motionless men watched over the breathless jigging of the fly-wheels, when a furnace suddenly released its collar of flame in a blaze of light.

And in spite of herself her gaze always went back up towards the ceiling, to the very life-blood of the machines, to the smooth flow of the belting, as with upturned eyes she watched its tremendous, silent power gliding past in the uncertain shadows beneath the roof.

Goujet, meanwhile, had stopped in front of one of the rivet machines. He stood there deep in thought, hanging his head, staring. The machine was forging forty-millimetre rivets with the placid ease of a giant. And in truth nothing could have been simpler. The stoker took the piece of iron from the furnace; the hammer-man placed it in the heading frame which a stream of water kept permanently wet so the steel would remain tempered; and that was that, the screw came down and the bolt fell out with its head as round as if it had been cast in a mould. In twelve hours this infernal machine produced hundreds of kilos of them. Goujet was not at all vindictive, but there were times when he'd gladly have picked up Fifine and bashed that iron contraption to bits, out of fury because its arms were stronger than his own. It filled him with real anguish which he was unable to reason away by telling himself that human flesh couldn't fight against iron. Certainly someday the machine would be the death of the manual worker; wages had already dropped from twelve to nine francs a day, and there was talk of further cuts; in fact, they weren't at all funny, these great brutes that turned out rivets and bolts as if they were making sausages. He gazed at this one in silence for a good three minutes with his brow furrowed and his handsome golden beard bristling threateningly. Then an expression of sweetness and resignation gradually softened his features. He turned to Gervaise who was close beside him, saying with a sad smile:

'That's got us beat alright, hasn't it! But perhaps one day it'll serve to bring happiness to everybody.'

Gervaise didn't care a hoot for everybody's happiness. She thought the machined bolts badly made.

'What I mean,' she cried eagerly, 'is that they're too perfect . . . I like yours better. You can at least see that they're the work of an artist.'

She made him very very happy by saying this, because for a moment he'd been afraid she might despise him, after seeing the machines. For indeed he might be stronger than Bec-Salé, alias Boit-sans-Soif, but the machines were stronger than him. When at last he parted from her in the yard, he was so exultant that he squeezed her wrists hard enough to break them.

Every Saturday the laundress went to the Goujets' home to deliver their washing. They still lived in the little house in the Rue Neuve de la Goutte-d'Or. Each month during the first year she'd regularly paid back twenty of the five hundred francs; in order to keep the accounts simple, they only totted everything up at the end of the month, and she'd add what was necessary to bring the amount up to twenty francs, because the Goujets' monthly laundry bill rarely exceeded seven or eight francs. So she'd paid off about half the sum when, one quarterly rent day, because some customers hadn't settled up as promised and she couldn't think what to do, she'd had to rush round to the Goujets' and borrow the rent from them. On two other occasions she'd also turned to them so she could pay her workers, with the result that the amount had gone back up again to four hundred and twenty-five francs. Now she no longer gave them a sou, but was simply paying off the debt by doing their washing. It wasn't that she was working less or that her business was going downhill. Quite the opposite. But she was often a bit short, money simply seemed to melt away and she was pleased when she could just make both ends meet. Lord, so long as you could get by, there wasn't anything to grumble about, was there? She was putting on weight, and giving way to all the little indulgences that went with getting fat, no longer finding the energy to be anxious about the future. Not to worry! The money would keep on rolling in, and hoarding made it rusty. But despite this Madame Goujet still treated Gervaise in a motherly way. Occasionally she'd lecture her gently, not on account of the money owed to her, but because she was fond of Gervaise and was afraid of seeing her go to the bad. As for her money, she never even mentioned it. In fact, on that subject she was the soul of tact.

It so happened that the day after Gervaise's visit to the forge was the last Saturday of the month. When she reached the Goujets', where she always insisted on going herself, her heavy basket had made her arms ache so badly that it took her a full two minutes to catch her breath. No one knows how much laundry weighs, especially when there's sheets.

'You're sure everything's here?' asked Madame Goujet.

She was very strict about that. She liked to get her laundry back with not a single piece missing, to keep things straight, as she put it. Another of her requirements was that the laundress should come the exact day that had been agreed on, and always at the same time; that way, nobody's time was wasted.

'Oh! It's all there,' answered Gervaise with a smile. 'You know I never leave anything behind.'

'That's true,' admitted Madame Goujet. 'You are picking up some little faults but that's not one of them yet.'

And, while the laundress emptied her basket and put the linen on the bed, the old lady sang her praises: she never burnt anything or tore anything like so many others did, or pulled off buttons with the iron; however she did use too much blue and she starched the shirt fronts too heavily.

'Here, this is just like cardboard,' she went on, making a shirt front crackle. 'My son doesn't complain, but it cuts into his neck . . . His neck'll be bleeding by the time we get back from Vincennes tomorrow.'

'Oh no, don't say that, please!' cried Gervaise, very upset. 'Dress shirts have to be a bit stiff, if you don't want to look as if you're wearing a rag. Think what gentlemen look like . . . I do all your things meself. My girls never touch 'em, and I take great care, really I do, I'd sooner do something over again ten times, because it's for you, I mean.'

She'd gone a bit pink, her voice faltering as she finished speaking. She was afraid of showing what pleasure she took in ironing Goujet's shirts herself. Of course she hadn't any dirty thoughts but nevertheless she did feel a bit ashamed.

'Oh, I'm not criticizing your work, you do everything quite perfectly, I know,' said Madame Goujet. 'Take this bonnet, for instance, it's a real gem. There's nobody else with your knack for making the embroidery stand out like that. And the goffering's so even! There, I can recognize your work instantly. If you only give a duster to an assistant to do, I can tell . . . So all I'm saying is that you should use a little less starch, please. Goujet has no wish to look like a gentleman.'

In the meantime she'd picked up the book and was crossing off the items. Everything was accounted for. When they added it all up and she saw that Gervaise was charging six sous for a bonnet, she protested, but then had to agree that actually it wasn't expensive, given today's prices: no, men's shirts five sous, women's drawers four sous, pillow cases a sou and a half, aprons a sou, no, it wasn't expensive, considering that lots of laundresses asked a half or even a whole sou more for all those things. Next Gervaise called out the items of dirty washing while the old lady listed them, and then she shoved it all into her basket, but she still didn't leave; she had a request to make that embarrassed her greatly.

'Madame Goujet,' she blurted out at last, 'if it's all the same to you, I'd be glad of the money for the washing, this month.'

As it happened, this time it was quite a large sum, the addition they'd just done together amounting to ten francs seven sous. Madame Goujet looked at her gravely for a moment. Then she said:

'Just as you like, my child. I don't want to refuse to give you this money if you need it . . . The only thing is, it's hardly the way to work off your debt; please believe I'm just thinking of you when I say that. You ought to be careful, really you ought.'

Hanging her head, Gervaise stammered a response to this rebuke. The ten francs would make up the money on a promissory note she'd signed for her coke dealer. But Madame Goujet waxed sterner on hearing the word 'note'. She cited herself as an example: she was cutting back her expenses, now that Goujet's daily wage had been reduced from twelve to nine francs. If you weren't prudent in your youth you'd starve in old age. She did not, however, tell Gervaise that the only reason she gave her her washing was to enable her to pay off her debt: she'd washed everything herself in the past, and she'd go back to doing her own washing if she was going to have to lay out sums like that on laundry. When Gervaise had the ten francs seven sous in her hand she thanked Madame Goujet and quickly left. Once out on the landing she breathed easily again and could have danced for joy, for she was already growing hardened to the worries and nastiness of money troubles, and

would remember nothing about them afterwards except the
satisfaction of solving them, until the next time.

It was that very Saturday that Gervaise had the oddest
encounter as she was going down the Goujets' stairs. She had
to stand to one side against the railing with her basket, to let a
tall bareheaded woman go past who was carrying on one hand,
on a bit of paper, a very fresh mackerel that was bleeding about
the gills. And lo and behold she recognized Virginie, the girl
whose skirts she'd pulled up in the washhouse. Each gave the
other a good stare. Gervaise closed her eyes, imagining for an
instant that she was about to get the mackerel right in her face.
But no, Virginie gave her a tight little smile. So then the
laundress, whose basket was blocking the stairs, felt impelled to
be polite.

'I beg your pardon,' she said.

'Don't mention it,' replied the tall brunette.

And they stood there in the middle of the staircase, chatting,
instantly reconciled though not venturing a single reference to
the past. Virginie, now twenty-nine, had become a very handsome woman, well built, with a rather long face framed by two
bands of jet-black hair. She told her story right away so there'd
be no doubt about her status: she'd been married that spring to
a former cabinet-maker who'd recently left the army and was
now trying to get an appointment in the police, because that
kind of position is more secure and more genteel. In fact she'd
just been out to buy him a mackerel.

'He adores mackerel,' she said. 'You really have to spoil the
brutes, don't you? . . . But do come on up. You'll see our place
. . . We're in a draught here.'

When Gervaise had also told the story of her marriage and
explained that she'd lived in those rooms once and had even
had her baby girl there, Virginie pressed her still more eagerly
to come up. It's always a pleasure, going back to a place where
you've been happy. For five years she herself had lived across
the river, in Gros-Caillou.* That was where she'd met her
husband, when he was in the army. But she was bored there
and used to dream of returning to the Goutte-d'Or neighbourhood where she knew everybody. And so she'd been living for
two weeks in the room opposite the Goujets. Of course

everything was still in a terrible mess; they'd get it straight bit by bit.

Then, on the landing, they finally told each other their names.

'Madame Coupeau.'

'Madame Poisson.'

And, from then on, they always called each other by their full titles, Madame Coupeau and Madame Poisson, just for the pleasure of being proper married ladies now, they who in the past had known one another in rather less orthodox circumstances. However Gervaise, deep down, still felt some mistrust. The tall brunette might perhaps be behaving in this friendly way so she could get her own back more easily for that washhouse thrashing, by plotting some devilishly two-faced scheme. Gervaise told herself she'd be on her guard. For the moment Virginie was being so nice that she must be nice too.

Upstairs in the room Poisson, the husband, a pasty-faced man of thirty-five with a red moustache and small beard, was sitting working at a table near the window. He was making little boxes. His only tools were a knife, a saw no bigger than a nail-file, and a pot of glue. He was using wood which came from old cigar boxes, thin strips of unpolished mahogany on which he carved fret-work and decorations of extraordinary delicacy. All day long, from one year's end to the other, he made the same kind of box, eight centimetres by six. But he'd embellish it with inlay, or think up a new kind of cover, or add compartments. He did it for amusement, as a way of killing time until his appointment to the police came through. All that remained of his former trade of cabinet-maker was this passion for little boxes. He didn't sell his work, he gave it away to acquaintances.

Poisson stood up and politely greeted Gervaise, whom his wife introduced as an old friend. But he was no talker, and promptly picked up his small saw again. From time to time, however, he cast a glance at the mackerel which was lying on the chest of drawers. Gervaise was very happy to see her former home again; she described how her furniture had been arranged and pointed out the place on the floor where she'd had her baby. But wasn't it funny how things worked out! When they'd lost sight of each other, long ago, they'd never have dreamt that they'd meet like this, living one after the other in the same room. Virginie added a few further details about herself and her husband; he'd inherited a little legacy from an aunt and would very probably set her up in business one day; for the present, though, she was continuing with her sewing, running up a dress now and again. Eventually, after a good half-hour, the laundress said she must leave. Poisson hardly turned round. Virginie, who saw her out of the door, promised to return her visit, and of course in any case she meant to give her their laundry to do. And as Virginie was keeping her chatting on the landing, Gervaise got the idea that she wanted to talk about Lantier and her sister Adèle the burnisher. The thought gave her quite a turn. But not a word was uttered about that upsetting subject, and their parting exchanges were as friendly as could be.

' 'Bye for now, Madame Coupeau.'

'Be seeing you, Madame Poisson.'

That was the beginning of a close friendship. By the end of a week Virginie never passed in front of Gervaise's shop without going in; she'd stop there and chat for hours and hours until a silent, putty-faced Poisson, worried that Virginie might have been knocked down in the street, came looking for her. Gervaise, seeing the dressmaker like this every day, soon became obsessed by a strange idea: she couldn't hear her start a sentence without imagining that she was about to speak of Lantier; she simply couldn't prevent herself thinking of Lantier the whole time that Virginie was there. It was really very silly, because after all she couldn't care less about Lantier and Adèle and what had become of them both; she never ever asked a question, indeed she didn't even feel any urge to hear news of them. No, it was something quite beyond her control. The idea of them was fixed in her head the way you keep on humming an irritating tune that simply won't leave you in peace. In any case she didn't bear Virginie any ill-will on that account, because it certainly wasn't her fault. She really enjoyed her company, and would call her back time and again before letting her go home.

Meanwhile winter had arrived, the fourth winter the Coupeaus had spent in the Rue de la Goutte-d'Or. December and

January were particularly severe that year. There was a terribly hard frost. After New Year's Day, the snow lay in the street for three weeks without melting. It didn't stop them working, quite the opposite, because winter is the nicest time of year in the laundry business. It was ever so cosy in the shop! You never saw any icicles on the windows, like those on the grocer's and the hosier's across the road. The stove, stuffed full of coke, kept the place as hot as a bath; the washing steamed away and it might have been the middle of summer; and it was really comfy with the doors shut and everywhere warm, so very warm that you could have dropped off with your eyes open. Gervaise would say with a laugh that she could imagine she was in the country. And indeed the carriages no longer made a sound as they rolled along on the snow; you could hardly hear the tread of the passers-by; only the voices of children rose up in the great frozen stillness, the clamour of a band of kids who'd made a big slide along the gutter outside the farrier's. Sometimes she'd go over to one of the glass panes in the door and, wiping away the steam with her hand, look out to see what the locals were up to in this fiendishly cold weather; but not so much as a nose ever emerged from any of the nearby shops; the neighbourhood, blanketed by snow, seemed to have become quite stand-offish, and she'd only exchange a little nod with the coal lady next door, who'd been going round bare-headed and grinning from ear to ear ever since the hard frost began.

What was especially nice, in this filthy weather, was having a good hot coffee at midday. The assistants certainly couldn't grumble: the boss made it very strong with hardly any chicory in it: not at all like Madame Fauconnier's coffee, which was absolute dishwater. Only, when Maman Coupeau volunteered to pour the water over the grounds it took forever, because she'd doze off beside the kettle. So after lunch the assistants would do a bit of ironing while waiting for their coffee.

And indeed, on the day after Twelfth Night, half-past twelve had struck and the coffee still wasn't ready. That day it just wouldn't go through. Maman Coupeau was tapping the filter with a little spoon; you could hear the drops falling one by one, slowly, not going any faster at all.

'Leave it alone,' said Clémence. 'It makes it muddy . . . Today we'll be having food as well as drink, I'm sure.'

Clémence was doing up a man's shirt, separating out its pleats with the end of her nail. She had a frightful cold, her eyes were swollen and her throat rent by fits of coughing which made her double up over the edge of the work-table. But in spite of this she hadn't even tied a scarf round her neck, and was shivering in her dress of thin cheap wool. Near her, Madame Putois, enveloped in flannel and wrapped up to her ears, was ironing a petticoat, turning it over on the dress board which had its narrow end propped on the back of a chair; they'd thrown a sheet underneath to stop the petticoat getting dirty when it brushed the floor. Gervaise took up half the work-table all by herself with some embroidered muslin curtains she was ironing, her outstretched arms moving the iron straight up and down to avoid making creases. All of a sudden she raised her head at the sound of the coffee running noisily. That cross-eyed Augustine had made a hole in the coffee grounds by pushing a spoon into the filter.

'Stop it, will you!' shouted Gervaise. 'Whatever's got into you? We'll be drinking mud, now.'

Maman Coupeau had set up five glasses in a row on a free corner of the work-table. The assistants put aside their work. The boss always poured the coffee herself, after placing two lumps of sugar in each glass. It was the moment they looked forward to every day. On this occasion, as each one was taking her glass and squatting down on a little stool in front of the stove, the street door opened and in came Virginie, shivering all over.

'Well my dears,' she said, 'it cuts you right in two! I can't feel my ears. The cold's something fierce!'

'Oh, it's Madame Poisson!' cried Gervaise. 'Lovely, you've come at the right moment . . . You must have some coffee with us.'

'My word, I won't say no . . . Just crossing the street, you get winter in your bones.'

Luckily there was some coffee left. Maman Coupeau fetched a sixth glass and Gervaise let Virginie help herself to sugar, out of politeness. The assistants moved along and made a little space for her near the stove. She shivered for a minute or two, her nose red, clasping her stiffened hands tightly round her glass to warm them. She'd just come from the grocer's, where you froze simply waiting for a little bit of cheese. And she exclaimed at how hot it was in the shop; really, it was like walking into an oven, it was enough to wake the dead, it made your skin tingle so wonderfully. Then, as she thawed, she stretched out her long legs. And all six of them slowly sipped their coffee, surrounded by their interrupted work, in the stuffy dampness from the drying laundry. Only Maman Coupeau and Virginie were on chairs; the others, on their little stools, seemed to be sitting on the floor; indeed cross-eyed Augustine had pulled over a corner of the sheet from under the petticoat and was stretched out on it. At first they didn't say anything but sat with their noses in their glasses, enjoying the coffee.

'It is good, after all,' declared Clémence.

But a coughing spasm nearly made her choke. She rested her head against the wall so she could cough harder.

'You've not half got a nasty one,' said Virginie. 'Wherever did you catch that?'

'Who knows!' replied Clémence, wiping her face with her sleeve. 'It must have been the other evening. There was a couple o' women having a set-to at the entrance to the Grand-Balcon. I wanted to see so I stayed there, in the snow. My, what a punch-up! I nearly died laughing. One of 'em had her nose almost torn off, there was blood streaming on to the ground. When the other one—a great tall skinny thing like me—saw the blood, she cleared out like greased lightning . . . An' then that night I started to cough. But also men are such fat-heads, aren't they, the way they pinch all the blankets when they sleep with a woman an' leave you uncovered all night long . . .'

'Nice goings-on,' muttered Madame Putois. 'You're killing yourself, my dear.'

'An' suppose I am killin' meself, so what, if I like it? . . . Life's not that wonderful anyway. You knock yourself out the whole bleeding day to earn fifty-five sous, you're boiling all the time because of the stove, no, really, I've had it up to here!

. . . Anyway, this cold won't do me the favour of finishing me off, it'll go just the same way it came.'

There was a silence. That no-good Clémence, who in sleazy dance-halls was always the first out on the floor, flinging herself about and shrieking her head off, at work gave them all the blues with her ideas about snuffing it. Gervaise knew what she was like and just said:

'When you've been out on the tiles you're never a ray of sunshine, the morning after, are you?'

The fact was that Gervaise would rather they didn't talk about women having fights. Because of the thrashing in the washhouse, it bothered her when she and Virginie were together and the talk turned to kicks on the shins and slaps on the face. And indeed Virginie was looking at her and smiling.

'Oh!' she murmured, 'I saw two women going at it yesterday. Were they ever bashing each other about . . .'

'Who was it?' asked Madame Putois.

'The midwife down the end of the street and that girl who works for her, you know, the short, fair one . . . A real bitch, that girl. She was yelling at the midwife: "Yes, yes, you got rid of that baby for the fruitshop woman, and I'll tell the police if you don't stump up." And she was carrying on like anything, you should have seen! Then the midwife landed her such a wallop, wham, right on the snout. And so the bloody little tramp went for her mistress's eyes, and scratched her and pulled her hair out; oh, it was first rate! The pork-butcher had to prize her out of the girl's paws.'

The assistants laughed obligingly. Then they all took a greedy little swallow of coffee.

'You think it's true, do you, that she got rid of a baby?' Clémence went on.

'Oh yes, the story was all over the neighbourhood,' Virginie replied. 'But I wasn't there, you know . . . Anyway, it's part of the job. They all get rid of 'em.'

'Really,' said Madame Putois, 'how can they be so silly as to trust those women. Letting yourself be mauled about! No thanks! . . . But you know there is a foolproof way. Every evening you drink a glass of holy water while making three

signs of the cross with your thumb on your belly. It just goes
away like a bit o' wind.'

Maman Coupeau, who everyone had supposed was asleep,
shook her head in disagreement. She knew a different way,
which really was infallible. You must eat a hard-boiled egg
every hour and put spinach leaves on your loins. The four
women didn't even smile. But cross-eyed Augustine, who
would roar with laughter all on her own without anybody ever
knowing why, made the sound like a hen clucking that was her
laugh. They'd forgotten her. Gervaise picked up the petticoat
and saw her on the sheet, rolling about like a little pig with her
legs in the air. Giving her a slap, she pulled her off the sheet
and made her stand up. Whatever was she laughing at, the silly
goose? What business had *she* listening to what the grown-ups
were saying? She was to leave that very minute for the
Batignolles and deliver the washing for a friend of Madame
Lerat's. As she spoke, the laundress was putting the basket on
to the girl's arm and pushing her towards the door. Grousing
and whining, Augustine set off, dragging her feet in the snow.

Maman Coupeau, Madame Putois and Clémence, meanwhile,
were debating the efficacy of hard-boiled eggs and spinach
leaves. So then Virginie, who'd been sitting dreaming with her
coffee glass in her hand, said very softly:

'Lord, you fight, then you kiss and make up, that's always
how it is when your heart's in the right place . . .'

And, leaning towards Gervaise and smiling:

'No, really, I don't bear you any ill-will . . . That business in
the washhouse, remember?'

The laundress was terribly embarrassed. This was what she'd
been afraid of. Now, she guessed, the subject of Lantier and
Adèle was bound to come up. The stove was roaring away, its
red-hot flue radiating more and more heat. In the drowsy
warmth the assistants, lingering over their coffee so they'd get
back to work as late as possible, were staring out at the snow in
the street, their faces languid and greedy. They'd reached the
stage of confidences; they were talking about what they'd have
done if they'd had ten thousand francs a year; they wouldn't
have done anything at all, they'd have spent whole afternoons
like this, keeping warm and letting work go to hell. Virginie had

moved closer to Gervaise so the others wouldn't be able to hear.
And Gervaise felt overcome by lethargy, perhaps because it was
far too hot, so weak and lethargic that she hadn't the strength
to turn the conversation; she was even waiting for what Virginie
was about to say, her heart bursting with a pleasurable though
unacknowledged emotion.

'I hope I'm not upsetting you, am I?' went on the dressmaker. 'Time and again it's been on the tip of me tongue.
However, now the subject's come up . . . It's something we can
chat about, isn't it? . . . Oh, of course not, I've no hard feelings
against you for what happened. Word of honour! I've not been
nursing a grudge on that account!'

She swished round the remains of her coffee in her glass so
as to get all the sugar, then drank the three drops, making a
little sucking sound with her lips. Gervaise still waited, her
heart in her mouth, wondering whether Virginie really had
forgiven that thrashing as completely as she claimed, for she
could see yellow glints gleaming in her black eyes. The great
big vixen must just have stowed her resentment safely away for
future reference.

'You had every excuse,' she went on. 'You'd just had a mean
trick played on you, a bloody filthy trick . . . After all, fair's fair.
I'd have used a knife if I'd been you.'

She drank three more drops, sucking at the edge of the glass.
And abandoning her drawl, she added rapidly, without pausing:

'What's more it didn't bring them any luck, Lord knows! No,
no luck at all! . . . They'd gone to live miles away, over by La
Glacière, in a dirty street where you're always knee-deep in
mud. A couple of days later I went over in the morning to have
lunch with them; a hell of a long omnibus ride, let me tell you!
Well, my dear, I found they were already having a set-to. Yes,
truly, as I went in they were clouting one another. How about
that for a pair of lovebirds! . . . Adèle's not worth the rope to
hang her with, you know. The fact that she's my sister doesn't
stop me saying that she's a real bitch. She's done the dirty on
me time and again; it would take too long to tell you everything,
and anyway that's for us to settle between ourselves . . . As for
Lantier, well you know him, he's certainly no angel either. A
real little gent, isn't he, as'll have the skin off your bum over

nothing at all! *And* he clenches his fist when he slugs you . . .
So they were roughing each other up good and proper. You
could hear 'em bashing one another as you went up the stairs.
The police actually came one day. Lantier had wanted olive-oil
soup—filthy stuff they eat in the south—and as Adèle thought
it disgusting, they'd thrown everything at each other, the bottle
of oil, the saucepan and the soup tureen, the whole works; in
fact, that dust-up was the talk of the neighbourhood.'

She told Gervaise about other rows, there was no stopping
her on the subject, she knew things about the couple that would
make your hair stand on end. Gervaise listened to the whole of
this tale without saying a word, her face pale, a nervous twitch
like a little smile at the corners of her lips. It was almost seven
years since she'd heard any mention of Lantier. Never would
she have believed that Lantier's name, murmured in her ear like
this, would have given her such a sensation of warmth in the
pit of her stomach. No, she'd had no idea she was so curious
to hear what had become of that wretch who'd treated her so
abominably. She could no longer be jealous, now, of Adèle, but
just the same she laughed to herself when she thought of the
couple bashing each other about, she imagined that girl's body
covered with bruises and felt avenged and amused. So she could
have stayed there all night long listening to Virginie's stories.
She asked no questions because she didn't want to appear that
interested. It was as if a blank in her life had been suddenly
filled in; her past, now, was directly connected to her present.

Virginie, meanwhile, had stuck her nose back into her glass;
she sucked at the sugar with half-closed eyes. So then Gervaise,
realizing that she ought to say something, assumed an air of
indifference and asked:

'And they're still living out at La Glacière?'

'Oh no!' answered the other; 'didn't I tell you? . . . It's a week
now since they split up. One fine day Adèle up and went, taking
all her stuff, and Lantier didn't go after her, you can take it
from me.'

The laundress gave a faint cry and repeated:

'They've split up!'

'Who's split up?' asked Clémence, breaking off her conversation with Mamam Coupeau and Madame Putois.

'Nobody,' said Virginie, 'people you don't know.'

But she was staring hard at Gervaise and thinking she looked ever so upset. She moved closer, seeming to take a malicious delight in going on with her stories. Then, quite suddenly, she asked Gervaise what she would do if Lantier started hanging round her again; for after all, men were so funny, Lantier was quite capable of returning to his first love. Gervaise drew herself up very straight and became very decisive and dignified. She was a married woman, she'd show Lantier the door, and that'd be that. There could never again be anything between them, not even so much as a hand-shake. Really, her heart would have to be made of stone for her ever to look at that man again.

'Of course I know that Étienne's his,' she said, 'and it's a bond I can't break. If Lantier wants to see Étienne I'll send him the kid, because it's impossible to stop a father loving his child. But as for me, well you see, Madame Poisson, I'd sooner be cut into tiny little bits than let him touch me with the tip of his finger. It's all over.'

When she uttered these last words she traced a cross in the air, as if to seal her oath for ever. And, wanting to put a stop to the conversation, she made a show of coming to with a start and shouted at the assistants:

'Hey, you lot! D'you think the clothes are going to iron themselves? . . . What a lazy bunch! C'mon, get going!'

But, drowsy and listless, the assistants didn't hurry, sitting with their arms limp in their laps, an empty glass with a few remaining coffee grounds still clasped in one hand. They went on chatting.

'It was that little Célestine,' Clémence was saying. 'I knew her. She was cracked about cat hairs . . . You know, she could see cat hairs everywhere, an' she was always rolling her tongue round like this, 'cos she thought her mouth was full of cat hairs.'

'Well,' went on Madame Putois, 'I was friendly with this woman who had a tapeworm . . . Oh, those creatures aren't half choosy! . . . It would twist up her insides when she didn't give it chicken. Just imagine, the husband earned seven francs, and it all went on treats for the worm . . .'

'I'd have cured her straight away, I would,' Maman Coupeau chipped in. 'Lord, you just swallow a grilled mouse. It poisons the worm on the spot.'

Gervaise herself had slipped back into her state of happy idleness. But, with a shake, she got to her feet. Oh well! A whole afternoon gone just lazing about! That was no way to make your fortune! She was the first to return to her curtains; but she found they were stained with coffee, and had to rub the spot with a wet cloth before starting ironing again. The assistants stretched themselves in front of the stove and hunted grumpily for their iron-holders. The minute Clémence moved, it brought on such a dreadful fit of coughing she nearly coughed up her tongue; then she finished her man's shirt and pinned the sleeves and the collar. Madame Putois had gone back to her petticoat.

'Well bye-bye,' said Virginie. 'I came out to buy a piece of cheese. Poisson'll be thinking the cold's turned me into a block of ice.'

But she'd only gone three steps along the pavement when she reopened the door to shout that she could see Augustine at the bottom of the street, sliding about on the ice with some boys. The little wretch had been gone two good hours. She ran up red-faced and out of breath with her basket on her arm, a lump of snow sticking to her coil of hair, and listened to her scolding with a shifty look, saying you couldn't walk because of the ice. Some kid must have shoved bits of ice into her pockets as a joke because a quarter of an hour later water began spouting out of them on to the shop floor.

Every afternoon was like that now. The shop became the refuge of everyone in the neighbourhood who couldn't bear the cold. The entire Rue de la Goutte-d'Or knew that it was cosy in there. There were always a bunch of women nattering, getting nice and warm by the stove, their skirts pulled up to their knees as they enjoyed a good gossip. Gervaise felt proud of this cosy warmth and she encouraged people to come in, she held court, as the Lorilleux and the Boches nastily put it. The truth was that she was kind and helpful, so much so that she'd bring in any of the poor she saw shivering outside. She took a particular liking to an old man of seventy, a former house-painter who lived in a garret in the building, where he was slowly dying of cold and hunger; he'd lost his three sons in the Crimea,* and, for the past two years, now that he could no longer hold a paintbrush, had been existing on whatever came his way. As soon as Gervaise caught sight of Père Bru stamping about in the snow to warm himself up she'd call him in and make room for him by the stove; often she'd even force him to eat a piece of bread and cheese. Père Bru, with his bent back and white bread and face as wrinkled as an old apple, would sit for hours without saying a word, listening to the crackling of the coke. Perhaps he was going over in his memory his fifty years of working on a ladder, half a century spent painting doors and whitewashing ceilings all over Paris.

'Well now, Père Bru,' the laundress would sometimes ask him, 'what are you thinking about?'

'Nothing, all sorts of things,' he'd answer in a dazed way.

The assistants teased him, saying he must be in love. But he wouldn't hear them, sinking back into silence and meditative gloom.

From then on, Virginie often spoke of Lantier to Gervaise. She seemed to enjoy making Gervaise think about her former lover, just for the pleasure of embarrassing her with her conjectures. One day she said she'd met him; but, as the laundress remained silent, Virginie said nothing more, and not until the following day did she let slip that he'd talked at length about Gervaise, and very tenderly. Gervaise was greatly troubled by these whispered exchanges in a corner of the shop. Lantier's name still brought on a burning sensation in the pit of her stomach, as if that man had left something of himself there, under her skin. Of course she didn't have any doubts about herself and was resolved to remain virtuous, because virtue and happiness go hand in hand. Nor did she think of Coupeau in this connection since as far as her husband was concerned, she had nothing to reproach herself with, not even in thought. It was of the smith that she kept thinking, with a faltering, uneasy heart. It seemed to her that the rekindling of her memories of Lantier, this slow repossessing of her by him, was making her unfaithful to Goujet and to their unspoken love, with its sweet companionship. She lived through some

miserable days, believing she was wronging her dear friend.
She'd have liked to feel affection for nobody but him, apart
from her own family. All this engaged the finest part of her
being, far above the base thoughts at which her cheeks flamed
with those blushes Virginie was watching for.

When spring came, Gervaise went often to see Goujet. She
could no longer just sit and think about nothing, now, without
the idea of her first lover instantly filling her mind; she pictured
him leaving Adèle, putting his clothes back into their old trunk
and returning to her with the trunk on the roof of the cab.
When she went out she'd be overcome by sudden, ridiculous
panics, right there in the street; she'd fancy she could hear
Lantier's step behind her and, trembling, not daring to turn
round, she'd imagine she could feel his hands grasp her about
the waist. He must certainly be on the lookout for her; one of
these days he'd pounce on her; and the thought brought her out
in a cold sweat, because he'd be sure to kiss her on the ear the
way he used to do, in the past, to tease her. It was this kiss that
terrified her; it deafened her, already, filling her head with a
buzzing through which she could hear nothing but the heavy
pounding of her heart. So, whenever she was gripped by these
terrors, the forge was her only refuge; there she'd regain her
smiling tranquility under the protection of Goujet, whose
ringing hammer drove away her bad dreams.

That was such a happy spring! The laundress took special
pains over her customer in the Rue des Portes-Blanches; she
always delivered her washing personally because this errand,
every Friday, was a perfect excuse to go by the Rue Marcadet
and drop in at the forge. As soon as she turned the corner she'd
feel as nimble and light-hearted as if she were going on a picnic,
there among those strips of waste land bordered by grey
factories; the road, black with coal dust, the plumes of steam
over the roofs, charmed her as much as a mossy path winding
away through clumps of dense greenery in a country wood; and
she loved the dim skyline, striped by tall factory chimneys, and
the heights of Montmartre blocking the sky with its chalky
houses pierced by their evenly-spaced windows. Then she'd
slow down as she drew near, jumping over the puddles and
finding it fun to pick her way through the deserted muddle of

the demolition yard. In the distance, even at midday, she could
see the forge glowing with light. Her heart would leap to the
rhythm of the hammers. She'd be very flushed when she went
in, with the little blond curls at her neck flying about, as if she
were a woman coming to meet her lover. Goujet would be
waiting for her, bare-armed and bare-chested, and on those
days he'd be hammering more loudly on the anvil so as to be
heard from further away. He'd know she was there, and would
greet her with a great silent laugh in his golden beard. But she
didn't want to interrupt his work, she'd beg him to take up his
hammer again because she loved him all the more when he
swung it with his big, heavily-muscled arms. She'd go over to
Étienne where he was working the bellows and give him a little
pat on the cheek, and then she'd stay there for an hour,
watching the bolts being made. They wouldn't exchange ten
words. They couldn't have better satisfied their love had they
been together in a room with the door double-locked. The
sniggering of Bec-Salé, alias Boit-sans-Soif, didn't bother them
at all, for they no longer even heard it. After she'd been there
about a quarter of an hour she'd begin to feel a bit breathless;
the heat, the strong smell, the smoke rising up made her dizzy,
while the dull thudding shook her from head to foot. There was
nothing more she could desire, her pleasure was complete. Had
Goujet clasped her in his arms it couldn't have moved her more
deeply. She'd step nearer to him, so as to feel the gust of air
from his hammer on her cheek and be part of the blow he
was striking. When sparks stung her soft-skinned hands she
wouldn't pull them back, on the contrary, she'd delight in the
fiery rain that made her skin smart. He, of course, sensed the
happiness she found there; he'd save the difficult tasks for
Friday, wooing her with all his strength and all his skill; he put
his whole being into his work, almost rending the anvil apart,
panting, his loins vibrating with the joy he was giving her. All
through the spring their love filled the forge with a tempestuous
thunder. They lived their idyll amid toiling giants and blazing
fires, in that great shed which would shake right through, even
to its creaking, soot-blackened frame. Every piece of the iron
he pounded and moulded into shape, as if it were red sealing-
wax, bore the rough imprint of their love. Each Friday when

Gervaise left Gueule-d'Or she'd walk slowly back up the Rue des Poissonniers, satisfied, weary, at peace in mind and body.

Little by little her fear of Lantier subsided and her common sense returned. At this period she would still have been very happy but for Coupeau, who was definitely going to the bad. One day as she was coming back from the forge, she thought she recognized Coupeau in Père Colombe's Assommoir, knocking back rounds of rotgut with Mes-Bottes, Bibi-la-Grillade and Bec-Salé, alias Boit-sans-Soif. She walked quickly past, so she wouldn't seem to be spying on them. But then she turned round: yes, it really was Coupeau, tossing his little glass of rotgut down his throat with a very practised air. So he was lying, he *was* on spirits now! She went home in despair, filled afresh with all her former horror of spirits. Wine she could excuse, because wine makes a workman strong; spirits on the other hand were vile things, poisons that destroyed a man's appetite for food. Oh, surely the government ought to prevent people producing that filth!

When she reached the Rue de la Goutte-d'Or she found the whole building in turmoil. Her assistants had left the work-table and were in the courtyard, looking upwards. She questioned Clémence.

'Old man Bijard's beating up his wife,' the girl told her. 'He was waiting for her in the entryway, pissed as a newt, to catch her when she came back from the washhouse . . . He forced her to climb the stairs, punching her the whole way, and now he's up there knocking her about in their room . . . There, can't you hear the screaming?'

Gervaise raced up the stairs. She was fond of her washer-woman, Madame Bijard, who was a very brave woman. She hoped she could stop the beating. When she got to the sixth floor she found the door to the room was open; there were some tenants on the landing, shouting, while Madame Boche stood in the doorway screaming:

'Stop it, stop it this minute! . . . We're going for the police, d'you hear!'

Not a soul dared go into the room because they all knew that Bijard was like a mad beast when he was drunk. In fact he was never really sober. On the rare occasions when he worked, he'd stand a litre bottle of spirits beside his locksmith's vice and take a swig from it every half-hour. That was what he lived on now, and he'd have gone up in flames like straw if you'd held a match to his mouth.

'But we can't let her be butchered!' said Gervaise, trembling all over.

And she went in. The attic room, though very clean, was cold and stark; Bijard's boozing had stripped it bare, for he sold the very sheets off the bed for drink. In the fight the table had been shoved right against the window and the two chairs overturned with their legs in the air. On the floor in the middle of the room lay Madame Bijard; her skirts were still soaking wet from the washhouse and clung to her thighs, her hair was pulled down, she was bleeding and giving great throaty groans, long-drawn-out "ohs!" each time Bijard kicked her. First he'd knocked her down with his fists; now he was stamping on her.

'Ah, you bitch! . . . You bitch! . . . You bitch! . . .' he kept grunting hoarsely, punctuating every kick with the word, working himself into a frenzy with the repetition, kicking harder as his voice grew hoarser.

Then his voice gave out but he went on kicking dully, stupidly, standing stiffly in his tattered smock and overalls, his face purple under his filthy beard, his bald pate covered with big red blotches. Out on the landing the neighbours were saying that he was beating her because she'd refused to give him a franc that morning. Boche's voice could be heard at the bottom of the stairs. He was calling to Madame Boche, shouting:

'Come on down, let 'em kill each other, it'll be good riddance!'

Père Bru had followed Gervaise into the room. The two of them tried to reason with the locksmith and get him over to the door. But he turned on them, quite silent, foaming at the mouth; in his pale, alcohol-inflamed eyes there blazed a murderous light. The laundress had her wrist badly mauled and the old workman was thrown against the table. On the floor Madame Bijard lay breathing more noisily, with her mouth wide open and her eyes closed. Bijard, now, was missing her when he kicked; he kept on trying frantically, kicking wide of his target, frenzied and blind with rage, even catching his own body with blows aimed into the thin air. And throughout this murderous scene Gervaise could see, in a corner of the room, little four-year-old Lalie watching her father as he battered her mother. The child was holding her recently-weaned sister Henriette in her arms, as if to protect her. Lalie stood there, her head tied up in a bit of printed calico, looking very pale and serious. The gaze of her big dark eyes was unwavering and deeply thoughtful, without a tear.

Eventually Bijard tripped over a chair and fell his length on to the floor; he was left there to snore while Père Bru helped Gervaise lift up Madame Bijard. She was now crying bitterly; Lalie, who'd moved closer, watched her mother cry, as if accustomed to such things and already resigned to them. When the laundress went downstairs again through the now quiet building she could still see that gaze, the gaze of a four-year-old child, as serious and unafraid as the gaze of a grown woman.

'Monsieur Coupeau's across there on the pavement,' Clémence shouted as soon as she caught sight of her. 'He looks absolutely plastered!'

Coupeau was actually just crossing the road. He very nearly smashed his shoulder into a pane of glass as he stumbled against the door. He was dead white from drink, with clenched teeth and a pinched look to his nose. And Gervaise instantly recognized the Assommoir's rotgut in the polluted blood that blanched his skin. She wanted to laugh about it and help him to lie down, as she always did when too much wine had made him a bit merry. But, pushing her aside without uttering a syllable, he raised his fist at her as he passed by on his way to bed. He was just like the other one, the drunkard who was snoring away upstairs, worn out with slugging. Gervaise felt an icy chill run through her as, stricken to the heart, she thought about men, about her husband and Goujet and Lantier, and despaired of ever being happy.

CHAPTER VII

GERVAISE'S saint's day was the 19th of June. The Coupeaus
spent money like water on these occasions, celebrating with
binges which left you round as a barrel, your belly stuffed full
for the week. Everyone's spare cash was scraped together. In
that household, the minute they'd saved up a few sous, they
blew them on food. They added imaginary saint's days to the
calender just as an excuse for a real spread. Virginie was all for
Gervaise cramming herself with goodies. When you've a man
who boozes it all away it serves him right, doesn't it, if you
don't let everything you've got be poured down his gullet, but
line your own stomach first. Since your money disappeared
anyway, it might as well go into the butcher's pocket as the
wine merchant's. And Gervaise, greedier than ever, readily
went along with this excuse. It couldn't be helped if they no
longer saved a bleeding sou: it was all Coupeau's fault. She had
put on even more weight and her limp was worse, because her
leg seemed to be getting shorter as it grew fatter.

That year they started talking about the party a month in
advance. Licking their lips in anticipation, they considered what
dishes they might have. The whole shop was absolutely dying
for a binge. It must be a bleeding knock-out of a spree,
something really different and damned good because—Lord
knows!—it's not every day a treat comes your way. Gervaise's
big problem was to decide who to invite; she wanted twelve at
table, no more, no less. Herself, her husband, Maman Coupeau,
Madame Lerat, that already made four from the family. She'd
have the Goujets and the Poissons as well. At first she thought
she certainly would not invite her assistants, Madame Putois
and Clémence, in case it made them too familiar; however, as
the party was always being discussed in front of them and they
looked so down in the mouth, in the end she said they could
come. Four and four's eight, and two's ten. Then, since she was
dead set on having twelve, she made it up with the Lorilleux,
who of late had been hanging round her; at least, it was
arranged that the Lorilleux would come down for the dinner
and they would all agree to let bygones be bygones over a glass.

After all, you can't keep family rows going for ever. And then, the thought of the party softened everyone's heart. You just couldn't miss a chance like that. The only thing was, when the Boches heard of the planned reconciliation, they promptly made up to Gervaise, all politeness and fawning smiles; so they had to be invited to the meal as well. There! That would make it fourteen, not counting the children. Never had she given such a dinner, and it made her feel all fluttery and triumphant.

As it happened, the anniversary fell on a Monday. This was a bit of luck: Gervaise could count on the Sunday afternoon to start the cooking. On the Saturday, as the assistants were dashing through the ironing, a long discussion took place in the shop to settle once and for all what they were going to eat. Only one dish had been decided on, three weeks ago: a fat roast goose. Their eyes glazed over with greed as they talked about it. The goose had even been bought already. Maman Coupeau went to fetch it so that Clémence and Madame Putois could feel its weight. They exclaimed at how huge it seemed, with its coarse skin swelling out over yellow fat.

'What about boiled beef before the goose?' said Gervaise. 'Soup and a bit of boiled beef, that's always good . . . Then we must have something with a sauce.'

Clémence suggested rabbit, but no, they ate that all the time, everyone was sick to death of rabbit. Gervaise fancied something classier. When Madame Putois mentioned veal in white sauce, they looked at one another with widening smiles. Now that *was* an idea: nothing could be more impressive than a blanquette of veal.

'After that,' resumed Gervaise, 'we'd still want something else with a sauce.'

Maman Coupeau thought of fish. But the others made a face, banging their irons down harder. No one liked fish; it didn't fill you up and there were all those bones. Cross-eyed Augustine dared to mention she was fond of skate, but Clémence snapped at her to shut up. Finally, when Gervaise had hit on chine of pork with potatoes, and they were all smiling broadly again, Virginie burst into the shop, her face flushed scarlet.

'You've come just at the right moment!' cried Gervaise, 'Maman Coupeau, show her the bird.'

Once again Maman Coupeau fetched the fat goose, and Virginie had to weigh it in her hands. She exclaimed. Christ! it wasn't half heavy! But she quickly put it down on the edge of the work-table, between a petticoat and a pile of shirts. Her mind was on something else, and she dragged Gervaise off into the back room.

'Listen, love,' said Virginie in a hurried whisper, 'I've come to warn you . . . You'll never guess who I bumped into down the street? Lantier, my pet! He's prowling about over there, all eyes . . . So I came here as fast as I could. It gave me quite a turn—on your account, I mean.'

Gervaise had gone white as a sheet. What could that wretch want with her? And what's more he'd turned up bang in the middle of the preparations for the party. She'd never had any luck, she couldn't enjoy a simple pleasure in peace. But Virginie told her she was very silly to get in a state about it. Heavens, if Lantier took it into his head to follow her, she should call a policeman and have him put away. Since her husband had joined the police a month before, Virginie had got very high and mighty and talked about arresting everybody. She went on to declare in a loud voice that she wished someone would pinch her bottom in the street, just so she could take the cheeky beggar to the station and hand him over to Poisson herself, and Gervaise with a gesture had to beg her to be quiet because the girls were all ears. Going back into the shop, and trying to sound very calm, Gervaise said:

'Now, what sort of veg?'

'How about peas with bacon?' said Virginie. 'I'd be happy with that and nothing else.'

'Yes, yes, peas with bacon,' the others all agreed, while Augustine, greatly excited, kept ramming the poker into the stove.

At three o'clock the next day, Sunday, Maman Coupeau lit their two cooking stoves as well as a third, earthenware one, borrowed from the Boches. By three-thirty the boiled beef was bubbling away in a large pot lent by the restaurant next door, their own pot being thought too small. They'd decided to cook the veal and the chine of pork the day before, because those dishes are better hotted up; only they wouldn't thicken the

sauce for the veal until they were ready to sit down to dinner.
There would still be more than enough to do on the Monday:
the soup, the peas with bacon, the roast goose. The back room
was all lit up by the fires in the three stoves; browning for the
sauces was sputtering in the pans, giving off a powerful smell
of burnt flour, while the big pot belched puffs of steam like a
boiler, its sides vibrating with deep, low-pitched gurgles.
Maman Coupeau and Gervaise, enveloped in white aprons,
filled the room with their bustle as they cleaned the parsley,
hunted for the pepper and salt and turned the meat over with
the wooden spoon. They'd sent Coupeau off to get him out of
their way. Even so they had people under their feet all
afternoon. There was such a delicious smell of cooking in the
building that the neighbours came down one after another,
inventing excuses to drop in just so they could find out what
was being cooked, and they stuck around in the room waiting
until Gervaise had to take the lids off the pans. Then, about
five, Virginie appeared; she'd seen Lantier again; really, you
couldn't set foot in the street without running into him.
Madame Boche had also just seen him, down at the corner,
peering about in a very shifty way. And Gervaise, who'd been
on the point of leaving to buy a sou's worth of roast onions for
the stock pot, came over quite trembly and didn't dare go out,
particularly as the concierge and the seamstress were scaring her
to death with terrible stories about men lying in wait for women
with knives and pistols hidden under their frock-coats. My
goodness, yes! You could read about it in the papers every day;
when one of those bastards is desperate to find an old flame
again, there's no telling what he might do. Virginie thoughtfully
offered to go for the onions herself. Women should stick
together, and she couldn't let this poor dear get her throat slit.
When she came back, she said Lantier had gone; he must have
realized he'd been spotted, and hopped it. Just the same, they
talked of nothing but him all afternoon, over the pots and pans.
When Madame Boche advised her to tell Coupeau, Gervaise in
a great panic begged her never to breathe a word about the
subject. Lord, that would be a fine mess! Her husband must
already have his suspicions about it, because for some days now,
on going to bed, he'd been swearing and bashing his fist into

the wall. Her hands were shaking at the idea that the two men
might come to blows over her; she knew Coupeau, he was
jealous enough to go for Lantier with his shears. And while the
four of them were engrossed in this drama the sauces were
simmering gently on the banked-down stoves; when Maman
Coupeau took off the lids, the veal and the chine of pork made
discreet little bubbling sounds while the stock-pot kept snoring
away like a big-bellied cantor asleep in the sun. In the end they
each had a drop of broth with bread in a cup, just to see what
it tasted like.

Monday came at last. Now that Gervaise was going to have
fourteen to dinner, she was afraid she wouldn't have room for
such a crowd. She decided to lay the table in the shop but, even
so, first thing in the morning she was taking measurements with
a tape, working out which way round the table should go. Then
they had to move all the washing out and take down the
work-table; it was the work-table, on different trestles, which
was to serve as a dining-table. But right in the middle of all this
commotion a customer turned up and made a scene, grumbling
that she'd been waiting for her washing since Friday, they
didn't give a damn about her, and she wanted her washing right
now. Gervaise apologized and lied like a trooper—it wasn't her
fault, she was cleaning the shop, and the girls wouldn't be back
till tomorrow; she calmed the customer down and sent her
away, promising to see to her stuff first thing in the morning.
But the minute she'd gone, Gervaise flew off the handle. Really!
If you listened to customers you wouldn't even take time off to
eat, you'd kill yourself all your life just for their sakes. After all,
you weren't a slave, were you? No, not if the Grand Turk
himself turned up with a collar to be done, not if it meant
earning a hundred thousand francs, she wouldn't do one stroke
of ironing that Monday, because when all was said and done it
was her turn for a bit of fun.

It took the whole morning to finish the shopping. Gervaise
went out three times and came back laden like a pack-horse.
But, when she was about to set out again to order the wine, she
realized she hadn't enough money left. She could easily have
got the wine on tick but the household couldn't be left without
any money, there'd be thousands of little things they'd need

that you don't think of. In the back room she and Maman
Coupeau worried themselves silly working out they'd want at
least twenty francs. Wherever could they lay their hands on
four five-franc pieces? Maman Coupeau, who'd once 'done' for
a second-rate actress at the Batignolles theatre, was the first to
mention the pawn shop. Gervaise laughed with relief. What a
fool not to have remembered the pawn shop! She quickly folded
up her black silk dress, pinning it into a bundle inside a towel.
She herself tucked this away under Maman Coupeau's apron,
urging her to keep it nice and flat against her stomach, because
of the neighbours—no need for them to know anything about
it. She came to the door and kept an eye to see if anyone
followed the old lady. But Maman Coupeau hadn't got as far as
the coal merchant's when Gervaise called her back.

'Mamma! Mamma!'

She made her come back into the shop and, slipping her
wedding ring off her finger, said:

'Here, take this as well. We'll get more.'

When Maman Coupeau brought back twenty-five francs
Gervaise jumped for joy. Now she could order six more bottles
of a good year to go with the goose. That'd be one in the eye
for the Lorilleux!

One in the eye for the Lorilleux had been the Coupeaus'
dream for the last fortnight. Really what a lovely couple they
were! So sly that the pair of them shut themselves up, didn't
they, if they were having something specially nice to eat, just
as if they'd pinched it? Yes, they covered the window with a
blanket to hide the light and make it look as if they were asleep.
Naturally, that kept people from going up there, and they
guzzled away all by themselves, wolfing down their food as fast
as they could and keeping their voices low. And they even took
good care the next day not to throw the bones on to the rubbish
heap, because then everyone would know what they'd eaten; no,
Madame Lorilleux would go to the end of the street and fling
them into a drain; one morning, Gervaise had caught her
emptying out a basketful of oyster shells down there. No, really,
you couldn't exactly call those cheese-parers open-handed, and
all their little dodges came from being dead set on appearing
poor. All right, she was going to teach 'em a lesson, she was

going to show 'em that everyone wasn't so stingy. If possible,
Gervaise would have set up her table right across the street, just
so she could invite all the passers-by. Money wasn't invented
to grow mouldy, was it? It looks pretty when it's all new and
glittery in the sunlight. She was so different from the Lorilleux
now that when she had five francs she did her best to give the
impression she had ten.

Maman Coupeau and Gervaise discussed the Lorilleux while
they were laying the table, at about three. They'd hung some
big curtains across the window, but as the afternoon was hot
they left the door open, and the whole street passed right by
the table. Not once did the two women put down a carafe, a
bottle, or a salt cellar, without dragging in the hope that it
would infuriate the Lorilleux. Their places at table were chosen
so they'd have a good view of the impressive array of silverware,
and Gervaise had saved the best china for them, knowing full
well that porcelain plates would be a nasty blow.

'No, no, Mamma, don't give them those napkins, I've two
damask ones.'

'Good,' muttered the old girl, 'that'll be the death of 'em, for
sure.'

And they smiled at one another, standing on either side of
the big white table, whose carefully aligned place settings made
them swell with pride. It was like a shrine in the middle of the
shop.

'And anyway,' went on Gervaise, 'why *are* they such pinch-
fists? You know, last month, they were lying when she told
everybody she'd lost a bit of gold chain while she was delivering
it. I ask you! As if that woman ever loses anything! . . . They
were just pretending they were poor so they wouldn't have to
give you your five francs.'

'So far I've only set eyes on 'em twice, me five francs,' said
Maman Coupeau.

'Want to bet? Next month, they'll think up another story . . .
That's why they cover up their window when they've rabbit for
dinner. You'd have the right to say to them, wouldn't you, "as
you've got rabbit, you can perfectly well give your mother five
francs." Oh, they're sly customers, they are! . . . What would've
become of you, if I hadn't taken you in with us?'

Maman Coupeau nodded. That day she hadn't a good word to say for the Lorilleux, because of the grand dinner the Coupeaus were giving. She loved cooking, and chatting over the pots and pans, and houses all topsy-turvy with preparations for parties. Besides, as a rule she got on quite well with Gervaise. There were times, though, when they had a little tiff, as happens in every family, and the old woman would grumble, saying she was horribly unlucky to be at her daughter-in-law's mercy in this way. Deep down, she must still have had a soft spot for Madame Lorilleux, who was her daughter, after all.

'Well?' Gervaise insisted. 'You wouldn't have got so plump, would you, with them? And no coffee, no snuff, no little treats! Tell me, would *they* have put two mattresses on your bed?'

'No, never,' answered Maman Coupeau. 'When they come in, I'm going to stand in front of the door so I can see the look on their faces.'

They were tickled to death at the prospect of the look on their faces. But they'd better not just stand there, gazing at the table. The Coupeaus had had lunch very late, at about one, off a bit of cold meat, because the three ovens were already in use and they didn't want to dirty the crockery they'd washed in preparation for the evening. By four o'clock the two women were hard at it. The goose was cooking in a portable roaster which had been put on the ground against the wall, beside the open window; the bird was so huge that they'd had to jam it in by force. Cross-eyed Augustine, seated on a little stool right in the blast of heat reflected from the roaster, was solemnly basting the goose with a long-handled spoon. Gervaise was busy with the peas and bacon. Maman Coupeau, in quite a dither because of all the different dishes, bustled about waiting for the moment to heat up the chine of pork and the veal. At about five the guests began to arrive. The first to appear were the two assistants, Clémence and Madame Putois, wearing their Sunday best, the first in blue and the second in black; Clémence brought a geranium plant and Madame Putois a heliotrope and Gervaise, whose hands just then were white with flour, gave each in turn two smacking kisses with her hands held out behind her. Then, close on their heels came Virginie, all got up like a proper lady in a printed muslin dress with a scarf and hat although she'd only come from across the street. She was carrying a pot of red carnations. She put her long arms round Gervaise and gave her an almighty hug. Finally Boche appeared with a pot of pansies, Madame Boche with one of mignonette, while Madame Lerat had a pot of lemon-scented verbena, the soil of which had dirtied her violet merino dress. All these folk kissed each other, crowding into the room where the heat from the three stoves and the roaster was asphyxiating. The noise of frying drowned people's voices. There was great excitement when someone's dress caught on the roaster. The smell of roast goose was so powerful that all the nostrils were flaring. Gervaise thanked each of them very sweetly for their flowers, while she went on mixing the thickening for the blanquette in the bottom of a deep-sided dish. She'd put the pots of flowers in the shop, at the end of the table, without removing their tall white paper frills. A fragrant scent of flowers mingled with the aromas of cooking.

'Would you like a hand?' said Virginie. 'To think you've been slaving away for three days making all this food and it'll all be scoffed before you can turn round!'

'Of course! It wouldn't get cooked just by itself . . .' Gervaise replied. 'No, don't dirty your hands. Look, everything's ready, there's only the soup to do . . .'

So they all made themselves at home. The ladies put their shawls and bonnets on the bed, and pinned up their skirts so they wouldn't get dirty. Boche, who'd sent his wife back to keep an eye on the lodge till dinner-time, was already nudging Clémence into the corner by the stove and asking her if she was ticklish; Clémence gasped and squirmed, her shoulders hunched up and her bosom almost bursting out of her bodice, for just the idea of being tickled made her feel shivery all over. The other ladies, so as not to be in the cooks' way, also went into the shop where they stood round the walls facing the table; but as they kept on talking through the open door and couldn't hear properly, they were forever returning to the back room, their voices filling it with sudden bursts of noise while they gathered round Gervaise who, clutching her steaming spoon, would forget what she was doing as she answered them. There was lots of laughter and outrageous remarks. When Virginie said she hadn't eaten anything for two days so she'd be good and empty, that disgusting Clémence outdid her with a cock-and-bull story about cleaning herself out that morning, like the English, with an enema. At that, Boche gave a recipe for instant digestion, namely to squeeze yourself in a door after each course; the English did that too, it meant you could eat for twelve hours without stopping and not upset your stomach. When you're invited out to dinner it's good manners, isn't it, to eat? People don't put veal, and pork, and goose on the table just to be looked at. Oh, the missus needn't worry, they'd polish everything off so thoroughly she wouldn't even have to wash up the dishes the next morning. And all the guests seemed to be whetting their appetite by coming in to sniff at the pans and the roaster. Then the ladies started carrying on like little girls: pushing and chasing each other from room to room so that the floor shook and their skirts fanned the cooking smells, mixing and spreading them, while they raised a deafening racket in which laughter mingled with the sound of Maman Coupeau's knife chopping the bacon.

At that very moment, when everybody was leaping about and shouting just for the hell of it, Goujet arrived. He didn't have the nerve to come in but stood abashed with a large white rose bush in his arms, a magnificent plant whose stem reached up to his face so that his golden beard seemed full of flowers. Gervaise rushed up to him, her cheeks aflame from the heat of the stoves. But he couldn't think what to do with his pot of roses; when she took it from him he stammered something, not daring to kiss her. It was she who stood on tip-toe and put her cheek to his lips, but he was in such a state that he kissed her on the eye, so roughly he might have blinded her. They were both trembling.

'Oh, Monsieur Goujet, it's too beautiful!' she exclaimed, setting the rose-bush beside the other plants, where its crown of foliage showed high above the rest.

'Not at all, not at all,' he kept repeating, tongue-tied.

And when, after a heavy sigh, he'd pulled himself together somewhat, he announced that they'd better not count on his mother, who was having one of her attacks of sciatica. Gervaise was very upset and declared she would put a bit of the goose aside, because she'd set her heart on Madame Goujet's tasting the bird. No one else was expected now. Coupeau must be hanging about somewhere in the area with Poisson, whom he'd gone to fetch after lunch; they'd be back any minute, they'd promised they'd be right on the dot at six. So, as the soup was almost ready, Gervaise called Madame Lerat and said she thought it was time to go up for the Lorilleux. Madame Lerat immediately became very grave for she it was who'd carried out all the negotiations and settled with the two families how things would be done. She put on her shawl and bonnet again and went upstairs, holding herself very straight and looking important. Downstairs, Gervaise went on stirring her noodle soup without saying a word. The guests, who'd suddenly turned serious, were waiting in solemn silence.

It was Madame Lerat who appeared first. She came round by the street, so as to give added consequence to the reconciliation. She held the door of the shop open wide, while Madame Lorilleux, in a silk dress, stood on the threshold. All the guests had risen and Gervaise came forward, kissing her sister-in-law as had been agreed and saying:

'Well do come in. It's over and done with now, isn't it? . . . We'll both of us be nice.'

And Madame Lorilleux replied:

'I hope it'll last forever; nothing would please me more.'

When she'd come in Lorilleux also stopped on the threshold, and also waited to be kissed before entering the shop. Neither of them had brought flowers; they'd decided not to, because it would look too much like knuckling under to Banban if they came with flowers the first time. Gervaise shouted to Augustine to bring in two litres. Then, at one end of the table, she poured glasses of wine and called the whole party over. Everybody took a glass and drank to family unity. There was a silence as the guests drank: the ladies drained their glasses right down, tilting them to get the last drop.

'Nothing nicer before grub,' declared Boche, smacking his lips. 'Better than a kick up the backside.'

Maman Coupeau had placed herself opposite the door, to see the look on the Lorilleux's faces. Pulling at Gervaise's skirt, she dragged her off into the back room, where the pair of them leant over the soup, talking in rapid whispers.

'What sour faces, eh!' said the old lady. 'You couldn't see 'em, you couldn't. But I was keeping my eye on 'em . . . When she saw the table, my word, her face got all twisted up like this and the corners of her mouth went right up to her eyes; as for him, it fair choked him, it made him cough . . . Now do look at 'em over there: they couldn't so much as spit, their mouths are that dry, and they're chewing their lips.'

'It's awful when people are as jealous as that,' Gervaise murmured.

It was true, the Lorilleux did look very queer. Of course, no one likes being put in the shade, and especially within a family, when one lot gets ahead it makes the others furious, that's only natural. But the thing is, most people hide their feelings, don't they? You don't make an exhibition of yourself. Well, the Lorilleux couldn't hide their feelings. It was more than they could stand, and they looked about disdainfully, with pursed mouths. In fact, it was so obvious that the other guests were staring at them and asking if they felt all right. Never would they be able to stomach the table with its fourteen place settings, its white linen, its bread sliced in advance. You might easily be in a fancy restaurant on the boulevards. Madame Lorilleux made the rounds, averting her eyes so as not to see the flowers and surreptitiously fingering the big tablecloth, tortured by the idea that it must be new.

'It's all ready!' cried Gervaise as she reappeared with a smile, her arms bare and little bits of golden hair blowing round her temples.

The guests, looking rather fed up, were milling about near the table. They were all hungry and kept giving little yawns.

'If only the boss was here,' their hostess went on, 'we could begin.'

'Well, the soup'll get cold,' said Madame Lorilleux. 'Coupeau always forgets everything. You shouldn't have let him take off.'

It was already half-past six. Everything was getting burnt, now, and the goose would be overdone. Gervaise, greatly put out, suggested sending someone to see if Coupeau might be in

one of the bars near by. Then, when Goujet offered, she said
she'd go too; and Virginie, worried about her own husband,
went along as well. The three of them, bareheaded, took up the
entire pavement. The smith, in his frock-coat, with Gervaise on
his left arm and Virginie on his right was, he said, a basket with
two handles, and they thought this so funny that they stopped
dead in their tracks, laughing so much they couldn't move.
Seeing their reflection in the pork-butcher's window, they
laughed even harder. Beside Goujet, who was all in black, the
two women looked like a pair of speckled hens, the seamstress
in her muslin gown with clusters of pink flowers, the laundress
in a short-sleeved dress of white percale with blue spots, and a
little grey silk scarf knotted round her neck. People turned
round to watch them as they passed along, looking so happy
and fresh, wearing their Sunday best although it was a weekday,
and pushing through the crowds which filled the Rue des
Poissonniers that warm June evening. But it was no laughing
matter. They went straight to the door of every tavern and
peered in, inspecting the customers in front of the bar. Could
that bastard Coupeau have gone right to the Arc-de-Triomphe
for his tipple? They'd already scoured the upper part of the
street, trying all the likely places: the Petite Civette, famous for
its brandied plums, Mère Baquet's, where you could get
Orléans wine for eight sous; the Papillon,* the haunt of cabbies,
who were very hard to please. No Coupeau. Then, on their way
down towards the boulevard, just as they were passing François's bar on the corner, Gervaise gave a little scream.

'What's the matter?' Goujet asked.

The laundress was no longer laughing. She'd gone deathly
white, and was so agitated she'd almost fallen. Virginie understood at once, on catching sight of Lantier calmly having
dinner at a table in François's bar. The two women rushed
Goujet on.

'I twisted me ankle,' said Gervaise when she could speak.

Finally, at the bottom of the street, they discovered Coupeau
and Poisson in Père Colombe's Assommoir. They were on their
feet, in the middle of a crowd of men; Coupeau, dressed in a
grey smock, was shouting, angrily waving his arms about and
banging his fist down on the counter; Poisson, wearing a tightly

buttoned old brown coat—he was off duty that day—was
listening to Coupeau, his expression leaden and withdrawn, his
red imperial and moustache bristling. Goujet left the women on
the pavement and, going up to the roofer, touched him on the
shoulder. But when Coupeau caught sight of Gervaise and
Virginie outside, he flew into a rage. Who the hell had sent
those bloody women after him! Now he was being chased by
some bits of skirt! Well he wasn't going to budge; they could
eat their fucking dinner all by themselves. To calm him, Goujet
had to accept something to drink and then Coupeau was mean
enough to drag it out for five long minutes at the counter.
When they finally did come into the street, he said to his wife:

'I don't like this, I don't. I'm stayin' if I feel like it, I've
things to do here!'

She didn't answer. She was trembling all over. She and
Virginie must have been talking about Lantier, because Virginie
pushed her husband and Goujet ahead, shouting to them to
walk in front. Then the women got one on each side of
Coupeau, to distract him and stop him from seeing. He was
more stupefied by all the shouting than really tipsy from drink.
Just to be a pest, because they seemed to want to follow the
left-hand pavement, he shoved them out of the way and crossed
over to the right. They ran after him in great alarm, and tried
to block his view of the door to François's bar, but Coupeau
must have known Lantier was there. Gervaise was stunned to
hear him snarl:

'Yes, my pet, there's a bloke in there we've met before. I
wasn't born yesterday, y' know! . . . Just let me cop you gaddin'
about again an' makin' eyes!'

And he used some crude words. It wasn't him, Coupeau, she
was looking for, with her arms bare and her mug all powdered,
it was her old fancy man. Then all of a sudden he began to rant
and rave at Lantier. The bloody sod! The shit! One of them
two would have to end up on the pavement, gutted like a rabbit.
Lantier, however, didn't seem to grasp what was happening and
went on slowly eating his veal with sorrel. A crowd began to
gather. At last Virginie led Coupeau away; he calmed down at
once, the minute he'd turned the corner. Even so, they returned
to the shop less cheerfully than they had left it.

The guests were waiting by the table, looking glum. The roofer went round shaking hands, preening himself a bit in front of the ladies. Gervaise, feeling rather subdued and speaking quietly, was showing everyone their places when she suddenly realized that because Madame Goujet hadn't come, a place would be empty, the one next to Madame Lorilleux.

'There's thirteen of us!' she said, very shaken by this fresh evidence of the bad luck she'd felt threatening her for some time.

The ladies had sat down but got up again, looking uneasy and annoyed. Madame Putois offered to leave because, in her opinion, this was not something to be trifled with; besides, she wouldn't touch a thing, her insides couldn't take any of the food. Boche, for his part, was sniggering: better be thirteen than fourteen, the helpings would be bigger, it was as simple as that.

'Just a minute!' continued Gervaise, 'I can fix it!'

And going out on to the pavement she called to Père Bru who happened to be crossing the road. The old workman came in, bent double, stiff and silent.

'Sit you down there, Père Bru,' said Gervaise, 'You'd like to have dinner with us, wouldn't you?'

He just nodded. He didn't mind if he did, it was all the same to him.

'Might as well be him as somebody else, eh?' she went on, lowering her voice. 'It's not often he can eat his fill. At any rate he'll have a square meal again . . . Now we needn't feel guilty, stuffing ourselves.'

Goujet's eyes were wet, he was so moved. The others also were very touched, and thought it a fine idea, adding that it would bring them all good luck. Madame Lorilleux, however, didn't seem too pleased at being next to the old man; she edged away, casting disgusted glances at his calloused hands and his patched and faded smock. Père Bru sat with his head hanging, really bothered by the napkin which lay over the plate in front of him. In the end he picked it up and placed it carefully on the edge of the table; it never entered his head to put it on his knees.

Gervaise was at last serving the noodle soup and the guests were picking up their spoons when Virginie pointed out that Coupeau had disappeared again: he'd probably gone back to Père Colombe's. At this, the assembled company got cross. They said that's that; no one was going to go running after him this time, he could stay out in the street if he wasn't hungry. However, just as all the spoons were scraping the bottom of the soup-plates, Coupeau reappeared carrying a pot of wallflowers and a pot of balsam, one under each arm. The whole table clapped. With a gallant gesture he placed his plants on either side of Gervaise's glass; then he leant down and kissed her, saying:

'I'd forgotten you, my pet . . . Still, we love each other just the same, don't we, especially on a day like today.'

'He's ever so nice, Monsieur Coupeau is, this evening,' Clémence murmured in Boche's ear. 'He's had exactly the right amount, just enough to make him agreeable.'

Coupeau's good behaviour restored the festive spirit which for a moment had seemed in danger. Gervaise, reassured, was all smiles again. The guests were finishing the soup. Next the bottles went the rounds and the first glass of wine was drunk, a good four fingers— without water—to help the noodles down. In the next room the children could be heard quarrelling: Étienne, Nana, Pauline and little Victor Fauconnier were there. It had been decided the four of them should have their own table and they'd been told to behave themselves. Cross-eyed Augustine, whose job it was to watch the stoves, had to eat off her lap.

'Mummy! Mummy!' Nana suddenly shouted, 'Augustine is dipping her bread in the roaster.'

Gervaise ran through and caught Augustine just as she was scalding her gullet by bolting a piece of bread soaked in boiling goose fat. She gave her a clout because the bleeding kid was yelling it wasn't true.

After the beef, when the veal appeared in a salad bowl because the household didn't have a big enough dish, a laugh ran round the table.

'We're getting down to serious business now,' declared Poisson, who rarely spoke.

It was half-past seven. They'd closed the door of the shop so as not to be spied on by the locals, especially the little watchmaker across the road who stared with eyes as big as saucers, practically snatching the morsels from their lips with his greedy gaze so that it quite spoiled their appetites. The curtains draped over the windows let in a strong, white, even light which cast no shadows and shone on the table with its still symmetrical place settings and its pots of flowers in tall paper collars; and this pale luminosity, this lingering twilight made the company seem quite distinguished. Virginie hit on the right word: she gazed round the room, all closed up and hung with muslin, and declared it looked classy. When a cart passed in the street, the glasses danced about on the tablecloth and the ladies had to shout as loudly as the men. But there wasn't much conversation, they were minding their manners and being very polite to each other. Coupeau was the only one wearing a smock, because, as he put it, there's no need to make a fuss when it's your friends, and anyway the smock is the working-man's garb of honour.

The ladies were tightly laced into their bodices; their hair, smoothed down from a centre parting, was so thick with pomade that it reflected the light; while the gentlemen sat well away from the table, thrusting out their chests and sticking out their elbows, for fear of spilling something on their frock-coats.

Christ almighty! What a hole they made in that bowl of veal! Though there wasn't much talking, there was a lot of serious chewing. The salad bowl was emptying fast; a spoon stood upright in its thick sauce, a rich yellow sauce which trembled like a jelly. People fished about for the chunks of veal; there were still some left, and as the bowl travelled from hand to hand, faces peered into it, hunting for mushrooms. The huge loaves of bread set against the wall behind the guests seemed to be melting away. Between mouthfuls, you could hear the sound of glasses being plonked down on the table. The sauce was a trifle too salty, and it took four litres to drown that bloody great blanquette, which slipped down like a custard but set your innards all afire. And before you could draw breath, the chine of pork, laid out on a deep platter and flanked by big round potatoes, arrived in a cloud of steam. A shout went up. Hell and damnation, what a brain-wave! Everyone loved pork and spuds. This time you really were going to work up an appetite, and out of the corner of your eye you watched the dish going round, wiping your knife on your bread so as to be ready. Then, when you'd taken some, you started poking your neighbour with your elbow, talking away with your mouth full. Wonderful, wasn't it, this bit of pork? It was that soft, but filling too, you could feel it slide all the way through your innards, right down to your boots! The spuds were a dream. It wasn't at all salty, but just because of the spuds a spot of watering was called for every minute or so. Four more litres were knocked off. The plates were wiped so clean they weren't changed for the peas with bacon. Oh well, vegetables hardly counted. You could down them by the spoonful, just to pass the time. A real dainty, a treat for the ladies, you might say. The best thing about them was the little bits of bacon, grilled to a turn so they smelled like a horse's hoof. Two litres did for the peas.

'Mummy! Mummy!' Nana suddenly called out, 'Augustine keeps sticking her fingers in my plate!'

'Don't bother me! Just give her a slap!' answered Gervaise, busy stuffing herself with peas.

In the next room, at the children's table, Nana was playing at lady of the house. She'd seated herself beside Victor and had placed her brother Étienne next to little Pauline; that way, they could play house, and be two married couples enjoying a party. At first Nana had served her guests very nicely, smiling at them like a grown-up; but she'd just given way to her love of bacon, and had kept it all for herself. Cross-eyed Augustine was sneaking about near the children's table and took advantage of this to grab handfuls of bacon on the pretext of sharing it out more fairly. Nana flew into a rage and bit her on the wrist.

'Ah! You know what, I'm going to tell your mother that after the veal you made Victor kiss you,' whispered Augustine.

But order was restored when Gervaise and Maman Coupeau arrived to take the goose off the spit. At the big table, people were leaning back against their chairs, breathing deeply. The men unbuttoned their waistcoats, the ladies wiped their faces with their napkins. There was a sort of lull in the meal, except that a few of the guests, their jaws still working, went on swallowing huge mouthfuls of bread without being aware of what they were doing. People were letting their food settle while they waited. Night had gradually fallen, and on the other side of the curtains the dirty, ashen greyness was growing thicker. When Augustine placed two lighted lamps on the table, one at each end, the bright light revealed the mess the table was in, with its greasy plates and forks and wine-stained cloth covered with crumbs. The powerful smell rising up made you gasp for breath. Meanwhile noses were turning towards the kitchen, enticed by savoury whiffs of warm air.

'Would you like a hand?' Virginie called.

She left her chair and went into the next room. One by one, all the women followed her. They stood round the roaster, watching with rapt attention while Gervaise and Maman Coupeau tugged at the goose. Then a hubbub arose; you could hear the children's shrill voices and the noise they made jumping about in glee. There was a triumphal procession back into the shop: Gervaise carrying the goose, her arms held straight out and her sweaty face lit up by a great silent laugh; the women walking behind, laughing like her; while Nana, at the very back, stood on tiptoe, round-eyed and staring. When the goose was on the table, enormous, golden-brown and juicy as they come, they didn't attack it right away. Amazement and awed surprise had silenced every tongue. The company was reduced to winks and thrusts of the chin to indicate the bird. Bloody hell, what a lady! What thighs! What a belly!

'That one didn't get fat licking the walls, not that one!' said Boche.

And then they started going into the details. Gervaise gave the facts: the goose was the very finest she could find at the poulterer's in the Faubourg Poissonnière; it had weighed twelve and a half pounds on the coal merchant's scales; they'd burnt a bushel of coal roasting it, and it had yielded three bowls of fat. Virginie interrupted her to boast that she'd seen the bird before it was cooked: you could have eaten it raw, she said, its skin was that delicate and white, just like a blonde's, really! All the men responded with a greedy, suggestive laugh, smacking their lips. Lorilleux and Madame Lorilleux, however, looked down their noses, choking with anger at seeing a goose like that on Banban's table.

'Well come on, we can't eat it whole,' Gervaise said at last. 'Who's going to carve? . . . Oh no, not me! It's too big, I'm scared.'

Coupeau offered. Good Lord, it was quite simple, you got hold of the limbs and pulled; the pieces were just as good that way. But there was a chorus of protest and the carving knife was forcibly taken from him; no, when he carved, he made a regular battlefield of the platter. There was a little pause while they looked round for a volunteer. Finally, Madame Lerat said in a gracious voice:

'Listen, it should be Monsieur Poisson . . . Yes, obviously, Monsieur Poisson.'

And as the gathering didn't seem to catch her meaning, she added in an even more flattering tone:

'Well of course it should be Monsieur Poisson, as he's used to handling weapons.'

And she passed the knife she was holding to the policeman. The whole table joined in a laugh of relief and approval. Poisson accepted with a stiff soldierly nod and placed the goose in front of him. His neighbours, Gervaise and Madame Boche, moved away to give him elbow room. He carved slowly, with exaggerated gestures, his eyes fixed on the bird as if to nail it to the bottom of the platter. When he thrust the knife into the carcass and it cracked, Lorilleux exclaimed in a burst of patriotic fervour:

'If only it was a Cossack,* eh?'

'Did you ever fight any Cossacks, Monsieur Poisson?' Madame Boche inquired.

'No, only Bedouins,'* the policeman replied, as he cut off a wing. 'There aren't any Cossacks any more.'

Complete silence fell. All heads were leaning forward, all eyes were following the knife. Poisson had a surprise up his sleeve. Suddenly, with a final stroke of the knife, the back half of the bird came away and stood upended, rump in air, revealing the parson's nose. At this, there were cries of admiration. No one could beat an old soldier at making the party go! Meanwhile, the bird had let loose a torrent of juice through the gaping hole in its rear, which set Boche laughing.

'I'll sign on, if someone'll pee that way in my mouth,' he muttered.

'Oh! The filthy thing!' cried the ladies. 'How can he be so filthy!'

'No, I don't know anyone more disgusting!' said Madame Boche, angrier than the others. 'Shut up, d'you hear! You're enough to disgust an army . . . Y'know he's doing it so he'll get it all to himself.'

At that point Clémence could be heard urgently repeating, above the din:

'Monsieur Poisson, listen, Monsieur Poisson . . . You'll save the parson's nose for me, won't you!'

'My dear, the parson's nose is yours by right,' said Madame Lerat in her discreetly suggestive way.

The goose had now been carved up. The policeman, after letting the company admire the parson's nose for several minutes, had just cut the slices loose and arranged them round the dish. People could help themselves. But the ladies were complaining of the heat and unfastening their dresses. Coupeau shouted that this was his home, he didn't give a spit about the neighbours, and he flung the street door wide open, so the party continued amid the rumbling of cabs and the bustle of passers-by on the pavements. Then, with everyone's jaws rested and fresh space in their stomachs, they began again on their dinner, falling on the goose with ferocity. Just having to wait and watch the goose being carved, as that wag Boche put it, had made the veal and the pork slide right down into his calves.

My word, that was one hell of a blow-out: in fact, not a single person there could remember ever having such good cause for indigestion. Gervaise looked enormous as she sat slumped forward on her elbows, eating great chunks of breast and never saying a word for fear of missing a mouthful; indeed she felt a bit ashamed in front of Goujet, a bit bothered at showing herself like this, as greedy as a cat. In any case Goujet, seeing her all rosy pink in the face from food, was himself eating too much. And then, even in her greediness, she was still so nice and so kind! She didn't say anything, but she went out of her way every other minute to look after Père Bru and pass something extra special on to his plate. It was quite touching to see her, loving food the way she did, take a bit of a wing she'd been going to eat and give it instead to Père Bru, who didn't know what he was eating and swallowed everything, his head hanging down, in a daze from all that guzzling when his own gullet had forgotten what even bread tasted like. The Lorilleux were working off their fury on the roast goose; they took enough to last three days, they would have devoured the platter, the table and the shop if that would have ruined Banban on the spot. All the ladies had wanted some of the carcass, well, the carcass is the ladies' portion. Madame Lerat, Madame Boche, Madame Putois were gnawing away at some bones while Maman Coupeau, who adored the neck, was tearing the meat off it with her last two teeth. As for Virginie, she liked the skin when it was nice and crispy and the men all gallantly passed her their skin, until Poisson, glaring severely at his wife, said that was quite enough and she must stop; once before, when she'd eaten too much roast goose, she'd had to stay in bed for two weeks with her belly all swollen up. This vexed Coupeau, who put one of the thigh joints on Virginie's plate, shouting that, bloody hell, if she couldn't polish that off she wasn't fit to be called a woman! When had goose ever hurt anyone? It was just the other way round: goose was a cure for spleen trouble. You could eat it by itself, without bread, like a dessert. As for him, he could stuff on it all night long and never feel a thing, whereupon he crammed a whole drumstick into his mouth, just to show 'em. Clémence, meanwhile, was finishing her parson's nose, smacking her lips as she sucked at it and squirming with laughter at the smut Boche was murmuring in her ear. Christ almighty! Yes, that was an amazing blow-out if ever there was one! Well, while you're at it, you're at it, aren't you? And if you only get a chance at a real spread once in a blue moon, you'd be a sodding half-wit not to stuff yourself up to the eyeballs! You could see their bellies swell up while they ate, you could really. The ladies looked in the family way. Every one of 'em bursting out of their skins, the bleeding hogs! With their mouths open and their chins dripping with grease, their faces were like backsides, and that red, you'd have said rich folk's backsides, bursting with prosperity.

And as for the wine, well, friends, the wine flowed round that table like water down the Seine, or like a stream when it's been raining and the ground is parched. When Coupeau poured he raised the bottle high, to see the red jet foam in the glass; and when a bottle was empty, he made a joke of up-ending it and squeezing its neck with his fingers the way women do when they milk a cow. Another litre'd turned its toes up! In a corner of the shop, the pile of dead men was growing bigger, making a cemetery of bottles where they dumped the rubbish from the tablecloth. When Madame Putois asked for water, the roofer indignantly took all the carafes from the table. Since when did decent folk drink water? Did she fancy a few frogs in her stomach, then? Glasses were being emptied in one go: you could hear the liquid flowing straight down people's throats, sounding like rainwater pouring down drainpipes on a stormy day. You could say, couldn't you, that it was raining wine, wine which at first tasted of old casks, but you'd no trouble at all getting used to it, so that soon it seemed quite nutty. Oh, what the hell, the Jesuits could say what they liked, the juice of the vine was a bloody good invention! The company laughed in approval; after all, a workman couldn't get along without wine, and old man Noah must have planted the vine specially for roofers, tailors and blacksmiths. Wine cleaned you up and refreshed you after work, and put fire in your guts when you didn't feel like doing anything; and when that jester played his little tricks on you, well, then you thought you were one hell of a feller, and Paris belonged to you. What's more a worker who was worn out and stony broke, and treated like scum by the rich, had a fat lot to cheer about, so it was a bit much, wasn't it, to grumble if he went on the booze now and again, just to make life seem a bit rosier! Right now, fr'instance, wasn't it true they didn't give a damn about the Emperor? Very likely the Emperor was pissed as well, but who cared, they didn't give a damn about him, they dared him to be more pissed than them or be having more of a blast. To hell with the nobs! If Coupeau had his way, everyone could go to hell. Still, not the ladies—the ladies were sweeties, and he tapped his pocket, jingling his three sous and laughing as if he were shovelling a pile of five-franc pieces. Even Goujet himself, ordinarily so sober, had taken quite a skinful. Boche's eyes were getting smaller and Lorilleux's paler, while Poisson glared more and more sternly, rolling his eyes about in his bronzed ex-soldier's face. They were already as tight as ticks. And the ladies were a bit high as well, oh, just a shade tiddly, their cheeks flushed with wine, with an urge to cast some clothing which made them strip off their shawls; Clémence was the only one who carried this rather too far. Suddenly, Gervaise remembered the six bottles of vintage wine she'd forgotten to serve with the goose; she brought them out and refilled the glasses. At that, Poisson got to his feet and said, glass in hand,

'I drink to the health of our hostess.'

Noisily scraping back their chairs, everyone stood up, stretching out their arms to clink their glasses amid the general hubbub.

'Here's to fifty years from now!' shouted Virginie.

'No, no,' protested Gervaise, smiling and very touched, 'I'd be too old. After all, the time comes when you're glad to go.'

Meanwhile, with the door wide open, the whole neighbourhood was watching and sharing in the goings-on. Passers-by stopped in the strip of light which fanned out over the cobbles, laughing happily at the sight of people tucking in with such enthusiasm. Cabbies, bent over on their boxes as they whipped their nags, would glance in and yell something funny: 'Hey, is that all going for free? . . . My, just look at Mamma fatty, I'll be right back with the midwife!' . . . The smell of roast goose brought good cheer and good will to the whole street; across on the opposite pavement the grocer's boys felt they were actually eating it, while the fruit merchant and the tripe-shop woman kept appearing in front of their doors and stood licking their chops as they sniffed the air. In fact the whole street was in the throes of indigestion. Madame Cudorge and her daughter, who kept the umbrella shop next door and who no one ever saw, now crossed the road one behind the other, casting sidelong glances, their faces as red as if they'd been cooking pancakes. The little clockmaker at his bench couldn't go on working, he was tipsy from counting wine bottles and sat there in quite a state amid his cheery cuckoo clocks. Yes, the neighbours were all quite steamed up, shouted Coupeau, so why bother to hide? Now they'd really got going the company no longer felt ashamed of being seen at table; quite the opposite, they felt flattered and excited, having all those people gathered round, gaping greedily; they would have liked to break down the shop-front and push the table out on to the street and enjoy their dessert there, under people's noses, amid all the bustle of the traffic. There was nothing nasty about the sight, was there? Well then, they didn't have to shut themselves up in that selfish way. Coupeau, seeing the little clockmaker thirstily licking his lips, held up a bottle. The other nodded his acceptance and Coupeau carried over a bottle and glass. Friendly ties were being formed between party and street. They toasted passers-by, and called out to mates who seemed like nice chaps. The binge was spreading, catching on little by little through the neighbourhood until the whole of the Goutte-d'Or smelled of the blow-out and was clutching its belly in a bacchanalian orgy to end all orgies.

Madame Vigouroux, the coal dealer, had been walking up and down in front of the door for several minutes.

'Madame Vigouroux! Hey, Madame Vigouroux!' the company bellowed.

In she came, giggling inanely, looking quite clean and so fat she was almost bursting her bodice. The men loved pinching her, because they could pinch her all over without ever finding a bone. Boche made her sit down by him and at once stealthily grasped her knee under the table. But she was used to that kind of thing and calmly drained her glass of wine, telling them the neighbours were watching from their windows and that some people in the building were beginning to get annoyed.

'Oh, that's our business, that is,' said Madame Boche. 'We're the concierges, aren't we? So peace and quiet's our job . . . Just let 'em come and complain, we'll give 'em something to think about.'

In the back room, a furious battle had just been raging between Nana and Augustine over the roaster, which they both wanted to scrape clean. For fifteen minutes the roaster had been bouncing about on the floor, clattering like an old stewpot.

Now, Nana was tending to little Victor, who had a goose bone in his throat; she was prodding him under the chin with her fingers and making him swallow huge lumps of sugar as a remedy. This didn't stop her keeping an eye on the big table. She was forever running over to ask for wine, or bread, or meat, for Étienne and Pauline.

'Here, take this, I hope it chokes you!' her mother said. 'Now for pity's sake let's have a bit of peace!'

The children couldn't swallow another bite, but they went on eating just the same, banging out a hymn tune with their forks for encouragement.

Meanwhile, in the midst of all the din, a conversation had got going between Père Bru and Maman Coupeau. The old man, still deathly pale despite the food and drink, was talking about his sons killed in the Crimea. Oh, if only those boys had lived, he'd have had something to eat every day. But Maman Coupeau, her voice slightly slurred, leaned over and said:

'Oh, but children can be a deal of trouble, y'know. Take me, fr'instance, I seem like I'm happy here, don't I? Well, it's often as I've a good cry . . . No, don't go wishing you'd children.'

Père Bru was shaking his head.

'No one wants to take me on, not any place,' he murmured. 'I'm too old to work. Now if I go into a workshop the young fellers laugh and ask if it was me as polished Henry IV's boots* . . . Last year, I could still make thirty sous a day painting a bridge; it meant lying on me back all the time, an' the river right below. It was then I got me bad chest . . . But now there's nothing doing, they've kicked me out, everywhere.'

He looked down at his poor stiff hands and went on:

'You can understand it, because I can't do nothing now. They're right, I'd do the same . . . My trouble, see, is I'm not dead. Yes, it's me own fault. When you can't work no more you should just lie down and die.'

'What I can't understand,' said Lorilleux who was listening, 'is why the government doesn't do something to help disabled workmen. I was reading about it in a newspaper the other day . . .'

Poisson thought he ought to stand up for the government.

'Workmen aren't soldiers,' he declared. 'The Invalides* is for soldiers . . . There's no point asking the impossible.'

The sweet had now been served. In the centre of the table stood a sponge cake in the shape of a temple with a dome made of melon slices; on the dome was an artificial rose with a silver paper butterfly alongside, dangling from the end of a wire. In the heart of the flower two drops of gum represented dew-drops. Then, to the left of the cake, a soup-plate held a lump of cream cheese swimming in liquid while on the right another plate was piled high with fat bruised strawberries dripping with juice. However there was still some salad left, large leaves of romaine drenched in oil.

'Come on now, Madame Boche,' said Gervaise invitingly, 'have a bit more salad. I know you adore salad.'

'Oh no thanks, I'm full to the brim,' replied the concierge.

Gervaise turned towards Virginie, who stuck her finger into her mouth as if she could touch the food.

'No, really, I'm completely stuffed,' she muttered. 'I've no more room. Couldn't manage another bite.'

'I'm sure, if you just try,' Gervaise repeated, smiling, 'there's always a bit of room somewhere. You don't have to be hungry when it's salad . . . Surely you'll not let this romaine go to waste?'

'You can have it tomorrow,' Madame Lerat said. 'It's tastier when it's been well soaked in the dressing.'

The ladies, breathing hard, gazed wistfully at the salad bowl. Clémence told how she had once got through three bunches of cress for lunch. Madame Putois could beat that, she ate heads of romaine just as they were, not trimmed or cleaned, munching them with only a sprinkle of salt. They could all live on salad, they could eat it by the bucketful. And, helped along by this conversation, the ladies polished off the salad.

'I'd go down on all fours in a field, I would' Madame Boche kept saying, her mouth full.

The sweet was treated as a joke. It didn't really count, the sweet didn't. It was a bit late appearing, but that didn't matter, you could still toy with it. Even if it meant you'd explode like a bomb, you couldn't let a few strawberries and some cake get the better of you. Anyway, what was the hurry, there was plenty of time, all night if you felt like it. So plates were filled with strawberries and cream cheese. The men lit their pipes and as the vintage wine was all gone, they went back to the ordinary, drinking while they smoked. But they wanted Gervaise to cut the cake straight away. Poisson got up and, picking off the rose, handed it to his hostess with a very gallant gesture, amid general applause. She had to use a pin to fix it on her left breast, near her heart. Every time she moved, the butterfly gave a flutter.

'Goodness me!' shouted Lorilleux, who'd just made a discovery, 'if it's not your work-table we're eating off! Well! There's probably never been so much work done on it before!'

This unkind crack was a huge success. A shower of witticisms followed: Clémence couldn't swallow a spoonful of strawberries without saying she was ironing them; Madame Lerat claimed the cream cheese tasted of starch, while Madame Lorilleux muttered between clenched teeth that it was a fine idea to gobble up the money so fast over the very same boards where it had been such a job to earn it. A storm of laughter and shouts arose.

All of a sudden, a powerful voice imposed silence on everyone. It was Boche, standing there in a rakish pose with a wicked twinkle in his eye, singing "The Volcano of Love or The Irresistible Trooper".

> I'm Blavin the trooper, wot the ladies can't resist . . .

A thunder of bravos greeted the first verse. Yes, yes, they'd have a sing-song, and everybody must oblige! There was nothing like a sing-song for a good laugh. They all put their elbows on the table or lolled against the chairbacks, nodding their heads at the best bits, taking a swig during the choruses. That bastard Boche was a real pro at comic songs. It was enough to make even the carafes laugh, when he was imitating the cheeky soldierboy, his fingers spread wide and his hat on the back of his head. After 'The Volcano of Love' he went straight on with 'The Baroness of Follebiche',* one of his star turns. On reaching the third verse, he turned towards Clémence and crooned slowly and voluptuously:

> The baroness was not alone,
> Her sisters four were there;
> One was blonde, three others dark,
> Eight eyes of beauty rare.

By now the whole company was quite carried away, and they took up the chorus, the men drumming their heels to the beat and the ladies tapping out the time on their glasses with their knives. They all bawled:

> Now who the hell will buy the drinks,*
> Buy the drinks for the pa . . . for the pa . . .
> Now who the hell will buy the drinks,
> The drinks for the whole patrol?

The glass in the shop-windows rang, and the singers' powerful breath made the muslin curtains fly about. Virginie, meanwhile, had vanished a couple of times, and on returning had bent over Gervaise to whisper something in her ear. When she came back the third time she said to Gervaise under cover of the din:

'My dear, he's still at François's, pretending to read the paper . . . I know there must be something fishy going on.'

She was talking about Lantier. It was Lantier she was keeping an eye on. At each fresh report, Gervaise looked worried.

'Is he pissed?' she asked Virginie.

'No' the tall brunette replied. 'He looks quite sober. That's what I don't like. I ask you, why's he hanging about in a bar if he's sober? . . . My God! I just hope nothing's going to happen!'

The laundress, very upset, begged her to be quiet. All of a sudden complete silence had fallen. Madame Putois had risen to her feet to sing "Pirate Ship Ahoy!". The guests, silent and intent, were watching her: even Poisson had put his pipe on the edge of the table, the better to hear her. Tiny and impassioned, she stood rigidly erect, her face white under her black bonnet; she kept thrusting her left fist forward with proud conviction as she boomed, in a voice bigger than she was:

> A pirate bold, my hearties,
> Is chasing us for slaughter;
> Damnation to the sea wolf!

We'll never give him quarter!
Man the guns, my hearties,
Here's rum to toast their doom;
Death to the bold sea rovers!
The sea shall be their tomb!

That was serious stuff, but, Christ in heaven, it made you
feel like you were there. Poisson, who'd been to sea, nodded
his agreement with the details. Besides, you could easily see
that the song fitted Madame Putois exactly. Coupeau leant over
and described how one evening in the Rue Poulet Madame
Putois had boxed the ears of four men who'd tried to molest
her.

By now Gervaise, helped by Maman Coupeau, was serving
coffee, although people were still eating the cake. They would-
n't let her sit down again, shouting that it was her turn. She
protested, looking so pale and uncomfortable that someone
asked if by any chance the goose had upset her. So she sang
'Oh! Let Me Sleep' in a slight, sweet voice, and when she
came to the refrain, to the wish for a sleep filled with lovely
dreams, her lids closed a little as she gazed vaguely out into the
darkness of the street. Immediately afterwards, Poisson made
the ladies a stiff little bow and embarked on a drinking song,
'The Wines of France', but he couldn't carry a tune; only the
last verse, the patriotic one, went down well, because at the bit
about the Tricolour, he raised his glass very high, waved it back
and forth and finally emptied it down his wide open mouth.
Then came a succession of sentimental pieces; Madame Boche's
barcarolle had Venice and gondoliers in it whereas Madame
Lorilleux's bolero had Seville and Andalusians, while Lorilleux
even managed to bring in the perfumes of Araby in singing of
Fatima the dancer's amours. In the heavy indigestion-laden
atmosphere round the grease-spotted table golden vistas were
conjured up, with ivory throats and ebony tresses, moonlit
kisses to the strumming of guitars and nautch-girls carpeting
the ground under their feet with pearls and precious stones; and
the men smoked away blissfully at their pipes, while the ladies
wore unconscious little smiles of sensual pleasure. They were
all far away, breathing in the perfumed air. When Clémence

began warbling 'Build Your Nest' with a tremolo in her voice, that was also much enjoyed, it reminded you of the countryside, and the dainty little birds, and dancing under the trees, and the nectar-laden flowers, in fact, what you saw in the Bois de Vincennes when you went there to eat rabbit. But they were soon splitting their sides again when Virginie started 'My Little Riquiqui',* taking off a vivandière, one arm akimbo while at the same time turning her other wrist as though pouring into an imaginary glass. This was such a success that they all begged Maman Coupeau to sing 'The Mouse'.* The old woman refused, swearing she didn't know that dirty song, but then she did begin it in her reedy, cracked voice, her wrinkled face and bright little eyes emphasizing the innuendos and the terrors of Mademoiselle Lise as she gathered her skirts close about her legs at the sight of the mouse. The whole table was roaring; the ladies couldn't keep their faces straight, and were flashing glances at the men beside them: it wasn't a naughty song, after all, there were no rude words in it. It's true that Boche was busy being a mouse up and down Madame Vigoureux's calves. Things might have got out of hand had not Goujet, at a glance from Gervaise, restored silence and good taste with 'Abd-el-Kader's Farewell',* which he thundered out in his deep bass. Now there was someone with a good pair of bellows if you like! The song rolled forth from his wide, handsome golden beard as if from a brass trumpet. When he cried out: 'Oh, my noble companion'—referring to the warrior's black mare—every heart beat faster and immediate applause drowned the end of the song, his voice had been so resounding.

'It's your turn now, Père Bru, your turn!' Maman Coupeau called. 'Sing yours now. The old ones are the best, aren't they?'

The guests turned to the old man, pressing and encouraging him. He sat there stupefied, his face a motionless mask of bronzed skin, staring at everyone and apparently not understanding. They asked him if he knew the 'The Five Vowels'. He hung his head: no, he couldn't remember it, all the songs from the good old days were jumbled together in his noddle. Just as they were deciding to leave him in peace, he seemed to remember, and began in a faltering, hollow voice:

> Tra la la, tra la la,
> tra la, tra la, tra la la!

His face lit up, as if this refrain awakened in him the memory of long distant revelries which only he could enjoy, and he listened with a child's delight to his own fading voice:

> Tra la la, tra la la,
> tra la, tra la, tra la la!

'I say, my dear,' Virginie whispered in Gervaise's ear, 'you know I've been back to François's again. It really bothered me . . . Well, Lantier's pushed off.'

'You didn't run into him outside?' asked Gervaise.

'No, I was walking fast, and I never thought of looking.'

But raising her eyes just then, Virginie exclaimed, stifling a gasp: 'My God! . . . There he is, on the pavement opposite; he's looking in here.'

Filled with dismay, Gervaise risked a quick glance. A crowd had gathered in the street, to listen to the party singing. The grocer's boys, the tripe woman and the little clockmaker had collected in a group as if watching a show. There were soldiers, and frockcoated gentlemen, as well as three little girls of five or six who stood holding hands in solemn amazement. And yes, Lantier was actually there, right in the front, watching and listening, as cool as could be. Proper cheek it was, this time! Gervaise felt a chill spreading from her feet up to her heart, and she sat not daring to move as Père Bru went on:

> Tra la la, tra la la,
> Tra la, tra la, tra la la!

'That'll do, old chap, that's enough for now,' said Coupeau. 'D'you know the whole thing? What about singin' us it another day, eh, when we've got a bit too jolly?'

There was some laughter. The old man stopped short, looking round the table with his faded eyes, then relapsed into his former state of brooding imbecility. The coffee was finished and Coupeau asked for more wine. Clémence had started on the strawberries again. The singing stopped for a moment and they talked about a woman who'd been found hanged that morning, in the house next door. It was Madame Lerat's turn, but there

were things she had to do in preparation. She wet the corner of
her napkin in a glass of water and pressed it to her temples,
because she was too hot. After that, she asked for a drop of
brandy, drank it, then wiped her lips with great care.

'How about "The Child of the Lord"?' she murmured. 'Yes,
"The Child of the Lord" . . .'

And tall, masculine-looking Madame Lerat, with her bony
nose and her square policeman's shoulders, began:

> Frightened and lost in the chill of the night,
> Forsaken by all save the merciful Lord,
> The motherless maid is preserved by His might,
> For a child that is lost is the child of the Lord . . .

Her voice trembled on certain words, lingering over the
palatalized notes; she slanted her eyes upwards to heaven, while
her right hand, hovering in front of her bosom, would sometimes press her heart with a fervent gesture. Gervaise, tormented by Lantier's presence, could not restrain her tears; she
felt as if the song was about her own suffering, as if she were
that lost, forsaken waif whom the Lord would take into his care.
Clémence, who was very tipsy, suddenly burst into sobs and sat
with her head on the edge of the table, muffling her hiccups in
the tablecloth. A quivering silence reigned. The ladies had all
pulled out their handkerchiefs, and were wiping their eyes, their
heads up, proud of their emotion. The men had bowed their
heads and stared straight ahead, blinking. Poisson, choking and
clenching his teeth, twice broke the end off his pipe, spitting
the bits on to the ground each time without stopping smoking.
Boche, whose hand still lay on Madame Vigoureux's knee, was
no longer pinching her, as, overcome by a vague feeling of
remorse and respect, he sat with two large tears running down
his cheeks. That bunch of boozers were all as tight as lords and
as tender as lambs. In fact, that was wine they were weeping!
When the chorus began again yet more slowly and mournfully,
they all gave in and blubbered into their plates, letting themselves go completely, wallowing in pity.

But Gervaise and Virginie couldn't help themselves, they
never took their eyes off the opposite pavement. Madame Boche
was the next to notice Lantier, and she gave a little cry, her face

still streaming with tears. Now all three of them were looking worried as they exchanged involuntary little nods. My God, what if Coupeau turned round, what if Coupeau saw him! There'd be blue murder! There'd be hell to pay! So that of course Coupeau asked:

'Whatever is it you're looking at?'

Bending round, he saw Lantier.

'Christ in heaven! That's too much,' he muttered. 'The sod, the fuckin' sod! No, that's the bleedin' limit, I'm goin' to put a stop to it . . .'

And, as he got up, spluttering out dreadful threats, Gervaise begged him in a low voice:

'Listen, oh please listen . . . Put that knife down . . . Stay right here, don't go and do something awful.'

Virginie had to grab the knife he'd taken from the table, but she couldn't stop him going out and walking up to Lantier. The company in its increasingly tearful and maudlin state was quite unaware of what was happening, as they listened to Madame Lerat singing, with a heart-rending expression on her face:

> She was lost, quite lost, poor orphan child
> And her plaintive cries went all unheard
> Save by the trees and the wind so wild.

The last line trailed away like the mournful moaning of the storm. Madame Putois, who was drinking just then, felt so overcome that she spilt her wine all over the tablecloth. Gervaise, meanwhile, sat frozen in her place, jamming a fist into her mouth to stop herself crying out and blinking with terror, expecting any minute to see one of the two men knocked senseless there in the middle of the street. Virginie and Madame Boche were also engrossed in the scene. Coupeau, unprepared for the fresh air, had nearly come a cropper in the gutter as he tried to leap at Lantier, who'd simply moved to one side, his hands in his pockets. Now the two men were yelling insults at one another, Coupeau especially letting Lantier have it good and proper, calling him a bleeding swine, and swearing he'd have his guts. You could hear their furious voices and you could see their violent gestures, they were swinging their arms about so much you'd have thought they'd come out of their sockets. Gervaise began to feel faint and she closed her eyes because it was going on too long and she felt they were sure to bite off each other's noses, their faces were that close. But then, hearing nothing more, she reopened her eyes, and was stunned to see they were chatting quietly.

Madame Lerat's voice arose, cooing and tearful, as she started on another verse:

> Next day they brought the poor child home,
> Frozen and faint and close to death . . .

'There are women who are real bitches, aren't there!' said Madame Lorilleux, in the midst of the general approbation.

Gervaise had exchanged glances with Madame Boche and Virginie. Were Coupeau and Lantier making it up, then? They were still on the pavement, talking. They were still jeering at each other, but in a companionable way, calling each other things like 'silly bugger' in tones which sounded almost friendly. People were looking at them, so they began walking quietly side by side along in front of the houses, turning round every ten steps or so. Their conversation had become very animated. All of a sudden it looked as if Coupeau was getting angry again, while Lantier was refusing to do something, something Coupeau wanted. Then the roofer actually pushed Lantier, making him cross the street and come into the shop.

'I tell you I really want you to!' he shouted. 'You must 'ave a glass of wine with us. Men are men, right? We're meant to get along together . . .'

Madame Lerat was finishing the last chorus. All the ladies joined in, twisting their handkerchiefs in their hands:

> For a child that is lost is the child of the Lord.

Compliments were showered on the singer as she sat down, claiming she was quite overcome. She asked for something to drink—she put too much feeling into that particular song and was always afraid she would wreck her nerves. The whole table, meanwhile, was staring at Lantier, who'd calmly settled down beside Coupeau and was already eating the last piece of the cake, dipping it in a glass of wine. Apart from Virginie and Madame Boche, no one knew him. The Lorilleux, certainly, could smell a rat, but they didn't know what exactly, and they sat there looking snooty. Goujet had noticed Gervaise's dismay, and was eyeing the new arrival disapprovingly. As an uncomfortable silence had fallen, Coupeau said simply:

'He's a friend.'

And, turning to his wife: 'C'mon, get movin'! . . . Maybe there's still some 'ot coffee.'

Gervaise was staring meekly and stupidly from one to the other. At first, when her husband had pushed her former lover into the shop, she'd clasped her head in her hands with the same instinctive movement she used during a bad storm every time a clap of thunder came. She just couldn't believe this was happening; surely the walls would collapse and bury them all? Then, seeing the two men sitting there, and not even the muslin curtains stirring, she had all of a sudden found it perfectly natural. The goose hadn't really agreed with her; she'd certainly eaten too much of it, and it was stopping her thinking. She was paralysed by a pleasing languor which kept her slumped over the table, wanting only to be left in peace. Why get all upset, for Christ's sake, when no one else was, and things seemed to be working out by themselves to everyone's liking? She got up to see if there was any coffee left.

In the back room, the children were fast asleep. Augustine had terrorized them all through the dessert, pinching their strawberries and scaring them stiff with dreadful threats. Now she was feeling very ill as she crouched on a little stool, white-faced and silent. Fat Pauline had let her head drop on to the shoulder of Étienne who was himself asleep over the table edge. Nana was sitting on the bedside mat beside Victor, holding him against her with one arm round his neck; half asleep, her eyes shut, she kept repeating in a feeble, monotonous voice:

'Oh, Mummy, it hurts, it hurts, Mummy . . .'

'No wonder,' muttered Augustine, her head rolling about on her shoulders, 'they're pissed; they were singing just like the grown-ups.'

Seeing Étienne gave Gervaise a fresh jolt. She felt she would suffocate when she thought that the kid's father was there, eating cake in the next room, and he hadn't even said he'd like to give the child a kiss. She nearly woke up Étienne, to take him through in her arms. But then, yet again, she decided it was quite all right that things were working out in this calm fashion. It wouldn't have done, she was sure, to make a scene at the end of the dinner. She came back with the coffee-pot and poured a cup for Lantier, who in any case didn't seem at all interested in her.

'Well now, 'smy turn,' mumbled Coupeau in a thick voice. 'You've been savin' me up, eh? Best for last! Now I'm goin' to give you "What a Pig of a Boy!" '*

'Yes, yes, "What a Pig of a Boy!" ' everyone at the table yelled.

The din was starting up again, Lantier was forgotten. The ladies placed their glasses and knives at the ready, to accompany the chorus. They were already laughing in anticipation as they watched Coupeau swaying about on his pins, with a devilish look in his eye. He put on a rasping voice, like an old woman's:

> Every mornin' when I wake
> I'm real queer in me tum,
> I send him down the Grève* to get
> A few sous' worth of rum.*
> He takes his time in comin' up*
> And when he brings me tot*
> I find he's supped the half of it,*
> What a pig of a boy I've got!

And the ladies, tapping on their glasses, took up the chorus in a tremendous explosion of gaiety:

> What a pig of a boy,
> What a pig of a boy,
> What a pig of a boy I've got!

The Rue de la Goutte-d'Or itself was joining in now; the whole neighbourhood was singing 'What a Pig of a Boy'. Across the street, the little clockmaker, the grocer's boys, the tripe-shop woman and the greengrocer, who all knew the song, joined in the chorus, exchanging slaps just for fun. The entire street was getting sozzled, and that's a fact; the mere smell of the spree going on at the Coupeaus was enough to make people stagger about on the pavements. And you had to admit that inside the shop they were all well and truly plastered. It had been coming on steadily ever since that first slug of unwatered wine, after the soup. Now they were going full blast, every one of them bawling out the song, fairly bursting with food as they sat in the reddish haze from the two smoking lamps. The racket from this stupendous jamboree drowned the rumbling of the last vehicles in the street. Two policemen came rushing up thinking it must be a riot, but on seeing Poisson they gave him a conniving little nod. Then they proceeded slowly on their way, walking together along by the darkened houses.

Coupeau had reached this verse:

> Sunday night, when it was cool,
> We went to P'tit-Villette
> To see my Unc the cess-pool man
> Who's known as old Tinette;*
> We ate cherries, 'twas our luck
> They were a stony lot,*
> And then he rolled in Uncle's muck,
> What a pig of a boy I've got!

Then, the house seemed to burst apart as a colossal bellow rose into the warm stillness of the night, so deafening that the revellers began to applaud themselves, for surely never would they be able to bellow any louder.

Not one of the company could ever remember exactly how the party ended. It must have been very late, that much was clear, because there wasn't even a cat about in the street. It's quite possible, all the same, that they joined hands and danced round the table. Everything was engulfed in a yellowish fog, in which red faces jumped about, grinning from ear to ear. They certainly did have some wine with sugar in it towards the end, the only thing was, they couldn't remember if someone hadn't gone and put salt in the glasses instead, for a lark. The children must have undressed and put themselves to bed. The next morning, Madame Boche boasted that she'd boxed Boche's ears on catching him chatting up Madame Vigoureux rather too cosily in a corner, but Boche couldn't remember a thing about it and treated it as a joke. What everyone agreed was *not* very nice, was the way Clémence had carried on. Obviously, she

wasn't the kind of girl you'd ask again: she'd ended up showing
off everything she'd got, and she'd puked all down one of the
muslin curtains and completely ruined it. At least the men did
go into the street to do it; Lorilleux and Poisson, when they felt
queer, managed to dash as far as the pork-butcher's shop.
Breeding always tells. For instance, when some of the ladies,
Madame Putois, Madame Lerat and Virginie, found the heat
too much for them, they simply went into the back room and
took off their stays; and Virginie even had a little lie down on
the bed, just for a minute, to avoid trouble later. Then the
company just seemed to melt away one behind the other,
disappearing together into the depths of the dark street, raising
a racket one last time with a furious quarrel between the
Lorilleux and a persistent, mournful 'tra la la, tra la la' from
Père Bru. Gervaise was pretty sure that Goujet had started to
cry when he left; Coupeau was still singing; as for Lantier, he
must have stayed till last. She could still remember feeling, at
one moment, something like breath in her hair, but she couldn't
be certain if it was Lantier or just the warm night air.

As Madame Lerat refused to walk home to the Batignolles at
that late hour, they took a mattress off the bed and spread it for
her in a corner of the shop, after pushing the table over. That
is where she slept, amid the crumbs from the dinner. And, all
night long, while the Coupeaus lay dead to the world, sleeping
off the binge, a neighbour's cat who'd taken advantage of an
open window crunched up the bones of the goose, quietly
gnawing away with its tiny teeth until it finally finished it off.

CHAPTER VIII

The following Saturday Coupeau, who hadn't come in for
dinner, brought Lantier home with him about ten o'clock.
They'd had a dish of sheep's trotters together at Thomas's in
Montmartre.

'You mustn't scold us, old lady,' said the roofer: 'We're
behavin' ourselves, as you see . . . Oh, you don't run any risks
with him, he makes you stick to the straight an' narrow.'

And he told her how they'd bumped into each other in the Rue Rochechouart. After dinner, Lantier had refused a drink at the Boule Noire,* saying that when you're married to a nice decent woman you shouldn't loaf around in all the seedy dives. Gervaise listened with a faint smile. No, certainly, it hadn't entered her head to scold him; she felt too uncomfortable. Ever since the party, she'd been expecting to see her former lover again some day or other, but at such an hour, just when she was about to go to bed, the sudden arrival of the two men had caught her off guard, and her hands were trembling as she pinned up her knot of hair which had been loose about her neck.

'Now how 'bout it,' Coupeau went on. 'Seein' as he was so considerate, refusin' a drink while we were out, you can give us one now . . . It's the least you can do!'

The assistants had long since left. Maman Coupeau and Nana had just gone to bed. So Gervaise, who'd already been holding one of the shutters when the men appeared, left the shop open and brought glasses and the remains of a bottle of cognac over to a corner of the work-table. Lantier didn't sit down, and avoided addressing her directly. However, when she poured his drink, he exclaimed:

'Just a drop for me, please, Madame.'

Coupeau stared at them, and came straight out with what he thought. Surely they weren't going to be silly, now! Bygones were bygones, weren't they? If you went on nursing grudges after nine or ten years, you'd end up not seeing anyone. No, no, he himself was being perfectly frank about his feelings. In the first place, he knew who he was dealing with, a good woman and a good man, two good friends, in fact! It didn't worry him, he knew he could trust them.

'Oh of course, of course . . .' Gervaise kept repeating, looking down and hardly knowing what she was saying.

'She's like a sister now, nothing but a sister!' murmured Lantier in his turn.

'Then for Christ's sake shake hands; we don't give a shit what bourgeois sods think!' yelled Coupeau. 'When you've got that into your nut, see, you're better off than a millionaire. As for me, I think friendship's more important than anything, 'cos friendship, well it's friendship, an' it's the best thing in the world.'

He kept pounding his stomach fiercely with his fist, his manner so excited that they had to calm him down. Then, in silence, they all three clinked glasses and drank up. Gervaise could now take her time looking at Lantier, for on the night of the party she'd seen him through a haze. He'd gained weight, and had become round and plump; because of his short height his arms and legs were too heavy. But his features, despite an overall puffiness due to his slothful life, were as handsome as ever, and as he still spent a lot of time on the care of his thin little moustache, he appeared exactly the age he was, thirty-five. That day, in grey trousers and a dark blue coat, with a round hat, he looked quite the gentleman; he even had a watch with a silver chain from which hung a ring, a keepsake.

'I'm off,' he said. 'My place is miles away.'

He was already out on the pavement, when the roofer called him back to make him promise he'd never pass their door without dropping in to say hello. Meanwhile Gervaise, who'd quietly disappeared, came back pushing Étienne in front of her. The boy was in his shirt, his face already heavy with sleep, but he smiled as he rubbed his eyes. When he caught sight of Lantier, however, he began trembling and looked uncomfortable, as he cast uneasy glances towards his mother and Coupeau.

'Don't you recognize this gentleman?' asked Coupeau.

The child hung his head without answering, then gave a slight nod to indicate that he did.

'Well, stop actin' the fool, go an' give 'im a kiss.'

Lantier stood waiting, grave and calm. When Étienne made up his mind to go up to him, he bent down and offered both cheeks, then himself planted a smacking kiss on the boy's forehead. At that, Étienne plucked up his courage and looked at his father. Quite suddenly, however, he burst into sobs and rushed off like a maniac, his clothes all awry, with Coupeau scolding him for his rudeness.

'He's upset,' said Gervaise, white in the face and shaken herself.

'Oh, as a rule he's very sweet-tempered and nice,' Coupeau was saying. 'I've done a good job bringin' 'im up, you'll see . . . He'll get used to you. He has to get to know people . . . Well, if only for his sake, we couldn't 'ave stayed enemies for ever, could we? We should 'ave made it up ages ago, 'cos I'd stick my head on the block sooner than keep a father from seein' 'is kid.'

And thereupon he proposed that they finish off the bottle. All three clinked glasses again. Lantier showed no surprise and seemed completely at ease. Before leaving, to return the roofer's courtesy, he insisted on helping him shut up the shop. Then, dusting off his hands, he wished the couple goodnight.

'Sleep well. I'm going to try and catch an omnibus . . . I promise I'll be back soon.'

From that evening, Lantier often turned up in the Rue de la Goutte-d'Or. He came when Coupeau was at home, and on arriving would immediately enquire after him, acting as though he came solely on his account. Then he'd sit by the window in his coat, nicely shaven, his hair well-groomed, and chat politely, with the manners of an educated man. That is how, bit by bit, the Coupeaus got to know something about his life. At one point during the last eight years he'd managed a hat factory, and when they asked him why he'd given it up, he only talked about the double-dealing of a partner, a southerner like himself, a scoundrel who'd squandered all the firm's money on women. But he still retained the consciousness of his former status as an employer, like a noble title which he could never deny. He always said he was on the point of bringing off a splendid business deal: hatmakers were going to set him up and entrust him with vast enterprises. In the meantime he did absolutely nothing, but strolled about in the sun with his hands in his pockets like the idle rich. Sometimes, when he complained, they'd venture to mention a factory that needed workers, and then he'd smile in a pitying fashion and declare he had no intention of starving to death while slogging away for other people. Still, as Coupeau said, the bugger certainly wasn't living on fresh air. He was a sharp one all right, he knew how to look after number one, he must be in on some sort of racket because after all he gave the impression of being quite comfortable, and

he must need money for those clean shirts and classy neckties
of his. One morning Coupeau had seen him getting his boots
shined in the Boulevard Montmartre. The truth of the matter
was that Lantier, who talked nineteen to the dozen about other
people, said nothing or told lies about himself. He didn't even
want to let on where he lived. No, he was putting up at a
friend's, miles away, until he found a good job, and he forbade
people to come to see him because he was never in.

'For every ten openings there's only one good one,' he'd
often explain. 'The thing is, there's no point in starting at a
dump where you won't stay twenty-four hours . . . For instance, one Monday I began at Champion's in Montrouge.*
That evening, Champion and I had a row about politics; he
didn't see things the way I did. So, on the Tuesday morning, I
took myself off, since slavery's over and done with and I don't
propose to sell myself for seven francs a day.'

It was the beginning of November. Ever courteous, Lantier
brought bunches of violets for Gervaise and her two assistants.
Little by little his visits became more frequent, until he came
almost every day. It seemed as if he wanted to make a conquest
of the household and of the entire neighbourhood: and he began
by making up to Clémence and Madame Putois, to whom he
paid the most assiduous attentions, without distinction of age.
In a month, the two assistants adored him. The Boches, greatly
flattered because he'd call at their lodge to pay his respects,
went into raptures over his politeness. As for the Lorilleux,
when they found out who it was who'd turned up at the party
at the dessert stage, at first they spewed out a torrent of abuse
against Gervaise for having the gall to bring her former lover
into her home in this way. One day, however, Lantier went up
to their place and made such a good impression on them as he
ordered a gold chain for a lady of his acquaintance, that they
asked him to sit down and kept him for an hour, delighted
by his conversation, even wondering how a man of such
distinction could ever have lived with Banban. After a bit,
Lantier's visits to the Coupeaus no longer upset anyone and
seemed quite natural, so well had he succeeded in ingratiating
himself with the whole Rue de la Goutte-d'Or. Only Goujet
kept aloof. If he happened to be there when Lantier arrived,

he'd make for the door, to avoid having to become acquainted with the fellow.

However, during those first weeks while Lantier was inspiring this warm regard all round, Gervaise felt deeply troubled. She was conscious of the same burning sensation in the pit of her stomach she'd felt the day of Virginie's revelations. Her terror came from a fear that she'd be quite unable to resist him, were he to take it into his head to kiss her if he caught her alone one evening. She thought about him too much, she was much too wrapped up in him. Slowly, however, she began to relax, as she saw how correctly he behaved, never looking straight at her, never touching her with so much as a fingertip when the others had their backs turned. And then Virginie, who seemed able to read her mind, made her feel embarrassed about her shameful thoughts. Why ever was she trembling like that? You couldn't find a nicer man. Of course there was nothing for her to be afraid of now. And one day the tall brunette manœuvred the pair of them into a corner where she turned the conversation to the subject of love. Choosing his words carefully, Lantier declared in a solemn voice that his heart was quite dead, and that all he wanted from now on was to devote himself to his son's happiness. He never mentioned Claude, who was still in the South. Every evening he'd kiss Étienne on the forehead, but he didn't know what to say to him if the boy hung about; Lantier would then forget all about him and bandy sweet nothings with Clémence. So Gervaise, her peace of mind restored, felt the past was dead and gone. Lantier's actual presence wore away at her memories of Plassans and the Hôtel Boncœur. Seeing him constantly, she no longer dreamt of him. She was even overcome by repugnance at the thought of their former relationship. Oh, it was all over, all quite over. If ever he dared ask her for that, she'd answer him with a couple of slaps, or better still, she'd tell her husband. And, once more, without feeling a single qualm, she let her thoughts dwell with extraordinary sweetness on Goujet's warm friendship.

One morning when she arrived at the laundry, Clémence reported that the previous evening at about eleven she'd seen Lantier with a woman on his arm. She talked about this very crudely, and not without a certain malice, curious to know how

her employer would react. Yes, Monsieur Lantier was walking
up the Rue Notre-Dame-de-Lorette;* the woman was blonde,
one of those worn-out street-walkers with a bare bum under
their silk skirts. And just for a lark she'd followed them. The
tart had gone into a pork-butchers' to buy some ham and some
shrimps. Then, in the Rue de la Rochefoucauld,* Monsieur
Lantier had waited on the pavement, staring up, till the girl,
who'd gone in alone, gave him the all-clear to join her. But it
was in vain that Clémence went on with her filthy remarks, for
Gervaise just continued calmly ironing a white dress. At
times the story made her smile slightly. Those southerners, she
said, were all wild about women; they had to have them no
matter what; they'd pick 'em off a dung heap with a shovel. And
that evening when Lantier turned up she was amused when
Clémence teased him with roundabout questions about his
blonde. Actually he seemed quite flattered at having been
noticed. Lord! it was an old friend he still saw from time to
time, when it wouldn't bother anyone; a girl with lots of style,
whose place was done up in rosewood; and he mentioned some
of her former lovers, a viscount, a wealthy dealer in china, a
notary's son. He himself adored women who smelt nice. He was
shoving his handkerchief under Clémence's nose— the girl had
scented it for him—when Étienne came back. At that he came
over all serious and kissed the child, adding it had just been a
bit of a laugh, didn't mean a thing, and his heart was dead.
Gervaise, leaning over her work, nodded in approval. And in
the end Clémence got what she deserved for being mean,
because she'd certainly felt Lantier pinch her bottom a few
times on the sly and she was dying of jealousy because she
didn't stink of musk like that street-walker.

   When spring came round again, Lantier, now quite one of
the family, spoke of coming to live in the neighbourhood so as
to be nearer his friends. He wanted a furnished room in a nice
house. Madame Boche and even Gervaise herself went to a lot
of trouble to find one for him. They combed all the nearby
streets. But he was too fussy, he'd like a ground floor, he must
have a large courtyard, in short he wanted every imaginable
convenience. And each evening now, at the Coupeaus', he
seemed to be calculating the height of the ceilings and studying

the layout of the rooms, as if longing for a place just like theirs. Oh, he couldn't think of anything that would suit him better, he'd gladly have built himself a little nest in a quiet warm corner. And each time he'd conclude his examination with these words:

'Good Lord! You've really a very nice set-up here, you know!'

One evening when Lantier had had dinner with them and then repeated his remark during dessert, Coupeau, who now called him by the familiar 'tu', suddenly declared:

'You must stay here, old man, if that's how you feel . . . We'll manage somehow.'

And he explained that where they put the dirty laundry would make a lovely room if it was cleaned up. Étienne would sleep on a mattress on the floor of the shop, that was all.

'No, no, I can't accept, you'd find it too much of a nuisance,' said Lantier. 'I know you really mean it, but we'd be too much on top of one another . . . And then, see here, we all want our privacy. I'd have to go through your room, and that wouldn't always be so funny.'

'What a fathead!' the roofer replied, choking with laughter and thumping the table as he tried to control his voice; 'he's always on about some rubbish like that . . . But, you silly bugger, we've got brains, haven't we? There's two windows in the room. Well, we open one down to ground level an' make it into a door. Then, y'see, you come in through the courtyard. We can even block up the communicating door if we want. We could all lead our own lives: you'd have your place an' we'd have ours.'

There was a silence. The hatter murmured:

'Well now, if it was like that, I'd not say . . . No, no, I'd still be too much in the way.'

He was careful not to look at Gervaise. Clearly, though, he was waiting for a word from her before accepting. She didn't like her husband's idea at all: not that the thought of Lantier's living with them upset or worried her particularly, but she couldn't imagine where she'd put her dirty washing. Meanwhile, the roofer was pointing out the advantages of the arrangement. The rent—five hundred francs—had always been a bit steep. Well, their mate could pay them twenty francs a month for the furnished room; he wouldn't find that dear, and it'd help them when the rent came due. He added that he'd see to rigging up a box under their bed big enough to hold the dirty washing of the whole neighbourhood. At that, Gervaise still hesitated, looking at Maman Coupeau as if to find out what she thought; but Lantier had won her over months ago by bringing her pastilles for her catarrh.

'You wouldn't be a bother to us, of course not,' she said at last. 'We could work things out . . .'

'Thank you, but no,' repeated Lantier. 'You're too kind, it'd be taking advantage.'

This time Coupeau blew up. How much longer was he going to go on being such a mug! When they kept telling him they really meant it! He'd be doing them a favour; there, could he get that into his head? Then, in a furious voice, he yelled:

'Étienne! Étienne!'

The boy had fallen asleep leaning on the table. Startled, he raised his head.

'Listen, tell him it's what you want . . . Yes, tell that gentleman . . . Tell him good an' loud: it's what I want . . .'

'It's what I want!' stammered Étienne, his voice thick with sleep.

They all started to laugh. However Lantier quickly resumed his grave, earnest manner, shaking Coupeau's hand across the table and saying:

'I accept . . . We're all good friends, aren't we? Yes, I accept for the sake of the boy.'

The very next day, when Monsieur Marescot, the landlord, dropped in to see the Boches in their lodge, Gervaise spoke to him about the plan. At first he seemed uneasy, and refused in some annoyance, as if she'd asked him to pull down a whole wing of his building. In the end, however, after a close inspection of the premises and a good look at the upper stories to make sure they wouldn't be weakened, he did give them permission, on condition that he wouldn't bear any of the expense; and the Coupeaus had to sign a paper committing them to restore everything to its original state when their lease expired. That same evening, the roofer brought over some pals of his, a bricklayer, a carpenter and a painter, nice blokes who'd polish off that little job after their day's work, just to help out. Even so, the fitting of the new door and the cleaning of the room still cost a good hundred francs, not counting the bottles to help the work along. Coupeau told his mates he'd pay them later, with his lodger's first lot of rent. Then they had to furnish the room. Gervaise left Maman Coupeau's cupboard there and added a table and two chairs from her own room; but there was no avoiding buying a wash-stand and a bed, complete with all the bedding, which came to a hundred and thirty francs, which she'd have to pay off at ten francs a month. But even though, for the first ten months, Lantier's twenty francs would be swallowed up by the debts they'd contracted, there'd be a nice profit later on.

Lantier moved in early in June. The day before, Coupeau had offered to fetch his trunk from his old place, to save him the thirty sous a cab would cost. But the hatter seemed embarrassed, saying his trunk was too heavy, as if wanting to hide where he lived from them until the end. He arrived in the afternoon, about three o'clock. Coupeau wasn't there. And Gervaise, standing at the entrance to the laundry, turned very pale as she recognized the trunk on the cab. It was their old trunk, the one she'd done the journey from Plassans with; it was scratched and broken now, and held together with rope. She was seeing it coming back to her just as she had often dreamed, and she could imagine that the same cab, the cab in which that bitch Adèle had cocked a snook at her, was bringing it back. Meanwhile Boche was giving Lantier a hand. Gervaise, rather dazed, followed them in silence. When they'd put down their burden in the middle of the room, she remarked, for something to say,

'Well, that's a good job done, eh?'

Then, seeing that Lantier was busy undoing the ropes and not even looking at her, she pulled herself together and added:

'Monsieur Boche, do have a drink.'

And off she went to fetch a bottle and some glasses. Just at that moment Poisson, in uniform, was passing by on the pavement. She signalled to him with a smile and a wink. The policeman understood perfectly. When he was on duty and he was winked at, that meant he was being offered a glass of wine. In fact he'd even walk up and down for hours in front of the laundry waiting for Gervaise to wink. Then, so no one would see, he'd go in through the courtyard and swig his wine on the sly.

'Aha!' said Lantier, seeing him come in, 'it's you, Badingue!'*

He called him Badingue as a joke, to poke fun at the Emperor. Poisson accepted this in his stiff-necked way, without letting on whether it actually annoyed him. Indeed the two men, although divided by their political convictions, had become very good friends.

'Y'know the Emperor was a policeman in London,'* Boche now remarked. 'It's true, I swear! He used to run in tipsy women.'

Gervaise had filled three glasses on the table. She herself didn't fancy a drink, she felt too queasy. But she stayed where she was, watching Lantier remove the last pieces of rope, gripped by the need to know what the trunk contained. She could remember, down in a corner, a bundle of socks, two dirty shirts and an old hat. Could those things still be there? Was she going to see those relics of the past again? Before raising the lid of the trunk Lantier took his glass and clinked it with the others.

'Your health!'

'And yours,' replied Boche and Poisson.

The laundress refilled the glasses. The three men wiped their lips with their hands. Then, at last, Lantier opened the trunk. It was full of a jumble of newspapers, books, old clothes and bundles of linen. One after another he pulled out a saucepan, a pair of boots, a bust of Ledru-Rollin* with its nose broken, an embroidered shirt and a pair of work trousers. And Gervaise, leaning over the trunk, smelled a tobaccoey smell, the smell of a sloppy man who only bothers about the top layer, the part of himself that people can see. No, the old hat wasn't in the corner on the left any more. There was a pin cushion there she'd never seen before, a present from some woman. At that, she grew calmer, feeling vaguely sad as she continued staring at the things as they emerged, wondering if they dated from her days or from the days of the others.

'Hey, Badingue, have you ever seen this?' the hatter went on.

He shoved a little book printed in Brussels* under the policeman's nose: *The Amours of Napoleon III*,* with illustrations. It contained, among other anecdotes, the story of how the Emperor had seduced the thirteen-year-old daughter of a cook, and the picture showed Napoleon III, bare-legged and clad only in the Sash of the Legion of Honour, chasing a little girl who was fleeing from his lust.

'There you are now!' exclaimed Boche, his furtive sensuality aroused. 'That's the way it always is!'

Poisson stood there struck dumb with consternation: he couldn't find a word to say in defence of the Emperor. It was printed in a book, so he couldn't deny it. Then, as Lantier kept jeering and brandishing the picture under his nose, he suddenly shouted, spreading out his arms,

'Well, so what? It's part of human nature, isn't it?'

This reply shut Lantier up. He arranged his books and newspapers on a shelf in the cupboard; and as he seemed very put out at not having a little bookshelf hanging on the wall above the table, Gervaise promised to get him one. He had Louis Blanc's *Histoire de dix ans*,'* minus the first volume, which in any case he'd never owned; Lamartine's *Girondins*,* in two-sous instalments, Eugène Sue's *Les Mystères de Paris* and *Le Juif errant*,* as well as a pile of philosophic and philanthropic books he'd picked up in junk shops. But what he cherished and valued above anything else were his newspapers. He'd been collecting them for years. Whenever, in a café, he read a good article which he agreed with, he'd buy the paper and keep it. In this way he'd amassed an enormous number of newspapers of every title and every date, which were all bundled together without any kind of order. When he'd taken this pile from the bottom of his trunk, he patted it in a friendly way, saying to the two men,

'See that? Well, that belongs to yours truly, and no one else can boast of anything to touch it. You just can't imagine what's in there. I mean, if you put half those ideas into practice, society'd be cleaned up in a twinkling. Yes, that Emperor of yours and all his narks 'ud be in the soup, all right . . .'

He was interrupted by the policeman, whose red moustache and beard were quivering on his white face.

'And the army? What'd you do with the army, I'd like to know?'

At that, Lantier flew off the handle. Thumping his fist down on his newspapers, he shouted:

'I'm for doing away with the military, I believe in fraternity among peoples . . . I want to abolish privilege, and titles, and monopolies . . . I want equal wages, profit-sharing, and the glorification of the proletariat . . . . All the liberties, d'you hear, all of them! Divorce* as well!'

'Yes, yes, divorce, for the sake of morality!' Boche chimed in.

Poisson had assumed a majestic air. He replied:

'But even though I don't want your liberties, I'm perfectly free just the same.'

'If you don't want them, if you don't want them . . .' stuttered Lantier, incoherent with rage. 'No, you're not free! I'd pack you off to Cayenne* if you don't want to be free, that's what I'd do, off to Cayenne with your fucking Emperor and his band of pigs!'

They went for each other like this each time they met. Usually Gervaise, who disliked arguments, would intervene. Rousing herself from the torpor produced by the sight of that trunk which reeked so sourly of her former love, she drew the men's attention to the glasses of wine.

'Yes, of course,' said Lantier, suddenly quite calm, picking up his glass. 'Here's to you!'

'To you!' Boche and Poisson replied, clinking glasses with him. Boche, however, was anxiously hopping from one foot to the other and glancing at the policeman out of the corner of his eye.

'This is just between ourselves, isn't it, Monsieur Poisson?' he murmured eventually. 'You've been shown things, been told things . . .'

Poisson didn't let him finish. He placed his hand on his heart, as if to indicate that everything would stay hidden there. He'd never tell on pals, not he. As Coupeau had now turned up, they downed a second bottle. The policeman then took off through the courtyard and resumed his beat, walking with measured pace, stiff and stern.

At first, after Lantier arrived, everything at the laundry was topsy-turvy. It was true Lantier had his own separate room, his own entrance and his own key, but as at the last moment they'd decided not to block up the communicating door, he usually came and went through the shop. The dirty washing also bothered Gervaise a lot, because her husband didn't do anything about the big box he'd talked of, and she was forced to stuff the clothes any old where, into corners and mostly under their bed, which wasn't very pleasant on summer nights. What's more, she didn't at all like having to make up Étienne's bed right in the middle of the shop; when her assistants worked late, the child would fall asleep on a chair, waiting. Therefore, when Goujet suggested sending Étienne to Lille where his former boss, a machinist, was looking for apprentices, the idea appealed to her, the more so because the boy, not too happy at home and eager to be his own master, begged her to agree. But she was afraid Lantier would refuse point blank. He'd come to live with them solely to be near his son, and he wouldn't want to lose him barely two weeks after moving in. However, when she nervously raised the matter with him, he gave it his strong approval, saying that young workers needed to travel about a bit. The morning Étienne set off Lantier made him a speech about his rights, then, embracing him, declared:

'Always remember that the worker who produces is not a slave, but that whoever produces nothing is a parasite.'

After that the household resumed its daily round, and things calmed down as they settled into new ways. Gervaise had got used to the muddle of dirty clothes and to Lantier's comings and goings. Lantier still talked of important deals; occasionally he'd go out with his hair carefully combed and his shirt spotless; he'd disappear and even stay away all night, claiming on his return to be worn out, with a splitting headache, as if he'd just spent twenty-four hours discussing matters of the gravest import. The truth was that he was taking things easy. Oh! No danger of him getting callouses on his hands! He usually got up about ten and would have a stroll in the afternoon if the sunshine was to his liking, or if it was rainy he'd stay in the laundry looking through his newspaper. He was in his element there; he adored being surrounded by skirts and would worm his way right in among the women, revelling in their crude language, egging them on to be vulgar while watching his own language carefully; that was why he so much enjoyed rubbing shoulders with laundresses, a very free-spoken lot. When Clémence let loose her tongue he'd sit there smiling fondly and fingering his little moustache. The smell of the workshop, the sweaty, bare-armed girls banging their irons down, the whole place like a bedroom littered with underclothes belonging to all the women of the neighbourhood, seemed to him the hideaway of his dreams, a long sought haven of indolence and pleasure.

At first Lantier went out for his meals to François's, on the corner of the Rue des Poissonniers. But of the seven days in the week he'd have dinner with the Coupeaus three or four times, so that in the end he suggested boarding with them properly, saying he'd give them fifteen francs every Saturday. After that he never stirred from the house, but settled in once and for all. From morning to night he was to be seen going to and fro in his shirt sleeves between the back room and the shop, shouting orders, even dealing with the customers, in fact running the whole outfit. As he didn't like the wine François sold, he persuaded Gervaise to buy hers in future from the coal merchant next door, Vigoureux, whose wife he and Boche enjoyed pinching when they called there to give an order. Next he pronounced Coudeloup's bread badly baked, and sent Augustine for bread to Meyer's, the Viennese bakery on the Faubourg Poissonnière. He also changed Lehongre, the grocer, only sticking to the butcher, big Charles in the Rue Polonceau, because of his political ideas. After a month, he wanted all the cooking done in oil. As Clémence put it, teasing him, no matter what you did you'd never get rid of the oil-stains on that bloody Provençal! He used to make the omelettes himself, cooking them on both sides so they were browner than pancakes and as hard as ship's biscuits. He stood over Maman Coupeau, insisting that the steaks be well done, just like shoe leather, putting garlic in everything and getting cross if they dressed the salad with herbs, shouting that herbs were weeds, and might easily include some poisonous ones.

But his great treat was a certain kind of soup, a thick concoction of vermicelli boiled in water into which he'd pour half a bottle of oil. Only he and Gervaise would eat this, because the others, the Parisians, had brought up almost all their guts one day when they'd risked trying it.

Little by little Lantier had also involved himself in the affairs of the family. As the Lorilleux always jibbed at parting with Maman Coupeau's five francs, he'd pointed out that they could be sued. Didn't they give a damn about anyone? It was ten francs a month, not five, they ought to be shelling out! And he went up to collect the money himself, his manner so agreeable yet so resolute that Madame Lorilleux didn't dare refuse. Madame Lerat gave ten francs now as well. Maman Coupeau could have kissed Lantier's hands, especially as he also took on the role of chief mediator when the old woman and Gervaise quarrelled. When the laundress lost patience and browbeat her mother-in-law, who would then take to her bed in tears, he'd bully them both till they kissed and made up, asking them whether they imagined everyone round them found such charming behaviour amusing. It was the same with Nana; in his opinion they were making a real mess of bringing her up. He was quite right there, because whenever the father pitched into her the mother took the kid's side, and whenever the mother went for Nana, the father hit the roof. Nana, delighted to see her parents at each other's throats, felt she was excused in advance and got away with murder. Her latest idea was to go and play in the blacksmith's yard across the street; all day long she'd swing from the shafts of carts or else hide, with a gang of ragamuffins, in the gloomy recesses of the courtyard, which the forge's glowing red fire lit up; suddenly she'd reappear, screaming, hair flying, mud-stained, racing along followed by her retinue, as if a volley of hammering had just put all those filthy little buggers to flight. Lantier was the only one who could tell her off and even so she knew exactly how to get round him. That little bitch of ten would mince about in front of him like a lady, swinging her hips and casting sidelong glances at him from eyes which were already viciously knowing. In the end he'd taken over her education; he was teaching her to dance and to speak his dialect.

A year went by in this fashion. In the neighbourhood it was believed that Lantier had private means, since this was the only possible explanation for the Coupeaus' fancy life style. Gervaise, of course, was still earning, but now that she was feeding two men who did nothing, the laundry alone was certainly not sufficient: and furthermore the laundry was becoming less good, customers were leaving and the assistants just fooled about all day long. The truth was that Lantier wasn't paying anything at all, neither rent nor keep. During the first months he'd paid something on account; after that, however, all he did was talk about a large sum he'd soon be laying his hands on which he'd use to pay off everything at once, later on. Gervaise no longer dared ask him even for a centime. She bought the bread, the wine and the meat on tick. Everywhere her bills were mounting up, every day it was three francs more here, four francs more there. She hadn't paid a sou to the furniture dealer, or to Coupeau's three mates, the bricklayer, the carpenter and the painter. Everyone was beginning to grumble and people were much less polite to her in the shops. But she behaved as if drunk with the frenzy of running into debt, madly choosing the most expensive things and surrendering to her greed now that she no longer paid for anything; at heart, though, she remained completely honest, dreaming of making hundreds of francs in one day, just how she didn't exactly know, so she'd be able to hand out fistfuls of francs to her tradesmen. In a word, she was going downhill, and the further she slid the more she talked of expanding her business. About the middle of the summer, however, Clémence left; there wasn't enough work for two assistants and she'd been waiting for weeks to get paid. Coupeau and Lantier were thriving on this growing disaster. Those two fine fellows, their knees well under the table, were gobbling up the laundry and growing fatter on the ruins of the business; and they egged each other on to take double helpings, then, giggling, they'd slap their bellies when it was time for dessert, to make their food go down faster.

The great subject of conversation in the neighbourhood was whether Lantier and Gervaise were really back together again.

Opinions were divided. According to the Lorilleux, Banban was doing her very best to get Lantier back, but he'd have nothing to do with her, she'd gone so much to seed and he'd got much prettier bits of stuff tucked away in town. The Boches, on the other hand, maintained that the laundress had gone back to her former lover the very first night, the minute that mutton-head Coupeau had started to snore. Whatever the facts might be, it all seemed rather unsavoury, but then there were so many nasty things in life, much worse things in fact, that in the end people thought the threesome quite natural, even rather nice, because there was never any rough stuff and the decencies were observed. No question about it, if you stuck your nose into some other homes in the neighbourhood, you'd smell something much more foul. At least, at the Coupeaus', it was all very good-natured. The three of them went in for their little games, getting plastered, then bedding down together nice and old-fashioned like, without ever keeping the neighbours awake. And then, the entire neighbourhood was won over by Lantier's good manners. He charmed all the wagging tongues into silence. And when, in discussing whether there was anything going on between Lantier and Gervaise, the greengrocer would tell the tripe-shop woman that there wasn't, the tripe-shop woman even seemed to think it a shame, because actually that made the Coupeaus less interesting.

Gervaise, meanwhile, was quite untroubled on this score, because such filthy ideas never crossed her mind. It even came to the point where she was accused of being cold-hearted. The family couldn't understand why she was so down on Lantier. Madame Lerat, that inveterate meddler in affairs of the heart, now dropped in every evening; Lantier's attractions were irresistible, she declared, and even the poshest of ladies would fall eagerly into his arms. As for Madame Boche, had she been ten years younger, she wouldn't have answered for her virtue. An unacknowledged but relentless conspiracy was spreading and spreading, slowly pushing Gervaise towards him, as if all the women round her must satisfy their own need by giving her a lover. But Gervaise, astonished, couldn't see what was so alluring about Lantier. He'd certainly changed for the better: he always wore a coat, and he'd picked up a bit of education in

the cafés and political meetings. But she, who knew him
through and through, could read his innermost soul through his
eyes, and much of what she saw there made her shudder.
Anyway, if the others found him so appealing, what was
stopping them from sampling the gentleman themselves? One
day she hinted as much to Virginie, who was the most
enthusiastic. Then, to get Gervaise worked up, Madame Lerat
and Virginie told her about the affair between Lantier and
Clémence. Of course she hadn't noticed a thing, but as soon as
Gervaise set off on an errand, Lantier used to take Clémence
into his room. Now they were sometimes seen together, so he
must be visiting her at home.

'Well what of it?' said Gervaise, her voice trembling a little,
'what's it got to do with me?'

And she looked into Virginie's yellow eyes with their golden
glints, like the eyes of a cat. Did this woman still have it in for
her then, since she was trying to make her jealous? But Virginie
replied, putting on an innocent air:

'It hasn't anything to do with you, of course . . . Only, you
should tell him to drop that girl, because he'll have trouble with
her.'

The worst of it was that Lantier, feeling he had supporters,
changed his behaviour towards Gervaise. Now, when he shook
her hand, he'd keep her fingers in his for a moment. She was
worn down by his stares, by his insolent gaze where she could
clearly read what he was after. If he passed behind her he'd
thrust his knees into her skirts and breathe down her neck as if
to lull her to sleep. Yet he still put off making a bald
declaration. One evening, however, finding himself alone with
her, without saying a word he pushed her before him up to the
wall at the rear of the shop, where she stood trembling as he
tried to kiss her. By chance, at that very moment Goujet came
in. Gervaise struggled free of Lantier's grasp. The three of
them exchanged a few words as if nothing had happened.
Goujet, white in the face, had lowered his eyes, imagining he
was intruding and that she'd struggled just to avoid being kissed
in public.

The next day Gervaise was drifting about the shop in great
distress, unable even to iron a handkerchief; she was desperate

to see Goujet and explain how it had come about that Lantier
had pinned her against the wall. But ever since Étienne had
gone to Lille, she no longer dared go into the forge, where
Bec-Salé, alias Boit-sans-Soif, would greet her with suggestive
titters. In the afternoon, however, she gave way to her longing
and took up an empty basket, declaring that she was going to
collect some petticoats from her customer in the Rue des
Portes-Blanches. Then, when she was in the Rue Marcadet, she
walked very slowly along in front of the bolt factory, hoping
she'd be lucky. For his part Goujet must have been expecting
her, for she hadn't been there five minutes when he appeared
as if by chance.

'Oh! You've been out on an errand,' he said with a feeble
smile, 'and now you're going home . . .'

He said that just for something to say. In fact, Gervaise was
standing with her back towards the Rue des Poissonniers. They
walked up side by side towards Montmartre, not linking their
arms. Their one idea must have been to get away from the
factory, so it would not appear they'd arranged to meet in front
of its doors. Heads down, they followed the rutted roadway,
amid the rumble of the factories. Then, some two hundred
yards farther on they turned quite naturally, still not speaking,
to the left, as if heading for a place they both knew of, and came
to a piece of waste land. Lying between a sawmill and a button
factory, this last remaining strip of green had yellow patches
where the grass was scorched; a goat, tethered to a stake, was
bleating as it circled round and round, while on the far side a
dead tree rotted away in the sunshine.

'Just look!' murmured Gervaise. 'You'd think you were in the
country!'

They went over and sat under the dead tree. The laundress
put her basket at her feet. Opposite them rose the heights of
Montmartre with its tiers of tall yellow and grey houses among
clusters of sparse greenery; when they tilted their heads farther
back, they could see the vast blazing purity of the sky above
the city, cut across to the north by a flight of little white
clouds. But, dazzled by the bright light, they turned their gaze
instead along the flat horizon, where the outskirts of the city
formed a chalky backdrop, staring in particular at the sawmill's

slim chimney from which came puffs of steam. The great sighs
of the chimney seemed to bring comfort to their stricken hearts.

'Yes,' Gervaise, embarrassed by their silence, went on, 'I was
on an errand, I'd come out . . .'

After desperately wanting to explain, suddenly she no longer
dared to speak. She felt deeply ashamed. But even so she knew
they'd come to this place of their own free will, in order to
speak of it: indeed they actually were speaking of it, without
needing to say a word. What had happened yesterday was there
between them like a heavy, awkward burden.

Then, overcome with unbearable sadness, her eyes full of
tears, she described the dreadful death of Madame Bijard, her
washerwoman, who'd died that morning after atrocious suffering.

'It was from a kick Bijard gave her,' she said in a soft,
monotonous voice. 'Her belly swelled up. He must'ave broken
something in her insides. My God! Three whole days she was
twisting about with the agony of it . . . There are villains sent
to the galleys for less than that. But the law would be too busy
if it bothered about women whose husbands had done 'em in.
One more kick's neither here nor there, is it, when you're
getting kicked every day. And what's more the poor woman
wanted to save her husband from the scaffold and said she'd
hurt her stomach when she fell on to a tub . . . She screamed
right through the night, before she went.'

Goujet said nothing, but tore up handfuls of grass, his fists
clenched.

'It's hardly a fortnight since she weaned her last, little
Jules,' Gervaise went on, 'That's a bit of luck, 'cos the baby
won't suffer . . . Still, it means that kid Lalie'll have two brats
to look after. She's not even eight yet, but she's as steady and
sensible as a proper mother. And her father's always knocking
her about . . . Ah well! some people are put into this world to
suffer.'

Goujet looked at her and suddenly said, with trembling lips:
'You really hurt me, yesterday, oh! you hurt me so badly . . .'

Turning pale, Gervaise clasped her hands together. But he
was still speaking:

'I know it was bound to happen . . . Only you should have

been frank with me and told me what was going on so I wouldn't be left thinking . . .'

He couldn't finish. She'd stood up, realizing that Goujet imagined she and Lantier were back together, as all the neighbours said they were. Stretching out her arms, she cried:

'No, no, I swear . . . He was pushing me, he was going to kiss me, it's true, but his face didn't even touch mine, and it's the first time he's tried . . . I swear it, on my life, on my children's, by everything I hold most sacred!'

But Goujet was nodding his head. He didn't believe her: women always denied things like that. Then Gervaise became very serious and spoke again, slowly:

'You know me, Monsieur Goujet, I've never been one to lie . . . And I'm telling you: No, it's not like that, word of honour! It never will be, d'you hear, never! The day that happened, I'd be the lowest of the low, I'd not deserve the friendship of a decent man like you.'

Her face, as she spoke, was so beautiful in its perfect honesty that he took her hand and made her sit down again. Now he could breathe freely, he could rejoice within himself. It was the first time he'd held her hand in this way, gripping it in his. They were both silent. Above, the flight of white clouds, like swans, moved slowly across the sky. In the corner of the field the goat had turned towards them and was watching them, bleating very softly at long, regular intervals. And without letting go of each other's fingers, their eyes wet with emotion, they gazed dreamily into the distance at the drab slope of Montmartre amid the tall forest of factory chimneys streaking the horizon, in that chalky, desolate city outskirt where the clumps of greenery growing round disreputable taverns moved them to tears.

'Your mother's vexed with me, I know,' Gervaise went on quietly. 'Don't deny it . . . We owe you so much money!'

But, quite roughly, he made her stop. He shook her by the hand hard enough to break a bone. He didn't want her to talk of money. Then, after hesitating, he finally stammered:

'Listen, I've been thinking for so long of suggesting something . . . You're not happy. My mother's sure things are going wrong for you . . .'

He stopped, unable to get the words out.

'Well then, we must go away together.'

She stared at him, at first not understanding clearly, taken aback by this sudden declaration of a love of which he'd never breathed a word before.

'What do you mean?' she asked.

'Yes,' he went on, looking down, 'we'd go away, we'd live somewhere or other, in Belgium if you like . . . That's almost like my own country. With both of us working, we'd soon be all right.'

At that she blushed scarlet. Had he pressed her to him and kissed her she couldn't have been more ashamed. What a strange chap he was, to propose eloping, like what goes on in novels and high society! Well, all round her she saw working men chasing after married women, but they didn't even take them to Saint-Denis, they carried on right there on the spot, without beating about the bush.

'Oh, Monsieur Goujet, Monsieur Goujet . . .' she whispered, unable to say anything more.

'That way there'd just be the two of us,' he continued. 'The others bother me, d'you see? When I care for a person, I can't bear to see that person with other people.'

But by now she'd pulled herself together and was saying no in a sensible way.

'It's impossible, Monsieur Goujet. It would be very wrong . . . I'm married, aren't I? I've got children . . . I know quite well that you're fond of me and that I'm hurting you. Only, we'd feel guilty, we'd never have any happiness . . . I'm fond of you also, too fond of you to let you do something silly. And it would be silly, I'm sure . . . No, you see, it's better to stay as we are. We respect one another, and we feel the same about things. That means a lot, it's helped me many a time. For folks like us, when you keep straight, in the end you do get your reward.'

He nodded as he listened to her. He thought she was right, he couldn't say different. Suddenly, there in the broad daylight, he took her in his arms and crushed her to him, kissing her furiously on the neck as if trying to bite her skin. Then he released her without asking for anything more, and he said not another word about their love. She gave herself a shake, not at all angry, feeling they both deserved that brief moment of pleasure.

Goujet, meanwhile, trembling violently from head to foot, pulled himself away from her to avoid the temptation of embracing her again; dragging himself along on his knees, not knowing what to do with his hands, he started picking dandelions and throwing them from where he was into her basket. Some magnificent yellow dandelions were growing there, in the middle of the parched grass. Gradually this little game soothed and even amused him. With fingers stiffened by constant hammering he delicately picked the flowers and flung them one by one; his kind dog-like eyes sparkled with fun each time a flower landed in the basket. Gervaise was leaning on the dead tree, cheerful and relaxed, raising her voice to make herself heard above the noisy wheezing of the sawmill. When they left the waste land, walking side by side and chatting about how much Étienne liked Lille, her basket was full of dandelions.

Deep down, Gervaise didn't feel as sure of herself with Lantier as she claimed. Certainly, she was determined not to let him touch her with so much as a finger-tip, but she was afraid, if ever he did touch her, of her former weakness, of that easygoing compliance, that desire to please others, that had such power over her. Lantier, however, didn't try again. He was alone with her on several occasions and did nothing. He now seemed to be interested in the tripe-shop woman, who was forty-five and very well preserved. Gervaise talked about the tripe-shop woman in front of Goujet, to reassure him. To Virginie and Madame Lerat she'd say, when they sang the hatter's praises, that he didn't need her admiration, since all the other local women were sweet on him.

Coupeau went about the neighbourhood loudly proclaiming that Lantier was a friend, the best there was. People could gab on about them, he knew what he knew, and didn't give a damn about the gossip, since right was on his side. When the three of them went out together on a Sunday, he'd make his wife and Lantier walk in front, arm in arm, just to cock a snook at the street; he'd keep an eye as they passed, ready to rough up anyone who dared even to snigger. It's true he thought Lantier a bit stuck-up, accused him of being snooty about rotgut and

pulled his leg because he could read, and because he talked like
a lawyer. But, apart from that, he declared he was a gutsy
bastard. There wasn't another to equal him in the whole of La
Chapelle.* In a word, they understood one another, they were
made for one another. Friendship between men is stronger than
love between man and woman.

Coupeau and Lantier, it must be admitted, used to go off
together on the most stupendous binges. Lantier, now, borrowed money from Gervaise—ten francs here, twenty francs
there—whenever he sensed there was money in the house. It
was always for important business he had on hand. He used
those occasions to get Coupeau off the straight and narrow,
taking him off on what he said would be a protracted errand;
then, seated opposite each other in the depths of a nearby
restaurant, they'd stuff their gizzards with dishes you never get
at home, washed down with vintage wines. Coupeau would
rather have gone on binges that weren't so fancy, but he was
impressed by the hatter's posh tastes, when he chose from the
menu sauces with extraordinary names. It was hard to credit a
man could be so finicky and fussy. It seems they're all like that
in the South. For instance, he wouldn't touch anything too
heating, he discussed everything in a made-up dish as to
whether it was good for you, and sent back meat if he thought
it too salty or peppery. Draughts were even worse; they scared
him stiff, and he'd bawl out the entire restaurant if a door was
left half-open. Along with that he was very close-fisted, tipping
two sous on a seven or eight franc meal. But Lantier put the
fear of God into waiters just the same, and he and Coupeau
were well known along the outer boulevards from Batignolles
to Belleville.* They frequented a place in the Grande Rue des
Batignolles where they ate tripe* served in small chafing-dishes.
They went to the Ville de Bar-le-Duc,* just below Montmartre,
for the finest oysters in the entire neighbourhood. When they
ventured up the hill as far as the Moulin de la Galette* the
kitchen would produce fried rabbit for them. The Lilas* on the
Rue des Martyrs specialized in calf's head, whereas the Lion
d'Or* and the Deux Marronniers* on the Chaussée Clignancourt served a sauté of kidneys that melted in your mouth.
Most often, however, they turned left towards Belleville, where

their table was kept for them at the Vendanges de Bourgogne,* at the Cadran Bleu,* at the Capucin, all reliable places where you could order anything whatever with your eyes shut. These were secret feasts which the next day they'd talk about in veiled language as they pecked at Gervaise's potatoes. One day Lantier even brought a woman to their table under the trees outside the Moulin de la Galette; when the dessert appeared, Coupeau left him with her.

Needless to say, you can't go on sprees and work as well. So, after Lantier joined the household, Coupeau, who already hardly raised a finger, got that he didn't so much as touch his tools. When, fed up with not earning, he did find himself a job, his mate would track him down at work and tease him mercilessly on seeing him hanging from a knotted rope like a ham that was being smoked; he'd shout to him to come down and have a quick one. That settled it, the roofer would walk off the job and start a binge that went on for days, for weeks. First rate, those binges were: a general inspection of all the bars in the neighbourhood, the morning's boozing slept off at lunch-time and resurrected in the evening; round after round of rotgut stretching right on into the night like chinese lanterns at a party, until the last candle and the last glass were consumed! Lantier, cunning bugger that he was, never stayed till the end. He let Coupeau get lit up, then left him to it, and went home smiling in his pleasant fashion. As for Lantier, he'd get sozzled in a nice way, without it showing. You could only tell, if you knew him well, because his eyes grew smaller and his behaviour towards women grew bolder. The roofer, on the other hand, became disgusting, he couldn't drink now without finishing up in a foul state.

And so it happened that early in November Coupeau went on a binge that ended in a really revolting way for himself and for the others. He'd found work the day before. On this occasion Lantier was full of high-flown sentiments, singing the praises of work, saying that work ennobles man. He even got up while it was still dark in order to escort his mate to work with due ceremony, in recognition of his being a labourer worthy of that title. But when they reached the Petite-Civette, which was just opening, they went in for a brandied plum, no more than one, intending simply to drink a toast together to their firm resolve of good behaviour. Across from the counter Bibi-la-Grillade was sitting on a bench with his back to the wall, glumly smoking his pipe.

'Hey! Look who's moochin' about!' said Coupeau. 'Don't you feel like workin', Bibi, old sod?'

'No, no,' their mate answered, stretching his arms. 'It's the bosses, they get up your nose . . . I walked out on mine yesterday. They're a lot of stinkers, a lot of shits . . .'

And Bibi-la-Grillade accepted a plum. He must have been sitting waiting on the bench for someone to buy a round. But Lantier stood up for the bosses; sometimes they had to put up with ever such a lot, he ought to know, having recently been in business himself. Workmen were a bunch of bastards, always going on benders, not giving a damn about their work, leaving you in the lurch right in the middle of an order and turning up again when they were broke. Why he'd had a little Picardy chap with a craze for gadding about in cabs; yes, as soon as he'd been paid for the week he'd spend days at a time in a cab. Did a taste like that go with being industrious? Then, suddenly, Lantier started attacking the bosses as well. Oh, he could see what was what, and he told everyone exactly what he thought. A foul breed they were, exploiting people shamelessly, living off human flesh. He himself, praise be, could sleep with a clear conscience, because he'd always been like a friend to his men, preferring not to make millions out of them the way others did.

'Come on mate, let's be off,' he said to Coupeau. 'We must behave ourselves, or we'll be late.'

Bibi-la-Grillade came out with them, swinging his arms. Outside, day was barely breaking, its dim glow clouded by the reflection of the muddy road; it had rained the previous evening and the air was very mild. The gaslights had just been put out; the Rue des Poissonniers, in which wisps of dark cloud, trapped by the tall houses, still lingered, was filling with the muffled tramping of workers going down into Paris. Coupeau, his roofer's bag on his shoulder, swaggered along like a chap who for once in his life felt on top form. He turned round and asked:

'Bibi, d'you want a job? The boss told me to bring a mate, if I could.'

'No thanks,' answered Bibi-la-Grillade, 'I've taken a purge . . . You'd better ask Mes-Bottes, he was lookin' for work yesterday. Wait, Mes-Bottes is sure to be in there.'

And as they reached the bottom of the street they did indeed see Mes-Bottes in Père Colombe's bar. Despite the early hour the Assommoir was ablaze, with the shutters down and the gaslights on. Lantier stayed in the doorway, telling Coupeau to hurry because they only had ten minutes.

'What! You're going to work for that rat Bourguignon!' yelled Mes-Bottes, when Coupeau had talked to him. 'You won't catch me in that dump again! I'd sooner be on me uppers for the rest of the year! But, let me tell you, old chap, you won't last three days there, you won't!'

'Really, it's that bad, is it?' asked Coupeau anxiously.

'Oh, it's as bad as they come . . . You can't move a muscle. The boss is on your back every minute. And such a way of doing things, too; his missus treats you like a sozzler, and they won't even let you spit in the place . . . I told them what they could bleeding well do with it the very first evening, I did!'

'Right! I've had fair warning. No chance I'll be spendin' the rest of my days with 'em. I'll give it a go this morning, but if the boss picks on me I'll lift him up an' dump him down on his old woman, I'll stick 'em together like a pair o' kippers!'

Coupeau shook his mate's hand to thank him for his useful advice, and was on his way out when Mes-Bottes turned shirty. Fucking hell! Was that Bourguignon going to stop them having a drop? So men weren't men any more, eh? Surely the bugger could wait five minutes. Accepting a drink, Lantier came in and the four workmen stood at the counter. Meanwhile Mes-Bottes, in his down-at-heel shoes, filthy black smock and cap squashed down on the top of his head, was roaring away full blast and glaring round the Assommoir as if he owned it. He'd just been proclaimed emperor of piss-tanks and king of hogs for having eaten a salad of live bugs and taken a bite into a dead cat.

'Come on, you bleeding Borgia,' he bellowed at Père Colombe, 'gimme some of the yellow stuff, your very best asses' piss.'

And when Père Colombe, pale and calm in his blue jersey, had filled the four glasses, those gents downed them in one go in case the drink might go off.

'It certainly does you a power of good on the way down,' muttered Bibi-la-Grillade.

But that devil Mes-Bottes was telling a good 'un. He'd been so pissed on Friday that his mates had stuck his pipe into his mouth with a handful of plaster. It would have done for anyone else; and he was swanking and swaggering about it.

'You gentlemen having another?' enquired Père Colombe in his oily voice.

'Yes, same again,' said Lantier. 'It's my round.'

They were talking about women now. Last Sunday Bibi-la-Grillade had taken his ball and chain to an aunt's in Montrouge. Coupeau enquired after Malle des Indes,* a laundress from Chaillot* who was well known in the Assommoir. They were just going to drink when Mes-Bottes yelled loudly to Goujet and Lorilleux who were passing outside. They stopped at the door but refused to come in. The blacksmith didn't feel the need of a drink. The chain-maker, wan and shivering, had the gold chains he was delivering stowed away in his pocket; he coughed and excused himself, saying that even a drop of brandy knocked him sideways.

'What a pair of humbugs!' grunted Mes-Bottes. 'I'll bet they have it on the quiet.'

He took a sniff at his glass and grabbed Père Colombe.

'You old shit-bag, you've switched bottles! When it comes to rotgut, it's no good trying to bamboozle me, y'know.'

It was morning now and a murky light filled the Assommoir, where the landlord was turning off the gasjets. But Coupeau was making excuses for his brother-in-law; after all, drink didn't agree with him, and you shouldn't hold that against him like a crime. He even approved of Goujet, seeing that it was a blessing never to feel thirsty. And he was talking about going off to work, when Lantier, putting on his best man-of-the-world air, read him the riot act: at the very least you paid for

your round before doing a bunk; you didn't just walk out on
your pals like a sponger, even if duty called.

'When's he going to stop being such a pain in the neck about
his job!' shouted Mes-Bottes.

'Then it's your round, is it, sir?' Père Colombe asked
Coupeau.

He paid for his round. But, when it came to Bibi-la-Grillade,
he leant forward to whisper to the landlord, who slowly shook
his head in refusal. Mes-Bottes understood and started blasting
that old chiseller Colombe again. What! A half-wit like him
taking the liberty of being rude to one of their friends! Every
booze merchant gave tick! Fancy being insulted in a boozer!
Quite unruffled, the landlord leant forward, his big fists on the
edge of the counter, politely repeating:

'Lend the gentleman some money, it'll be simpler.'

'Bloody hell! Yes, I'll lend him some,' bawled Mes-Bottes.
'Here, Bibi, shove his money down his throat, the fucking rat!'

By now Bibi was well away, and, irritated by the bag
Coupeau had kept on his shoulder, he said to him:

'You look like a nursemaid. Get rid of your baby. It makes
you hunch-backed.'

Coupeau hesitated a moment; then, as if it were something
he'd decided after careful reflection, he calmly put his tool bag
on the ground, saying:

'It's too late now. I'll go to Bourguignon's after lunch. I'll
say that the missus 'ad a belly-ache. Listen, Père Colombe,
I'll leave me tools under this bench and pick 'em up again at
noon.'

Lantier nodded his approval of this arrangement. A man has
to work, no two ways about it, only, when you find yourself
with friends, politeness comes first. Little by little all four of
them had been succumbing to the temptation of a binge, and
now, overcome with lethargy, they exchanged enquiring glances,
their hands hanging inertly by their sides. And then, at the
prospect of five whole hours of idleness, they were suddenly
filled with boisterous glee, slapping each other and bellowing
affectionately into each other's faces, none more so than Coupeau, who, relieved and rejuvenated, kept on calling the others
'me old cock'. They wet their whistles with another round and

then went to La Puce qui renifle,* a seedy little dive where you
could play billiards. Lantier sulked for a bit because the place
wasn't exactly spotless; the fire-water cost a franc a litre, or ten
sous the half, served in two glasses; the regulars had made
such a filthy mess on the billiard table that the balls stuck to
it. But, once the game had begun, Lantier, a dab hand with a
cue, was restored to charm and good humour as, puffing out
his chest, he accompanied each cannon with a wriggle of the
hips.

When it was time for lunch, Coupeau had an idea. Stamping
his foot, he shouted:

'Let's go an' get Bec-Salé. I know where 'e works. We can
take 'im along to eat trotters 'n parsley sauce at Mère Louis's
place.'

The idea was greeted with applause. Yes, trotters 'n' parsley
sauce must be just what Bec-Salé, alias Boit-sans-Soif, needed.
They set off. The streets were a yellowish colour and a fine
drizzle was falling, but they were too warm inside to feel this
gentle sprinkle on their limbs. Coupeau led them to the bolt
factory in the Rue Marcadet. Since they arrived a good
half-hour before the lunch hour, the roofer gave a couple of
sous to a kid to go in and tell Bec-Salé that the missus was in
a bad way and wanted him home right then. The smith came
strutting out at once, looking quite untroubled, as if he could
smell a good feed in the offing.

'Ah, so it's you lot of piss-tanks!' he said, catching sight of
them skulking in a doorway. 'I guessed as much . . . Well, so
what's for lunch?'

At Mère Louis's, while they sucked on the little bones in the
trotters, they started blasting the bosses again. Bec-Salé, alias
Boit-sans-Soif, was telling them there was a rush order at his
place. Oh, his boss didn't make a song and dance about the odd
quarter of an hour; you could miss the roll-call and he'd still be
friendly, he must reckon himself lucky that you came back at
all. In any case, there was no risk that an employer would ever
dare give him, Bec-Salé, the sack, because they just weren't to
be had, blokes as good as he was. After the trotters they had an
omelette. They drank a bottle apiece. Mère Louis got her wine
sent from the Auvergne,* it was the colour of blood and you

could have cut it with a knife. Things were warming up, the
binge was really getting going.

'Why's that flipping boss of mine such a pain in the arse?'
Bec-Salé was shouting when they'd got to the dessert. 'He's
taken it into his head to stick a bell up in his dump. A bell, like
you have for slaves. Hell, today it can ring! They bloody well
won't catch me back on that anvil! I've been slogging away for
five days so I can certainly give it a miss . . . If he belly-aches,
I'll tell him to fuck off.'

'I'm goin' to have to leave you,' said Coupeau importantly.
'I'm off to work. Yes, I promised the wife . . . Enjoy yourselves,
I'll be with all you mates in spirit, y'know.'

The others made a joke of it. But Coupeau seemed so
determined that when he said he was going to fetch his tools
from Père Colombe's, they all went with him. He took his bag
from under the bench and put it in front of him while they had
a final snifter. At one o'clock they were still there, standing each
other rounds. So Coupeau, with a peevish gesture, put the tools
back under the bench; they were in his way, he couldn't get
near the counter without tripping on them. It seemed too silly
to go now, he'd go to Bourguignon's tomorrow. The four
others, who were arguing about wages, didn't seem surprised
when the roofer suggested, without any explanation, that they
take a little turn on the boulevard to stretch their legs. The rain
had stopped. The little turn amounted to a couple of hundred
paces, walking in single file with their arms dangling; they were
stunned by the fresh air and disgruntled at being outside, and
couldn't think of a thing to say. Slowly, instinctively, without
even a poke from an elbow by way of consultation, they strolled
back up the Rue des Poissonniers and into François's for a glass
of the best. My, they really needed that to buck 'em up. It gave
'em the miseries, being in the street; the mud was so awful you
wouldn't even turn a policeman out into it. Lantier steered the
gang into the private bar, a cramped little place with only one
table and a frosted glass partition separating it from the public
bar. As a rule he liked to do his boozing in private bars, it was
more suitable. Weren't they all quite cosy there? It was just like
being at home, you could have a spot of shut-eye without
feeling embarrassed. He asked for the paper, and, spreading out

the sheets, skimmed it with a preoccupied frown. Coupeau and
Mes-Bottes had started a game of piquet. Two bottles of wine
and five glasses stood on the table.

'Well? So what does it say, in your paper?' Bibi-la-Grillade
asked Lantier.

He didn't reply immediately. Then, without looking up:

'This is the report on the Chamber. What a hopeless bunch
of republicans they are, those bleeding parasites on the left. Did
the people elect them just to dribble a lot of sugary nonsense?
. . . Here's one who believes in God, yet he's sucking up to
those sodding politicians! Now me, if I was elected, I'd get up
there on the rostrum and say: "Shit!" Yes, nothing else, that's
my opinion!'

'D'you know that Badinguet pitched into his missus the other
evening, in front of the whole Court,' Bec-Salé, alias Boit-sans-
Soif, was saying. 'Word of honour! And all over nothing, just
a squabble. Badinguet was pissed.'

'You're borin' us to death with your politics,' said the roofer.
'Read the murders, they're a lot more fun.'

And, returning to his game, he declared three nines and three
queens:

'I've got three nines an' three ladies . . . The skirts won't
leave me in peace.'

Glasses were emptied. Lantier started to read aloud:

'A shocking crime has brought terror to the commune of
Gaillon* (Seine-et-Marne). A son murdered his father by
striking him with a spade, to rob him of thirty sous . . .'

They all exclaimed in horror. Now there was one they'd have
been happy to watch being guillotined! But no, the guillotine
wasn't enough, he should have been chopped into little bits.
They were equally appalled by a story of infanticide, but
Lantier, taking a moral line, excused the woman, saying that
her seducer should get all the blame, for when all was said and
done, if some swine hadn't got the poor creature in the family
way, she wouldn't have been able to throw the thing down the
privy. But what they really got excited over were the exploits
of the Marquis de T.; leaving a ball in the Boulevard des
Invalides* at two in the morning, he'd got the better of three
layabouts; without even taking off his gloves, he'd polished off

the first two thugs by butting them in the belly, and had grabbed the third by the ear and marched him off to the police station. Now there's a man for you! Too bad he was a nobleman.

'Now listen to this,' said Lantier. 'I've got to the stuff about the nobs. "The Comtesse de Brétigny announces the marriage of her eldest daughter to the young Baron de Valançay,* aide-de-camp to His Majesty. The bridegroom's gift to the bride includes more than three hundred thousand francs' worth of lace" . . .'

'What the hell do we care!' interrupted Bibi-la-Grillade. 'We don't want to know the colour of their nightshirts . . . The girl can have as much lace as she wants, she'll still lose her cherry the same way as everyone else.'

As Lantier looked as if he meant to finish what he was reading, Bec-Salé, alias Boit-sans-Soif, grabbed the paper from him and sat on it, saying:

'Oh no, enough's enough! . . . It'll be nice and cosy there . . . That's all paper's any good for.'

Mes-Bottes, meanwhile, was studying his hand and gave a triumphant thump on the table. He'd got ninety-three.

'I've the Revolution,' he shouted. 'A flush, in clubs, that's twenty, right? . . . Then, a diamond straight, twenty-three; three gentlemen, twenty-six; three knaves, twenty-nine; three of Kelly's eye, ninety-two . . . And so when I play Year One of the Republic,* that makes ninety-three.'

'You're done for, chum,' they all yelled at Coupeau.

They ordered two more bottles. Glasses were never empty now and the whole party was getting more and more sozzled. By about five it was becoming disgusting, and Lantier, who'd quieted down, was thinking of slipping away; bellowing and slopping wine about on the floor wasn't the sort of thing he went in for. Coupeau stood up just then to make the boozer's sign of the cross. Tapping his head he pronounced Montpernasse, on his right shoulder Menilmonte, La Courtille on his left shoulder, Bagnolet* on his groin and then Fried Rabbit three times in the pit of his stomach. Lantier, taking advantage of the uproar which greeted this exercise, quietly took himself off. His mates didn't even notice his departure. He himself had

had quite a skinful. Once outside, however, he managed to pull himself together and walked calmly back to the shop, where he told Gervaise that Coupeau was with some friends.

Two days went by. The roofer had not reappeared. He was somewhere about in the neighbourhood, no one knew exactly where. People did say, however, that they'd seen him at Mère Baquet's, and at the Papillon, and the Petit Bonhomme qui tousse. But some declared he was all alone while others had met him in the company of seven or eight other drunks. Gervaise shrugged her shoulders resignedly. Christ! She'd just have to get used to it. She didn't run after her man; indeed if she caught sight of him in a bar she'd go the long way round so as not to make him angry; and she waited for him to come home, listening for him at night in case he might be snoring away outside the door. He'd fall asleep on a heap of rubbish, on a bench, on a bit of waste land, in the gutter, anywhere. In the morning, with the last night's binge only partly slept off, he'd start all over again, banging on the shutters of taverns and launching afresh into a frenzied bout of little drinks and bigger drinks and whole bottlefuls, losing his friends and then finding them, setting out on errands from which he'd return in a stupor, seeing the streets whirling round and night fall and day break with no thought in his head except drinking and sleeping it off right there where he happened to be. Once he'd slept it off, it would be over. Still, on the second day, Gervaise did go to Père Colombe's Assommoir to find out what she could; he'd been seen five times, and that was all anyone could tell her. She had to be satisfied with taking away his tools which were still under the bench.

That evening Lantier, seeing she was upset, suggested taking her to a *café-concert** for a nice change. The laundress refused at first, saying she wasn't in any mood for fun. She wouldn't have said no otherwise, because Lantier made his offer in too forthright a manner for her to suspect any funny business. He seemed concerned about her misfortune and his manner was quite fatherly. Coupeau had never stayed away two nights running. So every ten minutes, in spite of herself, she'd go to the door with her iron in her hand and look up and down the street to see if her old man mightn't be coming home. She said it gave her pins and needles in her legs, and she couldn't stand still. Of course, Coupeau could bleeding well bust a leg or fall under a cab and stay there; she'd think it good riddance, for she no longer had the slightest feeling in her heart for a dirty sod like him. But for all that it was maddening to be wondering all the time if he was coming back or not. And, when the gaslights were lit, and Lantier mentioned the *café-concert* again, she accepted. After all, she'd be a proper fool to refuse a treat when her husband had been out on the tiles for three days. Since he wasn't coming home, she'd go out as well. As far as she was concerned the place could bleeding well burn down. In fact she'd gladly have set fire to the dump herself, she was getting so pissed off with her bloody awful life.

They finished dinner quickly. At eight o'clock, as she set off escorted by Lantier, Gervaise begged Maman Coupeau and Nana to go to bed straight away. The shop had been closed up. She left by the courtyard door and gave the key to Madame Boche, asking her to kindly see that swine Coupeau to bed if he should turn up. Lantier was waiting for her in the entryway; he was nicely dressed and whistling a little tune. She was wearing her silk dress. They walked quietly along the pavement, close together; as they passed through the shafts of light coming from the shops you could see them chatting softly and smiling at one another.

The *café-concert* was in the Boulevard de Rochechouart; once a little café, it had been enlarged by building a wooden hut in the courtyard. Glass globes were strung round the entrance, outlining the doorway with bright lights. Some tall posters, stuck on to wooden boards, stood on the ground near the gutters.

'Here we are,' said Lantier. 'Tonight, first appearance of Mademoiselle Amanda, high-class singer.'

He caught sight of Bibi-la-Grillade, who was also reading the poster. Bibi had a black eye—someone must have hit him the previous day.

'Well, where's Coupeau?' asked Lantier, looking all round, 'you've lost Coupeau, have you?'

'Oh, ages ago, yesterday,' the other replied. 'We had a bit of a punch-up coming out of Mère Baquet's. Me, I don't like

fisting it out . . . We had a row, see, with the waiter at Mère
Baquet's about a bottle he wanted to make us pay for twice . . .
So I took meself off for a bit of a kip.'

He was still yawning, he'd slept for eighteen hours. But he'd
sobered up completely, though he looked dazed and his old
jacket was covered with fluff; he must have gone to bed fully
dressed.

'And you don't know where my husband is?' asked Gervaise.

'No, haven't the foggiest . . . It was five when we left Mère
Baquet's. That's it! He probably went further down the street
. . . Yes, I'm pretty sure I saw him going into the Papillon with
a cabbie . . . Oh, it's so stupid! Really, we're a lot of useless
sods!'

Lantier and Gervaise spent a very pleasant evening in the
café-concert. When the place closed at eleven they sauntered
back, taking their time. The cold was quite nippy and people
were making their way home in groups; you could hear girls
giggling their heads off, in the shadows of the trees, when their
fellows became rather too friendly. Lantier was humming one
of Mademoiselle Amanda's songs: 'My nose is where it tickles
me'.* Gervaise, her head swimming, half tipsy, took up the
refrain. It had been very hot in there. And then, the two drinks
she'd had, the pipe smoke and the smell of all those people
crowded together had made her a bit queasy. But her most vivid
impression was of Mademoiselle Amanda. Never would she
herself have dared appear in public with so little on. You had
to give the lady her due, she had a gorgeous skin. And she
listened with a sensual curiosity to Lantier as he went into
details about Amanda's person, in the style of a man who had
every reason to know what he was talking about.

'Everyone's asleep,' said Gervaise, after ringing three times
before the door-pull was released by Boche.

The door opened but the entryway was in darkness and when
she knocked at the lodge window for her key, a sleepy Madame
Boche shouted something to her which at first she couldn't
understand. Finally, she grasped that the policeman Poisson
had brought Coupeau home in a very bad state, and that the
key should be in the lock.

'Christ Almighty!' muttered Lantier when they were inside. 'Whatever's he been doing? The stink's revolting.'

And indeed it stank to high heaven. Gervaise, who was hunting for matches, kept stepping in something wet. When she finally managed to light a candle, a pretty spectacle lay before them. Coupeau had vomited his guts out; the room was covered in vomit; the bed was plastered with it, the carpet too, and even the chest of drawers was splashed. And what's more Coupeau had fallen off the bed where Poisson must have dumped him and was lying right in the middle of his filth, snoring. He was sprawled in it, wallowing like a pig, with one cheek all smeared, breathing foul breath through his open mouth, while his already greying hair brushed the puddle surrounding his head.

'Oh, the swine, the swine!' Gervaise kept repeating, fuming with indignation. 'He's got everything in a muck . . . No, not even a dog would have done that, a dying dog's cleaner than that.'

They neither of them dared move or take a step. Never before had the roofer come home so pissed or got the room into such an unspeakable state. Consequently, the sight was a harsh blow to any feeling his wife might still have for him. In the past, when he'd come home just a bit tiddly or absolutely plastered, she'd been sympathetic rather than disgusted. But this, this was too much; her stomach was heaving. She wouldn't have touched him with a barge pole. The mere thought of that lout's skin close to hers was as repugnant to her as if she'd been asked to lie down beside a corpse that had died of some foul disease.

'Still, I must go to bed,' she murmured. 'I can't go out and sleep in the street . . . Oh, I'll manage to climb over him somehow.'

She tried to step over the drunken Coupeau and had to catch hold of a corner of the chest to stop herself slipping in the filth. Coupeau completely blocked access to the bed. Then Lantier, who was grinning at the thought that she certainly wouldn't be having her shut-eye on her own pillow that night, took her hand and said in a fervent whisper:

'Gervaise . . . Listen, Gervaise . . .'

But she understood, and took away her hand, so disconcerted that she also reverted to the intimate 'tu' of the old days.

'No, leave me alone . . . I beg you, Auguste, go into your room . . . I'll find a way, I'll climb over the foot of the bed.'

'Come on Gervaise, don't be silly,' he kept saying. 'It smells too awful, you can't stay here . . . Come on, what are you afraid of? He can't hear us, can he?'

She struggled, shaking her head fiercely in refusal. In her agitation, as if to show that she meant to stay where she was, she was undressing and flinging her silk dress on to a chair, stripping frantically till she stood in her chemise and petticoat, with her white neck and arms bare. It was her bed, wasn't it? She wanted to sleep in her own bed. Twice more she tried to find a clean spot and get past. But Lantier didn't give up, he kept putting his arm round her waist, saying things that set her blood on fire. Oh, she was in a proper fix, with a good-for-nothing husband in front, stopping her from slipping decently between her own sheets, and a bloody shit of a man behind, whose one idea was to take advantage of her bad luck to have her again! As the hatter was beginning to raise his voice she begged him to be quiet. And she strained her ears towards the little room where Nana and Maman Coupeau slept. The child and the old woman must be asleep; she could hear someone breathing loudly.

'Leave me alone, Auguste, you'll wake them up,' she went on, clasping her hands. 'Be sensible. Another time, somewhere else . . . Not here, not in front of me daughter . . .'

He was saying nothing now, but just smiling and kissing her slowly on the ear, the teasing way he used to kiss her in the past, to make her head spin. A weakness came over her and she felt a great buzzing and shivering run through her body. Nevertheless she took a step away. And then had to step towards him again. It wasn't possible, her revulsion was too deep, and the smell was becoming so bad that she herself would have been taken ill in the bed. The drunken Coupeau was lying dead to the world with leaden limbs and mouth askew, sleeping off his binge as if he were on a feather mattress. The entire street could have walked in and had his wife without a hair on his body stirring.

'What's the point,' she muttered. 'It's his fault, I can't help it . . . My God, my God, he's turned me out of me own bed, I haven't a bed any more . . . No, I can't help it, it's his fault.'

She was trembling, and hardly knew what she was doing. And, while Lantier was pushing her towards his room, Nana's face appeared behind one of the panes of the glass door of the little room. The child had just woken up and had got quietly out of bed in her nightgown, pale with sleep. She looked at her father lying slumped in his own vomit; then, with her face pressed against the glass, she stayed there, waiting till her mother's petticoat disappeared into the other man's room opposite. She watched with grave attention. Her staring eyes, the eyes of a perverted child, were alight with sensual curiosity.

CHAPTER IX

THAT winter, a fit of wheezing almost carried Maman Coupeau off. Every year, in December, she could count on her asthma keeping her flat on her back for two or three weeks. She wasn't a young thing any longer, she'd be seventy-three come the next feast of Saint Anthony.* What's more she was a proper old crock, the slightest thing set her wheezing, even though she was still nice and stout. The doctor declared that one day her cough would do her in just like that.

When Maman Coupeau had to stay in bed she became as nasty as the pox. Of course, the hole she slept in with Nana wasn't exactly cheerful. There was just enough room for two chairs between the child's bed and her own. The old, faded, grey wallpaper hung down in tatters. From the round fanlight, up near the ceiling, came a murky, pale glow like the light in a cellar. You grew old bloody fast in there, especially if you had trouble breathing. At night when she couldn't drop off she'd listen to Nana sleeping and it passed the time. But by day, as no one came to see her from morning till night, she'd grumble and moan over and over again for hours on end, tossing about on her pillow:

'Lord, what misery! . . . Lord, what misery! . . . They'll have me end me days shut up here, yes, shut up here in prison!'

And when someone came to see her, Virginie or Madame Boche, to ask after her health, she wouldn't answer, embarking instead on her catalogue of woes:

'Dear oh dear! The bread I eat here don't half cost me! I'd suffer less with strangers! . . . Look, I wanted a cup of tisane, well they brought me a whole jugful, just to make me feel guilty about drinking too much tisane . . . Then that Nana, that kid I brought up, well she nips off barefoot in the morning and I never set eyes on her again. Anyone'd think I smell. But she sleeps like a log at night, she'd never wake up, not once, to ask me if me chest's bad . . . In fact, I'm a burden to them, they're waiting for me to pop off. Well, it won't be long now. I've no son no more, that laundress bitch has got him away from me. She'd wallop me, she'd finish me off, except she's scared of the law.'

Indeed Gervaise was a bit rough at times. The household was going to the dogs, they were all feeling sour and telling each other to fuck off at the slightest provocation. One morning when Coupeau had a hangover he'd shouted: 'The old girl's always sayin' she's goin' to die, but she never does die!' and this had struck Maman Coupeau to the heart. They reproached her for what she cost, calmly saying that if she weren't there they'd save a tidy sum. To tell the truth, she wasn't behaving very well either. For example, when she saw her eldest daughter, Madame Lerat, she'd tell a hard luck story, accusing her son and daughter-in-law of letting her die of hunger, just so as to get twenty sous out of Madame Lerat that she'd spend on sweetmeats. And she'd repeat frightful bits of tittle-tattle to the Lorilleux, describing how their ten francs would go on things Gervaise fancied, new bonnets, cakes eaten on the sly, and even nastier things she didn't dare repeat. On two or three occasions the family almost came to blows because of her. Sometimes she took one side and sometimes the other; in fact, it was a real mess.

At the very worst of her attack that winter, one afternoon when Madame Lorilleux and Madame Lerat met at her bedside, Maman Coupeau blinked her eyes as a sign that they should bend down close to her. She could barely speak. She whispered softly:

'It's disgusting! . . . I heard 'em together last night. Yes, yes, Banban an' the hatter! And were they ever carrying on! Coupeau's some fine fellow. It's disgusting!'

And, coughing and choking, she gasped out her story: her son must have been dead drunk when he'd come home the night before. And, as she wasn't asleep, she'd heard everything very clearly, Banban's bare feet scampering across the floor, Lantier's voice calling to her in a whisper, the communicating door stealthily opening, and everything else. It must have gone on till daybreak, she wasn't sure of the time, because despite her best efforts she'd dropped off in the end.

'And the nastiest thing about it is that Nana could have heard,' she went on. 'In fact she was very restless all night, an' usually she sleeps like a log; she was tossing an' turning as if she'd got live coals in her bed.'

The two women didn't seem surprised.

'Of course!' murmured Madame Lorilleux. 'It must have started the very first day . . . And as long as it suits Coupeau, it's no affair of ours. But still! It certainly doesn't do the family any credit.'

'If it were me now, and I was there,' said Madame Lerat, tight-lipped, 'I'd give her a real fright, I'd shout something, anything, like "I can see you", or "the cops are here" . . . A doctor's servant told me his master had told him that getting a fright at a certain moment could kill a woman stone dead. And if she was struck dead there on the spot, well it'd be a good thing, wouldn't it, her sin would've done her in.'

Soon the whole neighbourhood knew that Gervaise went in to Lantier every night. Madame Lorilleux was noisily indignant for the neighbours' benefit; she was sorry for her brother, that dolt whose wife was giving him such a fine pair of horns; and, according to her, if she still set her foot in a hole like that it was solely on account of her poor mother who was forced to live in the midst of such depravity. With one accord, the neighbourhood set upon Gervaise. It must have been she who'd corrupted Lantier. You could see it in her eyes. Yes, in spite of the ugly rumours, that sly devil Lantier was still everybody's darling, because he went on behaving to all and sundry like a real gent, reading his paper as he walked down the street, always obliging and attentive to the ladies, with a ready supply of pastilles and flowers to hand round. Lord! it was in his nature to chase skirts; after all a man's a man, you can't expect him to say no to women who throw themselves at him. But there was no excuse for her, she was a disgrace to the Rue de la Goutte-d'Or. And the Lorilleux, who were Nana's godparents, would entice the kid over to their place, to pump her for details. When they asked her roundabout questions Nana would put on her innocent air, masking her flashing eyes with her long soft lids.

Amid this general outrage Gervaise went placidly about her business, weary and half asleep. At first she'd felt dreadfully guilty and shameless and had been disgusted with herself. On leaving Lantier's room she'd wash her hands and, with a wet rag, scrub her shoulders hard enough to abrade the skin, as if to clean off the filth. If Coupeau tried to fool about she'd get angry and rush off shivering to the back of the shop to dress; nor would she allow the hatter to touch her when her husband had just kissed her. She'd have liked to change her skin when she changed men. But, slowly, she became inured. It was too tiring to wash every time. Her slothful habits sapped her will, her need to be happy made her find what happiness she could in her troubles. She was easy on herself and on the others, simply trying to arrange matters so that nobody would have too much bother. As long as her husband and her lover were happy, and the household's little ways went on undisturbed, and they all had a fine time from dawn to dusk, all of them plump and pleased with life, taking things easily, there wasn't really anything to grumble about, was there? For after all, what she was doing couldn't be so wrong, since it had settled into such a good arrangement, which suited them all; as a rule you're punished when you do wrong. So then her promiscuity simply became a habit. Now it was all as regular as eating and drinking; each time Coupeau came home drunk she went in to Lantier, and this happened at the very least each Monday, Tuesday, and Wednesday. She shared her nights. In the end she'd even taken to leaving Coupeau fast asleep, if he was snoring too loudly, and calmly going to finish her snooze on the pillow of the other. It wasn't that she preferred Lantier. No, it was just that she found him cleaner, and she slept better in his room where she felt as if she was having a bath. In short, she was like a cat who loves curling up for a nap on clean linen.

Maman Coupeau never dared say anything openly about all this. However when they had rows and Gervaise would shake her, the old girl dropped some pretty clear hints. She'd talk about knowing men who were real half-wits and women who were real sluts; and she'd mutter other, bawdier words, drawing on the crude vocabulary of a former waistcoat-maker. The first few times, Gervaise had stared hard at her without replying. Later, however, she defended herself, though never explicitly, giving general reasons. If a woman was married to a soak, a swine who wallowed in his own filth, then that woman had every excuse for looking around for someone cleaner. She went further, implying that Lantier was every bit as much her husband as Coupeau was, more so perhaps. Hadn't she known him when she was fourteen? Hadn't she borne him two children? Well, that being so, it was all excusable, nobody could cast a stone at her. What she was doing was only natural. Then, they'd better not start picking on her. She'd have no trouble showing them where they got off. The Rue de la Goutte-d'Or wasn't all that spotless! Little Madame Vigoureux let herself be tumbled from dawn to dusk on her coal-heap. Madame Lehongre, the grocer's wife, slept with her brother-in-law, a great big slob Gervaise wouldn't touch with a barge pole. That prissy clockmaker on the other side of the road was almost had up at the Assizes for something vile, going with his own daughter, a brazen hussy who worked the streets. And, with a wide sweep of her arm, she indicated the entire neighbourhood, she could have gone on for an hour just telling all those folks' dirty secrets, people who slept like animals all heaped together, fathers, mothers, kids, rolling about in their muck. Ah! there was plenty she could tell, the place was dripping with shit, it poisoned everything round about. Yes, yes, men and women were a foul lot, in this bit of Paris where people had to live all on top of one another because they were so wretchedly poor! If you dumped both sexes together under a grindstone, all you'd get for your pains would be something to fertilize the cherry trees on the plain of Saint-Denis.

'They'd do better not to spit into the air, it'll land back on their noses,' she'd shout when she couldn't stand any more. 'To each his own, eh? Live and let live . . . I think everything's just fine, as long as I'm not dragged in the gutter by folk who wallow about in it themselves, up to their ears in muck.'

And, one day when Maman Coupeau had said something more pointed, she'd answered her between clenched teeth:

'You're taking advantage because you're lying there in bed . . . See here, you're in the wrong, you know very well I'm good to you, I've never thrown your own life in your face! Oh! I know, a nice life all right, two or three men while Père Coupeau was still alive . . . No, you needn't start coughing, I've said my say. It's just to get you to leave me in peace, that's all!'

The old lady had almost choked. The next day, when Goujet came for his mother's washing while Gervaise was out, Maman Coupeau called him and kept him seated by her bed for a long time. She well knew what he felt for Gervaise, and she saw he'd been depressed and unhappy for some time, from wondering what ugly things might be going on. And, for something to chat about, and to get her own back for yesterday's row, she came out crudely with the truth, sobbing and complaining as if Gervaise's bad behaviour was above all an affront to herself. When Goujet emerged from her little room he was so overcome with distress he had to lean against the wall. Then, when Gervaise returned, Maman Coupeau shouted to her that she was wanted immediately at Madame Goujet's, with the washing whether it was ironed or not; and she seemed so excited that Gervaise could smell tittle-tattle and imagine the painful scene and the heart-break that lay in store for her.

White as a sheet, her legs already turned to jelly, she put the washing in a basket and set off. For years now she hadn't paid back to the Goujets one sou of the debt. It still stood at four hundred and twenty-five francs. She accepted payment for the laundry every time, saying she was hard up. She felt bitterly ashamed, because it looked as if she was using Goujet's friendship to make a mug of him. Coupeau, less scrupulous now, would snigger, saying Goujet must have been cuddling her on the sly and reckoned that as payment. But, despite her involvement with Lantier, Gervaise was outraged, asking her husband if that was what he really wanted. No one could speak ill of Goujet in front of her; she cherished her love for him like a part of her own integrity. So, each time she returned their washing to those good souls, Gervaise would feel a great pang as she started up the stairs.

'Oh, so you're here at last!' Madame Goujet said curtly, opening the door. 'When I want Death to call it's you I'll send to get him.'

Embarrassed, Gervaise went in, not daring even to mutter an excuse. She wasn't reliable any longer, she never came on time, kept people waiting as long as a week. Little by little she was letting everything go to pot.

'I've been expecting you for a whole week,' went on the lace-maker. 'And what's more you tell a lot of lies, you send your apprentice to me with trumped-up stories: my washing's being done, it's going to be delivered that very evening, or else there's been an accident, it's fallen into a bucket. And in the meantime my whole day's wasted, nothing ever arrives and I get all upset. No, really, you go too far . . . Well, let's see what you've got in your basket. Let's hope everything's here! Have you brought the pair of sheets you've had for a month, and the shirt that was left behind the last time?'

'Yes, yes,' murmured Gervaise, 'I've brought the shirt, here it is.'

But Madame Goujet protested. This shirt wasn't hers, she didn't want it. She wasn't getting her own things back now, it was the last straw! Last week she'd already had two handkerchiefs without her mark on them. That really put her off, getting linen from goodness knows where. And after all, she did like her own things.

'And the sheets?' she went on. 'They're lost, aren't they? . . . Well, my girl, it's your problem, but I want them tomorrow morning, d'you hear!' A silence fell. Gervaise sensed that the door of Goujet's room behind her was ajar, and this made her more upset than ever. He must be there, she felt sure of it; and how dreadful, if he was listening to all these well-deserved reproaches, to which she had no reply! She made herself be very submissive and meek, bending her head and putting the washing on the bed as quickly as possible. But it got still worse

when Madame Goujet began to examine the articles one at a
time. She picked each one up, then dropped it, saying:

'My, you've really lost your touch! It's no longer a case of
my always singing your praises! . . . Yes, these days, you do
things just anyhow, your work's really sloppy . . . Here, take a
look at this shirt front, it's scorched, the iron's left a mark on
the pleats. And the buttons, they're all torn off. I don't know
how you manage it, but there's never a single button left . . .
My word! Here's a bodice I'm not going to pay you for. D'you
see that? It's still dirty, you've just spread the dirt . . . Thank
you very much! If the washing isn't even clean now . . .'

She stopped, counting the articles. Then she cried:

'What! Is this all you've brought? There's two pairs of
stockings missing, and six napkins, a tablecloth, some dusters
. . . What do you take me for? I left word for you to bring me
everything, whether it was ironed or not. If your apprentice
isn't here within the hour with the rest, I warn you, Madame
Coupeau, you'll be in trouble.'

At that moment, Goujet coughed in his room. Gervaise gave
a little shudder. God, what a way to treat her in front of him!
And she stood there in the middle of the room, uneasy and
abashed, waiting to be given the dirty clothes. But, after settling
the account, Madame Goujet calmly took her place again by the
window, where she was mending a lace shawl.

'And the washing?' Gervaise enquired timidly.

'No, thank you,' replied the old lady, 'there's nothing this
week.'

Gervaise turned pale. Madame Goujet was taking away her
custom. At that she lost her head completely and had to sit
down on a chair, because her legs were giving way under her.
She made no attempt to defend herself, and all she could say
was:

'Is Monsieur Goujet ill then?'

Yes, he wasn't feeling well, he'd had to come home instead
of going to the forge, and he'd just lain down on his bed to rest.
Madame Goujet spoke in a grave voice, sitting there in her
inevitable black dress, her white face framed by her nun-like
headdress. Bolt-makers' wages had been lowered again; instead
of nine francs a day it was down to seven, because of the

machines which did all the work. And she explained that they were saving every way they could; she was going to do her own washing again. Naturally, it would have come in very handy if the Coupeaus had paid back the money her son had lent them. But she wasn't going to put the bailiffs on them, as they weren't able to pay. Since the old lady had begun speaking of the debt, Gervaise had kept her head bowed, apparently following the nimble play of the lace-maker's needle as one by one she formed the new stitches.

'Still,' continued Madame Goujet, 'if you tried to cut back a bit, you'd manage to pay it off. Because when all's said and done you don't skimp on meals, you must spend a lot, I'm sure . . . If you only gave us ten francs a month . . .'

She was interrupted by Goujet's voice, calling her.

'Mother! Mother!'

But when almost immediately she returned and sat down again, she changed the subject. Her son had undoubtedly asked her not to press Gervaise for money. However, in spite of herself, five minutes later she was back on the subject of the debt. Oh! She'd foreseen what was happening, the roofer was drinking up the whole laundry, and he'd take his wife down with him. So if he'd listened to her, her son would never have lent the five hundred francs. Today he'd be married, he wouldn't be fretting himself to death, with the prospect of being unhappy his whole life. She was growing angry, speaking in very harsh terms, accusing Gervaise openly of conspiring with Coupeau to take advantage of her simple son. Oh yes, there were some women who could play the hypocrite for years, but in the end their goings-on were exposed to the light of day.

'Mother! Mother!' Goujet's voice called a second time, more violently.

She stood up and on returning said, as she took up her lace-making again:

'Go in, he wants to see you.'

Trembling, Gervaise did so, leaving the door open. She felt deeply moved, because it was as if they were acknowledging their love before Madame Goujet. She was back in that quiet little room, with its walls covered in pictures and its narrow iron bed, like the room of a fifteen-year-old boy. Goujet, his huge body devastated by what Maman Coupeau had told him, lay on the bed, his eyes red and his handsome golden beard still wet. In the first moments of rage he must have battered the pillow with his formidable fists, for feathers were coming out through a tear in the cloth.

'Listen, Mother's wrong,' he told Gervaise in almost a whisper. 'You don't owe me anything, I don't want to hear it mentioned.'

He'd sat up and was looking at her. Immediately, his eyes filled again with large tears.

'Are you ill, Monsieur Goujet?' she asked softly. 'Please, please tell me what's the matter.'

'Thank you, but it's nothing. I got too tired yesterday. I'm going to sleep a bit.'

But then, his heart breaking, he couldn't stop himself from crying out:

'My God, my God, it never ought to have happened, never! You'd given me your solemn word! And now there it is, there it is! . . . Oh my God! It's more than I can bear, please go!'

And with a gentle gesture he entreated her to leave. She didn't go near the bed, she did as he asked and left, dazed, unable to say anything to comfort him. In the next room she picked up her basket; but still she stayed, from the need to say something, anything. Madame Goujet went on with her mending without looking up. In the end it was she who said:

'Well good night! Send me back my washing and we'll settle up later.'

'Yes, of course, good night,' stammered Gervaise.

She closed the door slowly, casting her eyes one last time round that clean, orderly home where, she felt, she was leaving behind some part of her own decency. She made her way back to the laundry automatically, like a dumb animal returning home, never giving a thought to where she was going. Maman Coupeau, out of bed for the first time, was sitting beside the stove. But Gervaise didn't tell her off; she was too exhausted, her bones ached as if she'd been beaten; life, she felt, was really too hard, and, unless you managed to do yourself in at first go, you couldn't tear your own heart out, now could you!

Gervaise, now, didn't give a damn about anything. She'd send everyone packing with a vague wave of the hand. Each time a fresh problem arose she'd plunge deeper into her sole pleasure, eating her three meals every day. The laundry could have collapsed and as long as she wasn't caught under it she'd gladly have buggered off without even a shirt to her name. And indeed the laundry was collapsing, not all at once, but bit by bit, every morning and evening. One after another the clients lost patience and took their washing elsewhere. Monsieur Madinier, Mademoiselle Remanjou, even the Boches themselves, had gone back to Madame Fauconnier, whom they found more reliable. Eventually people got fed up with asking for a pair of stockings for three weeks on end or bringing back shirts which still had grease spots on them from the previous Sunday. Gervaise never lost her appetite over these clients, she'd wish 'em luck and let 'em know exactly where they got off, saying she was bloody pleased not to have to paw through their filthy things any longer. All right! The whole neighbourhood could walk out, she'd be shot of a fine load of muck; and then, it was that much less work. Meanwhile the only customers she kept were those that paid late, and the tarts, or women like Madame Gaudron whose dirty clothes stank so much that not a single laundress in the Rue Neuve would wash them. The laundry was done for, she'd had to dismiss her last assistant, Madame Putois, and she was left alone with her cross-eyed apprentice Augustine who grew stupider as she grew older; and even so there wasn't always enough work for the two of them, they'd spend entire afternoons with their behinds draped over the stools. In short, a proper nose-dive. You could smell disaster a mile off.

Naturally, as fecklessness and poverty took over, so too did squalor. You'd never have recognized that lovely shop with its sky-blue paint which had once been Gervaise's pride and joy. The shop window's woodwork and panes, which they forgot to wash, were permanently spattered from top to bottom with dirt from passing carriages. Hanging from the boards of the brass sign were three grey rags belonging to clients who'd died in hospital. And the inside looked even seedier: the damp from clothes strung up near the ceiling to dry had made the

wallpaper come unstuck; the glazed chintz hung in shreds like
dusty spiders' webs; the ruined stove, pierced full of holes by
the poker, stood in its corner like a heap of cast iron in a junk
yard; you'd think an entire garrison had eaten off the work-
table, which was stained with wine and coffee, encrusted with
jam and covered in grease from their Monday blow-outs. And
along with all that there was a smell of sour starch and a stench
made up of mildew, burnt fat and filth. But Gervaise felt right
at home there. She'd never noticed the shop getting dirty; she'd
let herself go along with it and had grown used to the torn
paper, the greasy woodwork, in the same way that she took to
wearing skirts split at the seams and she no longer washed her
ears. The dirt itself was like a cosy nest it was lovely to snuggle
into. Just to let the whole thing go to hell, and wait for the dust
to stop up the holes and cover everything in velvet; to feel the
whole house growing heavier about her in a drowsy indolence,
was a truly sensual pleasure she found intoxicating. The great
thing was to be let alone: she didn't give a damn for anything
else. Her debts were still mounting up but they no longer
worried her. She was becoming less scrupulous: she would pay
them, or she wouldn't, the whole thing was vague, and she'd
rather not know. When a shop refused to give her tick any
longer she'd open an account at the place next door. She was
running out of credit in the neighbourhood, with bad debts
here, there and everywhere. Just to take the Rue de la Goutte-
d'Or, she no longer dared pass by the coal-merchant's, nor the
grocer's, nor the fruiterer's, which meant that to get to the
washhouse she had to go round by the Rue des Poissonniers, a
good ten minutes' slog. The shopkeepers called her names. One
evening, the man who'd sold her the furniture for Lantier
stirred up some of the neighbours, yelling that he'd pull up her
skirts and give her a good hiding if she didn't hand over the
cash. Of course scenes like that left her trembling; but she'd
just give herself a good shake like a dog that's been beaten and
it was over, she'd eat no less heartily that evening. What a
cheeky bunch, bothering her like that! She hadn't any money,
and she couldn't produce it out of thin air, now could she! And
then, shopkeepers stole enough, it was their place to wait for
their money. And she'd go back to sleep in her corner, carefully

not thinking of what was bound to happen one day. She'd be for it, all right! But until that moment, she wasn't going to let anyone plague her.

Maman Coupeau, however, got better. The household scraped along for another year. Of course during the summer there was a bit more work, the white skirts and percale dresses of the good-time girls from the outer boulevards. Disaster crept up on them slowly, as each week they sank further into the mire, although they still had their ups and downs, some evenings when they gazed at the empty larder, rubbing their bellies, others when they gorged themselves on veal. Maman Coupeau was always to be seen ambling along the pavements with parcels tucked under her apron, heading for the pawn shop in the Rue Polonceau. She walked with her shoulders hunched, wearing the self-righteous, oily expression of a devout churchgoer on her way to mass: for she didn't dislike the task, scratching around for money amused her, and haggling with old clothes dealers was right up the street of an old gossip like her. The assistants in the Rue Polonceau knew her well; they called her Mother 'Four Francs' because she always asked for four francs when they offered her three, for parcels the size of a knob of butter. Gervaise would have borrowed on the house itself; her mania for pawning things was so great she'd have shaved her head if they'd been willing to lend her something on her hair. It was too easy, how could you resist going there for cash when you needed a four pound loaf. The whole caboodle found its way to uncle, their linen, their clothes, even the tools and furniture. At first, if she had a good week, she'd take the opportunity to redeem her stuff, although back it'd go the following week. But later she got that she didn't give a damn and just let things go, and sold the pawn tickets. One thing only broke her heart, when she had to pawn her clock to pay a twenty-franc bill to a bailiff who came to serve a writ. Until then, she'd sworn she'd die of hunger sooner than touch her clock. When Maman Coupeau carried it off in a little hatbox, she sank down on to a chair, her arms slack and her eyes wet, as if she were losing her entire fortune. But when Maman Coupeau came back with twenty-five francs, a sum she'd never expected, the extra five francs consoled her; she sent the old woman off straight away to buy four sous' worth of booze in a glass, just to celebrate the five-franc piece. Now, when they were on good terms they often had a nip together, on a corner of the work-table, a mixture part brandy and part cassis. Maman Coupeau had the knack of bringing back the full glass in her apron pocket without spilling a drop. No need for the neighbours to know, was there? The truth was that the neighbours knew perfectly well. The fruiterer, the tripe-shop woman, and the grocer's boys would say: 'Hey! The old girl's going to see uncle,' or, 'Look! The old girl's got a glass of booze in her pocket'. And naturally that turned the neighbours even more against Gervaise. Everything was disappearing down her throat, she'd soon have polished off the whole lot. Yes, yes, just a few more mouthfuls and the place would be clean as a whistle.

Amid this general devastation Coupeau was flourishing. That bloody swillpot was in fine form. He positively thrived on plonk and rotgut. He ate a great deal and sneered at that weedy Lorilleux who held that booze was a killer, answering him by tapping his paunch whose skin was stretched by fat, like the skin on a drum. He'd play him a tune on it, sonorously belching and burping out the belly's vespers, with rumblings and rollings on his drum such as would have made a fortune for an itinerant tooth-puller. But Lorilleux, annoyed at having no belly himself, said it was yellow fat, unhealthy fat. No matter, Coupeau just got tipsier, for the sake of his health. His tousled hair, speckled now with grey, stood up round his face like flaming brandy. His boozer's face with its ape-like jawbone was seasoned brick red by alcohol, with tinges of winey-blue. And he was just as happy-go-lucky as ever: he'd shout at his wife to shut her trap, if she tried to tell him her troubles. Since when were men expected to get their hands dirty dealing with how-d'you-dos of that sort? There might be no bread in the larder but it was no business of his. He had to have his grub morning and evening and he never bothered about where it came from. When he spent weeks without working he became even more demanding. Moreover he'd still give Lantier a friendly slap on the back. To be sure, he didn't know a thing about his wife's misconduct; at least certain people, the Boches, the Poissons, swore to high heaven that he hadn't the faintest inkling, and that it'd be a great misfortune if he ever found out about it. But Madame Lerat, his own sister, would toss her head and declare she knew husbands who didn't object. One night Gervaise herself, as she was finding her way back in the dark from Lantier's room, was petrified to feel a slap on her behind; but in the end she decided she must just have banged into the bedstead. Really, the situation was too awful; surely her husband couldn't be amusing himself by pulling her leg.

Lantier wasn't wasting away either. He looked after himself very carefully, measuring his waistline by his trouser belt which he was always afraid he'd have to take in or let out; he liked himself just as he was, he didn't want to get fatter or thinner, out of vanity. This made him fussy about his food, because he chose every dish with a view to staying the same size. Even when there wasn't a sou in the house, he insisted on food which was nourishing but light, like eggs and cutlets. Ever since he'd begun sharing the wife with the husband, he'd thought of himself as an equal partner in the household: he'd pocket small change he found lying about, he had Gervaise trained to do his every bidding, he grumbled and bawled, more at home than was Coupeau in his own house. In fact, it was a household with two hubbies. And the backdoor, craftier hubby pulled the blanket over to his side, helping himself to the pick of the crop whether it be wife, food or anything else. In a word, he was skimming the cream off the Coupeaus! He no longer cared if people saw what he was doing. Nana remained his favourite, because he liked little girls who were nice. He bothered less and less about Étienne, saying that boys ought to be able to shift for themselves. If someone came asking for Coupeau, Lantier was always there in his slippers and shirt-sleeves; he'd appear from the back shop with the irritated air of a husband who's been disturbed, and he'd answer for Coupeau, saying it amounted to the same thing.

Life wasn't always a picnic for Gervaise, caught between these two men. She couldn't grumble about her health, thank God! She also was getting too fat. But to be lumbered with two men to take care of and please was often too much for her. Jesus Christ! Just one husband's enough to wear you out! The worst of it was that those bastards got on very well together. They never quarrelled; in the evening after dinner they'd sit at the table leaning on their elbows and grinning away at each other; all day long they'd play up to each other like a pair of pleasure-loving cats. On days when they came home in a bad temper, they took it out on her. Go on! Fetch the stupid bitch a good one! It was always she who got the blame; it made them better pals if they joined forces against her. And she'd better not take it into her head to answer back! At first, when one of them yelled at her, she'd give the other a beseeching look, hoping for a kind word. But it never did much good. Now she lay low and hunched her heavy shoulders, having realized that it amused them to knock her about, she was so round, as round as a ball. Coupeau was very foul-mouthed and called her revolting names. Lantier, on the other hand, chose his insults with care, thinking up expressions that people just don't use and which hurt her even more. Fortunately you get used to anything; in the end the abuse and unfair accusations the two men heaped on her just slid off her delicate skin as if it were oilcloth. She even reached the point where she preferred them cross, because on those occasions when they were being nice they pestered her more, they were always after her, so that she couldn't even iron a bonnet in peace any longer. They'd make her cook them little dishes, which they wanted salted, or not salted, they'd make her say first one thing then another, they'd make her coddle them and swaddle them in cotton wool. By the end of the week her head was spinning and her limbs aching, and she'd stare about her wild-eyed, in a complete daze. It uses a woman up, a job like that does.

Yes, Coupeau and Lantier were using her up, that's the right word, burning her at both ends like a candle. Of course, Coupeau had had no education, but Lantier had had too much, or rather he'd had an education the way dirty people have a white shirt, to cover the filth underneath. One night, she dreamt she was standing at the mouth of a pit; Coupeau was punching her to make her go forward while Lantier was tickling her bottom so she'd jump all the sooner. Well! Her life was like that. She was in expert hands, and it wasn't really surprising if she was going to the dogs. The neighbours were hardly fair when they blamed her for becoming such a slut, because her misfortunes were not of her making. Sometimes, when she stopped to think, a shiver would run through her. Then she'd reflect that things might have turned out even worse. For example, it was better to have two men than to lose your two arms. And, feeling her situation to be natural and not at all unusual, she did her best to find a modest measure of happiness in it. What proved how cosy and good natured the whole thing was becoming is that she didn't hate Coupeau any more than she hated Lantier. In a play put on at the Gaîté* she'd seen a trollop who'd loathed her husband and poisoned him because of her lover; and this had made Gervaise angry, because she didn't feel anything like that in her heart. Wasn't it more sensible for the three of them to rub along together in peace? No, no nonsense of that kind; it messed up your life, which wasn't exactly a picnic in any case. In short, in spite of the debts and the threat of destitution, she'd have said she was very tranquil and contented if the two men hadn't overworked her so dreadfully and bawled at her so much.

Towards autumn, unfortunately, things got even worse at the Coupeaus'. Lantier said he was losing weight, and went round with a long face which got longer every day. He groused about the slightest thing, and turned up his nose at potato casseroles and a ratatouille which he claimed he couldn't eat without getting a belly-ache. The least little squabble, now, turned into a real dust-up, when they'd all blame one another for the mess they were in, and it was a hell of a job to patch things up before they each went off for their bit of shut-eye. When the bran's all gone, the donkeys set upon one other, don't they? Disaster lay just around the corner, Lantier could smell it; it exasperated him that the household was already so skint, so thoroughly cleaned out, that he could see the day when he'd have to pick up his hat and look elsewhere for bed and board. He'd got so used to his little nest and to all the little habits he'd fallen into; he was pampered by everyone; it was truly a land of milk and honey, and he'd never find such comforts anywhere else. But you simply can't stuff yourself up to the eyeballs and still keep the victuals on your plate. It was his own belly he was angry with, because after all his belly was where the household now was. But he didn't think like that; he bore a terrible grudge against the others for letting themselves go down the drain in two years. It's true the Coupeaus didn't exactly think ahead. So he started bawling Gervaise out for being a bad manager. Christ in heaven! Whatever was going to become of him? His friends were leaving him stranded just when he was about to pull off a wonderful deal, a job in a factory that paid six thousand francs, enough to keep the entire little family in luxury.

One night in December there was nothing whatever for dinner. They hadn't a bean. Lantier, very gloomy, went out early and tramped around, sniffing out a place with a reassuring aroma of cooking. He spent hours beside the stove, thinking. Then, all of a sudden, he became very friendly with the Poissons. He no longer teased the policeman by calling him Badingue, and went so far as to agree that the Emperor was a decent chap, maybe. Above all he seemed to approve of Virginie, saying she was a capable woman who'd be very good at managing her own affairs. It was obvious he was buttering them up. You might even imagine he was planning to become their lodger. But Lantier's nut was full of secret twists and turns, and his scheme was much more devious than that. Virginie having told him she wanted to start some kind of business, he played up to her, declaring her plan to be first-rate. Yes, she must have been born to be a business woman, being so tall, nice-looking and energetic. Oh! She'd make as much money as she liked. Since the capital had been there for some time—an inheritance from an aunt—she was damn right to give up the four dresses she cobbled together every season, and get started in business; and he cited people who were making their fortunes, the woman from the fruit shop at the corner, and a little crockery vendor on the outer boulevard, for the timing was wonderful, you could have sold the sweepings off a counter. Virginie, however, hesitated: she was looking for a shop to rent, and didn't want to leave the area. At that, Lantier got her into a corner and they whispered together for ten minutes. It looked as if he was really urging something on her, and she wasn't refusing any longer, she seemed to be authorizing him to do something. It was like a secret between them, there were winks and rapidly muttered words, and even their handshakes suggested furtive machinations. From then on Lantier, as he ate his dry bread, observed the Coupeaus on the sly while battering them with his perpetual complaints—for he'd become very talkative again. All day long Gervaise had her nose rubbed in their poverty, the details of which he'd go over complacently. It wasn't for himself—Christ in heaven!—that he was saying all this. He'd starve to death with his friends if necessary. Still, it was only prudent to look at the situation squarely. They owed at least five hundred francs in the neighbourhood, to the baker, the coal merchant, the grocer and others. What's more they hadn't paid the rent for the last two quarters, so that made another two hundred and fifty francs; the landlord, Monsieur Marescot, was talking of evicting them if they didn't pay before the first of January. Then, the pawn shop had taken everything, they hadn't three francs' worth of odds and ends left to pawn, they'd cleaned the place out so thoroughly; the nails were still on the walls, that was all, maybe two pounds of them worth three sous. Gervaise, muddled by his arguments and stunned by this calculation, would lose her temper and bang her fists on the table, or else start to cry like a baby. One evening, she burst out:

'I'm going to hop it tomorrow, that's what I'm going to do! . . . I'd sooner put the key under the door and sleep on the pavement than go on like this, being scared stiff about what's going to happen.'

'It would be more sensible,' said Lantier cunningly, 'to transfer the lease, if someone could be found . . . When the pair of you decide you'd best give up the laundry . . .'

She interrupted him, saying more vehemently:

'This very minute! This very minute! Oh! That'd be a bloody good riddance, that would!'

Then Lantier became very practical. On transferring the lease they'd surely be able to get the two overdue rent payments from the new occupant. Next he ventured to mention the Poissons, reminding Gervaise that Virginie was looking for a shop; perhaps the laundry would suit her. Yes, he remembered now having heard her say she wanted one just like it. But on hearing Virginie's name Gervaise had suddenly calmed down again. She'd see; people always talked of walking out on everything when they were in a temper, but when you stopped to think, it wasn't all that easy to do.

It was in vain, during the next few days, that Lantier started holding forth again; Gervaise would reply that she'd been in worse pickles before and had managed to pull herself out of it. How in the world could she be better off, without her laundry? That wasn't the way to put food on their plates. She was going to do just the opposite, employ some more assistants and build up a new clientele. This was her way of resisting Lantier's reasoning; he pictured her as completely down, overwhelmed by debt, without the faintest hope of getting back in the saddle. But he was tactless enough to mention Virginie's name again, and at that she grew desperately stubborn. No, no, never! She'd always had her suspicions about Virginie's real feelings; if she had her eye on her shop, it was to make her eat humble pie. She might perhaps have handed it over to the first woman she met in the street, but not to that great big hypocrite who'd clearly been waiting years to see her fall flat on her face. Oh, that explained everything! Now she understood why those yellow sparks lit up in the bitch's cat-like eyes. Yes, Virginie still bore a grudge because of the washhouse thrashing, and all this time she'd been carefully nursing her grudge. Well! She'd be wise to put her grudge on ice, if she didn't want another thrashing. And that could happen very soon, she could be getting her bum all prepared. In reply to this tongue-lashing, Lantier at first went for Gervaise, calling her pig-headed, a bag of wind, Madame Bossy, and was so carried away that he even called Coupeau himself an oaf, accusing him of not being able to make his wife respect his friend. Then, realizing that being angry would put everything at risk, he swore that never again would he involve himself in other people's affairs, because you don't get any thanks for your pains; and indeed he seemed to give up trying to persuade them to part with the lease, while he waited for the right moment to raise the matter again and get the laundress to agree.

It was now January, and the weather was very nasty, damp and cold. Maman Coupeau, who'd coughed and wheezed all through December, was forced to take to her bed after Twelfth Night. This was her annuity and every winter she expected its arrival. But this winter everyone round her said she'd only leave her room feet first: and in truth her cough had a damned awful graveyard ring to it; she was still a big solid woman, though one eye was useless and one side of her face all twisted up. Of course her children wouldn't ever have finished her off; however, she'd been lingering on for so long and was such a burden that deep down they longed for her to die, as a deliverance for everybody. She herself would be much happier, because she'd lived out her time, hadn't she? And when you've lived out your time, you've nothing to regret. The doctor had been sent for once and didn't even bother to come a second time. They'd give her herb tea, they didn't abandon her completely. Every hour, they'd go in to see if she was still alive. She no longer spoke, her breathing was so bad, but with her one good eye, which was still clear and lively, she'd look hard at them; and that one good eye conveyed ever such a lot: yearning for her lost youth, sadness at seeing her family so impatient to be rid of her, and fury at that foul-minded little Nana who now quite shamelessly got up at night to stand watching through the glass door in her nightgown.

One Monday night Coupeau came home sloshed. Ever since his mother had become dangerously ill, he'd been in a perpetually maudlin state. When he'd gone to bed and was snoring his head off, Gervaise wandered round for a while. She usually sat up with Maman Coupeau part of the night. Nana, who by the by was being very spunky about it all, still shared the old woman's bed, saying that if she heard her dying she'd certainly call everybody. That particular night, as the child was asleep and the invalid seemed to be dozing peacefully, Gervaise finally gave in to Lantier, who was calling her from his room, urging her to come and get a bit of rest. They left just one candle alight, on the ground, behind the cupboard. But, about three in the morning, Gervaise suddenly leapt out of bed, shivering and overcome with anguish. She fancied she'd felt a cold breath pass over her body. The candle had burnt out and in the darkness Gervaise, flustered, tied on her petticoats with feverish hands. It was not until she reached the little room, after bumping into the furniture, that she could light a small lamp. The dark oppressive silence was broken only by the deep notes of

Coupeau's snores. Nana lay sleeping on her back, breathing gently through her full lips. When Gervaise lowered the lamp it set great shadows dancing and lit up Maman Coupeau's face which was quite white; her head had rolled over sideways and her eyes were open. Maman Coupeau was dead.

Chilled to the bone and moving cautiously, Gervaise returned softly to Lantier's room without uttering a single cry. He'd gone back to sleep. She bent down and murmured:

'Listen, it's all over, she's dead.'

At first, heavy with sleep and only half awake, he growled:

'For God's sake shut up and get back into bed . . . There's nothing we can do if she's dead.'

Then he raised himself on one elbow and asked:

'What time is it?'

'Three o'clock.'

'Only three o'clock! Well get back into bed then. You'll catch a chill . . . We'll see about it when it's morning.'

She didn't pay him any attention, but got fully dressed. So he snuggled back under the blanket, his face to the wall, muttering that women were bloody pig-headed. What was the hurry to tell all and sundry there was a death in the house? It wasn't exactly cheerful, in the middle of the night, and he was fed up at having his sleep spoilt by such nasty thoughts. Still, when she'd taken all her things, even her hairpins, back into her own room, she sat down and sobbed to her heart's content, no longer afraid of being caught with Lantier. Deep down, she really loved Maman Coupeau, she was conscious of a great sorrow, after feeling at first only fear and vexation because she'd picked such an inconvenient time to go. And, all alone, she continued sobbing noisily in the silence, while Coupeau snored on without interruption: he couldn't hear a thing, she'd called him and shaken him and had then decided to leave him in peace, reflecting that it would only be a fresh worry if he did wake up. When she went back to the dead body, she found Nana sitting up, rubbing her eyes. The child grasped what had happened and, shameless little brat that she was, leaned forward inquisitively for a better look at her grandmother; she didn't say anything, she was quite trembly, quite amazed and gratified at being in the presence of this death she'd been looking forward to for two days, knowing it was an ugly, forbidden thing which must be kept from children; and seeing this white mask so wasted by life's passions at the end of its journey, the pupils of her kittenish eyes dilated and she felt her spine tingle as it did when she stood riveted to the glass door, spying on things which chits like her had no business watching.

'Come on, get up,' said her mother in a low voice. 'I don't want you to stay there.'

She slid out of the bed reluctantly, keeping her head turned and not taking her eyes off the dead woman. Gervaise was quite bothered, not knowing where to put Nana for the rest of the night. She'd decided to make her get dressed when Lantier, wearing trousers and slippers, came into the room; he hadn't been able to get back to sleep and was rather ashamed of his behaviour. That solved everything.

'She can sleep in my bed,' he whispered. 'She'll have lots of room.'

Nana turned her big bright eyes on her mother and Lantier, and put on her stupid look, the way she did on New Year's Day when someone gave her a box of chocolate drops. She certainly didn't need telling twice; off she went in her nightie, her bare little tootsies hardly touching the floor; she slid like a snake into the bed, which was still nice and warm, and stretched her length there, snuggling down, her thin body scarcely making a bump in the counterpane. Each time her mother came in, she saw her lying there with her eyes gleaming in her flushed, still face, not sleeping, not moving, evidently thinking about something.

Meanwhile, Lantier had been helping Gervaise to dress Maman Coupeau; and it was no small task, because the dead woman was a good weight. You'd never have thought it possible that the old woman could be so fat and so white. They'd put stockings on her, and a white petticoat, a camisole and a cap; in short, her best things. Coupeau was still snoring away on two notes, one deep, which sank down low, the other rasping, which rose up; it sounded like church music, the kind they play on Good Friday. So, when the corpse had been dressed and decently laid out on the bed, Lantier poured a glass of wine as a pick-me-up, for he felt quite queasy. Gervaise was hunting through the chest of drawers for a little copper crucifix she'd brought with her from Plassans; but then she remembered that Maman Coupeau herself must have sold it. They'd relit the stove. They spent the rest of the night half asleep on their chairs, finishing the opened bottle, feeling worried and annoyed at each other as if they were to blame for this death.

Before daybreak, about seven, Coupeau finally woke up. At first, when he heard the bad news, he stood there dry-eyed and stuttering, vaguely supposing they were playing a joke on him. Then he flung himself down on to his knees beside the dead woman, kissing her and bawling his head off, his tears so copious that he wet the sheet wiping his cheeks on it. Gervaise had begun sobbing again, very touched by her husband's grief, quite reconciled with him; yes, he was a better man than she'd thought. Coupeau's despair was all mixed in with a blinding hangover. He kept running his fingers through his hair, he had a thickly-coated morning-after tongue, and he was still a trifle tipsy despite his ten hours' sleep. And, clenching his fists, he wailed and moaned. Damn it all! his dear mother, whom he loved so much, dead and gone! Oh, what a terrible head he had, it'd be the death of him! Just like a band of red-hot coals round his head, and now his heart was being torn out as well! No, it wasn't fair of fate to plague a man so!

'Come on, cheer up, old chap,' said Lantier as he helped him up. 'You must pull yourself together.'

He was pouring him a glass of wine, but Coupeau refused to drink.

'Whatever's the matter with me? I've a taste of brass in me mouth . . . It's Mamma, when I saw her, I could taste brass . . . Mamma, oh my God, Mamma!'

And he began crying like a child again. However, he did drink the glass of wine, to put out the fire burning in his chest. Lantier soon took off, on the pretext of telling the family and registering the death at the Town Hall. He needed some fresh air. So he didn't hurry but enjoyed a cigarette or two in the cold morning air. On leaving Madame Lerat's in the Batignolles he even went into a local dairy for a nice hot cup of coffee. And he stayed there for a good hour, thinking.

By nine o'clock, meanwhile, the family had gathered at the laundry, where the shutters were left closed. Lorilleux didn't shed a tear; in any case, he had an order that couldn't wait, and almost immediately went back up to his workshop, after standing about for a couple of minutes with a suitably long face. Madame Lorilleux and Madame Lerat had kissed the Coupeaus and were dabbing at their eyes, from which a few little tears were falling. But Madame Lorilleux, glancing quickly round the room where the corpse lay, abruptly raised her voice to say it wasn't at all the thing, you never left a lighted lamp beside a dead body; you had to have candles, and they sent Nana off to buy a packet of candles, tall ones. Well really! If you were to die at Banban's, she'd lay you out in ever such a funny way! What a dim-wit, not even to know what to do with a corpse! Had she never ever buried anyone then? Madame Lerat had to go up to the neighbours' to borrow a crucifix; the one she brought back was too big, a cross of black wood with a painted cardboard Christ nailed to it, which covered the whole of Maman Coupeau's chest and seemed to crush it with its weight. Then they wanted some holy water, but no one had any, and again it was Nana who had to run to the church to fetch a bottle. In the twinkling of an eye the little room was transformed: on a small table burned a candle, with a glass of holy water beside it in which stood a sprig of boxwood. Now, if anyone called, it would at least look decent. And they arranged the chairs in a circle in the shop, to receive callers.

Lantier didn't come in till eleven o'clock. He'd been to the undertaker's to make enquiries.

'The coffin's twelve francs,' he said. 'If you want a mass, that'll be ten francs more. Then there's the hearse, and the cost of that depends on the decoration . . .'

'Oh, that's quite unnecessary,' murmured Madame Lorilleux, raising her head in a surprised and uneasy way. 'It wouldn't bring Mamma back, would it? . . . We've got to think of what we can afford.'

'Of course, I quite agree with you,' replied the hatter. 'I only asked so that you'd have the facts . . . Tell me what you want and after lunch I'll go and see to everything.'

They talked in low voices, sitting in the dim light which filtered into the shop through the cracks in the shutters. The door of the little room stood wide open and through that gaping portal came the great stillness of death. Children's laughter rose from the courtyard, where a circle of kids was dancing round in the pale winter sunshine. Suddenly they heard Nana, who'd slipped away from the Boches' where she'd been sent. She was bossing the others in her shrill voice, while heels beat time on the paving stones and the words of this song rose up into the air with a sound like jabbering birds:

> Our donkey, our donkey,
> Has a pain in his leg.
> So Madame's had him made
> A pretty sock for his peg,
> And some lilac shoes la la,
> And some lilac shoes!

Gervaise waited, then said in her turn:

'We're not rich, of course, but all the same we want to do things right. Even if Maman Coupeau hasn't left us anything, that's no reason to shove her into the ground like a dog . . . No, we must have a mass, and a nice hearse . . .'

'And who's going to pay for it?' enquired Madame Lorilleux fiercely. 'Not us, we lost some money last week, and not you either, since you're skint . . . Surely you can see where it's landed you, this wanting to impress people!'

When Coupeau was consulted he mumbled something and made a gesture indicating complete indifference, as he dozed off again on his chair. Madame Lerat said she'd pay her share. She agreed with Gervaise, they ought to do things right. So the pair of them added up some figures on a bit of paper: it would come to about ninety francs all told, because they decided, after a long discussion, on a hearse decorated with a narrow valance.

'There are three of us,' concluded Gervaise. 'We'll each give thirty francs. It's not going to ruin us.'

But Madame Lorilleux burst out in a fury:

'Well for my part I refuse! Yes, I refuse! . . . It's not because of the thirty francs. I'd give a hundred thousand, if I had them, and if that'd bring Mamma back! But I can't stand people who give themselves airs. You have a shop, and you want to show off in front of the whole neighbourhood. But as for us, that's not our way. We don't pretend to be something we're not . . . Oh, you do as you like. Put plumes on the hearse if that's what you fancy.'

'No one's asking you for anything,' retorted Gervaise. 'I'd sooner sell myself than have anything to reproach myself with. I fed Maman Coupeau without your help and I can certainly bury her without your help . . . I told you straight out once before: I take in stray cats, so I'm not about to leave your mother in the gutter.'

At that, Madame Lorilleux burst into tears, and Lantier had to prevent her from leaving. The quarrel became so noisy that Madame Lerat, who was trying hard to hush them, felt the need to slip quietly into the little room where she gave the dead woman a troubled, uneasy glance, as if afraid of finding her awake and listening to what was being discussed so close by. Just then, the little girls started dancing round again in the courtyard, with Nana's piercing voice dominating the others.

> Our donkey, our donkey,
> Has a pain in his tum.
> So Madame's had him made
> A pretty band for his tum,
> And some lilac shoes la la,
> And some lilac shoes!

'My God! Those kids don't half get on your nerves, with their singing!' Gervaise said to Lantier. She was thoroughly upset and almost crying with exasperation and distress. 'Make 'em shut up, and send Nana back to Madame Boche with a good kick on her you-know-what!'

Madame Lerat and Madame Lorilleux went off to lunch, promising to return. The Coupeaus sat down at table and ate some cold meat, but without being hungry and not daring even to let a fork rattle. They felt very upset and bewildered, with that poor Maman Coupeau weighing heavily upon them and seeming to fill all the rooms. Their life had been turned upside down. At first, they shuffled about without being able to find things, aching all over as if they had a hangover. Lantier set off again immediately to the undertaker's, bearing Madame Lerat's thirty francs and sixty that Gervaise, bare-headed, had raced round like a madwoman to borrow from Goujet. A few callers came during the afternoon, neighbours consumed with curiosity who arrived heaving sighs and rolling tearful eyes; they'd go into the little room, stare at the corpse while making the sign of the cross and shaking the sprig of boxwood dipped in the holy water; then they'd take a seat in the shop and talk about the dear woman, interminably, never tiring of repeating the same phrase for hours on end. Mademoiselle Remanjou had noticed that her right eye was still open; Madame Gaudron kept on repeating that she was a lovely colour for her age, and Madame Fauconnier couldn't stop being amazed at having seen her take her coffee three days ago. Really, it didn't take a minute to croak, they'd all better be prepared to meet their Maker. Towards evening, the Coupeaus began to feel they'd had enough. It was far too hard on a family, to have to keep a corpse so long. The government really ought to have made a different law about it. There was still another whole evening, a whole night and a whole morning, oh no! Would it never end? When you can't cry any more your sorrow turns into vexation, and you might behave badly, isn't that the case? They were all more and more conscious, everywhere in the apartment, of the presence of Maman Coupeau, lying silent and stiff down there in the little room; the weight of that presence was crushing them all. And the family, in spite of her, began to go back to its ordinary ways, and show less respect.

'You must have a bite to eat with us,' said Gervaise to Madame Lorilleux and Madame Lerat when they reappeared. 'We're all too miserable, we should stay together.'

They laid the supper things on the work-table. Each one of them, on seeing the plates set out, was reminded of the blow-outs they'd had there. Lantier had returned. Lorilleux came down. A pastry-cook had just brought round a pie, because Gervaise didn't feel up to cooking. Just as they were sitting down, Boche appeared, saying that Monsieur Marescot would like to pay his respects, and the landlord came in, looking very serious and wearing his large decoration on his frock-coat. He nodded silently to them and went straight to the little room, where he knelt down. His piety was striking: he prayed in the collected way priests pray, then made a sign of the cross in the air, while sprinkling holy water on the body with the sprig of box. The whole family had left the table and stood watching, deeply impressed. Monsieur Marescot, having finished his devotions, came into the shop and said to the Coupeaus:

'I've come for the two overdue rent payments. Can you settle up?'

'No, Monsieur, not exactly,' stammered Gervaise, very put out at having this mentioned in front of the Lorilleux. 'You see, what with our sad loss and all . . .'

'Of course, but everyone has their troubles,' replied the landlord, spreading out his huge ex-workman's fingers. 'I'm very sorry but I can't wait any longer . . . If I'm not paid the day after tomorrow—in the morning—I shall be obliged to have you put out.'

Gervaise, her eyes full of tears, clasped her hands in silent supplication. He gave a decisive nod of his big bony head to indicate that any entreaty would be a waste of time. Besides, the respect due to the dead forebade all discussion. Walking backwards, he quietly withdrew.

'A thousand pardons for having disturbed you,' he murmured. 'Don't forget, the day after tomorrow in the morning.'

And as he passed the little room again on his way out, he once more paid his respects to the corpse with a devout genuflection through the wide open door.

At first they ate quickly so they wouldn't seem to be enjoying their meal. But they slowed down when they reached the dessert, overcome by a need for comfort. From time to time Gervaise or one of the two sisters, her mouth full, would get up and glance into the little room without putting down her serviette; and when she sat down again, still chewing, the others would look at her for a second to see if everything was all right in there. Then the ladies got up less often and Maman Coupeau was forgotten. They'd made a tubful of coffee, very strong, so they could stay awake all night. The Poissons came at eight. They were offered a drink. At that moment Lantier, who'd been watching Gervaise's face, seemed to grasp an opportunity he'd been waiting for since morning. While they were discussing the disgusting behaviour of landlords who came and demanded their money in a house where there'd been a death, Lantier suddenly said:

'That bastard's a real Jesuit, carrying on as though he was officiating at mass! . . . If I were in your shoes I'd tell him what he could do with his shop!'

Feeling deathly tired, weak and nervy, Gervaise replied, giving in:

'Oh, you're right, I don't plan to wait for the law to turn up . . . I've had more than I can stand, more than I can stand.'

The Lorilleux, delighted at the thought that Banban would no longer have a shop, agreed completely. Nobody had any idea what a shop cost. If she only earned three francs from someone else, at least she'd have no expenses, she wouldn't risk losing huge sums of money. They made Coupeau repeat this argument, pressing him: he was drinking a lot, and was still in a permanently maudlin state, crying all by himself into his plate. As Gervaise seemed to be coming round to his point of view, Lantier looked at the Poissons and winked. And Virginie, at her most amiable, stepped in.

'You know, we could settle this between us. I'd take over the rest of the lease and fix things for you with the landlord . . . Then you wouldn't have to worry any more.'

'No, thank you,' declared Gervaise, giving herself a shake as if she had the shivers. 'I know where I can find a loan, if I want. I'll work; I've me two arms, thank goodness, to get me out of this hole.'

'You can talk about that later,' Lantier said hastily. 'It's not suitable, this evening . . . Later, tomorrow for example.'

At that moment Madame Lerat, who'd gone into the little room, gave a faint cry. She'd had a fright, because she'd found the candle burnt out. They all busied themselves lighting another, shaking their heads and repeating that it wasn't a good sign when the light went out beside a corpse.

The wake began. Coupeau had lain down, not to sleep, he said, but to think, and in five minutes was snoring. When they sent Nana off to sleep at the Boches', she burst into tears; ever since morning she'd been looking forward to being nice and cosy in her good friend Lantier's big bed. The Poissons stayed till midnight. In the end they made some mulled wine in a salad bowl, because the ladies were a mass of nerves from drinking the coffee. The conversation turned very sentimental. Virginie talked about the country, she'd like to be buried by a wood, with wildflowers on her tomb. Madame Lerat already kept, in a cupboard, the sheet for her shroud, which she perfumed with a bunch of lavender; she wanted to have something nice to smell while she was pushing up the daisies. Then, with no sort of transition, the policeman described how he'd arrested a tall, beautiful girl that morning, for stealing from a pork-butcher's shop; when they'd undressed her at the police station, they'd found ten sausages hanging round her body, fore and aft. And, on Madame Lerat's saying disgustedly that she'd never eat any of *those* sausages, the whole company began laughing quietly. The wake was livening up, while still observing the proprieties.

But just as they were finishing the mulled wine a strange muffled sound of trickling came from the little room. They all raised their heads and looked at one another.

'It's nothing,' Lantier said calmly, lowering his voice. 'She's emptying.'

They all nodded, reassured by this explanation, and put their glasses down again on the table.

At length the Poissons left. Lantier went with them; he'd stay with his friend, he explained, so his bed would be free for the ladies, who could take turns resting on it for an hour. Lorilleux went upstairs to bed alone, repeating that this had never once happened since his marriage. Then Gervaise and the two sisters, alone now with the sleeping Coupeau, settled down round the stove, on which they stood the coffee to keep hot. They huddled there, bending forward with their hands under their aprons and their noses close to the fire, chatting very softly in the great silence which enveloped the neighbourhood. Madame Lorilleux was moaning that she had no black dress, and she'd have liked to avoid buying one, as they were very hard up; and she questioned Gervaise, asking whether Maman Coupeau hadn't left a black skirt, the one they'd given her for her birthday. Gervaise had to go and fetch the skirt. It would do if it was taken in at the waist. But Madame Lorilleux also wanted any old linen, and mentioned the bed, and the cupboard

...d the two chairs, looking round for any bits and pieces that would have to be shared out. There was nearly a quarrel. Madame Lerat smoothed things over: she was more fair-minded, saying that since the Coupeaus had had the care of Maman Coupeau, they were certainly entitled to the few odds and ends she'd left. And, gossiping monotonously, they all three dozed off again over the stove. The night seemed terribly long to them. Now and again they'd give themselves a shake and drink some coffee, peering towards the little room where the candle, which they mustn't snuff, was burning with a gloomy red flame made bigger by the wick's excrescences. Towards morning they began shivering, even though the stove was very hot. They were overcome with distress and exhaustion from talking too much; their mouths were dry and their eyes sore. Madame Lerat flung herself on Lantier's bed and began snoring like a man, while the other two, their heads drooping forward on to their knees, slept by the fire. They awoke with a shiver at dawn. Maman Coupeau's candle had gone out again. And as the muffled trickling sound was beginning once more in the darkness, Madame Lorilleux, to reassure herself, repeated the explanation aloud:

'She's emptying,' she said, lighting another candle.

The funeral was to be at ten-thirty. What a nice morning, coming on top of that night and the day before! In fact although Gervaise was flat broke, she'd have given a hundred francs to anyone who'd have come to fetch Maman Coupeau three hours earlier. No, however much you love someone, they weigh too heavily upon you when they're dead; and indeed the more you love them, the sooner you want to be rid of them.

Luckily the morning of a funeral is full of distractions. There are all sorts of preparations to be made. First of all they had breakfast. Then who should appear but Père Bazouge, the undertaker's assistant from the sixth floor, with the coffin and the sack of bran. A fine fellow, who was never sober. At eight that morning he was still in great spirits from the previous night's boozing.

'This is for 'ere, ain't it?' he said.

And he put down the coffin, which creaked because it was new.

But as he was throwing down the sack of bran beside it, he stopped short, wide-eyed and open-mouthed, on seeing Gervaise standing before him.

'Beg pardon, excuse me, I've made a mistake,' he stammered. 'They told me it was for 'ere.'

He'd already picked up the sack again, and Gervaise had to tell him:

'Leave it alone, it is for here.'

'Christ in heaven! Let's sort this out!' he went on, slapping himself on the thigh. 'Oh I see, it's the old lady . . .'

Gervaise had gone as white as a sheet. Père Bazouge had brought the coffin for her. He was still talking, jollying her along and trying to apologize:

'Y'see, they told me yesterday someone had gone, on the ground floor. So I got it into me head . . . Y'know, in our job, these things go in one ear and out at t'other . . . All the same, let me congratulate you. The later the better, eh? Even though life's not always so funny, Christ! No, not so funny.'

She was drawing away as she listened to him, fearful that he might seize her with his large dirty hands and carry her off in his box. Once before, on her wedding night, he'd told her he knew women who'd thank him if he came to take them away. Well! She hadn't got as far as that yet; the idea sent a shiver down her spine. Her life was in a mess but she didn't want to leave it so soon; no, she'd rather starve to death for years than kick the bucket just like that, in a couple of seconds.

'He's pissed,' she murmured, at once disgusted and frightened. 'At the very least they shouldn't send us boozers. We pay dear enough.'

At that he became sarcastic and insolent.

'Come on, dearie, we're just puttin' it off. I'm always at your service, y'know! All you have to do is gimme a nod. I'm the ladies' comforter. And don't go lookin' down your nose at Père Bazouge, now, 'cos he's held finer ones than you in 'is arms, who've let themselves be tidied up without grumblin', only too pleased to finish their snoozin' in the dark.'

'Be quiet, Bazouge!' said Lorilleux severely, drawn by the sound of voices. 'Those sort of jokes are quite uncalled-for. If

we complained about you, you'd get the sack. Come on, get out
of here, since you've no respect for principles.'

The man took himself off, but for a long time they could hear
him mumbling along the pavement;

'Principles, what sort o' principles! There ain't no such thing
as principles, there ain't. There's only fair dealin'!'

At length it struck ten. The hearse was late. There were
already people gathered in the shop, friends and neighbours,
Monsieur Madinier, Mes-Bottes, Madame Gaudron, Mademoiselle Remanjou; and every minute a man's or a woman's head
would be thrust out through the open doorway, between the
closely-shuttered windows, to see if that slowcoach of a hearse
was coming. The family was assembled in the back room,
shaking people's hands. As they waited in feverish agitation,
brief silences would fall, broken by rapid whisperings and
a sudden rush of skirts as Madame Lorilleux looked for a
forgotten handkerchief or Madame Lerat tried to borrow a
prayer-book. Each person on arriving saw the open coffin
standing in the middle of the little room, in front of the bed;
and however hard they tried they couldn't stop themselves
examining it covertly, calculating that fat old Maman Coupeau
would never fit in it. They were all thinking this as they looked
at one another, though they didn't put it into words. But
someone was pushing at the street door. Monsieur Madinier
came in and, holding out his arms, announced in a grave,
controlled voice:

'They're here!'

It still wasn't the hearse. Four undertaker's assistants came
in one behind the other, walking fast, with the red faces and
thickened hands of men who carry heavy things, their filthy
black garments worn thin and white from constantly rubbing
against coffins. Père Bazouge walked in front, very pissed and
very correct: as soon as he was on a job he recovered his
composure. They never said a word and held their heads down
a little, already weighing Maman Coupeau with their eyes. And
there wasn't any dilly-dallying; the poor old girl was parcelled
up in the twinkling of an eye. The smallest of the group, a
youth who squinted, had emptied the bran into the coffin and
was kneading it as he spread it out, as if about to make bread.

Another, who was tall and skinny and looked like a joker, laid the sheet on top of the bran. Then one, two, off you go, they all four grasped the body and lifted it, two at the feet and two at the head. You couldn't toss a pancake any faster. Those who were trying to see what was going on might have thought Maman Coupeau had jumped into the coffin on her own. She'd slid into it as if she belonged there, fitting quite perfectly, so perfectly that they'd heard her rub against the new wood. She touched on every side, just like a picture in a frame. But at any rate she was in it, which amazed those present; obviously, she must have shrunk since the previous day. The men, meanwhile, had stood up and were waiting; the little one with the squint took hold of the lid as an invitation to the family to make its last farewells, while Bazouge stuck some nails in his mouth and held the hammer at the ready. Then Coupeau, his two sisters, Gervaise and others as well fell to their knees and kissed the mamma who was departing, weeping profusely, their hot tears falling on to and streaming over that stiffened, ice-cold face. The sound of sobbing lasted a long time. The lid was lowered, Père Bazouge hammered in his nails with the skill of a baler, two taps for each; and they could no longer listen to themselves sobbing in that din which sounded like furniture being repaired. It was over. They were off.

'Fancy making a splash like this at such a time!' said Madame Lorilleux to her husband, on catching sight of the hearse in front of the door.

The hearse was the sensation of the neighbourhood. The tripe-shop woman was calling to the grocer's boys, the little clockmaker had appeared on the pavement, the neighbours were leaning out of their windows. And they were all talking about the valance with the white cotton fringes. Oh, the Coupeaus would have done better to pay their debts! But, as the Lorilleux said, when you're proud, it always shows, no matter what.

'It's shameful!' Gervaise was saying about the chain-makers, at the same moment. 'To think that those skinflints haven't even brought a bunch of violets for their own mother!'

It was true, the Lorilleux had come empty-handed. Madame Lerat had brought a wreath of artificial flowers. A wreath of immortelles and a bouquet, given by the Coupeaus, were placed

on the coffin as well. It must have taken an almighty heave for
the undertaker's assistants to lift up the body and load it on to
the hearse. The procession was slow to form. It was led by
Coupeau and Lorilleux, wearing frock-coats and carrying their
hats; Coupeau, whose overwrought state two early morning
glasses of white wine had helped sustain, was leaning on his
brother-in-law's arm, his legs like jelly and his head throbbing.
Then came the men, Monsieur Madinier very grave and all in
black; Mes-Bottes with an overcoat covering his smock; Boche,
whose yellow trousers hit you in the eye; Lantier, Gaudron,
Bibi-la-Grillade, Poisson and some others. The ladies came
next; in the first row walked Madame Lorilleux trailing the
corpse's made-over skirt and Madame Lerat wearing a shawl to
conceal her improvised mourning, a jacket trimmed with lilac;
behind them followed Virginie, Madame Gaudron, Madame
Fauconnier, Mademoiselle Remanjou and all the rest. When
the hearse set off slowly down the Rue de la Goutte-d'Or,
amid signs of the cross and bared heads, the four undertaker's
men took the lead, two in front of the hearse and the other
two on either side. Gervaise had stayed behind to close up the
shop. She left Nana under the archway in the care of Madame
Boche and ran to catch up with the procession, while the child,
held by the concierge, gazed with intense interest at her
grandmother disappearing down the street in that beautiful
carriage.

Just as Gervaise, quite out of breath, was catching up with
the end of the procession, Goujet came up from his side of the
street. He joined the men, but turned round and greeted her
with a little nod, so gently that she suddenly felt very unhappy
and was overcome again with tears. She was no longer weeping
only for Maman Coupeau, she was weeping for something
appalling, which she couldn't have put into words and which
was choking her. During the entire route, she held her handkerchief pressed against her eyes. Madame Lorilleux, whose
flaming cheeks were dry, kept giving her sidelong glances, as if
accusing her of putting on an act.

They soon raced through the ceremony at the church. The
mass dragged a bit, though, the priest being very old. Mes-
Bottes and Bibi-la-Grillade chose to remain outside, because of

the collection. Monsieur Madinier spent the whole time watching the priests and passing on his conclusions to Lantier: that bunch of Latin-spewing fakes didn't even know what it was they were rattling on about: they'd bury a person the same way they'd baptize or marry them, without it meaning a thing to them. Then Monsieur Madinier criticized all the ceremonial, those candles and doleful voices and all that show for the benefit of the families. Really, you lost your dear ones twice over, at home and again at church. And all the men agreed with him, because another painful moment came when, at the end of the mass, there was a mumbling of prayers and those present had to pass beside the body, sprinkling it with holy water. Luckily the cemetery* wasn't far away, the little cemetery of La Chapelle, a tiny garden which gave on to the Rue Marcadet. The procession arrived there in disorder with people stamping their feet and chatting about their own affairs. The hard ground reverberated under their feet and it would have been nice to be able to keep moving. The gaping hole, already completely frozen, beside which they'd put down the coffin looked pale and stony like some chalk quarry; and the company, grouped round heaps of gravel, didn't think it funny to have to wait in cold like that, not to mention the unpleasantness of staring at the hole. Finally a priest in a surplice emerged from a little house; he was shivering and you could see his breath steaming every time he uttered a 'de profundis'. After the last sign of the cross he dashed off, obviously unwilling to go through that again. The grave-digger took up his shovel but because of the frost he could only loosen great big clods which played a fine tune down there, a regular bombardment on the coffin, giving it such a pounding that you'd have thought the wood must surely crack. However self-centred you may be, that music wrings your heart. The weeping began again. They moved away, they even got outside, but they could still hear the bangs. Mes-Bottes, blowing on his fingers, loudly remarked that no, Christ almighty! Poor old Maman Coupeau certainly wasn't going to be very warm!

'Ladies, everyone,' said Coupeau to the few friends who were still in the street with the family, 'do allow us to offer you a little something . . .'

And he led the way into A la descente du cimetière,* a bar in the Rue Marcadet. Gervaise, remaining on the pavement outside, called to Goujet who was moving off after again nodding to her. Why wouldn't he have a glass of wine? But he was in a hurry, he was going back to the workshop. They stood looking at one another for a moment without speaking.

'I'm sorry about the sixty francs,' Gervaise murmured in the end. 'I was absolutely frantic, and I thought of you . . .'

'Oh, don't mention it, it's quite all right,' he interrupted. 'And you know I'm always at your service, if you're in trouble . . . But don't say anything about it to Mother, because she has her own ideas and I don't want to upset her.'

She was still gazing at him; and, seeing him so good, so sad, with his handsome golden beard, she was on the point of accepting his proposal of long ago, to run away with him so they could be happy together somewhere. Then another wicked thought came to her, to borrow the two quarters' rent from him, no matter what the price might be. Trembling, she continued in a caressing tone:

'We're still good friends, aren't we?'

He nodded as he replied:

'Yes, of course, we'll always be good friends . . . But you must understand, it's all over.'

And he took himself off with great strides, leaving Gervaise stunned, listening to his last words ringing in her ears like the tolling of a bell. As she went into the bar she seemed to hear a voice deep within her: 'It's all over, it's all over; well, there's nothing more for me to do, if it's all over!' She sat down, she swallowed some bread and cheese, she emptied a full glass she found standing in front of her.

It was a long low-ceilinged room on the ground-floor, with two large tables in it. Bottles of wine, quarter-loaves of bread and three plates with large wedges of brie were set out in a row. They were just having a snack, without plates or a tablecloth. Further away, beside the roaring stove, the four assistants were finishing their lunch.

'Heavens,' Monsieur Madinier was expounding, 'we all come to it. The old make room for the young . . . When you get home you'll find it'll seem very empty.'

'Oh, my brother's giving notice,' Madame Lorilleux interrupted quickly. 'It's ruination, that shop is.'

They'd been working on Coupeau. Everyone was urging him to give up the lease. Madame Lerat herself, who'd been well in with Lantier and Virginie for quite a while and was thrilled by the idea that they must fancy one another, talked of bankruptcy and prison, putting on an air of alarm. And then suddenly Coupeau got angry, his mawkishness giving way to rage under the influence of too much booze.

'Listen!' he bawled, shoving his face right up to Gervaise. 'You're to listen to me! You always bloody well have things your own way. But this time, I'm tellin' you, I'm goin' to do what I want.'

'Fine!' said Lantier. 'But when could anyone ever talk her round? You'll need a mallet to get it into her head.'

And they both went at her for a while. That didn't stop the jaws from working. The brie was disappearing, the wine was flowing like a fountain. Gervaise, meanwhile, was weakening under the attack. She said nothing in reply, her mouth permanently full as she bolted her food as if she'd been starving. When they began to flag, she quietly raised her head and said:

'That's enough, d'you hear? I don't give a damn for the shop. I don't want anything more to do with it . . . D'you understand, I don't give a damn for it! It's all over!'

Then they ordered more bread and cheese and got down to business. The Poissons would take over the remainder of the lease and be responsible for the two overdue quarters. Moreover Boche, with a self-important air, agreed to the arrangement in the name of the landlord. He even rented the Coupeaus a place there and then: the vacant rooms on the sixth floor, in the same corridor where the Lorilleux lived. As for Lantier, Lord! he'd like to keep his room, if the Poissons didn't mind. The policeman bowed: he didn't mind at all; friends always get on together, whatever their political ideas. And Lantier, like someone who has finally brought off his own little transaction, didn't trouble himself further in the matter of the lease, but cut himself an enormous slice of bread and brie; he sat back and ate with concentration, his blood coursing through his body as he glowed with furtive pleasure, half closing his eyes and surreptitiously watching first Gervaise then Virginie.

'Hey! Père Bazouge!' called Coupeau, 'come an' have a drink. We're not stuck up, we're all workers.'

The four fellows were leaving, but came back inside to enjoy a glass with the party. They didn't mean to complain, but the lady just now had weighed a good bit and was worth a glass of wine. Père Bazouge stared fixedly at Gervaise but said not a word out of place. Feeling ill at ease she got up and left the men, who were now well away. Coupeau, drunk as an owl, was beginning to blubber again, saying it was from grief.

Back home that evening Gervaise just sat on a chair in a daze. The rooms seemed empty and huge. Of course it was a real load off their backs. But in truth it wasn't only Maman Coupeau she'd left at the bottom of that hole in the little garden of the Rue Marcadet. Too much was missing; what she'd buried that day must be a part of her own life, her shop, her pride as an employer, and other feelings as well. Yes, the walls were bare, and so was her heart, it was a complete clear-out, a nose-dive into the gutter. And she felt too exhausted; she'd pull herself together later on, if she could.

When Nana was undressing at ten o'clock that night she burst into tears and made a scene. She wanted to sleep in Maman Coupeau's bed. Her mother tried to scare her, but the child was very precocious and the dead simply filled her with intense curiosity, so that in the end, for the sake of peace, they let her lie down where Maman Coupeau had lain. The kid liked big beds; she stretched out her arms and legs, rolling about. That night she slept wonderfully well in the cosy tickling warmth of the feather bed.

CHAPTER X

THE Coupeaus' new home was on the sixth floor, staircase B. You went past Mademoiselle Remanjou's and took the corridor on the left. Then you had to turn again. The first door was the Bijards'. Almost opposite, in an unventilated cubby-hole tucked

under a little stairway that led to the roof, slept Père Bru. Two
doors further on you came to Bazouge's. Finally, next to
Bazouge, were the Coupeaus, with a large and a very small
room looking on to the courtyard. And beyond, down the
corridor, there were only two more families before you reached
the Lorilleux right at the end.

One large and one very small room, no more. That was where
the Coupeaus were roosting now. And even the large room was
no bigger than your hand. They had to do everything there,
sleep, eat, the lot. Nana's bed just fitted into the little room; she
had to undress in her parents' room and they left the door open
at night so she wouldn't suffocate. It was so small that Gervaise
had left some things for the Poissons when she gave up the
shop, because she couldn't fit everything in. With the bed, the
table and four chairs the place was crammed. Even so, sick at
heart and unable to bear parting with her chest, she'd cluttered
up the floor space with the wretched great thing, blocking half
the window. This made it impossible to open one of the
shutters, so the place was much less light and cheerful. She was
getting very fat, and when she wanted to look down into the
courtyard there wasn't room to lean on the sill on her elbows,
she had to bend sideways and twist her neck to see.

During the first few days Gervaise just sat there and cried. It
seemed too cruel, not having room to move about in her home
after always being used to plenty of space. She couldn't breathe,
she stayed by the window for hours on end, squeezed between
the wall and the chest, getting a stiff neck. Only there could she
breathe. But the courtyard, as a rule, just made her feel more
down in the dumps. Opposite her, on the sunny side, she could
see her dream of long ago, that fifth floor window where scarlet
runners, every spring, wound their slender stalks round a
network of string. But the room she had was on the shaded side,
and her pots of mignonette died within a week. No, her life
wasn't turning out all that well, it certainly wasn't what she'd
hoped for. Instead of having flowers round her as she approached old age, she was spending her days among things that
were nasty. Leaning out one day she had a very strange
sensation, she thought she could actually see herself down there
under the archway, near the concierge's lodge, staring up,

examining the building for the first time; and that thirteen-year
backward leap stabbed at her heart. The courtyard hadn't
changed, the bare walls hardly looked any blacker or more
dilapidated; a stench was rising up from the rust-eaten drain
heads; washing was drying on lines strung across the casements,
and there were babies' nappies caked with filth; down below,
the broken paving stones were still messy with clinkers from the
locksmith's and woodshavings from the carpenter's; there was
even, in the damp corner by the tap, a puddle from the
dyeworks of a pretty blue, a blue as delicate as that of long ago.
But she herself, now, felt very different, very worn and shabby.
To begin with, she wasn't down there any longer, happy and
unafraid, with her face turned towards the sky, making plans
about a nice home. She was up in a garret in the slummy part,
in the very dingiest spot, where you never saw a ray of
sunshine. That was why she was crying, she just couldn't be
happy about the way her life had turned out.

Still, once Gervaise had got a bit used to it, the Coupeaus'
life in the new place looked quite promising at first. The winter
was almost over and the few francs from the furniture sold to
Virginie helped them settle in. Then, when the fine weather
came, they had a stroke of luck, Coupeau was taken on for a
job at Étampes,* in the country; and he was there for nearly
three months without drinking, cured for a while by the
country air. People don't realize how it quenches a boozer's
thirst just to leave the air of Paris where the streets positively
reek of brandy and wine. He returned looking fresh as a daisy,
and bringing four hundred francs with which they paid off the
two quarters owing on the shop, a debt the Poissons had agreed
to be responsible for; they also settled the most pressing of their
small debts in the neighbourhood. Gervaise could once again
walk along some streets she'd long been avoiding. Of course
she'd found work by the day, ironing. Madame Fauconnier,
who was a very nice woman as long as you buttered her up, had
willingly taken Gervaise back. She even paid her three francs,
the rate for a head assistant, out of consideration for her former
position as an employer. So it looked as if the household should
get by all right. And, if they worked and saved, Gervaise could
even see the day when they'd be able to pay off everything and

settle into quite a decent little way of life. But that was what she imagined when she was all excited over the huge sum earned by her husband. When she'd calmed down she was ready to take life as it came, and said that good times don't last.

What the Coupeaus found hardest to bear just then was seeing the Poissons move into their shop. They weren't very jealous by nature, but it was maddening the way people deliberately talked in front of them about the wonderful improvements made by their successors. The Boches and especially the Lorilleux never stopped carrying on about it. Listening to them you'd think there'd never been a more splendid shop. And they talked about the filthy state the Poissons had found the place in, saying that the cleaning alone had set them back thirty francs. After thinking it over Virginie had settled on a little shop selling fine groceries, things like sweets, chocolate, coffee, and tea. Lantier had strongly recommended that line of business, because according to him there was heaps of money to be made from such delicacies. The shop was painted black, picked out with gold lines, two classy colours. Three carpenters worked for a week to fit up racks and glass cases and a counter with shelves for the jars, such as you see in sweetshops. It must have left quite a dent in the little legacy that Poisson had put away. But Virginie was queening it, and the Lorilleux, aided and abetted by the two concierges, didn't spare Gervaise a rack, a glass case or a jar: they enjoyed watching her face fall. Even if you aren't the jealous type, it makes your blood boil to see others step into your shoes and then trample all over you.

There was also, at the bottom of this, something to do with sex. It was asserted that Lantier had left Gervaise. The neighbours declared that that was a very good thing. After all, it gave the street a bit more respectability. And the whole credit for the separation was given to that crafty hatter, who was still the darling of the ladies. People went into details, saying he'd had to box Gervaise's ears to get her to leave him alone, she was so crazy about him. Of course nobody told what was really going on, because those who might have known the truth thought it too simple and not sufficiently interesting. You could say that Lantier had indeed left Gervaise, in the sense that he no longer had her at his beck and call night and day; but there was no doubt that he climbed up to see her on the sixth floor whenever he fancied, for Mademoiselle Remanjou met him coming out of the Coupeaus' at the most peculiar hours. In short, their relationship still continued when the opportunity arose, in a haphazard way, without either of them finding much pleasure in it; a habit that lingered on, mutual convenience, nothing more. But what complicated the situation was that the neighbourhood, now, had Lantier and Virginie tucked up in the same pair of sheets. There again, the neighbourhood was in too much of a hurry. No doubt about it, Lantier had his cap set at the tall brunette; which was only to be expected, considering that she was replacing Gervaise in absolutely every respect in that apartment. In fact a joke was going the rounds about it, they said that one night he'd gone to fetch Gervaise from his neighbour's bed, and had brought back Virginie, keeping her with him without recognizing her until dawn, because of the dark. People had a good laugh over the story, but in reality he hadn't got that far, he daren't do more than pinch her bottom. But that didn't stop the Lorilleux gushing on in front of Gervaise about the love affair between Lantier and Madame Poisson, hoping to make her jealous. The Boches, as well, went round saying that they'd never seen a handsomer couple. The funny thing in all this was that the Rue de la Goutte-d'Or didn't seem to take exception to this new matrimonial triangle; no, morality, which had been so severe on Gervaise, was lenient towards Virginie. Perhaps the smiling indulgence of the street had something to do with her husband's being a policeman.

Luckily Gervaise wasn't particularly troubled by jealousy. Lantier's infidelities left her quite composed, because it was a long time since their relationship had in any way touched her heart. Without trying to find anything out she'd heard foul stories about the hatter's entanglements with girls of all kinds, dreadful-looking creatures you could pick up in the street at any hour, and it mattered so little to her that she'd gone on being accommodating, for she wasn't even able to feel angry enough to break off. However, she didn't find it so easy to accept her lover's new fancy. With Virginie, it was a different matter. They'd dreamt this up just so as to have some fun at her expense, and even though she didn't mind about the love-making, she did expect some consideration. So, when Madame Lorilleux or some other nasty bitch made a point of saying in front of her that Poisson was now wearing the horns, she'd go very pale, feeling a rending in her heart and a burning in her stomach. She'd press her lips together, she'd be careful not to lose her temper, determined not to give her enemies that pleasure. But she must have gone for Lantier, because one afternoon Mademoiselle Remanjou thought she heard the sound of a slap; anyway, there was certainly a row, because Lantier didn't speak to her for two weeks, but it was he who gave in first, and the affair seemed to start up again as if nothing had happened. Gervaise chose to make the best of a bad job; she didn't relish having a set-to with Virginie, for she didn't want to make an even worse mess of her life. No, she wasn't twenty any more and she no longer cared that much about men, not to the point of coming to blows over them and risking being run in. But she kept count of it all, along with the other things.

Coupeau was forever cracking jokes. That accommodating husband, who'd turned a blind eye to hanky-panky in his own home, laughed himself silly over Poisson's pair of horns. In his home cuckolding didn't count but when it happened to some-one else Coupeau thought it a huge joke, and he went to great lengths to spot that kind of thing, when a neighbour's wife had a roll in the hay. What a dope that Poisson was! And to think he wore a sword, and believed he'd the right to shove people about on the streets! Then Coupeau had the nerve to tease Gervaise about it. Well, well, her boyfriend had dumped her and no mistake! She hadn't any luck: her first go, she'd had no success with blacksmiths, and now on her second go it was hatters who were leaving her in the lurch. But then, she hadn't been setting her cap at the serious trades. Why not go for a mason, a dependable type, used to mixing nice solid plaster? Of course he said all this in fun, but that didn't stop Gervaise turning a sickly green as he pierced her with his little grey eyes as if he wanted to drill the words right into her. When he started to talk dirty she never knew if he was joking or not. A man who's on the booze from one end of the year to the other no longer has his wits about him, and there are husbands who are very jealous at twenty, whom drink has made very easy-going on the subject of marital fidelity by the time they reach thirty.

You should have seen Coupeau swaggering about in the Rue de la Goutte-d'Or! He referred to Poisson as the cuckold. That'd make those old gossips shut their traps! He, Coupeau, wasn't the cuckold any longer. Oh, he knew what he knew. If in the past he'd seemed not to hear, obviously that was because he didn't like tittle-tattle. Everyone knows what's going on in his own home and can scratch himself where it itches. Well he didn't have an itch and he couldn't scratch himself just to please other people. So what about the policeman, did *he* hear what was being said? Yet it was really true, this time; the lovers had been seen, it wasn't just an idle bit of chit-chat. And he grew indignant, he couldn't understand how a man, a government employee at that, could put up with such a scandal in his own home. The policeman must like other men's leavings, that's all you could say. On evenings when Coupeau was bored, all alone with his wife in their corner under the eaves, none of this stopped him going down to get Lantier and forcing him to come up. He found the place depressing now his mate was no longer there. Coupeau would talk Lantier round if he and Gervaise seemed pissed off with each other. Christ in heaven! Who gives a damn what people think, is there a law against enjoying yourself in your own way? He'd snigger, and his shifty boozer's eyes would shine with big-hearted ideas, with the urge to share everything with the hatter, so life would be more fun. And it was especially on those evenings that Gervaise no longer knew whether he was joking or talking seriously.

While all this was going on Lantier kept his dignity. His manner was fatherly and grave. On three occasions he'd prevented quarrels between the Coupeaus and the Poissons. It was important to his comfort that the two households should get on well. Thanks to the kind but firm eye he kept on Gervaise and Virginie, they continued to profess a great affection for one another. He ruled over blonde and brunette alike with the calm assurance of a pasha, flourishing on his own cunning. That scheming bastard was already consuming the Poissons while still digesting the Coupeaus. Not that it bothered him one little bit! He'd swallowed one shop and was getting started on a second. In short, it's only men of that kind who have any luck in life.

It was in June of that year that Nana made her first communion. She was nearly thirteen, she'd shot up like a stalk of asparagus and had a very cheeky manner; she'd been kicked out of her catechism class the year before because of bad behaviour and the priest had only accepted her this time for fear she'd never come back and he'd be letting yet another heathen loose on the world. Nana danced for joy at the thought of the white dress. The Lorilleux, as godparents, had promised the dress, and were talking about this present all over the building; Madame Lerat was to give the veil and bonnet, Virginie the purse and Lantier the prayer-book, so that the Coupeaus were looking forward to the ceremony without worrying too much. And the Poissons, who'd been meaning to have a house-warming party, even chose that very day for it, no doubt on Lantier's advice. They invited the Coupeaus and the Boches, whose little girl was also making her first communion. In the evening, they'd all have dinner together, a leg of mutton with a few nice veggies.

It so happened that the day before, just as Nana was gazing in amazement at the presents spread out on the chest, Coupeau came home in a disgusting state. The air of Paris was getting a grip on him once more. And he began bawling out his wife and child, using a drunkard's logic and filthy language which was very much out of place in the circumstances. Although in any case Nana herself was growing foul-mouthed, from constantly hearing dirty talk all around her. When there was a row, she'd think nothing of calling her mother a bitch or a cow.

'Soddin' hell!' the roofer was yelling. 'Gimme me food, you fuckin' bitches! Just look at those females with their rags! I'll shit on your bits 'n' bobs, y'know, if I don't get me food!'

'What a pain in the neck he is when he's pissed,' Gervaise muttered impatiently.

And, turning towards him: 'Stop bothering us, it's warming up.'

Nana was doing her modest little girl act, because she thought it appropriate for that particular evening. She went on looking at the presents on the chest, pretending to lower her eyes and not understand the filthy things her father was saying. But when he'd been on the binge the roofer could be a terrible pest. Right in her ear he said:

'I'll give you white dresses! So, I s'pose it's so you can make yourself tits by shovin' paper balls down your top, like last Sunday? Wait, I'm not done yet! Oh, I can see you wrigglin' your bum! They tickle your thighs, these fancy duds do. They go to your fuckin' little head . . . Get the hell away from 'em, you rotten little whore! Take your paws off 'em, stick 'em all in the drawer, or I'll use 'em to clean up your face!'

Keeping her head bent, Nana still didn't answer. She'd picked up the little tulle bonnet and was asking her mother what it had cost. And, as Coupeau reached out to grab it, Gervaise pushed him away, shouting:

'Leave the kid alone! She's being good, she's not doing anything wrong.'

Then he really let them have it.

'Oh you bitches! Mother 'n' daughter, what a pair. It's a fine thing to go an' eat the body of our Lord while you're makin' eyes at the men all the while! Just you try to deny it, you little slut . . . I'm gonna dress you in a sack, an' we'll just see if it scratches your hide. Yes, in a sack, to see if that'll put you off it, you 'n' your fuckin' priests. Why should I want 'em to teach you how to sin? Christ in heaven! Listen to me, will you, the pair of you!'

This time Nana turned on him furiously, while Gervaise had to stretch out her arms to protect the things Coupeau said he was going to tear to bits. The child stared hard at her father and, forgetting the submissiveness enjoined by her confessor, spat out between clenched teeth:

'Pig!'

As soon as the roofer had finished his supper he was snoring. Next morning he woke up in a very agreeable frame of mind. He was still a trifle hung over from the night before, but just enough to make him amiable. He watched the child being made ready and was moved by the white dress, observing that it took almost nothing to make that little bit of trash look like a real young lady. In short, as he put it, it was natural for a father to be proud of his daughter at a time like that. And you should have seen how stylish Nana looked, smiling like a self-conscious bride in her too-short dress. When they went down and she caught sight of Pauline, dressed like her, at the lodge door, she paused and studied her quickly with her clear eyes; and as she thought Pauline less well-dressed than herself—got up like a sack of potatoes, in fact—Nana was on her best behaviour. The two families left together for the church. Nana and Pauline walked in front, carrying their prayer books and holding down their veils which billowed in the wind; they didn't chat, they were bursting with pleasure to see people coming out of the shops to look at them; and when they heard people say as they passed that they looked very sweet, they put on pious expressions. Madame Boche and Madame Lorilleux hung back because they were exchanging views on Banban, a proper spendthrift whose daughter would never have taken her first communion if her relations hadn't given her everything, yes, everything, even a new chemise out of respect for the holy table. Madame Lorilleux was particularly concerned about the dress, a present from her, scolding Nana and calling her a 'filthy thing' every time the child got some dust on her skirt by going too near the shops.

In church, Coupeau cried the whole time. It was stupid, but he couldn't stop himself. He was overcome by the way the priest spread his arms out wide and the way the little girls, like angels, walked with their hands together; the organ music made him feel funny inside and the lovely smell of the incense made him sniff, as though someone had shoved his face into a bunch of flowers. In a word, he was knocked all of a heap, he was struck to the heart. There was one special hymn, something so sweet, while the kids were taking communion, which seemed to just wash over him, giving him the shivers up and down his spine. Anyway, all round him there were other soft-hearted people with wet handkerchiefs. Yes, it really was a wonderful day, the most wonderful day of your life. Only when they came out of the church and he went off for a drink with Lorilleux, who'd stayed dry-eyed and was teasing him, he started to gripe, accusing the black-coats of burning devilish herbs in their churches to soften up men. Anyway, he wasn't making a secret

of it, his eyes had melted into tears, which simply proved
that he hadn't a stone for a heart. And he ordered another
round.

The house-warming at the Poissons that evening was very
jolly. From the beginning of the meal to the end, nothing
happened to mar the reign of friendship. When things have
gone to the bad, happy evenings like that do occasionally come
your way, when people who loathe each other get on fine.
Lantier, with Gervaise on his left and Virginie on his right,
made himself agreeable to them both, showering them with
little attentions like a barnyard cock who wants peace in his
hen-house. Opposite them, Poisson wore his usual policeman's
look, dreamy, calm and stern, and maintained his habit, from
long hours on the beat, of looking down and thinking of
nothing. But the queens of the party were the two little girls,
Nana and Pauline, who'd been allowed to keep their dresses on;
they sat stiffly, afraid of staining their white gowns, and each
time they took a mouthful someone would shout at them to
hold up their heads and swallow properly. In the end Nana got
bored and dribbled her wine down the front of her dress; there
was a great fuss, her dress was taken off and the bodice rinsed
right away in a glass of water.

Then, over dessert, they talked seriously about the children's
futures. Madame Boche had made up her mind, Pauline was
going into a shop where they did pierced work in gold and
silver and you could earn five or six francs. Gervaise didn't
know yet; Nana hadn't any particular bent. Oh, she could run
wild all right, she was good at that, but as for anything else, she
was a proper butter-fingers.

'If I were you,' said Madame Lerat, 'I'd get her into artificial
flowers. It's a nice clean trade.'

'Flower-workers,' muttered Lorilleux, 'they're a lot of tarts,
they are.'

'Thank you very much! And what about me?' replied the tall
widow, pursing her lips. 'A proper gentleman, you are. Let me
tell you, I'm not a bitch, I don't roll over with my legs in the
air when somebody whistles!'

But everybody told her to shut up.

'Madame Lerat, oh, Madame Lerat!'

Meaningful glances were directed at the two first communicants, who'd stuck their noses in their glasses to keep from giggling. Until then, even the men had been keeping their language refined, for the sake of propriety. But Madame Lerat wouldn't pay any attention. What she'd just said she'd heard in the very best company. Besides, she flattered herself she knew her own language; she was often complimented on the way she could discuss any subject, even in front of children, without ever offending against decency.

'There are some very well-bred women in the flower trade, I'd have you know!' she shouted. 'They're made like other women, of course, they're not just skin all over. But they know how to behave, and they're choosy, when they decide to stray . . . Yes, they get that from the flowers. In my case, that's what's saved me . . .'

'Lor', interrupted Gervaise, 'I've no objection to flowers. But Nana must like them, that's all; you shouldn't go against what a child wants, in choosing a trade for her . . . Come on Nana, don't be silly, tell us. D'you like that idea, flowers?'

The child was bending over her plate, picking up cake crumbs with her wet finger which she'd then suck. She took her time answering. She was smiling in that wicked way of hers.

'Yes, Mamma, I like that idea,' she finally announced.

So it was all arranged right then. Coupeau was quite willing for Madame Lerat to take the child to her workshop in the Rue du Caire* the very next day. And the whole party talked seriously about life's responsibilities. Boche declared that Nana and Pauline were grown-up women, now that they'd taken communion. Poisson added that from now on they ought to know how to cook, mend socks, and run a house. There was even talk of their marriage and the children they'd bear one day. The little brats listened, giggling surreptitiously and rubbing up against one another, bursting with pride at being women and blushing self-consciously in their white dresses. But what excited them the most was when Lantier asked them teasingly whether they hadn't already decided on a hubby. And the grown-ups forced Nana to admit she was very fond of Victor Fauconnier, the son of her mother's employer.

'Well!' said Madame Lorilleux to the Boches as they were leaving, 'she's our goddaughter, but if they put her to making flowers we won't want any more to do with her. It'll be just one more hussy on the streets . . . She'll fly the coop in less than six months.'

As they went up to bed the Coupeaus agreed that everything had gone off well and the Poissons weren't bad people. Gervaise even thought that the shop had been nicely set up. She'd expected to mind very much, spending an evening like that in her former home where others, now, were swanking about, and she was amazed that she hadn't felt furious even for a moment. Nana, who was undressing, asked her mother whether the gown of the young lady on the second floor who'd been married last month was made of muslin like her own.

But that was the family's last happy day. During the next two years they went further and further downhill. It was the winters especially that did them in. There might be food on their table in the fine weather but, with the rain and cold of winter, hunger came as well, the cupboard was bare and they'd have nothing for dinner but memories, in their little Siberia of a home. That villain December would slip in under their door, bringing with him every kind of trouble, the closing down of workshops, the frozen idleness of hard frosts, the black misery of wet weather. The first winter they still had a fire sometimes, huddling round the stove, preferring warmth to food; the second winter, the stove was never even cleaned of its rust, but stood there like a mournful cast-iron relic, chilling the room. And what really finished them off, wiped them out, more than anything else was having to pay their rent. Oh! That January rent, when there wasn't a bean in the place and old Boche handed them their bill! It was even colder then, with a wind from the north. Monsieur Marescot turned up the next Saturday wrapped in a warm coat, his big hands stuck into woollen gloves; he was still talking of evicting them, while outside the snow was falling, as though preparing a bed for them on the pavement, a bed with white sheets. They'd have sold their own flesh to pay the rent. It was rent day that emptied the larder and the stove. Indeed, from the whole building there arose one great lament. There was weeping on every floor, a dirge of misfortune groaning down the stairway and along the corridors. If each of them had had a death in the family, it could not have produced a more dreadful music. A veritable day of judgement, the end of everything, life denied, the poor crushed under foot. The woman from the third floor went on the streets for a week, at the corner of the Rue Belhomme. One workman, the mason on the fifth, robbed his employer.

Of course, the Coupeaus had only themselves to blame. However hard life may be, you can always get by if you're methodical and economical, witness the Lorilleux who regularly handed over their rent on the dot, screwed up in scraps of dirty paper; but really those two lived like frugal spiders, it was enough to put you off work. Nana wasn't earning anything yet with her flowers; indeed her keep set them back quite a lot. Gervaise, working for Madame Fauconnier, was no longer highly thought of. She seemed to be losing her touch more and more, making such a mess of her work that her employer had cut her down to two francs, the rate for unskilled labour. But she was very proud and touchy just the same, quick to point out to all and sundry that she'd once had her own business. She'd miss whole days of work or else she'd walk out in a huff; once, for example, she'd been so cross with Madame Fauconnier for taking on Madame Putois and making her work side by side with her former employee that she didn't turn up again for two weeks. After capers like that she'd be taken back out of charity, which made her even more bitter. Naturally, at the end of the week her pay didn't amount to much, and she'd remark sourly that one of these Saturdays it would be she who'd be paying Madame Fauconnier. As for Coupeau, perhaps he did have work, but if so he was certainly making a present of it to the government; for since the job at Étampes Gervaise had never again seen the colour of his money. When he came home on pay-day she no longer looked at his hands. He'd turn up with his arms dangling, and often not so much as a handkerchief in his pockets; Christ, yes, he'd even lost his snot-rag, or else some swine of a mate of his had pinched it. At first he'd make up figures and think up whopping lies about ten francs gone on a whip-round, or twenty francs falling from his pocket through a hole that he'd show her, or else he'd paid over fifty for an imaginary debt. Then he stopped bothering. Money just vanished, so it did! It was no longer in his pocket, it was in his belly, another way of bringing it home to the missus that didn't strike her as funny. Gervaise, on the advice of Madame Boche, would sometimes lie in wait for her man at the work-shop door so she could nab the newly-laid nest-egg, but that didn't do her any good because his mates warned Coupeau, and the money vanished into his shoes or into some other carrying-place that was even less clean. On this topic Madame Boche was craftiness itself, because Boche had a way of doing the disappearing trick with ten-franc coins, which he hoarded to stand treats to certain accommodating ladies of his acquaintance; she'd inspect the minutest corners of his clothes and generally find the missing coin in the peak of his cap, stitched between the leather and the cloth. But goodness knows the roofer wasn't the sort to pad his duds with gold! He stuffed his into his flesh. Gervaise could hardly take her scissors and unpick the skin of his belly.

Yes, they'd only themselves to blame if they sank lower every season. But you don't ever admit things like that to yourself, especially not when you're down in the gutter. They blamed it on bad luck, declaring that God had it in for 'em. These days their place was a regular bear-garden. They squabbled all day long. Still, they hadn't yet come to blows, except for a slap or two exchanged in the heat of an argument. The saddest thing about it all was that now that they'd opened the cage door and let affection fly away, other feelings had flown off too, like canaries. The kindly warmth of a little family, when father, mother and child are closely bound to one another, had deserted them, leaving them alone and shivering in their separate corners. The three of them, Coupeau, Gervaise and Nana were all as cross as two sticks, at each other's throats over nothing at all, their eyes full of hate; it was as if something had snapped, the basic mechanism of the family which when people are happy makes hearts beat in unison. Oh, long gone were the days when Gervaise would be scared stiff if she saw Coupeau working on the edge of a roof, twelve or fifteen metres above the road! She wouldn't have given him a push herself, but if he'd simply fallen, Christ! it would have rid the earth's surface of a good-for-nothing. On days when the fur was flying, she'd

scream that she'd never have the luck to see him carried home
on a stretcher. She lived in hopes of that, that'd make her day.
What use was he, the drunken sod? Only to make her weep,
bleed her white and drive her into doing wrong. Well then; with
men as useless as that you shoved them into a hole in the
ground as fast as you could, then you danced a polka over them
to celebrate your freedom. And when the mother said 'kill!', the
daughter answered 'bash his brains in!'. Nana would read the
accident column in the paper and make remarks that were
most unnatural in a daughter. Her father had such luck that
he'd been knocked down by an omnibus and it hadn't even
sobered him up. When in the world was the bastard going to
croak?

Amid the torments of her poverty-ridden existence, Gervaise's suffering was made worse by the groans of hunger she
could hear all around her. That corner of the building was the
corner of the have-nots, where three or four families seemed to
have made a pact to have nothing in the larder some days. Their
doors might open but they almost never let out any smell of
cooking. The silence of death reigned all along the corridor, and
the walls rang hollow, like empty bellies. Occasionally you
could hear a row going on, with women bawling and starving
kids wailing, when families went at each other as a way of
forgetting their hunger. Cramp had set in in every throat, every
famished mouth gaped open; chests grew hollow simply from
breathing that air where not even a midge could have lived for
want of nourishment. But what Gervaise found most heart-
rending of all was Père Bru in his hole under the little stairway.
He crawled in there and rolled himself into a ball like a tiny
animal, to keep out the cold; he'd stay there for days on end,
on a heap of straw, without budging. Not even hunger drove
him out any more, for there was no point in going out and
working up an appetite when no one had invited him to a meal.
When he hadn't been seen for three or four days the neighbours
would push open his door and look, in case he'd kicked the
bucket. No, he was still alive, not much but a bit, just in one
eye: death itself had forgotten him! Whenever Gervaise had any
bread she'd throw him some crusts. Even if she was turning
nasty and beginning to hate people, because of her husband, she

still felt truly sorry for animals; and Père Bru, the poor old thing, who because he could no longer hold a tool was simply being left to croak, was like a dog in her eyes, an animal that could no longer work and not even the knackers wanted for its skin or its fat. It weighed on her heart to know he was always there, on the other side of the corridor, abandoned by God and man, feeding solely on himself, reverting to the size of a child, wizened and withered like an orange left to shrivel on a mantelpiece.

Gervaise also suffered greatly from being so close to Bazouge, the undertaker's man. A simple partition, very thin, separated the two rooms. He couldn't stick a finger in his mouth without her hearing. From the moment he came home in the evening she just couldn't stop herself keeping track of his little routine, listening to the black leather hat landing on the chest with a thud like a spadeful of earth, and the black coat as he hung it up brushing against the wall like the wing of a nightbird; then all his black clothing would be flung on to the floor, making a funeral pile that filled the middle of the room. She could hear him tramping about, and listened uneasily to his slightest movement, jumping out of her skin if he bumped into the furniture or clattered the dishes. The wretched old soak became her obsession, in which furtive terror mingled with a longing to know. He was a joker all right, always pissed and in a muddle, forever coughing, spitting, singing idiotic songs, swearing foully, and fighting with the four walls before managing to find his way to bed. She'd go as white as a sheet, wondering what kind of trade he was getting up to in there; she imagined horrifying things, convincing herself he must have brought in a dead body and was stuffing it under his bed. Lord! After all there was a story in the paper about an undertaker's man who'd collected the coffins of little children in his room, to save himself trouble and only have to make a single trip to the cemetery. One thing was certain, when Bazouge came in you really could smell death through the partition. You could imagine you were living right by Père Lachaise in among the graves. He was a frightening devil the way he laughed when he was by himself, as if he found his trade amusing. And even when he'd finished his roistering and was flat on his back, he snored in an extraordinary fashion that made Gervaise hold her breath. She'd lie there straining her ears for hours on end, sure there must be funeral processions moving through her neighbour's room.

Yes, and the worst of it was that even in her terror Gervaise was so fascinated that she'd stick her ear to the partition to get a better idea of what was going on. Bazouge affected her the way handsome men affect decent women: they'd love to touch but don't dare; their upbringing prevents them. Well! If fear hadn't held her back, Gervaise would have liked to touch death and see how he was made. She behaved so funnily sometimes, holding her breath, engrossed, hoping some movement of Bazouge's would reveal the secret, that Coupeau would ask her jokingly if she had a crush on the undertaker's man next door. She'd get cross and talk of moving, she so disliked living near him; but in spite of herself, as soon as the old man came in bringing with him his cemetery smell, she'd be back to her musing, looking excited and nervous like a wife dreaming of tearing up her marriage vows. Hadn't he twice offered to wrap her in a shroud and take her off with him somewhere, to sleep a sleep of pleasures so intense that all your woes are instantly forgotten? Perhaps those pleasures really were wonderful. Gradually, the temptation to put it to the test became fiercer. She'd have liked to try it for a fortnight, for a month. Oh, to sleep for a month, especially in winter, the month when the rent was due, when life's troubles wiped her out! But it wasn't possible, you had to go on sleeping for ever, if you began sleeping for an hour; and that thought chilled her to the marrow, and her infatuation with death would vanish in the face of the everlasting and implacable friendship demanded by the earth.

Nevertheless, one evening in January she did bang on the partition with both fists. She'd had a dreadful week, knocked about by everybody, with nothing in her pocket and no hope in her heart. That evening she was sick, shivering feverishly, with lights dancing before her eyes. So instead of throwing herself out of the window, as she'd thought of doing for a moment, she began knocking and calling:

'Père Bazouge! Père Bazouge!'

The undertaker's man was taking off his shoes and singing 'There once were three pretty girls'. Business must have been brisk that day, because he seemed even more pissed than usual.

'Père Bazouge! Père Bazouge!' shouted Gervaise, more loudly.

Couldn't he hear her then? He could have her straight away, he could just put her over his shoulder and carry her off wherever it was he took his other women, rich and poor alike, for comfort. She was upset by his song, 'There once were three pretty girls', because she could see in it the contempt of a man with too many girls at his beck and call.

'What is it? What is it?' stammered Bazouge. 'Who's been took bad? I'm coming, missus!'

But at the sound of that hoarse voice Gervaise woke up as if from a nightmare. Whatever had she done? She must have knocked on the partition. Then, like the thwack from a cane across her behind, terror made her tighten her buttocks and she stepped back, imagining she could see Bazouge's great hands coming through the wall to grab her by the hair. No, no, she didn't want to, she wasn't ready. If she had knocked it must have been with her elbow, as she turned, without meaning to. And a shiver of horror ran through her from her knees up to her shoulders at the thought of herself all stiff, with a face white as chalk, being lugged away in the old man's arms.

'Well, so now nobody's at home, eh?' the undertaker continued in the silence. 'Wait a tick, I'm always happy to help a lady out.'

'No, it's nothing,' Gervaise finally managed to gasp. 'I don't need anything, thank you.'

While Bazouge was dozing off, grumbling, she stood tensely there, listening to him and not daring to move, afraid he might think he'd heard her knock again. She swore to herself that she'd be much more careful now. Even if she was at death's door she wouldn't ask her neighbour for help. She said that to reassure herself, for at certain moments, in spite of the panic she'd been in, she did still feel the same terrified fascination.

In her poverty-ridden attic, surrounded by her own troubles and the troubles of her neighbours, Gervaise nevertheless found a fine example of courage in the home of the Bijards. Tiny eight-year-old Lalie, who was no bigger than two sous' worth of butter, kept house as neatly as a grown-up; and it wasn't an easy task, for she had charge of two little mites, her brother Jules and her sister Henriette, tots of three and five, whom she had to keep an eye on all day long while she swept the floors and washed the dishes. Since the time when Père Bijard had killed his missus with a kick in the belly, Lalie had become a little mother to them all. Without saying a word, all by herself, she'd taken the dead woman's place, so much so that her brute of a father, no doubt to make the likeness perfect, now beat up the daughter just as he used to beat up the mother. When he came home pissed he just had to have women to batter. He didn't even notice that Lalie was really very small; he couldn't have struck harder if she'd been some old trout. A single clout of his would cover her whole face, and her flesh was still so delicate that the marks left by his five fingers would be visible for two days. The thrashings were shameful, she was beaten over the least little thing; it was like a mad wolf falling on a poor gentle, frightened kitten, who was pitifully skinny and gazed meekly at him with her lovely eyes, never uttering a word of complaint. No, Lalie never rebelled. She'd bend her neck a bit to protect her face, but she'd stop herself crying out so as not to upset the people living nearby. Then, when the father got sick of sending her flying into the four corners of the room with his kicks, she'd wait till she felt strong enough to stand and she'd get back to work, cleaning up her babies, making the meal and not leaving a speck of dust on the furniture. It was all part of her daily round, being knocked about.

Gervaise had taken a great liking to her neighbour. She treated her as an equal, a grown woman, who understood about life. You should know that Lalie had a pale, serious face, and an expression like an old maid's. Listening to her talk you'd have thought she was thirty. She knew all about shopping, mending, and looking after her home, and she spoke of the children as if she'd already borne two or three herself. It made you smile, to hear an eight-year-old talk like that, but then it caught at your throat and you'd turn away so as not to cry. Gervaise asked her in as much as possible and gave her all she could, things to eat, old dresses. Once when she was trying an old jacket of Nana's on Lalie, she was appalled to see her back black and blue, her elbow grazed and still bleeding, all her innocent flesh tortured and sticking to her bones. Well! Père Bazouge could get his box ready, she wouldn't last long at this rate! But the child begged Gervaise not to say anything about it. She didn't want her father bothered on her account. She stuck up for him, insisting that he wouldn't have been so cruel if he hadn't been drinking. Drinking drove him mad, and he no longer knew what he was doing. Oh, she forgave him, you have to forgive mad people for everything.

From then on the laundress kept an eye on Lalie and would try to intervene when she heard Bijard coming up the stairs. But as a rule she herself simply got a slap for her pains. When she went in during the day, she often found Lalie tied to the end of the iron bedstead; this was an idea of the locksmith's, who before he left would truss her legs and belly with a thick rope, no one knew why; the whim of a mind crazed by drink, a way, probably, of bullying the kid even when he wasn't there. Lalie, stiff as a post, with pins and needles in her legs, would be tied to the bedpost for a day at a time; she even spent a night like that, when Bijard forgot to come home. When Gervaise indignantly spoke of untying her, Lalie begged her not to touch any of the ropes because her father became so enraged if he didn't find the knots made just the way he'd left them. She wasn't uncomfortable, really, it was restful; and she'd smile as she spoke, her little cherub's legs swollen and numb. What upset her was that she couldn't get on with her work, tied to the bed like that, having to stare at the muddle the place was in. Her father really ought to have thought of something else. Even so, she looked after Henriette and Jules, making them do as they were told, and calling them over so she could wipe their noses. As her hands weren't tied she'd knit while waiting to be set free so her time wouldn't be completely wasted. The worst thing was when Bijard untied her; she'd crawl about on the floor for a good quarter of an hour, unable to stand up because her circulation wasn't working.

The locksmith had thought up another little game as well. He heated coins till they were red hot in the stove and then put them on the end of the mantelpiece. Calling Lalie, he told her to go and buy some bread. The unsuspecting child picked up the sous but instantly dropped them with a scream, shaking her burnt little hand. At that, he flew into a rage. Whatever had he done to deserve a little tramp like her! Now she was losing their money! And he threatened to have the skin off her bum if she didn't pick up the money right then. While the child was hesitating she was given a first warning, a clout of such force that it made her see stars. In silence, her eyes brimming with two large tears, she picked up the coins and went out, tossing them up and down in her palm to cool them off.

No, you'd never believe what fiendish ideas can take root in a boozer's head. One afternoon, for example, Lalie was playing with the children after she'd finished tidying up. As the window was open there was a draught from the corridor which kept opening the door with a little rush of air.

'It's Monsieur Hardi,'* the child kept saying. 'Do come in, Monsieur Hardi. Be so good as to come in.'

And she'd curtsey to the door, greeting the wind. Henriette and Jules, behind her, curtsied and bowed as well, delighted with the game, roaring with laughter as if they were being tickled. Lalie'd gone quite pink from seeing them enjoy themselves so much, and she was even enjoying it herself as well, which was something that happened to her once in a blue moon.

'Good afternoon, Monsieur Hardi. And how are you, Monsieur Hardi?'

But a brutal hand pushed the door open and Bijard came in. At that the whole scene changed; Henriette and Jules fell backwards on to their behinds, against the wall, while Lalie, petrified, was caught right in the middle of a curtsey. In his hand the locksmith held a large new drayman's whip, with a long handle of white wood and a leather lash finishing in a length of thin string. He put this whip down on the corner of the bed, but didn't reach out with his boot to kick the child as usual; she meanwhile had turned her behind towards him defensively. He was grinning and showing his black teeth; he was very cheerful, very pissed, his noggin all afire with an idea for a bit of fun.

'So, pretendin' we're a tart, are we, you fuckin' little darlin'! I could hear you dancin' from way down there . . . Alright, come here! Nearer, for Christ's sake! an' turn round, I don't want to smell your arse. Why're you shakin' like that, I'm not touchin' you, am I? Take me shoes off.'

Lalie, terrified at not getting her usual thrashing, and once more very pale, took off his shoes. He'd sat down on the edge of the bed, and now he stretched out fully dressed, his eyes wide open, watching the little girl as she moved round the room. She was so paralysed by his stare that little by little her limbs became rigid with fear and in the end she broke a cup. Then, without moving, he picked up the whip and showed it to her.

'Well now, me little calf, just look at this: it's a present for you. Yes, that's another fifty sous you've cost me . . . With this toy, I won't have to run no more, and it won't do you no good to hide in corners. Wanna have a go? . . . So we're breakin' cups, are we! . . . C'mon, get a move on, dance! Make your bob to Monsieur Hardi!'

He didn't even sit up, but lay spread-eagled on his back, his head pressed down into his pillow, cracking the big whip all round the room with a sound like a postilion whipping up his horses. Then, bringing down his arm, he lashed Lallie round the middle of her body, winding her in the thong then unwinding her like a top. She fell and tried to get away on all fours, but he lashed her again and set her upright.

'Gee up! Gee up!' he screamed. 'It's a donkey's race! Hey, it's a bleedin' brainwave for a winter morning: I can stay in bed, I won't get cold, an' I can round up me little calfs without bangin' me chilblains . . . In the corner there, got you, you trollop! And in the other corner, got you again! And again in that one! Oh, if you crawl under the bed I'll hit you with the handle! . . . Gee up, gee up! Ride a cock horse!'

There was a slight froth on his lips and his yellow eyes bulged in their dark sockets. Lalie, crazed and screaming with pain, leapt into the corners of the room, curled into a ball on the floor, clung to the walls; but the big whip's slender thong reached her wherever she was, cracking in her ears like gunshot and leaving long weals in her flesh. It was like the leaping of some animal being trained to do circus tricks. You should have seen that poor little kitten waltz about, with her heels in the air like kids skipping who are trying to skip faster. Completely out of breath, blinded, bouncing about like a rubber ball, she let herself be thrashed, worn out with trying to find shelter. And that wild beast her father was exultantly calling her a trollop, and asking whether she'd had enough and whether she did finally understand that this time she hadn't a hope of getting away from him.

But suddenly Gervaise rushed in, attracted by the child's screams. She flew into a fury of indignation at the sight that greeted her.

'Oh you shit of a man!' she yelled. 'Leave her alone, you brute! I'll set the police on you, I will!'

Bijard growled like an animal that's thwarted. He stammered: 'Listen, old Stumpy, mind your own fuckin' business. D'you expect me to wear gloves to flog her? I'm just givin' her a warnin', that's all it is you see, just so she knows I've a long arm.'

And he let fly with a last lash of the whip that caught Lalie on her face. Her upper lip split and blood streamed out. Gervaise had picked up a chair and was on the point of attacking the locksmith. But the child stretched out her hands towards her, begging her, saying it was nothing, it was all over. She was wiping the blood with the corner of her apron and hushing the children who were bawling their heads off as if the lashes had landed on them.

When Gervaise thought of Lalie she felt she herself couldn't complain. She wished she had the courage of that eight-year-old kid, who alone had to bear as much as all the women on the staircase put together. She'd seen her with nothing but bread to eat for three months, and not even enough of that to satisfy her hunger, so skinny and weak she had to lean against the walls when she walked; and when Gervaise secretly took her scraps of meat, she thought her heart would break, watching the child weep great silent tears as she swallowed a tiny bit at a time, because food could no longer pass through her shrunken gullet. But despite all that she was always gentle and devoted, and sensible beyond her years, carrying out her duties as little mother even to the point of sacrificing her own life to maternal instincts which were premature in someone of such frail childish innocence. So Gervaise watched the suffering of that sweet forgiving creature, trying to learn from her to keep silent about her own agony. All that remained of Lalie now was her wordless gaze; her great dark eyes were full of resignation; in their depths you could read nothing but endless misery and pain. Not a word, ever, only those great dark eyes, open wide.

The fact is that the Assommoir's poison was beginning its ravages at the Coupeaus' as well. Gervaise could see the time coming when her man would pick up his whip, like Bijard, to make her dance about. And the evils threatening her naturally made her more sensitive to the evils of the child's life. Yes, Coupeau was in a bad way. Gone were the days when the rotgut put colour in his cheeks. No longer could he slap himself on the belly and boast that the bleeding firewater made him fat, for the ugly yellow fat of past years had melted away and he was growing skinny, his complexion turning a leaden grey tinged with green, like that of a stiff rotting in a pond. His appetite, too, had vanished. Little by little he'd lost his taste for bread and he'd even turn up his nose at cooked food. You could put the tastiest stew in front of him, his stomach went on strike and his weakened teeth refused to chew. To keep going he needed his pint of spirits every day; that was his ration, his meat and drink, the only food he could digest. In the morning, as soon as he got out of bed, he'd be bent double for a good quarter of an hour, coughing so his whole frame shook, holding his head and spitting up phlegm, phlegm bitter as aloes which brought everything in his throat up with it. It never failed: you might as well keep the pisspot at the ready. He didn't feel steady on his pins again until he'd had his first little drop of comfort, a real medicine that cauterized his innards with its fire. But as the day went on his strength would come back to him. In the beginning he'd felt tickling and tingling on the skin of his hands and feet and he used to giggle, saying they were playing tricks on him, the missus must have put itching powder in the sheets. Then his legs became heavy and the tickling changed into awful cramps that gripped his flesh like a vice. Now that struck him as much less funny. It didn't make him laugh any more; he'd come to a sudden halt on the pavement, his head swimming; there'd be buzzing in his ears and he'd see stars. Everything turned yellow, the houses were dancing about, and he'd stagger around for a few seconds, terrified of falling flat on his back. Other times, when he was out in hot sunshine, a shiver would come over him like iced water pouring from his shoulders to his bum. But what really got his goat was the way both his hands shook; his right hand in particular must have done something very dreadful, it had such nightmares. Christ! Wasn't he a man any longer, was he turning into an old woman! He'd tense his muscles frantically and grasp his glass, declaring he could hold it so steady you'd think his hand was made of marble, but no matter what he tried the glass would still do its jig, jumping to the right, jumping to the left, with tiny, rapid, regular jerks. So then he'd empty his glass down his gullet in a fury, yelling that what he needed was a few dozen of 'em and then he'd undertake to carry a barrel without a single finger shaking. Gervaise would tell him that on the contrary he ought to stop drinking if he wanted to stop shaking. But he'd tell her to go to hell, get through a few more litres and try again, flying into a rage and accusing the passing omnibuses of joggling the booze in his glass.

One March evening Coupeau came in soaked to the skin; he'd been coming home with Mes-Bottes from Montmartre where they'd treated themselves to a bellyful of eel soup, and he'd been caught in a downpour which lasted the whole bloody long way between the Barrière des Fourneaux and the Barrière Poissonnière. During the night he was taken bad with a hell of a cough; he was very red in the face, had a raging fever, and his chest was pumping away like a pair of worn out bellows. When the Boches' doctor saw him the next morning and had listened to his chest, he shook his head and, drawing Gervaise aside, advised her to have her husband taken to the hospital right away. Coupeau had pneumonia.

Of course this didn't bother Gervaise in the least. Time was when she'd have let herself be chopped into little bits sooner than hand her man over to the quacks. At the time of the accident in the Rue de la Nation she'd used up their nest-egg so she could coddle him. But such fine feelings soon die away when men turn rotten. No, she'd no intention of saddling herself again with that kind of carry-on. They could take him away and never bring him back to her and she'd say a big thank-you. Even so, when the stretcher arrived and they loaded Coupeau on to it like a piece of furniture, she turned pale and bit her lips; and though she still muttered grumpily that it was a good thing, her heart wasn't in it, she wished she had just ten francs in her drawer so as not to be forced to let him go. She went with him to Lariboisière and watched the male nurses put him to bed at one end of a long room, where rows of patients with corpse-like faces raised their heads and watched this new mate being brought in; death was right at home there, it really was, with that suffocating smell of fever and that consumptive music that made you want to cough your own lungs out; and anyway the ward was just another Père Lachaise cemetery in miniature, with its lines of white beds like rows of graves. Then, as he just lay there flat on his pillow she took herself off, not finding anything to say and unfortunately having nothing in her pocket to comfort him. Outside, opposite the hospital, she turned round and looked at the building. And she remembered the time so long ago, when Coupeau, perched on the edge of the eaves, would be setting in his zinc plates and singing up there in the sunshine. He didn't drink, in those days, his skin was like a girl's. She'd look for him from her window in the Hôtel Boncœur and see him there, right in the middle of the sky, and they'd both wave their handkerchiefs, smiling at each other by telegraph. Yes, Coupeau had worked up there, never dreaming he was working for himself. Now he wasn't on the roof any longer, like some cheerful, randy sparrow; he was down below, he'd built his little nest in the hospital and had come there to croak, his hide coarse with fever. Christ, didn't their courting seem far away, now!

Two days later when Gervaise went to enquire after Coupeau, she found his bed empty. A sister explained to her that they'd had to take him to the Sainte-Anne asylum* because all of a sudden, the day before, he'd gone round the bend. Oh, he'd gone quite out of his mind, trying to bash his head in against the wall, and shrieking so that the other patients couldn't sleep. Apparently it was the drink. Drink, lying in wait in his body, had grabbed its chance while he was flat on his back and weak as a baby with the pneumonia, to attack him and wreck his nerves. The laundress went home in a terrible state. Her hubby was a loony now! Life was going to be really fun if they let him out. Nana kept shouting that they must leave him in hospital as otherwise, one day, he'd do them both in.

It wasn't until the Sunday that Gervaise could go to Sainte-Anne. It was a real expedition. Luckily, the omnibus from the Boulevard Rochechouart to La Glacière passed right by the hospital. She went down the Rue de la Santé* and bought two oranges so as not to go in empty-handed. Yet another vast public building, with grey courtyards and endless corridors that smelled of stale medicines: it didn't exactly fill you with good cheer. But, when they'd shown her into a cell, she saw with some surprise that Coupeau looked quite chipper. He happened to be sitting on the throne, which was very clean and made of wood, and didn't smell at all; and they had a good laugh at her finding him doing his business, with his arsehole taking the air. Well, everyone knows, don't they, what to expect when someone's sick. He sat there in state, like the Pope, gabbing away just the way he used to. Oh, he was much better now, he was going regularly.

'And the pneumonia?' enquired Gervaise.

'Packed up!' he replied. 'They got rid of that by hand. I still cough a bit, but I don't have to clear me tubes out any more.'

Then just as he was getting off the throne to return to bed, he giggled again.

'Your nose is good and tough, a pong don't worry you, not you!'

And they laughed even more. They felt very happy, deep down. Sharing a good laugh about Coupeau taking a crap was their way of showing one another they were happy, without saying a whole lot. It's only when you've had dealings with sick people that you know how wonderful it is to see them in proper working order again.

When he was back in bed and she gave him the two oranges he was really touched. He was his nice old self again, now that he was drinking tisanes and could no longer leave his better feelings behind on the counter of a bar. She was surprised to hear him talk sensibly, just like the old days, and finally plucked up her courage to mention his going off his rocker.

'Oh, yes,' he said, making fun of himself, 'I carried on something dreadful . . . Just imagine, I was seein' rats and rushin' about on all fours to stick salt on their tails. And you, you were yellin' for me, because some men were tryin' to do you. All sorts of rubbish, in fact, ghosts in broad daylight . . . Oh, I can remember it clearly, so me loaf's still doin' its stuff . . . It's over now, I dream a bit when I'm droppin' off, I've nightmares, but everyone has nightmares.'

Gervaise stayed with him until evening. When the doctor came on his rounds at six he made Coupeau stretch out his hands; they hardly trembled at all now, just a little tremor of the fingertips. However, as night began to fall, Coupeau gradually became more and more uneasy. Twice he sat up, staring at the floor in the parts of the room which lay in shadow. Suddenly he reached out and appeared to squash some creature against the wall.

'What is it?' asked Gervaise, frightened.

'The rats, the rats,' he muttered.

Then, after a silence, when he'd seemed to be drifting off to sleep, he began to thrash about and talk in broken snatches.

'Christ in heaven! They're nibblin' holes in me skin! Oh, the filthy brutes! Hold still, pull your skirts close! Watch out for that bugger behind you! Bloody hell, they've got her on her back, just look at 'em sniggerin'! You swine! You devils! You thugs!'

He was hitting out into the void; then pulling at his blanket he rolled it into a bundle against his chest, as if for protection against the bearded men he could see. An attendant had rushed in so Gervaise went home, appalled by this scene. But when she returned a few days later she found Coupeau quite better. Even the nightmares had gone; he slept like a child, ten hours at a stretch, never budging. So they let his wife take him away. The doctor, however, did give him the usual sensible advice on leaving, and urged him to think it over carefully. If he went back to drinking the trouble would start all over again; eventually it would be the death of him. Yes, it was entirely up to him. He'd seen for himself how you got back your health and happiness when you weren't on the booze. Well then! At home he must continue the sober life he'd led at Sainte-Anne, and pretend that he was still under lock and key and that bars didn't exist.

'He's right, that doctor is,' said Gervaise as the omnibus was taking them home to the Rue de la Goutte-d'Or.

'Of course he's right,' replied Coupeau.

Then, after thinking for a moment, he continued:

'Oh, you know, the odd glass now an' then, that won't kill you, it's good for your digestion.'

And that very evening he downed a tot of firewater, for the sake of his digestion. Nevertheless for a week he was quite sensible. He was a great coward at heart and had no desire to end up in Bicêtre.* But his craving carried the day, the first tot inevitably leading to a second, to a third, to a fourth; so that by the end of a fortnight he was back to his usual ration of a pint of rotgut every day. Gervaise, exasperated, could have clobbered him. To think, when she'd seen him come to his senses in the asylum, that she'd been stupid enough to dream of having a decent life once again! That was the end of another dream of happiness, and surely it would be her last. Oh, now that nothing could make him change, not even the fear of soon kicking the bucket, she swore not to bother any more: their home could go to pot, she didn't give a damn, and she announced she was going to have what fun she could. They were back once more to their hellish existence, only they'd sunk deeper into the mire and now there wasn't a glimmer of hope of fairer weather ahead. When her father slapped her Nana would ask furiously why the swine hadn't stayed in the hospital. She was looking forward to earning money, she said, so she could buy him brandy and he'd croak all the sooner. Gervaise, for her part, flew into a rage one day when Coupeau was belly-aching about having married her. Oh, so she'd brought him other men's leftovers, had she, she'd picked him up in the street, had she, trapping him with her innocent country looks. Bloody hell! What a nerve! Not a word of truth in it. The real truth was she hadn't wanted him. He'd grovelled at her feet begging her to agree, while she'd kept telling him to think it over. And if she had it to do over again, just wouldn't her answer be "no!". She'd sooner they cut her arm off. It was true she'd lost her cherry before meeting him, but a woman who's lost her cherry and is a hard worker is worth more than a lazy sod who drags his own and his family's honour in the dust of every bar. That day, for the first time at the Coupeaus', they really slugged it out, so fiercely in fact that an old umbrella and the broom were broken.

Gervaise kept her word. She became even more slovenly; she stayed away from the laundry more often, spending entire days jabbering, and went limp as a rag when there was work to be done. If she dropped something on the floor it could bloody well stay there, couldn't it, she certainly wasn't going to be the one to bend down and pick it up. She became a proper lazy-bones. She'd no intention of wearing herself out. So she took things easy and never even swept the floor until she was practically falling over the mess. The Lorilleux, now, made a show of holding their noses when they passed her room; they called her a filthy cow. They led a furtive existence at the end of the corridor, shutting themselves away from all the miseries that whined through that part of the building, keeping their door closed so as not to have to lend a few sous. Such good-hearted folk! Such kind, helpful neighbours! Oh that noise at the door was only the cat! You just had to knock and ask for a match, a pinch of salt or a jug of water, and you could be sure their door would slam in your face. And what poisonous tongues! If it was a matter of helping a neighbour, they'd declare loudly that they never meddled in others' affairs, but if it was a matter of mud-slinging then they certainly meddled in others' affairs, and from dawn to dusk. With the bolt securely home and a blanket hung up to block the cracks and the keyhole, they'd settle down to an orgy of tittle-tattle, never laying aside their gold wire for one second. Banban's downfall in particular set them purring all day long like cats being stroked. On her beam ends, y'know, and as for her looks, what a wreck! They'd watch her set off to the shops and snigger at the tiny bit of bread she'd bring back under her apron. They worked out which days she had nothing to eat. They knew how thick the dust was in her home and how many dirty plates were left lying about, they knew about each fresh concession to poverty and sloth. And her clothes! Filthy odds and ends that an old-clothes dealer wouldn't stoop to pick up! Lord! Business was in a very bad way now for that wonderful blonde, that trollop who was always wiggling her bum down in her lovely blue shop. Just look at where it got you, being mad on guzzling and bingeing and stuffing yourself. Gervaise, who suspected them of pulling her to bits, would take off her shoes and stick her ear against their door, but the blanket prevented her hearing. Just once did she manage to overhear them calling her "Big Boobs" no doubt because she was still quite big up there despite the bad food that was making her flesh fall away. Anyway, she didn't give a damn about them; she went on speaking to them, as otherwise people would talk, but she expected nothing but snubs from those bastards and could no longer even be bothered to answer back and leave them standing there like a pair of dummies. In any case, sod it, she meant to do as she pleased, either stay put and twiddle her thumbs or else get moving if there was some fun to be had, but not otherwise.

One Saturday, Coupeau had promised to take her to the circus. Now that really was worth stirring your stumps for, to see ladies galloping round on horses and jumping through paper hoops. Coupeau had just had a fortnight's pay, so he could part with forty sous; and they were even going to have a meal out, as Nana had to stay at her boss's very late that evening because of a rush order. But seven o'clock came and no Coupeau; eight, and still no Coupeau. Gervaise was furious. Clearly her pisstank was with his mates, blueing his wages in the nearby bars. She'd washed a bonnet and had spent the whole day struggling with the holes in an old dress, so she'd look presentable. Finally, about nine, ravenously hungry and purple with rage, she made up her mind to go down and hunt for Coupeau around the neighbourhood.

'Looking for your husband are you?' asked Madame Boche when she saw Gervaise's face. 'He's at old Colombe's. Boche's just been having brandied cherries with him.'

Gervaise thanked her. She dashed off along the pavement, meaning to go and claw Coupeau's eyes out. A fine rain was falling, which made the expedition even less fun. But when she reached the Assommoir, the fear that she herself would cop it if she pestered her man quickly calmed her down and made her cautious. The bar was ablaze, its gas-lights burning, the mirrors shining brightly like suns, the flasks and jars decorating the walls with their glass of different colours. She stood there a moment, craning forward to peer through the window between two of the jars, sneaking a look at Coupeau at the back of the room: he was sitting with some friends at a little zinc table; they looked blurred and blueish in the haze of pipe-smoke and, as she couldn't hear them shouting, it struck her as funny the way they were flinging their arms about and thrusting out their chins, with their eyes popping out of their heads. How the hell could men leave their wives and their homes to shut themselves up like that in a hole where they couldn't breathe! The rain was dripping down her neck; she stood up and set off along the outer boulevard, turning things over in her mind, not daring to go in. Coupeau would have given her a bloody nice reception, he loathed being badgered. Then again, to be honest, she didn't think it a proper place for a decent woman. Nevertheless, passing beneath the sodden trees, still undecided, she began to shiver slightly, and she thought she must be coming down with a really nasty chill. Twice she went back and stationed herself in front of the window, sticking her eye to it once again, vexed to see those blasted sozzlers still sitting there in the dry, shouting and drinking. The light from the Assommoir was reflected in the bubbling, rain-dimpled surface of the puddles on the pavement. When the door opened and closed with a rattle of its strips of brass, Gervaise would quickly move away, splashing through the puddles. In the end, telling herself she was behaving like an ass, she pushed open the door and walked straight up to Coupeau's table. After all, it was her own hubby she was coming for, wasn't it? And she'd a perfect right to, since he'd promised to take her to the circus that evening. She didn't care! She didn't fancy melting away like a cake of soap, out there on the pavement.

'Lor'! It's you, old girl!' bellowed the roofer, choking with laughter. 'What a hoot! Now I ask you, ain't she a friggin' hoot!'

They were all laughing, Mes-Bottes, Bibi-la-Grillade, Bec-Salé, alias Boit-sans-Soif. Yes, they thought her a hoot, but they didn't say why. Gervaise stood there feeling a bit dazed.

As Coupeau seemed in such a nice mood she plucked up her courage to say:

'We're going down to the circus, you know. We'd better get a move on. We'll still be in time to see something.'

'I can't get up, I'm stuck, honest I am,' replied Coupeau, still giggling. 'Try, you'll see: pull me arm, as hard as you can, no, sod it, harder'n that, come on, pull! . . . There, what did I tell you, it's that bugger Colombe, he's screwed me to the seat.'

Gervaise had entered into the game and when she let go of his arm they all thought it such a good joke that they flung themselves one upon the other, shouting and rubbing their shoulders together like donkeys being curry-combed. The roofer had his mouth open in such a huge laugh that you could see right down his gullet.

'Come on, you flippin' moron,' he said finally, 'sit down for a couple o' minutes, can't you! We're better off here than splashin' about outside. Well yes, I didn't come home, I'd things to do. No use pullin' a long face, it won't get you nowhere . . . Move over a bit, chaps.'

'If Madame would like to sit on my knee it would be cosier,' said Mes-Bottes gallantly.

Not wishing to attract attention, Gervaise took a chair and sat down at a few feet from the table. She looked at what the men were drinking: rotgut, gleaming like gold in the glasses; there was a little pool of it on the table, and Bec-Salé, alias Boit-sans-Soif, wet his finger in it as he talked and wrote a woman's name, Eulalie, in big letters. She thought that Bibi-la-Grillade looked dreadfully haggard and skinnier than a plucked chicken. Mes-Bottes's nose was quite florid, a real Burgundy dahlia. All four of them were filthy, their disgusting beards stiff and yellow as a chamber-pot brush, their smocks all ragged, their nails funeral-black as they reached out with their dirty paws. But in fact it was all right be seen with them, because even if they'd been knocking it back since six, they were still behaving properly, though now just on the brink of being sozzled. Gervaise noticed two other men boozing at the counter who were so pissed they were tipping their drinks down their fronts and drenching their shirts, in the belief that they were wetting their whistles. Big old Colombe was calmly serving rounds, displaying those mighty arms that ensured proper respect among his customers. It was very warm, pipe-smoke swirled up like a cloud of dust in the blinding gas-light, engulfing the customers in a slowly thickening fog; and out of this fog came a din, a deafening, chaotic din, of cracked voices, clinking glasses, oaths, and fists banging on tables with a sound like guns going off. So Gervaise had a snooty expression on her face because that kind of place isn't very nice for a woman, especially when she's not used to it; she was suffocating, her eyes were smarting and her head already throbbing from the reek of alcohol that the whole room gave off. Then, suddenly, she sensed there was something yet more disturbing behind her back. She turned round and saw the still, the booze-machine, working away under the glass roof of the narrow little court-yard, its devil's kitchen vibrating deep inside it. At night the copper pipes looked more dismal than ever, lit up solely by big, red, star-shaped reflections on their curved surfaces, and the shadow cast by the apparatus on the wall behind it conjured up obscene shapes, figures with tails, monsters opening wide their jaws as if to devour the world.

'Hey, you old bag of wind, don't sulk!' yelled Coupeau. 'To hell with wet blankets. What'll you have?'

'I don't want anything at all,' replied Gervaise. 'I've not had any dinner.'

'Well, all the more reason; a little drop of somethin' keeps you goin'.'

As she didn't seem to be brightening up, Mes-Bottes turned his charm on her once again.

'I'm sure Madame likes something sweet,' he murmured.

'I like men who don't get pissed,' she replied rather crossly. 'Yes, I like people to bring home their pay and to keep their word, when they've promised something.'

'Oh, that's what's eatin' you!' said the roofer, still laughing. 'You want your whack. So, you great dummy, why won't you have a drink? Have one, it's your perks.'

She stared at him long and seriously, a deep line creasing her forehead. Then she answered with deliberation:

'Yes, you're right, it's a good idea. That way, we'll drink the wages up together.'

Bibi-la-Grillade stood up to fetch her a glass of anisette. She pulled her chair over to the table. While she was sipping her anisette she suddenly remembered something, she remembered the brandied plum she'd had with Coupeau, long ago, sitting by the door, when he was courting her. In those days she never drank the syrup of brandied fruits. And now here she was drinking spirits again. Oh, she knew herself only too well, she hadn't a smidgen of will-power. All she needed was a little push on the behind to send her lurching back on to the booze. Why she even thought this anisette very good, though maybe a little too sweet, a little sickly. And she drained her glass, listening to Bec-Salé, alias Boit-sans-Soif, telling them about his affair with great big Eulalie, that woman who sold fish in the street; bloody artful she was, able to nose him out in a bar while she was pushing her barrow along the pavement; it was no good his mates tipping him off and hiding him, she often nabbed him; why only yesterday she'd flung a sole in his face to learn him not to skip work. Now did you ever hear anything so funny? Bibi-la-Grillade and Mes-Bottes, laughing fit to bust, kept giving Gervaise slaps across the shoulders, and now she was laughing as well, as if they were tickling her and she couldn't stop herself; and they advised her to do like Eulalie, to bring her irons and iron out Coupeau's ears on the bar counter.

'Thanks very much!' bellowed Coupeau, up-ending his wife's empty glass. 'Hell, you can't half get outside it! Just take a look at this, chaps, she don't fiddle about.'

'Would Madame like another?' enquired Bec-Salé, alias Boit-sans-Soif.

No, she'd had enough. But just the same she hesitated. The anisette made her feel queasy, and she'd have liked some neat spirits to settle her insides. And she kept casting sidelong glances at the boozing machine behind her. That bloody great pot, as round as the belly of a fat tinker's wife, with its thrusting, twisting snout, sent shivers down her back, shivers of fear mixed with longing. Yes, it was like the metallic innards of some gigantic whore, of some sorceress who was distilling, drop by drop, the fire that burned in her gut. A pretty source of poison, an operation so shameless, so foul, it should have been buried away deep down inside a cellar! But in spite of what

she felt, Gervaise would have liked to get her nose right in it,
to sniff the smell and taste the filthy stuff, even if it burned her
tongue and made it peel like an orange.

'What's that you're drinking there?' she asked the men
craftily, her eyes lighting up at the lovely golden colour in their
glasses.

'That, old girl, is Père Colombe's rotgut,' Coupeau replied.
'Now don't be silly, will you? We're just goin' to give you a
drop to try.'

And when they'd brought her a glass of it, and her throat
contracted at the first sip, Coupeau went on, slapping his thigh:

'There, that scours your windpipe for you, don't it! . . .
Swallow it in one go. Every drink of that you down is one less
coin in the doctor's pocket.'

After her second glass Gervaise was no longer plagued by
hunger pangs. She'd made it up with Coupeau now, she wasn't
cross with him any more because he'd broken his word. They'd
go to the circus some other time; it wasn't all that funny, just
people doing tricks while they galloped round on horseback. It
wasn't raining in Père Colombe's bar, and even if your wages
were melting away in firewater, at least it was going into your
own belly, clear and shiny like lovely liquid gold. Oh, everyone
could go to hell! She didn't get that much pleasure from life,
and anyway, it was a consolation to have her share in blueing
their money. She was quite comfy there, wasn't she, so why
shouldn't she stay? They could let off a cannon if they wanted,
she wasn't going to budge, not now she was nicely settled. She
was stewing away in the lovely warmth, with her bodice stuck
to her back, filled with a sense of well-being that made her
limbs feel heavy. She sat there giggling to herself, staring into
space with her elbows on the table, much amused by two
customers at a nearby table, a great big lout and a little midget,
who were so pissed they were hugging each other enthusiasti-
cally. Yes, the Assommoir made her laugh, and so did Père
Colombe's big round fat face, like a lump of lard, and so did
the customers smoking their nose-warmers and yelling and
spitting, and so did the big gas-jets which lit up the mirrors and
the bottles of spirits. The smell no longer bothered her; quite
the opposite, it made her nose tickle and she thought it smelt

good; her lids had closed a bit and although she didn't feel at all short of breath, she was breathing very shallowly and savouring the pleasure of being slowly overcome by drowsiness. Then, after her third tot, she dropped her chin on to her hands so she could only see Coupeau and his mates; and she remained face to face with them like that, very close, her cheeks warmed by their breath, staring at their dirty beards as if she were counting the hairs on them. By now they were very sozzled. Mes-Bottes, his pipe between his teeth, dribbled as he sat there, silent and grave as a sleepy bullock. Bibi-la Grillade was telling a story about how he could sink a litre at one go, by holding the bottle arse over tip and pouring it straight down his throat. Meanwhile Bec-Salé, alias Boit-sans-Soif, had fetched the gaming wheel from the counter and was playing Coupeau for the price of the drinks.

'Two hundred!. . . . You're rakin' it in, you get the high ones every time.'

The wheel turned and the pointer squeaked, while under its piece of glass the picture of Fortune, a big woman in red, turned also, until it was nothing but a red splash in the centre, like a splash of wine.

'Three hundred an' fifty! You must 'ave kicked it, you rotten bugger! Hell! I'm not playin' any more!'

Gervaise was fascinated by the gaming wheel. She was really hitting the bottle now and calling Mes-Bottes 'sonny boy'. Behind her the booze machine was still working away, rumbling like an underground stream; and, having no hope of stopping or exhausting it, she was filled with a cold rage, with an urge to leap on the huge still as if it were a wild beast, to stamp on it with her heels and smash in its belly. Everything was growing foggy and she could see the machine moving and feel its copper claws clutching her, and the stream flowing now through her own body.

Then the room began dancing round and the gas-lights were flying about like shooting stars. Gervaise was plastered. She could hear a furious argument going on between Bec-Salé, alias Boit-sans-Soif, and that chiseller Colombe. The thief of a landlord had padded the bill! What a shit-house of a place! Suddenly there were scuffles and yells and the racket of tables being overturned. It was Père Colombe, unceremoniously kicking everyone out with practised ease. They jeered at him from outside, calling him a bloody swindler. It was still raining and there was a nasty cold wind blowing. Gervaise lost Coupeau, found him and then lost him again. She wanted to get home and groped her way along the shops, trying to find where to go. She was quite astonished by the sudden darkness. At the corner of the Rue des Poissonniers she sat down in the gutter, and thought she must be in the washhouse. Her head was spinning: all that flowing water was making her feel deathly ill. Finally she reached home and hurried past the lodge door; inside she could clearly see the Lorilleux and the Boches sitting at table and frowning in disgust at the fine mess she was in.

She never understood how she got up those six flights of stairs. At the top, just as she was turning into the corridor, little Lalie, hearing her step, ran up holding out her arms affectionately and saying with a laugh:

'Madame Gervaise, Papa isn't home yet, do please come in and look at my babies sleeping . . . Oh, they're so sweet!'

But on seeing Gervaise's dazed expression she stepped back, trembling. She recognized that smell of spirits, those lack-lustre eyes, that twisted mouth. Then Gervaise staggered past her without a word, while the child stood at her door, silently gazing after her with her dark, serious eyes.

CHAPTER XI

NANA was getting taller and becoming quite a dish. At fifteen she'd grown like a young calf and was very fair-skinned and well-rounded, in fact as plump as a pin cushion. Yes, that was Nana at fifteen, fully developed but no corset as yet. A pretty, trollopy little face, with a creamy complexion, skin velvety as a peach, a funny nose, a rosy kisser and eyes so bright that men longed to light their pipes at them. Her mass of blond hair, the colour of ripe oats, seemed to have dusted her temples with golden freckles that lay across her brow like a band of sunshine. Oh, she was a hot number, as the Lorilleux put it, a kid who still needed telling off but whose big body was curved and full, with the ripe smell of a grown woman.

No longer did Nana stuff balls of paper down the top of her dress. She'd got her own tits now, a brand new pair, white and satiny. And she wasn't in the least bashful about them either, she wanted great big ones, and dreamt of having tits like a wet-nurse's; that's how the young are, heedless and grasping. What made her particularly fetching was an awful habit she'd developed of poking the tip of her tongue out between her little pearl-white teeth. She'd probably decided, after admiring herself in mirrors, that she looked sweet like that. So, to make herself pretty, she'd stick out her tongue all day long.

'Tuck away your fibber!' her mother would yell at her.

And often Coupeau had to join in, banging with his fist and bellowing and swearing:

'Stick that red rag back inside, for God's sake!'

Nana had become very vain. She didn't always wash her feet, but she bought such narrow boots that her tootsies gave her hell; and if anybody asked her why she'd gone purple in the face she'd say she had a belly-ache, sooner than confess her vanity. When there was nothing to eat at home it was difficult for her to doll herself up but she did the impossible, bringing ribbons home from the workshop and getting herself up in dirty old dresses covered with bows and rosettes. Summer was her season of glory. Each Sunday, dressed in her six-franc percale dress, she filled the Goutte-d'Or neighbourhood with her golden beauty. Yes, she was well known everywhere from the outer boulevards to the fortifications, from the Chaussée de Clignancourt to the Grande Rue de la Chapelle. They called her the 'little chick' because she really had the tender flesh and freshness of a young chicken.

There was one dress in particular that suited her to perfection. It was white with pink spots, very simple, without any kind of trimming. The skirt was on the short side and showed her feet; the loose, wide sleeves revealed her arms to the elbow; the neckline, which she'd enlarge with pins into a heart-shape, working in a dark corner of the stairs so as to avoid her father's slaps, set off her snowy neck and the golden shadow between her breasts. Nothing more, nothing except a pink ribbon tied round her blond hair with its ends floating down the back of her neck. Dressed like that she was as fresh as a bunch of flowers. She smelt good, she smelt of youth, she smelt of a child's nakedness, and of a woman's.

At that time Sundays were, for her, days when she could mingle with the crowds and with all the men who walked past giving her the glad eye. All week long she looked forward to Sunday, filled with little titillating urges, feeling stifled indoors, longing to get into the fresh air and go for a walk in the sunshine, amid the throng of local people decked out in their Sunday best. She'd start getting ready early in the morning, and would spend hours in her chemise in front of the bit of mirror that hung above the chest of drawers; and as the whole building could see her through the window, her mother would get cross, asking how much longer she meant to parade about giving everyone an eyeful. But Nana would calmly go on sticking kiss-curls on to her forehead with sugar and water, sewing her boot-buttons on again or putting a stitch in her dress, sitting there with bare legs, her chemise slipping off her shoulders, her tousled hair all over the place. Oh, she was a knock-out like that, Père Coupeau would say sneeringly, to tease her; a proper Mary Magdalene! She could have gone on show as a wild woman and charged a couple of sous. He'd yell at her: 'Cover yourself up, so I can eat me bread!' She looked bewitching, pale and delicate under her tumbling golden mane, but she'd turn quite pink with rage, although she didn't dare answer her father back, and she'd break her thread between her teeth with an angry jerk that would send a shudder through her lovely young nakedness.

As soon as they'd finished lunch she'd take off down the stairs to the courtyard. The building was dozing in the warm Sunday peace; down below, the workshops were shut and you could see, through the wide open windows of people's rooms, tables already set for the evening meal, waiting for couples who were out working up an appetite on the fortifications; on the third floor a woman was using the day to scrub out her room, rolling up the bed, shoving the furniture about, and singing the same song for hours on end in a soft, whining voice. And, amid the silence of the idle workshops, in the empty, echoing courtyard,

Nana, Pauline, and some of the other big girls would start playing a game of shuttlecock. There were five or six of them who'd grown up together and were now the queens of the building, sharing between them the admiring glances of the gents. Whenever a man crossed the courtyard soft laughter would be heard, and the girls' starched skirts would rustle like a sudden gust of wind. Above them blazed the holiday sky, scorching and heavy, as though languid from idleness and bleached white by the dust of Sunday walkers.

But the games of shuttlecock were simply a sham to help them make a getaway. Quite suddenly a great silence would fall on the building. They'd just slipped out into the street, heading for the outer boulevards. Off they went, the six of them, taking up the whole width of the road, arm in arm in their light dresses, with only ribbons on their bare heads. Casting brief glances from under primly lowered lids, their quick eyes missed nothing, and they'd laugh, throwing back their heads and displaying their plump throats. When, during these noisy bursts of gaiety, they passed a hunchback or met an old woman waiting for her dog beside a mile-post, their band would divide, some of them staying behind while the others would pull violently at them; and they'd sway their hips, clustering together or flopping awkwardly about, so as to attract attention and make their bodices stretch tightly over their swelling bosoms. The street belonged to them; they'd grown up in it, hauling up their skirts to pee beside the shops; and they still pulled their skirts up, up to their thighs, to refasten their garters. They raced helter-skelter through the dawdling, pasty-faced crowd, between the scraggy trees of the boulevard, from the Barrière Rochechouart to the Barrière Saint-Denis, bumping into people, barging sideways through groups, turning round to make remarks amid ripples of laughter. And their flying dresses left behind them a sense of their insolent youth; they displayed themselves there in the open air, in the glaring sunlight, with the crude vulgarity of young hooligans, yet seemed as captivating and tender as virgins* returning from bathing with their hair curling damply about their necks.

Nana would walk in the middle, her pink dress glowing in the sunshine. She'd take the arm of Pauline, whose dress of yellow flowers on a white background also shone brightly, spangled with tiny flames. And as the two of them were the biggest, the most womanly and the boldest members of the band, they were its leaders, swaggering about and enjoying the stares and the compliments. The others, the younger girls, trailed along to right and left, trying to puff out their chests so as to be taken seriously. In actual fact Nana and Pauline had worked out some very complicated manœuvres for catching the eye of the boys. If they ran so fast, it was so they could show off their white stockings and make their hair-ribbons fly out in the wind. Then when they stopped, pretending to gasp for breath and displaying their heaving bosoms, if you looked around you'd be certain to see someone they knew nearby, some lad from their neighbourhood, and then they'd walk on languidly, whispering and laughing among themselves, on the lookout, their eyes carefully veiled. These chance encounters among the jostling crowd of walkers were really why they raced along the way they did. Tall lads all dressed up in jackets and round hats would stop them for a moment on the edge of the pavement, giggling and trying to squeeze their waists. Twenty-year-old workmen in untidy grey smocks would chat to them in a leisurely way, standing there with arms crossed, blowing the smoke from their clay pipes in the girls' faces. It didn't amount to anything, those boys had grown up alongside them in the street. Nevertheless the girls were already making their choices from among them. Pauline always met one of Madame Gaudron's sons, a carpenter of seventeen who bought her apples. Nana could spot Victor Fauconnier, the laundress's son, from the other end of the avenue; they used to meet in dark corners for a kiss and cuddle. It didn't go any further than that; they were too sharp to do anything silly through ignorance. But they did go in for bawdy talk.

Then, when the sun went down, what those little devils loved best was to stop and watch the street entertainers. Conjurers and muscle-men turned up and spread out their threadbare carpets on the road. A gaping crowd would gather and make a circle round the performer who, clad in a faded singlet, was rippling his muscles. Nana and Pauline would stand for hours in the thick of the crowd. Their pretty, cool dresses were crushed between overcoats and dirty smocks. Their bare arms, their bare necks, their bare heads were warmed by hot, foul breath, and bathed in a stench of wine and sweat. And they'd laugh, finding it great fun, not in the least disgusted, their faces a little pinker, as if they felt quite at home amid all that filth. On every side they could hear swearing, coarse obscenities and drunken remarks. This was their language, they knew it all, and they'd turn round with a smile, brazenly composed, the delicate pallor of their satiny skin quite undisturbed.

The only thing that bothered them was if they bumped into their fathers, particularly when the men had been drinking. They kept their eyes peeled and warned each other.

'Hey, Nana, look out, there's Père Coupeau!' Pauline would suddenly shout.

'Oh, great, and not half sozzled, is he, either!' Nana would reply, very put out. 'Well I'll piss off; I don't want a whacking . . . Hey, look, he's taken a nose dive. Hell, if only he'd break his bloody neck!'

Other times, when Coupeau was making straight for her without giving her a chance to escape, she'd crouch down, whispering:

'Come on, you lot, hide me . . . He's looking for me, he swore he'd give me a kick up me arse if he caught me hanging about here again.'

When the drunken Coupeau had gone past, she'd stand up again and they'd all follow him, exploding with laughter. He'll catch her! No he won't! It was a proper game of hide-and-seek. One day, however, Boche had come and marched Pauline off by the ears, and Coupeau had kicked Nana all the way home.

The sun was setting and they took one last turn before walking home in the dim twilight, surrounded by the exhausted crowd. The dust in the air was denser, blanching the leaden sky. The Rue de la Goutte-d'Or might have been in a country village, with women standing at their doorways and bursts of chatter breaking the sultry silence of the traffic-free streets. The girls would stop for a moment in the courtyard and pick up their racquets, hoping to make it look as if they'd never budged from there. And they'd climb up the stairs to their homes, thinking up some story which often they didn't need, finding their parents in the middle of a set-to over a supper that was too salty or not properly cooked.

Nana had a job now at Titreville's, the firm in the Rue du Caire where she'd served her apprenticeship; she was earning a wage of two francs. The Coupeaus didn't want to move her, preferring that she remain under the watchful eye of Madame Lerat, who for ten years had been forewoman in the workshop. Each morning the mother would note the time on the cuckoo clock and the child, looking very sweet, would set off on her own, her shoulders squeezed into her old black dress that was too tight and too short; Madame Lerat had to remember the time she arrived and later tell Gervaise. She was allowed twenty minutes to get from the Rue de la Goutte-d'Or to the Rue du Caire, which was enough, because those little lassies have legs like deer. Occasionally she'd arrive exactly on time, but so red and out of breath that she must surely have come tearing down from the Barrière in ten minutes, after dawdling along the way. Most often she'd arrive seven or eight minutes late; and all day long she'd make a great fuss of her aunt, staring at her imploringly and trying to get round her and stop her telling. Madame Lerat, who understood the young, would lie to the Coupeaus, but she treated Nana to interminable lectures about it, talking of her own responsibility and the dangers a young girl ran in the streets of Paris. God almighty! Why even she herself was always being followed! She'd gaze fondly at her niece, her eyes gleaming with her own perpetually prurient obsessions, all worked up at the thought of protecting and coddling the innocence of that poor little darling.

'Now listen,' she kept saying to her, 'you must tell me everything. I'm too good to you, and I'd just have to throw myself in the Seine if something bad happened to you . . . You do understand, don't you, my pet, that if men speak to you, you must tell me everything, everything, and not leave a single word out . . . D'you swear that nobody's said anything to you yet, d'you swear it?'

And Nana would laugh, screwing up her mouth in a funny way. No, no, men didn't speak to her. She walked too fast. Anyway, what would they have said to her? No reason for her to have anything to do with men, surely! And she'd explain, in her guileless way, why she was late, saying she'd stopped to look at some pictures, or else that she'd been with Pauline, who had something to tell her. They could follow her if they didn't believe her; she even stayed all the time on the left pavement; and she walked at a spanking pace, overtaking all the other girls, just like a carriage. In fact Madame Lerat had once caught her loafing about in the Rue du Petit-Carreau* with three other flower girls, trashy little things, and they were all having a good laugh because a man was shaving at a window; but Nana had angrily protested that she'd been just about to go into the corner bakery to buy a roll.

'Oh don't you worry, I'm keeping an eye on her,' the tall widow would tell the Coupeaus. 'I'm as sure of her as I am of myself. If some bastard tried to so much as pinch her, I'd shield her with my own body.'

The workshop at Titreville's was on the mezzanine level; it had a big table standing on trestles that took up all the middle of the room. Along the four empty walls, where plaster showed through the tears in the dingy grey paper, stretched shelves laden with old boxes and parcels and abandoned flower designs, lying forgotten there under a thick blanket of dust. The gas-lights had painted the ceiling with a coating of soot. The two windows opened so wide that without leaving the work-table the girls could watch the world go by on the opposite pavement.

Madame Lerat, to set a good example, would arrive first. Then the door would swing to and fro for a quarter of an hour as the little flower workers came rushing in, perspiring, their hair in a mess. One morning in July Nana turned up last, which moreover happened quite frequently.

'Well I certainly won't be sorry when I've a carriage of my own,' she said.

And without even taking off her hat, a black affair she called her cap and that she was fed up with mending, she went up to the window and leant out to left and right, to see into the street.

'What are you looking at?' enquired Madame Lerat suspiciously. 'Did your father come with you?'

'No of course not,' Nana replied calmly. 'I'm not looking at anything . . . I'm looking at how bleeding hot it is. It's hot enough to make you ill, having to run like that.'

It was a stiflingly hot morning. The girls had lowered the blinds but kept watch through the slats on the activity in the street; they'd finally settled down to work, seated along the two sides of the table with Madame Lerat all by herself at the top end. There were eight of them, and each had her own pot of glue, pincers, tools, and embossing cushion in front of her. The table was littered with a jumble of pieces of wire, cotton reels, cotton wool, green and brown paper, and leaves and petals cut out of silk, satin or velvet. In the middle of the table stood a large carafe, and into its neck one of the girls had stuck a cheap little spray of flowers that had been wilting on her dress since the evening before.

'Oh, I must tell you,' said Léonie, a pretty brunette, as she leaned over her cushion to emboss some rose petals, 'well, that poor Caroline is ever so miserable with that chap who used to wait for her in the evenings.'

Nana, who was busy cutting thin strips of green paper, exclaimed:

'Well of course! A two-timing shit who's forever cheating on her!'

A surreptitious titter ran round the table, and Madame Lerat felt a reprimand was called for. Screwing up her nose she said:

'You're not too particular, are you, my girl, with the words you use! I'll tell your father what you said, and we'll see how well he likes it.'

Nana puffed out her cheeks as if she was holding back a guffaw. Her father, what a joke! How about the words he used! But Léonie suddenly said, in a very rapid, soft whisper:

'Watch out! The boss!'

And sure enough Madame Titreville, a tall, spare woman, had walked in. As a rule she remained downstairs, in the shop. The girls were really frightened of her, because she never ever joked. She went slowly round the work-table, where now all heads were bent in silent activity. She called one of the girls a bungler and made her start a daisy all over again. Then she went out as starchily as she'd come in.

'Oops! Oops!' exclaimed Nana, amid general groans.

'Really, young ladies, young ladies!' said Madame Lerat,

doing her best to look severe. 'I shall be obliged to take steps . . .'

But they didn't pay any attention to her, nor were they in the least afraid of her. She was too easy-going, getting a real kick out of the company of these young things whose eyes sparkled with fun, taking them aside to pump them about their lovers and even telling their fortunes when there was space for the cards on the end of the work-table. Madame Lerat was an inveterate gossip, and her leathery skin and policeman-like body quivered with pleasure whenever the talk turned to love affairs. The only thing she found offensive was crude words; as long as you avoided crude words you could say anything you liked.

No doubt about it, the workroom was doing a fine job rounding out Nana's education! Oh, she had a natural bent in that direction, of course. But constantly rubbing shoulders with a lot of girls who were already broken in by poverty and depravity was the finishing touch. They were all on top of one another at Titreville's, and went to the bad together; exactly like the story of the baskets of apples, when some of them are rotten. Of course they behaved properly in company and were careful not to seem too bitchy, or use language that was too foul. In a word, they posed as well-brought-up young ladies. But when they huddled into corners, whispering, it was nothing but bawdy talk. As soon as two girls got together, they'd immediately start screaming with laughter and talking filth. Then in the evening, walking home, they'd tell each other things, stories that would make your hair stand on end; and the pair of them, all worked up, would hang about chatting on the pavement amid the jostling of the crowd. And there was also, for those girls like Nana who were still virgins, a bad atmosphere in the workshop, a smell of low dance-halls and unconsecrated nights, brought in by the girls on the make, which clung to their hastily combed hairdos and skirts so crushed that they looked as if they'd been slept in. The slothful languor of mornings-after, eyes circled in black, those black circles that Madame Lerat politely called love's bruises, undulating hips and hoarse voices together created an atmosphere of perversion that hung over the work-table above the brilliance and delicacy

of the artificial flowers. Nana would sniff, intoxicated by
the smell, if she sensed she was next to a girl who'd already
lost her cherry. For a long time she chose to sit beside big Lisa,
who was said to be pregnant; and she'd cast bright, side-long
glances at her neighbour as if expecting to see her swell up
and burst all of a sudden. It was hardly a case of her finding
out anything new. The little wretch had learnt everything
on the pavements of the Rue de la Goutte-d'Or. It was simply
that in the workshop she could watch it going on, and she
was gradually developing the urge and the nerve to do it
herself.

'You can't breathe,' she murmured, going up to one of the
windows as if to lower the blind further.

But she bent down, looking again to left and right. At the
same moment Léonie, who was keeping her eye on a man
standing on the opposite pavement, cried:

'Whatever's that old chap doing over there? He's been spying
on this place for a quarter of an hour.'

'Some dirty old man or other,' said Madame Lerat. 'Nana,
come over here and sit down! I've forbidden you to stand at the
window.'

Nana picked up the violet stalks she was rolling and the entire
workshop began discussing the man. He was a well-dressed
gentleman of about fifty, wearing a coat, with a pale, dignified,
grave face fringed by a neatly trimmed grey beard. He stood for
an hour in front of a herbalist's shop, staring up at the blinds
of the workshop. The girls kept giving little giggles that were
swallowed up by the noises from the street; they bent very
diligently over their work, glancing out from time to time so as
not to lose sight of the gentleman.

'Goodness! He's got a monocle,' observed Léonie. 'He's ever
so smart . . . It must be Augustine he's waiting for.'

But Augustine, a tall, plain blonde, sourly replied that she
didn't go in for old men. And, tossing her head, Madame Lerat
murmured with a prim smile full of innuendo:

'There, my dear, you make a mistake; old men are more
loving.'

At this point Léonie's neighbour, a plump little thing,
muttered something in her ear; and Léonie suddenly leant right

back in her chair, laughing uncontrollably, writhing about, glancing towards the gentleman and laughing even louder. She gasped:

'Yes, that's it, that's it! . . . . Oh what a filthy mind our Sophie has!'

'What'd she say? What'd she say?' they all asked, bursting with curiosity.

Léonie was wiping the tears from her eyes and didn't answer. When she'd calmed down a bit she picked up her embossing again and declared:

'It's something I can't repeat.'

They kept on asking and she'd shake her head, overcome by gales of giggles. Then Augustine, on her left, begged her to whisper it to her. And in the end Léonie agreed, putting her lips to Augustine's ear. Augustine in her turn leant back in her chair, splitting her sides. Then she herself passed on the remark, and it did the rounds from ear to ear to the tune of gasps and stifled laughter. When they'd all heard Sophie's dirty joke, they glanced at one another and burst out laughing in unison, though they did look rather flushed and embarrassed. Only Madame Lerat hadn't heard it. She was very annoyed.

'What you're doing is very bad manners, young ladies,' she said. 'You should never whisper when you're with other people . . . It was something indecent, wasn't it? A fine thing, I must say!'

But she didn't dare ask to be told Sophie's dirty remark, although she was desperate to hear it. Nevertheless, keeping her eyes down in a dignified manner, she listened for a moment with relish to the conversation of the girls. No one could say anything, not even something completely innocent, about her work for instance, without the others immediately seeing something dirty in it; they'd twist the word's sense round, giving it a suggestive meaning, reading the most amazing innuendos into simple remarks like: 'my pincers have got a crack in them', or 'who's been poking about in my little pot?'. And they made everything apply to the gentleman who was cooling his heels across the street, it was he who turned out to be the point of every allusion. How his ears must have been

burning! They ended up saying really silly things, so determined were they to be clever. But that didn't stop them finding
this game very amusing, and their eyes flashed with excitement
as they came out with things that were more and more
outrageous. There was nothing for Madame Lerat to get angry
about, they weren't saying anything vulgar. She herself set
them off into gales of mirth by asking:

'Mademoiselle Lisa, my flame's gone out, would you pass me
yours?'

'Oh, Madame Lerat's flame's gone out!' shouted the workshop.

She tried to begin an explanation:

'When you're my age, young ladies . . .'

But they weren't listening to her, they were talking about
calling the man over to relight Madame Lerat's flame.

You should just have seen Nana doing her share of all this
screaming and laughing! Not one double meaning escaped her.
She too said some pretty outrageous things, sticking out her
chin to emphasize them, ever so proud and pleased with herself.
She was completely in her element amid all that smut. And
while she was squirming about with mirth on her chair, she
went on very competently rolling her violet stalks. Oh, she had
a marvellous knack, she did it faster than you could roll a
cigarette. She'd just pick up a thin strip of green paper and, lo
and behold, the paper had wound itself round the wire; then a
drop of glue at one end to fix it and there it was, a fresh,
delicate sprig of green, just the thing to pin on a lady's breast.
The knack was in the fingers, in those tapering, harlot's fingers
which looked so pliant, so supple and coaxing. That was the
only part of flower-making that she'd been able to master. She
was given every stalk in the workshop to make, she did them
so well.

Meanwhile the gentleman on the opposite pavement had left.
The girls were settling down and getting on with their work in
the extreme heat. When it struck noon, time for lunch, they all
roused themselves with a shake. Nana, who'd rushed to the
window, shouted that she'd pop down and run the errands, if
they liked. And Léonie asked for two sous' worth of shrimps,
Augustine a bag of chips, Lisa a bunch of radishes, and Sophie

a sausage. Then just as she was setting off, Madame Lerat, who'd thought Nana's interest in the window that day rather odd, raced after her with her long stride, saying:

'Wait, I'll go with you, there's something I need.'

And who should she see standing there in the alley-way but the gentleman himself, giving Nana the glad eye! The kid went very red. Her aunt grabbed her arm and made her hurry along the pavement, with the individual following close behind. So, the old letch was after Nana, was he! Well! A nice thing that was, to have men hanging round your skirts at fifteen and a half! And Madame Lerat pressed her with questions. Oh, Lord, Nana'd no idea; he'd only been following her for five days, she couldn't put her nose outside without finding him under her feet; she thought he was in business, yes, that was it, he made bone buttons. Madame Lerat was very impressed. She turned round and gave the man a quick glance.

'You can tell he's rolling in it,' she muttered. 'Listen, my pet, you must tell me everything. You've nothing to be scared of now.'

As they chatted they hurried from shop to shop, to the pork-butcher's, the fruiterer's and the cook-shop. Their purchases, wrapped in greasy paper, were piling up in their arms. But despite that they managed to look appealing, swaying their hips, giving little laughs and casting flashing glances behind them. Madame Lerat herself turned on the charm and came over all girlish for the benefit of the button manufacturer, who was still dogging their footsteps.

'He looks very distinguished,' she declared, as they turned back into the alley. 'Now if only his intentions were honourable . . .'

Then, as they were climbing the stairs, she suddenly seemed to remember something.

'By the way, tell me what those girls were whispering to each other, you know, Sophie's dirty joke?'

Nana didn't bat an eyelid. However she grabbed Madame Lerat by the neck and forced her to come down two steps, because really and truly it couldn't be repeated out loud, not even on a staircase. She whispered the word. It was so obscene that her aunt, with eyes wide and lips pursed, just tossed her head. Anyway, now she knew, and it wouldn't bug her any more.

The flower workers ate on their laps, so as not to dirty the table. They thought eating was a bore, and bolted their food, preferring to spend the lunch hour watching the passers-by or telling each other secrets in corners. That particular day they were trying to find out where the man they'd seen that morning had hidden himself, for he certainly seemed to have vanished. Madame Lerat and Nana caught each other's eye but never said a word. It was already ten past one, and no one seemed in a hurry to take up her pincers again, when Léonie, with a little psst! sound of her lips such as house-painters use to call each other, signalled the approach of the boss. They were all instantly on their chairs, heads bent over their work. Madame Titreville came in and walked austerely round the table.

From that day forward Madame Lerat positively revelled in her niece's first affair. She never left her side and went with her in the mornings and evenings, talking about her own responsibilities. Of course Nana found that a bit of a nuisance, but it did also fill her with pride to be guarded like a treasure, and the conversations that the two of them had in the street, with the button manufacturer close behind, excited Nana's imagination and if anything made her long to take the plunge. Oh, Madame Lerat understood the tender passion; in fact the button manufacturer—no longer young and so respectable—touched her because, after all, love in those of mature years is always more deeply rooted. But just the same, she kept an eye. Yes, he'd have to climb over her own body in order to get to the child. One evening she went up to him and told him straight out that what he was doing wasn't right. He, old goat that he was, must have been used to rebuffs from relatives, and he just bowed to her politely without replying. She couldn't really be angry, he was too well-mannered. And she went on giving practical advice about love, and hinting that men were filthy bastards, and telling all sorts of stories about little trollops who repented bitterly of giving men what they wanted, all of which left Nana pining for love, with her eyes gleaming wickedly in her white face.

But one day in the Rue du Faubourg-Poissonnière the button manufacturer had dared to stick his face between the niece and the aunt and murmur things that you just don't say. Madame Lerat, alarmed and declaring she no longer even felt safe herself, dumped the whole matter in her brother's lap. Things were very different after that. There were some tremendous ructions at the Coupeaus'. The first thing the roofer did was give Nana a good hiding. What was this he'd been told? The little tramp was running after old men, was she? Well, just let him catch her canoodling out there in the street and he'd break her neck in two shakes, he would, she could bet on it! Did you ever hear the like! A brat who was dragging her family down into the gutter! And he'd give her a good shaking, saying that Christ!, she'd better watch her step, 'cos he'd be the one to keep tabs on her in future. The minute she came in he'd examine her, looking carefully at her face to see if she hadn't had a little kiss—one of those quick quiet ones on the eye that are easy to sneak. He'd sniff at her, he'd turn her round. She got another thrashing one evening because he found a black mark on her neck. The little bitch dared to say it wasn't a love-bite! Yes, it was a bruise, she said, just a bruise she'd got larking about with Léonie. He'd give her bruises, he'd stop her carrying on, he would, he'd put a spoke in her wheel. At other times, when he was in a good mood, he'd make fun of her and tease her. She was just what a man wanted, as flat as a pancake, with salt-cellars big enough to put your fist in! Nana, beaten for filthy things she hadn't done and dragged in the mud of her father's foul accusations, behaved with the sly and enraged submissiveness of a hunted animal.

'Just leave her alone!' Gervaise, who was more reasonable, would say. 'You'll make her want to, if you carry on about it all day long.'

Oh yes, she wanted to all right! Her whole body itched with longing to run away and try it, as Coupeau said. He kept the idea so constantly before her that even a decent girl would have felt the urge. And by yelling at her the way he did he even taught her things she didn't yet know, which was quite astonishing. So little by little she took to doing some funny things. One morning he noticed her messing about with a screw of paper and sticking something on her mug. It was rice powder, which a freakish fashion dictated she plaster over her delicate, satiny skin. He rubbed her face with the paper, so roughly that he scratched her skin, and called her the miller's daughter. Another time she brought in some red ribbons to refurbish her hat, that old black cap she was so ashamed of. He asked her angrily where she'd got the ribbons. Well? She'd earned 'em on her back, hadn't she? Or maybe she'd pinched 'em? She was either a tart or a thief, perhaps both, by now. On several occasions he caught her like that with pretty things in her hands, a cornelian ring, a pair of cuffs edged with narrow lace, one of those little plated hearts—"come hithers"—that girls wear between their tits. Coupeau tried to smash everything, but she defended her things furiously, they were hers, some ladies had given her them, or else she'd swapped them for something at work. The heart for instance she'd found in the Rue d'Aboukir. When her father ground the heart under his heel, she stood there very straight, very white and tense, while underneath rebellion raged, making her long to fling herself on him and claw at his flesh. She'd been dreaming of that heart for two years, and there he was stamping on it! No, it was too much, it couldn't go on like that.

Indeed Coupeau, in his attempts to keep Nana under control, was governed more by the fun of needling her than by concern for her proper behaviour. He was often wrong and his unfairness exasperated the girl. She even started missing work, and when Coupeau gave her a licking she laughed at him, telling him she didn't want to go back to work for Titreville because they sat her next to Augustine who must have eaten her feet, her breath stank so foully. So Coupeau himself took her down to the Rue du Caire, and begged the boss to always put her next to Augustine, as a punishment. Each morning for two weeks he took the trouble to walk with Nana from the Barrière Poisson-nière to the door of the workshop.* And he'd wait for five minutes on the pavement so as to be certain she'd gone in. But one morning, stopping off with a friend at a bar in the Rue Saint-Denis, he saw the little wretch ten minutes later making tracks down the street, jiggling her behind. She'd been hood-winking him for two weeks by climbing up two floors instead

of going into Titreville's, and sitting on a step until he took off.
When Coupeau tried to complain about this to Madame Lerat,
she replied sharply that it wasn't her responsibility; she'd told
her niece everything she ought to tell her about how awful men
were, and it was no fault of hers if the kid still hankered after
the bastards; now she was washing her hands of the whole affair,
she swore she'd have nothing further to do with anything,
because she knew what she knew, the mud-slinging in the
family, yes, there were those who dared accuse her of going to
the bad along with Nana and taking a filthy pleasure in
watching her niece being debauched before her very eyes.
What's more Coupeau found out from the proprietress that
Nana had been led astray by another worker, that little bitch
Léonie, who'd walked out on flower-making to go on the game.
No doubt what really interested the greedy kid were the goodies
on the street vendors' stalls and she could still be married with
a wreath of orange blossom on her head. But Lord! they'd
better get a move on if they wanted to give her to a husband
without anything torn, with everything nice and clean and
intact, the way it should be in a self-respecting girl.

In the Goutte-d'Or building they talked about Nana's old
gent as if they all knew him. Oh, he was always very polite,
even rather timid, but as persistent and obstinate as the devil,
following ten paces behind her like a small obedient dog.
Occasionally he'd even walk right into the courtyard. Madame
Gaudron came upon him one evening on the second-floor
landing; he was racing up the stairs with his head bent, looking
randy and scared. And the Lorilleux were threatening to move
if their chit of a niece brought any more men in after her,
because it was becoming disgusting, the staircase was full of
them, you couldn't go downstairs any longer without seeing
them on every step, sniffing about and waiting; really you'd
have thought there was a bitch on heat in that part of the
building. The Boches felt sorry for the poor gentleman, such a
respectable man, who'd lost his head over a little tart. After all,
he was a business man, they'd seen his button factory in the
Boulevard de la Villette,* and if he'd fallen for someone decent
he could have set her up very nicely. Thanks to the details
furnished by the concierges, all the neighbourhood, even the

Lorilleux themselves, treated the old man with the greatest respect when he passed by close on Nana's heels, with his mouth hanging open in his pale face and his frill of grey beard neatly trimmed.

For the first month Nana thought her old gent was a huge joke. He was quite a sight, hanging round her all the time, scared stiff. A real bottom pincher, who'd stroke her skirts from behind, in a crowded street, with the most innocent air. And his legs! Spindle-shanks he had, proper matchsticks! Bald as an egg, with just four hairs hanging down his neck, so that she was always tempted to ask him the address of the barber who made his parting. What an old fuddy-duddy! Nothing very thrilling about *him*!

But then, seeing him always there, she began to think he wasn't all that funny. Secretly she was afraid of him, and she'd have screamed if he'd come up to her. Often when she stopped in front of a jeweller's window she'd suddenly hear him mumbling something behind her. And what he'd be saying was true, she'd have loved a cross on a velvet ribbon to hang round her neck, or else some little coral earrings, so tiny you'd have thought they were drops of blood. But even apart from longing for jewels, she really couldn't go on looking like a rag, she was fed up with using the sweepings from the Rue du Caire workshops to do her clothes up, and she was especially sick of her hat, that old thing on which the flowers she pinched from Titreville's dangled like so many gobs of dirt, the way bells dangle from a beggar's backside. Then as she trudged along in the mud, splashed by passing vehicles and dazzled by the splendour of the window displays, she'd feel cravings that wrenched at her stomach like hunger pangs, she'd long to be well dressed, to eat in restaurants, to go to the theatre, to have a room of her own with beautiful furniture. Pale with desire, she'd stop in her tracks, feeling the warmth of the Paris paving stones creeping up her thighs, feeling a fierce urge to taste all the pleasures that pressed in upon her in the crowded street. And always, without fail, it was at those moments that her old man would murmur his propositions in her ear. Oh, how readily she'd have said yes, if she hadn't been afraid of him, if deep down she hadn't felt, in spite of all her faults, a rebellious, angry disgust with the mystery of masculine desire, which stiffened her refusals.

But, with the arrival of winter, life at the Coupeaus' became impossible. Nana got a belting every evening. When the father was tired of beating her, the mother would box her ears to teach her how to behave. And it often turned into a family brawl, for the minute one parent hit her the other would defend her, so that all three would finish up rolling about on the floor among the broken crockery. What's more there was never enough to eat and it was deathly cold. If Nana bought herself something nice, like a bow made of ribbon or some cuff buttons, her parents would confiscate it and turn it into cash. She had nothing to call her own except her ration of blows, before creeping under the raggy sheet where she'd lie shivering with only her little black skirt spread out as a coverlet. No, this bloody awful existence couldn't go on, she didn't want to end her days like this. It was a long while since her father had meant anything to her; when a man's on the booze the way her father was, he's not a father, he's a filthy brute you long to be rid of. And now Nana was rapidly losing her feeling for her mother too. Gervaise also drank. She liked going to fetch Coupeau from Père Colombe's bar, because then someone would stand her a drink; she'd sit down very readily these days, never turning up her nose the way she did the first time, and she'd polish off her drinks in one go, hanging around in the place for hours and coming out glassy-eyed. When Nana went past the Assommoir and caught sight of her mother sitting in the back there with her nose stuck in her glass, looking like a slut with all those bawling men round her, she'd be furiously angry, because the young are greedy for a different kind of pleasure and don't understand about drink. On those evenings a pretty sight would greet her: a drunken Papa, a drunken Mamma, a home like the wrath of God, not a bite to eat and a filthy stink of booze. In a word, even a saint wouldn't have stayed there. It would be just too bad if one of these days she did a bunk; her parents could say their *mea culpa* and admit that they themselves had shoved her out.

One Saturday Nana came home to find her parents in a revolting state. Coupeau was sprawled across the bed, snoring.

Gervaise sat hunched up in a chair, rolling her head about and gazing at nothing with a vacant, unsettling stare. She'd forgotten to warm up the dinner, some left-over stew. An untrimmed candle lit up the poverty-stricken squalor of the room.

'Is that you, you little slut?' muttered Gervaise. 'You'll catch it from your Papa, you will!'

Nana, very pale, said nothing, but stood there looking at the unlit stove, the unlaid table, and the dismal room to which the drunken stupor of those two white-faced soaks added a note of horror. Without taking off her hat she walked round the room, and then, gritting her teeth, opened the door again and went out.

'You going back down?' asked her mother, unable to turn her head.

'Yes, I've forgotten something. I'll be back . . . Bye-bye.'

She did not come back. The next morning when the Coupeaus sobered up they had a proper set-to, each blaming the other for Nana's flight. Oh, she'd be far away now if she was still running! As people say to children about sparrows, if her parents put a grain of salt on her tail maybe they'd be able to catch her. This was a dreadful blow which brought Gervaise down even lower for, despite the sorry mess she'd become, she still knew perfectly well that her child's going off the rails like that and losing her cherry meant that she, her mother, would sink still lower now she was on her own, without a child to think of, without anything to stop her downward slide. Yes, Nana, that unnatural little bitch, had gone off with the last scraps of Gervaise's decency in her dirty skirts. And Gervaise spent three days in a drunken rage, her fists clenched and her mouth spewing foul abuse about her whore of a daughter. Coupeau, after strolling round the outer boulevards and having a good look at every tart he passed, took up his pipe again as calmly as you please; however sometimes when they were at table he'd spring to his feet clutching a knife and, waving his arms, would scream that he'd been dishonoured; but then he'd sit down again to finish his meal.

In that building, where not a month went by without girls taking off like canaries from an open cage, the Coupeaus' misfortune surprised nobody. But the Lorilleux were full of glee. Oh, they'd always said that the kid would give 'em the slip! The Coupeaus deserved no better, flower girls always went to the bad. The Boches and the Poissons sniggered about it too, making a tremendous parade of their virtue. Only Lantier, indirectly, stuck up for Nana. Lord! he'd declare in his strait-laced manner, no question but that a young girl who flew the coop offended against every law of decency; but then he'd add with a gleam in his eye that, heaven knows, the kid was too pretty to be scrabbling about for a crust at her age.

'Have you heard the latest?' cried Madame Lorilleux one morning in the Boches' lodge, where they were all having coffee, 'Well! Banban's sold her daughter, it's the gospel truth. Yes, she's sold her, I can prove it! . . . That old gent, the one that we were always bumping into on the stairs, well he was already paying them instalments. It was as plain as the nose on your face. And then yesterday someone saw the pair of them, the little madame with her old goat, at the Ambigu. Word of honour! So you see, they're together, no question about it!'

They talked it over while they finished the coffee. After all it was possible, still worse things than that went on. And in the end even the most level-headed in the neighbourhood went round saying that Gervaise had sold her daughter.

Gervaise, now, had become a real slattern, and didn't give a damn about anybody. If someone had yelled 'Thief!' at her in the street she wouldn't have turned her head. It was a month since she'd stopped working for Madame Fauconnier, who'd had to kick her out to prevent rows. Within the space of a few weeks she'd started at eight different laundries, staying in each for two or three days before getting the sack, because she bungled her work so badly, was careless and dirty and so out of it that she was even forgetting the skills of her trade. Realizing this, she'd given up ironing, and taken work by the day washing in the Rue Neuve washhouse; splashing about, beating the filth out of clothes, slipping back into the roughest, easiest kind of laundry work was still within her powers, and this change took her a further step down the slope to degradation. And the washhouse certainly did nothing for her looks, either. Just like a bedraggled dog she was when she came out of there, soaked through and showing bits of discoloured flesh. And at the same time she was getting even fatter, despite the days when the cupboard was bare, and her leg was so deformed that now she couldn't walk beside another person without almost knocking them down, she limped so badly.

Naturally when someone lets herself go as badly as that she loses all her feminine self-respect. Gervaise had cast aside her former pride, her vanities, her need for affection, decency and respect. You could give her a kick anywhere, front or back, and she wouldn't feel it, she was too flabby, too limp. So Lantier had dropped her completely; he no longer even went through the motions of giving her a pinch; and she seemed unaware of this end to a long relationship that had dragged slowly on then finally petered out in mutual weariness. For her it was one less chore. Even the relations between Lantier and Virginie left her absolutely cold, she now felt such complete indifference to all that nonsense that in the past had driven her so wild. She'd have held the candle for them if they'd asked her. Everybody now knew about the hatter and the shop-keeper, who were carrying on in a big way. And it couldn't have been easier for them; the cuckold of a husband was on duty every other night, shivering along the deserted pavements while his wife and his friend kept each other's feet warm at home. Oh, they could take their time over it, listening to the sound of his boots as he paced slowly past the shop-front in the dark empty street, without needing to stick their noses out from under the blanket. A policeman always puts duty first, doesn't he? And they'd stay calmly there till morning, tampering with his property while that unbending man went about protecting the property of others. The entire Goutte-d'Or neighbourhood sniggered over this good joke. When authority wears the horns, now that really is funny. Besides, Lantier had earned a right to that little spot. The shop and the shop-keeper went together. He'd just gobbled up a laundress and now he was munching on a grocer; and even if he set 'em up in a row one after the other, drapers, stationers, dress-makers, his jaws were big enough to devour them all.

No, when it came to wallowing in sugary things, no one had ever seen the likes of him. Lantier had certainly known what he was doing when he advised Virginie to go in for confectionery. He was too much of a Southerner not to love sweets; in fact he could have lived on pastilles, gum, dragées* and chocolate. The dragées especially— he called them "sugared almonds"—left a little froth on his lips, they tickled his gullet so. He'd been living on nothing but sweetmeats for a year now. When Virginie asked him to look after the shop he'd open the drawers and gorge on sweets all by himself. Often, while chatting, with five or six people watching, he'd take the top off one of the jars on the counter, stick in his hand and eat something; the jar would stay open and empty itself. He said it was just a little mannerism of his, and now no one took any notice. Then, he'd hit upon the idea of a perpetual cold, a tickle in his throat that he said needed soothing. He still wasn't working, but had projects in mind that were more ambitious than ever; for the moment he was mulling over a marvellous invention, the umbrella-hat, a hat that changed into a brolly on the wearer's head, at the first drops of rain; and, promising Poisson half the profits, he'd even borrow the odd twenty francs from him, for the experiments. Meanwhile the shop was melting away on his tongue; that was where all the merchandise ended up, even the chocolate cigars and the red toffee pipes. When, crammed to bursting with sweets and feeling very loving, he'd treat himself, in a quiet corner, to a last little guzzle of the shop's owner, he'd seem all sugary to her, with lips like pralines. He was a lovely man to kiss! Just like pure honey. The Boches said that all he had to do was dip his finger in his coffee to turn it into syrup.

Mellowed by this everlasting dessert, Lantier's manner towards Gervaise became quite fatherly. He'd give her advice and scold her for no longer liking work. What the hell! A woman of her age ought to know how to rise to the occasion! And he'd accuse her of having always been greedy. But, as you have to give people a helping hand even if they don't really deserve it, he tried to find her little jobs. So he'd persuaded Virginie to get Gervaise in once a week to wash the floors in the shop and the other rooms; scrubbing things with lye was right up her alley and she'd earn a franc and a half each time. Gervaise would turn up on Saturday mornings with a scrubbing brush and pail, not appearing to mind coming back to do a dirty and demeaning job, a charwoman's job, in this establishment where she herself had ordered people about in the days when she was the pretty blonde proprietress. It was a final humiliation, the end of all her pride.

One Saturday she had a dreadful time getting her job done. It had rained for three days and the customers seemed to have brought all the mud of the neighbourhood into the shop. Virginie stood behind the counter doing the grand lady act, with her hair nicely arranged, wearing a little lace collar and lace cuffs. Beside her on the narrow bench covered in red imitation leather Lantier was taking his ease, looking quite at home as if he were the real owner of the place, and as usual his hand was absent-mindedly reaching into a jar of mint pastilles for something sweet to munch.

'Now then, Madame Coupeau!' shouted Virginie as with pursued lips she watched Gervaise working, 'you're leaving some dirt over there, in that corner. Give it a bit more of a scrub, will you!'

Gervaise obeyed. She went back into the corner and started scrubbing again. She knelt on the floor in the dirty water, hunched right over, with her shoulder-blades poking out and her arms purple and rigid. Her old skirt was soaked and clung to her buttocks. There on the floor she looked like a heap of something rather dirty, with her hair all tousled and her bulging flesh visible through the holes in her bodice, a mass of flab that rippled, rolled and twitched under the vigour of her scrubbing; she was sweating so heavily that it poured off her sopping wet face in big drops.

'The more elbow grease you put into it, the more it shines,' said Lantier sententiously, his mouth full of pastilles.

Virginie, her head thrown back majestically and her eyes half closed, was still watching and commenting on the floor cleaning.

'A little more on the right. Now do be careful of the woodwork . . . You know, I wasn't all that pleased, last Saturday. The marks were still there.'

And they both put on an even more majestic air, as if they were on thrones, while Gervaise dragged herself about at their feet in the black mud. Virginie must have been enjoying herself, for yellow glints showed for an instant in her cat-like eyes, and she gave Lantier a little smile. Yes, now she had her revenge for the pasting of long ago, in the washhouse, that pasting she'd never ever been able to forget!

Meanwhile, whenever Gervaise stopped scrubbing, a faint sawing sound could be heard from the back room. Through the open door you could see, outlined against the wan light of the courtyard, the profile of Poisson who was off duty that day and was using his free time to indulge his passion for making little boxes. He was sitting at a table, very skilfully cutting arabesques in the mahogany of a cigar box.

'Listen, Badingue!' cried Lantier, who, to be friendly, had started calling him by that nickname again; 'I'll have that box of yours, it's a present for a young lady.'

Virginie gave him a pinch but the hatter, with an unwavering smile, most gallantly returned good for evil by playing at mouse up her leg, under the counter, removing his hand in the most natural way when the husband glanced up, his little beard and red moustache bristling on his ashen face.

'As a matter of fact I was making it for you, Auguste,' said the policeman. 'A souvenir of our friendship.'

'Well in that case, dammit, I'll hang on to your little thingummy!' replied Lantier, laughing. 'You know, I'll wear it on a ribbon round my neck.'

Then suddenly, as if this idea led to another one:

'By the way,' he exclaimed, 'I bumped into Nana last night.'

The sudden shock of this news made Gervaise sit back into the puddle of dirty water that covered the shop floor. She waited, sweating and breathless, her scrubbing brush in her hand.

'Oh!' she murmured simply.

'Yes, I was going down the Rue des Martyrs, watching a young thing jiggling about in front of me on the arm of an old man, and thinking: "now there's a little backside that looks familiar . . ." So I speeded up a bit and found myself staring straight at our precious little Nana . . . Well, no need to feel sorry for her, she's right as rain, a pretty woollen dress on her back, a gold cross on her neck, and looking as saucy as they come!'

'Oh!' repeated Gervaise more faintly.

Lantier, who'd finished the pastilles, took a piece of barley sugar from another jar.

'She's a sharp one, that kid is!' he continued. 'Just imagine, she signalled to me to follow her, as cool as a cucumber. Then she dumped her old boy somewhere, in a café . . . And was that old boy ever a sight! Completely knackered! . . . She came back and met me in a doorway. Talk about being artful! As nice as can be, chattering away, and fawning on you like a little dog. Yes, she gave me a kiss and wanted to hear about everybody . . . Anyway, I was ever so pleased to bump into her.'

'Oh!' said Gervaise a third time.

She still sat there in a heap, waiting. Hadn't her daughter even mentioned her? In the silence, you could once more hear Poisson's saw. Lantier, very cheerful, was vigorously sucking his barley sugar and smacking his lips.

'Well, for my part, if I see her, I'll cross over to the other side of the street,' remarked Virginie, who'd just given the hatter another fierce pinch. 'Yes, it'd make me blush, to be greeted in public by one of those girls . . . I'm not saying this just because you're here, Madame Coupeau, but your daughter's nothing but trash. Poisson runs in girls every day who're worth more than she is.'

Gervaise went on staring into space, not saying anything, not moving. Eventually she gave a little nod, as if in response to some private thoughts, while Lantier muttered, with a greedy expression on his face:

'I wouldn't mind getting a belly-ache from trash of that sort. It's as tender as chicken . . .'

But Virginie was giving Lantier such a terrible look that he had to shut up and placate her with an affectionate gesture. He glanced up and, seeing the policeman bent over his little box, he took the opportunity to pop some barley sugar into Virginie's mouth. She gave a complacent laugh. Then she turned her anger against Gervaise.

'Get a move on a bit, can't you? You'll never finish the job if you just sit there like a lump of stone. Come on, jump to it, I don't fancy paddling about in water all day long.'

And, lowering her voice, she added nastily:

'Is it my fault if her girl's gone on the streets?'

Probably Gervaise didn't hear her. With aching back she'd begun scrubbing again, kneeling low on the floor and dragging herself about with sluggish, frog-like movements. Both hands were clutching the wooden back of the brush as she pushed before her a pool of filthy water, which splashed her with specks of mud right up to her hair. She only had to rinse the floor now, after sweeping the dirty water out into the gutter.

After a short silence Lantier, who was getting bored, raised his voice.

'I haven't told you, Badingue,' he shouted, 'I saw your boss yesterday in the Rue de Rivoli.* He looks as haggard as the devil, I wouldn't give him more than six months* . . . But then, with the life he leads!'

He was speaking of the Emperor. The policeman replied curtly, without raising his eyes:

'If you were the government you wouldn't be as fat as you are.'

'Oh, if I were the government, old chap,' replied the hatter, abruptly putting on a serious air, 'you can bet your boots that things would be going rather better . . . Just look at the foreign policy they've had for some time now, well it makes you sick, it really does. Now me, yes me, if only I knew even one journalist that I could get to take up my ideas . . .'

He was growing excited, and as he'd finished his barley sugar he'd opened a drawer and was taking out pieces of marshmallow that he gulped down while he gesticulated.

'It's very simple . . . First of all I'd reorganize Poland, and I'd establish a great Scandinavian state to keep the giant of the North in its place . . . Then I'd turn all those little German kingdoms into a republic . . . As for England, there's no need to be afraid of her; if she made a move, I'd send a hundred thousand men to India . . . And then I'd send the Grand Turk back to Mecca at gun point, and the Pope to Jerusalem . . . Well? Europe would be cleaned up in a jiffy.* There you are! Now just watch, Badingue . . .'

He stopped to take a handful of five or six pieces of marshmallow.

'There! It wouldn't take any longer than swallowing that.'

And, one after another, he threw the sweets into his open mouth.

'The Emperor has a different plan,' said the policeman after spending two full minutes in thought.

'Don't make me laugh!' Lantier replied savagely. 'We know all about his plan! Europe's thumbing its nose at us . . . Every day the Tuileries' flunkeys drag your boss out from under the table, along with a couple of high-class whores.'

But Poisson had got to his feet. He walked forward and said, with his hand on his heart:

'You're hurting me, Auguste. Don't bring personalities into your arguments.'

Virginie interrupted at that point, telling them to shut up. She didn't give a damn about Europe. How in the world could two men who shared everything else be constantly at each other's throats over politics? They went on muttering crossly for a few minutes. Then, to show there were no hard feelings, the policeman brought in the lid of the little box which he'd just finished: written across it in inlay were the words: 'To Auguste, in friendship.' Very flattered, Lantier leant back and stretched himself, so that he was almost on top of Virginie. And the husband looked at them, his bleary eyes expressionless in his plaster-coloured face; but the red bristles of his moustache would occasionally twitch all by themselves, in a very funny way, which might have worried a man less sure of himself than the hatter.

That bastard Lantier had the kind of cool-headed nerve that women find attractive. As Poisson had his back to them, Lantier thought it would be a great joke to plant a kiss on Madame Poisson's left eye. As a rule he behaved with cunning prudence, but when he'd been arguing about politics he'd take all kinds of risks just to show that he could do as he pleased with Poisson's wife. Those greedy caresses, shamelessly filched behind the policeman's back, were his revenge against the Empire which was turning France into a whore-house. Only this time he'd forgotten that Gervaise was there. She'd just rinsed and wiped over the floor of the shop, and was standing by the counter waiting to be given her thirty sous. The kiss on the eye left her quite unruffled, as if it were a perfectly natural thing that shouldn't concern her. Virginie looked a trifle upset.

She flung the thirty sous on to the counter in front of Gervaise. The latter never moved, but still seemed to be waiting, exhausted by her scrubbing, sopping wet and unsightly like some dog that's been fished out of a sewer.

'So she didn't say anything else?' she finally asked the hatter.

'Who?' he exclaimed. 'Oh, you mean Nana . . . No, nothing else. What a mouth the little tramp has! Like a tiny pot of strawberries!'

And Gervaise went off with her thirty sous in her hand. Her worn-down slippers squirted water like pumps: real musical slippers they were, playing a tune and leaving the prints of their broad wet soles all along the pavement.

The other women in the neighbourhood who were sozzlers like Gervaise now said that she drank to forget her daughter's disgrace. She herself, as she downed her tot of booze at the counter, would put on dramatic airs and say, while knocking it back, that she hoped it would finish her off. And on those occasions when she came home pissed as a newt, she'd mumble that it was on account of her troubles. But decent folks shrugged their shoulders; they'd heard that one before, drunks saying it was on account of their troubles that they'd got pissed on the Assommoir's rotgut; at any rate, you could call them troubles in a bottle. Of course, at first, she'd found Nana's flight hard to swallow. What was left of her sense of decency was outraged; and then, in general, a mother doesn't like having to admit that her daughter, that very minute, may be carrying on with just any man she happens to run into. But Gervaise was already too befuddled, her mind too sick and her heart too crushed, to feel that shame for long. In her case, it came and went. She'd be fine for a week at a go, never giving a thought to her tart of a daughter, then suddenly—she might be sober or again she might be sozzled—she'd be overcome with tenderness or fury, with a fierce need to drag Nana into some private little spot where she could either take her in her arms or beat her black and blue, depending on the whim of the moment. Eventually she no longer had a very clear idea of what was right and proper. But the thing was, Nana belonged to her, didn't she? Well, when something belongs to you, you don't want to see it vanish into thin air.

So, when thoughts like these gripped her, Gervaise would search the streets with the eyes of a policeman. Ah! If she'd caught sight of her little bit of trash, she'd have marched her straight back to the house, wouldn't she just! That year the entire neighbourhood was being turned upside down. The Boulevard Magenta and the Boulevard Ornano* were being built, they went right through where the Barrière Poissonnière had been, carving a hole in the outer boulevard. Really, you no longer knew where you were. All of one side of the Rue des Poissonniers had been razed. Now, from the Rue de la Goutte-d'Or, you could see an immense open space, full of sunshine and fresh air; and, where there used to be hovels blocking the view on that side, a veritable mansion rose up on the Boulevard Ornano, a six-storey affair decorated, like a church, with carvings, whose bright windows, hung with embroidered curtains, reeked of money. It seemed as if, from that pure white building standing exactly opposite, a beam of light shone out, illuminating the street. Every day, Lantier and Poisson would argue about the place. The hatter never stopped talking about the demolitions going on in the city; he'd accuse the Emperor of putting up places everywhere, so the workers would have to move out to the provinces; and the policeman, white with anger, would reply that on the contrary the Emperor was thinking first and foremost of the workers, that he'd pull Paris down, if necessary, simply in order to give them work. Gervaise, too, was fed up with these improvements, they were messing up this dismal little corner of Paris she'd grown used to. Her annoyance came from the fact that the neighbourhood was being beautified just when she herself was on the skids. When you're down in the gutter you don't like having a sunbeam shining right on you. So on those days when she was hunting for Nana, she'd get furious when she had to step over piles of building materials or squelch along unfinished pavements, or when she found her way blocked by palings. The beautiful big building on the Boulevard Ornano made her fly off the handle. Buildings of that sort were for tarts like Nana.

Still she did hear news of the girl on several occasions. There'll always be well-meaning folks who can't wait to pass on something nasty. Yes, they'd told her that Nana had dumped her old gent, just the kind of silly thing an inexperienced girl would do. She'd been very well off with him, pampered and adored and her own boss, even, if she'd gone about it the right way. But the young are silly, she must have gone off with some young smoothie or other, they didn't exactly know who. It *was* certain, however, that one afternoon in the Place de la Bastille she'd asked her old boy for three sous because she needed to pee, and he was still waiting for her. In the best circles they call that pissing off. Some people swore they'd seen her since, dancing a wild dance at the Grand Salon de la Folie* in the Rue de la Chapelle. That was when Gervaise got the idea of hanging round the neighbourhood dance-halls. Now she never went by one without going in. Coupeau went too. At first they simply did the rounds of the places and stared at the floozies jigging about. Then one evening when they had a bit of cash, they sat down and drank a bowl of mulled wine to refresh themselves while they waited to see if Nana might turn up. After a month they'd forgotten about Nana, they treated themselves to the dance-hall because they enjoyed it, they liked looking at the dancing. They'd spend hours sitting there in a daze, their elbows on the table with the floor shaking under them, never saying a word to each other; apparently they really enjoyed gazing with their lack-lustre eyes at the local tarts dancing past in the stifling red glare of the hall.

It so happened that one November evening they went into the Grand Salon de la Folie for a warm-up. Outside, a nasty cold wind was stinging the faces of the passers-by. But the hall was full to overflowing. There was the most bloody amazing swarming mass in there, people at all the tables, people in the middle, people up in the air, a real mountain of offal, yes, quite a treat for anyone fond of tripe. When they'd gone round the room twice without finding a table they decided to stay and wait for someone to leave. Coupeau, in his dirty smock, his old cloth cap without a peak squashed on to the back of his head, was swaying about on his feet. He was standing in people's way, and noticed a small, thin young man wiping the sleeve of his overcoat where he'd bumped his elbow into him.

'Hey, you,' he shouted furiously, removing his nose-warmer from the black hole of his mouth, 'can't you say excuse me? . . . And turnin' up your nose too, just because someone's got a work smock on!'

The young man had turned round, and was looking the roofer up and down as Coupeau went on:

'Lemme tell you, you fuckin' little sod, that the smock's better'n anythin', 'cos it's what the worker wears! . . . I'm gonna give you a couple o' clouts to dust you off, if that's what you want . . . Did you ever see the like, one of those fruits insultin' a workin' man!'

Gervaise tried in vain to calm him. He kept flaunting his rags, tapping on his smock and bellowing:

'Inside this there's a real man!'

The young man vanished into the throng, muttering:

'What a filthy feller!'

Coupeau tried to go after him. He wasn't going to stand for being put down by an overcoat! Probably not even paid for, neither! Some secondhand thing or other to help the sod make a play for a floozie without spending a centime. If he, Coupeau, ran into him again, he'd shove him on to his knees and make him pay homage to the smock. But the suffocating crush was too great, you couldn't move. Gervaise and he went slowly round the edge of the dance-floor; the spectators were squashed together three deep, their faces lighting up when a man came a cropper or a woman kicked up her leg and showed everything she'd got; and as they were both short, they had to stand on tiptoe to see anything at all, even just a glimpse of women's hairdos or of hats as they bobbed up and down. The band was madly playing a quadrille on its cracked brass instruments, making a thunderous racket that set the hall shaking, while the dancers, stamping their feet, were raising a cloud of dust that turned the gaslight murky. The heat was something fierce.

'Hey, look!' Gervaise said suddenly.

'What?'

'That velvet hat over there.'

They stood on tiptoe. Over to the left they could see an old black velvet hat, with two tatty feathers waving about on it like plumes on a hearse. But they could see nothing except the hat, which was dancing a diabolically wild dance, leaping and twirling, bobbing down and springing up. They'd lose it in the wild whirl of heads, then spot it again as it wobbled about above the others hats, so cheeky and so comical that people near them started chuckling as they watched, just to see that hat dancing, without knowing what was underneath it.

'Well?' asked Coupeau.

'Don't you know that coil of hair?' Gervaise managed to whisper. 'I'd lay my life it's her!'

With a single thrust the roofer pushed the crowd aside. Christ, yes, it was Nana! And what a get-up! She'd nothing covering her bum but an old silk dress all mucky from rubbing up against bar tables, with tattered flounces spewing out all over the place. No jacket, and not so much as a wisp of a shawl round her shoulders, so you could see her bodice with its split buttonholes. And to think that the little tramp had had an old man spoiling her to death, and she'd fallen this low just to be with some good-for-nothing who probably beat her up! But even so she still looked very fresh and appetizing, with her hair frizzed up like a poodle's and her rosebud mouth under that jaunty great hat.

'Just wait, I'll make 'er dance!' said Coupeau.

Naturally, Nana hadn't an inkling. You should have seen the way she was twirling! Shoving her bum out this way and shoving it out that way, curtseying so low you'd think she'd break in two, then kicking up her foot into her partner's face as if she was about to do the splits! People had gathered round in a circle and were clapping her; and, well away now, she hauled up her skirts to her knees, her whole body rocking to the motion of the dance as she whirled round like a top being whipped, fell flat on to the floor in the splits then went back to dancing a modest little dance, rolling her hips and bosom in an immensely stylish manner. It made you long to carry her off into a corner and devour her with kisses.

Coupeau, meanwhile, had barged right into the quadrille, where the dancers were shouting at him angrily because he was obstructing their moves.

'I tell you she's me daughter!' he yelled. 'Let me through!'

Just at that moment Nana was moving backwards, letting the feathers of her hat sweep the floor while she rounded her behind and gave it little jiggles to make it more appealing. She caught the most tremendous boot just where it counts, and, straightening up, turned white as a sheet on recognizing her father and mother. Did you ever see such bloody bad luck!

'Kick 'em out!' the dancers were screaming.

But Coupeau, who'd just realized that his daughter's partner was the thin young man with the overcoat, didn't give a damn about anyone else.

'Yes, it's us!' he bellowed. 'You weren't expectin' us, were you now! Aha! So this is where we find you, an' with a little snot who insulted me just now!'

Gervaise gave him a push, saying between clenched teeth:

'Shut up! . . . There's no call to go into all that.'

And, moving forward, she fetched Nana a couple of well-placed slaps. The first knocked the hat with the feathers sideways and the second left a red mark on the dead white cheek. Nana stood there in a daze, neither crying nor resisting. The band was still playing and the crowd, growing restive, kept roaring:

'Kick 'em out! Kick 'em out!'

'Come on, get moving!' said Gervaise. 'You go first, and don't even think of taking off, neither, or I'll have you put in jug!'

The snotty young man had prudently vanished. So Nana walked in front, very upright, still stunned by her bad luck. Any sign of resistance was met by a belt from behind which made her keep heading for the door. The three of them left like that, amid the gibes and boos of the hall, while the band finished playing the quadrille, making such a thunderous row that you'd have thought the trombones were spitting out cannon-balls.

Life began again. Nana slept for twelve hours in her old cupboard of a room, and behaved very nicely for a whole week. She'd patched up a prim little dress and wore a bonnet with the ribbons tied under her coil of hair. In the first flush of enthusiasm she even declared she wanted to work at home: you could earn what you liked on your own, and you didn't have to listen to the workroom smut; she found herself some work and settled down at a table with her instruments, getting up at five, during the first few days, to roll her violet stalks. But, after she'd delivered a few gross of them, she sat in front of her work stretching out her arms, with her hands racked by cramps; she'd lost the knack of making stalks and felt she was suffocating, shut up indoors after the six months of lovely fresh air she'd treated herself to. So then the glue-pot dried up, the petals and green paper got spots of grease on them and the owner himself came three times and made a scene, demanding the return of the materials he'd supplied. Nana would lounge about the place, still getting clouts from her father, while she and her mother squabbled all day long, yelling filthy insults at each other. It couldn't go on like that; on the twelfth day the little bitch skipped, taking nothing by way of luggage except the prim little dress on her back and the little bonnet on her head. The Lorilleux, who'd greeted the girl's return and repentance with glum looks, were practically rolling on the floor and exploding with mirth. Second showing, second disappearance, this way for Saint-Lazare!* No, it was really too funny. Nana was a whiz at taking off! Well if the Coupeaus still wanted to keep her now, all they had to do was sew up her thing and stick her in a cage!

In public, the Coupeaus pretended to be well rid of her. Privately they were furious. But fury doesn't last for ever. Soon, they heard without batting an eyelid that Nana was working the neighbourhood streets. Gervaise, who declared she was doing it to bring disgrace upon her parents, claimed to be above gossip; if she bumped into her girl in the street she wouldn't even soil her hand by slapping her; yes, it was all over, if she'd found her pegging out, lying naked there on the pavement, she'd have passed by, never letting on that the little bitch was flesh of her flesh. Nana was the centre of attraction in all the local dance-halls. She was well-known from the Reine-Blanche* to the Grand Salon de la Folie. When she went into the Elysée-Montmartre,* people would climb on to the tables to see her doing the backwards shimmy, in the quadrille. As they'd twice kicked her out at the Château-Rouge* she'd just hang about the entrance until someone she knew turned up. The Boule-Noire on the boulevard and the Grand-Turc in the

Rue des Poissonniers were fancy places where she went when she had the clothes. But what she liked even better among the neighbourhood hops were the Bal de l'Ermitage,* in a damp courtyard, and the Bal Robert,* in the Impasse du Cadran, two sleazy little dives lit by just half a dozen lamps, simple, cheerful, easy-going places, where no one minded or interfered if chaps had it off with their girls, round the back of the dance-floor. And Nana certainly had her ups and downs; Fortune would wave her wand and she'd be all dolled up like a smart lady, then she'd be trailing about in the gutter like a slut. Yes, it was a lovely life she was leading!

On several occasions the Coupeaus thought they saw their daughter in unsavoury spots. They'd turn their backs and take off in the other direction so as not to have to recognize her. They no longer felt like having an entire dance-hall jeering at them, just so they could bring a trollop like her back home. But one evening about ten o'clock, just as they were going to bed, someone knocked at the door. It was Nana, calmly saying she wanted to go to bed; and Lord, what a state she was in: bare-headed, dress in tatters, down-at-heel boots, looking just the sort the police might run in. She got a thrashing, of course, and then pounced greedily on a piece of stale bread; she fell asleep, exhausted, with the last of the bread still in her mouth. Then the routine started all over again. When she felt a bit perkier, one morning the kid disappeared. No warning of any kind, the bird had simply flown. Weeks and months would go by, she seemed lost for ever, when she'd suddenly reappear without ever saying where she'd come from, sometimes so dirty you wouldn't touch her with a pair of tongs, with scratches all over her body, at other times smartly got up but so limp, so drained by fast living that she couldn't keep on her feet. The parents just had to get used to it. The strap had no effect. They beat her black and blue, but that didn't stop her from using their place like an inn where you could have a bed by the week. She knew that the price of her bed was a thrashing, and she'd take stock of her situation and have the thrashing if it suited her. Besides, you get sick of hitting someone. In the end, the Coupeaus learnt to put up with Nana's binges. She'd come home, or she wouldn't come home, but as long as she didn't leave the door open that was OK. Christ! Habit will wear away at decent behaviour just like anything else.

One thing only made Gervaise see red. That was when her daughter turned up again wearing dresses with trains and hats covered in feathers. No, she couldn't stomach that kind of display. Let Nana go on the spree if she wanted, but when she came home to her mother she must at least dress the way a working girl should dress. The dresses with trains set the building buzzing; the Lorilleux sniggered, Lantier, all excited, would hang round the girl, sniffing her nice smell; the Boches had forbidden Pauline to go near that tart with her cheap finery. Another thing that made Gervaise angry was the way Nana slept like a log after one of her binges; she'd lie there fast asleep till midday, with her bosom uncovered and her coil of hair, the pins still in it, all loose, looking so white and breathing so shallowly that you'd think she was dead. Gervaise would shake her five or six times during the morning, and threaten to chuck a jugful of water over her stomach. It exasperated her to see that beautiful, lazy, half-naked girl, so sexy and voluptuous, lying like that sleeping off the lusts her flesh was still heavy with, unable even to wake up. Nana would open one eye, close it again, and stretch out more comfortably.

One day Gervaise, while giving her the rough side of her tongue about her way of life and asking whether she came back so done in because she was going with soldiers now, finally carried out her threat and shook her wet hand over the girl's body. Infuriated, Nana rolled herself up in the sheet and shouted:

'Just stop it, will you, Mamma? Don't let's talk about men, it's better not to. You did what you wanted, I'm doing what I want.'

'What? What?' stammered the mother.

'Yes, I've never said anything about it 'cos it wasn't my business, but you didn't put yourself out, I've seen you many a time going off in your chemise, down there, while Papa was snoring . . . Now you don't fancy it any longer, but others do. Leave me alone, you shouldn't have set me the example!'

White in the face, her hands trembling, Gervaise turned away without knowing what she was doing, while Nana lay on her stomach with her pillow clutched in her arms and fell back into a leaden sleep.

It no longer entered Coupeau's head to beat his daughter; he just groused. He was going completely off his rocker. Indeed, there was little point in accusing him of having no principles as a father, because booze was robbing him of any sense of right and wrong.

It had settled into a routine, now. He'd be drunk for six months on end, then he'd collapse and go into Sainte-Anne's; it was like a little country outing for him. The Lorilleux said that the Duke of Rotgut was retiring to his estates. After a few weeks he'd emerge from the asylum, patched up and tacked together, and then he'd set about wrecking himself again, until the day he fell apart and had to go in for repairs. In this way he went into Sainte-Anne's seven times in three years. It was said in the neighbourhood that they kept a cell specially for him. But the horrible thing about the whole affair was that this persevering boozer was making a worse wreck of himself each time, so that, as relapse followed relapse, you could see the eventual disintegration coming, the final break-up of this decaying barrel as its hoops snapped apart one after the other.

What's more he wasn't getting any handsomer, either; looked just like a ghost, he did! The poison was having a terrible effect on him. His alcohol-saturated body was shrivelling up like those foetuses in jars displayed in chemists' windows. He was so gaunt that when he stood in front of a window you could see the daylight through his ribs. With his hollow cheeks and eyes that oozed enough wax to supply a cathedral, the only thing about Coupeau that flourished now was his schnozzle: it was like a lovely red carnation in the middle of his ravaged mug. Those that knew his age, just forty, would give a little shiver when he went by, bent and doddery and old as the streets themselves. And the shaking of his hands was getting worse, his right hand especially shook so wildly that some days he had to grasp his glass with both fists to raise it to his lips. Oh! Those bloody awful shakes! The shakes were the only thing that could still get a rise out of him, in his apathetic state. You could hear him muttering ferocious curses at his hands. Other times, you'd see him staring at his hands for hours, watching them dance and jump about like frogs, not saying anything, no longer getting angry, seemingly trying to discover what internal mechanism could make them play about in that way; and one evening Gervaise had found him like that with two large tears rolling down his drunkard's scaly cheeks.

That last summer, when Nana still lounged about in her parents' place on her occasional free nights, was especially bad for Coupeau. His voice changed completely, as if the rotgut had set up a new kind of music in his throat. He went deaf in one ear. Then, in the space of a few days, his eyesight failed: he had to hang on to the staircase railing to avoid falling down the stairs. As for his health, you could say it had gone away for a rest. He suffered from dreadful headaches, and from dizzy spells when he'd see stars. He'd get sudden, sharp pains in his arms and legs; he'd turn pale and have to sit down, staying on his chair in a complete daze for hours at a time; once, after an attack of this kind, his arm had been paralysed for a whole day. On several occasions he took to his bed; he'd huddle up, hiding under the sheet and breathing loud and fast like an animal in pain. Then, the Sainte-Anne craziness would begin again. Distrustful, apprehensive, racked by a high fever, he'd be gripped by uncontrollable fits of rage, he'd rip his smocks and bite the furniture, foaming at the mouth; or else he'd be wallowing in self-pity, whining like a girl, sobbing and complaining that no one loved him. One evening Gervaise and Nana, coming in together, found he was no longer in his bed. He'd put the bolster in instead. And when they found him, lying between the bed and the wall, his teeth chattering, he told them that some men were coming to murder him. The two women had to put him back to bed and reassure him, like a child.

As far as Coupeau was concerned there was only one cure, to down his slug of rotgut; it was like a punch in the belly that got him up on his feet. That was how he cured his catarrh every morning. His memory had taken wing long ago, and there was nothing inside his noddle; the minute he was on his feet, he'd scoff at the notion that he was ill. He'd never been ill. Yes, he'd got to the point where you peg out while declaring you're as right as rain. Anyway, he'd gone off his noddle in every other way too. When Nana came home after six weeks on the tiles, he seemed to imagine she was returning from doing an errand round the corner. Often, clinging to some man's arm, she'd meet him in the street and have a giggle; he wouldn't recognize her. In fact, he no longer counted for anything, and she'd have used him to sit on if she hadn't been able to find a chair.

It was when the first frosts came that Nana took off once again, on the pretext of going to see if the fruit shop had any baked pears. She could feel the winter coming and didn't fancy sitting by the empty stove with her teeth chattering. The Coupeaus just called her a swine, because they were waiting for the pears. She'd come back all right; last winter, she'd gone down for two sous' worth of tobacco and stayed away three whole weeks. But months and months passed and the girl didn't reappear. She must have really gone on the spree this time. When June rolled round, she didn't turn up along with the sun, either. It really was over this time; she must have found herself a cushy spot somewhere. One day when the Coupeaus were on their beam ends they sold their kid's iron bedstead for six nice franc pieces that they drank at Saint-Ouen. It had been in their way, that bed had.

One July morning Virginie called to Gervaise as she was passing and asked her to lend a hand with the dishes; Lantier had invited a couple of friends in to a real spread the night before. And, while Gervaise was washing the dishes—and they weren't half greasy from Lantier's blow-out—the latter, who was still engaged in digesting his dinner, suddenly shouted from the shop:

'Hey, old girl, you'll never guess what, I saw Nana the other day.'

Virginie, sitting at the counter and gazing worriedly at the emptying containers and drawers, tossed her head furiously. She was keeping her tongue in check for fear of saying more than she ought, but there was something a bit fishy about it all. Lantier saw Nana very often. Oh, she wouldn't take her oath on it, he was capable of even worse, when a bit of skirt caught his fancy. Madame Lerat had that moment walked in, she was very thick just then with Virginie, who was always confiding in her, and she enquired, with that suggestive look of hers:

'In what sense d'you mean saw her?'

'Oh, in the good sense,' replied the hatter, very flattered, laughing and twirling his moustache. 'She was in a carriage and I was splashing along in the road . . . It's true, I swear! No need to get up in arms about it, 'cos those fine young gents who're having it off with her are damn lucky!'

His eyes gleaming, he turned towards Gervaise who was standing in the back of the shop drying a plate.

'Yes, she was in a carriage, and wearing ever such a smart get-up! I didn't recognize her, she looked so much the grand lady, with her pearlies shining in her fresh little rosebud face. But she did give me a tiny wave with her glove . . . I think she's landed a viscount. Oh, she's made it, all right! She can thumb her nose at the lot of us, she's got all she could want and more, the little tramp! What a darling! No, you've never seen anything like that sweet little darling!'

Gervaise was still polishing her plate, although it had long been perfectly clean and shiny. Virginie was thinking anxiously about two bills due the next morning that she didn't see how she could pay, while Lantier, plump and portly and exuding the sugar he lived on, prattled about well-turned-out little sweet-hearts, his enthusiasm bubbling over and filling that fancy food shop which was now almost totally consumed, and where you could smell disaster in the air. Yes, there were only a few pralines left to munch, a few barley sugars left to suck, and the Poissons' business would be completely cleaned out. Suddenly Lantier caught sight of the policeman going past on the opposite pavement; Poisson was doing his rounds, all buttoned up in his uniform with his sword slapping against his thigh. That added to his mirth. He made Virginie look at her husband.

'Well now!' he murmured, 'he looks a bit of a mug this morning, does Badingue! . . . Careful, he's tightening his buttocks too much, he must have stuck a glass eye somewhere up it to catch people out with.'

When Gervaise climbed back upstairs, she found Coupeau sitting in a daze on the edge of the bed; he was in the middle of one of his attacks. He was staring dully at the floor. She herself sank on to a chair, tired in every limb, her hands dangling down her dirty skirt. And she stayed like that, facing him, saying nothing, for a quarter of an hour.

'I've had some news,' she muttered finally. 'Your daughter's been seen . . . Oh, she's ever so posh and doesn't need you any more. Yes, she's bloody all right, she is, that's for sure . . . Christ, what wouldn't I give to be in her shoes!'

Coupeau was still staring at the floor. Then he raised his wreck of a face and, laughing inanely, stammered:

'Well, dearie, don't lemme stop you . . . You still ain't so bad when you clean yourself up. Y'know what they say, there's no pot too old to find its lid . . . Christ, why not, if that'd make life a bit easier!'

CHAPTER XII

It must have been the Saturday after rent day, something like the twelfth or thirteenth of January, Gervaise wasn't really sure. She was going off her nut because it was such ages since she'd had anything warm in her belly. Oh, what a bloody awful week! They were totally cleaned-out: two four-pound loaves on Tuesday that had lasted till Thursday, then a dry crust she'd come across yesterday, and not a crumb for the last thirty-six hours, talk about living on air! One thing she *was* sure of, damn sure, because she could feel it on her back, was that the weather was foul, deathly cold, with a sky as black as the bottom of a frying pan, and heavy with snow that just wouldn't come down. When you can feel both winter and hunger in your guts, you can tighten your belt, but that doesn't do much to fill up your belly.

Perhaps Coupeau would bring home some money that evening. He said he was working. Anything's possible, isn't it? And Gervaise, despite having been taken in so very often, was really counting on Coupeau's money this time. She herself, after all sorts of to-dos, could now no longer find so much as a rag to wash in the neighbourhood; even an old lady she'd been charring for had just given her the sack, accusing her of swigging her liqueurs. Nobody, nowhere, wanted her: she was done for; and deep down this suited her, because she'd been reduced to such a sottish state that she'd rather croak than raise a finger. Anyway, if Coupeau brought home his pay, they'd have something hot to eat. And, while she was waiting, as it wasn't noon yet, she lay there on the mattress, because you feel cold and hunger less when you're lying down.

Gervaise called it the mattress but in actual fact it was only a heap of straw in a corner. Bit by bit their bed had made its way to the neighbourhood second-hand dealers. At first, whenever they were skint, she unpicked the mattress and pulled out handfuls of wool which she then carried off under her apron and sold for ten sous a pound in the Rue Belhomme. Then when the mattress was empty she'd got thirty sous for the cover, to buy herself coffee one morning. The pillows had followed, then the bolster. There remained the wooden bedstead, which she couldn't carry off under her arm because of the Boches who'd have roused the whole building if they'd seen the proprietor's surety disappearing. One evening, though, with the help of Coupeau, she kept an eye till the Boches were feeding their faces and then calmly moved the bed out piece by piece, the sides, the ends and the frame. They were able to stuff themselves for three days on the ten francs from selling that off. Wasn't the palliasse, the under-mattress, quite enough? And even the case for the palliasse had gone the same way as the one for the top mattress, so that they'd eaten up every bit of their bed, and got cramps from wolfing all that bread after being famished for twenty-four hours. They'd give the straw a shove with the broom, so you could say the flea-bag had been turned, and it was no dirtier than everything else.

Gervaise lay curled up on the heap of straw, fully dressed, with her feet tucked under her ragged skirt for warmth. Huddled up like that, her eyes wide open, she was thinking some very gloomy thoughts, that particular day. No, sod it! They couldn't go on like this, living without eating! Her hunger no longer bothered her, but she had a lump of lead in her stomach while her head felt empty. And she certainly couldn't see anything to laugh about when she looked round that wretched hole! A real dog-kennel, now, but one where those greyhounds you see in the streets, wearing coats, wouldn't dream of staying. With lack-lustre eyes she stared at the bare walls. It had all long since gone to uncle. The chest, the table, and one chair were still there, but the chest's marble top and its drawers had vanished by the same route as the wooden part of the bed. A fire couldn't have done a better job of cleaning the place out: the little odds and ends had all melted away, from the ticker—a twelve-franc watch—to the family photos, which a dealer had bought for the frames; a dealer who was ever so obliging, to whom she'd taken a saucepan, an iron, a comb, and who'd dish out five sous, three sous, two sous depending on the object; enough, anyway, so she'd go home with some bread. All that was left now was a broken old pair of candle-snuffers for which the dealer refused her a sou. Oh, if she'd known of someone who'd buy the rubbish, dust, and muck, she'd have quickly set up shop, because the room was such a filthy mess! She could see nothing but spiders' webs in the corners, and spiders' webs may be good for cuts but there still aren't any dealers who buy them. So, turning her head the other way and giving up any hope of finding something to sell, she curled herself up more tightly on her palliasse, preferring to look through the window at the snow-laden sky and the gloomy daylight that chilled the very marrow of her bones.

How bloody awful everything was! What good did it do to get all worked up and worry yourself sick? If only she could get a bit of shut-eye! But this bear-garden, this dump she called home, kept running through her head. Yesterday Monsieur Marescot, the landlord, had himself come to tell them that unless, within the week, they paid the two quarters' rent they owed, he'd turn them out. Oh well, let him turn 'em out, they certainly wouldn't be worse off on the streets! Did you ever see the like of it, that fucking swine with his overcoat and woolly gloves coming up to talk about paying the rent, as if they had a nest-egg tucked away somewhere! Jesus Christ! First thing she'd have done in that case would have been to shove something down her gullet, instead of tightening her belt. He was too fucking mean by half, he was, the fat so-and-so, and she knew where she'd stick him, yes, and right up there too! It was the same with her Coupeau, the stupid sod, who never came home, now, without beating her up; she stuck him in the same place as the landlord. Right now that place of hers must be bloody big, for she shoved everybody up there, she wanted so badly to be shot of 'em all, and of life itself. She was becoming a proper punching-bag. Coupeau had a stick that he called his arse-fanner; you should just have seen him fanning his old woman, he'd go at it something dreadful, and she'd be drenched in sweat afterwards. She wasn't all that nice either, she'd bite and scratch. Then they'd thrash around in the empty room, forgetting, while they slugged it out, that they were hungry. But eventually she got that she didn't give a damn about anything at all, including being beaten. Coupeau could stay away from work for weeks at a time, could go on binges that lasted for months and come home crazed with booze and itching to bash her about, she'd become used to it and thought him a hell of a pest, nothing more. And those were the times that she just shoved him up her arse. Yes, up her arse with her swine of a hubby, up her arse with the Lorilleux, the Boches and the Poissons! Up her arse with all the neighbours that looked down their noses at her! The whole of Paris went in there too, propelled by a little slap, a gesture of complete indifference, although sticking everyone in there did give her a nice feeling of revenge.

Unfortunately, even though you can get used to anything, nobody's yet got into the habit of not eating. That was the only thing that put Gervaise out. She didn't give a damn about being the lowest of the low, right there in the gutter with the riff-raff, and seeing people brush off their clothes when she passed nearby. Bad manners no longer bothered her, whereas hunger still twisted her guts. Oh, she'd said bye-bye to tasty little titbits, she'd come down to wolfing anything she came across. Now, on days when she was living it up, she'd pay the butcher four sous a pound for blackening scraps of meat that had being lying about too long on a tray; she'd put them with a potful of potatoes and slosh the lot around together in the bottom of a pan. Or perhaps she might cook up an ox heart, a dish she really fancied. Other times when she had some wine, she'd give herself a treat and make bread soaked in wine. A couple of sous' worth of liver sausage, a kilo of potatoes, a quarter of dried beans cooked in their liquid were other goodies she couldn't often afford now. She was reduced to buying the messes sold in disreputable eateries, where for a sou she'd get a heap of fish bones mixed up with scraps from a roast that had gone off. She came down lower still, and begged from a kindly restaurant owner the crusts left by his clients, which she made into a bread soup, letting them simmer as long as possible on a neighbour's stove. And on those mornings when she was ravenous she even stooped to prowling about with the dogs near shopkeepers' doors, before the dustmen came along; that was how she sometimes ate rich folk's food, over-ripe melons, mackerel that had gone bad, cutlets she'd have to examine for maggots. Yes, she'd sunk that low; finicky people find the idea revolting, but if those finicky people hadn't had even a crumb to eat for three days we'd soon see if they'd ignore their bellies, no, they'd be down on all fours and eating refuse like the others. Oh! The poor dying of starvation, their hollow bellies groaning with hunger as they cram unspeakably foul things between their chattering teeth like so many desperate animals, in this great golden city of Paris that blazes with light! And to think that Gervaise had once stuffed herself on fat goose! Now she'd just have to manage without. One day, when Coupeau had pinched two bread tokens from her and sold them for booze, she'd almost done him in with a blow from a shovel, she'd been so famished and enraged by this theft of a bit of bread.

Meanwhile, through staring at the pallid sky, she dropped off into a restless little doze. Because the cold was so biting she dreamt that the heavy sky was emptying its snow out on to her. Suddenly she jumped to her feet, startled into wakefulness by a terrible spasm of anguish. God! Was she going to die? Hollow-eyed and shivering, she saw it was still daylight. Night would never come! How slowly time passes when you've nothing in your belly! Her stomach was waking up as well, and torturing her. She sat slumped on a chair, with her head down and her hands between her thighs for warmth, already planning what she'd get for dinner as soon as Coupeau brought the money: bread, wine, and two portions of tripe fried with onions. Three o'clock struck on old Bazouge's cuckoo clock. It was only three. She burst into tears. She'd never have the strength to wait till seven. She sat doubled up, squeezing her stomach so she would no longer feel it, rocking her whole body to and fro like a little girl trying to lull a very bad pain. Oh, childbirth's easier to bear than hunger! And, finding no relief, she stood up and stamped in a fury round the room, hoping to settle her hunger as one settles a baby by walking it around. For half an hour she charged about from corner to corner in the empty room. Then, all of a sudden, she stopped, her eyes intent. What the hell! They could say whatever they liked, she'd lick their boots if they wanted, but she was going to borrow ten sous from the Lorilleux.

In winter, on that staircase of the building, the have-nots' staircase, people were forever borrowing ten sous here, twenty there—little favours the starving did one another. But they'd all sooner die than ask the Lorilleux, who were known to be too close-fisted. Gervaise showed great courage, going to knock at their door. She was so frightened in the corridor that she felt a sudden sense of relief as she knocked, just as people do when they knock at the dentist's door.

'Come in!' called the chain-maker in his testy voice.

How lovely it was in there! The forge was blazing away, its bright fire lighting up the cramped workshop where Madame Lorilleux was setting a ball of gold wire to reheat. Lorilleux, seated at his work-bench, was so hot he was sweating as he soldered links with his blowpipe. And there was a nice smell, some cabbage soup was simmering on the stove, giving off an aroma that turned Gervaise's stomach and made her feel faint.

'Oh, it's you,' muttered Madame Lorilleux, not even asking her to sit down. 'What d'you want?'

Gervaise didn't reply. That week things weren't too bad between her and the Lorilleux. But the request for ten sous stuck in her throat, because she'd just noticed Boche nicely settled beside the stove, enjoying a good gossip. What a nerve the bastard had! An arsehole—that's what he looked like when he laughed, with his mouth a round hole and his cheeks so puffed out they hid his nose; yes, an arsehole, exactly!

'What d'you want?' repeated Lorilleux.

'You haven't seen Coupeau?' Gervaise finally stammered. 'I thought he was here.'

The chain-makers and the concierge all laughed unpleasantly. No, of course not, they hadn't seen Coupeau. They weren't free enough with the drink to see much of Coupeau. Gervaise pulled herself together and managed to stammer:

'It's just that he'd promised me he'd come home . . . Yes, he's going to bring me some money . . . And as there's something I absolutely must get . . .'

A heavy silence had fallen. Madame Lorilleux was vigorously fanning the forge, Lorilleux had lowered his head over the bit of chain that was growing between his fingers, while Boche still grinned like a full moon, his mouth such a round hole that it made you want to stick your finger in there, to see.

'If I just had ten sous,' Gervaise mumbled in a low voice.

The silence continued.

'I suppose you couldn't lend me ten sous? . . . Oh, I'd give 'em back this evening!'

Madame Lorilleux turned round and gave her a hard stare. Trying to get round them with her wheedling, was she! She'd touch 'em for ten sous today and tomorrow it would be twenty, there'd be nothing to stop her, ever. No, thank you very much. Maybe Tuesday, if the moon is blue!

'But my dear,' she cried, 'you know very well we've no money! Here, look in my pocket. Search us if you want . . . We'd be only too willing, naturally.'

'We're always willing,' grunted Lorilleux, 'only, if you can't, you can't.'

Very humbly, Gervaise nodded in agreement. However she didn't leave, she was casting sidelong glances at the gold, at the coils of gold hanging on the walls, at the gold wire the wife was pulling through the drawplate with all the strength of her short arms, at the gold links heaped under the knotty fingers of the husband. And she was thinking that one little bit of that ugly black metal would be enough to buy her a good dinner. That day it didn't matter how dirty the workshop looked, with its old iron tools, its coal dust and its grime from carelessly wiped oil spills, in her eyes it seemed to glow with riches like some money-changer's shop. So she dared to say again, in a gentle voice:

'I'd pay it back, I'd pay it back, of course I would . . . Ten sous, that wouldn't put you out.'

With a lump in her throat she struggled not to tell them that she'd had nothing to eat since yesterday. Then, feeling her legs giving way beneath her and afraid she'd burst into tears, she once again stammered out:

'It would be so kind of you . . . You can't have any idea . . . My God, what have I come to, what have I come to . . .'

At that the two Lorilleux pursed their lips and exchanged a little look. Now Banban was actually begging! Well, her come-down was complete. Begging—that was something they really didn't hold with. If they'd known they'd have bolted their door, because you must always be on your guard with beggars, who find some excuse to get into your home and then make off with your valuables. And all the more in their case as they did have something worth stealing; you could put your fingers down anywhere and carry off thirty or forty francs' worth simply by closing your fist. They'd had their doubts several times already on noticing Gervaise's funny expression when she stood staring at the gold. This time they really were going to keep an eye on her. And as she was coming closer, so she was standing on the wooden slats, the chain-maker shouted at her brusquely, giving no further answer to her entreaty:

'Now then, watch what you're doing, you'll be carrying off bits of gold on your soles again . . . Really, anybody'd think you'd got grease on them to make things stick.'

Gervaise slowly retreated. She'd leant on a shelf for a second, and seeing that Madame Lorilleux was examining her hands, she opened them very wide and showed them, saying softly, not getting angry, like someone who's fallen so low she'll submit to anything:

'I haven't taken anything, you can look.'

And she went out, because the strong smell of the cabbage soup and the lovely warmth of the workshop were making her feel too ill.

There wasn't much danger the Lorilleux would ask her to stay! Good riddance, and the devil take 'em if they ever let *her* in again! They'd seen quite enough of her face, and they'd no wish to have other people's misery in their home, especially when that misery was well deserved. And they settled down to an orgy of self-satisfied enjoyment—weren't they clever, and wasn't it nice and cosy, with that wonderful soup to look forward to. Boche too was showing off, and puffing out his cheeks even more, so that his laugh was quite unsavoury. They all felt they'd well and truly got their own back on Banban for her former fancy ways, her blue shop, her great spreads and all the rest. It was too perfect, it just showed where a love of grub could land you. Let's sling out all the greedy-guts, the lazy-bones and the floozies!

'What d'you think of that! Coming here and begging ten sous!' said Madame Lorilleux the minute Gervaise's back was turned. 'Yes, fat chance I'd lend her ten sous just like that so she could go and get herself a nip or two of booze!'

With heavy limbs and bowed shoulders Gervaise shuffled down the passage. When she reached her own door she didn't go in, her room frightened her. It was better to walk, she'd feel warmer and get through the time better. She peered into Père Bru's little nook under the stairs as she went past; there was someone else who must have a good appetite as it was three days since he'd had anything but memories for lunch or dinner; however he wasn't there, there was just his hole, and she felt a pang of jealousy, imagining that perhaps he'd been invited somewhere. Then, hearing moaning as she came up to the Bijards', she went in; the key, as usual, was in the lock.

'What's the matter?' she asked.

The room was very clean. It was clear that Lalie had swept the floor and tidied everything that very morning. Even though the wind of poverty blew through there, carrying off clothes and depositing its endless load of filth, Lalie still followed on behind, cleaning everything and making the place look nice. Her home might not be a rich one but you could tell it was well looked after. That day the two children, Henriette and Jules, were in a corner, quietly cutting out some old pictures they'd found. But Gervaise was amazed to find Lalie lying in her narrow trestle bed, very pale, with the sheet up to her chin. Lalie in bed, whatever next! She must be really ill!

'What's the matter?' Gervaise repeated anxiously.

Lalie was no longer moaning. She slowly raised her pale lids and tried to form her pain-racked lips into a smile.

'It's nothing,' she whispered very softly, 'oh, really, it's nothing at all.'

Then, closing her eyes again she said with an effort:

'All these last days I've felt so terribly tired, so I'm being lazy, I'm coddling myself, you see.'

But her childish face, covered in livid blotches, had taken on such an expression of unbearable agony that Gervaise, forgetting her own suffering, clasped her hands together and fell on her knees beside her. For a month now she'd been seeing Lalie lean against the wall when she walked, doubled up by a cough that had a graveyard ring to it. The child couldn't even cough any more. She gave a kind of hiccup, and trickles of blood seeped from the corners of her mouth.

'I can't help it, I don't feel at all strong,' she whispered, as if relieved by the admission. 'I did manage to get round and tidy up a bit . . . It's clean enough, isn't it? And I wanted to wash the windows, but my legs gave out. Isn't it silly! Well, anyway, when you've finished your work, you go to bed.'

She broke off to say:

'Please watch to see my babies don't cut themselves with their scissors.'

She stopped talking and began to tremble, listening to a heavy step coming up the stairs. Père Bijard abruptly thrust the door open. As always, he'd been at the bottle, and his eyes were blazing with a frenzied alcoholic rage. When he caught sight of Lalie lying in bed he slapped his thighs, gave a nasty laugh and, unhooking the big whip, growled:

'Bloody hell, this beats anything! We're gonna have some fun! . . . So now we're lazin' about in the middle of the day, are we! Are you takin' the Mickey out of us all, eh, you bleedin' slug-abed? C'mon, ups-a-daisy, out of there!'

He was already cracking the whip over the bed. But the child kept imploring him:

'No, Papa, I beg you, don't hit me . . . You'd be sorry, I'm certain you'd be sorry . . . Don't hit me.'

'Get movin', will you,' he yelled more loudly, 'or I'll tickle your ribs . . . C'mon, get movin', you fuckin' bitch!'

Then she said softly:

'I can't, d'you see? I'm going to die.'

Gervaise had flung herself at Bijard and grabbed the whip from him. Stunned, he stood there beside the bed. Whatever was the kid carrying on about? Who ever heard of dying as young as that, when you hadn't even been ill! It must be a trick to get herself given something nice. Well, he was going to find out, and if she was lying . . .

'It's true, you'll see,' she went on. 'I tried not to bother anybody, as long as I could . . . But now please be nice, and say goodbye to me, Papa.'

Bijard was pulling at his nose, afraid of being had. Still, it was true that her face looked funny, very long and serious, like that of an adult. The presence of death could be felt in the room, and was sobering him up. Like a man awakening from a long sleep, he gazed all round and saw how tidy the place was, with the two children nice and clean, laughing as they played. And he sank on to a chair, stammering:

'Our little mother, our little mother . . .'

That was all he could find to say, but for Lalie, who'd never been so indulged, it sounded very loving. She comforted her father. What bothered her most was having to go like this before she could finish bringing up her children. He'd take care of them, wouldn't he? And with her dying voice she gave him details on how to dress them and keep them clean. Quite stupefied, he'd sunk back into his alcoholic daze and rolled his head about, round-eyed, watching Lalie die. It was stirring up all sorts of memories in him but he could no longer pin anything down and his hide was so tough he couldn't cry.

'There's something else,' Lalie went on after a silence. 'We owe the baker four francs seven sous, you'll have to settle that . . . Madame Gaudron has an iron of ours you'd better get back . . . For this evening I couldn't make any soup but there's some bread left and you can warm up the potatoes . . .'

Right up to her last breath that poor sweet love never stopped being a little mother to her family. Lalie was someone who could never be replaced, that much was certain! She was dying because, though only a child, she had the heart and mind of a true mother, while her breast was still too frail and small to bear such a heavy burden of maternity. And it was certainly the fault of that ferocious brute her father, if he was losing this treasure. After kicking the mother to death, hadn't he now just murdered the daughter! His two good angels would be in their graves, and there'd be nothing left for him to do but die like a dog on some street corner.

Gervaise, meanwhile, was trying her best not to burst into tears. She reached out with her hands, wanting to comfort Lalie, and as the ragged sheet was slipping off she pulled it right down, intending to remake the bed. The poor little body of the dying child was thus exposed. Lord Jesus, what a heart-rending, pitiable sight! The stones themselves would have wept. Lalie was quite naked, with only the remnants of a bodice round her shoulders to serve as a nightgown; yes, quite naked, the nakedness of a martyr, bleeding and tortured. There was no longer any flesh on her, her bones poked through her skin. From her ribs to her thighs thin purple weals reached down, where the whip's bite had left its vivid imprint. A blue-black bruise circled her left arm, as if the jaws of a vice had crushed this delicate limb, no thicker than a matchstick. On her right leg there was a gash that hadn't healed, some nasty wound that must have reopened each morning as she hurried round doing her chores. She was nothing but a bruise from head to toe. Oh, what butchery of childhood—that dear little chick crushed under a man's heavy foot; what infamy—that feeblest of creatures dying under the burden of such a cross! People in churches venerate martyred virgins whose naked flesh is not so pure. Gervaise had crouched down again, forgetting to pull up the sheet, overcome by the sight of this pitiful nothing, lying there sunk into the bed, as, with trembling lips, she tried to say some prayers.

'Please, Madame Coupeau . . .' whispered the child.

In her great modesty, and full of shame for her father's sake, she was trying to pull up the sheet with her short little arms. Bijard stood there stupidly, staring at the corpse he was responsible for, and rolling his head about slowly like an animal that's bothered by something.

Gervaise, after she'd covered Lalie up, could stay no more. The dying child was growing weaker and now was no longer speaking; all she had left was that gaze of hers, that familiar dark gaze, pensive and resigned, that she'd fixed on her two little ones who were cutting out their pictures. In the room the shadows were lengthening, and Bijard, bewildered by Lalie's death, sat there dozing off his hangover. No, no, life was too abominable! How foul, how unspeakably foul! And Gervaise went out of the room and down the stairs without knowing what she was doing, in such a state, so overwhelmed by how bloody life was that she'd gladly have flung herself under the wheels of an omnibus, to end it all.

As she ran along, railing against the hellishness of fate, she found herself at the door of the place where Coupeau said he was working. Her legs had taken her there, and her stomach was starting up again, intoning its never-ending lament for hunger, a lament she knew by heart. This way, if she caught Coupeau on the way out, she'd get her hands on the cash and she'd be able to buy food. Just an hour to wait at the most, she could easily stand that, she who'd been sucking her thumbs since yesterday.

She was at the corner of the Rue de la Charbonnière and the Rue de Chartres, a god-awful crossroads where the wind blew from every direction. Jesus! It wasn't exactly warm, walking up and down that road. Not so bad if you had some furs! The sky was still a nasty leaden colour and the snow collecting up there had covered the whole neighbourhood with a sheet of ice. Nothing was coming down, but a heavy silence filled the air, preparing a fancy-dress costume for Paris, a pretty ballgown, white and new. Gervaise raised her head, begging the good Lord not to let His white muslin come down just then. She stamped her feet, looking at a grocer's shop across the road, then turned round because it was silly to get too hungry, too soon. There wasn't anything at the crossroads worth looking at. The few passers-by, enveloped in scarves, hurried by, because obviously you don't hang about when the cold's nipping your bum. However Gervaise did notice four or five other women who were keeping guard as she was at the master-roofer's door; they must be poor wretches like herself, wives on the watch for the pay-packet so as to stop it vanishing into the boozer. There was a great tall, skinny woman with a face like a policeman's, who'd flattened herself against the wall, ready to jump out and collar her man. A small, very dark girl, with a meek, frail air, was walking about on the other side of the road. Then there was another, ungainly-looking woman, who'd brought her two little tots and was dragging them along, shivering and crying, on either side of her. And they all, Gervaise and her fellow sentries, passed each other again and again, exchanging sidelong glances but never speaking. A really delightful get-together, oh yes, not half! They didn't need to make each other's acquaintance, they already knew every detail. They were all in the same boat, a boat called Hunger and Cold. It made you feel even colder, watching them tramping to and fro and passing each other in silence, in that terrible January weather.

Meanwhile not so much as a cat had emerged from the door. In the end, however, a workman did show up, followed by two, and then three; but those were probably good chaps, who faithfully took home their wages, for they shook their heads when they saw the shadowy figures prowling round the workshop. The tall, skinny woman flattened herself even more into the wall beside the door; all of a sudden she pounced on a peaky-looking little man who was cautiously sticking his head out. It was all over in a jiffy! She'd frisked him and raked in the cash. Nabbed, no more lolly, won't get a drop to drink! So, mortified and despairing, the little man went off behind his policeman, weeping big, childish tears. Workmen were still appearing, and as the large woman with the two kids had come closer, a tall, dark, crafty-looking man shot back inside on seeing her, to warn her husband; so that when the latter came strutting out, he'd stowed away two lovely new five-franc coins—rear coach-wheels, they're known as—one in each shoe. He picked up one of his kids and walked off, cooking up some rubbish or other to tell his nagging wife. There were some cheerful chaps who bounded into the street, rushing away to blew their wages on a meal with their mates. And some had very long faces and looked in a bad way, as they clenched their fists tightly over the three or four days' money they'd earned in a fortnight, calling themselves lazy buggers and making drunkards' promises. But the saddest sight was the distress of the dark little woman, the meek, frail one: her chap, a real good looker, had raced off under her very nose, passing by her so roughly that he'd nearly knocked her down; and, all alone, she walked off unsteadily past the shops, her face streaming with tears.

The procession had finally come to an end. Gervaise stood in the middle of the road watching the entrance. Things were beginning to look bad. Two more workers showed up belatedly, but still no Coupeau. And when she asked the men if Coupeau was coming out they jokingly replied—for they knew what was going on—that he'd nipped out the back way that very minute with old So-and-so to see about this and that. Gervaise understood. Another of Coupeau's lies, and she could just go and take a running jump! Trailing along in her worn-out shoes she went slowly down the Rue de la Charbonnière. Her dinner was running away in front of her, and she gave a little shiver as, in the yellow twilight, she watched it disappear. This time, it was all over. Not a bean, nothing to hope for, nothing but night and hunger. And what a perfect night to croak, a night as vile as this one that was closing in round her now!

She was dragging herself up the Rue des Poissonniers when she heard Coupeau's voice. Yes, there he was in the Petite-Civette, being stood a drink by Mes-Bottes. That joker Mes-Bottes, towards the end of the summer, had actually managed to get himself married—yes, really and truly married—to a lady who was well past her prime but even so still quite an eyeful; and she was a lady from the Rue des Martyrs, furthermore, not one of your local floozies. You should just have seen the lucky devil, living like the idle rich with his hands in his pockets, well-dressed and well-fed. He'd grown so fat you could hardly recognize him. The chaps said that his wife got as much work as she wanted from the gentlemen of her acquaintance. A wife like that and a house in the country, what more could anyone wish for to make life agreeable! So Coupeau kept giving Mes-Bottes little admiring glances. Why the bleeder was even wearing a gold ring on his little finger!

Gervaise put her hand on Coupeau's shoulder just as he was coming out of the Petite-Civette.

'See here, I'm still waiting . . . I'm hungry. Aren't you going to give me any money?'

But he shut her up in no uncertain fashion.

'Hungry, are you? Well eat your fist! . . . And keep the other one for tomorrow.'

What a pain in the neck she was, making a fuss like that in front of other people. Well, OK, so what! He hadn't been working, but the bakers had baked bread just the same. She must think he was some kind of sissy, trying to lean on him like that with her gripes.

'So you want me to steal,' she muttered in a dull voice.

Mes-Bottes was stroking his chin in a conciliatory way.

'No, no, that's prohibited,' he said. 'But when a wife knows how to make the best of herself . . .'

Coupeau interrupted him to shout 'Bravo!'. Yes, a wife should know how to make the best of herself. But his had always been a wreck, a mess. It would be her fault if they croaked in the gutter. Then he went back to singing Mes-Bottes' praises. What a dandy the bastard was! Looked just like a landlord, he did, with his white linen and natty dress shoes! Damn it! Nothing cheap or trashy about him! At any rate here was one chap whose old lady was a good manager!

The two men were making for the outer boulevard. Gervaise followed them. After a silence she said again, from behind Coupeau:

'I'm hungry, y'know . . . I was counting on you. You've got to find me something to fill me gut.'

He didn't answer, and she repeated in a heart-rending tone:

'So, ain't you going to give me any money?'

'For Christ's sake, I've not got any!' he screamed, turning round in a fury.

'Leave me alone, d'you hear? Or I'll fetch you one.'

He was already raising his fist. She shrank away, then, apparently, made up her mind.

'All right, I'll leave you alone, I'll get myself a man.'

At that, the roofer gave a laugh. He pretended to take it as a joke, but was goading her on without seeming to. Now that really was a terrific idea! At night, by lamplight, she could still make a catch. If she got off with someone, he recommended the Capucin, which had little private rooms where they served a smashing dinner. And as she was setting off along the outer boulevard, pale and wild-eyed, he shouted again:

'Listen, bring me back some dessert, I'm fond o' cakes . . . An' if your gent's well-turned out, ask him for an old coat, that'd do me fine.'

Gervaise walked fast, pursued by this infernal gabbing. Then, when she found herself alone in the middle of the crowd, she slowed down. She was quite determined. Between stealing and doing that, she preferred doing that, because at least she wouldn't be hurting anyone. She wasn't going to dispose of anything that wasn't hers. Of course it wasn't at all nice, but just now what was and what wasn't nice were all mixed up in her noddle; when you're dying of hunger you don't natter about philosophy, you eat what comes to hand. She'd walked back up to the Chaussée Clignancourt. Night was taking forever to fall. So, while she waited, she strolled along the boulevards, like a lady enjoying the air before going home for supper.

This district, which was becoming so splendid that she now felt uncomfortable in it, was being opened up to the air in every direction. The Boulevard Magenta which led up from the heart of Paris and the Boulevard Ornano which stretched on out into the country had left a hole behind them where the city wall used to stand, marked by a great mass of demolished houses; these two vast avenues, still white with plaster dust, were closely flanked by the Rue du Faubourg-Poissonnière and the Rue des Poissonniers. The latter were cropped and scarred at the points where they joined the boulevards, and twisted away as dark, serpentine alleys. The demolition of the octroi wall had long since widened the outer boulevards, with pavements on the sides and a central strip for pedestrians, planted with four rows of small plane trees. It was now a huge crossing leading to the distant horizon, along interminable streets that swarmed with people; everywhere there was chaos from the building operations. But, alongside the tall new houses, many rickety shacks were still standing; between the carved façades there remained blackened gaps where jumbled hovels flaunted their dilapidated windows. Beneath the ever-increasing luxury of Paris the dreadful poverty of the slums forced itself upon the eye, defiling these sites where the new city was being so hastily erected.

Lost among the people thronging the broad pavement beneath the young plane trees, Gervaise felt alone and abandoned. Those glimpses of the distant avenues made her feel even emptier; and to think that in all this crowd of people, which surely must include some who were well-off, there wasn't one Christian soul who would guess at her plight and slip ten sous into her hand! Yes, it was all too grand and too fine, her head was spinning and her legs buckling under her, beneath this enormous expanse of grey sky that stretched out over such a vast space. The twilight was that dirty-yellow colour typical of Parisian twilights, a colour which makes you long to die that very instant, so ugly is the life of the streets. It was that uncertain time of day when distant prospects merge together in a murky haze. Gervaise, already worn out, had reached there just when the workers were returning home. At this point in the evening the ladies wearing hats and the well-dressed gentlemen who lived in the new houses were swallowed up by the crowds of workers, processions of men and women still pasty-faced from the bad air of the workshops. Band upon band of them surged out from the Boulevard Magenta and the Rue du Faubourg-Poissonnière, catching their breath after the climb. Surrounded by the muffled rumbling of omnibuses and cabs, amid the drays and closed wagons and carts that were galloping home empty, an ever-growing stream of smocks and overalls covered the road. Porters were going home, their luggage hooks over their shoulders. Two workers walking side by side were taking great strides, talking loudly and gesticulating but not looking at each other; others, all alone, wearing coats and caps and keeping their eyes down, walked along the edge of the pavement; others came in groups of five or six, following close behind one another but never exchanging a word, their eyes bleary, their hands in their pockets. The odd one had an unlit pipe clenched between his teeth. Four masons had hired a cab between them; their hods bounced about on its roof and as it passed you could glimpse their pale faces through the door-curtains. Painters were swinging their paint-pots; a roofer was carrying a long ladder and nearly poking people's eyes out with it; a tardy fountain workman, his tool-box on his back, came along playing the 'Good King Dagobert'* on his little trumpet, a melancholy air that rose up from the disconsolate twilight shadows. Oh, such a sad tune it was, just the thing to accompany the herd as it trampled past, as the beasts of burden dragged themselves along in their exhaustion! Another day ended! But in truth the days were long and began again too often. There was barely time to fill your belly and to sleep off your meal, it was daylight again, it was time to take up the yoke of poverty once more. But even so, strapping young fellows whistled and stamped their feet down smartly as they raced past, their faces turned towards supper. And Gervaise, heedless of being bumped into and jostled from left and right, borne along in the middle of the stream, let the mob flow past her, for men have no time to be polite when they're deathly tired and driven by hunger.

Suddenly, looking up, the laundress saw the former Hôtel Boncœur in front of her. The little building had become a shady café and been closed by the police; it now stood empty, its shutters covered with posters and its lantern broken, its entire façade crumbling and rotting away in the rain, its filthy, wine-coloured paint mouldering. And nothing in the area seemed to have changed. The stationer's and the tobacconist's were still there. Behind you could still see, above the low buildings, the scabrous fronts of some five-storey houses whose tall, dilapidated silhouettes reached up into the sky. The only thing that had gone was the Grand-Balcon dance-hall; in the hall where the ten windows used to blaze with light, a loaf sugar-cutting business had just been started and you could hear the continuous whirring sound coming from it. Yet it was there, in that wretched dump the Hôtel Boncœur, that this bloody life of hers had begun. She stood there staring at the first-floor window where a broken shutter hung down, remembering her youth with Lantier, their first rows, and the disgusting way he'd walked out on her. No matter, she'd been young then and it all seemed quite fun, looked at from afar. God, only twenty years, and here she was on the streets. The sight of the building upset her and she climbed back up the boulevard in the direction of Montmartre.

In the gathering darkness there were kids still playing on the heaps of sand between the benches. The procession continued, with working girls going past at the double, hurrying to make up time spent staring at shop windows; there was a tall one who'd stopped, her hand still held by a youth who was accompanying her to within three doors of her home; others as they said goodbye were arranging to meet later that evening at the Grand Salon de la Folie or the Boule Noire. In the groups there'd be an occasional jobbing tailor, making his way home with his delivery bag folded under his arm. A stove-setter, strapped into a harness and pulling a barrow loaded with rubble, was almost crushed under an omnibus. Now, in the lessening crowd, there were hatless women who'd come back down after lighting the fire and were hurrying to get the dinner; they pushed past people, rushing into the baker's and the pork-butcher's and setting off home again without delay, carrying their shopping. There were little eight-year-old girls who'd been sent on errands, wandering along past the shops and hugging to their chests great four-pound loaves, as tall as themselves, that looked like lovely yellow dolls; they'd forget, for five minutes at a time, what they were supposed to be doing as they gazed at some picture, one cheek resting on the big loaf of bread. Then the stream became thinner and the groups less frequent as the workers reached home; and under the flaring gaslight, now the day was ended, sloth and self-indulgence were rousing themselves and beginning their long-suppressed revenge.

Ah, yes, Gervaise's day was ended! She was more weary than all that mass of workers who'd pushed her about as they went past. She might as well lie down there and croak, for work no longer wanted her, and she'd toiled hard enough in her lifetime to say: 'Who's next? Me, I'm all in.' At this hour everyone was eating. It really was the end, the sun had blown out its candle and the night would be a long one. My God! To stretch out comfortably and never get up again, to know you've laid down your tools for good and can laze about for all eternity! Now that'd be a bit of all-right, after wearing yourself to death for twenty years! And Gervaise, her guts twisted by hunger cramps, couldn't stop herself remembering the red-letter days, the binges, and the good times she'd had in her life. There was one day in particular, a mid-Lent Thursday that was bitter cold, when she'd had the most marvellous fun. In those days she'd looked so pretty, so fair-haired and young. Her wash-house in the Rue Neuve had chosen her as queen, in spite of her leg. So they'd larked about on the boulevards in carts decorated with greenery, in amongst all those nobs who weren't half giving her the glad eye. The gents had brought out their monocles, as if she was a real queen. In the evening they'd had one hell of a blow-out, and then had danced till daybreak. Queen, yes, queen, with a crown and a sash, for twenty-four hours, twice round the clock! And, tormented by her hunger, she stared in bewilderment at the ground, as if searching for the gutter into which her lost majesty had fallen.

She raised her eyes again. Now she was in front of the slaughterhouses that were being demolished; their façade had been torn away, revealing dark and stinking courtyards still damp with blood. And on reaching the bottom of the boulevard, she could also see the Lariboisière Hospital with its high grey wall, above which the building's gloomy wings with their evenly spaced windows fanned out; there was a door in the wall that terrified the locals, the door of the dead, made of solid oak without a crack, implacable and silent as a tombstone. So to get away from there she went on, right down as far as the railway bridge. The tall parapets of heavy bolted sheet metal hid the line from her view; all she could see was the wide angle formed by the station's huge roof,* black with coal-dust, against the brilliant Paris skyline; she could hear, across that enormous empty space, the whistle of engines and the rhythmic jolting of turntables, a whole vast, hidden world of activity. Then a train came by on its way out of Paris, puffing along, its rumbling gradually getting louder. She didn't see the train, only a white plume of smoke that suddenly spouted up round the parapet and then vanished. But the bridge had been shaken and she could still feel the momentum from this departure at full speed. She turned round as if to follow the now invisible engine as its roar died away. Looking from that side Gervaise fancied she saw country and open sky, through a gap between some tall, isolated houses that rose up haphazardly to left and right, and whose unplastered façades and walls, some with enormous advertisements painted on them, had all been turned the same dirty yellow by the soot from the engines. Oh, if only she could have gone away, gone far away, away from these dwelling-places of poverty and suffering! Perhaps she would have begun to live again. Then she found she'd been automatically reading the posters stuck on the parapet. They were in every colour. A pretty little blue one offered a reward of fifty francs for a lost dog. Now there was an animal that must have been loved!

Slowly, Gervaise set off again. Gaslights were being lit as the foggy, smoke-laden darkness fell; and the long avenues that had been gradually disappearing into the engulfing blackness were re-emerging aglow with light, stretching out and streaking through the night as far as the dimly shadowed horizon. You could feel a great breath of life as the neighbourhood staked out its increased size with cordons of little flames, under the huge moonless sky. It was now that the line of bars, sleazy dance-halls and bawdy-houses stretching from end to end of the boulevards blazed brightly, lighting up the good cheer of the first drinks and the first dances. The fortnightly pay-day filled the pavement with jostling groups of idlers looking for a good time. There was a feeling in the air that made you think of binges, terrific binges, but nothing nasty yet, just getting a bit lit up, nothing more. In the small cafés people were sitting stuffing; through the lighted windows you could see them eating their supper, their mouths full, laughing without even bothering to swallow. In the bars the pisspots were already settling in, shouting and gesticulating. The noise was tremendous, a din in which voices—some yapping, some oily—could be heard above the non-stop drumming of feet on the pavement. 'Oy! You comin' for a nosh? . . . Get a move on, you lazy bum, I'm buyin' a round o' the best . . . Hey, there's Pauline! Now for a good laugh!' The doors swung wide, letting out fumes of wine and snatches of airs played on the cornet. People were queuing up outside old Colombe's Assommoir, which was lit like a cathedral for High Mass, and, my God, you'd have thought there really was a mass going on, for the chaps were singing away in there looking exactly like choristers, with puffed-out cheeks and rounded bellies. They were celebrating

Saint Pay-Day, a very kind saint, who must look after the till
in paradise. Only, seeing with what zest it was all getting going,
the solid citizens out for a stroll with the wife shook their heads,
remarking that there'd be an awful lot of drunks in Paris that
night. And above all the racket stretched the night, black, still
and icy-cold, broken only by the blazing lines of the boulevards
leading out towards the four corners of the sky.

Gervaise stood there in front of the Assommoir, deep in
thought. If she'd had a couple of sous, she'd have gone in for
a quick one. Maybe a tot would have taken the edge off her
hunger. Oh, she'd downed plenty of tots in her day! And she
certainly liked it. And, from afar, she stared at the booze
machine, feeling that it was the source of her misfortune and
dreaming of doing herself in with brandy when she had the
necessary. But the chill air ruffled her hair and she saw that the
night was very dark. Come on, it was now or never. This was
the moment to have some guts and make 'em think she was
nice, if she didn't want to croak right there in the midst of all
these high jinks. Especially as watching other people stuffing
themselves didn't exactly fill her belly. She slowed down again
and looked round. The shadows lingering under the trees were
deeper. The passers-by were few, and walked very briskly,
hurrying down the boulevard. And, on this wide, dark, deserted
pavement, where the sounds of revelry from nearby streets died
away, women were standing, waiting. They'd stay there for
minutes at a time, never stirring, as patient and upright as the
meagre little plane trees; then, slowly, they'd move off, dragging their worn shoes over the frozen ground, walking ten paces
then stopping again as if rooted to the spot. One woman with
a yellow scarf on her head had an enormous body and insect-
like arms and legs: she was rolling along, overflowing her
tattered, black silk dress; another creature, tall, dried-up,
bare-headed, was wearing a servant's apron; and then there
were still more of them, some old and tarted-up, some young
and very dirty, so dirty, so squalid that not even a rag-and-bone
man would have given them a second look. Meanwhile Gervaise, not knowing how to set about it, tried to learn by doing
what they did. Her heart in her mouth, she felt as agitated as a
child; she couldn't tell whether she was ashamed, for it all

seemed like a horrible dream. For a quarter of an hour she stood there, very upright. Men hurried along without turning round. So then she roused herself, and found the nerve to accost a man who was passing by with his hands in his pockets, whistling; her voice hoarse, she whispered:

'Excuse me, Sir . . .'

The man gave her a sidelong glance and continued on his way, whistling more loudly.

Then Gervaise grew bolder. She forgot to be self-conscious in the desperation of this chase as, with empty belly, she doggedly pursued her ever-elusive supper. For a long while she roamed around, unaware of time and place. All round her the silent dark figures of the women marched about beneath the trees, confining their movements to those of caged animals pacing back and forth. They'd emerge from the shadows with the uncertain slowness of a ghost; they'd pass into the sudden light of a lamp-post, where their wan, mask-like features would loom into clear view, then they'd vanish once more, reclaimed by the darkness, the white edge of a petticoat swinging as they slipped back into the disturbing, enticing shadows of the pavement. Some men let themselves be stopped and just for fun would have a chat, then go on their way, laughing. Others would set off unobtrusively, keeping ten discreet paces behind a woman. Coarse murmured exchanges could be heard, and quarrelling in hushed tones, and fierce bargaining followed by sudden, total silence. And Gervaise, no matter how far she walked, could see these women sentries spaced out through the night as if the outer boulevards had been planted with women from end to end.

Twenty paces away from one she could always see another. The line of them went on forever, the whole of Paris was guarded by them. Exasperated at being ignored she kept changing her position, finally moving from the Chaussée de Clignancourt to the Grande Rue de la Chapelle.

'Excuse me, Sir . . .'

But the men passed by. She moved away from the slaughter-houses, with their rubble that stank of blood. She gave the former Hôtel Boncœur, closed and disreputable-looking, a quick glance. She walked along the front of the Lariboisière

Hospital, automatically counting the lighted windows in the façades, windows that glowed pale and calm like so many night-lights for the dying. She crossed the railway bridge as the trains jolted past, rumbling and rending the air with the desperate screech of their whistles. Oh, how sad night made it all seem! Then she turned on her heels and again let her eyes pass over those same buildings and that same sweep of this end of the avenue; she did this ten, twenty times, without let-up, without resting for one moment on a bench. No, nobody wanted her. It seemed to her that this contempt made her shame the greater. Once more she walked down towards the Hospital and up towards the slaughterhouses. This was her final walk, between the blood-drenched yards where the slaughtering went on and the dimly-lit wards where death laid out your stiffened corpse in a common shroud. That space had encompassed her life.

'Excuse me, Sir . . .'

Suddenly, she noticed her shadow on the ground. When she came near a lamp-post the blurry shadow would concentrate and sharpen, becoming a huge, squat mass, so round it looked grotesque. It would spread out, the belly, breasts and rump sliding and flowing into each other. She was limping so badly that the shadow did a somersault at every step: a real clown! Then when she moved away the clown would grow larger, gigantic, filling the boulevard, making bows that hit its nose against the trees and the houses. Christ! How comic and how frightening she looked! She'd never so completely grasped how far she'd come down. So then she couldn't stop herself watching it, waiting for each gas-lamp and following the antics of her shadow. Oh, what a fine floozie she'd got walking beside her! What a sight! That must really draw the men! And she lowered her voice, not daring to do more than mumble at the backs of passers-by.

'Excuse me, Sir . . .'

But it must be getting very late. Things were becoming unsavoury, now, in the neighbourhood. The little cafés were closed and in the bars, from which came voices slurred with drink, the gaslight had grown dim and red. The fun was turning into quarrels and fights. One great slovenly devil kept yelling: 'I'm gonna take you apart, so count your bones!' A tart was going for her lover at the entrance to a dance-hall, calling him a filthy bastard and a dirty swine, while he could only repeat 'Up yours!' over and over again. The boozing had filled the streets with a craving for violence, a savage mood that made the few remaining passers-by look white-faced and terrified. In one fight, a boozer fell flat on his back and just lay sprawled there, while his mate, thinking he'd done him in, ran away, his heavy boots clattering. There were gangs bawling dirty songs, then heavy silences, broken by the hiccupping of drunks or their muffled thuds when they fell. The fortnightly pay-day binge always ended like this, with the wine that had been flowing so freely for six hours flowing out on to the pavements. Oh, glorious puddles of vomit, throw-up that spread right over the middle of the road so that anyone fussy who was out that late had to take great strides to avoid stepping in it! Oh yes, the neighbourhood was lovely and clean! A stranger seeing it before the early morning sweeping-up would have gone away with a pretty impression. But right now the drunks were king of the castle, and didn't give a damn about the rest of the world. Jesus Christ! Knives were being pulled out of pockets, the evening's little spree was winding up in bloodshed. Women walked fast, wary-eyed men prowled about, and the thickening night was big with dreadful deeds.

Gervaise was still staggering along, up the street then down again, with no thought in her head save that of walking forever. Overcome with sleepiness she'd doze off, rocked into slumber by her limp; then she'd give a start and look around, realizing she'd walked a hundred paces quite unconsciously, as if she were dead. Her dog-tired feet were becoming more and more swollen inside her wornout shoes. She could no longer feel anything, she was so exhausted and empty. The last clear thought she'd had was that her bitch of a daughter was perhaps eating oysters that very moment. After that everything became mixed up, and although she kept her eyes open, she found it too great an effort to think. The only sensation she was still aware of, in her utter prostration, was one of perishing cold: a biting, deathly cold such as she had never before experienced. Surely the dead lying in the ground didn't feel that cold. She

raised her head heavily and felt an icy stinging on her face. It
was the snow which had finally made up its mind to come down
from the murky sky, a fine, dense snow, that swirled about in
the light wind. It had been expected for three days. It had
picked the right moment to fall.

Gervaise, startled into wakefulness by that first squall, quick-
ened her pace. There were men running, in a hurry to get
home, their shoulders already white. And, seeing a man approaching slowly under the trees, she moved closer, saying once
more:

'Excuse me, Sir . . .'

The man had stopped. But he didn't seem to have heard. He
held out his hand, saying in a low voice:

'Spare a coin, mum.'

They stared at each other. My God! They'd come down to
this, old Bru begging, Madame Coupeau street-walking! They
stood there open-mouthed, gazing at one another. Now indeed
they were companions in misfortune. All evening long the old
workman had wandered about, not daring to speak to anyone,
and the first person he stopped was a down-and-out like
himself. Lord, wasn't it pitiful? To have worked for fifty years,
and now be begging! To have been one of the best laundresses
in the Rue de la Goutte-d'Or and end up in the gutter! They
went on staring at each other. Then, without exchanging a
word, they each went off alone into the driving snow.

It was a real blizzard. Up on the heights there, with virtually
open space on every side, the fine snow whirled about as if
being blown simultaneously from the four corners of the sky.
You couldn't see ten paces in front of you, everything was
vanishing under this flying powder. The surrounding buildings
had disappeared and the boulevard seemed dead, as if the
squall's white shroud had silenced the hiccups of the last
remaining drunks. Blinded and lost, Gervaise still plodded
painfully on. She felt her way from tree to tree. As she
advanced, the lamp-posts emerged from the pale air like torches
that had been extinguished. Then, quite suddenly, when she
was on a cross-roads, even those lights were gone; she was
caught up and enveloped in a ghostly whirlwind, unable to
make out anything to guide her. The uncertain white ground

gave way beneath her feet. Grey walls imprisoned her. And, when she stopped and looked round in hesitation, she could sense, beyond that icy veil, the great expanse of the avenues, the endless lines of lamp-posts, the dark, deserted, unmeasurable vastness of the sleeping city.

She'd reached the junction of the outer boulevard with the Boulevards Magenta and Ornano, and was thinking she might simply lie down there on the ground, when she heard the sound of steps. She began to run, but the snow got in her eyes, and the steps were drawing away without her being able to tell whether they were heading left or right. Eventually she saw the broad shoulders of a man, a dark shifting smudge that was disappearing into a fog. Oh, this one she must have, she wouldn't let this one go! And, running faster, she caught up with him and grabbed hold of his smock.

'Sir, sir, excuse me . . .'

The man turned round. It was Goujet.

So now it was Gueule-d'Or she was accosting! What had she done to so offend the good Lord, for him to torture her like this to the very end? It was the final blow, to be flinging herself at the blacksmith's feet, to let him see her as a neighbourhood whore, white-faced and importunate. They were under a street-lamp, and she could see her misshapen shadow clowning about on the snow like some travesty. You'd have said it was a drunken woman. Christ! Not to have a morsel of bread or a drop of wine in your body and to be taken for a drunken woman! It was her own fault, why did she drink? Of course Goujet must think that she'd been drinking and was making a real orgy of it.

Goujet meanwhile was looking at her, while the snow sprinkled his handsome yellow beard with daisies. Then, as she moved away, hanging her head, he stopped her.

'Come,' he said.

He walked in front. She followed him. The pair of them went through the neighbourhood's hushed streets, slipping silently along close to the walls. Poor Madame Goujet had died in October of rheumatic fever. Depressed and lonely, Goujet still lived in the little house in the Rue Neuve. On that particular day he'd stayed out late looking after an injured workmate.

When he'd opened the door and lit a lamp, he turned towards Gervaise who was waiting humbly out on the landing. He said very softly, as if his mother could still hear them:

'Come in.'

The first room, Madame Goujet's, had been piously preserved just as she'd left it. The embroidery frame lay on a chair near the window, beside the big armchair that seemed to be waiting for the old lace-maker. The bed was made up and she could have slept in it if she'd left the cemetery to spend the evening with her son. The room still kept its air of serenity, decency and kindness.

'Come in,' repeated the blacksmith more loudly.

She went in timidly, like a tart going into a respectable place. He was very pale and agitated at bringing a woman into his dead mother's room in this way. They crossed the room on tiptoe as if ashamed of being heard. Then when he'd urged Gervaise into his own room he shut the door. There he was at home. It was the little room she knew, the room of a school-child, with the narrow, white-curtained iron bedstead. But now there were more cut out pictures on the walls, reaching right up to the ceiling. Gervaise did not dare trespass into this purity and she hung back, out of the light. Then without a word, in a frenzy of passion, he tried to seize her and crush her in his arms. But, almost fainting, she murmured:

'My God! . . . Oh my God! . . .'

The stove was still alight under a covering of coke dust, and the remains of a stew that the blacksmith had left to keep warm for his return were simmering by the ashes. Gervaise, thawing out now in the intense heat, could have gone down on all fours to eat straight out of the saucepan. It was more than she could bear, her stomach was being rent apart, and she collapsed with a moan. But Goujet had understood. He put the stew on the table, cut some bread, and poured her some water.

'Thank you! Thank you!' she kept saying. 'Oh, how good you are! Thank you!'

Unable to get the words out, she could only stammer. She was trembling so when she picked up the fork that she dropped it again. The hunger clenching at her throat made her head wobble as if she was senile. She had to eat with her fingers. At the first potato that she stuffed into her mouth she burst into tears. Great tears rolled down her cheeks and fell on to her bread. She went on eating, greedily devouring her tear-soaked bread, breathing very loudly, her chin jerking spasmodically. Goujet made her drink so she wouldn't choke, and her glass rattled a bit against her teeth.

'D'you want more bread?' he asked in a low voice.

Weeping, she said no—yes—she didn't know. Lord, how good and how sad it is to eat when you're dying of hunger!

He was standing in front of her and looking at her. He could see her properly now, in the bright light cast by the lamp-shade. How she'd aged and gone to seed! The warmth was melting the snow on her hair and clothes and she streamed with water. Her poor wobbling head was completely grey, grey clumps of hair tangled by the wind. She was sitting in a huddle with her shoulders hunched up, looking so ugly and fat that it made you want to cry. And he remembered when they were in love, when she used to be all rosy as she slapped down her irons, with her little baby-crease like a pretty necklace round her neck. In those days he used to go and gaze at her for hours, satisfied just to see her. Later, she'd come to the forge, and there they'd known great happiness, while he hammered on his iron and she stood close by, watching his hammer dance about. And afterwards, at night, how often had he lain there biting his pillow, longing to have her in his room like this! Oh, he'd have broken her in two if he'd taken her, he wanted her so much! And now she was his, he could have her. She was finishing her bread, wiping up her tears from the bottom of the saucepan, those huge silent tears which were still falling into her food.

Gervaise got to her feet. She'd finished. For a moment she stood there with bent head, embarrassed, not knowing if he wanted her. Then, thinking she saw a flash of desire in his eyes, she raised her hand to her bodice and undid the top button. But Goujet had knelt down and was taking her hands, saying softly:

'I love you, Madame Gervaise, oh I still love you in spite of everything, I swear I do!'

'Don't say that, Monsieur Goujet!' she cried, appalled at seeing him kneeling before her like this. 'No, don't say that, it hurts me too much!'

And, as he was repeating that he could never love anyone else, she became still more distressed.

'No, no, I don't want to hear any more, it makes me too ashamed . . . Get up, for God's sake! I'm the one who should be kneeling.'

He stood up, trembling all over, and said in a halting voice:

'Will you let me kiss you?'

Overcome with astonishment and emotion, she could find nothing to say. She gave a nod. Good God, she was his, he could do what he wanted with her. But he simply leaned forward to kiss her.

'That's all you and I need, Madame Gervaise,' he whispered. 'Everything we feel for each other is here, isn't it?'

He kissed her on the forehead, on a lock of her grey hair. He hadn't kissed anyone since his mother's death. His dear friend Gervaise was all he had left in life. Then after kissing her with such reverence he drew back and fell across his bed, gulping down his sobs. And Gervaise couldn't stay there any longer: it was too sad, too horrible, to be together again in circumstances like these, when they loved each other. She exclaimed:

'I love you, Monsieur Goujet, I love you too, so much . . . Oh, I know it's impossible . . . Goodbye, goodbye, it would be more than either of us could bear.'

She ran across Madame Goujet's room and found herself in the street. When she came to her senses, she'd pulled the bell in the Rue de la Goutte-d'Or and Boche was opening the door. The building was in complete darkness. Going in there was like going into mourning for herself. At this time of night the gaping, dilapidated entryway looked like a pair of open jaws. To think that long ago she'd dreamed of living in this cadaverous barracks of a place! In those days her ears must have been blocked up, so she didn't hear the hellish chorus of despair droning behind its walls! From the day she first set foot in the sodding place she'd been on the skids. Yes, it must bring you bad luck to be right on top of one another like this, in these wretched great working-class tenements; you caught poverty in them, like the cholera. That night you'd have thought every-body had croaked. All she could hear was the Boches snoring to her right, while Virginie and Lantier, to her left, were purring like a pair of cats who aren't asleep but are lying cosily with their eyes closed. In the courtyard it felt as if she was in a real cemetery; the snow lay on the ground in a pale square; the tall, leaden grey façades, where no light showed, loomed up like the walls of some ruin; not even a sigh could be heard, it could have been the tomb of a whole village that had died of cold and hunger. She had to step over a black stream, a pool from the dye-works which steamed as it melted a muddy bed for itself in the whiteness of the snow. The pool was the colour of her thoughts. Those pretty pale blue and pink waters had long since flowed away!

Then, climbing the six floors in the darkness, she couldn't help laughing—a nasty laugh, that hurt her. She was remembering what had been her ideal, all those years ago: to be able to get on with her work, always have something to eat and a half-decent place to sleep, bring up her children properly, not be beaten, and die in her own bed. No, really, it was too funny, the way it was all working out! She was no longer working, she was no longer eating, she slept on filth, her daughter was on the make, her husband beat her up; the only thing left for her was to snuff it down there on the paving-stones, and she'd do it right now, if she had the guts to throw herself out of the window when she reached her own room. Wouldn't you have thought that she'd asked heaven for thirty thousand a year and to be fussed over? Oh, it really makes no difference at all in this life, even if your dreams are modest ones, you can still just whistle for 'em. Not even a crust and a bed, that's the common lot. And her nasty laugh grew even louder when she remembered her wonderful dream of retiring to the country, after twenty years of ironing. Well, that was where she was going, to the country. She wanted her bit of green in Père Lachaise.

By the time she turned into her corridor she was like someone crazy. Her poor head was spinning. Deep down, her dreadful distress came from having said goodbye forever to the blacksmith. It was all over between them, they would never meet again. Then all her other reasons for misery came piling in on top of that one, to the point where she was going round the bend. As she passed the Bijards' she poked her nose in and saw Lalie lying there dead, looking as if she was pleased to be

resting and to be able to pamper herself for ever more. Well
now! Children were luckier than grown-ups! And as a ray of
light was streaming from under Père Bazouge's door, she
walked straight into his room, gripped by a fierce craving to
take the same journey as the child.

That old clown Bazouge had come home that night in an
amazingly cheerful state. He'd got so sozzled that, in spite of
the cold, he was lying snoring on the floor; and evidently that
didn't stop him having a lovely dream because his belly seemed
to be shaking with laughter while he slept. The lamp was still
burning and lit up his gear—his black hat flattened in a corner,
his black coat pulled up over his knees as a covering.

On seeing him Gervaise suddenly began to moan so loudly
that he woke up.

'Jesus Christ! Shut the door, it's bloody freezin'! . . . Oh, so
it's you! . . . What's goin' on? What d'you want?'

So then Gervaise, her arms outstretched, hardly knowing any
more what she was saying, launched into a desperate, incoherent entreaty.

'Oh, take me away, I've had enough, I want to go . . . You
mustn't bear me a grudge. My God, I didn't know! You don't
know, not until you're ready . . . Oh, yes, there comes a day
when you're glad to go . . . Take me away, take me away, I'll
be ever so grateful.'

And she went down on her knees, trembling all over and pale
with longing. Never had she grovelled like this at the feet of
any man. Père Bazouge's boozy mug, with his screwed-up
mouth and his leathery skin clogged by graveyard dust, seemed
to her as beautiful, as glorious as a sun. But the old man, only
half awake, thought she was playing a mean trick on him.

'C'mon now,' he muttered, 'don't try it on with me.'

'Take me away,' Gervaise repeated more urgently. 'You
remember when I knocked on the wall that night, but then I
said I hadn't, 'cos I was still too stupid . . . But see here, gimme
your hands, I'm not frightened any more . . . Take me away so
I can go bye-byes, I won't stir, you'll see . . . Oh, there's
nothing else I want, an' I'll love you so much!'

Ever gallant, Bazouge felt he ought not to upset a lady who
seemed to have such a crush on him. She was going bats, but

she was still worth looking at, especially when she got all
worked up.

'You're bloody right,' he said with conviction, 'why only
today I packed up three who'd 'ave given me a ruddy great tip
if they'd been able to put their hand in their pocket . . . But
trouble is, sweetheart, it can't be done just like that . . .'

'Take me away, take me away,' Gervaise was still bawling, 'I
want to go . . .'

'But see here, there's a li'l something has to happen first . . .
You know, *cric*!'

And he made a noise in his throat as though swallowing his
tongue. Thinking this a good joke, he tittered.

Gervaise had slowly stood up. So he couldn't help her,
either? In a daze she went into her own room and threw herself
on the straw, regretting that she'd eaten. No, no, poverty
certainly didn't finish you off fast enough!

CHAPTER XIII

THAT night Coupeau went off on a bender. The next day
Gervaise got ten francs from her son Étienne, who was now an
engine driver on the railway; the boy, knowing money was short
at home, sent her a few francs from time to time. She made a
stew but ate it by herself, because that bastard Coupeau didn't
turn up the next day either. Monday came and no Coupeau:
Tuesday, still no Coupeau. The whole week went by. Hell! If
some lady had taken him away with her, now that'd be a bit of
luck! But, on the Sunday, Gervaise received a printed piece of
paper which gave her a fright at first, because it looked like
something from the police. But she soon calmed down, because
it was just to let her know that her swine of a hubby was
croaking, over at Sainte-Anne. The paper put it more politely
but really that's what it amounted to. It was indeed a lady
who'd taken Coupeau away with her, and her name was Sophie
Snuff-it, the very last of a drunkard's girlfriends.

Gervaise certainly didn't put herself out. He knew the way,
he could come home from the asylum on his own; they'd cured

him there so often that they'd surely do the dirty on him again and set him back on his pins. Hadn't she heard that very morning that for a whole week Coupeau, pissed as a newt, had been seen doing the rounds of the Belleville bars, along with Mes-Bottes! Yes, and Mes-Bottes had even footed the bill; he must have got his hooks into his missus's nest-egg that she'd earned playing at you-know-what. Oh, they were drinking up nice clean money, they were, money that could give you every kind of horrible disease. So much the better, if Coupeau had got a belly ache from it! What really made Gervaise see red was that it hadn't even entered the heads of those two selfish buggers to take her out for a glass or two. Did you ever see the like! A week-long booze-up and never a thought of treating the ladies! When you drink by yourself you croak by yourself, and good riddance!

However, on the Monday, as Gervaise had a nice little meal ready for the evening, some left-over beans and a drop of wine, she told herself that an outing would give her an appetite. That letter from the asylum lying on the chest of drawers bothered her. The snow had melted and the day was clement, overcast and mild, with just a nip in the air to buck you up. She left at noon because it was a long way: you had to go clear across Paris and her leg always slowed her down. What's more the streets were thronged, but she found the crowds entertaining and she made her way there quite pleasantly. When she identified herself they told her the weirdest story: it seemed Coupeau had been fished out of the river at the Pont Neuf;* he'd thrown himself over the parapet in the belief that a bearded man was barring his way. Quite a jump, wasn't it, and as for what Coupeau was doing on the Pont Neuf, that was something he himself couldn't explain.

An attendant took Gervaise to Coupeau. As she was climbing the stairs she could hear some shrieking that made her blood run cold.

'Just listen to that row he's kicking up!' said the attendant.

'Who?' she asked.

'Your old man, of course! He's been yelling like that since the day before yesterday. And dancing; well, you'll see.'

God! What a sight! She stood there paralysed. The cell was padded from top to bottom; on the floor there were two mats, one on top of the other; in a corner lay a mattress and bolster, nothing else. And in there was Coupeau, dancing and screaming. A proper carnival masker from La Courtille,* with his tattered smock and his limbs beating the air; but not a comic one, oh no! A masker whose frightful capering made your hair stand on end. He was got up to look like a dying man. Jesus Christ! Talk about a one-man show! He'd charge into the window then back away from it, beating time with his arms and shaking his hands as if he wanted to break them off and fling them into someone's face. In dance-halls you can see comics imitating what Coupeau was doing; only they imitate it badly, you really have to see a drunk hopping through that jig if you want to appreciate how stylish the dance can be when it's the real thing. The song also has style to it, a carnival bawling-out that goes on and on, a wide open mouth that belts out the same rusty trombone notes for hours on end. The sound Coupeau was making was like an animal whose foot's been crushed. Come on, the band's striking up, swing your partners!

'Lord, whatever's the matter with him? Whatever's the matter with him?' Gervaise, scared stiff, kept repeating.

A young house physician, a big, fair, rosy-cheeked man in a white overall, was sitting there calmly taking notes. The case was unusual and he never left the patient.

'Stay a while if you wish,' he said to the laundress, 'but keep still . . . Try and speak to him, but he won't recognize you.'

Indeed Coupeau didn't even seem to notice his wife was there. She hadn't had a good look at him when she first arrived, he'd been flinging himself about so much. Now that she could see him properly, her arms fell limply to her sides in shock. God, was that really him, with those blood-shot eyes and scab-encrusted lips? She'd certainly never have recognized him. In the first place, he was making so many faces, without any reason, his kisser suddenly turned inside out, his nose all screwed up, his cheeks sucked in, just like the mug of some animal. His skin, which shone like polished hide, was so hot that the air round him was steaming, and heavy sweat poured off him constantly. But all the same you could tell, as he danced his crazed buffoon's dance, that he didn't feel comfortable, that his head ached and his arms and legs hurt.

Gervaise had gone up to the doctor, who was strumming a tune with his fingers on the back of his chair.

'It's serious, is it, Monsieur, this time?'

The doctor nodded without answering.

'Tell me, isn't he jabbering about something under his breath? What is it, can you hear?'

'Things he can see,' whispered the young man. 'Be quiet, let me listen.'

Coupeau was talking in a staccato voice. But his eyes were gleaming with fun. He was looking down, and to right and left, and turning around, as if he were strolling about in the woods at Vincennes, chattering to himself.

'Oh, now that's nice, first rate . . . Look at the booths, it's a proper fair. An' nifty music. What a blow-out! They're makin' quite a splash in there! Absolutely great! Oh, look, it's lightin' up, there's red balloons in the air, bobbin' about, flyin' off . . . Oh! Oh! What a lot o' lanterns in the trees! It's bloody wonderful. An' lots o' water pissin' down everywhere, springs, waterfalls, an' it sounds like singin', like a choirboy singin' . . . They're damn good, the waterfalls!'

And he stood up straight, as if to hear the delightful singing of the water better; and he breathed deeply, believing he was drinking in the fresh spray flying off the springs. But, little by little, his face resumed its anguished expression. Then he bent over, and began walking faster round the walls of his cell, uttering muffled threats.

'That there's all just a fuckin' put-on! I thought as much . . . Shut up, you friggin' bastards! Oh, you don't give a damn about me. All that drinkin' an' singin' with your tarts in there, you're only doin' it to get on me wick . . . I'm gonna give you a thrashin', I am, in your bloody booth! . . . Jesus Christ, fuck off, will you!'

Clenching his fists, Coupeau gave a hoarse scream, began to run, then tripped and fell. His teeth were chattering with terror as he gasped:

'It's so I'll kill meself. No, no, I won't jump! . . . Not into all that water, I haven't the guts. No, I won't jump!'

The falls receded as he approached and advanced when he stepped back. And suddenly he stared round stupidly and stammered, his voice barely audible:

'I don't believe it, they've gone an' brought some doctors to do me in!'

'I'm going, Monsieur, good night!' Gervaise said to the doctor. 'It's more than I can take, I'll come back later.'

She'd gone dead white. Coupeau went on with his one-man show, back and forth between window and mattress, mattress and window, dripping with sweat, wearing himself out, beating time always to the same rhythm. She made her escape. But even though she raced down the stairs, the bloody awful racket her old man was making followed her all the way to the bottom. Christ, how lovely it was outside, where you could breathe!

That evening, the whole Goutte-d'Or building was talking about old Coupeau's strange illness. The Boches, who now treated Banban in a very cavalier way, did nevertheless invite her into the lodge for a cassis, so they could hear all the details. Madame Lorilleux turned up, and so did Madame Poisson. The discussion was endless. Boche had known a woodworker who'd stripped naked in the Rue Saint-Martin* and had died dancing the polka; absinthe was what he drank. The ladies squirmed with laughter, because although of course it was sad, it was funny all the same. Then, as they didn't quite understand, Gervaise pushed them all back, calling for room, and there, in the middle of the lodge, while they all watched, she did Coupeau, bawling, leaping, thrashing about, and making fright-ful faces. Yes, word of honour, that was exactly it! The others were flabbergasted: no, it wasn't possible! No one could have lasted three hours, carrying on like that. Well, it was so, Coupeau'd already lasted thirty-six hours, since yesterday; she swore it on everything she held most sacred. Besides, they could go there and see, if they didn't believe her. But Madame Lorilleux declared that she'd had quite enough of Sainte-Anne, thank you very much, and what's more she'd see to it that Lorilleux didn't set foot in the place either. As for Virginie, whose shop was going from bad to worse and who looked grim as death, she just muttered that life wasn't always a bed of roses, no, it damn well wasn't! They finished the cassis and Gervaise said good-night to everyone. As soon as she stopped talking she looked like one of the Chaillot* loonies, with staring eyes. No doubt she was still seeing her husband waltzing about. When she got up the next morning she told herself she wouldn't go there any more. What was the point? She didn't want to go off her onion too. However, every few minutes she found she was thinking about it again; she was only half present, as they say. Wouldn't it be funny though, if he was still hoofing it round the room! When noon struck, she couldn't stand it any longer; she didn't even notice how far she had to walk, her head was so full of curiosity and fear of what awaited her.

Oh, there was no need to enquire after him. From the bottom of the staircase, she could hear Coupeau's song. Exactly the same tune, exactly the same dance. It was as if she'd just that minute come down the stairs and was now going back up. The attendant she'd seen yesterday was carrying some jugs of tisane along the corridor, and he winked in a friendly way when he saw her.

'Still at it, eh?' she said.

'Yes, still at it,' he replied without stopping.

She went in but stayed in the corner by the door, because there were some people with Coupeau. The fair, rosy-cheeked doctor was standing, having given his chair to a bald, elderly, weasel-faced man with a ribbon in his lapel. He must be the hospital's senior specialist, for he had narrow, piercing, gimlet eyes. All your dealers in sudden death have eyes like that.

Anyway, he wasn't the person Gervaise had come to see, and she peered over his skull, devouring Coupeau with her gaze. That maniac was dancing and bellowing even more frantically than yesterday. In the past she'd often seen, at Mardi Gras* dances, great big lads who worked in the washhouse keep it up for a whole night; but never, never in all her born days, would she have imagined that a man could go on enjoying himself for such a long time; when she said enjoy himself, it was just a manner of speaking, because you don't enjoy somersaulting about uncontrollably as if you'd swallowed a powder magazine. Coupeau, drenched in sweat, was steaming even more than before, that was all. His mouth seemed bigger, from all that shouting. Oh, pregnant woman did right to keep away! He'd walked so much from the mattress to the window that you could see his tracks on the floor; the mat had been worn down by his slippers.

No, it certainly wasn't a pretty sight, and Gervaise, trembling, wondered why she'd come back. To think that last night at the Boches' they'd accused her of overdoing her imitation! When in fact she hadn't done the half of it! Now she could see better just how Coupeau went about it, and never again would she forget how he looked, with his wide-open eyes staring into space. But she could hear remarks passing between the house doctor and the specialist. The former was going into details about the night, using words she didn't understand. Her Coupeau had jabbered and pirouetted the whole night long, that was what he really meant. Then the bald old gentleman, who indeed was not very polite, suddenly seemed to notice her presence; and when the doctor told him she was the patient's wife, he started to question her, rather roughly, like a policeman.

'Did this man's father drink?'

'Yes, Monsieur, a little, like everyone else . . . He was killed when he fell off a roof one day when he'd been having a few.'

'And did his mother drink?'

'Lord, Monsieur, like everyone does you know, just a drop now and again . . . Oh, it's a very good family! There was a brother who died very young, from convulsions.'

The doctor stared at her with his piercing gaze. He continued in his rough voice:

'And you, d'you drink too?'

Gervaise stammered a denial, swearing it was the truth with her hand on her heart.

'You do drink! Watch out, just look at where drink lands you . . . Sooner or later you'll die like this!'

She stood rooted to the spot, by the wall. The doctor had turned his back. He squatted down, quite unconcerned whether he might be getting dust from the mat on his tail-coat; for a long time he studied Coupeau's tremors, waiting for him to go past, following him with his eyes. That day it was the legs' turn to jerk, for the tremors had passed down from the hands to the feet; a proper Punchinello,* he was, that you could have worked with strings, having fun with the legs and arms while the trunk stayed as stiff as a board. The disease was spreading little by little. You could say it was a kind of music under the skin; it would begin every three or four seconds and play for an instant; then it would stop and then start again, like the tiny shudder of cold a stray dog gives, as it shelters from the winter in some doorway. The belly and the shoulders were already quivering, like water just coming to the boil. But wasn't it a funny way to croak, to go off wriggling, like a girl who can't stand being tickled!

Coupeau, meanwhile, was moaning in a low voice. He seemed to be suffering much more than the day before. His disjointed moans suggested all kinds of torments. Thousands of pins were pricking into him. Something was pressing down heavily all over his skin; a cold, wet creature was dragging itself over his thighs, digging its fangs into his flesh. And then there were other beasts, clutching at his shoulders, tearing the flesh from his back with their claws.

'I'm thirsty, I'm thirsty!' he kept grunting.

The doctor took a pot of lemonade from a small shelf and gave it to him. He grabbed the pot with both hands and greedily sucked up a mouthful, splashing half the liquid down himself; but then he promptly spat it out in angry disgust, screaming:

'Jesus Christ, it's brandy!'

Then, at a sign from the specialist, the young doctor tried to make him drink some water, keeping hold of the carafe. This time he swallowed the mouthful, shrieking as if he'd swallowed fire.

'It's brandy, Jesus Christ, it's brandy!'

Everything he'd drunk since the day before had been brandy. It made his thirst even worse and he could no longer drink, because everything burnt him. They'd brought him some soup, but it was clear they were trying to poison him because the soup tasted of rotgut. The bread was sour and rotten. Everything round him was poisoned. The cell reeked of sulphur. He even accused people of striking matches under his nose to make him ill.

The specialist had just stood up and was listening to Coupeau, who now was seeing ghosts in broad daylight again. He fancied he could see spider's webs as big as ships' sails on the walls! And then the spider's webs became nets with mesh that shrank and stretched, like some funny kind of toy! There were black balls bouncing about in the mesh, magic ones that at first were the size of billiard balls and then the size of cannon balls; and they'd swell and then they'd shrink, on purpose, just to madden him. All of a sudden, he screamed:

'Oh, the rats, the rats are here now!'

The balls were turning into rats. The filthy beasts grew and grew, came through the net and leapt on to the mat, where they vanished. There was also a monkey which came out of the wall then went back into it, each time coming so close to him that he'd jump back for fear of having his nose bitten off. Suddenly, everything changed again: the walls must have been capering about, because he was saying, choking with terror and rage:

'Ow, ow, go on! Yes, fling me about, see if I care! Ow! Ow! The whole place is fallin' down, it's fallin' down . . . Yes, ring the bells, you black crows, bash the organ so I can't call for help . . . The scumbags have gone an' stuck somethin' round behind the wall, I can hear it rumblin' away, they're gonna blow us up . . . Fire, fire! Jesus Christ, fire! There's a fire! What a blaze! Oh, it's so bright, so bright! The sky's all on fire, there's red flames, an' green, an' yellow . . . Help, help! Fire!'

His shrieks died away in a throaty rattle. Now he could only mumble incoherently, frothing at the mouth, his chin wet with saliva. The specialist was rubbing his nose with his finger, a habit of his, no doubt, when faced with serious cases. He turned towards the young doctor and quietly asked him:

'And the temperature's still a hundred and four, is it?'

'Yes, Monsieur.'

The specialist pursed his lips. He stood there another couple of minutes, gazing at Coupeau. Then he added with a shrug:

'The same treatment, broth, milk, lemonade, weak extract of quinine in liquid form . . . Don't leave him, and call me.'

He went out, and Gervaise followed, to ask him whether there was no longer any hope. But he was walking down the corridor so quickly that she didn't dare speak to him. She stayed where she was for a moment, reluctant to go back in to her hubby. The visit had already seemed so bloody awful. Hearing Coupeau shouting again that the lemonade tasted of brandy, she simply took to her heels; she'd had quite enough for one performance. In the streets the galloping of the horses and the noise of the carriages made her think she had all of Sainte-Anne chasing after her. And the warning that doctor'd given her! Really, she felt as if she'd already caught the disease, too.

Needless to say the Boches and the others were waiting for her in the Rue de la Goutte-d'Or. The instant she appeared in the entrance they called her into the lodge. Well? Was old Coupeau still hanging on? Lord, yes, still hanging on. Boche looked astonished and dismayed: he'd bet a bottle that old Coupeau wouldn't last till evening. What! Still hanging on! And, slapping their thighs, they all expressed amazement. Now there was a chap who could hold his own! Madame Lorilleux worked out how many hours it had been: thirty-six and twenty-four made sixty. Damn it! Sixty hours he'd been at it, bouncing about and bellowing! Never before had such a feat of strength been seen. But Boche, with a sickly smile on account of his bet, was questioning Gervaise in a doubting way, asking whether she was quite certain that he hadn't pegged out behind her back. Oh, no, he was leaping about too much, he didn't want to die. So then Boche, even more insistently, begged her to imitate Coupeau a bit again, so they could see. Yes, yes, again, just a bit! By popular demand! They all kept telling her it would be so kind, because here were two ladies who hadn't seen it yesterday and who'd just popped down specially to watch. The concierge was shouting at everyone to get out of the way, and, aquiver with curiosity, they were all elbowing one another to clear a space in the middle of the lodge. But Gervaise stood there hanging her head. Really, she was afraid she'd make herself ill. However, to prove she wasn't just trying to make them keep on asking, she began with two or three little jumps, but it did make her come over queer, and she sprang back: no, she couldn't, honestly! A murmur of disappointment ran through the group; what a shame, she did Coupeau to perfection. Well, after all, if she really couldn't! And, as Virginie went

back to her shop, they dropped Coupeau in favour of a good
old gossip about the Poisson household, which was a regular
bear-garden these days: yesterday the bailiffs had come; the
policeman was going to lose his job; as for Lantier, he was
hanging round the girl from the restaurant next door, a
splendid-looking creature who talked of setting up in the tripe
business. Yes indeed! They all had a good laugh about it,
already picturing a tripe-seller installed in the shop; he'd had
the titbits first, and now wanted something solid. That cuckold
Poisson looked a bit of a mug in all this: how the devil could a
man who needs to be cunning in his job be such a dope in his
own home! But they suddenly shut up on noticing Gervaise,
whom they'd stopped watching, trying it out all by herself at
the back of the room, shaking her hands and her feet, doing
Coupeau. Bravo! That was the way, that was just what they
wanted. She broke off, looking bewildered, as if she'd just come
out of a dream. Then she rushed away. Good night everyone,
she was going up to try to get some shut-eye.

The next day the Boches saw her leaving at noon, like the
other two days. They wished her a pleasant time of it. At
Sainte-Anne's Coupeau's yelling and stamping was making the
corridor shake. While her hand was still holding the rail on the
stairs, she could hear him howling:

'Bugs, now it's bugs! . . . Just come back 'ere a sec an' lemme
work you over . . . Aha, they wanna do me in, do they!
But you'll never get the better of me . . . Fuck off, for Christ's
sake . . .'

She stopped a moment outside the door to catch her breath.
So now he must be fighting an army! When she went in she
saw that it was getting more complicated and more marvellous
than ever. Coupeau had become a raving loony, a runaway from
Charenton!* He was flinging himself about in the middle of the
cell, lashing out with his fists in every direction, hitting himself,
the walls, the floor, falling head over heels, slapping at empty
air; he'd try to open the window, he'd hide, he'd defend
himself, he'd call, he'd answer; he was making this incredible
racket all by himself, his manner exasperated, like a man who's
being hounded by a whole bunch of people. Then, Gervaise
realized that he fancied he was on a roof, putting down sheets

of zinc. He'd do the bellows with his mouth, he'd move the soldering irons about in the brazier, and then kneel down to run his thumb round the edges of the mat as if he thought he was soldering it. Yes, his trade was coming back to him when he was just about to croak; and if he was yelling so loudly and fighting tooth and nail up there on his roof it was because some bastards were stopping him doing his job properly. On all the adjacent roofs there were sons of bitches plaguing the living daylights out of him. And what's more those jokers were setting hordes of rats at his legs. Oh, the filthy beasts, he could see 'em wherever he looked! It was useless to squash 'em, pounding his foot on the floor as hard as he could, fresh packs of rats kept coming, the roof was black with 'em. And there were spiders as well, weren't there! He'd grab fiercely at his trouser leg to squash against his thigh the huge spiders that had crawled up there. Soddin' hell! He'd never get through his stint for the day, they were trying to ruin him, his boss would send him to jug.* Then he started to hurry and, believing he had a steam engine in his belly, he puffed steam out of his wide open mouth, thick steam that filled the cell and went out of the window; bending over, still puffing, he watched the band of steam unwinding and rising upwards in the sky, where it hid the sun.

'Hey, look!' he shouted, 'it's that troupe from the Chaussée Clignancourt, dressed up like bears, makin' quite a show . . .'

He stayed crouched in front of the window, as if he were watching a procession in a street, from a rooftop.

'Here comes the parade, with lions an' panthers pullin' awful faces . . . And some little kids dressed as dogs 'n' cats . . . There's that great Clémence with her mop full o' feathers. Oh, lord, just look at her, gone arse over tip, showin' everythin' she's got! Hey, sweetheart, lets you 'n' me make tracks together, eh? Oh, you fuckin' cops, leave her alone, will you! Don't shoot, Christ, don't shoot! . . .'

His voice rose, hoarse and terrified, as he quickly flung himself on to the floor, repeating that the cops and the soldiers were down below aiming at him with their rifles. In the wall he could see the barrel of a pistol pointed at his chest. They were coming to take the girl away from him again.

'Don't shoot, for God's sake! Don't shoot . . .'

Then all the houses were caving in, and he was making crashing noises as if a whole neighbourhood was collapsing; everything was vanishing and fading away. But before he could draw breath there were other scenes racing by with extraordinary speed. A desperate urge to speak filled his mouth with words, which came bubbling up from his throat in a meaningless jumble. His voice grew louder and louder.

'Hey, it's you! Hallo! Don't fool about, I don't want your hair in me mouth.'

And he passed his hand over his face, blowing to get rid of the hairs. The doctor asked:

'Who is it you can see?'

'Me wife, of course!'

He was staring at the wall, with his back to Gervaise. This didn't half scare Gervaise, and she too stared at the wall, to find out if she could see herself there. He chattered on:

'Oh, don't try to pull the wool over me eyes . . . I don't want to be tied on to a rope . . . Hell, you're lookin' real nice, that's a smart get-up. Where d'you get it, you bitch? You've been out on the streets, you slut! Just you wait, I'll fix you! Ah, you're hidin' your fancy man behind your skirts! Who the hell is it? Come on, bob down a bit, let's see . . . Jesus Christ! Him again!'

With one terrible leap he crashed his head against the wall, but the padding deadened the blow. The only sound was the thud of his body landing on the mat, where he'd been thrown by the shock of the impact.

'Who is it you can see?' repeated the doctor.

'The hatter! The hatter!' screamed Coupeau.

In response to the doctor's questions Gervaise just stuttered, unable to answer: this scene was bringing back all the greatest troubles of her life. The roofer was hitting out with his fists.

'It's just you an' me now, mate. This time I'm gonna finish you off, I am. You roll up here as large as life with that hag on your arm to make fun of me in front of 'em all. Well I'm gonna choke the life out of you, that's what I'm gonna do! And I won't put me gloves on neither! I've had enough of your swaggerin' . . . Take that! And that! And that!'

He was hitting at the empty air. Then a terrible rage took hold of him. He'd bumped into the wall as he backed away and thought he was being attacked from behind. He turned and set upon the padding. He sprang about, leaping from corner to corner, hitting out with his belly, with his buttocks, with one shoulder, rolling over, jumping up again. His bones were getting soft and his flesh resounded dully, like wet wadding. And he was playing this lovely game to the tune of frightful threats and guttural, savage screams. But the battle must have been going badly for him, for he was breathing faster and his eyes bulged in their sockets; little by little he seemed to be falling prey to childish terrors.

'Murder, murder! . . . Fuck off, the pair of you. Oh, the dirty bastards, they think it's funny. Just look at her, the slut, with her legs in the air! . . . She's for it, that's certain . . . Oh, the brute, he's slaughterin' her! He's cuttin' off one of her legs with his knife. The other's lyin' there on the ground, her belly's split open, there's blood everywhere . . . Oh, my God! oh my God! oh my God! . . .'

Drenched in sweat, his hair standing on end, Coupeau was a frightening sight as he backed away, lashing frantically about with his arms as if to fend off the ghastly vision. He let out two harrowing cries and, his heels catching in the mattress, fell backwards on to it.

'Monsieur, Monsieur, he's dead!' said Gervaise, clasping her hands.

The doctor had stepped forward and was pulling Coupeau on to the middle of the mattress. No, he wasn't dead. They'd taken off his shoes and his bare feet stuck out over the end, and all on their own, side by side, keeping time, those feet were dancing a fast, rhythmic little dance.

The specialist came in just then. He was with two colleagues, one thin and one fat, who like him were wearing decorations. The three of them bent down without saying anything and examined the man all over; then they conferred rapidly in undertones. They'd stripped Coupeau from the shoulders down to the thighs and by standing on tiptoe Gervaise could see his naked torso lying there. Well, the process was complete, the tremors had moved down from the arms and moved up from the legs, and now the trunk itself was joining in the fun! It really looked as if Punchinello's paunch was having a good giggle as well. There were ripples of mirth right down the ribs, and the tum was panting with laughter fit to bust. And everything was doing its stuff, no question about it! The muscles took their places opposite their partners, the skin vibrated like a drum, the hairs waltzed about, nodding to each other. In a word, it was like the grand finale at a dance, a sort of last galop round when dawn's breaking and all the dancers hold hands, stamping their heels to the beat.

'He's asleep,' murmured the specialist.

And he drew the attention of the others to the face. Coupeau's eyes were closed and his whole face was jerking with tiny nervous twitches. He looked more ghastly than ever, lying flattened in that way, his jaw-bone protruding, his features contorted like those of a corpse haunted by nightmares. But, noticing the feet, the doctors scrutinized them with an air of the greatest interest. The feet were still dancing. Coupeau might have fallen asleep but his feet were dancing. Oh, let their boss snore, that was no concern of theirs, they jogged on in their own little way, not hurrying and not slowing down. Proper mechanical feet, feet that took their fun where they found it.

Seeing the doctors put their hands on her old man's torso, Gervaise wanted to touch him herself. She went quietly up to him and put her hand on his shoulder. She left it there for a minute. Lord! Whatever was going on inside there? She could feel dancing, deep down in his flesh; his very bones must be skipping about. From somewhere far away came quiverings and ripplings that flowed like a river under the skin. When she pressed a bit she could sense cries of pain coming from the marrow of his bones. All you could see with the naked eye were tiny wavelets that left the skin dimpled, as happens on the surface of a whirlpool, but just imagine the havoc underneath! What a devilish business! A sapper's job, really! The Assommoir's rotgut was at work with its pickaxe down there. His entire body was steeped in it, and Christ! the job would soon be finished, Coupeau would fall to pieces, he'd be done in by this complete, continuous shaking of his whole body.

The specialists had left. After an hour, Gervaise, who'd stayed with the doctor, said again in a low voice:

'Monsieur, Monsieur, he's dead . . .'

But the doctor, who was watching the feet, shook his head. The bare feet, sticking out over the end of the mattress, were still dancing. They were not at all clean and the nails were long. Hours passed. Suddenly the feet stiffened and were still. Then the doctor turned to Gervaise and said:

'That's it.'

Death alone had stopped the feet.

When Gervaise got home to the Rue de la Goutte-d'Or, she found a lot of women at the Boches', gossiping excitedly. She thought they were waiting for her to hear the news, like the other days.

'He's croaked,' she said, calmly pushing open the door, her face dazed and exhausted.

But nobody was listening. The whole place was in an uproar. Oh, the funniest thing had happened! Poisson had nabbed his wife with Lantier. They didn't know the exact details, because everyone had their own version of the story. Anyway, he'd walked in on them just when the pair least expected it. And there were even some details that made the ladies purse their lips as they repeated them. Naturally, a sight like that had shocked Poisson out of his true nature. An absolute tiger! That silent man, who walked as if he'd a poker up his arse, had begun to roar and leap about. Then nothing more was heard. Lantier must have explained it all to the husband. Anyway, things couldn't go on like that any longer. And Boche told them that the girl from the restaurant next door was definitely going to take over the shop to sell tripe. That artful hatter adored tripe.

Meanwhile, seeing Madame Lorilleux come in with Madame Lerat, Gervaise repeated in a feeble voice:

'He's croaked . . . My God! Four whole days of jigging about and yelling . . .'

At that the two sisters couldn't do other than pull out their handkerchiefs. Their brother had certainly had his faults, but after all he was their brother. Boche shrugged, saying loud enough to be heard by everyone:

'Bah! One drunkard the less!'

From then on, as Gervaise often seemed to go a bit round the bend, one of the pastimes in the building was to watch her do Coupeau. You no longer had to press her, she did the imitation for nothing, the shaking of the feet and the hands, the little involuntary cries. No doubt she'd picked that up at Sainte-Anne, from watching her husband for too long. But she didn't have any luck, she didn't die of it like him. All she did was pull faces like a monkey that's broken loose from its cage, and what she got for that was cabbage stumps thrown at her by kids in the street.

Gervaise lasted like that for months. She sank lower and lower, suffering the vilest humiliations, dying a little each day from hunger. The minute she had a few sous, she'd spend them on drink and start rambling on like a loony. She was given the filthiest jobs in the neighbourhood to do. One evening they bet she wouldn't eat something really disgusting, and she did eat it, to earn ten sous. Monsieur Marescot decided he'd have to evict her from the room on the sixth floor. But as they'd just found Père Bru dead in his nook under the stairs up there, the landlord was willing to let her have that. So now she lived in Père Bru's tiny hole. There, on some old straw, her belly empty, frozen to the marrow, she lay and starved to death. It seemed as if the earth itself didn't want her. She grew quite simple-minded, and never even thought of finishing it all by throwing herself from the sixth floor on to the courtyard below. Death had to take her little by little, bit by bit, dragging her along to the bitter end of the miserable existence she'd made for herself. They never even knew exactly what she did die of. Some spoke of a chill. But the truth was that she died from poverty, from the filth and the weariness of her wretched life. She rotted to death, as the Lorilleux put it. One morning there was a bad smell in the corridor and people remembered that she hadn't been seen for two days; they found her in her hole, already green.

It so happened that it was Père Bazouge who came, with a pauper's coffin under his arm, to pack her up. That day he was, as usual, pretty sozzled, but a decent bloke just the same, and as cheerful as a lark. When he saw who his client was he indulged in some philosophizing while making his little preparations.

'We all go the same way . . . No need to push an' shove, there's room for everybody . . . And it's silly to rush 'cos you don't get there no sooner . . . As for me, all I want is to please folks. Some want to, some don't want to. Now just let me take a little look 'ere . . . This 'ere's one that didn't want to, an' then did want to. But then she 'ad to wait . . . Anyway, that's that, she's got what she wants! Off we go!'

And as he seized Gervaise in his huge filthy hands he was filled with tenderness, very gently lifting this woman who for so long had harboured such a craving for him. Then, laying her down with fatherly care in the coffin, he stammered between two hiccups:

'Y'know . . . listen to me . . . it's me, Bibi-la-Gaieté, that they call the ladies' comforter . . . There now, that's better. Go to bye-byes, my pretty one!'

EXPLANATORY NOTES

5   *Veau à deux têtes*: literally the Two-Headed Calf; but, in working-class slang, a *veau* was a young woman predisposed to prostitution.

    Grand-Balcon: situated on the northern side of the Boulevard de la Chapelle; in working-class slang, 'faire le balcon' meant a young woman was accessible to visitors, a state of readiness signalled by an item of clothing left on her balcony.

    outer boulevards: the Boulevard de Rochechouart and the Boulevard de la Chapelle, immediately adjacent to the city-limit formed by the octroi wall (cf. note to p. 6).

6   *Claude . . . Étienne*: Claude Lantier appears as a young artist in Zola's *Le Ventre de Paris* (1873) and is the hero of *L'Œuvre* (1886); Étienne becomes the leader of the striking miners in *Germinal* (1885) (see Introduction, p. ix).

    Barrière Poissonnière: one of sixty toll-houses which controlled access to the city through gateways in the octroi wall. The Barrière Poissonnière was sited at the present-day intersection of the Boulevard Barbès (formerly Ornano) and the Boulevard de Rochechouart, a development referred to at the end of the novel (p. 406).

    Boncœur: the Good Heart.

    Lariboisière Hospital: major Parisian hospital, very near the Gare du Nord, founded in 1846 by the widow of the Napoleonic general Jean-Antoine Lariboisière (1759–1812); it was completed in 1854.

    octroi wall: from the French verb *octroyer* (to grant), this eighteenth-century wall of the Fermiers-généraux (an organization responsible for raising royal taxes until 1791) allowed Paris to enforce its right to levy customs duties on goods brought into the city (cf. note to p. 71).

7   *Montmartre and La Chapelle*: when the novel begins, in 1850, these were still independent *communes* beyond the northern edge of the octroi wall and thus outside the administrative boundary of Paris. This was extended in 1859 (the legislation came into effect on 1 January 1860) to the military fortifications

(cf. note to p. 71), and the number of *arrondissements* was increased from twelve to the present twenty.

7   *Eugène Sue*: (1804–57), popular serial-novelist, elected as an opposition deputy on 28 April 1850 (cf. note to p. 243).

Bonaparte: Charles-Louis-Napoléon-Bonaparte (1808–73), nephew of Napoléon I, President of the Republic between 1848 and 1851; after his *coup d'état* on 2 December 1851 he became Napoléon III (cf. note to p. 108).

8   *Faubourg-Poissonnière*: the Rue du Faubourg-Poissonnière (as it is more correctly referred to on p. 65) leads due south towards the centre of Paris, continuing the Boulevard Barbès across the line of the octroi wall.

10   *Provençal accent*: the most recognizable feature of which is the accentuation of terminal vowels and consonants which remain silent in standard French.

La Glacière: district on the southern outskirts of the city, in the thirteenth *arrondissement*, a distance of at least 6 km. We are later told that Lantier goes to live there with Adèle after abandoning Gervaise (p. 184).

14   *sous*: the expression has outlived the actual coin, worth five centimes. Monetary denominations are notoriously difficult to translate into modern values. They make more sense in relative terms. In 1860, for example, the average male wage in Paris was about five francs per day, while female workers were paid less than half that amount, even when doing the same job. A laundress could expect to earn well under two francs at a time when a 2 kg. loaf of bread cost sixty centimes. All the figures in *L'Assommoir* are authentic, the result of Zola's careful documentation in this area.

18   *Plassans*: Zola's fictionalized version of Aix-en-Provence is the setting for the provincial novels of the Rougon–Macquart series, most obviously in *La Conquête de Plassans* (1874).

19   *Rue Montmartre*: running through the first and second *arrondissements*, distinctly more up-market than the area in which Gervaise now finds herself.

27   *Belhomme*: this plays with the meaning of the Rue Belhomme as Handsome Gent.

31   *Viorne*: Zola's invented name for the Arc, the river which flows to the south of Aix-en-Provence (cf. note to p. 18).

34   *Assommoir*: see Introduction, p. xi.

37   *Bibi-la-Grillade*: nickname which defies translation; 'griller' is slang for 'to down' (drink or food); 'bibi' is a term of affection, but the dictionary used by Zola also refers us to 'bibine' (a mediocre drink), 'biberonner' (to tipple), 'biberonneur' (a drunk), as well as 'bibi' meaning the tool of a thief or a small hat.

40   *Mes-Bottes*: another nickname which Zola found in one of his principal sources about working-class idioms; it is probably derived from the Italian ('botte') and Provençal ('bota') for bottle, and could be translated as 'in my cups'; but Delvau's *Dictionnaire de la langue verte* also notes that 'botter' is slang for 'to please' and that 'proposer la botte à quelqu'un' means to 'propose sexual intercourse'.

       Cadet-Cassis: Coupeau's nickname is explained on pp. 44: 'he was the youngest' ('cadet') and drinks cassis, the blackcurrant liqueur.

41   *Rue Coquenard*: now the Rue Lamartine, in the ninth *arrondissement*.

43   *Petit bonhomme qui tousse*: the Coughing Little Fellow.

       Barrière Saint-Denis: located in what is now the Place de la Chapelle.

       Rue des Moines . . . Batignolles: the latter was also an independent *commune* until 1859 (cf. note to *Montmartre and La Chapelle*, p. 7), north-west of the Place de Clichy; the Rue des Moines runs from the Avenue de Clichy to the Rue de la Jonquière, in the present-day seventeenth *arrondissement*.

58   *Paris to Versailles*: a distance of 23 km.

64   *Moulin-d'Argent*: the Money Mill, or the Silver Mill, equally ironic in view of the poverty of its clientele.

65   *Saint-Denis*: the Saint-Denis plain now forms part of the industrial suburbs north of Paris.

67   *Code*: the relevant section of French law which was systematized into five 'codes' during the Napoleonic regime.

       town hall to the church: French weddings have separate civil and religious components.

71   *fortifications*: built 1840–4, creating a new fortified boundary just outside the line of the present-day *boulevard périphérique*; beyond it was a (military) zone on which no building was officially allowed; but between the octroi wall (cf. note to p. 6)

and the fortifications there also existed rural spaces which have long since disappeared.

72 *Père Lachaise*: the main Parisian cemetery, named after, and built within the gardens of, the Jesuit confessor of Louis XIV; also known as the Cimetière de l'Est, which the characters could reach by going east along the Boulevard de la Chapelle.

Héloise and Abélard: legendary victims of the power of love; Héloise's (1101–64) secret marriage to Abélard (1079–1142), her spiritual mentor, led to the latter being castrated as punishment for their transgression of monastic vows of chastity; the authenticity of their joint tomb in the Père Lachaise cemetery is doubtful.

73 *museum*: the Louvre.

74 *Banban*: slang for someone with a limp.

boulevard: the present-day Boulevard Bonne-Nouvelle.

75 *Louis XIV*: King of France from 1643 to 1715. The statue (1822) has him on a rearing charger and dressed as a Roman emperor.

Assyrian Gallery: opened in 1847.

76 *Raft of the Medusa*: painted by Théodore Géricault (1791–1824) in 1819.

Gallery of Apollo: only reopened in July 1851 (after substantial restoration); the wedding-party's visit supposedly takes place a year earlier.

Salon Carré: it was in this room, otherwise known as the Grand Salon, that an annual art exhibition (thus called the Salon) was held between 1725 and 1848. Only in 1852 was the Salon Carré reorganized, on the model of the Tribune in the Uffizi, in order to accommodate the most prestigious works in the Louvre's collections. Here again, Zola's fictional chronology is not strictly accurate.

Charles IX: King of France between 1560 and 1574; the most notorious event of his reign was the St Bartholomew's Day Massacre (24 August 1572) of Protestants. The balcony pointed out by Monsieur Madinier was in fact designed during the reign of Henri IV, from 1589 to 1610.

77 *Wedding at Cana*: painted in 1562–3 by Paolo Veronese (1528–88); this huge painting (660 x 990 cm.) remained in the Salon Carré until 1951.

thighs: more likely those of the *Pardo Venus* by Titian (1489–1576).

Virgin: there are a number of such paintings in the Louvre by the Spanish artist Bartolé Esteban Murillo (1618–82); the one Zola had in mind is the *Immaculate Conception of the Virgin*, purchased from the Soult collection in 1852 for so scandalous a sum that, for a generation, guides to the Louvre named the price—right up to the last of the 615,300 francs it had cost the nation.

Titian's mistress: also known as *Young Woman at her Toilet*, with Venetian auburn rather than yellow hair.

La Belle Ferronnière: a painting in fact by Leonardo da Vinci (1452–1519); and the lady in question was reputed to be the mistress not of Henri IV but, at best, of François I (King of France, 1515–47) and, more probably, of Ludovico Sforza (1452–1508).

play at the Ambigu: Monsieur Madinier's general incompetence makes it unsurprising that no trace of any such play can be found. It was at the Théâtre de l'Ambigu, on the Boulevard St-Martin, that a very successful adaptation of *L'Assommoir* was staged in 1879.

78 *Kermesse*: composed in 1635 by the Flemish painter Peter-Paul Rubens (1577–1640).

79 *Pont-Royal*: bridge across the Seine, between the Rue du Bac and the western end of the Tuileries Palace.

80 *Marne*: major river, rising north of Dijon and flowing through the Champagne region before joining the Seine at Charenton-le-Pont in the southeastern suburbs of Paris.

column: the Vendôme column is 44 m. high. It was made from 1200 bronze cannons captured from the Austrians and Russians, erected in 1810 and dedicated to the veterans of the battle of Austerlitz (1805). As an emblem of Napoleonic glory (it originally had a statue of Napoleon on the top), it was a target for the revolution of the Commune; it was pulled down in May 1871 and rebuilt in 1874.

81 *Invalides . . . Tour Saint-Jacques*: moving anti-clockwise, this sweeping panorama takes in the most visible markers of the Parisian skyline: the Hôtel des Invalides (cf. note to p. 220); the Panthéon, with its 80 m. high cupola rising above the Latin Quarter, used once again as a church during the Second Empire

but housing the remains of the great men of France after 1871; the cathedral of Notre-Dame; and the Tour Saint-Jacques on the Rue de Rivoli, all that now remains of the church of Saint-Jacques-la Boucherie.

86 *Bernard Palissy*: (1510–89), famous ceramist credited with the discovery of how to make enamel, and also well-known because of having had to resort to burning the floor and contents of his house in order to keep his wood-stove burning to conduct his experiments.

87 *law of May 31st:* an attack on radicalism, the electoral law of 31 May 1850 required three years' residence (not two, as Madinier states) in one place in order to be eligible to vote, to be attested by a tax receipt or employer's affadavit. This effectively disenfranchised a very large number of workers forced to move in order to find a job.

loves the people: Louis-Napoléon (cf. note to *Bonaparte*, p. 7) had gained this reputation through his early writing: his *Rêveries politiques* (1832) and *Les Idées Napoléonniennes* (1839) both stressed the sovereignty of the people; his pamphlet *L'Extinction du paupérisme* (1844) was repeatedly cited in his campaign for the presidential elections of 10 December 1848. Together with his promise to restore France to her former (Napoleonic) glory, this assured him of massive popular support. He would again pose as the friend of the people—betrayed by the legislature—in staging his *coup d'état* of 1851 (cf. note to *second of December*, p. 108), immediately followed by the proclamation of universal suffrage.

Elysée Palace: official residence of the French head of state, in the Rue du Faubourg-Saint-Honoré. Louis-Napoléon was the first President of the Republic to occupy it, the Tuileries palace having been damaged in the 1848 Revolution (cf. note to *February and June*, p. 108).

Lyons: Louis-Napoléon made a highly-publicized trip to eastern France in July 1850, including Lyons and Strasbourg, in an effort to persuade the provincial electorate of his republican credentials.

Count of Chambord: (1820–83), grandson of Charles X, who had abdicated in 1830, and last surviving member of the senior branch of the Bourbons. The Legitimist party (supporters of the 'legitimate' Bourbon line and its pretender to the throne as Henri V) came closest to achieving the restoration of the monarchy in the period 1871–3.

92   *'Le Marchand de moutarde'*: Zola's work-notes make it clear that he was perfectly familiar with the obscene connotations of this title which translates as 'shit merchant'.

94   *Queue-de-Vache*: literally, cow's tail; an idiomatic expression used of unpleasantly brownish, or mousy, hair.

95   *Saint-Ouen*: small rural town on the Seine just north of Paris, long since swallowed up by the metropolis.

98   *Pascal*: Blaise Pascal (1623–62), celebrated philosopher and writer, best known as the author of *Les Pensées*.

     Béranger: Pierre Jean de Béranger (1780–1857), popular poet and writer of patriotic songs.

105   *Nord*: the *département* of which Lille is the administrative centre.

106   *Gueule-d'Or*: in colloquial French 'gueule' means face or mouth.

107   *savings account*: the original French here is the *Caisse d'epargne*, a state-controlled and non-profit-making savings institution set up in 1835 with the deliberate aim of encouraging thrift in the less well-off.

     Vincennes: area to the east of Paris, beyond the line of the fortifications (cf. note to p. 170).

108   *second of December*: on 2 December 1851, Louis-Napoléon—who was nearing the end of a four-year presidency under a constitution which did not permit two consecutive terms of office—staged a *coup d'état*. The date in question was no accident: it was the anniversary of Napoléon I's victory at Austerlitz (cf. note to p. 80). During the next few days, a group of republican deputies tried to organize popular opposition, in the shape of barricades which went up in the Faubourg Saint-Antoine between the Bastille and the Place de la Nation. Such limited resistance was brutally suppressed. The *coup d'état* itself was massively endorsed by a plebiscite, thus confirming Louis-Napoléon's skilful manipulation of the electorate (cf. note to *loves the people*, p. 87).

     February and June: the two revolutions of 1848. Rioting in Paris between 22 and 24 February led to the abdication of Louis Philippe, King of France since 1830, and the proclamation of the Second Republic. In the following months, newly-won liberalization was checked by conservative forces. A further insurrection between 23–26 June witnessed the bloodiest street-fighting Europe had seen and the definitive triumph of the so-called moderate republicans. Historians are agreed that both revolutions increased the power of the bourgeoisie at the expense of the workers who had manned the barricades.

108   *twenty-five francs*: reworking of the famous response made by Alphonse Baudin (1811–51) to criticism of parliamentary allowances. Baudin, who had been elected as a left-wing deputy in 1849, was killed on the barricades in the Faubourg Saint-Antoine on the morning of 3 December 1851, after an abortive attempt to organize resistance to the *coup d'état*. His 'You'll see, citizens, how one dies for 25 francs' became a rallying-cry for the Republic.

112   *Grenelle*: to the south-west, in the fifteenth *arrondissement*, where the Avenue Émile-Zola is to be found today.

113   *Moulin Rouge*: *not* the one notoriously associated with 'gay Paree' which only opened in 1889. There existed a dance-hall, the *Bal du Petit-Moulin-Rouge*, in the Place Constantin-Pecqueur, also in the eighteenth *arrondissement*.

126   *Rue de la Paix*: one of the roads which leads to the Place de l'Opéra, in the wealthy second *arrondissement*.

130   *Pompadour*: furnishing and decor from the reign of Louis XV associated with his influential favourite at court, Madame de Pompadour (1721–64).

133   *Zouave*: Berber name for the indigenous troops of the French army of North Africa. By 1852 there were three regiments of these native recruits who were to gain a reputation for their fierceness and bravery during the military campaigns of the Second Empire.

137   *Capucin*: the Restaurant des Capucins, named after the monastic order and the cowl worn by its members, was located on the righthand side of the Rue de la Chapelle.

151   *Petite Civette*: famous tobacconist's, deriving its name from the even more famous *La Civette*, in the Rue Saint-Honoré. The latter sold tobacco perfumed *à la civette*, i.e. like the scent of a civet.

165   *Bec-Salé*: meaning literally 'salty mouth', i.e. (and as his alias suggests) someone who drinks without ever slaking his thirst.

166   *Fifine and Dédèle*: affectionate versions of Joséphine and Adèle.

167   *Elysée-Montmartre*: dance-hall located, since 1807, on the corner of the Boulevard de Rochechouart and the Rue des Martyrs.

170   *Bois de Vincennes*: a park was developed there after 1857, consciously designed to complement the Bois de Boulogne in the west and to ensure that the working-class inhabitants of the east end of Paris would therefore not need to 'trespass' on the playground of the rich.

176   *Gros-Caillou*: area on the Left Bank, in the seventh *arrondissement*.

188   *Crimea*: reference to the Crimean War, with its high number of French and British casualties in the winter of 1854–5, ended by the Treaty of Paris in 1856 which thereby confirmed what Napoleon III presented as a major foreign policy success.

206   *Papillon*: *Au Papillon* was a wine merchant on the corner of the Rue Doudeauville and the Rue des Poissonnièrs; as well as referring to a butterfly, *papillon* was slang for a laundry, and for 'laundering' (in the criminal sense).

213   *Cossack*: famed for their military prowess and therefore recruited as mercenaries in northern Europe, the Cossacks were an autonomous people of the south Russian steppes before being finally incorporated into the Tsar's army in 1764.

      Bedouins: nomadic tribe of north Africa and the Arabian peninsula.

219   *Henry IV's boots*: i.e. at least 250 years ago (cf. note to *Charles IX*, p. 76).

220   *Invalides*: the Hôtel des Invalides, in the seventh *arrondissement*, was built by Louis XIV in 1670 to house wounded soldiers. It subsequently became a museum celebrating French military exploits. Napoléon I's remains were transferred there in 1840.

221   *Follebiche*: plays on a notorious term (*biche* meaning high-class prostitute) invented in 1857 by Nestor Roqueplan. Roqueplan (1804–70) was a writer, journalist, theatre administrator, and editor of *Le Figaro*.

222   *drinks*: the French term here is *goutte*, which also means sperm in slang; given the context, it is worth noting that *la goutte militaire* also meant the secretion associated with gonorrhoea.

224   *Riquiqui*: with its sexual innuendoes, this translates as someone 'poorly endowed'.

224 *Mouse*: this is explained immediately below and later in the
     novel when Zola uses the term *souris*: 'a little kiss—one of those
     quick quiet ones on the eye that are easy to sneak' (p. 363).

     Abd-el-Kader's Farewell: the Emir of Mascara (1807–83) finally
     surrendered to the French on 23 December 1847, having been the
     main obstacle to their conquest of Algeria. Contrary to promises
     made to him, Abd-el-Kader was sent to prison in France but
     later released by Napoleon III. The grandiose spectacle of his
     formal surrender inspired a number of paintings too.

230 *What a Pig of a Boy*: the French title is *Qué cochon d'enfant*
     while *être cochon*, in contemporary slang, meant to be sexually
     unrestrained or 'to make copious use of the virile member' (see
     Alfred Delvau, *Dictionnaire érotique moderne*). Such obscene
     connotations are reinforced by the word-play in the song itself
     (cf. notes to *rum*, *comin' up*, *tot*, *half of it* below).

     Grève: the water's edge, but also the Place de la Grève—the site
     of the guillotine and the place where workers congregated in the
     hope of getting a job for the day.

     rum: the original French here is *poisson*, meaning both a drink
     and a pimp.

     comin' up: an alternative translation would be 'to get back up'.

     tot: the French is 'en r'montant', playing with the erotic sense
     of 'mounting'.

     half of it: the original French is 'la moitié d' ma goutte' (cf. note
     to p. 222).

231 *Tinette*: slang for a lavatory or a foul-smelling orifice (not
     always a mouth).

     cherries . . . stony lot: in the coprophagous sense.

233 *Boule Noire*: well-known dance-hall at no. 120 Boulevard de
     Rochechouart, founded in 1822 by a legendary courtesan who
     gave it her own nickname of 'Belle-en-Cuisses' (literally 'beau-
     tiful thighs'). The sign outside this establishment figured a large
     ball, originally white but gradually blackened by dirt.

236 *Montrouge*: a district outside the city-limits, south west of Paris.

238 *Rue Notre-Dame-de-Lorette*: leads from the Rue du Faubourg
     Montmartre, through the ninth *arrondissement*, up towards the
     Boulevard de Clichy.

     Rue de la Rochefoucauld: cuts into the Rue Notre-Dame-de-
     Lorette at the intersection with the Rue Pigalle.

242 *Badingue*: abbreviated version of Badinguet, the nickname given to Napoléon III by his political opponents as a result of his having disguised himself in the clothes of a workman of that name when he escaped from the fortress of Ham (50 km. south-east of Amiens) on 26 May 1846, where he had been imprisoned since 1840 after an abortive attempt to seize power.

London: although the anecdote is apocryphal, it is true that Napoléon III had spent many of his years of exile in London, both before (May–August 1831; Nov. 1832–May 1833; 25 Oct. 1838–4 August 1840; 27 May 1846–23 Sept. 1848) and after (1870–3) being in power; he died in England on 9 January 1873.

Ledru-Rollin: Alexandre Ledru-Rollin (1807–74) was elected to the Assembly in May 1849 as a Reformist Radical, having been Minister of the Interior immediately after February 1848 (cf. note to *February and June* on p. 108). On 13 June 1849 he tried in vain to organize a left-wing revolution and fled to England. As he had also previously been a failed candidate for the Presidency in 1848, his 'broken nose' here seems appropriate.

243 *Brussels*: there was a long nineteenth-century tradition of having published in Belgium books and articles that the French authorities would have censored.

The Amours of Napoleon III: though the particular book is not identifiable, the subject in question would fill many volumes.

Histoire de dix ans: violent attack on the first ten years of the July Monarchy (1830–48) published in 1841 by the journalist and radical politician Louis Blanc (1811–82), a member of the provisional government of February 1848 who went into exile during the Second Empire, returning to serve as a left-wing deputy between 1871 and 1876.

Girondins: the *Histoire des Girondins* (1847) exalts the ideals of the First Republic while reconstructing the struggle between the Montagnards and the Girondins (the right-wing party briefly in power in 1792–3) at the time of the crisis of Thermidor (27 July 1794). As well as being a famous poet, Alphonse de Lamartine (1790–1869) was a deputy after 1834, foreign minister in the provisional government of February 1848, but after June 1848 as marginalized a figure as Lantier's other liberal heroes.

243   *Les Mystères de Paris and Le Juif errant*: published in 1843 and 1844–5 respectively. Partly because these novels evoked a world far from middle-class respectability, but mainly as a result of his *Le Berger de Kravan ou Entretiens socialistes et démocratiques* (1848–9), Eugène Sue (cf. note to *Eugène Sue* on p. 7) had a reputation as a socialist. His election in 1850 terrified conservative politicians. After the *coup d'état* of 1851, he went into exile.

244   *Divorce*: although allowed by the Revolution, renewed Catholic influence under the Restoration meant that divorce remained illegal during the whole of the period between 1816 and 1884.

   Cayenne: notorious penal colony on the coast of French Guyana.

256   *La Chapelle*: cf. note to *Montmartre and La Chapelle*, p. 7.

   Belleville: working-class district in the eastern outskirts of Paris, now in the twentieth *arrondissement*.

   tripe: the original French here is the untranslatable but well-known *tripes à la mode de Caen*, still available in restaurants; to be prepared at home: simply add ox feet, cider, Calvados, carrots, onions, and herbs; and cook in the oven for at least twelve hours!

   Ville de Bar-le-Duc: less a restaurant in the modern sense than a cheap eating-house, the A la Ville de Bar-le-Duc (named after the city 230 km. to the east of Paris) was located in the Rue de l'Empereur, subsequently renamed the Rue Lepic.

   Moulin de la Galette: in the Rue des Abbesses, at the corner of the Rue Lepic and the Rue Tholozé, and captured for posterity in Renoir's *Le Moulin de la Galette* (1876).

   Lilas: La Maison des Lilas was virtually opposite the Boule Noire (cf. note to p. 233).

   Lion d'Or: the Golden Lion.

   Deux Marronniers: the Two Chestnuts.

257   *Vendanges de Bourgogne*: the Burgundy Wine-Harvest; in 1880 a big restaurant called Aux Nouvelles Vendanges de Bourgogne opened at the same address in the Rue Jessaint.

   Cadran Bleu: the Blue Dial (as in sundial, or the face of a clock); located on the corner of the Rue Charlot, at no. 27 Boulevard du Temple.

260   *Malle des Indes*: an expression first recorded in France only in 1867, referring to the English mail-steamer to and from India; but there is also a pun here on *mâle* (male) and *mal* (disease).

      Chaillot: formerly a village north-west of Paris, now part of the sixteenth *arrondissement*.

262   *La Puce qui renifle*: the Drinking Flea.

      Auvergne: region in the middle of the Massif Central.

264   *Gaillon*: small town in the Seine valley west of Paris and 24 km. south-east of Rouen, in fact in the *département* of the Eure.

      Boulevard des Invalides: in the seventh *arrondissement*, running up past the Hôtel des Invalides (cf. note to p. 220).

265   *Comtesse de Brétigny . . . Baron de Valançay*: names invented by Zola.

      Republic: at the end of the phase known as the Terror, the surviving leaders of the French Revolution had recast the calendar starting with 1793 as Year One. These are all slang expressions for the game of piquet.

      Montpernasse . . . Bagnolet: more or less garbled allusions to: Montparnasse, in the fourteenth *arrondissement*; Menilmontant, on the eastern edge of Paris; La Courtille, part of Belleville (cf. note to *Belleville* on p. 256 and note to p. 425); and the eastern suburb of Bagnolet, lying beyond the fortifications.

266   *café-concert*: place of entertainment where spectators could drink, smoke and walk around during the performance of singers, acrobats and other kinds of popular artists. The one mentioned here may well have been the Théâtre de la Gaîté-Rochechouart, at no. 15 Boulevard de Rochechouart.

268   *'My nose is where it tickles me'*: this song ('C'est dans l'nez qu'ça me chatouille') was banned in 1874, a decision on the part of the Censor astonishing only to those naïve enough not to confuse one orifice with another in a manner popularized by Charles Colmance's *Le Nez CULotté*.

271   *feast of Saint Anthony*: i.e. 17 January.

287   *Gaîté*: the Théâtre de la Gaîté, on the Boulevard du Temple, was famous in the nineteenth century for its staging of popular melodramas. In 1862, the original building was destroyed to allow the creation of the Place du Château d'Eau and replaced by the Théâtre de la Gaîté-Lyrique on the Rue Réaumur.

307 *cemetery*: the Marcadet Cemetery, behind the church of Saint-Denis de la Chapelle.

308 *A la descente du cimetière*: On the Way Down from the Cemetery.

312 *Étampes*: town 49 km. south of Paris.

321 *Rue du Caire*: just off the Boulevard de Sébastopol in what is known as the *quartier des fringues*, traditionally an area with a large concentration of workshops devoted to clothes.

331 *Hardi*: meaning daring or audacious.

336 *Sainte-Anne asylum*: was, and remains, a psychiatric hospital set in huge grounds in the fourteenth *arrondissement*. The distance to La Glacière (cf. note to *La Glacière* on p. 10) explains why going there is 'a real expedition' for Gervaise.

337 *Rue de la Santé*: this divides the thirteenth and fourteenth *arrondissements* and borders one side of the Sainte-Anne hospital; the name of this road suggests, with tragic irony, the notion of health.

339 *Bicêtre*: vast hospice in Sceaux, south of Paris, for the old and the mentally ill. The French expression, *un echappé de Bicêtre*, means a lunatic, and Zola's 'finir à Bicêtre' here retains that added figurative dimension.

351 *virgins*: a comparison which only makes sense in the context of the pictorial tradition alluded to here, namely the depiction of nymphs bathing in bucolic surroundings.

355 *Rue du Petit-Carreau*: now the Rue des Petits-Carreaux (in the plural), near the Rue du Caire (cf. note to p. 321).

364 *from the Barrière Poissonnière to the door of the workshop*: a good 2 km.

365 *Boulevard de la Villette*: this divides the tenth and nineteenth *arrondissements*.

371 *dragées*: sugared almonds.

375 *Rue de Rivoli*: adjacent to the Tuileries palace.

   six months: Napoléon III's health deteriorated throughout the 1860s. He was often in visible pain caused by bladder problems. By 1868, medical writers were called in by opposition papers to regale their readers with intimate details of how he would die.

   First of all . . . in a jiffy: this paragraph reads as a not altogether parodic version of Napoléon III's *politique des nationalités*, a

foreign policy consisting of the reorganization of Europe roughly in accord with the principle of nationalities. This did indeed
include a union of the Scandinavian countries (Sweden was 'the
giant of the North'), and in both 1856 and 1863 France was
actively involved in the internal affairs of Poland. There is the
added irony, in retrospect, that the Second Empire would be a
victim of moves towards German unification, with Napoléon III
himself having to abdicate in 1870 after defeat in the Franco-
Prussian War. Turkey had no place in his design for a Christian
Europe, and in this respect he was at odds with the British who
wanted to preserve the integrity of the Ottoman Empire.

378   *Boulevard Magenta, Boulevard Ornano*: (cf. note to *Barrière
Poissonnière* on p. 6) the Boulevard Ornano was opened in 1863
though only named as such in 1867. The section of it in
question here, between the Rue Marcadet and the Boulevard
Rochechouart, was renamed the Boulevard Barbès in 1882; it
continues south-east across the line of the octroi wall as the
Boulevard de Magenta, commemorating the French victory
over the Austrians in the battle of that name on 4 June 1859.

379   *Grand Salon de la Folie*: many music-halls, etc. included the
term *folie* in their names, as is testified by the Folies-Bergère. It
derives from the seventeenth-century folly, with its connotations of extravagance and a house built solely for pleasure. But
a *folie* is also a sort of comic vaudeville, which explains why so
many theatres catering for light entertainment were given such
a title. *Faire une folie* and related expressions catch these
multiple associations of behaviour freed from the constraints of
judgement and common sense.

383   *Saint-Lazare*: originally for lepers in medieval times, this remained a women's prison from the Revolution until 1935, a
large section of which was reserved for prostitutes and with a
hospital annexe for the treatment of venereal diseases. Located
in the Faubourg Saint-Denis, it was destroyed in 1942.

Reine-Blanche: the Bal de la Reine-Blanche, famous since the
Romantic period, was situated at no. 82 Boulevard de Clichy.

Elysée-Montmartre: i.e. the Bal Élysée-Montmartre (cf. note to
p. 167).

Château-Rouge: otherwise known as the Bal du Nouveau-Tivoli
because of its gardens, the Bal du Château-Rouge was extremely
fashionable between 1848 and 1864; it was located on the
Chaussée de Clignancourt.

384   *Bal de l'Ermitage*: at no. 6 Boulevard de Clichy.

        Bal Robert: otherwise known as the Folies-Robert; the Impasse du Cadran was just off the Boulevard de Rochechouart. Zola visited it during the preparation of *L'Assommoir* and noted that it was 'very disgusting'.

408   *'Good King Dagobert'*: last Frankish king of the Merovingian dynasty, King of all France, 628–38. The burlesque song about him, which probably dates from before the Revolution, came into vogue in 1814 and was given new impetus by the return of the Bourbons. The habit of inserting satirical couplets into the original song led to it being banned by the police.

410   *station's huge roof*: formerly the *embarcadère du Nord*, built in 1845, the Gare du Nord aquired its present monumental dimensions in 1863.

424   *Pont Neuf*: built between 1578 and 1606 at the western end of the Ile de la Cité. It was lined with buildings, the last of which disappeared in 1854, which made it the very heart of the capital. Its appearance at the time of Zola's novel is celebrated in Renoir's painting (1872) of the same name.

425   *La Courtille*: (cf. note to *Montpernasse . . . Bagnolet* on p. 265) what was known as *la descente de la Courtille* was the most celebrated and picturesque Mardi Gras procession at the end of Carnival, so called because of the vast crowds wending their way down from the heights of Belleville wearing masks, etc. Although it never regained the status it enjoyed between 1830–8, the event remained in the collective memory throughout the nineteenth century.

427   *Rue Saint-Martin*: now runs from the Pompidou Centre to the Boulevard Saint-Denis.

428   *Chaillot*: for reasons which remain unclear, this was so generally considered to be a place populated by fools that the common expressions *un ahuri de Chaillot* (a madman from Chaillot) and *envoyer à Chaillot* (to send to Chaillot) are used by Zola himself in their figurative sense elsewhere in the novel (cf. note to *Chaillot* on p. 260).

        Mardi Gras: literally Fat Tuesday (more suggestive than Shrove Tuesday), this is the last day of Carnival and the occasion for a final outburst of festivities prior to Lent.

430   *Punchinello*: from the Italian Pulcinella and known as Punch in English, with the same personality and physical features.

433   *Charenton*: major psychiatric hospital near the Bois de Vincennes (cf. note to p. 170).

434   *send him to jug*: the original French here is 'l'envoyer à Mazas'. Located on the Boulevard Mazas (now the Boulevard Diderot), the Mazas was the first French prison with a cellular system. Not a single prisoner escaped from it during its existence (1850–98).

THE WORLD'S CLASSICS

A Select List

HANS ANDERSEN: Fairy Tales
Translated by L. W. Kingsland
Introduction by Naomi Lewis
Illustrated by Vilhelm Pedersen and Lorenz Frølich

JANE AUSTEN: Emma
Edited by James Kinsley and David Lodge

Mansfield Park
Edited by James Kinsley and John Lucas

J. M. BARRIE: Peter Pan in Kensington Gardens & Peter and Wendy
Edited by Peter Hollindale

WILLIAM BECKFORD: Vathek
Edited by Roger Lonsdale

CHARLOTTE BRONTË: Jane Eyre
Edited by Margaret Smith

THOMAS CARLYLE: The French Revolution
Edited by K. J. Fielding and David Sorensen

LEWIS CARROLL: Alice's Adventures in Wonderland
and Through the Looking Glass
Edited by Roger Lancelyn Green
Illustrated by John Tenniel

MIGUEL DE CERVANTES: Don Quixote
Translated by Charles Jarvis
Edited by E. C. Riley

GEOFFREY CHAUCER: The Canterbury Tales
Translated by David Wright

ANTON CHEKHOV: The Russian Master and Other Stories
Translated by Ronald Hingley

JOSEPH CONRAD: Victory
Edited by John Batchelor
Introduction by Tony Tanner

DANTE ALIGHIERI: The Divine Comedy
Translated by C. H. Sisson
Edited by David Higgins

VIRGIL: The Aeneid
Translated by C. Day Lewis
Edited by Jasper Griffin

HORACE WALPOLE : The Castle of Otranto
Edited by W. S. Lewis

IZAAK WALTON and CHARLES COTTON:
The Compleat Angler
Edited by John Buxton
Introduction by John Buchan

OSCAR WILDE: Complete Shorter Fiction
Edited by Isobel Murray

The Picture of Dorian Gray
Edited by Isobel Murray

VIRGINIA WOOLF: Orlando
Edited by Rachel Bowlby

ÉMILE ZOLA:
The Attack on the Mill and other stories
Translated by Douglas Parmée

A complete list of Oxford Paperbacks, including The World's Classics, OPUS, Past Masters, Oxford Authors, Oxford Shakespeare, and Oxford Paperback Reference, is available in the UK from the Arts and Reference Publicity Department (BH), Oxford University Press, Walton Street, Oxford OX2 6DP.

In the USA, complete lists are available from the Paperbacks Marketing Manager, Oxford University Press, 200 Madison Avenue, New York, NY 10016.

Oxford Paperbacks are available from all good bookshops. In case of difficulty, customers in the UK can order direct from Oxford University Press Bookshop, Freepost, 116 High Street, Oxford, OX1 4BR, enclosing full payment. Please add 10 per cent of published price for postage and packing.